Winter's Maiden

Winter's Magic Season 1 Collection

L. STARLA

Winter's Maiden 1

Winter's Magic Part 1

L. STARLA

Dedication

- This one is for Mum, the woman who brought magic into my world.

Epigraph

"This is why magic is worse even than quantum physics.
Because, while both spit in the eye of common sense, I've never
yet had a Higgs bosun turn up and try to have a conversation
with me."
   —Ben Aaronovitch

Book 1 Playlist

"So Say We All" by Landroid
"Run" by Dan White
"Stay" by The Score
"Believer" by Imagine Dragons
"The Hype" by Twenty One Pilots
"Night Time" by The Birthday Massacre
"Evoke" by Grey Hearts Red
"Art of Doubt" by Metric
"Legends are Made" by Sam Tinnesz
"Only Bones" by RedHook
"Wonderful Life" by Bring Me the Horizon
"Hallelujah (So Low)" by Editors
"Blood Like Lemonade" by Sneaker Pimps
"In This Moment" by Reside
"Born for This" by The Score
"The Hunter" by Adam Jensen
"Deceiver" by The Beautiful Monument
"Despicable" by grandson
"Alligator" by Of Monsters and Men

Playlist available on Spotify & YouTube.

Prologue

Nine Years Ago

'So, I will be a knight of Camelot, Lana will be the princess,' Liam lunged forward with his plastic sword pointed at his brother, 'and Brendan, you can be the roguish bandit. It will be my mission to rescue Lana from you.'

Brendan crossed his arms, scowling. 'Why can't I be the knight for a change?'

Stepping back, Liam frowned. 'Because I'm the older brother. Besides, I'm the one with the warrior's name.'

Alannah looked at both cousins hoping they were not about to start fighting again.

'That's a stupid reason. I wanna turn at being the hero.' Brendan stamped his foot and maintained his stance.

Liam shook his head. 'You make a much better rogue than I do. I don't know how to be a bad guy.'

Brendan looked at Alannah. 'What do you think? Who do you want to rescue you?'

She sighed. 'You know I love you both, but you do make a better rogue, Brendan.'

Liam beamed. 'Well, that settles it. Lana, you can go hide now.'

Turning to face the house, Brendan huffed, closed his eyes, and started counting.

Alannah took off, running across the lawn, into the scrubland bordering her family's rural property on the Fleurieu Peninsula. She passed gum trees, wattles, grevilleas, and bottlebrushes until she reached another manicured section of garden with lawn, flower beds, and a fenced enclosure full of smelly plants Mum called herbs. She ducked behind the giant weeping willow forming a centrepiece and providing ample concealment.

'Ready or not, here I come,' Brendan's faint voice cried out in the distance.

Her heart was pounding as she leaned back against the rough bark of the tree trunk. *I should have a few minutes to catch my breath before needing to leave this refuge.* She thanked the Goddess for the cool breeze and comforting shade. Despite the recent break in the weather, Alannah's pale skin was already blistering from an hour of playing in the sun.

Liam sped past her hideout and took cover behind the Moreton Bay Fig several metres away. He looked at her, bringing a finger to his lips to keep her quiet and turned his attention to the front of the yard.

Wondering how far away Brendan was, Alannah chanced a peek around the tree. *Oh Gods!* He was coming straight for her.

'*Run, Princess!* I will protect you!' Liam cried.

She surged on, approaching the rear boundary, and running out of ground to put between herself and Brendan. Stopping behind the Mulberry tree, she watched as Liam jumped out, sword in hand.

He took a fighting stance. 'En garde!'

Brendan drew his own plastic blade, and the battle began. Alannah waited with bated breath. Brendan's technique was improving, and he was forcing Liam back. Her knight was losing this battle. Knowing it was only a matter of time before the rogue reached her, she decided to take advantage of his distracted state to circle back, so she flew past them.

It did not take long for Brendan to realise what she was doing, and his own footsteps were rapidly gaining on her. In no time, he caught up, wrapping his arms around her. Tackling her to the ground, he laughed. 'Gotcha! Now you're mine, Princess.' Rolling Alannah onto her back, he straddled her, pressing a kiss on her lips, and winking.

Alannah's cheeks flushed as she squealed. '*Help me!* Sir Liam, where are you?'

'*Fear not, Princess, I'm coming!*' With that, Liam grappled the rogue away from her, pinning him to the ground. 'Run back to the castle!'

She did not hesitate to sprint back to the house, where she wrapped her arms around one of the steel pillars on the porch.

Liam was not far behind and he rushed to hug her. 'Are you okay, Princess? Did that rogue hurt you?'

Returning the embrace, she smiled, looking up into his beautiful blue eyes. 'I am fine, thank you, oh brave and honourable knight.' She planted a kiss on his cheek.

Blushing, he returned the favour with a quick peck on the lips and cried out as he thrust his sword in the air, 'Victory for Camelot once again!'

With the game over, the three of them sat around the outdoor table to enjoy a cool softdrink.

'I want to marry you one day, Lana,' Liam declared, grinning at her.

She smiled warmly. 'I would be honoured.'

'But *I* want to marry Lana!' Brendan protested.

'Don't be silly, brother, I'm the one she wants. Right Lana?' They both looked at her with unwavering focus.

Oh hell! She loved them both. *How can I choose?* 'Well…'

'*Alannah! Come here please sweetie. Daddy and I need to talk to you.*' Her mother Aileen's voice called from inside.

Answering her summons, she found her parents sitting in the family room. 'Yes, Mummy?'

Aileen smiled. 'Take a seat, honey. We have some important news to share.'

She sat between them.

'Hey beautiful girl,' Dennis, her father, kissed her on the forehead. 'I received a really good job offer, which I have decided to accept. This will mean a lot more money for toys and outings.'

'That's great Daddy! Congratulations.'

'Thanks sweetheart. There's one catch though…' He paused a moment and Alannah's stomach twisted into knots. 'The job is in Melbourne, so we are going to have to move.'

Tears brimmed in her eyes. 'But why, Daddy? I love living here with the boys.'

Mummy put her arm around Alannah. 'I know you do, darling, but this is an important opportunity for Daddy.'

'Well I don't want to go!' Storming off to her room, she slammed the door. She flung herself on her bed and cried her heart out.

Chapter One
The Present

Alannah jumped out of her dad's Mercedes and marched across the freshly cut lawn in front of her Melbourne high school. She stopped at a picnic table to meet her two best friends, Emma and Melissa. The three of them, dressed head to toe in black, wore matching pale foundation, thick black eyeliner, and blood red lipstick. The trio had adopted the look after a sudden aneurysm had ended Alannah's mother's life three years ago. Not that Alannah's porcelain complexion required any cosmetics to achieve the pallor she wanted.

As they made their entrance, fellow students stepped aside and gawked at them.

Zac, a rugby player who also happened to be the hottest guy in year eleven (according to an official poll), moved to block their path. 'Oh look, it's the Graveyard Girls!' Gesturing toward his groin with a lewd grin, he continued, 'Hey vamp tramps, you wanna suck my blood?' He high fived his mate Bryce and they bent over laughing.

Rolling her eyes, Alannah pushed past them and continued walking along the corridor.

Emma followed suit, turning to her, and pretending to stick her fingers down her throat. 'Zac is so gross!'

'Yeah, but you'd bone him given the chance,' Melissa added.

When they reached their lockers, Alannah dumped her bag inside. She was about to retrieve her books when she felt a hand on her backside. Grabbing the offending limb, she spun around and pushed its owner against the neighbouring lockers. Her breathing eased when she saw who he was.

'Jumpy much?' Cole grinned at her beneath his long, choppy fringe.

'Sorry.' She smiled coyly, following up on her apology with a heated kiss on her boyfriend's mouth, savouring the cool mint taste on his breath and the smell of his earthy fragrance.

'Ick, get a room you two!' Emma complained.

Alannah broke away from the kiss, pressed her head against Cole's chest, and turned to face her friend. 'You're just jealous you're not getting any.'

'Damn straight! I'm…' A loud horn cut her off. 'Hey, I've been saved by the bell. Come on, let's get moving.' Emma closed her locker and took off.

After planting one more kiss on Cole's lips, Alannah took her books and chased after Emma. She made it to homeroom in the nick of time, yawning her way through the roll call and morning announcements. Her first period was Ancient History, the only subject she had any interest in at school. Given her Irish heritage, she was eager to learn about the Celts. As part of her research assignment, she had decided to raid the attic and dig out some of her mother's old books and papers. Casting her mind back to the previous night…

She was rifling through a pile of musty papers containing crests and pedigree diagrams. When she put them aside, she found a large ornate trunk made from polished wood, with brass filigree designs embellishing the corners of the locked lid. Brass medallions shaped in Celtic knots, adorned the chest and a moonstone sat in the middle of each one. When she attempted to unfasten the clasps, they did not budge.

There must be a trick to this. *Studying the box for some time, the intricate patterns in the knotwork entranced her. Almost without thinking, she ran a finger beneath the central fastening and drew it back with a start when she pricked herself. A small drop of blood fell upon the moonstone adorning it and she heard the catch mechanism release. When she tried each of the other closures with her bloodied finger, they opened.* 'How strange. They must be in a state of disrepair. Simply needed a bit more work to open.'

Alannah gasped as she lifted the lid, discovering several tarnished, silver trinkets, including a small dagger, a carved wooden stick, a mirror, and a chalice. There were also various crystals and gems. One item caught her attention: a book bound in black leather and embossed with a silver symbol depicting two crescent moons either side of a circular design.

Before she had much time to investigate further, she heard Dad calling her, so she tucked the book and the family history papers in her bag, closed the box and ran downstairs.

Sitting at her desk in History, she retrieved the mysterious black volume from her bookbag and read the title page: '*Leabhar Scáthanna an Clan Gheimhridh*'. *Is that Gaelic?* Alannah recognised *Gheimhridh* as the original form of her surname, Winters. After starting up her laptop, she plugged the words into a translator. 'The Winters Clan's Book of Shadows.'

'Cool book. What is it?' Emma asked from the seat next to her.

'I don't know exactly, but it was my mum's. I think it might be a family heirloom or something. It's all in Gaelic, so I need to work on translating it.'

'Neat. I wish I had some family history stuff that was relevant.' Emma ran her finger over the symbol on the cover. 'What's this mean?'

'No idea. I'm gonna Google it now.' Alannah looked for 'Celtic knot with crescent moons and circle.' The references to witchcraft did not surprise Alannah. Her mum had been interested in all that wiccan stuff and owned a shop that had sold crystals and new age music. Alannah's search results suggested the knot was probably a Triple Moon, also known as the Triple Goddess symbol, although she could not find an exact match for the central dendriform motif.

As she delved deeper into her research on Celtic knots, she came across a familiar design known as the 'Shield'. The symbol, commonly used for protection, resembled the medallions on the old chest in the attic. She started taking down notes on symbology, deciding this would be her focus for the assignment.

She was engrossed in her work when Emma nudged her. 'You gonna respond to that?'

Alannah blinked at her friend. 'What?'

'You got called to the front office.'

'Really?' Alannah stood up. Before she left, she decided to put her mum's book in her bag. She did not want to take any chances leaving something so valuable lying around. When she reached the reception desk, her heart stopped at the sight of two uniformed police officers.

'Step into my office, please Alannah.' Principal Daniels gestured with his gnarled hand.

'But I haven't done anything wrong, I swear,' Alannah protested.

'No one is accusing you of anything, Alannah. Now please come in and take a seat.' He stepped through the door and moved behind his black particle board desk.

Alannah sat in one of the visitor's chairs, and the police officers followed. She noticed Cathy White, the school counsellor, sitting within. When the second officer—a woman with a permanent scowl on her face and upright, rigid posture—closed the door, Alannah's heart rate quickened. Directing her gaze at Mr. Daniels, she asked, 'What's this about?'

'I'm afraid these officers have some bad news for you. I'm terribly sorry, Alannah,' replied Mr. Daniels.

'Are you Alannah Winters, daughter of Dennis Wagner?' The other officer asked. She adopted a more casual pose than her partner and the delicate features of her face focused on Alannah.

'Yes. Why, what's wrong?'

'There was an incident at your home this morning. I'm sorry, Miss Winters, but your father's injuries were fatal,' the kind one replied.

Tears threatened to rain down Alannah's face for the first time in three years. Her jaw was too slack to speak, so she stared at the ladies in blue with wide eyes.

'We understand this can be a very difficult time and would like to offer a free counselling service for victims of crime in addition to the support I'm sure you will get from Mrs. White here.'

One word stood out to Alannah. 'Crime?' Her voice was barely more than a whisper.

'Yes. I'm afraid your dad stumbled upon a robbery in progress when he returned home this morning. The thief must have been armed. I'm so sorry, Miss. We have organised a safe place for you to stay until more permanent living arrangements can be made. When you are ready, we will drive you there. Take your time, we will wait outside.' She stood and left the room, along with her colleague.

Cathy put her arm around Alannah. 'Would you like me to call your friends up here to support you?'

Still unable to speak, Alannah simply nodded.

The rest of the day passed in a haze of tears and Alannah, vaguely moving from one set of arms to another until she arrived at a foster home.

Luna, the fluffy white Siberian cat, meowed and rubbed up against Alannah, who sat on the window seat of the living room. Over the last few days, she had come to share the feline's favourite pastime of watching the world go by. They had also developed a special bond, which Alannah knew was dangerous because her foster home was only temporary, but Luna, the cat, had been a great comfort to her.

Alannah was grateful the school had excused her for the time being. It would be impossible to focus on her studies in her state of mind. She sighed, gathering the fluffball up into her lap. After a little patting, Luna drifted off to sleep and Alannah returned to her trance. Memories of happier times with both of her parents filled her thoughts.

The doorbell rang, breaking Alannah from her reverie. She heard Marjorie rushing from the backyard with an infant attached to her hip. Her foster carer had been kind and considerate, but as a family day-care worker, she always had her hands full with the tiny tots and Alannah did not want to impose. At sixteen, she was generally capable of looking after herself during the day.

Marjorie ushered in the visitor and Alannah recognised the kind policewoman's voice. 'Alannah dear, Officer Smith is here to see you.' Her voice preceded her as they both walked into the room before returning to her duties with the kids outside.

'Hi Alannah. How are you holding up?' Smith asked.

Alannah shrugged. 'Surviving.'

'I see you've made a new friend here.' She looked at the cat in Alannah's lap.

This brought a slight smile to Alannah's face. 'Yeah. Luna's a sweetie.'

'I have some news for you, Alannah. Social Services have arranged a permanent home for you. I know this is likely to be a big change, but we all believe this is the best option.'

'Oh?' Alannah's heart started pounding *What sort of home am I going to?*

'It is policy to place minors with family wherever possible, so long as those family members are capable of course. The only family we have been able to track down for you are your South Australian Uncle and Aunt. I understand you lived with them as a child?'

'Yeah, that's right.' Alannah's heart quickened. *Moving interstate means leaving all my friends behind.* Her lip trembled as she turned her attention to the cat in her lap. But memories of her time in Gaeilge Shores surfaced. When she thought about living with her cousins again, her frown morphed into a smile.

'Right, well your Uncle and Aunt will be coming over for the funeral tomorrow. They will take you home with them.'

Shit! Tomorrow is too soon. Once Officer Smith left, Alannah updated Marjorie. Returning to her spot by the window, she sent Cole and her friends a message: Please come over 2nite. We need to talk.

Alannah's friends entered the lounge room and Marjorie gave them some privacy. After a round of hugs, Alannah slumped on the couch beside her boyfriend.

Cole drew Alannah into his arms. 'So, what's going on? Have the police caught the bastard yet?'

She sighed. 'I haven't heard any more about that.' Taking a deep breath, Alannah continued, 'But they made a more permanent living arrangement for me. I move tomorrow.'

'What?' Emma sat up. 'Move to where?'

Alannah felt Cole's grip around her tighten. She looked at him with tears in her eyes. 'I'm moving back to South Australia, to live with my Uncle Ross and his family.'

'Oh, fuck!' Cole closed his eyes and pressed his forehead against hers.

'That totally sucks balls!' Melissa cried. 'Why can't they find you somewhere in Melbourne?'

Alannah sat back and looked at her friends. 'Because these people are my only remaining family,' she conceded. 'We can still keep in touch and visit during school holidays and whatnot.'

'Yeah, but it won't be the same. School is gonna stink without you!' Emma sought Melissa's embrace and they sobbed into each other's arms.

'I'm sorry guys. It's not like I have a choice in the matter.' Alannah's own tears broke free and Cole pulled her closer.

'It's okay babe, we know. It's just, being separated from you will hurt like hell.' Cole hugged her tight.

His arms feel so good. Why do I have to leave them?

After several minutes, Melissa spoke up. 'Well, I don't fancy crying away our last night with Alannah. We should make the most of our time together. I say we watch some tacky movies and stuff ourselves with pizza for old times' sake.'

Emma wiped her eyes. 'I second that.'

'Good idea. Thanks guys.' Alannah settled in to enjoy the B-grade entertainment.

As *Sharknado*, their second film, finished, Emma stretched her arms. 'I think we need to change things up a bit before I fall asleep. How about we all share our favourite Alannah moments?'

'Brilliant,' Melissa agreed.

Alannah snorted. 'Oh gawd, guys. Please don't embarrass me!'

'Hey, this'll be good. I promise.' Emma smiled.

'Fine.' Alannah directed her gaze to Cole. 'But nothing too personal, please.'

He gave them an impish grin. 'I'll try my best.'

'Right, well I'm gonna start,' Emma declared. 'I remember the first time Alannah got drunk.'

Shaking her head, Alannah face palmed. 'Oh God, no!'

Emma giggled. 'It was at Hayley's party last year. She started touching everyone's hair and telling us how nice it felt.'

'Yes! I remember. That was hilarious.' Melissa laughed.

'Right up until she started on the other guys anyway. That's when I had to drag her away before they got any ideas,' Cole added. 'But since we're on funny moments, let's not forget the time Alannah got us to glitter bomb Zac and his buddies.' He kissed her on the cheek. 'Their reactions were priceless. I was so proud of you that day.'

'Yeah, I'm pretty sure those guys are still sparkling,' Alannah agreed.

'Hey, what about the time Alannah was giving that oral presentation where she accidentally said sex instead of six?' Melissa chuckled.

Emma bent over in hysterics.

Alannah grinned. 'That was pretty funny.'

Once Emma had recovered from her fit, she sat up. 'Okay, now for our most treasured moments. Mine was the day Alannah bought me this best friend charm.' She held up her half of the broken silver heart a small tear escaped her eye.

Melissa started to sniffle too. 'I will never forget the day I started at our school and Alannah found me sitting alone at lunch, so she dragged my arse over to sit with you guys.'

Alannah felt her eyes watering.

'Well since I probably can't mention any of the amazing sex, I guess I'll have to be soppy too.' Cole squeezed Alannah's hand before continuing, 'For me it was *my* first day of High School, which was also when Alannah started.' He looked directly into her eyes. 'The moment I saw you walk through our homeroom door; I knew I was in love. You were and still are the most beautiful girl I have ever seen.'

'Jesus, Cole.' Alannah's lips collapsed against his in a desperate kiss.

'On that note, we'll leave you lovebirds to it. See you tomorrow chickadee.' Emma stood and walked out with Melissa in tow.

Alannah stealthily led Cole to her bedroom where they spent the next few hours making love as if their lives depended upon it.

At about three in the morning, he looked at her with tearful eyes and whispered, 'Where do we go from here?'

Alannah sighed. 'I'd like to think we could make things work long-distance, but that wouldn't really be fair on either of us. We both need to move on.'

'I was worried you'd say that.' He closed his eyes as a tear trickled down his cheek. 'Can we still be friends and stay in touch?'

'Yes, of course. But please don't hold onto any hopes. Let's take life as it comes, okay?' She kissed his forehead.

''Kay.'

With that, they fell asleep in each other's arms.

It was the day of the funeral and Alannah would soon be leaving Melbourne. She had chosen to wear her favourite black lace dress and one of her mum's Celtic pendants. After running a brush through her long, black hair, she grabbed the last of her bags and dawdled to the front door.

She gave her foster parents a civil goodbye and stepped outside. Dark clouds filled the sky. They resembled her eyes; heavy with tears aching for release. She needed to hold it together a little longer, at least until she reached her father's coffin.

As soon as she spotted Aunt Nora, Alannah rushed to embrace the tall woman with brown hair and blue eyes. Her aunt's arms were warm, easing some of the tension in Alannah's muscles. 'Hi sweetheart. I'm so sorry about your dad.'

When Alannah stepped back, Uncle Ross came forward. 'Hey kiddo.' He hugged her briefly, took her bags and put them in the rental car. The family resemblance was so obvious with Ross that she looked more like him than her actual dad. She knew it was because they shared the Winters colouring: pale skin, black hair, and green eyes.

The three of them walked silently into the funeral home together and took their seats. Alannah was the last of her dad's surviving family, so the only other people in attendance were Emma and Melissa along with a few of her dad's friends and business associates. Cole had agreed it would make things harder for them both if he made an appearance, so he gave her the space she had asked for.

Once the service concluded, Alannah said her final farewells to her two best friends.

Nora turned to Alannah. 'We ought to get moving if we're gonna get our flight in time. Have you packed all of your essentials, sweetie?'

'Yeah, but what about everything else?'

'The police will box up the rest of the house and send it across. They said it isn't safe for us to go back there.' Nora placed a hand on the small of Alannah's back and led her to the car.

Ross took the driver's seat. 'Having you back home will be good, Alannah. The boys are looking forward to seeing you again.'

'Yeah, I'm excited to see them,' Alannah replied in a lacklustre tone. It was a shame they could not be there to pay their last respects to her dad, but she understood they were busy with school. She had not seen her cousins since her mother's funeral when she was thirteen and wondered what sort of men they had grown into.

Chapter Two

The journey only took a few hours overall, but it was tiring after such an emotional day. Alannah was glad to be stepping through the familiar doors of the Federation house at the heart of Cailleach Estate. She walked along the hallway, letting the warm glow of the vintage filament globes on the timber interior soothe her.

When she reached the living room, she dumped her handbag on the table and took a moment to regard the two young men who stood to attention the moment she entered. *Christ! How much have they grown?*

Liam was easily six feet tall with arm muscles bulging from beneath the short sleeves of his Quicksilver shirt. He wore his brown hair short on the sides and spiked on top, a style that flattered him almost as much as the gorgeous smile radiating from his blue eyes and full lips. *When did he become so hot?* She could not stop looking at him, despite the smug grin taking over his visage.

Closing the distance between them, Liam caught her in a bear hug, speaking gently into her ear. 'It's good to see you again, Lana. Although I'm sorry for the circumstances that brought you here.'

Alannah's chest fluttered when Liam used the diminutive of her name, something she only liked her cousins doing. She breathed in his fresh scent, which reminded her of the ocean. 'Thanks. It's good to see you and to be home again.'

They released each other hesitantly when Brendan cleared his throat. 'Bring it Cuz.' He held his arms out and grinned.

She moved into Brendan's firm hold and the first thing she noticed was his musky cologne. He was slightly shorter than his older brother, but still taller than Alannah by at least five inches. Slimmer than Liam too, but still toned and strong enough to lift her off the ground and spin her around, prompting her to laugh for the first time all day. His black hair was medium length with an angled fringe almost covering his right eye but exposed the eyebrow ring on his left, along with a matching sleeper through his left ear.

Brendan resembled Uncle Ross the most, right down to the green eyes and porcelain skin, while Liam took after his mother more. After releasing his hold on her, Brendan led Alannah to a couch and sat beside her. Liam took a seat in one of the armchairs and kept his gaze pinned on Alannah, compelling her to do likewise.

'Would you like a cup of tea, Alannah dear?' Nora asked.

Wrenching her eyes away from Liam, Alannah faced her aunt. 'Yes please. White and one, thanks.' She watched as Nora and Ross walked into the kitchen.

'Whadda ya know, Liam, our little Lana's all grown up.' Brendan's gruff voice brought Alannah's attention back to her cousins.

Liam smiled. 'Yes, I can see that.'

'Hey, I'm not little. I'm only one week younger than you, Brendan.' It was her usual comeback.

'But you've always been shorter than us. The goth look suits you, by the way.'

She raised an eyebrow. 'Are you being facetious?'

Brendan raised his hands in supplication. 'Nope, all genuine here. Seriously, you look good.'

'Thanks, I guess.' Alannah was glad she took the time to touch up her makeup after all the crying.

Nora returned and handed Alannah her tea. 'Right, I'll leave you kids to it. I'm going to prepare dinner.'

Liam waited for his mum to leave the room before questioning his cousin. 'So, Lana, tell us about yourself. What are you into these days?'

'Come on man, she must be exhausted after the day she had. Surely the twenty questions can wait?' Brendan rebuked Liam.

'It's okay, Brendan, I don't mind. I'd rather focus my thoughts elsewhere anyway.' Alannah returned her gorgeous green eyes in Liam's direction and smiled.

It was enough to jolt his heart into overdrive. Liam could not believe how stunning Alannah had become. She had always been a pretty girl, but in the years since he had seen her last, she had grown into a woman with thick, glossy hair, high-cheekbones, plump heart-shaped lips, and a curvaceous, hourglass figure. Even though he did not usually find goths attractive, Alannah was exceptional.

'I like listening to alternative rock music and going to parties.' Her voice was deep and husky.

Brendan leaned back and stretched his arms across the back of the couch. 'Awesome, a party girl. You're looking at your ticket into the best parties in town.'

Liam frowned. *Brendan sure isn't holding back. He must be loving how much more Alannah has in common with himself than me.*

If she were anyone else, he would have left them to their own devices. But Liam was not about to give up on Alannah.

'What about sport?' Liam continued.

'Can't say I'm a fan. You're clearly athletic though, Liam. What do you play?' She glanced at his chest and arms briefly.

Liam's blood superheated as it rushed throughout his body. He shifted uncomfortably in his chair, fighting the growing bulge in his pants. 'I like water sports, especially surfing.'

'That explains the tan. You're lucky you didn't inherit the Geimhreadh complexion, otherwise you'd look like a lobster.'

He laughed. 'I guess so. I take it you don't spend a lot of time in the sun?'

'Too right. I gotta lather on the sunblock if I get more than a few minutes of exposure. I tend to be pretty nocturnal though.'

'Ah, a woman after my own heart,' Brendan chimed in, bringing his arm down to her shoulders, grinning at Liam in the process.

She glanced at Brendan. 'Oh? And what keeps you up at night?'

'Wouldn't you like to know?' The filthy little flirt winked at her.

Alannah laughed. 'I'm sure I'll find out soon enough.'

Liam coughed. 'So, Lana, what do you channel the most?'

When she looked at him again, her brow furrowed. 'What do you mean?'

'You know, what's your favourite power source?'

She blinked a few times. 'Um, that's an odd question. I suppose any form of renewable energy is fine by me. The environment could use a break.'

Brendan shot him a wide-eyed look. *Has he drawn the same conclusion as me? Alannah's parents raised her ignorant of her heritage.* When Brendan began to open his mouth, Liam jumped up and smiled at Alannah. 'Well, I think we have probably overwhelmed you enough with our interrogation.' He turned to Brendan. 'I think we should let Lana rest for a bit. Let's see if Mum needs a hand.'

'But—' Brendan started to protest.

'Come on, brother.' He grabbed Brendan's arm, dragging him into the kitchen and out into the backyard.

As soon as they were outside, Brendan broke free of Liam's grip. 'What the fuck, man? That hurt.' He peered down at the red finger marks on his arm and glared at Liam.

'I could see you were about to open a seriously big can of worms on her. Obviously, she doesn't know anything about what we are, so we need to tread carefully.'

Brendan sighed. 'I guess you're right. *Shit!* I can't believe Aunt Aileen would hide the truth from her.'

'She must have had her reasons.'

'I suppose. So how do you want to handle this? It's not fair to keep her in the dark anymore.'

'I know.' Liam closed his eyes to think. As much as he hated to admit it, Brendan was the best equipped to tell her. 'I think you should break it to her gently, but not tonight.'

He shook his head. 'Nuh, uh! Why me?'

'You have a better chance of getting through to her with your attunements.'

'Wait, are you admitting I'm better than you at something?' He grinned.

Liam shrugged. 'Just this once, yes. Don't get used to it though.'

Brendan punched him lightly in the arm. 'Excuse me while I savour this feeling.' He closed his eyes and took a few deep breaths. When he opened them, he was beaming. 'Don't worry bro, Lana will be in safe hands.' He started walking toward the house.

Liam called after him, 'So long as you keep your actual hands off her.'

Brendan waved his arm in a dismissive gesture before disappearing inside.

Brendan made a point of sitting next to Alannah at dinner so he could breathe in her sweet musky perfume and admire her beauty at close range. He did not even care that their proximity meant her emotional state was playing havoc with his senses. 'What's your fave band, Lana?'

'Hmm. If I had to narrow it down, I'd say both The Score and Metric rate pretty high for me.' She faced him as she replied, and this was when he first noticed the sexy little diamond stud in the right-hand side of her nose.

I wonder if she has any other piercings. 'No shit? They are up there with my faves too.'

'They're okay, I guess,' Liam interjected, 'although my preference is for punk and grunge bands.' Unfortunately, he chose the seat on Alannah's other side and kept drawing her attention. This time he locked her gaze.

'So, Alannah, I can probably get tomorrow off work if you'd like some company.' His mum interrupted them from their visual disrobing of each other and Brendan could have kissed her for it.

'Oh, I was hoping to start school tomorrow.'

Brendan snorted. 'Seriously? Mum's offering you time off school and you're not taking it? No offence, but I didn't have you pegged for the academic type.'

'Brendan!' Dad scolded him, piercing him with his green eyes.

'It's okay, Uncle Ross. He's right. I'm not very studious, but I miss being around people and I'm looking forward to meeting Liam and Brendan's friends.'

Brendan smiled. 'Well, I'm not sure about Liam's mates, but you'll love mine.' He placed his hand on her shoulder. 'Stick with me and mine, Cuz, and we'll look after you.'

Alannah gave him a lascivious glance that made his pulse race. 'Thanks, *Cuz.*'

'Are you not hungry, Alannah?' Mum asked.

Alannah had barely touched her dinner and was pushing the remains around her plate. 'Uh, not really. Sorry. It was nice, but I haven't had much appetite with everything that's happened.'

'Understandable.' Mum took Alannah's plate. 'Here, I'll pop it in the fridge, and you can reheat it if you get peckish later.'

'Thanks. Let me help with the dishes.' Alannah stood up and started to follow Mum.

'Don't be silly. This is your first night here and you've had such a hard day. Relax. Besides, it's Liam's turn anyway.'

'That's right, go and make yourself comfortable. I'll be with you shortly.' Liam grinned as he cleared the plates.

Alannah was drooling as she watched Liam leave the room carrying a stack of dishes.

Brendan grabbed her hand. 'Come on, I'll show you how to work the entertainment system.' He led her into the family room. 'What sort of TV shows and movies do you like?'

'Anything occult, horror, or thriller.' She took a seat on one end of the couch.

He zeroed in on the spot next to her. 'Gods damn, woman, you keep makin' me hard.'

She laughed. 'You sure know how to make a girl feel special.'

He nudged her side before reaching for the remote controls. 'Believe me, "special" doesn't even begin to cover it.'

After showing her how to connect to the various streaming services, they settled on watching *A Quiet Place*.

When Liam entered the room and observed the seating arrangements, he scowled at Brendan, who gave him a smug grin in response.

Alannah was fast asleep by the time the movie ended, so Brendan took in the sight of her precious face resting peacefully. The view was such a contrast to the spark that existed when she was awake. 'I'll carry her up to bed.' He moved in, preparing to gather her into his arms.

'Get your smutty paws away from her.' Liam pulled him back by his t-shirt neckline. 'I'll put her to bed. At least then I know her slumber won't be disturbed.'

'Bah! I'm not that disturbing, and I haven't received any complaints yet.'

Liam's eyes blazed as he bared his teeth. 'I mean it when I say, "keep your hands off." This is Lana, not some random slut. If you hurt her, you *will* face my wrath.'

'Oh wow, you've got it bad for her, don't you?'

'You of all people shouldn't need to ask.' Liam scooped Alannah into his arms and carried her out the room.

Shit! Brendan knew what Liam was capable of and he did not fancy going head-to-head with such power.

Chapter Three

Alannah beelined for the coffee machine and guzzled half her cup before she even registered someone else's presence in the kitchen.

When she looked up, Brendan was grinning as he watched her with twinkling green eyes. 'You know, with Dad being a doctor, we could probably get our hands on an I.V. drip so you can mainline that coffee and be done with it.'

A hearty laugh spilled out of Alannah. *God it feels good to laugh so much.* 'Morning, Brendan.' Grabbing a banana, she headed back to her room to get ready. She decided on an off-the-shoulder black tank-top with a whiskey logo, short black skirt, fishnet stockings, Dr. Martin boots and her usual goth makeup. Once she was ready, she raced back to an empty kitchen. Her heart thumped loudly against her ribs. *I hope I don't need to find my own way to school.*

'Ready?' Brendan's voice startled her.

She spun around to look at him in his black skinny jeans and an Imagine Dragons hoodie. 'Where's everyone else?'

He gasped at the sight of her, scanning her attire. Nodding with approval, he licked his lips and gave her a lop-sided grin. 'The folks both had early shifts. Liam is doing his morning workout at the gym. So, it's just us.'

Alannah ignored the way his expression stirred tingles through her body. 'How do we get to school?'

'The bus, of course. Come on. We'd better get going or we'll miss it.' Brendan moved toward the front door.

'Oh.' Alannah had never caught a bus to school.

After she followed Brendan out the door, he locked up and gave her a set of house keys. 'These are yours.' They walked a few kilometres to a roadside rest stop, enough to leave Alannah breathless, yet Brendan did not show signs of tiring. He dumped his bag on the picnic table and sat next to it, with his feet on the bench seat.

Alannah looked around. Big old gum trees and a few wattles surrounded their gravel-covered island. There was no bus signage of any sort. 'This is a bus stop?'

'Yup.' Brendan's eyes narrowed as he studied her, then a smile dawned. 'Oh right, you've turned into a city chick. We don't have metro buses out here, but this is a school bus route. Don't worry, it'll be here soon.'

She breathed out a sigh. 'So, you mentioned Liam is at the gym. When do you work out?'

He smirked. 'Good of you to notice, Lana.' Brendan gazed upon her intensely for a silent moment and her pulse raced. He leaned forward, elbows on his knees and chin in his hands. 'Like you, I'm not a morning person, so, I exercise after school.' In that moment, a large yellow bus drove up beside them. Brendan jumped up, bag in hand. 'Follow close behind me—we sit up the back.'

After climbing the steps, she peered down the aisle of seats, most of them filled with teenagers. With all eyes on her, she gulped. Alannah had grown used to drawing attention to herself, but this crowd was a lot rougher than that of her Melbourne school. *I may not have made the best choice of attire.* She was going for a 'don't mess with me' vibe, but she may as well have stamped the word 'whore' on her forehead for the leering looks she was getting.

To begin with, she passed a few loners before reaching a small group of nerds. The middle of the bus was full of bogans and rednecks, dressed in flannelette shirts or footy guernseys, who offered several lewd remarks as she passed. Finally, they reached the back of the bus. Numerous counterculture kids mingled in the rear seats, including goths, emos, punks, hipsters, and metalheads. The scene surprised Alannah. She had not ever seen so many piercings and tattoos in one place. The clique that had been an outcast minority in her Melbourne school was clearly the majority here. This was where Brendan greeted a bunch of his friends with fist bumps and other odd handshakes, before taking the very back seat and pulling her down beside him.

He put his arm across her shoulders. 'This here is my cousin, Alannah.'

Everyone had turned to stare at her, but she tried to ignore most of them, instead focusing on Brendan's friends.

Brendan smacked a hand on one guy's shoulder. 'This is my mate, Jacob.'

Jacob had dark red hair, chubby cheeks and a build that implied a love of food rather than exercise. 'Hi, Alannah. It's good to meet you.' He offered her a mischievous grin.

She smiled at him. 'Hi Jacob.'

Brendan gestured to the girl next to Jacob. 'And this is Cara.'

Cara beamed. 'Hi Alannah. It's so good to finally meet you.' This girl had the most incredible dye job. The ombre effect ran from dark red on top to yellow at the tips resembling flames.

'Thanks, Cara.'

The introductions continued. 'Locky, Ben, Bianca, Nick, Amy, Connor, Bailey, Caleb…' Too many names washed over her in quick succession.

Alannah breathed easily again when they reached their destination.

'I'll take you to the front office so you can enrol in your classes.' Brendan blew the long, black strands of his fringe out of his eyes as he threw his protective arm across her shoulder and led them away from the hordes.

The school was smaller than her last one, but unfamiliarity gave the impression of increased size. When they reached the reception desk, a woman with orange-red hair and a flowing, floral dress looked up and smiled at them.

Brendan puffed his chest out as he spoke. 'Hi Miss O'Leary. This is my cousin, Alannah Winters. She's starting school today.'

'Thanks Brendan. Hi Alannah. Welcome to Gaeilge High.' She reached for a bunch of paperwork and handed it to Alannah. 'Take a seat and Mrs. Burke will see you shortly. She will help with your subject selection and enrolment papers.'

'Is it okay if I wait with Alannah and help her find her classes?' Brendan asked.

'Yes, that should be fine. Thank you, Brendan.' She filled out a slip of paper and handed it to him. 'Here's a hall pass.'

Mrs. Burke, the Careers Counsellor, called Alannah into an office a minute later. 'I received your transfer papers from Melbourne. You can probably take the equivalent subjects here, although you might like to have a look at our other courses to see if you'd like to try any of those instead.' She opened one of the booklets sitting in front of Alannah and pointed to the social sciences syllabus. 'It might interest you to know that a number of our students have chosen to learn Irish Gaelic with Language & Culture. Could tie in well with your project on The Celts.'

'That would be good actually. I've been wanting to learn the language anyway. The Women's Studies course also intrigues me.'

Mrs. Burke smiled. 'I thought it might.'

That's presumptive of her. 'Why do you say that?'

'Let's just say, your family's reputation precedes you.'

Who is this woman referring to? I can't imagine my cousins having feminist tendencies. 'Right, well I'll take it, along with the Gaelic subject. I want to stick with Ancient Studies and obviously I have to continue with English and Maths.'

'Certainly. Please fill out those forms while I arrange your classes.' She moved to her computer.

Brendan jumped up from his chair the moment Alannah emerged from the office. 'Give us a look at your schedule.'

She handed the page to him.

'Sweet! We're in the same Language class. You wanna learn Gaelic with me?'

'That was the plan. Do we have any other classes together?'

'Yup. Homegroup and English. Oh, and I'm pretty sure you'll find Cara in your next two lessons. Speaking of which, I should probably get you there, although I'd rather play hooky with you.' Brendan's face lit up and he fluttered his extraordinary lashes.

She grabbed her timetable back from him. 'Sorry to disappoint, but I'm not wagging on my first day.'

He pouted a moment before exhaling dramatically. 'Fine.' When he started striding away, Alannah struggled to keep up.

'What about textbooks?'

'I'll take you to the library at morning break.' He did not even slow down when replying. His abrupt mood change turned Alannah's stomach upside down.

Did I say or do something wrong?

'We've already missed Homegroup, so here's your classroom for first period. I'll meet you back here after.' He walked off.

What the hell? Brendan's behaviour could be the topic of a mystery novel. She shrugged, deciding to focus on more pressing issues.

'Hey Alannah! Are you in this class too?' Cara entered the empty room and took the desk next to her, lighting up the room with her blazing hair. The girl had pale skin too, but aside from mascara, she didn't appear to be wearing much makeup.

'Yeah. I don't have any books yet though. Mind if we share?'

'No probs, hun. I'd be happy to catch you up on stuff too. We've been working on a text using this gender analysis framework.' She handed Alannah her notebook.

'Thanks.' She took the book and started making her own notes as the room filled with the buzz of other students. The din ceased, and Alannah looked up to see her teacher and the rest of the class staring at her.

'Hello Alannah. I'm Irene Dempsey.' She smiled. 'It is so good to have a Winters woman in my class. Perhaps we can start to have some more intelligent group discussions.'

Alannah returned the smile. 'Um, thanks, Ms. Dempsey.'

During the personal study time, Alannah turned to Cara and whispered, 'Why do people keep staring at me?'

'They're in awe of you. You have a powerful presence and you're the first Winters woman they have met in person.'

'Oh. But what about my Aunt Nora?'

Cara's brow shot up as her head jerked back. 'Doesn't count. She married into the family. You're the one with Winters blood coursing through your veins.'

I am going to have to ask my cousins to fill me in on some family history.

By the time lunch started, Alannah had seen most of the campus thanks to Cara who had established herself as Alannah's new best friend.

When they reached the lunch tables, Brendan gave Alannah a huge grin. 'I see Cara has taken you under her wing. Thank you, Cara.'

Cara beamed and her fiery hair practically glowed as she sat down. 'It's been an absolute pleasure.' She gestured for Alannah to sit between herself and Brendan.

Brendan leaned in, tickling her neck with his breath. 'So, Lana, are you surviving your first day okay?'

She looked at Brendan and returned his smile. 'So far, so good.'

'Oh great, it's the fuckin' townies,' one of Brendan's mates complained. He was the one with scruffy brown hair and lots of stubble. *Was his name Connor?*

'Townies?' Alannah asked.

'The rich and famous. Most of them live in town, but there are a few from rural estates who think they're better than the rest of us,' Connor replied.

When she faced the direction of his gaze, Alannah saw a group of attractive people in brand-name clothes approaching. Her heart stopped when she realised who led the group.

'There you are. How are you today, Lana?' Liam's blue eyes pierced her with their intensity.

Alannah's heart leaped out of her chest, making way for the butterfly invasion. 'I'm okay, thanks.'

'Glad to hear it. Would you like to join me for lunch?'

She glanced at Liam's friends, catching a few glares. The tanned blonde girl standing next to him gave Alannah an icy stare, sending chills down her spine. Alannah gulped.

Cara cleared her throat. 'Listen, jerk. Alannah is fine with us, so you can all take your fancy threads elsewhere.'

Liam scowled at her, turning back to Alannah. 'You don't really want to sit with this riff-raff, do you?'

Alannah sensed Brendan stiffen beside her. *Oh God!* She hated being in the middle of conflict. Part of her desperately wanted to go with Liam, but his friends were not exactly welcoming. And she did not want to hurt the friends she had already made. 'Actually, I think I'm good where I am, but thanks for the invite, Liam. I'll see you after school.'

Liam's eyes bugged out before he adopted a cold, detached mask. 'Very well. Later then.' He turned and strode away, posse in tow.

Cara flipped them off as soon as they turned their backs. 'Ugh. Elitist pricks.'

Brendan laughed. 'Nice burn, Lana. I could kiss you right now.'

In any other circumstances Alannah might have felt good about sticking up for herself and her friends but refusing Liam left her nauseous. As she watched him leave, she kept picturing that awful mask going up. 'I can't believe Liam would associate with people like that.'

'Sorry to burst your bubble, Lana, but Liam's a bit of a golden boy.'

'You must be Alannah.' A tall guy with a buff build drew her attention back to the group. Standing across the table from her, he must have arrived recently. He was stunning: long black hair framing a chiselled face with a sexy five o'clock shadow. 'Is everything okay? You look as though someone ate your puppy.' A pair of large, bright blue, luminescent eyes were peering down at her.

How could this man be young enough for school?

Brendan answered for her, 'She just discovered what my brother dearest is really like. Alannah, this is Austin.'

Austin sat down and looked directly into her eyes. 'I'm sorry Liam's upset you, Alannah. I know it's not much consolation, but at least you learned the truth sooner rather than later.'

He makes a good point. Alannah's stomach fluttered under Austin's scrutiny. *By God, those eyes were incredible!*

'So, what subjects are you studying Austin? Am I likely to see you in any of my classes?'

His smile dropped. 'Unlikely, I'm afraid.'

'Austin's a senior and a prodigy to boot. Loves all that friggin maths and science crap,' Brendan explained.

'Really? It's a pity we won't be studying together.' Licking her lips, she grinned at Austin.

He glanced at her mouth before returning his intense gaze to her eyes. 'Yes, that is a shame.'

Liam's chest ached. It was an unfamiliar feeling, and he could not stand it. *I can't believe Alannah rejected me.*

'I don't see what's so great about her anyway.' Monique was still walking alongside him, her long blonde hair flowing in the breeze. 'So what if she's a Winters chick. I bet she'll end up on the left-hand path anyway.'

Liam turned to confront his ex. 'Shut your damn mouth, Monique. You don't know what you're talking about.'

'Hey, I'm just calling it as I see it. Besides, what hope does she have with company like that?' She threw her hand back in the direction of Brendan's friends.

As much as he hated to admit it, Monique had a point. Brendan's friends would be a bad influence. *But what else can I do? I hope I get enough time with her to set her on the right path.* He sighed. 'I'm sorry for snapping at you, Monique, but you should know I don't take kindly to anyone hurting or insulting Lana. She means a lot to me.'

Monique huffed. 'Fine, whatever.' She stormed off to join the rest of the girls in their crew.

'Hey bro, I wouldn't worry about her.' Blake, his best mate and cousin from Mum's side, stood close by with his usual can of cola in hand. He took a sip of the drink, adding, 'She's jealous.'

'That's what worries me. Envy can be a dangerous emotion.'

Blake's blue eyes dipped as he furrowed his brow. 'Right. You want me to watch her? Distract her a little? I bet Steve could help.'

'Good idea. Thanks man.' Liam released some tension as he exhaled. Not having to deal with Monique would ease his burdens considerably. He had broken up with Monique the moment news of Alannah's return reached his ears, but Monique was still behaving like she had a claim.

'You still wanna hit the boats after school?' Blake asked as his fingers combed through his mid-length brown hair.

Liam almost confirmed with an affirmative out of habit, but hesitated. 'I dunno. It depends on what Lana's plans are.'

'Right. Of course. I hope you don't miss too much training because of her.'

'If things go according to plan, I'll be practising with her. Problem is, I think I need a new plan.'

Blake snorted. 'You think? The way things look right now, your brother has more hope of becoming her training partner, among other things.'

Liam growled. 'Don't remind me. I never thought I'd see the day Lana chooses him over me.' *That little twerp is becoming a huge thorn in my side.*

'So how much Gaelic do you know, Lana?' Brendan asked as he sat at the desk next to Alannah.

'Not much.' Alannah flicked through her textbook, feeling herself grow cross-eyed. 'Wow, this grammar stuff looks complicated.'

Brendan grinned at her. '*Is é[1].*'

'Jesus, what have I gotten myself into?' Alannah shook her head.

'Don't worry. This is like the one school subject I'm good at. I'll help you out.'

'Thanks. I'm kinda hoping for some help with translating this.' She pulled her mum's old book from the bottom of the pile.

The moment it hit the desk, Brendan's eyes and mouth opened wide. He lowered his voice to ask, 'Where the hell did ya find that?'

She tried to match his volume. 'In a box of Mum's stuff, hidden away in the Melbourne attic, along with a bunch of old artefacts and jewellery. Unfortunately, this was the only treasure I was able to retrieve before Dad…' She paused to choke back the threatening tears. 'I hope the burglar didn't get to the rest of that trunk.'

---

[1] It is

'*Oh shit!*' Brendan whispered. He glanced around the room. 'You better put that book away for now. I'll help you with it at home.'

'Why? What is it?' Alannah's heart started racing.

'Just put it away. I'll tell you everything later,' Brendan hissed at her.

'Oh-kay.' She slid it beneath the stack on her desk and glowered at Brendan. The whole situation puzzled her. *Is the leather-bound volume forbidden? Why would Mum have anything illicit or scandalous in her possession? She had always been an upstanding citizen with a caring heart.*

Brendan leaned in to whisper. 'Look, there's nothing wrong with the book per se, but it's not the sort of thing to show in public. You shouldn't advertise having it either. Please trust me on this.'

She forced a smile. 'Yeah, okay. So, what are you working on?'

'An analysis of a film called *The Guard*. You need to watch an Irish movie and write a report on it. I recommend using the same as me. It's not bad, plus the lead actor has a pretty good name.' He smirked as he handed her the details.

Alannah giggled.

'Do I need to find you a new seat, Miss Winters?' Mr. Dougherty frowned.

She bit her lip. 'Sorry, Sir.' Opening her textbook again, she tried to focus on reading the first chapter. A few minutes later she glanced at Brendan and caught him still looking at her. 'What?' she mouthed silently.

He shook his head and returned to his work.

After school, Alannah walked through the library, the sound of papers shuffling and computers humming filling the air. She had agreed to stick around and wait for both of her cousins to get a lift with them. Given the amount of study she needed to catch up on, she figured this was an opportune time to do so. A familiar face was sitting at a table beneath the flickering of the bright fluoro lights. Her heart was racing as she approached him. 'Hi, Austin. Mind if I join you?'

He gave her an alluring smile when he looked up from his work. 'Please, by all means.' His soft, husky voice and glowing blue eyes were enough to make her weak at the knees.

She took the seat across the table to avoid disturbing the ordered mess of books surrounding him. 'Do you always study here after school?'

'Most afternoons, yes. I find this place more peaceful than home, where I have three younger siblings.'

'Fair call. I hope my presence isn't too disruptive. I can find another table if—'

'Please,' Austin cut in, 'you are a welcome distraction from the monotony of these calculus equations. My eyes were starting to blur anyway.' He glanced at the book about the Celts she had placed on the table. 'Reading up on a bit of family history, I see.'

'How did you know?'

'That you're Irish? Come on, this is an Irish settlement, and everyone knows the Winters clan was one of the founding families.'

'Oh, I didn't realise.' *Explains some of my family's reputation.*

The trace of a frown fled his face almost as soon as it had appeared. 'You really don't know much about your heritage, do you?'

'No, unfortunately. I'd like to learn more though. Especially given the apparent significance of my surname.'

'I'd be happy to help. I know a local expert on the families here.' He paused for a moment, locking in her gaze. 'It might interest you to know that the first Winters woman to set foot in this town was an Alannah. I'm guessing you were named after her.'

'That is curious.' Lowering her gaze, Alannah tapped her pen on the table as she became lost in thought. *It is a little disturbing that this guy I only just met knows more about my family history than I do, but apparently most of the town is more clued in than me.* Pushing those thoughts aside, she looked up into his eyes again. 'What about your family? How long have they been in Gaeilge Shores?'

'Almost as long as yours. The Pearce family arrived in 1865, twenty years after settlement. We have a couple of properties in town.'

'Did they come from Ireland too?'

'No. They were from Somerset, England. Wait there a second.' He stood up and moved into the reference shelves. When he emerged a few minutes later, he was carrying a book about their town. 'Here, this has some of the basics.'

A brief inspection of the contents revealed a compilation of names, dates, and family crests. 'Wow, this is awesome. Thanks, Austin.'

'Anytime.'

She became so absorbed in reading about the town's history that she lost track of time.

'Hey Lana, it's time to go.' Brendan's voice startled her.

When she looked up, she caught a glimpse of the clock on the wall behind him. It was nearly half past five. 'Okay. I gotta return this first.' She closed the book and stood.

'Here, allow me.' Austin held his hand out.

She gave him a warm smile. 'Thanks. See you tomorrow.'

'No worries.' Austin raised his hand for a fist bump with Brendan.

'Laters man.' Brendan threw his arm over Alannah's shoulder and led her out to the car park.

Liam watched as Brendan escorted Alannah out of the library toward his SUV. Seeing Brendan's possessive arm draped across her made Liam's blood boil. As they drew closer, Liam moved to the front passenger door, holding it open for Alannah. 'Hey Lana.'

The moment she looked at him, her smile disappeared, and she averted her gaze. 'Thanks, Liam,' she whispered as she lowered herself into the car.

Is she sensing my mood? Once Alannah took her seat, Liam closed the door, glaring at Brendan before returning to the driver's side.

They travelled for a few kilometres before Brendan spoke up. 'You can drop me at Bianca's.'

What an unexpected turn of events. Liam looked at Brendan in the rear-view mirror with a cocked brow. 'Are you sure?'

'Of course I'm bloody sure. What's it to you, anyway?'

Liam sneered into the mirror. 'I'm not complaining, just surprised.' *Have I misjudged Brendan's feelings for Alannah?* He looked across to gauge her reaction, but her expression was blank.

Brendan snorted. 'Right, whatever.' When they pulled into Bianca's drive, he leaned forward. 'Don't wait up for me.' He jumped out, pausing to stick his head back in the door. 'Night, Lana.'

She turned and smiled at him. 'Night.'

As they were driving away, Alannah turned to Liam. 'So, what's the deal with Bianca?'

Liam kept his face forward to hide his smug grin. 'She's been Brendan's main squeeze for years.'

'I didn't know he had a girl.' Her neutral tone did not betray disappointment.

Maybe Lana doesn't fancy Brendan after all, Liam thought. 'I probably shouldn't tell you this, but…'

'But what?'

'I guess you'll probably find out eventually… Brendan sleeps around, and I mean a lot.'

'Oh.' She fell quiet for the rest of the journey.

Liam's shoulder's hunched. *Then again. Perhaps Lana was hiding her feelings initially.*

As they entered the living room together, Alannah broke the silence. 'Hey Liam…'

His muscles tensed as he looked at her. 'Yeah?' *Please quit talking about Brendan,* he silently pleaded.

'Why is it being a Winters woman has people staring at me?'

He jolted. *Talk about left field.* After a deep breath he faced her head on. 'You should ask Brendan about that.'

Alannah collapsed on the couch. 'Well he's not here, so I'm asking you. Do you know the reason?'

Liam bit his lip. 'Yes, but I don't want to talk about it with you.'

Crinkling her nose, Alannah crossed her arms, her eyes glistening with unshed tears. 'Why? What's the problem? Did my choice of lunch companions offend you so much that you don't even want to talk to me now?'

He sighed as he settled into one of the armchairs. 'No, it's nothing like that. Look, I'm sorry Lana, but it's difficult for me to explain. I really think you should wait for Brendan on this one.'

The moment Brendan stepped into Bianca's bedroom, she launched herself at him and kissed him deeply.

A few minutes later, Brendan pulled back from her. 'I want to try something different tonight.'

Pressing her hands against his chest, Bianca's darkly lined eyes became sultry. 'Is it kinky? I like kinky.'

He laughed. 'That's not what I had in mind.'

Bianca stepped back and pouted. 'What? You don't want to have fun tonight?'

She looks fucking adorable pouting at me like that with those long, turquoise pigtails. After pulling her back into his arms, Brendan smiled. 'Okay, maybe we can still have a little fun, but only after I've had a chance to try my new party trick.'

She yelped and clapped her hands. 'Oh? And what does that involve?'

Brendan pressed a finger to her forehead. 'I want you to let me in here.'

'That's pretty ambitious. Are you sure about this?'

'Absolutely positive. I'm sick of living in my brother's shadow, so it's about time I upped my game. But this stays between us, okay? You can't tell a soul.'

Bianca offered him a sly grin. 'Ooh, you are a sneaky one. I promise you my lips are sealed.'

'Good. Now let's get comfortable because this is gonna be a long night.'

Chapter Four

When Alannah entered the party, she recognised The Score's "Stay" blaring from the stereo. Being one of her favourite songs, it did wonders to calm her racing heart as she took in the sights. The rich, earthy aroma of beer wafted across the front lounge room, where bodies crowded together, filling the space with the din of chatter.

Apparently, 'gatherings' like this were a regular occurrence on Friday nights. Brendan had explained their size could vary depending on the host, who on this occasion was a Senior named Lucas who floated between groups. His home was a huge country estate, comparable to Cailleach.

Brendan had brought Alannah to the party, entering with his protective arm over her shoulder. 'Hey Lana, let's do shots.'

She smiled. 'Sounds great.'

Brendan grabbed her hand and dragged her into the kitchen. 'Greetings my lads and ladies. It's time to get this party started.' He set the box he had been carrying with his other arm on the bench. Reaching inside, he retrieved a bunch of plastic shot cups and a bottle of Jose Cuervo tequila.

Jacob stepped forward, with dimples showing in his chubby cheeks as he grinned. 'You're an absolute champ, Brendo.'

Alannah knew the drill. She spied the bowl of lemons near the sink, so she set about slicing them into wedges.

'Let me help with that.'

Glancing up, Alannah spied Nick's smiling eyes. 'Um, sure.'

The massively muscular punk, with a bright pink sidecut, wore a plain black t-shirt stretching tight across heavily inked arms. Picking up the sharp knife, he looked ready to step onto the set of a crime show, but the impression eased with such a domestic task. Nick smiled at Alannah as he chopped the lemons. 'You settling in okay?'

'I guess so. You guys have all been great.' Alannah finished slicing the last of the lemons and threw them in a bowl.

'Glad to hear it.'

She grabbed a saltshaker and placed it on the central counter with everything else.

Brendan grinned at her. 'I love a girl who knows how to drink.'

Cara snorted. 'I pegged you more for liking the cheap drunks.'

'Lowered inhibitions certainly don't hurt,' Brendan agreed.

'Ugh.' Cara flicked back her flaming red hair as she rolled her eyes.

Caleb and Locky, the two goth guys in the group, sniggered. They made an interesting pair standing together. Caleb's locks were long and black, while Locky kept his bright green hair short and messy. Both were skinny with soft, delicate facial features that were almost feminine. Given their proximity to one another, she wondered if they were a gay couple.

'Right, let's line 'em up.' Bailey—the guy with two-tone spiky hair—poured the drinks like a pro. He handed Alannah the salt, indicating she should start.

'Wow, where'd you learn to do that?' she inquired.

'My folks own the only pub in town,' Bailey explained.

After seasoning her wrist, she handed the salt to Brendan, who had been watching her closely, only looking away to apply the salt to his own wrist and pass it on. Once everyone else had followed suit and grabbed their drink, Brendan raised his cup and drew her attention again. 'I toast to Lana's return. Welcome home, Cuz.'

'To Alannah!' The rest of the group cried.

Brendan kept his gaze locked with hers as he licked his wrist slowly. Alannah remembered their old game of Sleazy Chicken and felt compelled to imitate him. He did not back down. Her attempt only sparked a salacious gleam in his eyes. The moment was intense, and Alannah realised Brendan was probably leagues ahead of her in this game. She felt her cheeks flush, breaking their trance when she threw back her shot, welcoming the burn of the liquor down her throat.

She heard Brendan laughing beside her before he whispered in her ear, 'Making you blush has become too easy.'

Alannah could not turn down a challenge like that. She turned so her lips were touching his ear. 'Don't get used to it, I'm just out of practice.'

'Right, next round!' Brendan poured more tequila for everyone. As Alannah went to lick the salt from her wrist, Brendan grabbed her hand. 'Uh, uh. Here.' He presented her with his own salted wrist.

Narrowing her eyes at him, she drew his arm toward her mouth and whispered close to his ear. 'Game on.' When she licked Brendan's wrist, Alannah sensed his body stiffen. Her pulse quickened at the thought of possible victory. *I got a reaction out of him. Perhaps he did not expect me to rise to his challenge.* But when she looked up, he kept a straight face, no hint of colour. *Dammit!*

After sculling her drink, she picked up a wedge of lemon, but Brendan plucked it from her hand and placed it between his teeth for her. *By God! He is relentless.* She looked around to see who was watching. Only a few friends remained in the kitchen and they preoccupied themselves with their own conversations. She took a deep breath and started moving closer to him. His eyes lit up when he saw her approach. *Crap! What does he plan to do when I retrieve my piece of fruit?*

'Hey gorgeous, guess who!' A curvy brunette walked up behind Brendan and clamped her hands over his eyes.

After withdrawing the citrus wedge, Brendan grinned. 'Hi Chelsea.' He spun around and drew the girl into his arms, kissing her passionately.

When Chelsea wrapped her legs around his waist and Brendan's hand climbed beneath the girl's skirt, Alannah wondered if they were about to start fucking then and there. It was fortunate Brendan could not see Alannah's face, because the display reddened her cheeks.

'Come on, let's find the beer kegs.' Cara was standing beside her with a hand on Alannah's left shoulder.

'Good plan,' Alannah agreed, as she followed Cara into the rear living room.

'Thanks.' Alannah took the cup of beer from Cara. 'Is it true, Brendan's a womaniser?'

Cara bit her lip. 'Is that what Liam told you?'

'Yeah. Is it wrong?'

After sipping her drink, Cara sighed. 'No. It's true, although womaniser is a pretty harsh term. It's not like he promises any form of commitment. The girls know what they're getting. Are you disappointed in him?'

'Not really. It's not like it's any of my business really, I was merely curious. Have you ever—'

'Oh, Gods no! That's a line I've never wanted to cross in our friendship, not that it stops him trying every so often. I kinda pride myself on being one of the few girls in our year who hasn't succumbed to his charms.'

Alannah shook her head. 'Is he really that promiscuous?'

''Fraid so. But hey, at least in you, I now have a friend in the minority, right?' Tilting her head forward, Cara's brows rose as she looked at Alannah with wide, unblinking eyes.

Alannah laughed. 'Trust me, Brendan's not the cousin I'm interested in.'

Cara's jaw dropped. 'What the hell? Wait, are you and Liam...?'

She shook her head. 'No, not yet. I'm not entirely sure if he likes me in that way. Besides, I'm still getting over my ex.'

'Oh, what happened with your ex?' Cara led her to a couch and sat down.

'It was a mutual agreement to split when I had to move here. We decided it would be too hard to maintain a long-distance relationship.'

Solemn clouds marred Cara's features. 'Oh man, that's tough. How long were you guys together?'

Alannah looked down into her beer. 'About eighteen months. Although Cole was one of my best friends before we hooked up. He'd had a crush on me since we first met in Year Seven.'

'I'm so sorry, Alannah. It sounds like you guys had something special.'

'Yeah, I suppose we did. But I need to move on with my life and Liam's always been pretty special to me too.'

'I get your need to move on, but Liam? Seriously? He is such a douche.' She clapped a hand to her mouth. 'Sorry, I don't mean to offend.'

'It's okay. I get you don't see eye to eye with him. But I've always known a different side of Liam.'

'Speaking of the devil,' Cara gestured toward the front door.

When Alannah looked up, she saw Liam enter with his townie friends who strode in like they owned the place. The moment Liam's baby blue eyes locked with hers, he smiled and moved toward her.

Cara whispered in her ear, 'I can see he has a soft spot for you.'

Liam reached her in a matter of seconds. 'Hi Lana. Can I get you a drink?'

After finishing the last of her ale, she handed him the cup and smiled. 'Yeah sure. I'll have a beer, thanks.'

His hand brushed against hers as he took the cup, sending sparks through her nerves. His smile turned into a wide grin. 'Great. I'll be right back.'

Once he moved away, Alannah's eyes landed on the fierce glare of a tall blonde. 'Cara, who's that tanned Barbie doll sending me the deadly daggers?'

'That's Queen Bee Monique, Liam's girl…' The moment Cara caught the pain in Alannah's eyes, she realised what she'd said. 'Oh, shit! Sorry, hun. I forgot to mention… fuck!'

Alannah's heart sunk. 'Of course he has a girlfriend. I was stupid to think otherwise.'

Liam returned a moment later and handed Alannah another beer. His own drink was a can of cola.

'Thanks.' Alannah accepted the drink. Squeezing onto the sofa, Liam surprised her. She chanced another glance at Monique and saw the girl huff and turn away. Alannah turned back to Liam. 'Monique doesn't look very happy.'

He shrugged. 'She'll get over it.'

She gaped at him. 'Isn't she your girlfriend, though?'

Liam's head jerked back as his eyes narrowed. 'Not anymore.'

'Oh.' *Oh. A recent breakup coinciding with my arrival. Could she feel threatened?*

'Wow—did you finally dump her bony arse? When did that happen?' Cara laughed.

Liam scowled at Cara. 'I broke up with her on Monday. Looks like you're out of the loop, Hughes.'

Cara returned the scowl. 'Forgive me for not showing an interest in the rumour mill, Winters.' She stood. 'Excuse me Alannah, I'm gonna mingle some more.' She walked away.

Liam sighed. 'I'm sorry, Lana, I know she's your friend. It's just…'

Raising her hand, Alannah cut him off. 'I get it, okay. Please leave me out of it. How about we change the subject?'

That made him smile. 'Sure. How are you?'

'Okay, I suppose… all things considered. The last week's been pretty rough.'

He placed a comforting hand on her shoulder blades. 'You've been through a lot. I'm impressed by how well you're holding up.'

'It probably has more to do with my ability to ignore my emotions. I got good at it when Mum died.'

A frown formed on his face. 'That doesn't sound healthy. You know you can talk to me about anything at any time, right?'

'Yeah, thanks.' Alannah forced a smile as she looked into Liam's eyes. A buzzing noise in her bag drew her attention. She pulled her phone out and exhaled sharply when she saw who was calling: Cole. 'Excuse me a minute, Liam.'

He glanced briefly at her phone and frowned.

'Hi Cole. Give me a sec.' Alannah walked upstairs in pursuit of some peace and quiet. She found a storage room and shut herself inside. 'Sorry about that. I'm at a party.'

'No probs. How are you?'

'I'm coping. My family here have been a great comfort. How about you?'

'Bored and missing you like crazy. But otherwise, I've been great.'

'The sarcasm is still strong with you,' Alannah replied with an amused tone before sighing. 'But yeah, I miss you too.'

'You sure you don't wanna try and make things work between us?'

Alannah closed her eyes, and an image of Liam came to her mind. 'I'm sorry, Cole. I don't think it's a good idea.'

'I s'pose you're right.' The pain in his voice was evident. 'So, how's your new school?'

'It's pretty crazy. The kids here make your school look tame. There's a lot of schoolyard fights and the detention room's often full.'

'Damn. Now I really wish I could move there. That party you're at sounded pretty wild too.'

'It's alright.'

'I guess I'd better let you get back to it. I'll catch you later.'

'Yeah, sure. See ya.' After signing off, Alannah made her way back down the corridor.

Before she reached the stairs, Monique and three other girls cornered her. 'Hey Winters, I was hoping to get a moment alone with you.'

Alannah glanced at the other girls. 'Well in that case, you might want to send your minions away.' If they were hoping to intimidate her, they were not doing a very good job. Alannah had dealt with her fair share of bitches at her last school and she never took crap from anyone.

Monique's friends tittered.

'Not what I meant, Winters. I wanted to warn you to stay away from Liam. He's mine and if you touch him, I will end you.'

The empty threat made Alannah laugh hysterically. 'Oh my God, you're so funny.' She paused to regain her composure. 'Listen, Monique, Liam doesn't want you anymore, so get over yourself and suck it up.'

A chorus of knuckle cracking came from the four girls. 'You have no idea who you're dealing with. Mess with us and we will break you so hard, your dear Uncle won't be able to put you back together.'

'Alannah?' A familiar voice broke through the group.

Alannah looked up and the other girls spun around to face Austin.

Pursing his lips, Austin focused his eyes on Alannah. 'Everything okay here?'

Monique grinned. 'Fine, thanks Pearce. We were simply becoming more acquainted with Alannah here.'

Austin furrowed his brow, studying Monique a moment before returning his attention to Alannah. Pushing past Monique, he placed an arm around Alannah's shoulders and glowered at the bullies. 'I apologise for interrupting, but I'd like a word with Alannah.' He drew her away from them and out on a balcony down the hall.

'Are you okay?' Austin's stunning blue eyes locked with hers.

'I'm fine, but thanks for the intercept.'

He smiled. 'Anytime. Be careful of those girls, though; they're trouble.'

Breaking from his gaze, she placed her hands on the railing and looked out over the immaculate cottage gardens. 'I'll be fine. I've dealt with their sort before.'

'Oh, and what sort do you think they are?'

'Pretentious snobs who get their kicks from pushing their weight around.'

He laughed. 'I can see why you get along better with your younger cousin. It's rare for anyone in the founding families to be so down to earth, but you and Brendan are definitely the exceptions.'

'Is that what those girls are? Members of the founding families?'

'Yes, they are. Which is why you need to watch your back around them. They're very… powerful.'

'I'm sure I can handle myself with the likes of them, but thanks for the warning.' Alannah remembered what she had wanted to ask him earlier. 'I missed you at lunch today, So I'm glad I caught you tonight 'cause I have a favour to ask.'

'Oh?'

'I was hoping for some help with maths. I've fallen seriously behind, with everything that's happened, and I'm struggling to catch up. Would you mind tutoring me?' Alannah was starting to feel the cold.

'I'd love to. Anytime you need help, seek me out in the library after school.' He turned to face her, removing his coat.

'Here, looks like you need this more than me.' As he stepped up to drape it over her shoulders, a door slammed behind them.

'That won't be necessary. It's much warmer inside anyway.' Liam stood at the door, glaring at Austin, who was equally unimpressed.

Did Austin growl at Liam?

Liam turned his attention to Alannah. 'I've been looking everywhere for you, Lana. You've been gone a while.'

Shit. She forgot she had left him hanging when she took that call from Cole. Alannah's eyes lowered as she brought her hand up to cover her mouth. 'Sorry Liam. I had a run in with Monique, but Austin came to my rescue.' She turned back to Austin. 'Thanks again. I'll see you on Monday, okay?'

'No worries. See you then.'

Liam led her back inside. They were walking through the downstairs crowd when Liam stopped and put his hand on her shoulder. 'Are you okay? You mentioned an altercation with Monique. Did she hurt you?'

'I'm fine. Nothing really happened. They merely expelled a bunch of hot air.'

'Oh look, isn't that precious? A touching family moment for the Winters clan.' A deep, gruff voice behind Alannah startled her and she spun around to find one of the flannel-clad red necks staring down at her, a lewd grin on his face. 'Not that I'd mind touching a piece of that arse.'

A few loud sniggers came from the four blokes standing behind him.

'Back off, Chad, and keep your hands to your filthy selves.' Liam's tone was serious.

'Or you'll what? You don't scare us, Winters. None of your kind do.' Chad—the muscular behemoth—stepped a sizeable stride forward, closing the gap between himself and Alannah, his mates filing in around her.

'I'm warning you, Chad. Get away from her.' Liam's body pressed into her back, his hand still on her shoulder.

Chad reached out to grab Alannah and the next moment became a blur as Liam pulled her out of the way and dived at the guy.

'*Liam!*' She screamed as the five burly blokes piled in and started pummelling Liam.

A series of shouts and crashing noises followed and a few seconds later some of Liam's friends were pulling the brutes off him and throwing their own punches.

Alannah felt hands grab her, trying to pull her away from the fray, but she resisted. She could not see Liam and her mind raced through all the horrid possibilities.

Brendan was fastening the belt on his pants when he heard the ruckus coming from downstairs. He shot Chelsea a look. 'Stay here.' Without further ado, he sped off toward the racket. As he approached the stairs, he heard Alannah's shrieking. Drawing closer, he felt her panic, prompting him to pick up the pace.

Shit! It's the fucking ogres. He noticed Blake trying to restrain Alannah, who was protesting and shouting something about Liam. *Where is Liam?* A bright flash from the middle of the skirmish answered his question a second later. *Fuck!* Things were about to get ugly. He needed to step in and do something.

When Blake spotted him, he cried out, 'Brendan! Get Alannah out of here.'

'But I…'

'*No! Get her to safety*. We can't fight properly with her here.' Blake pushed Alannah into his arms, before jumping into the scuffle.

Alannah was frantic. '*Liam's in there*. He's been hurt!'

Brendan pinned her flailing arms to her sides with his own. 'He'll be fine. Now let's get you home.'

'*No, Brendan*, you've got to help him!' She tried to push away from him.

But Brendan picked her up and threw her over his shoulder. 'He has enough backup, and he will fight better knowing you're safe. Now come on.'

She continued to thrash at him, even gouged at the bare skin on his back as he walked her out to the carpark.

Brendan was relieved to find Austin outside, standing by his car. 'Need a lift?'

'Yup. Thanks man.'

Austin opened one of the back doors and Brendan piled in with Alannah, grappling her to prevent her escape.

Once the car was moving, Austin laughed. 'Your cousin's pretty feisty, Brendan.'

He looked at Alannah, still struggling in his arms, and grinned. 'Yeah, she's a Winters alright.' Once away from the fight, Brendan was able to focus on calming her, stroking her arms as he whispered, 'Hush. It's okay, Lana. Liam will be okay, I promise.'

She went limp in his arms, curling up and resting her head against his naked chest.

The skin-to-skin contact was thrilling. Brendan pulled her into a tighter embrace and stuffed his face in her strawberry scented hair. *Gods, it smells good!* Brendan started imagining those locks wrapped around his hands as he kissed her, as he fucked her. He knew he should not be having these thoughts about her, especially with her in this condition. But she pressed her sexy body up against him, rendering him powerless to resist. Feeling her trembling and the faint sound of sobbing switched his thoughts back to concern for her wellbeing.

'Hey, everything will be okay. I promise.' He continued to whisper soothing words for the rest of the drive home.

Chapter Five

Alannah jumped out of bed with a thumping heartbeat. First her sleeping mind then her waking thoughts fixated on the fight the night before and she teared up when she thought about Liam. She had to find him and make sure he was okay. A quick check of her alarm clock told her it was only 6AM. She put on her white silk dressing gown and grey slippers, before making her way down the hall.

There was a good chance the boys were still asleep, so she found Liam's room and knocked lightly on the door. No response. She tried the door handle: unlocked. After gently opening the door, Alannah peeked inside. Liam was sleeping soundly in his bed. Wanting to see the extent of his injuries, she stepped inside.

As soon as Liam's form came into full view, Alannah gasped. He had pushed his quilt down to his hips, revealing a chest of sun-kissed skin. *Wow, that looks like an eight pack!* She could also see most of his happy trail. *He sleeps naked!* It was tempting to tug the quilt a little lower, but she remembered why she was invading his privacy. This was the second reason for her gasping. There was not a single scratch on his perfect body, not even a bruise on his face. *How did he escape so unscathed? Did I imagine last night?*

She slipped out of the room and crept back toward her own. But she paused outside Brendan's. Waking him at such an ungodly hour was tempting fate, but she needed to ask him some questions. She sighed. The questions would have to wait. But she could not move away. Perhaps it was perverse curiosity leading her to open his door.

Apparently both guys overheated in their sleep. Brendan, unlike his big brother, was lying on his side, with the quilt tangled around his legs. He also slept naked. Some marks on his back drew Alannah's attention, so she moved closer to inspect them. There were a series of deep gouges, likely from a girl's finger nails. She grinned. *Kinky fucker!* But a flashback from the party smacked her in the face. Brendan had picked her up and carried her away from the fight. Those marks were her doing. *Shit!*

Brendan moaned and rolled onto his back. Alannah jumped back and stumbled when her feet landed on a pile of clothes. She righted her balance and started for the door.

'Mm, Lana.'

Alannah froze. *I'm so busted! How do I explain this?* She slowly turned around to face the music.

But Brendan's eyes remained closed. *Is he dreaming about me?* That was when she noticed the impressive tent he made with the quilt. *Geeezuuus!* She stood there gobsmacked. *No wonder he is so popular with the girls.* His quilt started moving down and she bolted.

After Ross and Nora joined Alannah for breakfast, they both left for work and the house fell silent again because the boys were still in bed. She decided to take the opportunity to video call her two best friends in Melbourne.

'Alannah! It's so good to see you,' Emma cried.

'We've missed you so much,' Melissa added.

'Hi guys. I've missed you too.'

Emma frowned. 'How have you been? Are they treating you okay over there?'

'My family here have been very supportive. Aunt Nora's an absolute gem.'

'Oh good,' Emma replied. 'And what about school? Cole mentioned you thought it was crazy there.'

'It is, but I haven't had any real problems other than falling behind with my studies. The worst thing that's really happened was a run in with the popular girls at a party last night. You know the type, like Olivia's group. Of course, I put them in their place.'

'You go girl.' Emma clapped her hands with delight.

'So, have you made friends with any hot guys?' Melissa asked.

'A few.'

Emma's eyes lit up. 'Oooh. Are any of them viable hook-ups or boyfriend material?'

'I suppose a couple are.'

'Alannah, you dirty minx,' Melissa giggled.

Alannah rolled her eyes. 'Please don't tell Cole though, in case the news hurts him. I'm not ready to start dating any of the guys here, but still. I miss Cole heaps and I know it'd kill me to think he'd moved on already.'

Emma nodded. 'Yeah, yeah. We get it. So, what are your dreamboat cousins like these days?'

Alannah let out a sigh. 'Well let's just say Liam is one of those hot prospects who I mentioned before. Like seriously out of this world hot.'

Emma laughed as Melissa replied, 'O. M. G. Seriously?'

Beaming, she nodded. 'Yeah, seriously. That said, he's also the most popular guy at school and hangs out with a bunch of A-holes, so I don't like my chances. I'm not really his type.'

Emma shrugged. 'Hm, pity. What about the younger cousin? The totally fuckable one. His name was Brendan, right?' Emma had met both the guys at Alannah's mum's funeral and Brendan left the biggest impression on her friend.

'He's cool. A lot like me, except funnier and a hell of a lot sluttier. I hang with his friends at school.'

'Do you agree with Emma? Is he totally fuckable?' Melissa asked with an impish grin.

Alannah blushed again, remembering the eyeful she had copped earlier that day. 'Yeah. He's slept with most of the girls in our year level; so, they clearly think so too.'

Melissa furrowed her brow. 'So, is he one of your choices?'

Alannah sighed. 'Brendan and I are too close, like best friends. Always have been. It's different with Liam, though. I grew up crushing on him and now…' She fanned her face for effect.

'Makes sense to me,' Emma admitted with a giggle, but Melissa shook her head.

The conversation shifted to gossiping about her old school for a while, which was followed by the tear-jerking farewells with promises to meet up in the winter break.

The scent of fried food drew Alannah to the kitchen at midday. When she entered, she found Liam and Brendan both stuffing their faces with the makings of a full Irish breakfast. It smelled incredible.

Liam looked up at her, smiling once he finished his mouthful. 'Morning, Lana. Did you pull up okay?'

'Yeah. I've been up for hours, so good afternoon to both of you.'

Brendan laughed and scoffed another mouthful.

'I guess I overslept a bit,' Liam agreed. 'Help yourself to the leftovers.'

She filled her plate with bacon, sausages, hash browns, mushrooms, and beans. Sitting at the table across from Liam, she cast her eyes over him again, looking for battle scars.

When he looked up, his eyes focused on her. 'You didn't get hurt from the fight last night, did you?'

'No. Not a scratch.' Alannah blushed at her choice of words and glanced at Brendan.

Of course, Brendan noticed. He narrowed his eyes at her.

She turned her attention back to Liam. 'I'm surprised you don't have any bruises. I hope you didn't end up with any internal injuries.'

'I'm fine. Don't worry about me. I can hold my own in a fight. I'm glad you're okay.' After finishing his food, he stood and put his plate and cutlery in the dishwasher. He turned back to her. 'Sorry, but I gotta fly. I need to get to a study session at Blake's. I'll see you tonight.'

Alannah tried to hide her disappointment, instead focussing on her meal. It was her first weekend with the boys in years and Liam was already bailing. After swallowing her mouthful, she looked at him. 'Sure, no probs. See ya.' She watched him go with a sigh and continued eating.

'Hey, Lana… have any good dreams lately?' Brendan inquired after dropping his plate in the dishwasher.

She shot him a sidelong glance.

He sat down again, this time directly across from her. 'I had a great dream this morning.'

Alannah felt the colour in her cheeks rise. 'Oh? What was it about?'

Brendan leaned forward. 'A girl with long black hair, dressed in white entered my room while I slept.'

Her eyes grew wider. 'You knew?'

'I sensed you enter my room. It woke me up. What were you doing there, Lana?'

'I uh… um, I… just wanted to check on you after last night, to make sure you weren't badly injured.'

'Right. You do realise, I didn't get involved with the fighting?' Brendan paused to gather a moment of awkward silence. 'So, did you like what you saw?'

Alannah's cheeks turned crimson.

He smirked. 'I got you good, this time.'

'Yeah, I guess you did.' She burst into laughter and Brendan joined in. Alannah felt weeks of tension releasing from her muscles. Regaining her composure, Alannah realised she had not been the subject of one of his twisted wet dreams. *At least not this morning anyway. Am I relieved or disappointed?* She finished eating and headed into the living room.

Brendan followed her. 'You wanna know how I detected your presence when I was asleep?'

Alannah slumped down on the couch. 'I suppose.'

'I used magic.'

'Ha ha. Very funny. You gonna give me the real answer?' Alannah replied playfully.

'I'm serious. I'm a mage. So is Liam and every other member of our bloodline. That includes you. You're not initiated, so you can't use your powers yet.'

Alannah's brow furrowed as she glanced at him askew. In a rare serious moment, intense focus replaced the usual impish glint in his eyes.

'You still don't believe me? Go grab that book of your mum's.'

'Fine.' Alannah retrieved the black leather binder. When she returned to the sofa, she sat next to Brendan and placed the book on the coffee table in front of them.

'This was your mum's Book of Shadows. It's both a spell book and reference guide for our practices. All mages have one, but this one is special because our ancestors handed it down the line from the original Winters woman. See this page?' He flicked to the second leaf which had a long list of names and signatures. 'These are the dedications of each mage who has used this book. They were all women, and they signed this page on the day of their initiation.'

'Wow, this is an incredible piece of family history.'

'Yes, it is. My own Book of Shadows is not an impressive heirloom.' He stood and found his own leather-bound volume. It was much thinner and the symbol on the front was different, but otherwise it looked similar. The title on the front page was in English: *Brendan's Book of Shadows*. 'Most mages need to create their own from scratch. The women of the Winters clan, however, wanted to hand down their knowledge to the first-born daughter of each generation. What you have there is a collection of very powerful spells and rituals from centuries of mage craft.'

Alannah was gobsmacked. She took another look at the list of names. 'So, who was the first Winters woman? This list of names goes on for pages.'

'Yup. That's because the first Winters mage was the daughter of the Goddess Cailleach. She was born in the Bronze Age.'

She stared at Brendan, completely dumbfounded. *Is he pulling my leg? How can that be true?* 'I didn't think the Celts had any written records. How could this book be from that time? not to mention the pages couldn't have survived for so long.'

'I understand your scepticism. It took me a while to believe some of our history when I started training. From what I understand, our ancestors created most of the book much later, when a written form of the Gaelic language emerged. They passed the knowledge down orally at first. But the dedication pages start with Bébinn Gheimhridh, our first Ancestor. Look here.' He pointed to a name. 'This was an archaic form of writing created by mages. All of the pages in this book have been magically treated to preserve them.' Brendan paused a moment. 'I'll get you a drink and give you a moment to process things. I imagine you will have some questions for me when I get back.'

Alannah was still unsure about the whole magic side of things, but the family history she was learning was fascinating. She wanted to know more.

When Brendan returned, he handed her a cup of tea.

'Thanks.' She took a few sips in silence before questioning him. 'So, are the Winters clan the only mages? Is that why Winters women have a reputation for being powerful?'

'No. There are millions of mage families around the world, all dating back to around Eight Hundred B.C. Mages are essentially demigods, the result of powerful beings from the celestial realms coupling with humans. We have come to call these beings Gods and Goddesses and they were worshipped by various pagan cultures.' He took a sip of his own tea.

Enthralled by his explanation, Alannah waited silently for him to continue.

'The Creator God, Lugh, fathered most Irish mage families. But Cailleach, the creator Goddess, gave rise to the Winters clan.

This is why we are the only matriarchal clan of Celtic origin. Being matriarchal is the reason we carry the surname of our Grandmother rather than our Grandfather, and why your mum didn't change her name when she married your dad.'

'Wait. Does that mean I'm like the head of the family now?'

'Not yet. Get initiated and became a full magus. Then you'd own me.' Brendan waggled his brows.

Alannah grinned. 'Sweet. So, what's the deal with magic? How does it work?'

'Mages channel different sources of mana, or magic power. Most of us focus on attuning ourselves to a couple of power sources, which we refer to as our attunements. It allows us to specialise so we can graduate to full magus status when we turn eighteen. These days, most mages use their attunements to guide their career choices. The spells we cast make use of our own attunements. Rituals, on the other hand, tend to be a joint effort. They involve a group of mages and are either a more powerful version of a spell, or they are a form of worship. We still pay homage to the Celtic Gods and Goddesses in this town.'

Alannah nodded. She was beginning to understand all the references to the Goddess Cailleach. 'So, are there any other mages at our school?'

He sat back and put his feet up on the ottoman. 'Yup. There's a bunch of 'em. In fact, mages make up about thirty-five percent of the town's population.'

Wide eyed, Alannah gaped at him. 'So, who are the mages I know at school?'

'Well, there's Cara for one, plus Connor and Bailey. Most of Liam's friends too.'

She sipped her tea as she digested this information. 'And each of you have different power source thingies?'

Brendan smiled. 'Attunements, yup. They are the main mana sources we can channel. As initiates, we spend a lot of time learning what mana we are most attuned to. Once we have identified our two primary sources, we hone our skills by practising basic spells and rituals that use them.'

'So, what are your attunements?'

Brendan stiffened and hesitated for a moment. 'Emotions and the five senses, which means I will most likely become an enchanter when I reach full magus status.'

Alannah wondered why he became uncomfortable with the conversation. 'Why do I get the feeling you're not happy about being an enchanter?'

He sighed. 'It's not that I mind being one, we just get a bad rap these days. There have been some notorious enchanters throughout history.'

'Really? Like whom?'

'Well Hitler's the first who comes to mind. I swear a few bad eggs and the rest of us are in the doghouse.'

'Oh wow.' Alannah started thinking about all the historical figures she knew about and wondered how many of them were mages. 'Can you demonstrate your powers?'

Relaxing, Brendan gave her a wicked grin. 'I'd love to, but Liam would totally kick my arse if he caught me.'

Her curiosity piqued. 'Why? What can you do?'

He leaned closer and held her gaze. 'I can read and manipulate emotions and enhance the senses. Makes for some pretty wild times in the sack.'

She blushed. 'Oh. So, uh… what can, uh… Liam do?'

Brendan laughed. 'Well, he is attuned to the elements and energy forces, which he uses for offensive magic like fireballs and lightning bolts. He is training to become a warlock.'

'What about your parents? What are they?'

He sat back again. 'Dad's an abjurer, like your mum was. They do healing and protective magic. Mum's a shaman who can channel elemental and emotional mana. She mostly uses it to help animals, which is why she's such a damn good vet. Cara's training to be a shaman too, although she's more interested in working with plants.' He paused and studied her. 'I'm sorry, I've overwhelmed you. I think we should leave all further talk of magic for another day.'

'Not a bad idea. Thanks.'

'You wanna watch a movie?'

Alannah picked up the DVD of *The Guard*. 'Actually, I do need to start studying this.'

The moment Liam walked into the living room late that afternoon, Alannah accosted him. She leaped up from the couch and blocked his path. *What the hell?*

'So, is it true?' she asked.

Feeling completely bewildered, he bit. 'Is what true?'

'That you can lob lightning bolts and shit.' She used an odd hand gesture to demonstrate her idea of a lightning bolt.

Liam let out a sigh of relief. 'So, he finally told you.'

'Yeah, Brendan told me what we are and all about what you can do. I'm still not sure I believe it though.'

He raised his eyebrows in surprise. 'So, he didn't give you a demonstration of his own powers?'

Alannah shook her head. 'No. That would've been inappropriate, and he said you'd kick his arse if he did.'

'Well he's not wrong. Come on.' He started walking out.

'Where are you going?' she asked, trailing him.

'The training room. It's safer to demonstrate in there.'

Liam led her into the cellar that had been built especially for training and group rituals. She gasped as she took in the sights. He had forgotten how awe inspiring the room had been for him the first time he entered. The most obvious feature was the enormous pentagram painted on the stone floor, each point marked with the symbols of the five elements of ritual magic: earth, air, fire, water, and Aether.

As her eyes shifted from the decorated floor, they scanned the bookshelves, lining the North wall, and locked behind bulletproof glass. Next, her attention wandered to the East where a series of shadow boards held various magic tools and weapons. She turned to him. 'How did I not know about this room before? Has it always been down here?'

'The house was built around this room. Our parents kept it locked tight and hidden from us until our initiation. I probably shouldn't be bringing you down here yet, but you deserve to learn the truth.'

She ran her hands along Liam's ritual robe.

'Oh, I should ask you to refrain from touching anything at this stage. We have consecrated most of our tools for individual use.'

Alannah snapped her hand back and offered him an apologetic smile. 'Sorry.'

He moved further into the room and picked up his staurolite elemental talisman ring. 'This ring has been charged with the four physical elements.' After giving Alannah a glimpse, he slipped it on his right index finger. He stood back from the target on the South wall, pulling Alannah back with him by a gentle tug of her arm. Taking aim, he fired a bolt of electricity from his pointed finger straight at the bullseye of the grounded target.

'*Fucking hell!*' Alannah cried. Her mouth gaped open when he looked at her.

Liam smiled. 'Are you okay? I hope that wasn't too *shocking* for you.'

Clenching her mouth shut, she slapped him lightly on the arm. 'The only thing that was too shocking for me was your terrible attempt at humour.'

'Right, well I hope you are okay because things are about to heat up in here.' This time when he aimed at the target, he shot a fireball about the size of a golf ball at a heatproof target. It sizzled out as soon as it hit the bullseye.

'Wow. That's incredible. So, it is true! Magic is fucking real.' Alannah gasped, her eyes wide like a kid in a toy store.

'Yes, it is most definitely real.' Liam smiled at her amazement.

Chapter Six

Alannah decided there was no time like the present to broach the topic with Ross and Nora. They sat at the dining table for a family meal, both boys backing her up. 'So, I've been thinking, I'd like to be initiated.'

Nora's fork fell to her plate as she gawked at Alannah.

Liam and Brendan both shot her reassuring smiles.

Ross clenched his jaw as he purposefully placed his cutlery along the side of his plate. 'No.'

'*What, why not?*' Brendan jumped to her defence. 'She has the r—'

'Because it is too dangerous,' Ross interjected.

Alannah could see Brendan was about to speak on her behalf again, but she put a hand up to silence him. 'With all due respect, Uncle Ross, don't you think I'd be more equipped to defend myself from said dangers if I trained properly?'

'Alannah makes a very valid point, Dad.' This time it was Liam who had her back.

'Becoming initiated would expose Alannah to a greater set of risks. Things none of you could even begin to fathom.' He sighed and drank a large mouthful of his wine. 'Listen, Alannah. Your mother removed you from the magic world for a good reason and I'm not willing to disrespect her wishes after all the sacrifices she made to protect you.'

The room fell silent for a moment.

Liam cleared his throat. 'Look, Dad. Aunt Aileen might have been able to hide her safely in Melbourne, but Alannah is now living in a predominantly magical town and she can't even see what she's up against. How is ignorance going to protect her here?'

'I expect the four of us should be able to handle that for her. With your abilities and proximity, Liam, you are well positioned to defend her should the need arise.'

Alannah could see the fierce intensity in Brendan's glare, and she expected to see smoke billowing out of his nostrils any moment. 'But she's a Winters woman, for Christ's sake! And the first-born of her generation at that. She's entitled to her birthright. Shouldn't this be her decision?'

Ross turned to Brendan, scowling. 'Being a Winters woman is exactly why she shouldn't be initiated. I will not have any more shame brought upon this family.' He stormed out of the room.

Blinking from her uncle's outburst, Alannah turned her attention to Nora.

Nora shook her head. 'I'm sorry dear. It's a touchy subject for him.'

'But why? What happened?' Alannah asked.

After a pregnant pause, Nora sighed. 'Your grandmother and great aunt grew power-hungry and tried to overthrow the Arch Mage. They were both outlawed for practising forbidden magic.'

'Oh.' Alannah did not know what else to say. *Is that what Ross fears will happen to me?* She did not think she was a bad person, nor was she ambitious. Perhaps she could convince him things would be different for her.

They all finished their dinner in silence. After cleaning up, Brendan approached her. 'Hey, Lana. Connor's having a few friends over tonight. Wanna join me?'

'Sounds great, but…' Alannah looked toward Liam, wondering what his plans were.

Shrugging, Liam forced a smile. 'I've got a heap of study to do this weekend, so I won't be much company. Sorry.'

'Right. I'm gonna change. Our ride will be here in half an hour.' Brendan walked out of the kitchen.

As Alannah was about to head to her own room, Liam stopped her. 'Wait a sec, Lana.'

She turned to find Liam biting his lip. 'What's up?'

'Please be careful. Brendan has some pretty shady friends. I don't trust them, and I hate not being there to protect you tonight. Do me a favour and either stick with Brendan or Cara, okay?'

This surprised her. 'I thought you hated Cara?'

'There's some bad blood between us, but that has more to do with our relationship history. She's still a good person and one of the few people in that group I trust.'

'I'll be careful. I promise.'

'Good.' He relaxed and smiled slightly. Walking up, he hugged her, taking her by surprise.

She returned the embrace, savouring the contact. Pressing up against his rock-hard abs felt incredible and the ocean-fresh scent surrounding her was intoxicating.

He whispered in her ear, 'Have a good night.' Releasing her, he swiftly left the room.

✽

'Good evening, Alannah. You look stunning tonight.' Austin was holding the front passenger door of his car open for her.

Alannah wondered who said chivalry was dead. She took the opportunity to look at his wheels properly for the first time. Austin drove a black Lexus with heavily tinted windows that blocked any view of the occupants from the outside. The vehicle was sleek and sexy, much like the driver. 'Hey, Austin. Thanks.' She climbed in and noticed the heavy music playing through the stereo.

'Ah man, I love these guys!' Brendan declared as he jumped into the back.

When she glanced at the streaming display on Austin's phone, Alannah saw the band was Grey Hearts Red. 'They sound good. Who are they?'

'A local hard rock band. They put on a great live show too,' Austin replied as he sat behind the wheel.

'Nice.' Once the car was moving, Alannah gazed out the window and let her mind wander. After the unbelievable day she'd had, chilling out and having some fun was exactly what she needed.

Five minutes later, they stopped, and Cara burst into the back of the car. 'Hi guys! Oh my God, Alannah, I'm so glad Brendan finally told you about magic!'

So much for an easy night, Alannah thought. She spun around and focussed on Cara. 'Wait, you knew about me being in the dark?'

Cara looked sheepish. 'Yeah, Brendan wanted us all to keep our mouths shut until he'd had a chance to explain things. It's been a hard secret to keep, believe me.'

Alannah turned to Austin, then back to Cara and whispered, 'Does Austin know about this stuff?'

'Yes, Alannah, I know that you are all mages.' Austin's raspy voice startled her.

'But you're not a mage, are you?'

He laughed softly. 'No, I'm not.'

When they arrived at Connor's house, Alannah discovered 'a few friends over' was not an accurate description for the gathering. It was a full-fledged party, though smaller than the one on Friday night.

As they approached the door, Cara linked arms with Alannah. 'Come on girl, let's get tanked!'

They filed into the hallway when Brendan walked up behind Alannah and Cara. 'Excuse me ladies, this house is full of lusty hotties just waiting for me.' He put his arms around them both. 'That is unless either or both of you want to learn first-hand how magical I am.'

'*Ugh, gross!*' Cara cried, pushing him away. 'You are such a man-slut. Why don't you try using your powers for good occasionally?'

Directing his gaze at Alannah, Brendan grinned. 'What can I say? Once a rogue, always a rogue.' He took off and threw his arm around some redhead standing by the beer keg.

Alannah leaned in to whisper to Cara, 'The way he uses his powers to seduce girls; isn't that wrong?'

'It's one of those moral grey areas. He doesn't make them do anything they don't want to, so it's not like rape or anything, but it is a more selfish use of his powers. He isn't hurting anyone, so it's not outlawed behaviour,' Cara explained. She poured a beer and handed it to Alannah before getting herself one.

They found their host surrounded by a few other friends. The short, spunky red-headed Amy engaged Connor in conversation. Alannah recognised the signs well enough to know Amy would not appreciate any disruptions.

The other couple in the room was Ben and Bianca. Ben's long, golden locks had fallen forward, blocking his face, but he's body language was enough to suggest his intentions and Bianca was every bit as complicit in the flirting.

Everyone was pairing off and Alannah's thoughts shifted to Austin. *Where did he disappear to? Is he hooking up with someone?* A pang of jealousy pinched at her gut, startling her. *Why should I care, especially when Liam is still a prospect?*

After finding a couch away from the crowds, Alannah needed to ask, 'Um, Cara…'

Cara sighed. 'Ugh, Brendan warned me you might try to bombard me with mage questions. What would you like to know?'

'No, this isn't about magic. It's about Liam.'

This time, Cara rolled her eyes, but Alannah also noticed her stiffen a little. 'Go on.'

She put on her best pleading face as she addressed Cara. 'He briefly mentioned your ill feelings were the result of something that happened between the two of you. I was hoping you could fill me in.'

'Oh, that.' Cara sipped her drink. 'We used to be good friends when I moved here in Year Seven.' She paused a moment, taking another swig of beer before elaborating. 'I developed a pretty big crush on him during that time. Then one night, he kissed me.' She let out a derisive laugh. 'The next day he acted like nothing happened and when I questioned him, he told me we could never be more than friends, that I needed to get over him.'

'Shit, Cara, I'm so sorry. I had no idea Liam could be like that. That's a horrid thing to do.' Alannah's opinion of Liam had taken a bit of a plunge on her first day at Gaeilge High, but Cara's story was sending it to rock bottom. 'He was such a sweet kid when we were younger. What the hell happened to him?'

Cara's head drooped. 'Truth is, he was still sweet then too, but he let his need for social status and the approval of his parents get the better of him.'

'What do you mean?'

She looked back up at Alannah. 'I'm not a pure mage, so his parents would not have approved of me dating him. Your family, along with several other clans, are pretty strict about only coupling with full mages, to keep the bloodline pure.'

Alannah's jaw hit the floor. 'That's so archaic!'

'You're telling me. I'm kinda thankful in a way, that I'm not a pure mage. I can't imagine being forced into an arranged marriage. At least in your case, the guy you like is on the pre-approved list, so your Uncle probably won't need to organise a spouse for either of you.' She clapped her hand over her mouth for a moment. 'Oh shit! That probably sounded really rude.'

Still reeling from the revelation, Alannah barely took notice of Cara's tone. 'It's okay. Don't worry about it. But hey, what about Brendan? He doesn't seem to care about how pure a girl's bloodline is.'

'That's true and I respect him for it. He doesn't care for status. That said, I doubt your Uncle would let him openly date a non-pure. I'm guessing that's part of the reason Brendan doesn't commit to one girl. When the time comes, I bet he'll elope to spite his folks.'

Alannah laughed. 'You're probably right.'

'Hey Cara, Alannah.' Jacob approached them with Austin in tow. 'You wanna join us for a game of beer pong?'

'Sounds great,' Alannah agreed. It was exactly what she needed.

Cara jumped up. 'Absolutely!' She pulled Alannah up from the sofa and they headed outside.

Ugh! Damn hangovers. Alannah dragged her sorry arse out of bed and glanced at the clock: 11AM. Wondering if it was too late to join the others for breakfast, she threw some warm clothes on and made her way downstairs.

Liam stood at the island bench drinking a smoothie. He raised a single eyebrow and gave her an amused grin when she entered the kitchen. 'Morning sunshine. Drink a bit, did you?'

Her splitting headache had her in a foul mood, so she replied by flipping him off.

Laughing, he grabbed a green concoction in a clear glass bottle, along with a shot glass and handed them to her. 'Here, have some of this.'

Alannah eyed the elixir in the fancy flask doubtfully.

'It's Dad's magically enhanced hangover cure. Perfectly safe, trust me.'

Thankfully, she did trust Liam, so she poured some of the potion into the glass and sculled it. '*Yuck!*' It tasted like a disgusting mix of wheatgrass and bitter herbs. She handed the bottle back to Liam, sitting down to wait for it to kick in. Amazingly, it only took a couple of minutes for the fog to clear and her stomach to settle. She smiled. 'Wow, that stuff's incredible. Your dad ought to sell it.'

'He does, but only to magic folk. Like most potions, it's toxic for humans.'

'Oh.' It was going to take a long time to wrap her head around the magic world. 'Must be handy having a father with magical healing abilities.'

'More than you'd realise,' Liam agreed. 'He fixes me up good whenever I get in fights.'

'Oh my God! That's why you looked unharmed after the fight on Friday night!'

Liam nodded.

She wondered how bad his injuries were before Ross healed him. Another thought struck: *Why didn't Brendan get his dad to tend to the scratches I left on his back? Did he enjoy that?* Pushing those questions to the back of her mind, she grabbed some toast and made her way to the table.

A few minutes later, Brendan sauntered in with messy hair, wearing a stupid grin and the same clothes from last night. *Trust Brendan to make the walk of shame look so hot.*

Wait, what? Alannah blinked away the ridiculous thought. *Casual, I mean* casual!

Liam glared at Brendan. 'Did you just get home?'

'Yup. Morning Lana.' He shot her a wicked grin before raiding the fridge.

'You were meant to keep an eye on Lana last night.' Liam clenched his jaw.

After grabbing the milk, he shut the fridge. 'I did, right Cuz?' He winked at her. 'I made sure she got home safe before heading over to Bianca's.'

Liam gave her a sidelong glance. 'Lana?'

'It's true. I stuck with Cara all night and Brendan was never far.'

As he exhaled, Liam's shoulders relaxed. 'You've been spending a lot of time with that nymph lately. Be careful Brendan, people might start thinking something serious is going on.'

'People can think what they like. Bianca's only a friend… with a lot of benefits.' Brendan poured a huge bowl of cereal and a coffee. He sat across from Alannah at the table. 'Where are the folks?'

Liam sat next to her. 'Council meeting. Which reminds me, Lana, we need to talk about getting you initiated.'

Brendan sprayed the remnants of his mouthful of coffee across the table, staring at Liam. 'This is a first! Liam defying Dad's orders. Never thought I'd see the day.'

'Well, this is the first time I've disagreed with him so adamantly. I really do think Lana needs to be initiated.' Turning to Alannah, he continued, 'That is, of course, if you want to do it.'

She did not know what to think. Uncle Ross' downright refusal to discuss the issue had infuriated her, but it also got her thinking about the reasons her mum had for hiding her. 'I dunno, to be honest. I don't know what the risks are.'

Liam sighed. 'I think staying in the dark is a bigger risk, especially in this town. You can't see past glamour, so you don't know who you're dealing with when you're out in public. Plus, it could be good to learn some protective spells.'

'Wait, what do you mean see "past glamour?"' Alannah inquired.

Liam shot Brendan a stern glance. 'You didn't tell her about other magicals?'

'Not yet. You told me to break things to her slowly. She was already reeling from the little I covered yesterday.'

Alannah raised a hand. 'Hang on a minute, guys. Firstly — Liam — you told Brendan to tell me about magic? Why couldn't you do it?'

Liam groaned. 'Because Brendan would be able to read your emotions and gauge when it was appropriate to tell you. Plus, if you got hysterical, he would have been able to calm you down.'

Alannah directed a piercing gaze at Brendan. 'You've been reading my emotions?'

He nodded.

'All of them?'

He lowered his gaze and nodded again.

She felt so violated. *How many private feelings has he witnessed me experience?*

Liam hung his head. 'If it's any consolation, half the time he can't switch it off. Besides, I was the one who asked him to read you.'

Narrowing her eyes, she spoke in a deadly serious tone. 'Brendan, have you told anyone about my feelings?'

He sat upright, shaking his head. 'Gods no! I keep that shit to myself. I do have a moral code, fuzzy as it may seem.'

'Well I still don't like it. Please refrain from reading me where possible in future.'

'Duly noted.' Curling his top lip, Brendan wrinkled the bridge of his nose.

Why is he taking offence when he wronged me? Alannah sighed. 'Now tell me, what are these other magicals?'

'Other supernatural creatures. They hide behind magic known as glamour to disguise their true form from humans and the uninitiated. Fairies, or fae as we tend to call them, are the most common,' Liam explained.

She was utterly gobsmacked. 'Uh, so… what else is there?'

'Almost anything you can recall from myth or legend is likely to be real to some extent, although humans tended to twist the truth in their versions of the stories,' replied Liam.

'But if these creatures are hiding with… what's that magic called?'

Brendan returned to the conversation. 'Glamour.'

Alannah nodded. 'Right, if they use glamour, how did these so-called myths come about?'

After a nod from Liam, Brendan answered, 'We used to all coexist openly with humans, but they started to hunt us like monsters when they developed monotheistic religions.'

'So, if fairies are real, what about elves and dwarves?'

'They exist,' Brendan confirmed. 'You familiar with *The Lord of the Rings*?'

'Yeah, of course.' Alannah knew the books and movies inside out.

'Tolkien was a mage, so he described them pretty accurately.'

'Orcs and goblins?' Alannah asked.

Brendan nodded. 'Yup, both real.'

'Wow,' she whispered. Then raising her voice, 'What about unicorns?'

Brendan smiled. 'You still got a thing for them, huh? You'll be pleased to know they are real, although rare. Apparently only virgin mages can see them though.'

Alannah felt a wave of disappointment and tried her hardest to keep a neutral face.

Brendan snorted. 'Kidding. About the virgin thing anyway. They are rare though. I had you there for a moment.' He gave her a knowing grin.

Shit! Brendan must have been reading her. 'Yeah, you got me good.'

Liam cleared his throat. 'It would take a long time to explain everything to you, so I think you would benefit from a structured training plan, much like what Brendan and I have undergone. You would start with the theory. When you are ready, you can be initiated and begin the practical lessons.'

Alannah sighed. 'You mean if I want to? I'm still not sure about learning magic.'

'Think about it. But remember, there are some real monsters out there, Lana, and you are safer seeing people for what they are.'

<h1 style="text-align:center">Chapter Seven</h1>

Austin looked up at Alannah from his homework and smiled. His eyes were almost glowing, and the effect was incredibly alluring. 'Did you need some help with maths today?'

Sitting down next to him at the library table, Alannah became overwhelmed by his strong, spicy fragrance. Everything about this man's appearance was such a contrast to Liam's beauty, yet she still found him insanely sexy. 'Yeah, I do, if that's okay?'

'Of course. What topic is stumping you?'

She laughed. 'All of them. But let's start with angle geometry.' After opening her textbook, she found the section that had been frustrating her the most.

Austin was a brilliant teacher, so patient and clear in his explanations. Within an hour, she had the concepts down pat.

'Wow! I totally get it now. Thank you, Austin, you're amazing.'

He was beaming from her praise. 'No problem. You should try some more practice questions to consolidate your understanding.'

Alannah attempted to do that, but after a couple of questions, her mind started to wander. She dropped her pen and gazed upon the gorgeous guy sitting next to her. He had gone back to his own maths, which looked beyond complicated. 'Austin?'

His focus returned to her. 'Yes?'

'Are you some kind of magical person? I get the sense you are super-human somehow.'

A soft laugh escaped his luscious lips. 'I'll take that as a compliment.' Leaning closer, he dropped his voice to a whisper. 'But, yes, you are right. I am not human. If you can detect that before initiation, I imagine you'll be a very powerful mage one day.'

Alannah frowned, remembering what she learned of her grandmother. 'Not too powerful, I hope.'

The comment earned her a sidelong glance. 'Would you like to know what I am?'

Curiosity dangled a length of twine in front of her, and like an impulsive kitten, Alannah almost reached out to grab it. But this world was still too new to her. 'No, not yet. I want to learn more about the true nature of magical people first. That way I won't let pop culture influence me with prejudice.'

He gave her a nod. 'That's a very noble approach. Perhaps you could try teaching the word "tolerance" to your cousin, Liam.'

The thought of Liam's attitudes made her sigh. 'I wish I could. Why does he behave like such an arse around you guys?'

'Most pure mages do. You and Brendan are the exceptions, I'm afraid.'

Interesting. Why did Brendan turn out different? Alannah grew up in the human world, ignorant of her heritage, so that explained her position. *But Brendan?* She made a mental note to question him later. 'So, why does having a higher concentration of mage blood make them such pompous pricks?'

Austin laughed heartily, prompting a scowl and shush from the librarian. 'Your colourful language is delightful, Alannah.'

She grinned.

'Pure mages take their position as magic law keepers very seriously.'

'Law keepers?'

'The Gods created mages for the purpose of bringing order to the magic world and ensuring our peaceful coexistence with humans. It is literally your God-given right to rule over us. It is why they make a point of keeping the bloodlines pure, to maintain their power. That's also why it is so common for mage cousins to marry one another.' Austin's tone was verging on bitter.

'Well shit. No wonder you're jumping to help me with my maths.'

His expression softened. 'You think I don't want to do this? I'll take any opportunity to spend time with you, Alannah.'

Those words alone knocked the air out of her, but his gleaming eyes also enchanted her. Alannah could not breathe, let alone speak or move. It was like his gaze trapped her and she savoured every second of it.

'Alannah? Are you okay? You look like you're about to faint.' Austin's voice broke her trance.

Her lungs remembered they needed oxygen and she sucked in a huge breath. 'Yeah, I'm fine.' She gave him a coy smile as she extracted some strands of hair from the side of her face and tucked them behind her ear.

'Hey Lana, time to go.' Brendan appeared out of nowhere, with Liam at his side.

Did Austin use magic? She looked up at her cousins.

Liam was glaring at Austin.

'Give me a sec.' While packing her books away, she took a moment to contemplate Liam's behaviour. *Is he jealous of Austin? But if he really wants me, why hasn't he made his move yet?* 'Okay, I'm ready. Thanks for your help, Austin.'

Another award-winning smile. 'It was a pleasure.'

'I'd like to begin my training tonight,' Alannah announced, breaking the uncomfortable silence that had set in on the drive home.

'That's great, Lana!' Brendan shifted forward on the back seat. 'I'm sure we'll have you initiated in no time. I can't wait to see what your attunements will be.'

She laughed. 'Easy, tiger. I haven't even started with the theory yet. I was hoping to begin with reading up on the different magical people.'

'Let me guess, you want to learn all about Austin's filthy race.' Liam's tone cut to the bone.

Turning to face him, Alannah tried to read his expression, but his attention was still on the road. *How dare he talk to me like that!* 'I don't know what Austin is yet and I don't want to know until I've read up on all the magic races. Same goes for the rest of my friends. I want to learn the facts first before I let the myths cloud my judgement. Besides, I thought *you* were the one who wanted me to know about the *monsters* out there.'

Liam scoffed. 'I wanted you to learn who the *monsters* are so you'd avoid them, not run into their arms.'

'I don't know what your problem is, Liam, and frankly I don't give a crap.' She huffed and crossed her arms, wishing she wasn't sitting next to him in a moving vehicle.

Brendan whistled through his teeth. 'Man, you two are already acting like an old married couple and you haven't even…'

'Shut up, Brendan!' They both snapped at him.

The car fell silent again. Alannah kept her focus fixed on the lush green hills and bushland passing them by as they approached Cailleach Estate. It was such a beautiful part of the world.

When they got home, Liam stormed off to his room and slammed the door.

Brendan laughed at his brother's temper, putting his arm around Alannah's shoulders. 'Come on, Lana, let's get some food, then start on your training.'

There was a remarkable number of books in the cellar. They were organised by subject matter, with one full shelf devoted to the magical races. There were also books dedicated to each of the magus specialisations, others on paganism and spirituality, and an extensive history collection of the Irish mage clans. And all the books sat behind locked, durable glass doors.

Brendan unlocked one of the bookcases and picked out a few volumes for her. 'These are all the beginner guides.'

Alannah flicked through each of the large, hard-cover reference books as he placed them on the reading desk next to her. *Preparing for Initiation*, *A Compendium of Magical People and Beasts*, *The Celtic Pantheon*, and *Celtic Traditions in the Modern Age*. She looked up at Brendan with a wry smile. 'So just a little light reading then.'

'Fear not, Lana. I'm sure you'll power through them. And if nothing else, they'll help you build muscle tone in your arms.' He grinned as he pushed the pile of books toward her.

Her weedy arms sank under their weight and she almost dropped a couple, but Brendan caught them. 'Bloody hell, Brendan, are you trying to kill me, or destroy the books?'

'You're gonna have to start working out, too. Mages need to be physically fit and strong.'

Alannah groaned. 'Seriously?'

Brendan gestured for her to head back upstairs. 'Yup. When we channel mana, we become a conduit for that power, and it can put a lot of stress on the body. Physical and mental endurance are essential. It also pays to prepare for all manner of challenges.'

'I'm not so sure I wanna be a mage anymore,' she complained. Alannah had always hated P.E.

When they returned to the living room, he turned to her and flashed a wicked smile. 'Hey, on the plus side, you could exercise with me and check out this glorious body in action.' He flexed his biceps as he spoke.

She rolled her eyes and continued making her way to her room, where she planned to conduct her research away from her uncle's prying eyes.

'There you go.' Brendan dropped the two books he had carried on her desk. 'Enjoy.'

Alannah looked up at him. 'So, you're not gonna guide me through any of my reading?'

He raised his eyebrows, sat on the edge of her bed and held his hands out to her. 'You want me to hold your hand through the process?'

She moved forward and gripped his hands in hers, digging her nails into his palms. 'I probably need my hands to hold those damn books.'

Wincing a little, he pulled her onto his lap such that she was straddling him. 'I could spoon you while you read in bed.'

Alannah narrowed her eyes on him. 'Oh sure, then when I fall asleep from boredom, you can wake me up by poking me in the arse.'

Brendan sucked in a breath, flipping her onto the mattress, he pinned her down. His expression was ferocious and wild. 'Don't fucking tempt me, Lana.'

Her face went bright red.

Standing up, Brendan clapped his hands together victoriously. 'My win streak continues.' He made his way to her door, pausing with a hand pressed against the frame, speaking without turning, 'I'll be here to answer any questions you have from your studies.'

Alannah's skin blazed, so she pulled off her jumper and grabbed the compendium to commence her reading.

Chapter One: The Origin of Magical Races.

Little is known of the time before the first mages.

There were no written records and most magical people were secretive about their own histories, but over time many of them assimilated with humanity and came to trust their new overseers.

Most accounts agree dragons were the first of the demigods, created from the primordial by the God of Wisdom and Knowledge, and they took to the skies. Elves — the offspring of Sun, Moon, and nature Gods and Goddesses — soon followed and they claimed the forests. Then came the giants of the plains, the dwarves of the mountains, the orcs of the hills and pastures, mermaid/mermen of the seas, and the gorgons of the deep, dark places of the world.

Magical people's souls leaving the mortal plane either ascended to the Celestial realm as spirits, or the Gods cursed and banished them to the underworld as demons.

Each of these races ruled in their own domains and rarely strayed from their homes, until humans began to populate the world. Trade and commerce became the means through which these people mingled and interbred, learning to live in harmony. But some of them also sought to increase their power and wealth.

A new generation of magical people arose. The most common hybrids were the faeries, or fae, the result of prolific mating between elves and other races. The other hybrids that came about during this time were the gnomes, and nāga.

In the Ninth Century B.C. the first mages were created to bring order to the magic world and establish peace among magical people and humans. With the mages came a new range of hybrids, including endarkened fae, enlightened fae, and were-creatures.

Not all mages were content to carry out the will of the Gods, however. Some went dark, disregarding the laws of society entirely and becoming obsessed with power. But the worst perpetrators were those who practised forbidden magic, bringing a curse upon themselves and their descendants: the ghouls, the liches, the succubi/incubi, and the vampires.

Liam found Brendan watching television in the living room. Knowing Alannah was busy studying, he approached his younger brother. 'Should the time Lana spends with Austin worry me? He hangs with your group; do you know if something's going on between them?'

Brendan looked up from his viewing. 'Austin's definitely hot for her, that much is obvious to everyone; but I haven't seen them kiss or anything.' He returned to watching his show, some dumb occult rubbish.

After collapsing on the sofa next to Brendan, Liam grabbed the remote and muted the volume.

'Hey, I was watching that.' He tried to grab it back, but Liam was too quick.

Holding the controller behind his back, he pressed on. 'What sort of a read have you got on her feelings?'

Brendan glared at him. 'I can't tell you that. You know it goes against my code.'

'Come on man. It's not like I'm asking how she feels about *me.*'

He shook his head, but Brendan's resolve was slipping at the sight of Liam's pleading eyes. 'Okay, fine, but you owe me one if this bites me in the arse.'

'Answer the bloody question.'

'Yes, she likes him.' Brendan's own pain was evident in his eyes.

Jumping up, Liam threw the remote control at one of the armchairs. '*Shit!*' He began pacing the room. 'Do you think her interest in him will wane when she learns the truth?'

'Probably. I get the sense she has a thing for bad boys. If you don't watch out, she might come after me next.'

Liam could not think of anything worse. 'Yeah right. Seriously though, I don't trust Austin. Beside his race or history — I still get a bad vibe from him.'

'Since when are you attuned to emotions? That's *my* specialty.'

Liam laughed. 'It's not like you ever use your powers constructively.'

'Touché.' Brendan put his feet up and stretched out.

'You know Mum channels emotions for the greater good. Wouldn't hurt you to give it a go sometime.'

'My approach is more fun though.' He slapped Liam on the leg. 'You know fun? You should try it sometime. It can't be good for you to keep walkin' around with that stick up your arse.'

'Please keep an eye on Austin, for Lana's sake,' Liam snarled.

Brendan adopted one of his rare serious expressions. 'Fine. Not that I've ever seen or read anything to give me cause for concern, not since he reformed. But if you're worried about Lana, so am I.'

Chapter Eight

'*Alannah Winters and Brendan Winters to reception.*'

Alannah was in second period English on Friday when the call came over the P.A. She froze in a panic. Her last summons over loudspeaker was because of her dad. Images of the whole incident flashed through her mind.

'Lana, it's okay. I got you. Lana?' Brendan's hand on hers brought her back to the present. 'Come on.' He helped her up and led her down the hall.

Alannah continued holding onto his hand for dear life. When they reached the front office, Aunt Nora was there, talking to Liam, and they were both in good spirits. When they turned to face Alannah and Brendan, both of their gazes shot to the vice grip between them.

Nora appeared curious, but Liam's countenance darkened, so Alannah quickly released Brendan. She did not want Liam to get the wrong idea. Things had been tense enough between them since her study session with Austin at the start of the week. At least they started talking again on Tuesday.

'Mum? What are you doing here?' Brendan asked.

Facing Alannah, she smiled. 'I thought you might like to help me with the boxes that arrived from Melbourne. The principal has agreed to let me take you home early.'

Relief washed over her. There was no bad news. 'That sounds great. Thanks.'

'And you boys are coming to help with the heavy lifting.'

Brendan's passive expression lifted, and he grinned. 'Any excuse to get off school's fine with me.'

As the four of them walked out to the car park, Alannah overheard the boys talking in hushed voices behind her.

'What the hell was *that* about?' Liam growled.

'Don't get your jocks in a knot. She freaked out when Miss O'Leary called her name over the P.A. Lana needed my support.'

'I don't need to warn you again, do I?' Liam's tone was serious.

'Fuck you, bro. I'm the least of your concerns right now.' Brendan shot forward to walk alongside Nora.

So, Liam *was* jealous. It gave Alannah a perverse sense of satisfaction.

Liam appeared to her left. 'You okay, Lana? Brendan told me you had a scare.'

'Yeah, I'm fine now. It's just… the last time someone beckoned me to the office like that… it was the day Dad…'

'Oh, shit, I'm sorry Lana.' He drew her into his arms.

They reached Nora's Mazda SUV and Liam pulled Alannah into the back seat with him.

'What about your car?' she asked him.

'I left it at home and rode with Mum today.' After fastening both of their seatbelts, he drew her back into his arms.

Alannah had not realised how much she missed Liam holding her. He used to hug her all the time when they were kids, but their physical contact had been less frequent since her return. Being this close to his warmth was one of her favourite feelings.

They spent the rest of the day moving and unpacking boxes. Nora stored most of the household items in the shed for Alannah to retrieve when she established her own home later.

But there were a few items, like photos and ornaments, she put around the place.

When they reached the boxes marked 'attic', Alannah called it: 'I'm exhausted. Let's leave these for later.'

'Okay, sweetheart. Let's order some takeaway for dinner.' Nora sounded relieved to finish.

After their meal, Alannah retired to the living room with the boys to watch movies.

Liam beelined for the couch and looked up at Alannah in anticipation. When she sat next to him, she curled up in his arms and fell asleep during the first film.

Nora and Ross were busy with work the next day, but Alannah was keen to get stuck into the rest of the boxes and both of her cousins were happy to help. They had been sorting for hours and only a handful of cartons remained.

'I expect the last of these boxes to contain my parents' magic gear,' Alannah explained.

'Sweet.' Brendan rubbed his hands together in anticipation.

The first two were full of old family photos. She avoided the temptation to linger along memory lane. Yet she still paused and smiled when she came across a framed picture of her with the boys on her seventh birthday. That had occurred nine months before she left South Australia. Both boys draped their arms around Alannah and they were looking at her while she smiled for the camera.

'I remember that day.' Liam kneeled close to her, his chin on her shoulder. 'They were good times.'

'Yeah, they were,' she agreed. Much simpler, too.

'Give us a look,' Brendan stuck his hand out.

Alannah handed him the photo.

'Oh Gods, I was such a weed back then. No wonder Liam was always kicking my arse.'

Liam laughed. 'I can still kick your arse, bro.'

'Not if it's a fair fight, without magic,' Brendan grinned.

Alannah moved on, leaving them to their pointless debate. When she opened the next carton, she gasped. The strange, decorated trunk. It was too heavy to lift, so she cut the cardboard from around it.

'*Wowsers!*' Brendan drew closer and exhaled sharply. 'Is that a mystic chest?'

'A what?'

Liam joined them. 'Yes, it is. A mystic chest is a magically sealed box used to protect powerful artefacts. The trick will be working out how to open it.'

'I managed to open it back in Melbourne. This was where I found the Winters Clan Book of Shadows.'

'You what?' Liam's head jerked back as his jaw gaped open. 'You have the family's Book of Shadows?'

'Uh, yeah. I told you I had my mum's book.'

'I assumed it was one of Aunt Aileen's notebooks. I didn't realise you meant *that* book. I thought our grandmother took it.' Liam shook his head. 'We should probably lock it up in the Cellar, along with the contents of this trunk, especially now you've broken the seal on it.'

Brendan tried to lift the lid of the chest, but it did not budge. 'Um, I don't think Lana broke the seal.'

After his own attempt, Liam's eyes narrowed on Alannah. 'But how?'

'I dunno. I fiddled with these Celtic knot thingies. Like this.' She ran her fingers under the medallions as she had done before, pricking her finger like last time. '*Ouch!* Damn thing got me again.' Drawing her injured hand up, she looked at the cut on her finger and it dawned on her. 'After doing that, I touched this moonstone.' Which she did with her bloody finger and the catch released.

'A blood seal,' Brendan pointed out. 'Only the person who made the seal, or a direct descendent, can open one of those.'

Liam frowned. 'A gamble though: Aunt Aileen risked bringing down the vampiric curse on herself and Alannah by using it.'

'I'm guessing you aren't cursed, Lana, although you are pale enough to be a vampire.' He bumped her with his shoulder. 'You don't get cravings to drink blood, do you Cuz?'

Giggling, she returned the shove. 'Not yet, but I'll be sure to bite you first if I do.'

A huge grin formed on Brendan's face. 'Have you read the chapter on vampires yet?'

'No, why?'

He leaned in to whisper in her ear. 'Because vampire bites feel orgasmic.'

Alannah would have pushed Brendan further, but she looked at Liam, whose fists clenched while his face reddened, so she decided against it. Clearing her throat, she returned her attention to the mystical box. Everything was still there.

'Looks like a full set of magic tools,' Liam observed. 'You could have them consecrated for your own use when you're initiated.'

'They seem pretty old,' Alannah replied.

Brendan peeked inside the chest and whistled. 'That's 'cause they are. I read about these in one of our clan's history books. Our ancestors forged them in the Middle Ages.'

Too astonished for words, Alannah closed the trunk and moved on to the next carton. It was full of files and folded papers. She pulled out a sheet.

'An updated family tree. Nice.' Liam was behind her.

'It's in Gaelic, though. Can you read it?'

'Yes, of course,' Liam replied. 'That's you, 'Alannah Geimhreadh, born thirtieth of July 2002, not yet tested.' He pointed to her name. 'And your parents.' His finger slid up the page. He froze. When Alannah looked at him, his face had gone almost as white as hers and he dropped the page.

'Liam? What's wrong?' she asked in a small voice.

Brendan grabbed the chart and finished translating it for her. 'Daughter of Aileen Geimhreadh, born sixth of June 1980, one hundred percent mage; and Dennis Wagner, born seventeenth of April 1978, one hundred percent human… Well shit! Your old man was human. We always assumed he was one of the German pure mages.'

Remembering what Cara had told her, Alannah understood Liam's reaction and her heart sank. Her blood was not pure. Liam stood and left the room without a word. It was enough to break her. Tears burst from her eyes as she collapsed on the floor.

'*Oh shit!*' Brendan sat beside her and pulled her into his arms. 'I guess you know about the whole stupid bloodline crap.' He tried stroking her back and mumbling soothing words, but he sounded too distraught to be calming her. '*Fuck!* Dammit, I'm sorry Lana.'

An hour later, Brendan was still embracing Alannah. Her tears had dried and she felt ready to stand, desperately needing a drink of water.

When she moved into the kitchen, Brendan followed her. 'My parents won't be back until well after midnight, apparently. Did you want to order pizza and watch stupid movies?'

Three guzzled glasses of water later, Alannah replied, 'Pizza sounds great.' She slumped into one of the dining chairs and dropped her head onto the table, supporting it with her folded arms. Moving on from Cole had been hard enough. *How am I going to get over a lifetime's worth of feelings?*

'Right, well dinner is on its way.' Brendan had rung through the order without her even noticing.

'Thanks.'

He sat beside her. 'You wanna talk about it?'

'Not really.' She sighed, turning her head to face him.

Brendan was watching her intently, concern plastered to his face. 'Okay…'

'I always imagined ending up with Liam and it really fucking hurts to know that can never be a reality.' She shot up from the table. 'Where do your folks stash their booze? I need to get shit-faced.'

He grinned. 'That's the spirit. Follow me.' Brendan led her out to the guest house, situated about two-hundred metres back from the main house on the left side of the block. After opening the antique cupboard behind the bar, he stepped aside. 'Help yourself.'

'Oh good, there's whiskey. Grab us some glasses, will you?' She retrieved the bottle of liquid gold and took it to the lounge area of the guest house. When Brendan placed the glasses in front of her, she poured them both a drink.

'What, no shot measure?'

'Too much effort.' She held her glass out to clink with Brendan's before throwing it back in synchronisation with him.

The sudden burn in her throat was just the ticket. But, requiring more, she poured another round.

'Gods, that stuff is good,' Brendan declared after his second shot.

The doorbell sounded through the guest house intercom speaker.

'Pizza!' His voice was verging on melodic. 'I'll be right back.' He jumped up and dashed out the room.

Alannah downed two more shots and finally welcomed the first signs of alcohol numbing her emotions. She was working on another when Brendan returned.

'Jesus, woman, save some for me.' He sank into the seat next to her with two pizza boxes in hand.

She shot him a rueful smile and dived for the food. 'Thanks for the grub.'

After shovelling a few slices into her mouth, she looked up to see Brendan grinning as he watched her. 'What?' she asked.

'Are you inhaling that food?'

'This is how I eat when I've been drinking. Does the sight disgust you?'

'Hell no! If anything, it turns me on.' He gave a lewd grin.

Alannah punched him in the arm, but she hit solid muscle and it only made him laugh.

Once they finished the pizza, the drinking continued.

'How's the reading going?' Brendan asked after a few more shots each.

'Smashish…smashging…great.' She giggled as she bumbled about with words. *'Words' is such a funny word. Words, words, words.* 'I'm halfway through the one about magical people.'

'That's good. Is it all making sense?'

'Mostly. Although I don't get how gorgons could mate to create those snake people if their gaze always turns humans to stone.'

'Blindfolds. Where do you think BDSM originates from?'

'BD what now?'

Brendan's jaw dropped. 'You don't know what BDSM is? I figured you for someone with an extensive sex vocab. It means bondage/discipline, domination/submission, and sadomasochism. It's how gorgons have sex with humans and make baby nāga.'

This time Alannah was gobsmacked. 'Are you for real?'

'Yup. No way I'd lie about shit like that.'

'Well there was the unicorn thing.'

'Hey that was one time, and I came clean *almost* straight away. Besides, it was a very *educational* experience.'

Alannah snorted. 'How was it eduma…educational?'

'Well, you learned the whole virgin thing is a myth and I learned you're not a virgin.' He beamed, apparently pleased with himself for such a deduction.

She burst into laughter and Brendan joined a moment later. After several minutes, they calmed down and had another drink.

'Have you read anything in the other books yet?' he asked her.

'I read a bit about the different types of mages and channelling stuff, but it looks pretty complicated. I haven't gotten to the other books yet. There's so-o much to get through. Why do I have to read about paganism to learn magic, anyway?'

'Imagine it like this, yeah?' Brendan was up out of his seat, clearly enthused by the topic. 'You've got this guy, so he's a dude, but he's not all that well-endowed physically, right? He's barely six inches on his own—'

'Does it always have to be a sex analogy?' Attempting to appear wearied, Alannah secretly praised herself for pronouncing analogy right in one go.

'Yup, it does. Also, shoosh. So, you've got this poor guy—let's call him Liam for argument's sake—*but* he's an illusionist. So well attuned in fact, that not only can he make himself look nine inches, but he can also make it *feel* like nine. So, for all intents and purposes, what is he actually packing? Is it barely-six or a nine?'

Pausing only a couple of times to giggle and burp, Alannah answered, 'Oh, I know where this is going. This is about how reality is subjectsh…subjunc…how it is what we see it as, right? So, the answer is nine.'

'Well sure, but the point of the question is, magic is not its own self-contained thing. It's all bound up in science and religion and philosophy.' Brendan gave Alannah the most unsteady bedroom eyes she had ever seen, before saying, 'Really. Philosophically. Deep.'

She glared at him levelly. 'You're such a slut.'

'I am a lover…' Brendan countered quickly, before misjudging the position of his seat and falling to the floor: 'Of knowledge.'

They fell silent a moment. Brendan sighed and looked at Alannah with a furrowed brow and pursed lips. 'Ya know what? I reckon you ought to say, "to hell with Liam." You're a beautiful woman and there's plenty more fishes in the sea.'

'Thanks, Brendan, you're tha best. What would I do without ya?'

'W-e-l-l, luckily for you, I aint goin' anywhere, so you'll never have to know.' He tried to stand, but staggered and fell again. 'Nope, nowhere.'

Alannah giggled. 'I don't think I should even try getting up. My arms and legs feel glued to this couch.'

'Well in that case, I'm joining you.' Brendan crawled around behind the sofa. Suddenly, the backrest collapsed, prompting a squeal from Alannah. He followed this up by climbing onto the futon bed and collapsing beside her.

A blanket and two pillows appeared out of nowhere and before she knew it, Brendan had tucked her in. She snuggled up alongside him and promptly fell asleep.

A morning run and workout left Liam soaked through to the bone with sweat and rain. He walked into the kitchen to grab a bottle of water for his parched throat and found Alannah knocking back a shot of Dad's hangover cure. 'I didn't know you went out last night.'

She gave him an irritated glance, moving over to the coffee machine. 'I didn't go anywhere. Brendan and I raided the liquor cabinet.'

Images of Brendan taking advantage of a drunk Alannah started flashing through his mind and he had to work hard at shaking them off. 'Lana?'

'What?' Her tone was curt as she poured her espresso.

'I'm sorry about how I reacted yesterday. It's just…'

Alannah cut him off. 'Enough, okay? I get it. My blood is tainted. Let's move on.'

Liam gasped at her dismissal. 'But…'

'I mean it, Liam, please drop the subject.' She stormed off as quickly as she could without risking a spill of her hot beverage.

Brendan strolled into the room as soon as she left, his scruffy hair suggesting he'd recently gotten out of bed. 'So, the moment you find out she's not pure, you drop her like a sack of potatoes. Nice… real nice.'

Liam filled his tone with equal contempt. 'Like you can talk. When have you ever done more than use girls?'

'At least I know when I'm on to a good thing, and I'd never let anything petty, like rules, get in the way of going after what I want.'

'Oh, is that why you string Bianca along?'

'Bianca's only a friend and she knows it.' He poured himself a shot of the hangover cure and sculled it before smirking at Liam. 'It sure is good that Lana has *my* shoulder to cry on.'

Liam had him up against the wall a second later, clutching the neckline of his top. 'Stay the *fuck* away from her.'

'Or you'll what, stretch my favourite shirt out of shape? What's it to you, anyway? You don't even want her anymore.' Brendan pushed him back and straightened his Bring-Me-The-Horizon t-shirt.

'I *do* still care about her.'

'Newsflash, Brother: you can't have everything your way. Either grow a pair and get the girl or let her go. But don't take too long to decide, else you might find she's moved on.' Brendan took a few steps toward the door. He paused, still facing away. 'By the way, it might interest you to know she didn't sleep alone last night.' As if anticipating the chase, he took off at a sprint.

Liam tried to chase him along the hall, but Dad stepped out of the study in time to catch him.

'By the Gods. What's gotten into you? Aren't you a bit old to be playing chasey in the house?' Ross stood firm, crossing his arms over his chest.

After letting out a huge sigh, Liam stepped back. 'Sorry, Dad. That brat's really pissing me off today.'

'I can see that. Listen, I need your help with some Council business. Come on.' He stepped back in the study, gesturing for Liam to follow.

Chapter Nine

'Mm, something smells divine,' Alannah commented as she walked through the front door, the smell of roasting food filling her nose. It was Friday and she had managed to avoid Liam for most of the week thanks to a busy study schedule and by opting to have Austin drive her home. Things were developing well with him, but she had not had a chance to make a move. Brendan always showed up whenever she attempted to get a moment alone with Austin.

Shadowing her into the house, Brendan placed a hand on her shoulder. 'It's the Winter Solstice early tomorrow morning, so Mum's cooking up a feast for us to enjoy tonight.'

'Nice. I better go see if I can help with anything.'

'No, don't go in there!' Brendan almost yanked her arm off when he pulled her back from her approach toward the kitchen. 'She's turned the kitchen into a sacred space. Mum treats the food preparation for such occasions as a ritual process.'

'Oh. Is the eating a ritual too?'

He dragged her into the front lounge area so they could take the long way around the house. 'There are some ritual elements, like prayer, but it's mostly a feast. A lot like Christmas for Christians. We celebrate the Triple Goddess tonight.'

Alannah simply nodded as she took in the ambience. She noticed a fire was burning in the hearth, and there were decorations all about the place, putting her in mind of the

Christmas in July celebrations Emma's family had invited her to. There were fairy lights strung up around the room, along with boughs of greenery. They walked through the formal dining room next, which only added to her impressions. The table display included a Yule log as the centrepiece, surrounded by candles. A scattering of fruits, berries, and pinecones completed the look.

'Mum and Dad are going to one of their friend's houses after dinner to perform a group ritual.' They had reached the living room and Brendan slumped onto the couch. 'Liam and I are both inviting a few mage friends over tonight to perform our own ritual. You should join us; would be a great opportunity to see what the spiritual aspect of mage life is like.'

'Really? I didn't think I could attend rituals before initiation.' She sat beside Brendan.

'It's only for worship, not to perform magic, so you don't need access to powers to participate,' Brendan explained.

'Would Liam mind my being there?'

'Would I mind you being where?' Liam entered from the backyard, dripping with sweat from one of his many workouts, which had become more frequent of late.

Alannah gulped, trying to quell the tingle she felt between her thighs at the sight of him. 'At your ritual gathering tonight.'

He smiled. 'Of course you're welcome. I planned on asking you myself, but you've been a hard woman to catch this week.'

When Alannah gazed upon the curve of his full lips, her disposition toward him softened. 'Great, count me in.'

'Excellent. I'm gonna hit the shower, but I'll see you at dinner.' Liam strode out with a renewed pep in his step.

Alannah was waiting with Brendan in the ritual space of the cellar. She was thankful Cara and Connor had also joined them because she was anxious about Liam's friends coming.

'What's *she* doing here?' As if on cue, Monique entered the room, took one look at Alannah and spun around to challenge Liam.

'Hey bitch, I'm right here. If you have a problem, take it up with me directly,' Alannah spat. 'And to answer your question, I *live* here, or did you forget that little detail?'

Monique turned her glaring eyes on Alannah. 'You don't belong down here though. You're not even initiated yet.'

Stepping beside her, Liam put a hand on her shoulder. 'Give it a rest, Monique. Brendan and I both invited her. She is family after all, and she has started her training.' The physical contact appeared to ease Monique's mood, but it did little for Alannah's.

Brendan must have read her apprehension because he put his arm across her shoulders and pulled her deeper into the room. 'Come on Lana.' He stood back from the pentagram marked on the floor, leaving a space for her between him and Cara.

'Here, take this.' Brendan handed her a small dagger with a jewelled hilt. 'It's an athame. Once the circle has been cast, you may only leave it by cutting yourself away. Do this by drawing the blade across the line on each side of your position.'

'Thanks. This was my mother's, wasn't it?'

He nodded.

With everyone standing in place, Monique directed proceedings. She walked around the perimeter of the circle with her own athame before lighting the red candle positioned at a pentagram point. 'I call upon the Guardians of the North to watch over us and grant us the blessing of fire. We invoke the name of Belenus. May your energy and willpower guide us.'

At this point everyone except Alannah responded with, 'Belenus, we invoke thee.'

Monique moved to the yellow candle. 'I call upon the Guardians of the East to watch over us and grant us the blessing of air. We invoke the name of Ecne. May your knowledge and wisdom guide us.'

'Ecne, we invoke thee.'

Lighting a green candle, she continued, 'I call upon the Guardians of the South to watch over us and grant us the blessing of earth. We invoke the name of The Dagda. May your endurance and strength guide us.'

Alannah knew the drill by this point and joined the chorus. 'The Dagda, we invoke thee.'

She lit a blue candle. 'I call upon the Guardians of the West to watch over us and grant us the blessing of water. We invoke the name of Cliodhna. May your passion and emotion guide us.'

'Cliodhna, we invoke thee.'

Finally, she stood before the silver candle at the apex of the star. 'I call upon Lugh, the father of mages, to watch over us and to grant us the blessings of Aether. We invoke you and pray that you guide us on the right path.'

'Lugh, we invoke thee.'

Monique moved to each participant and asked, 'How do you enter the circle?'.

Each person responded, 'With love and peace.'

To which Monique replied, 'Blessed be.' She hesitated slightly when she reached Alannah, but she put her grievances aside.

Once inside the circle, Alannah joined her companions on the floor, grateful for the small cushion protecting her backside from the cold stone.

Their ritual leader kneeled at the altar in the centre where she crossed her arms and looked to the ceiling, a gesture copied by everyone else. 'Cailleach, Goddess of Winter, we praise you in all of your forms. You are the Beautiful Maiden, the Blessed Mother, and the Divine Crone. The vessel from which all life springs forth. We ask you to honour us and allow us to feel your presence in our hearts.'

She lifted her arms and began chanting. 'I am the Maiden, the Mother and the Crone, and I live within you.'

The girls in the group, including Alannah, followed suit, repeating the mantra several times. As she spoke, Alannah felt a tingling sensation followed by an almost orgasmic rush of power flow through her. It was intoxicating. She looked around her and found everyone staring at her in amazement. When she drew her hands down, she noticed a faint glow emanating from her skin. *What the hell?* Overcome by the inexplicable need to touch something, she placed her fingers on her athame and a jolt of energy shot through her and into the knife.

Cara gasped. 'Alannah, did you just perform magic?'

Monique concluded the ritual and closed the circle in a rushed manner. She walked over to Alannah. 'How did you do that?'

Alannah shook her head, still reeling from the high she was on. 'I don't know. I don't even understand what I did.'

'My guess is, you imbued your athame with the power of the Goddess. May I examine it a moment?' Monique's attitude toward her had done a one-eighty-degree turn.

'Um, sure.' Alannah handed her the blade that had become luminescent.

'Wow, that's incredible. You made yourself a very potent magic tool.' She handed it back to Alannah. 'I've never seen or heard of an uninitiated mage being able to do this. It normally takes years of practice to infuse an object with the most basic of powers.'

Alannah smiled. If magic felt this good, she wanted more. 'I guess that settles it then. I better get myself initiated.'

Brendan headed toward the living room. Most of their guests had left by this stage, but Cara had remained and was chatting animatedly with Alannah on the couch. He stood in the doorway to admire the woman who had not only drawn down the moon without an inkling of how to do it but invoked the full power of the Goddess and transferred it to a Medieval dagger.

'She's remarkable, isn't she?' Liam had moved up behind Brendan and spoke quietly.

'That's a fucking understatement,' he whispered back.

Alannah looked up at them, beaming, probably still buzzing from the rush.

Witnessing her channel that power had been a huge turn-on, and Brendan still felt stirrings at the sight of her. 'She's definitely a Winters woman, pure blood or not.' He walked into the room and sat on one of the armchairs facing the sofa.

Liam took a seat too. 'So how are we going to do this without involving The Council of Mages? Because getting Alannah initiated without Mum and Dad knowing will mean going behind the backs of the whole Council.'

'We simply need to find experienced specialists in each field, right?' Cara pointed out.

'And a High Magus. Although, in theory an ex-High Magus would do.' Brendan was beginning to formulate a plan. 'I think I have the answer. I know a guy who can get us some specialists to help on a no questions asked basis, for the right price, of course.'

'I dunno,' Liam countered. 'They sound like shady people if they would work like that.'

'That's kinda the point, Brother. We're not looking to invite these folks into our home for tea and scones. We only need them to perform their part of the ritual, then they will bugger off.'

'But what if they try to harm Lana?'

Brendan should have figured Liam would not like his plan. 'That's unlikely, but we will protect her. You could even call on your goon squad. Monique seems to have changed her tune. Did you see the look of awe in her eyes tonight? With her on board, I imagine the rest of them would be happy to help Lana. Just don't tell those girls about Lana's human parentage.'

'Wait, what?' Cara broke in.

Brendan glanced at Alannah. 'You didn't tell Cara?'

The smile vanished from Alannah's face as she shook her head and Brendan could have kicked himself for being such a mood killer.

'Tell me what?' Cara demanded.

'My dad was human, so I'm not a pureblood.' Alannah's tone sounded so defeated it tore at Brendan's heart.

'Oh.' Cara's lips pulled back in a sympathetic grimace.

Liam huffed. 'I'm not planning on telling anyone, and I suggest the rest of you keep it under wraps too. The fewer people who know, the better.' He heaved a sigh. 'I don't like your proposal, Brendan, but it's probably our only option.'

Brendan shot up from his seat. 'Right then. Lana, continue reading those prep books. Liam and Cara: you guys can work out the venue. Leave the rest to me.'

'Hey, Austin. You got a minute?' Alannah had found the guy hiding in the library at lunch on the Monday following the Solstice.

Grinning, he spoke in a hushed tone. 'For you, Alannah, I have all day.'

His admission sent a thrill through her blood stream. She sat down next to him and whispered. 'The most awesome thing happened on Saturday night at the Solstice ritual. I performed magic! I'm not even initiated yet and I channelled power.' Alannah explained what had happened.

Austin's beautiful blue eyes were wide and his jaw agape by the time she finished. 'That's amazing.'

'I know, right. So now the guys are gonna setup a covert initiation ritual for me.' She had already told him about her uncle's stubborn attitude, and he'd agreed it was ridiculous. 'I still need to finish reading all my prep books though.'

'That's great news. Have you finished that book on magical people yet?'

'Yes, I have. Only three other huge volumes to get through.'

'Come on, there's something I want to show you.' He grabbed her hand and led her into a secluded spot behind the shelves where he pushed one of the bricks in the wall. A hidden passageway opened in the floor.

Alannah gasped. 'What's this for?'

'Safe travel between buildings. Because of this…' Austin walked along the wall until he reached a window where he held his hand out into a beam of sunlight. He withdrew his limb quickly as it started to burn.

'By the Gods.' Alannah kept her voice to a whisper as she took his burned hand and looked at the speed with which it healed. When she stared into his eyes, she understood their appeal. 'You're a vampire.'

'Yes,' he agreed. 'Does that scare you?'

'No. It fascinates me.'

Austin gave her a sly smile. 'Good. Now come with me.'

They entered the secret passage and Alannah found herself becoming thrilled by a rush of uncertainty and a sense of being somewhere dangerous and forbidden. The entranceway closed over, leaving them in complete darkness and making her jump.

Austin pulled her nearer, surrounding her in a cloud of his strong, spicy fragrance. 'Now you're afraid. I can smell it. Sorry, it's easy to forget others can't see in the dark. I take my vision for granted. Here.' A small light emanating from his smartphone lit the subterranean corridor. It was not much, but it was enough to calm her nerves.

'Thank you.' She looked up at him with wide eyes. 'Were you born this way, or did you…'

'The curse has been in my family for hundreds of years,' he explained.

Nodding, she pressed herself against him, brushing her fingertips along the side of his face. His eyes flickered at her touch. 'I know vampires can hypnotise people with their gaze. Is that what you've been doing to me?'

'No, at least not intentionally. Like an initiate mage, I'm not in full control of my powers, but I have tried hard to avoid impressing my will on you.'

Her eyes felt locked to his in that moment. 'Is your hypnotism power active now?'

'No.' He pressed his lips to hers, gripping the nape of her neck with a firm hand to draw her closer.

Alannah yielded without hesitation. His full lips were strong and demanding and the kiss soon heated, becoming full of need. When he opened his mouth to her probing tongue, she was grateful he had used breath mints to disguise the taste of his liquid lunch.

His other arm encircled her waist and just like that, his phone was forgotten, dropping to the ground and sending them back into pitch black. Only this time, Alannah did not mind at all.

The bell sounding the end of lunch brought an end to their moment of passion.

'Wow,' Austin whispered.

'Yeah.' Alannah's vision had adjusted slightly to the dark, enough to make out the gorgeous features on Austin's face by the light of his glowing eyes. She pressed her lips to his chiselled jawline. 'I guess we should get to class, huh? Not that I want to. It's only Mindfulness anyway.'

'You make a good point. Kissing you is much more therapeutic than meditation.' Austin stooped to pick up and pocket his phone. He grabbed her hand. 'I still want to show you something though.' After walking a few metres, they reached a door opening into a plush living area and neat dining space, illuminated by a few warm light globes. 'The vampire common room. Don't open the fridges if you get faint at the sight of blood.'

'Nice. So, is this where you hide most lunch times?'

'I try to join our friends when the sky is overcast, but yes, this is where I come when the sun is out. Unless I have study to do in the library, of course.' He moved into the room and pulled her down onto a couch.

'Does anyone else use this room much?'

'Only my cousins, but they don't come here often. My brother doesn't start high school until next year and there are no other vampires attending the school.'

Alannah climbed across his lap to straddle him. 'Are you telling me we have this place to ourselves?' She fluttered her lashes.

His hands pressed across her hips and he grinned. 'Pretty much. Please don't tell anyone else about it.'

They made out for the rest of fifth period.

Austin walked Alannah to her locker so she could collect her books for Ancient Studies.

'There you are. I missed you in Mindfulness.' Brendan was waiting at her locker. He nodded to Austin. 'Hey man.'

'Hi Brendan. I better get going, Alannah, but I'll see you after school.' He embraced her and they kissed briefly.

Her body was humming as she watched Austin's shapely backside moving away.

When she turned to Brendan, his eyes were wide. 'Did you guys skip class for a nooner?'

She laughed. 'Things were pretty heated, but they didn't go *that* far.'

'Geez, woman.' He shook his head. 'Why didn't you tell me about hooking up with Austin?' His brow creased.

'Relax, Brendan. It only just happened at lunch today. As if you didn't see this coming anyway.'

'Okay, fine.' Smiling, Brendan added, 'You're right though, I totally called it. Congrats, Lana.' He threw his arms around her, pulling her into a hug and whispered in her ear, 'I can't wait to see the look on Liam's face when he finds out.'

She pushed him back and slapped his arm. 'You're a horrible brother.'

'Yup. But I'm an awesome cousin.' He winked as he took a few backward steps before spinning around and walking away.

Liam was waiting for Alannah when she left her classroom at the end of the day and there was no sign of Austin. *Shit.*

He grabbed her arm, hauling her into an empty classroom and slammed the door. 'Is it true?'

Annoyed that he manhandled her roughly, she shook her arm loose from his grip. 'Is what true?'

'Don't play dumb with me, Lana. Did you kiss Austin?' His eyes blazed as he pursed his lips.

'Who told you?' *Had Brendan been that eager to rub it in Liam's face?*

'Does it matter? Word travels fast in these halls and several people claim to have seen the two of you. But I'm still not inclined to believe them over you. So, tell me the truth, Lana.'

'Yeah, it's true. I really like him, okay. I don't see what the big deal is.'

Unshed tears glistened in Liam's eyes a moment before his face reddened. 'You wouldn't say that if you knew what he was.'

Alannah crossed her arms in defiance. 'I know he's a vampire. That doesn't worry me.'

'It fucking well should, Lana. He's dangerous. How do you know he isn't coercing you with hypnotism?'

'Because he told me he isn't.'

Liam shook his head in disbelief. 'And you're gonna take his word for it?'

'Yeah, I am. I trust him. He hasn't done anything to hurt me even though he's had multiple opportunities to do so.' Alannah walked to the door, pausing as she gripped the handle. 'And he doesn't seem to mind how tainted my blood is.'

He moved at lighting speed, pulling Alannah back from the door and spinning her around with a hand on her shoulder. 'Has he fed on you?' Fear had overtaken his countenance.

This was getting ridiculous. 'You're overreacting, Liam. If I were to let Austin bite me, that would be my prerogative and it wouldn't be any of your business. Now let me go.'

His hand slipped away from her shoulder, but his brow remained creased.

Alannah turned and stormed out the room. It was time to move on and put Liam behind her.

Chapter Ten

It was a frosty August night when Alannah followed her cousins into the middle of a forest, carrying a velvet bag full of her mother's magic tools. She wore a long, white ritual dress, looking forward to the presentation of her ceremonial robe to help combat her shivers. Butterflies were having a dance party inside her stomach, but she also wore a smile a mile wide. Months of study had brought her to this point, and she was about to experience one of the most important rites of passage in her life. There would be no turning back once she opened herself up to the magic world.

She wished Austin could be there to support her. Their relationship had progressed well, and she felt herself finally letting go of the pain of an unrequited love. Liam had been cold and distant around her for a few weeks when she started seeing Austin, but things had returned to some form of normality between them in the last month. He even put in considerable effort to be civil around Austin at her seventeenth birthday party.

'Here we are.' Liam stopped beside the makings of a bonfire in the middle of a clearing. He looked toward a line of trees and called out, '*Táimid an Geimhreadh*[2]. You can show yourselves.'

---

[2] We are Winter

Eleven mages in robes of various colours stepped forward. They ranged in age from late twenties to approximately eighty. One elderly man with long white hair walked right up to them and addressed her. 'You must be Alannah. I am Magus Ciardha. It is an honour to direct proceedings for you tonight.' He took her hand and pressed a chaste kiss to her knuckles.

'Thank you, Magus,' Alannah replied softly as her spare hand twisted in the folds of her dress.

'Do you have your magic tools ready for me?' He took the bag she offered him, turning to the boys to discuss logistics. The man wore black robes with a gold Celtic trinity knot emblem on the back.

Liam and Brendan both shook his hand. Liam ushered Magus Ciardha to the altar next to the wood pile. The magus busied himself with preparations while Liam lit a fire with the click of his fingers.

'How are you feeling, Lana?' Brendan stood beside her as she watched Liam perform his magic. She knew Brendan did not need to ask, but since he had learned to control his powers more, he had been respectful enough to avoid reading her without permission.

'Seriously fucking nervous. But I'm hyped too. I really want this, Brendan. I know there are risks, but I'm sure I'll handle them with you and Liam alongside me.'

'That's my Lana.' He smiled and threw an arm across her shoulders and pulled her in close to him.

Alannah savoured the warmth emanating from his body as they waited.

Before long, a ritual circle was cast and Ciardha consecrated her tools. He beckoned them forward. 'Who seeks to enter this sacred space?'

Brendan, who Alannah had chosen as her guide, presented her. 'I bring the daughter of a mage who wishes to know the wonders of the magic world and to honour the Gods and Goddesses of the Celtic faith.'

'What is your name, daughter of mages?' Ciardha asked her.

'Alannah,' she replied.

'Please kneel before the Gods and Goddesses.'

Brendan helped her to her knees, standing behind her.

Ciardha continued, 'Are you ready to be purified?'

'Yes, I am.'

The magus placed a candle in her hand, encircled her with a cloud of incense, drew a line of dirt across her forehead, and sprinkled her with water. 'As a mage you will join a spiritual society. Do you vow to honour all the Gods and Goddesses by observing the Sabbats and the Esbats?'

'Yes, I do.'

'As a mage you will contribute to a peaceful magic community. Do you vow to uphold the laws of the magic world and do your best to protect the human world from the forces of magic?'

'Yes, I do.'

'We accept you as a member of our society.' He handed her a feather quill and inkwell.

She used them to sign the dedication page of her mother's book of shadows, claiming it for herself.

'It is time to open yourself up to the mysteries of the world.' Ciardha stepped back to form a circle with the other mages.

Alannah blew out the candle she was holding and set it aside. Closing her eyes, she reclined back against her calves and sank into a meditative state. The chanting began. It was an eerie sound, and she could feel a warm breeze circle about her as the voices rose in a crescendo.

Austin watched the ritual from the vantage of an elevated gum tree branch nearby. While he had seen numerous mage ceremonies, he had never witnessed an initiation before. It was a fascinating sight to behold and Alannah looked gorgeous in her white dress. She wore her long black hair in a partial braid, leaving strands cascading down her back in loose curls. He wished he could pull her into his arms and run his fingers through those locks, breathing in their strawberry scent.

She sank back against her bent legs and the assorted group of outcast mages began reciting various mantras. Supposedly, the man in the role of High Magus was lifting the veil, allowing her to see past glamour, while the other ten mages would open her up to the different mana sources. There was a twelfth mage in black robes a short distance beyond the tree line who was also chanting, but none of the other ritual participants were aware of her presence, nor did they know the woman's intentions.

As the chanting ended, the mysterious woman left her position among the trees. The head magus presented Alannah with her dark blue robe, adorned with the Winters matriarchal emblem: The Tree of Life flanked by the Triple Goddess. He returned Alannah's consecrated tools and concluded the ritual.

Austin jumped down from his hiding spot and made his way out of the forest. When he reached the roadside, the strange woman who had gate-crashed Alannah's party approached him. 'Hello Austin.'

He stopped abruptly, startled by her forward manner. 'How do you know my name?'

She slipped her hood back. 'Because I know all my subjects by name.'

Gasping, he dropped to one knee as a sign of proper respect for royalty. 'I'm sorry My Lady, I did not recognise you.'

'You may stand. I wish to speak with you in my car.' She gestured to the limousine parked a few metres down the road.

Austin followed her promptly. After opening the door for her, he made his way around to the other rear passenger seat.

They had moved several kilometres away when the Duchess spoke again. 'It would appear you have become close to the Winters girl, yes?'

'Yes, my Lady. We are… extremely close.'

'This will indeed please her Majesty. Our Queen will join us soon. She has an important job for you, relying on your relationship with this girl. I assume I do not need to remind you that your loyalty to your sovereign comes before all other alliances.'

'Of course, my Lady.'

'Very well. Expect contact from one of Her Majesty's messengers shortly.' She fell silent, dismissing him when they reached his parked car.

The first change Alannah noticed was the fields of different coloured light surrounding everyone. She blinked several times to be sure she was not hallucinating, but they remained even after she arrived home.

'Are you sure you're okay, Lana?' Liam asked again when they entered the living room.

She had been quiet and withdrawn since the ritual ended, insisting she was fine when the boys asked after her. 'What are those colours surrounding everyone?'

Brendan and Liam exchanged wide-eyed looks. They turned back to her.

'You can already see coloured auras?' Brendan asked.

'Is that what they are?'

'Yup. What colours can you see surrounding us?'

'Liam's aura is mostly deep red with a hint of bright pink, while yours is yellow and bright pink.'

Brendan smiled and the pink light around him pulsed a bright red. 'Damn girl, you're channelling *and* reading emotions. Now you know what it's like for me most of the time.'

'Most mages can only see people's auras as a bright white light, and they can tell how powerful another mage is by the size of their aura,' Liam explained. 'Colour reading is an enchanter's power.'

'So, Lana, you want to tell us whose is bigger?' Brendan smirked.

She rolled her eyes, directing her question at Liam. 'Does that mean I'm going to be an enchanter?'

Liam shook his head. 'It's too early to tell. You need to spend time channelling other mana sources to find what you are most attuned to.' He yawned. 'It's been a long day and we have school tomorrow, so I think we should call it a night.'

'Yeah, I guess. I don't know if I'll manage sleep though.' Alannah stood and followed her cousins up the stairs.

After Liam wished them goodnight and disappeared in his room, Alannah stopped at Brendan's room. 'Hey Brendan, can I ask you something?'

He smiled. 'You wanna know what the colours mean, don't you?'

'Yeah.'

'The main colour represents a person's personality, while the outer part of the aura indicates their current emotions. Liam's deep red aura shows he is strong-willed and stubborn, but also honest and loyal.' He paused for a moment to think. 'No one else ever told me the colour of my aura. I was a little surprised to learn my personality is yellow. That usually means someone is intelligent, but also easy-going, optimistic and friendly.'

'Sounds about right. You are smart when you apply yourself, Brendan.'

'I suppose.'

'What's my main colour?'

'Orange, meaning you are bold, courageous and creative. Definitely all true.'

Alannah snorted. 'Right. So, what does the bright pink emotion aura mean?'

'Feelings of love and affection, although the nature of the love can be difficult to read and generally requires more advanced insights. For example, it can be hard to distinguish between the love felt for a friend or relative and romantic love merely by looking at the colour. With practice, an enchanter can *feel* the emotions of the person they are reading, or they can read a person's thoughts.'

'I see. Well, thanks for explaining that. Good night, Brendan.'

'Night, Lana.' Brendan opened his door.

Before she moved away, she popped her head into his room before the door closed. 'One last question.'

After pulling off his shirt, he looked up at her. 'What's that?'

The sight of his bare, muscular chest momentarily distracted Alannah. Heat pulsed between her thighs and she clenched them. Biting her lip, she glanced up. 'What about the bright red emotion?' The colour had continued pulsing around

Brendan most of the time they had been speaking and she was curious.

He closed in on her with an impish grin. 'Why don't you tell me, Lana? It just flashed in your aura too.'

Blushing, she made a quick exit.

Alannah's stomach did backflips when she thought of Brendan, so she decided to avoid him the next morning. Getting up early, she was able to catch a ride to school with Liam after leaving a brief note with some excuse about needing to study at the library before school.

'Are you still seeing coloured auras?' Liam asked her on the drive.

'No. Yours is only bright white now. It's kind of a relief to be honest. I don't know how Brendan can stand it. There are some things I'd rather not know about people's feelings.'

Liam laughed. 'When you put it that way, and knowing what blokes can be like, I can appreciate it might be a bit much. But it could also be useful for gaining insight into people you don't know well.'

'I suppose. Like most powers, it's probably better when you can control it. Did you have problems controlling your fireballs in the beginning? I imagine a power like that could be dangerous.'

'Not exactly. Offensive magics like that are what we call activated spells. I always trained under controlled conditions, so I didn't set the house on fire. It's the passive powers most mages struggle with in the beginning. The biggest issue I had was in controlling my passive channelling of physical forces. It was a little awkward when I turned myself into a magnet in year eight.'

Alannah laughed. 'I bet. Oh crap, what's it gonna be like when I start passive channelling?'

'You'll be fine. The trick is to use mindfulness to switch it off. Not so easy for a thirteen-year-old, of course, but I'm sure you will manage fine, especially now we have classes in it at school.'

'Speaking of controlling powers, you have your eighteenth birthday coming up later this month. Doesn't that mean you'll be sitting the magus test soon?'

He sighed. 'Yes, preparations start next week. It's annoying that they can't wait until I've finished my high school studies. Graduating to full magus, makes me a deployable warlock.'

'Shit. Is that like compulsory enlistment?'

'More like being in the Reserves. Signing on as a registered warlock in the first place is optional and it won't be a full-time job, but they will call me up if the need arises.'

'That's kinda scary.'

'That's life as a mage. It's what we all sign up for in some form. Although, warlocks and conjurers are more likely to see active combat than other specialists. Deployment of Abjurers is just as likely in the event of magic war, but they work behind the scenes. Thankfully, outright war is rare. We usually only have law enforcement issues in our own backyards.'

Alannah realised Liam had been referring to her as part of his world. The fact that she was an active mage was going to take some getting used to.

When they arrived at school, Liam looked at her a moment. 'Today is going to be a challenge for you. Go easy on yourself, okay? If you need timeout, take it.'

'Thanks.'

They both headed straight for the gym. Alannah had started working out on the advice of both her cousins. Fitness was essential for all mages and more so for those who ended up doing combat training. Thankfully the only other people using the gym that morning were a couple of humans, so Alannah was able to work out in relative peace.

It was when she made her way down the corridor, heading to homeroom, she became overwhelmed with what she saw. There were so many non-humans! Nothing could have prepared her for what they looked like with the veil lifted. She thought fairies would be pretty (and sure some of them were) but there were so many sharp teeth and claws, some with skin in shades of green, grey, silver, or gold and all of them with pointed ears. Then there were the orcs with their horns and olive-green skin.

But the most horrifying of the lot were the ogres: they were grotesque, with mammoth-sized muscles, droopy skin like a Shar-Pei puppy (without the cute), and protruding fangs that leered at her. The moment she spotted them, she yelped and ducked into an empty classroom, locking the door behind her.

There was a knock.

'Go away,' she shouted.

'Alannah, it's me,' Austin's voice called from beyond the door.

Gods, she had forgotten about seeing his true form for the first time. She was not ready. Could not deal with it yet. 'Leave me alone, Austin.'

'Alannah, please. It's only me. Let me help you.'

'No, Austin. I'm not ready.' Slumping to the floor, she leaned her back against the wall next to the door. *Why did I decide it was a good idea to attempt this without Brendan to calm me down?* Remembering last night, she blushed again. *Oh, that's right! Fuck, fuck, fuck!*

'I promise, I'm not that scary to look at. Please let me in so I can help you.'

She heard muffled voices talking beyond the door. Another knock.

'Lana, it's Liam. I've sent Austin away to cool down. Can I come in?'

She flicked the lock, opening the door for him.

Liam fastened it again after walking into the room. 'Come here.' He opened his arms for her.

She entered his embrace. 'Is there a way to turn the glamour back on?'

'Yes, with practice, you can learn to distinguish between someone's true form and glamoured appearance. You wanna tell me what happened with Austin?'

Alannah sighed. 'Nothing really. I freaked out when I saw so many magical people and the ogres were the last straw. I haven't even seen Austin yet and I'm afraid of what he will look like. I'm worried it will alter my feelings and I'm not ready for that.'

Liam took her hand and drew her over to a desk. After pulling a chair out for her, he sat on the table. 'I'll probably come to regret saying this, but in this instance, you don't have anything to worry about with Austin. Vampires don't show their true form unless they are feeding. Most of the time you only see their glowing eyes and pale skin. Even their true form isn't as disturbing as an orc or ogre's face.'

'Really?'

'Yes, really.'

'Lana, are you in there?' Brendan tapped gently on the door.

'*Shit,*' she cursed under her breath.

Liam raised an eyebrow in response. 'Are you avoiding Brendan?'

She bit her lip and nodded.

'You gonna tell me why?'

'No,' she replied promptly as her cheeks flushed.

'I see…. Do you want me to send him away too?'

'No.' She sighed again. 'Facing him is inevitable. Leaving it longer will make things more awkward. Besides, I could use his help with facing the horrors out there.'

'Okay.' He walked over to the door and let Brendan in the room. 'Go easy on her. She's struggling with seeing people's true forms.'

'No shit, bro. I can sense her emotions a mile away.' Brendan crossed the room and pulled a chair up alongside her. 'Do you want me to help?' he asked in a soft tone.

Avoiding eye contact, she nodded.

Brendan began rubbing her back and she could feel a sense of calm pouring through from where his finger touched her. It was incredible how easily he soothed her. 'Do you feel ready to brave the crowds again?'

'Yeah, but can you stay with me in case I freak out again?'

'Of course.'

Alannah stood, ready to leave, but hesitated a moment. 'Can you get Austin for me first?'

'Sure, no probs.' Brendan left the room.

Liam locked the door again and walked up to her. 'Hey, I know I don't have Brendan's magic calming powers, and we are in different groups at school, but if you ever need anything, please don't hesitate to call on me, okay? I'll always be here for you.'

'Thanks, Liam.' She hugged him, holding on until she heard the door.

Liam left the room for her to have a few minutes alone with Austin.

Alannah chose to await his entrance with her back to him. She wanted him to come to her first. He did, placing his hands on her shoulders.

'I'm sorry, Alannah,' he whispered.

She turned around slowly and looked at him. To her surprise, he appeared exactly the same. 'No, I'm sorry. I shouldn't have shut you out.' She ran her fingers along his face, marvelling at how she had always seen him for what he is. 'You're the same.'

'Well I'm not about to feed, so I'm not showing you my true form. But aren't my eyes different?'

'They've always been a striking luminescent blue to me. And your skin has always been pale, but I never thought your complexion was strange considering my own pallor.'

He smiled. 'That means you've been able to see me through the glamour even before your initiation. I knew you were special.' Pulling her close, he pressed his lips to hers.

After kissing for a few minutes, a knock at the door interrupted them. Alannah looked up and saw Brendan through the window where he mimed being sick. 'Come on guys, I'd tell you to get a room, but since you're already in one, I figured that would be asking for trouble.'

Laughing, Alannah unlocked the door. She was ready to face the world.

To make things easier on Alannah, her friends had agreed to join the lunch table one at a time, while Brendan continued to soothe her with his magic touch. The mages came first. The only significant change she observed were the large white auras surrounding them, which varied in size to indicate their relative power levels. Bailey was the strongest—though nothing compared to a pure mage like Brendan or Liam. Connor was next, followed by Cara who also used cosmetic glamour to achieve her flaming red 'dye job'. Her natural hair colour was an orange red.

Amy was a dwarf, so the main feature she hid was her muscular bulk, something considered less desirable among human girls. Amazingly, her dark red hair was a true colour, as was Bianca's turquoise hair. But the nymph's skin colour was interesting: where she chose a pallor like Alannah's, piercing the veil showed a tan with a green vine pattern running along her arms and legs. Being fae, she also had pointy ears.

Bianca smiled at Alannah's gaping mouth and wide eyes. 'You should see my brother if you think I look interesting. We call the males of my race satyrs and they have stag horns.'

'I recall reading about you guys, but words on a page did little to prepare me for the reality of seeing you in the flesh.'

Bianca nodded her understanding.

Caleb sat in front of her next, with a smirk on his face. 'Hey Alannah. Top marks if you can pick what I am.'

'Hm, pointy ears and silvery grey skin, so probably fae?' *And such a pretty face, but I'm not about to say that out loud.*

'So far so good. Go on.'

'Your teeth and nails aren't especially sharp, so you aren't a boggart. That leaves sídhe or endarkened, right?'

'Yes, but one's seelie, the other unseelie. So, which am I?'

'The dark tint in your skin makes me think endarkened.'

He leaned forward with an intense gaze. 'You aced the test. Does my being unseelie scare you?'

'No. Why would it? My boyfriend is a vampire, remember?' She glanced at Austin, who sat to her left, offering him a warm smile. Fortunately, the wintry weather was doing a great job of blocking out the sun.

Caleb sat back smiling. 'Good point. That said, unseelie fae get a bad rap because we are usually prone to corruption. I'm not a part of any criminal syndicates, but most unseelie are.'

'Gee thanks for spilling those beans,' Jacob added as he sat beside Caleb.

Sucking in a sharp breath, Alannah took a moment to process the revelation that aside from his chubby build, Jacob was nothing like his glamoured form. Grey skin, short black hair, pointy ears, sharp teeth and claws. 'Boggart?'

'Yeah. For the record, I only do petty theft for the family.'

She laughed. 'Good to know.'

When Locky sat down she understood his choice of hair dye. It was a good match to his green skin tone. Aside from that, he looked similar to Jacob. He grinned. 'Yeah, so I'm a goblin. For the record I don't know who my dad is, and I hate all ogres.' The subtext she took from that was Locky's ogre father had raped his elven mother. That was generally how ogres bred with folk outside their own cursed race.

'It's all good, Locky. I'm not one to judge, but thanks for clarifying.'

Alannah laughed when Ben approached. 'Are you even magical?'

Aside from his faint aura, that could have been on a human, Ben was exactly the same. 'Way to wound a guy's ego, Alannah.' He grinned to show he was jesting. 'I bet my true form would terrify you though. I prefer to avoid the shape shifting if I'm not hunting.'

'Werecreature?' she asked with wide eyes.

'Yep, weredingo to be precise.'

Nick was the last of her friends to join the table and Alannah understood why he went to the back of the queue. She could feel a strong wave of calming magic pour into her from Brendan's hand as the orc sat down. The most obvious feature was his stag horns which made him look especially scary when combined with his olive green, leathery skin. Still, he was generally more attractive than those nasty ogres.

'Thanks for being patient with me, guys. It's been a big day.'

'I think I speak for all of us here,' Austin explained, 'in saying we totally understand, and we are glad you are willing to look past our monstrous features and focus on what lies beneath the skin.'

There was a chorus of consensus around the table.

With an arm across her shoulder, Brendan pulled her into his side. 'I'm so damn proud of you, Lana.'

The following night Alannah snuck Austin into her room, a feat made easier by his ability to levitate. She had managed to get through a full day without freaking out much and felt pleased with herself. With that in mind, she had invited her boyfriend over for a late-night rendezvous, although she had kept her intentions to herself, in case she lost her nerve.

Grinning at the sight of her in a skimpy black silk negligee, he pulled her into a firm hold the moment her window closed. 'You are full of surprises, Alannah.'

'You ain't seen nothing yet,' she whispered, offering him a cheeky smile. Alannah lured Austin down to her bed, where she straddled and kissed him deeply. A few minutes later, she came up for air and took a deep breath. 'I want to see your true form.'

'What? Are you sure? After everything you went through these last two days?' Stroking her hair gently, Austin focused on her with unwavering eyes and pursed lips.

'I'm sure, but I don't want you to simply show me. I want you to bite me. I want you to taste me as you make love to me.'

Austin was completely gobsmacked. 'I… I can't, Alannah. I mean, I'll absolutely make love to you tonight if that's what you want, but not the feeding. I don't want to hurt you and I'm afraid of draining too much of your blood.'

She put a finger to his lips. 'Shh. It's okay. I'll stop you if I start to feel faint. I want this, Austin. I want all of you.'

'Do you promise to stop me?'

'Yes, I promise.'

That was all the convincing Austin needed. He flipped Alannah onto her back and stood up to undress, removing everything except his silk boxers. Her breathing quickened at the sight of his arousal. *I'll never get over how sexy Austin is. I can't believe I've held out this long.*

They kissed more before he removed her satin slip; at which point he sat back to take in the view of her naked body. 'You are absolutely gorgeous, Alannah.' Clutching her breasts, he brought his mouth down on her nipples.

Arching her back, Alannah moaned softly. It felt like years since she had last had sex, even though it was only months. Her body was more than ready, even before he slipped his fingers inside her. She came after two thrusts of his hand, colours dancing across her closed lids.

'Gods, I love how responsive your body is to me, Alannah.' A moment later, Austin sat back, and she heard the unmistakable sound of foil ripping. When he shifted back atop her, he looked into her eyes a moment before pushing into her. As soon as Alannah felt Austin inside her, she groaned.

They moved together, slowly at first to continue kissing. As Alannah's core clenched around him, Austin pulled back. 'Are you sure about this?'

'Yes. Show me who you are, Austin.'

He thrust hard into her and buried his face against her neck. When he looked at her again, his visage had changed. His forehead creased, red rings surrounded his eyes, and his canines protruded into sharp fangs. After giving her a moment to register his true form, Austin sank his teeth into her jugular.

After a brief sting, Alannah felt nothing but pure ecstasy coursing through her blood: blood that was slowly draining from her body and nourishing the man who was also bringing her countless orgasms.

Brendan drank his coffee and waited in anticipation of Alannah's entrance into the kitchen. 'Good Morning, Lana.'

'Morning,' she replied blearily.

After waiting for Alannah to pour her own caffeinated beverage and join him at the table, he added, 'And what a fine morning it is after having such a good night.' He winked at her.

She cursed under her breath. 'Could you stop reading me for like one day at least?'

'Come on, Lana, any numpty could read that afterglow radiating on your face.'

Alannah simply glared at him.

But Brendan was not going to let something like the evil eye deter him. 'But it was pretty good, right? Let me guess: you let him bite you?'

'What, how?'

He grinned in satisfaction. 'With orgasms so intense, they woke me up, they'd either have to be from sex with an enchanter or a feeding vampire. And since I was alone in my own bed last night and your boyfriend *is* a vampire, I'm going to guess it was the second option.'

Alannah's eyes were wide. '*Shit!* You felt that?'

'Yup.' He took a sip of his coffee for effect before continuing: 'It's a good thing Mum sleeps at the other end of the house and not two doors down from your room, else you might have rocked her world too.' The sight of her face turning bright red gave him a thrilling sense of victory even though he was not trying to get a Sleazy Chicken win.

'I guess I'll have to do it elsewhere in future,' she conceded.

'By all means, let me live vicariously.'

Alannah scoffed. 'You get enough of your own action; you don't need to share mine.' She sighed. 'Please don't tell Liam.'

'Don't tell him what? That you're sleeping with Austin? Because we all saw that coming, pun totally intended. Or do you mean the fact that it was kinky vampire sex?'

That earned him a famous Alannah eyeroll. 'Both, but especially the fact that I let Austin feed on me. Liam would totally freak out.'

'And for once I wouldn't blame him for overreacting. I'm a little surprised Austin agreed to your request, to be honest.' He could see Alannah was about to cut him off, but he held a hand up to hush her. 'I know you asked because he never would have instigated something like that. Not after working so hard on his rehab. You ought to know you're playing with fire, Lana. Your lover hasn't always been a boy scout.'

'What? Why are you only telling me this now?' Fear oozed from her and it was about damn time.

'Because until now, I didn't think you would have been stupid enough to ask a vampire to bite you. I had intended to leave Austin's past where it belongs and let him fill you in if he so desired. Besides, his story interweaves with mine and it's not something I'm proud of either. They were very dark times for both of us.'

Alannah blinked at him. 'So, what was it you guys did?'

'Nuh, uh. I'm not going there. Ask Austin if you want the sordid details.'

'Please, Brendan? You can't drop a bombshell like that and leave me hanging.' Her pouting was almost enough to do him in.

'I can't, Lana. It's not my place to tell you.'

'But it's your story, too.'

'If it was only about me, I'd tell you in a heartbeat. But I'm not going to betray Austin.' Having finished his coffee, Brendan rose from the table and left the room.

Emma and Melissa's beaming faces appeared on Alannah's laptop screen. 'Hi Alannah.'

'Hi guys. Has it really been a month?' Their video calls had declined in frequency from weekly at first to monthly. They had all agreed it would be easier that way.

'I know, right. How's that tall, dark, and handsome hunk of yours?' Emma asked.

'Have you fucked him yet?' Trust one-track-mind Melissa to ask.

'Things have been good with Austin and yes, we've had sex.' Alannah sighed, remembering what Brendan had warned her about. *Why did he have to go and throw a wet blanket on my mood? I was looking forward to telling the girls about my phenomenal night.*

Melissa frowned. 'Oh, so he's not much of a performer?'

'Actually, he's incredible. It was the best sex of my life.'

'But?' Emma prompted.

'But I just learned that Austin has some skeletons in his closet. Brendan warned me to be careful. It pisses me off that he waited this long to tell me because Austin hasn't even hinted at having a troubled past. So, now I'm worried about trusting Austin and I don't know if I should ask him to fess up.'

'Oh wow. That's heavy. Do you have any suspicions about what Austin might have done in the past?' Emma's brow furrowed.

'I have an inkling, but it doesn't gel with the man I know. Austin is so kind and gentle.'

'Well maybe he is a changed man, and he didn't tell you about his past because he has moved on and put it behind him,' Melissa suggested. 'Do you think knowing what he did in a past life will make you feel better?'

'I don't know. Probably not if it is really as bad as Brendan implied.'

'Then don't ask him about it. Heed whatever caution Brendan has given you and let Austin open up when he's ready,' Emma advised.

'I suppose you're right. So, any word on how Cole is doing? I haven't heard from him for a couple of months now.'

The girls looked at each other and Emma's shoulders hunched.

'Come on guys, what's going on?'

'I'm sorry, hun, I wanted to wait until I knew you had moved on before telling you.'

'Well clearly, I have moved on, so tell me. Who has he hooked up with?'

'It was only one night, and he felt super guilty for betraying your memory. I'm sorry, Alannah. We were drunk and it just happened.' Emma blurted out her confession at lightning speed.

'Woah, Emma, relax. It's okay. If you like each other, go for it. I want him to be happy and I'd rather see him with one of you girls than some slag.'

'Really? Are you sure?' Emma's eyes lit up.

'Yeah, I'm sure.'

Chapter Eleven

rendan stepped into the training room and closed the door. Given that Liam had already grabbed his supplies for the graduation ceremony that night, he figured he should have the room to himself for a few hours.

After donning his robe, he cast the circle, sat at the altar, and began with a few minutes of meditation to clear his mind. He opened himself up to the emotions in the house, a process that had become second nature. Liam's heightened state came to him straight away: a mix of excitement and pride. Brendan reached out for Alannah next and felt her cheerful mood laced with an underlying anxiety that had been with her for a couple of weeks, ever since he had told her about Austin's dark past.

Liam's parents were both happy and pleased with their eldest son. *Of course they are. Liam has never screwed up or disappointed them.* But he was not going to be the only one to make them proud. Brendan gradually extended the range of his awareness, picking up on the people living in the country estates first. Most of their dispositions were pleasant, with the occasional frustrated child. Brendan let each of their emotions fill him with power.

He pushed himself further than ever before. This was the real test. *Can I reach into town?* The outskirts hit him first and he felt a rush of energy surge through his body. One last push. *By the Gods! So much emotion! It's... too much.* All the fear, the sadness, the greed, the anger. Brendan felt overwhelmed by the rush. *'Fuck!'* The pain became unbearable. Suddenly, he went numb and darkness took him.

'Have you seen Brendan?' Liam asked Alannah as she joined him in the living room.

'No. You want me to go check his room?'

He shook his head. 'I did that. Come on, let's go. He can catch a ride with Mum and Dad. I'm not letting that wretch ruin my night by making me late.'

'Yeah, okay.' She made her way to the front door, a breathtaking vision in her new dress of blue and white velvet: a perfect match for the robes she had draped over her arm.

Liam wore a basic suit that he would cover in robes at the ceremony. They jumped in the car and took off toward the estate of the High Magus.

'Are you excited?' Alannah asked him.

A huge smile filled his face. 'Hell yeah. I aced those tests, Lana. After tonight, I'm gonna be a full magus. It kind of makes high school graduation an anti-climax.'

'Yeah, it's pretty awesome. I'm so proud of you, Liam.'

'Thanks. How have you been getting on with your training? I'm sorry I've been too caught up with the tests to check-in before now.'

She sighed. 'Quite slow. So far I've only been able to consistently connect with one source.'

'It's early days yet, Lana. Don't lose hope. The fact that you have a consistent attunement already is impressive. It took me a full year to get to that stage. What source have you attuned to?'

'The invocation of names.'

'Curious. Makes sense though, considering what happened at the Winter Solstice ritual. It'd be pretty cool if you ended up becoming a conjurer.' The thought filled him with hope. It'd be great to work closely with Alannah.

'Yeah, I guess it would. Honestly, though, I'd be happy with almost any specialisation, except necromancy. The thought of talking to ghosts scares me.'

Liam laughed. 'Of all the aspects of necromancy to freak you out.'

'Well, it's pretty much the only useful thing a registered necromancer is allowed to do.'

'I suppose.' Liam pulled into the driveway of the Lane family estate.

They made their way to the ritual grounds behind the grand Georgian style manor where High Magus Kieran greeted them personally. 'Good evening Initiate Winters.' The man gave Liam a firm handshake.

Liam gestured to Alannah. 'High Magus Kieran, this is my cousin, Alannah Winters.'

Kieran took Alannah's hand and kissed her knuckles. 'It's good to finally meet you, Miss Winters.' The smile he wore did not suit his hard features.

'Thank you, Your Honour,' she replied awkwardly, clearly unimpressed by Kieran's charms.

Liam noticed Monique approaching, having stepped out from the house during the introductions.

Kieran continued addressing Alannah, 'It is not customary for the uninitiated to attend official ceremonies, but I think we can make an exception for a Winters lady.'

'That won't be necessary, Dad, because Alannah *is* an initiate.'

'Monique!' Liam hissed.

'Oh, I'm sorry. Was that meant to be a secret still? Oops.' Monique's tone was facetious.

Alannah glared at her.

Fucking great! What's with Monique? I thought she'd put her pettiness behind her at the Winter Solstice.

'Is that so?' Kieran inquired. 'And how did such an event escape my notice?'

'I'm sorry, Your Honour, but Alannah went elsewhere because my father thought it unsafe to initiate her. A covert ceremony was necessary for her protection.'

Kieran frowned. 'This is most irregular. Alannah, I do hope you will register through the proper channels when you come of age.'

'That is my intention, Your Honour.' Alannah's knees wobbled as she toyed with a strand of her hair.

'Good. I do not abide maverick mages in my town.'

'Nor can we tolerate rogues, right Daddy?' Monique piped up, still looking at Alannah.

'That's right, sweetheart. We adhere to all magic laws here. Now Liam, we need to prepare for your graduation. Please come with me.'

Liam hesitated, not wanting to leave Alannah alone with Monique, but it was not like he had a choice. He followed the High Magus to the sacred circle.

'What's your problem, Monique?' Alannah snapped the moment Kieran and Liam were out of earshot.

'You are, Winters. I can't stand you and all that your line of bitches stand for. You think you're so good. You might think you're powerful, but I have a theory your bloodline has reached saturation. You'll probably go rogue like the others, and when you do, I'll be here to put you down.' Monique turned and strode away.

Alannah shook her head. *The bitch must be jealous still.* She looked around the crowd of gathering guests, spotting Ross and Nora, but caught no sight of Brendan. She approached her Aunt and Uncle. 'Hi.'

'Hi Sweetie,' Nora replied with a brief hug.

'Where's Brendan?' Alannah asked.

Nora frowned. 'We were hoping you'd tell us. Didn't he come with you and Liam?'

'No, we couldn't find him, and Liam was in a rush, so we assumed he would catch a ride with you.'

Ross grumbled. 'I'm getting fed up with that boy's insolent attitude. I know he and Liam aren't exactly best friends, but to miss his brother's graduation is extremely disrespectful.'

Nora sighed. 'I hope he's late and getting a lift with a friend.'

The three of them found seats in the front ring of chairs surrounding the sacred circle. It was time to watch Liam advance to full magus.

Liam was still buzzing when they arrived home. *I am a magus!* And it was the dawn of his eighteenth birthday to boot.

'I'm going to make some coffee,' Mum declared. 'I don't think I'll be able to sleep now anyway.' She walked up to Liam and hugged him. 'I'm so thrilled for you, sweetheart.'

Dad slapped his shoulder. 'You have made us both proud, son.'

When his parents disappeared into the kitchen, Alannah approached him with a big smile. She threw her arms around him. 'Congratulations and happy birthday, Liam.'

'Thanks, Lana.' Their embrace was probably longer and closer than appropriate, but Liam was not going to complain. 'I'm gonna put my stuff away, then I'll join you all in the kitchen.' He pulled away from her arms hesitantly, making his way down to the cellar.

The illumination beneath the door was the first clue something was wrong. *Is someone in our ritual space?* Liam readied a lightning bolt before bursting into the room, stopping dead in his tracks. *Oh Gods! 'Brendan!'* he cried as he ran to his brother's collapsed form. He checked the boy's pulse. *Fuck!* It was there, but too faint. He ran back upstairs in a panic. *'Dad! Come quick! It's Brendan!'*

Three sets of eyes doubled in size when they stared at him. They followed promptly.

Mum and Alannah both yelped at the sight of Brendan on the floor. Alannah even threw herself at him and started sobbing hysterically.

'I need you to move aside, Alannah,' Dad instructed. 'I can't heal him with you in the way. Please.'

But she would not budge.

Liam had to remove her by force, but he did so as gently as possible, pulling her into his arms. She continued to sob, and he wished he could comfort her, but he felt helpless. Brendan would have been able to soothe her nerves. *Shit!* All this time he assumed his brother had shirked out on Liam. *How long has he been lying here unconscious?* It made him feel like such an arsehole.

'He's suffered from some sort of magic overload,' Dad announced. 'I'm going to take him to bed and continue working on him there. Mind out.'

Liam drew Alannah aside so his father could carry Brendan through. They followed him upstairs.

After several torturous moments, Dad sat back on the edge of the bed. 'I've done all I can. His body needs to rest, but he's stable. It should only be a matter of time before he comes 'round.'

A chorus of relieved sighs filled the room.

Dad walked to the door, pausing to speak. 'I'm completely drained of magic and energy, so I'm going to bed. I suggest all of you get some rest too.'

Liam shook his head. 'I'm not going anywhere until Brendan wakes up.'

'Me neither,' Alannah chimed in.

'Suit yourselves. Nora?'

Mum, who had been quiet the whole time, stood and accepted Dad's hand with a yawn. They closed the door behind them.

Liam and Alannah sat on either side of Brendan and settled into their vigil.

When Brendan awoke, he needed to blink a few times. 'Lana?'

She was in bed, lying beside him and staring straight at his face. A smile tugged at her lips. 'Hi.'

He reached out a hand to touch the side of her face. 'Am I still dreaming?' But he heard someone clear their throat behind him. Rolling over, he found Liam sitting up against the bedhead. 'What the fuck? Please tell me I'm not dreaming because if I am, my subconscious is far more disturbed than I realised.'

Liam laughed. 'Oh, you're plenty disturbed, but you're not dreaming. You gave us one hell of a fright there, Brother.'

'Why? What happened?'

'We found you unconscious on the practice room floor. You wanna tell us what you were doing in there?'

Memories of his training exercise came back to him. '*Shit!* I guess I overextended myself. I was trying to increase the reach of my emotional channelling. When I tapped into everyone in town, all the negativity overwhelmed me.'

Liam's eyes bugged out. 'By the Gods, Brendan! How did you even reach that far? That's insane, especially for a mage of your age.' Squinting, he huffed. 'You could have killed yourself tapping into so much power at once. That was really fucking stupid.'

'Gee, thanks for the brief moment of sympathy there, bro. So how long was I out cold for? I hope we aren't gonna be too late for your graduation.'

Liam's demeanour changed in a flash as he averted his eyes. 'I'm sorry, Brendan. I didn't know where you were.'

'What do you mean, why are you sorry?'

Liam fell silent.

He felt Alannah's hand on his shoulder. 'Liam graduated already.'

'Wait, did you leave me passed out on the floor all that time? For what… five hours at least?' He could feel his muscles tensing and heartbeat rising. *That selfish bastard!*

'I'm sorry, okay. I had no idea where you were and assumed you weren't coming.' Liam sounded genuine, but Brendan's blood was too hot to back down.

'Christ, Liam! Of course, you wouldn't think to check I was okay. Your head is too far up your arse to worry about little ol' me.'

Alannah's grip tightened on him. 'Brendan, please. Liam already apologised. You need to calm down and rest.'

'He's right, Lana. And I feel like shit because of it,' Liam conceded.

Holy crap! Liam never admitted to his faults. At least not to him.

Liam stood up. 'I should let you rest.' He hesitated before adding, 'Brendan, please don't take risks like that without someone else present.'

Once Liam had gone, Brendan turned to face Alannah. He noticed her eyes were blood-shot and puffy. 'Hey, are you okay, Lana?' he whispered as his thumb skimmed under one of her eyes.

'I'm fine. You're the one I'm worried about.'

Her level of concern touched his heart, deep. It made him want to kiss away all her fears. *Fuck! I'm falling for her again, falling hard.* He pushed that thought aside to reassure her. 'I feel perfectly healthy. I promise.'

'Good. I'll let you get some sleep. Night.' She pressed her lips to his forehead.

The intimate touch caused stirrings that were not only physical. *God damn!* It took all his willpower to refrain from dragging her back to his bed as she stood and left his room.

Chapter Twelve

familiar tapping sound had Alannah out of bed and rushing to her window. She still got such a thrill from sneaking around with her boyfriend and their late-night escapades had only intensified since Brendan's warning. She wondered if it was possible to become addicted to feeding a vampire. 'Hey, you.'

'Hi beautiful.' Austin wrapped his arms around her and drew her into a deep kiss. After stepping back to look at her more closely, his eyes narrowed. 'Hey, what's wrong?'

'Brendan had a near-death experience tonight. He overreached with his channelling and blacked out. It took everything Uncle Ross had to bring him back from the brink.'

'Oh Gods, is he okay?' Austin's concern warmed her heart. *Who would have thought vampires were loving, caring people?* Mythology and pop-culture had a lot to answer for. They were not even undead. Austin's body was as warm and living as Alannah's. The main difference: he was immortal and would stop ageing at twenty-one, that and he had heightened senses, an aversion to sunlight, and a need to drink blood. Most of his other powers were much like those of mages.

'Brendan is fine now, thank the Gods.'

Visibly relaxing, he let out a sigh of relief. 'Good. I'll understand if you're not in the mood tonight. We can just—'

She hushed him with a finger on his lips before kissing him.

Austin responded avidly, lifting her so he could carry her to bed. Before long, clothes flew across the room in a frenzy between their impassioned touches, scratches, and bites.

Gods did Alannah love those bites!

Dawn approached as Austin carefully extricated himself from Alannah's bed, making a stealthy exit through her window. He would have to hurry back to his car if he was going to avoid the sun.

As he stepped onto the roadside, the faint sound of a twig snapping alerted him to someone else's presence. Human hearing would not have picked up on the sound. His pulse started racing and he let his hunting instincts take over.

He scouted the perimeter and found a woman leaning against a large wattle, facing the road with her back to him. She wore floral perfume and a long red velvet cape with a hood covering her face.

A few more silent steps forward. He froze.

The woman laughed. 'Stand down, vampire.' She turned and revealed her face.

Austin gasped and dropped to his knees. 'Pardon me, Your Majesty.'

The Queen of the Cursed. She was both as beautiful and terrifying as the rumours had suggested. Her once black hair had turned as white as the colourless eyes staring back at him, with only the tiniest slits of black for pupils. But her skin was perfect and her features well defined. She did not appear a day over twenty, even though she had been closer to thirty when she stopped ageing.

'Please, get up.' She looked him over a moment once he was standing. 'You have performed your part exceptionally well, Austin Pearce. A little too well perhaps.'

Mystified, he blinked silently.

'My sister instructed you to win Alannah's trust so you could feed on her. That did not mean falling in love with the girl.'

'What? How did you know?'

'I am attuned to all emotions, remember? I felt the two of you together tonight.' She grinned and glanced up to the house. 'And I am not the only one.'

Cursing silently, Austin staggered and fell against a nearby tree. 'I'm sorry, Your Majesty. I didn't mean to.' The sun started to touch the southern hemisphere with its first rays, so he moved into the shade of the canopy.

The Queen had no reason to fear the dawning light. She was not a vampire or ghoul. 'It matters not. I think we can work this new angle to my advantage. I imagine you will not fancy an eternity alone. Few of us do. Win her heart over and invite her to join our ranks. That is your new mission.'

Austin felt relieved. The thought of having Alannah killed—or worse, having to do so himself—would have broken him. This way, he would always have her by his side. 'I am most grateful, Your Majesty. Shall I turn her into a vampire? Or will you want to make her one of the undead, such as you are?'

'The nature of her curse matters little to me. If you want a vampire lover, make her yourself. If you have not the guts, send her to me. Now get out of here before you burst into flames.'

'Yes, Your Majesty.'

'I think we ought to all train together. Now my magus exams are over with, I should be able to devote more time to helping you both.' Liam's declaration, along with his sudden appearance in the kitchen, startled Brendan.

He had just taken his first sip of coffee and the jolt caused him to spray it all over the table. Brendan glared at Liam. 'Hold up there, Brother, do you want to train *with* us? Or do you want to supervise *my* training?'

Liam slapped his hand on Brendan's shoulder. 'I want to train *with* you both. I think it would be advantageous to work as a group. And I'm sure Lana would benefit from the process too.' The guy was dripping with perspiration, clearly back from a recent workout. He smelled like the boys' change room at school. *Ick!*

Alannah looked up from her breakfast and smiled. 'Sure, sounds good.' Aside from her initial greeting, it was the first thing she had said that morning.

Brendan knew what she had spent the rest of her night doing and much like any other morning following such activities, she was avoiding eye contact and any conversation that might earn her a reprimand or further embarrassment. The fact that she continued the kinky sex in such proximity to Brendan was curious, however. *Is she doing it for safety reasons? Or did she enjoy sharing the experience with me?* In either case, he was glad she kept him close and not simply because it gave him a thrill.

'Brendan?' Liam fixed unwavering eyes upon him.

'Sure. Fine. Whatever.' He kept his tone indifferent; secretly pleased Liam cared enough to watch out for him.

'Great. I'll meet you both in the ritual room after you've finished breakfast.' He walked off, hopefully to shower.

Sliding off her chair, Alannah took her dishes to the sink. 'This is going to be fun. The three of us working together.'

'Are you a masochist, Lana? Because if not, you clearly have a different interpretation of fun than I do.'

She was faux pouting. 'What? You don't want to work with me?'

He could not help but laugh as he rinsed his own dishes. 'Nice duck lips. For the record, I am going to love working with you. It's just, Liam is an Antarctica-sized wet blanket.'

Alannah stood close behind him and whispered in his ear, 'To answer your question, of course I'm a masochist. But I'm also a sadist, so Liam won't be the only one whipping you into shape.' She slapped his arse with a loud *smack* before taking off toward the cellar at breakneck speed.

The brutal slap stung like hell and Brendan's dick was rock hard because of it. Taking a few minutes to breathe deeply, he calmed himself before following her. He found Alannah alone and kneeling before the altar. 'I wonder if you enjoyed that as much as I did.'

She laughed. 'You're losing your touch if you think that'll turn me red.'

'Who said I was playing?'

'Playing what?' Liam asked as he appeared in the doorway.

'Nothing.' Brendan grabbed his practice robes and got ready for their training session.

'Right. So, Lana, would you like to draw the circle today? It is traditionally your role as matriarch.'

Alannah began to tremble. 'Um. I'll give it a go. I've only ever done it for my own private training, so I don't know if I'm any good at it.'

Liam placed a hand on her shoulder. 'It's okay, we will help you if you need any prompting.'

They began the ritual and Brendan gaped at her with wide eyes. Alannah's recitation was perfect. The three of them converged at the altar to meditate for several minutes.

Liam broke the silence. 'Lana, what mana source did you want to open up to today?'

'I'd like to try matter again.'

Brendan knew she was pushing herself to become a conjurer and her success with invocation had suggested this as her most likely direction, but she had been struggling with matter.

After retrieving several rings from their locked box beneath the altar, Liam handed one to Alannah. The gold band with a bright orange citrine crystal contained the power of matter. He placed three rings in front of Brendan. The usual two: Botswana agate for channelling emotions, and blue lace agate for attunement with the senses. Brendan picked up the third ring, which he did not recognise, and examined it. The crystal, set in a thick metal band, was a swirl of blue, purple and green.

'Fluorite. It should help you work with large doses of power,' Liam explained.

'Thanks.' Brendan did not know what else to say.

Liam chose the peridot for himself. That could mean only one thing: he was opening himself to all mana and would channel the first source he connected with. It was the type of ring they had all used as new initiates. As a registered warlock, Liam was attuned to all the mana sources he needed. Expanding his repertoire was not necessary, not unless he had ambitions of becoming High Magus. He must have noticed Brendan's scrutiny. 'I'm testing the waters. It was Dad's suggestion.'

'Figures.' Pushing envy aside, he chose to work with the Botswana agate and put the fluorite on his other hand.

They sank back into their meditative states, but this time the three of them focused on their respective sources. Brendan pushed his reach into town again. It was painful at first, but this time he found himself able to control the flow of power. He used it to manipulate his own emotions, switching between each one (except for the forbidden: gluttony, greed, and pride) and finishing in a state of calm.

When he opened his eyes, Alannah and Liam were both looking at him.

Smiling, he nodded. 'It worked.'

'That's awesome!' Alannah threw her arms around him.

Breathing in the scent of her hair, he tried to draw in deep breaths to maintain his tranquillity, but that was never going to happen in Alannah's arms. 'So, uh, how did you go, Lana?'

'I did it. I was able to stay attuned to matter. I guess the next step is to work with my attunements, right?'

'Right,' he replied, releasing her reluctantly.

Liam was eyeing him warily a moment. He turned his attention to Alannah. 'Normally an initiate conjurer would start with basic summoning, but given your experience at the Winter Solstice, you could skip straight to imbuing items. Up to you, really.'

'I'd like to try summoning. How did you go, Liam?'

'Nothing new for me today,' Liam shrugged. 'No big deal. It's early days yet.'

Brendan removed his rings and placed them in the trinket box. 'I'd like to start practising something new next week.'

'Oh?' Liam looked at him with wide, unblinking eyes.

'Yup. I think it's time to try my hand at telepathic communication.'

Alannah grinned. 'Sounds like fun.'

'With you, I'm sure it's gonna be.' He winked at her.

A few days after their group training session, Liam sat at the dining table with Brendan, books on magic spread out in front of them. Learning any new power required a lot of theory study to start with. While Brendan was reading up on telepathy, Liam was learning about defensive energy circles.

When he looked up at the clock, the passing of hours surprised him. Alannah should have been back from her date by now. The sound of the front door slamming halted his hammering heart. That was until his father stepped into the room.

Steam was billowing out of Dad's ears, and his face resembled the tomatoes on the kitchen bench. 'I just had an interesting chat with High Magus Kieran. Can you guess what he told me, Liam?'

Brendan looked up at the sound of Dad's voice. He turned to Liam and the twerp started to grin.

Liam had not yet told Brendan what Kieran knew about Alannah. He shook his head, returning his attention to their father. 'It was her choice, Dad.'

'*Shit, Liam!* You told the High Magus about Lana?' Brendan roared.

'Of course not. Monique tattled.'

Dad stepped closer and fixed Liam with an icy gaze. 'And when were you going to enlighten your parents, who also happen to be Alannah's guardians?'

'Whenever Alannah was ready.' Liam refused to stand down on this issue.

'All three of you have been very foolish and insolent.' Dad leaned against the wall and crossed his arms. 'By initiating her into the magic world, you have made her presence known to someone her mother and I were trying to hide her from.'

Standing to face Dad square on, Liam also crossed his own arms. 'How does initiation make her presence known? And who are you hiding her from?'

A smooth, deep voice spoke from the doorway. 'The Queen of the Cursed.'

They all spun to face the vampire.

'Austin?' Dad asked. 'Where did you appear from? And what do you know about the Queen?'

Austin stepped into the room. 'I was dropping Alannah home after our date and heard you talking.' When Dad glanced around, Austin added, 'Don't worry, she went straight upstairs. As for the Queen, I know plenty about her because she married the Vampire King. I also know she's in town now and wants Alannah. Word travels fast among the cursed.'

Brendan finally stood up to join the conversation. 'Hold up. Who is this Queen? And what the hell does she want with Lana?'

'The Queen wants to eliminate Alannah's magic potential because she is the last female mage in her line and the only real threat to the Queen's power. Knowing that, who do you think the Queen is?' Austin replied.

Brendan shot Dad an alarmed look. 'No way! Dad, you said she was dead and gone.'

'Technically both true statements. She's undead and she left the country.' Dad's tone was cold, and bitter.

Liam shook his head. 'So, does that mean she succeeded in the most forbidden of all magic rituals? Is she a lich?'

Dad nodded gravely. 'Yes, I'm afraid so.'

His clammy palms itched as bile rose from his unsettled stomach. '*Shit!* I'm sorry Dad. I had no idea this was why you were so adamant about Lana. Why didn't you tell us?'

'I intended to eventually. I was waiting until you were full magus, Liam. It is not a matter I wanted to burden either of you with before you were mentally and physically ready to handle it.

But you were both reckless and now we have the consequences of your actions on our doorstep.'

'What do we do now?' Brendan asked.

Dad sighed. 'For now, I need you both to keep an eye on her. I'm going to bring this issue up with the Council and see what we can do. *Damn it!* Kieran will not be happy with me for letting this happen.' He started pacing. 'Liam and Brendan, until further notice, you're both grounded, along with Alannah. This is both your punishment and for Alannah's safety.'

Liam groaned, but he knew he deserved it. 'Understood, Sir.'

Brendan nodded in silent compliance.

'Also, please refrain from telling Alannah about the Queen. I need to work out how best to broach this very delicate topic with her.'

As soon as Dad left the room, Brendan cursed under his breath. 'I can't believe he kept this from us.'

Liam comprehended his father's reasoning but staying in the dark over something so serious still stung like a bitch. 'I can believe, but I don't like it.' He looked at Austin still standing in the room. At least the grounding meant Alannah would have more time with himself and less with her dubious boyfriend. He could not help but smirk. 'Sorry Austin, I guess this'll be a bit of a dampener on your relationship with Lana for a while.'

Austin returned the smug grin. 'Oh, don't worry about me. I'm sure I'll be fine.'

Brendan snorted. 'I'm sure you will, filthy bastard.' He narrowed his eyes. 'But let this be a warning, friend. If you harm her, I will put you in a world of pain and not the enjoyable sort.'

Liam could not believe Brendan was threatening his best mate. He wondered if something had transpired between the two of them. *Whatever. It's none of my business.* Brendan was clearly on board with protecting Alannah and that was all that mattered.

Turning to Brendan, Austin smiled. 'Don't worry, friend, I love her too. I also know your dirty little secret. It's almost like old times, huh? Almost, but not quite.' He swiftly left the house.

Curiosity piqued; Liam could not help himself. 'What "dirty little secret" was he referring to, Brendan?'

'Why should I tell you?' he huffed.

'Does it involve Lana? If so, spill it or I'll kick your arse. If not, I probably don't want to know.'

Brendan sighed. 'I kinda promised Lana I wouldn't tell you.'

Heat surged through Liam's veins as his temper started to rise. *If Brendan has touched Alannah, so help him Cailleach.* 'You had better tell me.'

'Fine. Don't tell her I told you. And please don't get mad at her or do anything rash.'

He could feel his face turning red. 'Spit. It. Out.'

Backing away from Liam's arm swinging range, he put his hands up in surrender. 'Okay, okay. Lana has been letting Austin feed on her when they have sex.'

Liam was utterly gobsmacked. *That stupid, stupid girl!* 'How are you okay with this?'

'I'm not and I told her as much. I warned her she was playing a dangerous game. I guess that's why she only does it at home.'

'Wait, what? How have I not noticed Austin coming here all this time? And how is it any safer here? Austin could lose control and drain her regardless of where she is.'

Brendan hesitated to answer. 'Lana lets him in through her window, which he can levitate to. They usually meet in the middle of the night when the rest of us are asleep. Well mostly asleep… I usually wake up when….' He started squirming.

'When what, Brendan?' Liam's tone was firm.

'When I feel her, uh, intense emotions.'

All the blood that had been boiling in Liam's face drained away, and he imagined his complexion was as white as Alannah's. 'You felt her orgasm?'

Brendan laughed a little. 'Yup. It's almost as good as being inside her myself. Almost, but not quite.'

Liam glared at him. 'By the Gods, Brendan! Have you no shame? You've got to tell Lana. If you don't, I will.'

'She knows. I told her after the first time it happened. Doesn't seem to stop her wanting to share her most personal experiences with me,' he grinned.

Liam tried to ignore how much his brother enjoyed provoking his jealousy. 'Do you at least switch off the channelling as soon as possible?'

'That's the thing. If you were in my shoes and knew there was a risk the vampire feeding on her might take too much blood, would you turn it off, or would you pay closer attention to make sure she's safe?'

Fuck! This is so sick and twisted! 'If it were me, I'd storm in there and kick the shit out of said vampire.' Liam sighed. 'But I know he's your friend and I get your point. Thank you for watching her back. I can't say I like your methods. In fact, I detest them. But at least you have her safety in mind.' Yawning, Liam left the room and made his way to bed.

Chapter Thirteen

lannah's grounding had continued for four weeks and counting. As she scuffed her feet in the dirt and bark chips beneath her swinging legs, she wondered how long this punishment would drag on. It was a Friday and most of her friends were partying. Even Austin would be out. He never stuck around to study in the library on Fridays, which was why she decided to wait for her cousins in the empty playground next to the school's parking lot once she had finished her own workout.

'Hello Alannah.'

She looked up and gasped at her mother's likeness. All except for the white hair and red gown. Aileen Winters never wore red. 'Do I know you?' she asked cautiously. The woman had a very powerful aura, so she was probably magical.

'Not formally. But I know you, dear child. My name is Tara Winters and I'm the Queen of the Cursed.'

Alannah's blood turned to ice. She remembered reading the name Tara on her family tree, but the woman before her did not look a day over thirty. 'That means you're…'

'Immortal, yes. And I would like to spend some time getting to know you better. Once you join the ranks of the cursed, that is.'

Frozen by her fear of this woman, Alannah barely whispered, 'What do you mean?'

'Alannah, you are a Winters mage of the first-born line. The shackles of mage society are stunting your potential. If you broke free of those constraints and embraced your true nature, you'd be much better off.' She advanced forward.

Alannah jumped off the swing and backed away. *Shit!*

'Choose your curse and join me. Return to your real family.'

Brendan was up to his last repetition of the bench press when a sudden sense of intense fear struck him. *Oh Gods! Alannah.* Caught off guard and distracted by his concern for her, Brendan didn't even notice the bar dropping across his chest.

'That's gotta hurt.' Ben's voice broke his trance.

Awareness returning, the pain set in. 'Ah, fuck!' *It feels like I've cracked a couple of ribs.*

'Here, let me help you.' Thankfully, Ben was spotting him and removed the weights. He tugged Brendan's shirt up to inspect the damage, wincing at the massive bruises already forming. 'Should I get Connor?'

'No time. Alannah's in trouble. I'll get Dad to look at it later.' He shot up from the bench and ran from the school gym. Using her fear as a beacon, he tracked Alannah's whereabouts to the primary school's playground. He sent Liam a quick SOS text, before approaching the two figures standing alone among the children's play equipment.

Once he was able to make out the conversation and get a closer glimpse of the woman in red, he understood exactly why Alannah was afraid.

'Choose your curse and join me. Return to your real family.'

Brendan shot out from behind a tree and stood next to Alannah. 'I am her real family. Leave us the hell alone, *Grandmother*.' He almost retched as he used her familial title. The thought of a relative wanting to harm Alannah turned his stomach.

'Oh Brendan. How noble of you to jump to your cousin's aid. Why do you would bother trying to be the hero after all the years you have spent in your brother's shadow? You always made a better rogue, did you not?' Tara's grin was vicious.

He glared at the evil woman. 'I told you to leave us alone.'

'I heard you, but I have not quite finished talking to my granddaughter.' She turned back to Alannah. 'You have two options, dear child. Become one of the cursed or face my wrath. You have until Beltane to decide.' Tara magiported away.

As soon as the Queen of the Cursed left, Brendan turned his attention to Alannah as she fainted. He grabbed her before she hit the ground. He cried out in pain as she collapsed against his cracked ribs.

'*Brendan!*' Liam came running from the seniors' block. As soon as he found Alannah unconscious in Brendan's arms, his visage paled. 'By the Gods! What happened?'

'Our grandmother gave her quite a fright. Oh, and something about joining the ranks of the cursed or facing the bitch's wrath, which I assume means death.'

'So, she's finally shown her hand. Poor Lana. We should get her home immediately. Are you okay? It looks like you're grimacing in pain?'

'I'll live. I think I busted a couple of ribs when Alannah's fear overwhelmed me in the gym.' He tried to carry Alannah's weight towards the carpark, but almost crumpled from the added weight against his chest.

'Christ, Brendan. Please, let me carry Lana.'

Brendan handed her over hesitantly. He would have tried supporting Alannah with all his ribs broken, but Liam insisted.

Once Dad had checked on Alannah, concluding that aside from some shock, she was fine, he put her to bed. He examined Brendan's injuries. 'How much were you pressing?'

'One hundred and thirty-two kilos.' He squirmed as Dad's fingers probed around the damaged area.

Liam whistled through his teeth. 'That's the same as me. You shouldn't be doing that much at your weight.'

'Elites of my weight can do one forty-five. I normally handle it fine; Lana's predicament distracted me.'

'I'll fix you up, then you'd better rest in bed until dinner.'

Alannah woke in a dark room with visions of her grandmother haunting her fleeting dreams. She sat up startled, relaxing when the familiarity of her own room sank in. A cursory glance at the clock told her it was nearly midnight. She noticed a couple of sandwiches on her bedside table, along with a note:

> *Dear Lana,*
> *Didn't have the heart to wake you for dinner. You looked*
> *so peaceful sleeping. I'm sorry the evil witch gave my*
> *princess such a fright. Rest well. I'll talk with you about*
> *things when you've had some time to recover.*
> *Love from Liam.*

Alannah scoffed the food and reread the note. She might have considered it romantic if she did not know better. Thoughts of Tara filled her mind, and she recalled her ultimatum: 'Become one of the cursed or face my wrath.' The memory of her icy tone sent shivers down Alannah's back. There was no way she would survive a fight with the Queen of the Cursed this early in her training. She needed to explore her options.

There was one cursed person she knew and trusted. She sent him a quick message: JUST MET MY GRANDMOTHER, QUEEN OF THE CURSED. NEED TO TALK. PLEASE MEET ME AT MY WINDOW ASAP.

Austin's prompt reply made her smile. ON MY WAY. LOVE YOU.

He arrived fifteen minutes later and pulled her into a firm embrace. 'Are you okay?'

'Physically, I'm fine. But I'm pretty freaked out.'

'I can imagine.' He pulled back slightly to look into her eyes. 'What did she do?'

'Only talked. Brendan found us together and told her to leave. I don't know what would have happened if he hadn't arrived.'

Pulling her back into his arms, he exhaled sharply. 'I'm so glad you're okay.'

'Austin…what's it like being a vampire? Do you like it?' With their proximity, Alannah could feel his heart begin to race.

'It's… complicated. Why do you ask?'

'Tara wants me to become cursed. I don't much fancy becoming undead like her and the thought of feeding on people's flesh puts me off the idea of becoming a ghoul, but vampirism… Maybe I'm biased, but it seems kind of… exciting… and sexy.'

'I'm not going to lie to you, Alannah. There's a big difference between starting life a vampire and becoming one. I've grown up learning the ropes and I'm part of a noble family. But a mage who chooses to become a vampire… they'll exile you from your current family.'

Shit! She had not considered that aspect.

Squeezing her even tighter, Austin continued, 'That said, my family would welcome you with open arms and I would absolutely love to share my world with you. And I'm sure Brendan would still hang out with you.'

'Yeah, Brendan's good like that.' *But Liam? Then again, it's not like I can be with him anyway.* 'I have time to think about it. Tara gave me two full months to decide. Right now, I just want to make out with my sexy vampire boyfriend.'

Austin groaned pleasurably, picking her up and carrying her to the bed. They kissed passionately for a while before the clothes started coming off. Alannah stripped his shirt off first. Her own t-shirt and bra followed, falling in a pile beside the bed.

The pressure of Austin's mouth sucking on her nipples made Alannah moan audibly. Perhaps too loudly because her door flung open a minute later and Liam entered her room. 'Right, Austin, I want you gone. I need a word with Alannah.'

Remaining atop Alannah, Austin merely turned to face the intruder. 'Screw you, arsehole! Can't you see we're busy here?'

Liam continued to advance toward the bed. 'I don't care. I have important family business to discuss. Now go before I hurt you.'

Austin moved after a moment's hesitation, grabbing his t-shirt from the floor. After snarling at Liam, he climbed out the window, letting it slam shut behind him; the glass pane rattling in its wake.

Alannah sat up as Liam perched on the edge of her bed. 'This better be good.' It took a moment for Alannah to realise Liam was staring at her naked breasts.

'Would you uh… mind covering up?' he asked, still mesmerised by the view of her firm C-Cups.

A smile started to tug at the corner of Alannah's lips. 'Why? Do you find my bare body distracting?'

'Yes, Lana, I do.'

Alannah's grin widened. Knowing Liam found her attractive was a huge turn-on, even if she knew she could not have him. Leaning across his lap, Alannah stretched out her arm to grab her top from the floor. He let out an audible gasp as she did so. After sitting up again, she pulled the garment down over her chest and Liam's eyes locked with hers.

There was an uncomfortable silence between them for a few seconds. Liam cleared his throat. 'Brendan told me about your meeting with our grandmother earlier. I was planning on letting you rest before having this talk, but apparently you have recovered well enough.' He paused a moment to look at the window. His gorgeous blue eyes turned to her with a fierce intensity she had never seen before. 'I hope you weren't about to make any rash decisions.'

Did he think… 'What? Gods no! You thought I was gonna get myself cursed tonight?' She waited for his nod to confirm what his fears had been. *So that's why he barged in.* 'Liam, even I'm not that impulsive! Yeah, I talked about it with Austin, but I'm going to take my time with such a life-changing decision.'

Pain filled Liam's eyes. 'But you are considering it? Christ, Lana! How could you think vampirism is even an option? You ought to know you will have the entire mage community of Gaeilge Shores to back you up if our grandmother attacks you. Given who this woman is, they might even mobilise an entire army to remove her from the face of the earth once and for all.' He pressed his forehead against hers. 'Please don't become cursed. If not for your own sake, then for mine.'

Alannah froze. 'Okay, I won't.'

'Are we training today?' Alannah asked the guys as she walked into the living room. 'I'm keen to step things up to daily sessions in light of yesterday's events.' *And not so big on dying,* she added silently.

Liam looked up from his book on magic theory. 'Sounds like a good plan, although my schoolwork will make it hard to attend every day. But I will come as often as possible.'

'I'm in,' Brendan replied simply.

'Great, let's get to it.' She started walking toward the cellar.

'Give me a sec,' Liam called after her. 'I need to finish this chapter first.'

Alannah sighed as she turned back to face her cousins and leaned against the doorframe. 'Don't take too long. I know what you're like with reading. One chapter becomes five, ten minutes becomes an hour, et cetera, et cetera.'

Brendan snorted. 'Impatient much, Lana?'

'Always. Also, I have a date tonight, so I'd like to finish at a reasonable time.'

Slamming his book shut, Liam's brow creased as he narrowed his eyes on her. 'Austin's coming again? Tonight? He was here last night.'

'Yeah, he is. I want to apologise for last night because *you* who rudely interrupted us.' She stood upright and crossed her arms.

Liam scowled. 'Oh, I'm so-o sorry for showing concern about your wellbeing, Lana.' He paused a moment to drop the sarcasm from his tone. 'I don't like how much time you spend with Austin and I hate seeing the two of you together.'

'That's too bad, because you don't get any say when it comes to my love life, Liam.' Alannah noticed Brendan had abandoned his own reading and was watching her and Liam intently.

Liam shot up abruptly and crossed half the distance between them. 'What if I want to be part of your love life? Do I get a say then?'

Dumbfounded, Alannah needed to lean against the doorframe for support. 'What are you saying, Liam?'

'Do I have to spell it out for you? I'm. In. Love. With you, Lana. I always have been.'

Gasping for much needed air, Alannah closed her eyes. When she opened them a moment later, a single tear escaped before the steam poured out from her ears. '*Why the hell couldn't you have told me this four months ago? Like before I fell for Austin. And what's the fucking point of telling me now when you know you can't have me and my tainted blood?*'

'I don't give a shit how pure your blood is, Lana. I might have told you that earlier had you not spent a week avoiding me as soon as you found out about your father. And just because I haven't said it in so many words, I've been trying to express my feelings ever since you returned home.'

'Sorry I'm not a mind reader. Maybe I should try to become an enchanter instead. Your timing really sucks, Liam. I'm with Austin now.'

'So you keep reminding me.' Liam spat with bitter contempt. 'But it's not like you're married to the guy.'

'No, but I am in love with him.'

Liam blanched, pushing past her. 'I'll meet you both in the ritual room when you're ready.'

Alannah turned on Brendan, closing in on him. '*You!* You've known how Liam felt all along, right?'

Shaking his head rapidly, he threw his hands up in a protective gesture. 'Nuh, uh. Don't put this on me, Lana. You know I have a code. How would you like it if I told other people how you felt about them?'

'But you must have known the feelings were mutual in the beginning. Surely it's not so bad in that case?'

He sighed. 'Don't twist things to suit yourself. I don't *ever* get involved in other people's relationships. It's my rule.'

She slumped down on the couch next to Brendan, tapping her foot as she ran her fingers through her hair. 'I'm so damn confused. Why didn't he tell me in the first place?'

'He did try, Lana. Men aren't good at talking about emotions. When it comes to love, we prefer to show, not tell how we feel.' He placed a comforting arm over her shoulders.

Alannah glared at him. 'Wait, so you're siding with Liam on this?'

He shook his head. 'No, I'm merely suggesting you might need to pay more attention to what guys do rather than what they say.'

Alannah scoffed. 'And what would a slut like you know about love?'

'You might be surprised… Oh, and have you forgotten about the whole emotion channelling thing I do? Speaking of which, we should get on with our training.' Brendan stood and left the room.

Exhaling heavily, Alannah braced herself for the awkward magic session ahead.

If it was possible to call sitting around feeling sorry for oneself work, Alannah was having a very productive Sunday. Whenever she attempted any study, whether it be for school or magic, her mind wandered to her two huge predicaments. Tara wanted her cursed or dead and Liam was in love with her.

Knowing how Liam felt made her heart rate quicken and her girly parts tingle, but other thoughts nagged at her. She had spent years fantasising about him, practically placing him on a pedestal like some hot celebrity. For most of her life they had lived in separate states, where their only real connection had been through social media. But everything had changed, and she did not know how to reconcile her dreams with the reality of being with him. There was also the fact that Uncle Ross would never allow it to happen.

And what about Austin? I love him, sure, but do I love him and want him more than Liam? So many questions cycled through her thoughts that she wound up grinding her teeth.

The knocking on her door was almost a reprieve. Brendan stood on her threshold when she answered it. 'Hey Lana. Dad's called a family meeting. Wants us all in the dining room pronto.'

'Okay, give me a sec to change.'

Brendan's gaze travelled down to her black satin negligee. 'I don't see what's wrong with what you're wearing.' When his eyes returned to hers there was an impish gleam to them.

Alannah scowled as she berated him, 'You are such a pervert!' She slammed the door on his laughter.

Having dressed more appropriately, she found the rest of the household waiting for her at the dinner-table. Alannah could smell Nora's Sunday roast baking in the oven, and it was driving her empty stomach crazy.

Ross smiled at her as she took her seat. 'Thank you for joining us, Alannah.'

She briefly glanced at Liam but found his expression blank and unreadable.

'Right, well to start with, I have decided to lift the grounding from all of you,' said Ross.

'Halle-fucking-lujah!' Brendan exclaimed.

Nora frowned. 'Language, Brendan!'

'Sorry, Mum.'

'As I was saying,' Ross continued, 'the grounding is over, however...' He paused, focusing his intense gaze on her. 'Alannah, your safety is still at risk, which is why I am going to impose a strict curfew and place some conditions on your outings.'

Pushing her chair back, she rose abruptly. 'What? That's so not fair! I've never had a curfew in my life!'

'Lana, please sit down and listen to him,' Liam pleaded.

With a sigh, she sank back in her chair. 'Sorry, Uncle Ross.'

'Please understand, this is for your safety, Alannah. Your grandmother is a very dangerous woman. I don't think any of you realise how much of a threat she poses. Her powers rival those of the Arch Mage himself. I would go so far as to say they exceed his powers because she is attuned to every single mana source.'

'I thought the Arch Mage was fully attuned,' queried Alannah.

'Not quite. There is one source the council forbids entirely,' Ross replied.

'Holy shi—' Brendan paused mid curse as Ross glared at him. '—ishkabob. You mean she's attuned to nether as well?'

'I'm afraid so. And the implications of such power are that she can summon and command demons. The Council has suspected the Queen of the Cursed had been biding her time and waiting for an opportunity to launch an outright assault on the Arch Mage, to take his seat by force. I know she feared the possibility Aileen might have challenged her because while she was not fully attuned, she was able to channel all other sources competently, something she kept a secret even from the Council. Alannah, your mother was probably the only mage who had any chance of defeating Tara outright. That was, until your initiation.'

'So why didn't Mum initiate me earlier? And why didn't she try to take on Tara?'

Closing his eyes, Ross exhaled heavily. He looked at Alannah again with his head hung low. 'Aileen did confront our mother, and she died trying.'

Alannah and the boys all gasped at the revelation. 'But I thought Mum died of—'

Ross cut her off. 'Of an aneurysm, yes. That's what her injuries looked like to the forensic pathologist. Regular humans don't know how to diagnose magic overload. Aileen pushed herself too hard and the surge of power she drew into herself destroyed her brain before she could direct her killing blow.'

The room fell quiet for a moment.

Ross sighed. 'Alannah, your mother didn't want you to become a mage and end up like her; or worse, like your grandmother. You weren't so much as a blip on Tara's radar before your initiation, but now she knows you have become a mage, she sees you as the only real threat to her power.'

She shook her head in disbelief. 'But I can't even do much with my magic.'

'Not yet but given time your power could outgrow hers. She wants to prevent that possibility from arising.'

'Dad, if Tara is such a threat to the Arch Mage, why hasn't he coordinated an attack on her?'

'Two reasons. Firstly, Tara hasn't done anything to warrant an outright assault. Her only real crimes thus far have been the use of forbidden magic. Curse and exile from mage society are punishment enough for this. And the second reason: she is impossible to ambush. Without the element of surprise, the Arch Mage's army won't stand a chance.'

'So, what do we do?' Liam asked.

'I want the three of you to continue with your daily training to prepare yourselves for the inevitable battle ahead. In the meantime, Alannah, I want to restrict your outings to reduce Tara's access to you. On school nights, I want you home before sunset and on weekends and during the school holidays, your curfew is 1AM.'

'Okay, but what happens if I break curfew?'

'I'll ground you again. I don't want to be unfair, Alannah, but I need to know you are safe. If unforeseen circumstances mean you might be home late, I want you to ring me before your deadline. But imposing time limits won't be enough. Except for classroom time at school, I don't want you leaving this house without Liam guarding you.'

'What?' Alannah shot Liam a look. He wore a smug grin. *What the hell? Was this his suggestion?*

She wondered if Ross knew about Liam's ulterior motives. There was no way she was going to enlighten her Uncle. 'What about getting to school in the morning? Can I still take the bus?'

'No, Alannah. Liam will drive you. Now, there are two other matters of business to discuss before dinner, so I'm not going to argue with you Alannah. My terms are final. Do you understand?'

'Yeah, I understand. Curfew times are sunset on school nights, 1AM otherwise, and Liam is now my shadow.'

Brendan laughed until Alannah's death-stare shut him up.

'Good. Next order of business is the Spring Equinox gala. This year the High Magus is inviting all active mages from across the state to attend and he insists on our presence. It is a cocktail reception tomorrow night, and you will all dress accordingly.'

Brendan groaned. 'I hate wearing suits.'

Alannah sympathised. 'Um, I don't really have any fancy dresses.'

'Don't worry, sweetheart, you can borrow one of mine.' Nora smiled.

'What's the final thing you wanted to talk about?' Liam prompted.

'Your mother and I have planned a family camping trip for the October long weekend. We will join several other mage families for a magic retreat at Deep Creek.'

'Sounds good. We haven't been camping in ages,' Liam beamed.

Brendan nodded. 'Camping is much more my style. Finally, something fun to look forward to. Can we eat now? I'm starving.'

Eating her meal in silence, Alannah paid little attention while the others reminisced about previous camping trips. She had not been on any of them anyway. Her thoughts were elsewhere and the intense looks Liam gave her on a few occasions did not help.

As Alannah made her way along the upstairs hallway that night, Liam stepped out of his room and stopped her, halting only a hair's breadth away. 'Better reset your alarm, Lana. I want to leave by seven in the morning.'

'So now I have to fit in with your schedule? What happens when you're off surfing or something? Do I have to stay home?'

A glimmer of amusement appeared in his eyes. 'Or you could come with me and learn how to surf. Seriously though, what's so bad about spending time with me? Your lack of enthusiasm cuts me to the bone.' His tone was light and humorous, but Alannah heard the truth in his words.

'It's not that I don't want to spend time with you, Liam. We lead very different lives. You have your friends and I have mine. You play water sports and I... well I like to party.'

'I go to most of the same parties as you, Lana.'

'That's not exactly what I meant.'

'Oh…. Well, I think more time together is a good thing.' He leaned in closer to whisper in her ear, 'Imagine that we're dating.'

'But we're not dating, and I have a boyfriend. How the hell am I supposed to get time alone with Austin now?'

Liam grinned. 'Who's Austin?'

Alannah whacked his bicep with the back of her hand. 'Not funny.'

'You know how I feel about you, Lana, and I know you want me too. When are you going to stop messing around with that vampire git and give us a chance?'

She stood agape and speechless. Deciding it was safer to go to bed than reply with some snide remark, she pushed past him.

He caught her hand before she was out of his reach, forcing her to turn and face him. 'Good night, Lana.' Liam's thumb caressed the back of her knuckles as he gazed into her eyes for several seconds. He released her and returned to his room.

After running into her room, Alannah leaned against her closed door and released a huge lung full of air. *What am I going to do about Liam?*

'Liam, was it your idea to shadow me?' Alannah asked, having decided to break the uncomfortable silence in the car. She was still half asleep and already regretted her decision to hold out until after her workout for breakfast.

'Not entirely. Dad was adamant you should have a warlock bodyguard before lifting your grounding. I simply volunteered for the job.'

'Why not let Uncle Ross hire someone with more experience? Were you looking for an excuse to get closer to me?'

Liam sighed. 'Believe it or not, Lana, Dad has faith in my abilities as a mage and he thinks I stand as much chance of protecting you as any other warlock in the state. I'll admit, the opportunity to spend more time with you is a huge bonus, but I genuinely care about your wellbeing. I intend to take my duties seriously.'

Knowing that helped Alannah relax. 'Thank you, Liam.'

He glanced at her briefly and smiled. 'You're welcome.' When his eyes returned to the road, they were pulling into the school driveway.

It was odd how the knowledge of Liam watching her made Alannah self-conscious in the gym. Being such a confident woman, she rarely felt embarrassed. Brendan was the only guy who had ever made her blush before, because of their game. But that morning, as Alannah used the machine weights, it felt like Liam's eyes were boring a hole through to her soul and her cheeks flushed.

'Did you want me to spot for you?' Liam asked as she approached the bench press.

'You may as well since you have to watch me anyway.' She adjusted the weights down to twenty kilos. She knew both her cousins could manage over six times her limit, but she wasn't trying to get ripped.

Liam observed her first lift intently. 'Your strength building is progressing well, and you've got some good muscle tone, Lana.'

'Um… thanks.' Her increased heart rate was not due to the exercise alone.

'We should start your combat training soon. It looks like you're ready.'

She gave up after her second set of reps. It was less than her usual four, but she could not deal with Liam's scrutiny. As soon as she was on her feet, she felt her breathing settle.

'My turn.' Liam set the weights up to one-thirty-two.

'What sort of combat?' Alannah asked.

'A mix of martial arts and weapon fighting.' Liam straddled the bench. 'As a mage, you will learn to use enchanted blades. They will give you a real edge in combat.' He flashed her a wicked grin before laying back to commence his exercises.

Alannah groaned at the pun. But she found her eyes drawn to the sight of Liam's muscles as they tensed and quivered. The tight shirt he wore left little to the imagination and she could not help but speculate what sex would be like with such a well-built man. Austin's figure was slim and toned, but he owed much of his strength to his vampire heritage and lacked the definition apparent in Liam's abs. *Shit!* She was already betraying Austin with her mind. Pushing such thoughts aside, she tried to refocus on their conversation. 'Training with swords sounds rather deadly.'

Liam took a few deep breaths between sets before replying. 'Don't worry. We'll start with blunt practice weapons.'

'What about guns?'

'Mages don't use guns or other explosives. Too risky when an opponent could use magic to set them off and injure the person holding them.'

After their gym session and a quick breakfast, Liam walked Alannah to her locker. When they reached her stretch of corridor, she spied Austin waiting for her and her stomach churned. 'I don't suppose you could leave me here?' she asked Liam.

'Not a chance.'

She sighed and advanced toward inevitable awkwardness.

Austin pulled her into his arms the moment she was in his reach. 'Hey beautiful.' As he leaned in for a kiss, the sound of Liam clearing his throat interrupted them. 'Beat it, Winters,' Austin growled.

'Sorry, I can't. Would you like to explain, Lana, or should I?'

Alannah felt Austin tense and his grip on her tighten. 'Explain what?' His tone was apprehensive.

'Liam is now my bodyguard. He will follow me everywhere except around the home and into classes. I'm sorry, Austin. I know this is a serious buzzkill for us. I don't fancy having a chaperone on our dates.' She leaned in to whisper so softly that only Austin's vampire ears had any chance of hearing her: 'But you can still meet me at my window.' She pecked him on the lips and pulled out of his hold.

Austin's expression was a closed book and Alannah feared what he thought of the situation. For once, she wished she could turn her aura reading powers back on. 'I can't say I like the idea of hanging out with Liam, but protecting you is of the utmost importance. I will work around whatever you need.'

'Thank you, Austin. Will I see you at lunch?'

'Unlikely. Too much sun today.'

Alannah's heart sank. If it was only her, she would have joined him in the vamp's common room, but Austin clearly didn't want Liam to see his secret tunnels. 'Damn. Tomorrow then, I guess?'

'I guess so. Bye for now.' He stole one last kiss from her before heading to class.

Liam was waiting outside her English lesson at recess.

Alannah's treacherous eyes could get used to seeing the hottest guy in school this much and they were not the only part of her body feeling that way.

Brendan huffed as he walked out of the room with her. 'Seriously, bro. What trouble do you think Lana could get in within fifteen minutes?'

'If she's spending the time with you? A hell of a lot, I'm sure.'

Brendan laughed. 'Not the sort of trouble I was referring to, but I'll pay that.'

'So how are we going to do this?' Alannah asked. 'Will you join our group, or do I have to hang with your friends?'

'I thought we could alternate. Recess with your friends today, mine tomorrow. Lunch with mine today, yours tomorrow. How does that sound?'

'I guess that's fair. Try to play nice, okay?'

He grinned. 'Don't worry, Lana. I'll be on my best behaviour.'

After dumping their books in their lockers, they made their way to Alannah and Brendan's usual table outside. A few of her friends gave Alannah sidelong glances when they observed Liam standing close beside her and even a few surprised gasps when he sat next to her.

'What are you doing here?' Caleb asked Liam. As an endarkened fae, he had a strong dislike for purists like Liam, and with good reason. The endarkened were the offspring of elves and dark mages and usually practised illegal magic like their dark mage parents.

Alannah sensed Liam tensing, so she shot him a warning look.

'I'm spending time with my favourite cousin,' he replied, still facing Alannah.

Locky, the goth goblin in the group, scoffed. 'What, you don't get enough time with her at home? You have to come and spoil our fun?'

'I'm not here to spoil anything—unless someone tries to hurt Lana.'

Everyone glanced at Alannah with wide eyes and arched brows. Cara, who was sitting on her left side, leaned in close to whisper, 'Are you guys, you know…?'

Alannah turned to her best friend and replied in a hushed voice. 'No. I'll fill you in later.'

A few people tried to carry on with their conversations and Jacob even attempted some small talk with Alannah and Cara, but a nervous energy filled the rest of their morning.

Lunch was not much better, except this time Alannah was the unwelcome party crasher. Liam led her into a private dining hall and rest area that struck her with awe.

'This is the Founding Families' Lounge,' Liam explained.

Yet another common room for the exclusive use of magicals. Alannah wondered how many other such areas existed around campus. This room was much more elaborate than the underground hideout which Austin used. Dark timber tables filled the centre of the room, with matching desks and shelves lining one wall and dark red sofas along another. There was even a kitchenette with a fridge, microwave, kettle, and small sink.

While Liam went about reheating some leftovers, Alannah sat at one of the empty tables to avoid a confrontation with the girls who had been glaring at her since she entered. But she was out of luck. After they giggled and whispered amongst themselves for a minute, Monique made her way over to Alannah.

The queen bee sat next to Alannah and leaned in close. 'Rumour has it that you're cheating on your vampire boyfriend with Liam. One guy not enough for you? But why stop at two when you could so easily jump into your other cousin's bed too? Or have you already been there?'

Alannah narrowed her gaze on Monique. 'You shouldn't believe everything you hear. You might earn a reputation for being dumb and gullible.'

'Everything okay, Lana?' Liam asked as he moved close and placed a protective hand on her shoulder.

Observing the way Liam touched Alannah, Monique's prying eyes searched her blank expression. It made Alannah thankful the bitch was not an enchanter.

'Everything's fine. Monique, you were just catching me up on some school gossip, right? Thanks for the intel, by the way.'

Monique smirked. 'Of course.' She rose and returned to her friends.

Most of Liam's other mates had joined the girls by this point.

'Come on, Lana. Let's sit with them. Don't worry, they won't mind.'

Doubting the truth in that, Alannah followed Liam hesitantly. It was not that she was afraid of them or lacked the nerve to approach the popular kids. Alannah simply disliked conflict.

When they reached the table, more wide-eyed looks greeted Alannah and Liam. At least this time Liam offered an explanation, 'Listen guys, we have a situation. I know you're all wondering why I am following Alannah everywhere.' A few of them nodded. 'There's no easy way to say this, so I'm gonna be blunt…' he paused a moment. 'Tara Winters is back in town and she has threatened Alannah's life.' All of Liam's friends gasped. 'I've taken on the role of Alannah's bodyguard and I expect the rest of you will help me watch out for her.'

Liam's best mate, Blake, clapped him on the shoulder. 'No worries, man. Welcome, Alannah. Sorry about the whole death-threat thing, but don't worry, we've got your back.'

Smiling, Alannah decided she liked Blake, thinking that perhaps sitting with this group would not be so bad, even if the rest of Liam's friends were arseholes.

'Here sweetheart, I picked up a little something from the shops on my way home. I hope I got your size right.' Nora gave Alannah a dress bag as she entered the kitchen.

'Oh, wow, you didn't have to do that. I could have borrowed one of yours—' she began to protest.

But her aunt put her hand up to silence her. 'You ought to have at least one of your own. It was no trouble, really.'

'Um, thanks.' Alannah whistled as she pulled the garment out of the bag. 'It's stunning.' She was holding a short, emerald green A-line dress with a low plunging V-neck. Elaborate beading covered the bodice, while a lace design started halfway down the top layer of the lined skirt.

'I figured it would bring out your eye colour. Oh, and here are some matching heels. Now you'd better go get ready.' She handed Alannah a pair of black strappy shoes.

After hugging Nora, she made her way to her room. The dress was a perfect fit and as Alannah looked in the mirror, she barely recognised herself. She rarely wore anything that was not black and certainly nothing so fancy. *But hey, I look pretty damn good!* When she contemplated what to do about jewellery, she remembered the set she had inherited from her mother. She retrieved the emerald pendant on its silver chain, along with the matching teardrop earrings. The colour was a perfect match.

Must be fate, she decided as she adorned her neck and ears with the precious gems.

As she stepped out into the hall, she found Brendan emerging from his own room, still struggling with his tie. Looking up at her, he stopped dead, eyes almost popping out of their sockets. '*Wowsers, Lana!* You are smokin' hot.'

'Thanks. You've scrubbed up pretty well too. Here, let me help you with that. I used to fix Dad's ties after Mum…' she left the rest hanging. It was not a night for mournful reminiscing. Taking Brendan's black satin tie in hand, she redid the botched double Windsor. 'There, much better.'

Brendan's eyes stared at her. 'Thanks, Lana.'

For a moment, electricity charged the air between them and Alannah's grip lingered on the tie. As much as Brendan hated dressing in suits, he pulled the look off superbly and it was easy to forget he was not the Winters man she had the hots for.

A closing door at the other end of the hallway broke the spell between them. When Alannah turned toward the noise, she spied Nora heading towards the stairs. She joined her aunt.

'Oh my gosh!' Nora clamped a hand over her mouth. 'You look gorgeous, sweetie.' She touched the emerald pendant. 'Was this your mum's? It's beautiful.'

'Yeah. She liked wearing green.'

'Yes, I remember that now. You look so much like her, Alannah. She would be proud of you. Come on, let's go knock the socks off the rest of the mage community.'

After taking a moment to wipe away a rogue tear, Alannah followed Nora and Brendan downstairs. Liam was waiting with Ross on the ground floor landing and as soon as he spotted her, his eyes lit up. She thought of all those cliché stairway scenes in American teen movies. At least he was not about to present her with a corsage and take her to prom.

Liam in a suit was a breathtaking sight. As they made their way to the car, he grabbed Alannah's arm to hold her back and whispered, 'I think I've just fallen in love with you all over again. You look incredible.'

She smiled back at him. 'Thanks.'

They all travelled together in Ross' Land Rover, with Alannah sandwiched in the back between her cousins. She was conscious of two sets of eyes on her for the duration of the journey. *Liam, I understand; but what is up with Brendan?* She shrugged it off, putting it down to his hormones responding to her attire.

Alannah discovered Cara at the buffet. She was sporting a striking red chiffon maxi dress, with a thigh high split, matching the colour of her hair. Grinning from the relief of finding a friendly face, she hugged Cara. 'Looking good.'

'Speak for yourself, Alannah. That outfit is amazing on you.' She leaned in closer and gestured towards a group of guys. 'Liam can't keep his eyes off you, and he's not the only one.'

A cursory glance told her Cara was right. All of Liam's mates were checking her out too. She spotted Brendan standing with his friends. Three of them were looking her way, but she noticed one set of eyes on Cara. 'Liam has to watch me. He's my bodyguard now and he also ordered his friends to help protect me.'

'Watch you, sure; but that's more than a look of concern for his charge. You've got every guy in this place drooling over you, girl.'

'Not quite. Bailey's got his eyes on you.'

'Yeah, well he's had a crush on me for years, poor guy. He knows I'm not interested. I've got my heart set on someone else.'

'Oh? Who?'

'Promise not to tell?'

'My lips are sealed.' Alannah zipped her mouth shut with a gesture.

Cara took a deep breath. 'Jacob. I love that impish smile of his and he always makes me laugh.'

Alannah giggled. 'You guys would make the cutest little redhead babies.'

'Would if we could!' Cara grinned.

Recollections from her reading on fae came to mind. *Hybrid races can only breed with their own kind or those of their precursor races.* For boggarts that meant elves or gorgons. 'Oh right, I forgot boggarts can't breed with mages.' She offered an apologetic smile.

'Honestly, it doesn't bother me at all. I'm not looking to breed, at least not yet. But seriously, getting back to Liam: you've got to tell me what's going on with you two.'

She sighed. 'He confessed his undying love to me on Saturday, admitting he doesn't care about my tainted blood. Problem is, I'm still in love with Austin. Plus, I know Uncle Ross would never approve of the relationship, despite what Liam says.'

'Well shit! That's huge. For Liam to be willing to break tradition and ignore his father's wishes… he's got it for you bad, Alannah. What are you going to do?'

'I dunno. I'm so damn confused!'

The High Magus called everyone to attention, ending Alannah's conversation as he summoned them into the ballroom. He stood in front of a band who had set up on the stage. After tapping on his microphone, he began his speech: 'I'd like to start by thanking you all for coming tonight. I know some of you have travelled across the state to get here. Thank the Gods for ley lines.'

A few people in the crowd chuckled, but Alannah did not find his attempt at humour very funny.

'The Spring Equinox is a special time of year, marking a season of rebirth and fertility in nature. This is especially important for the shamans among us. But today also represents the struggle between light and dark within all of us. As much as I hate to put a dampener on our celebration, it is crucial that I remind you all of this and the consequences of slipping into the left-hand path. Some of you may have heard an old threat has returned to Gaeilge Shores and I'm afraid I must confirm the rumours. Tara Winters, Queen of the Cursed, walks among us once again and she has already threatened a member of our community.'

Alannah heard gasps and murmurs among the audience. She scanned the crowd and saw the pale, aghast faces of the people surrounding her. *If my grandmother incites such terror among so many full-fledged mages, what hope do I have?* Her shoulders hunched and it felt as though someone had replaced her stomach with rocks.

Liam stepped closer to put his arm around her shoulders and whispered in her ear. 'Don't worry, Lana. I won't let anything happen to you.'

Kieran continued addressing them. 'This woman is very dangerous, and I advise against approaching or engaging her in direct combat without backup. If any of you have information on her whereabouts, please contact me directly.' He paused for several seconds to let everyone process his words. 'Now, with that unpleasant news out of the way, I invite you all to enjoy the festivities here tonight. Thank you.' The High Magus left the stage and the band started up with some classic rock covers.

'Wanna dance?' Liam asked her.

'No. I don't dance. Not to this music anyway.'

Liam arched his brow. 'What sort of music will you dance to?'

'Anything that's good and heavy. Even then, I only get into it if there's a decent mosh pit.'

'Fair enough. Come on, let's get a drink.' Liam led her outside, swiping a couple of beers from the bar on the way and handed her one. 'Don't let my folks see you drinking.'

Alannah smiled. 'Were you always this rebellious, or is it my bad influence?'

'Hey, I'm eighteen now, I'm allowed to drink. But I'd have to say some of your defiance has rubbed off on me.'

She snorted. 'Right. So, you never partook in underage drinking?'

'Sure, I did. But only with Dad's permission and supervision.' Liam stopped beside the bonfire and took a seat.

Alannah rolled her eyes as she perched beside him. 'So, what's the naughtiest thing you've ever done?'

'Well getting you initiated behind Dad's back is definitely right up there.'

'Yeah, I guess it would be. But come on, was there anything from before my return?'

Liam took several minutes to ponder his answer, leaving Alannah to watch a pair of fire dancers who had started performing nearby. The magic they cast was impressive in its own right, but the way their bodies whirled about was a fascinating sight to behold.

'There is one thing I can think of.'

'Huh, what?' The dancers still mesmerised Alannah and she was only vaguely aware of Liam talking.

He laughed. 'That's Claudia and Clayton, twin fire channellers. They're good, aren't they?'

'Brilliant. Sorry, what were you saying?'

'I can think of something I did that was technically naughty, and I certainly didn't tell my parents about it.'

'Well now you have my attention.' She eyed him expectantly.

'Underage sex.'

That made her grin. 'I had wondered about that. How old were you?'

'You wondered about my sex life, huh?' His eyes sparkled with a hint of mischief. 'I lost my virginity at fifteen. I'd planned to wait longer, but Monique was eager, and Brendan kept bragging about having sex. I guess I let my competitive nature get the better of me.'

'Of course Brendan started young.' She cast her eyes in her other cousin's direction. He was sitting on the opposite side of the fire, laughing, and drinking shots poured from a hipflask with Connor, Bailey, and Cara. Brendan turned to face her, tilting his head, and looking at her from beneath arched brows. She lifted her cup in a toast and he smiled, returning the gesture.

'How old were you, Lana?'

'Eleven,' she replied casually, her gaze still locked with Brendan's.

'So, you started young too.'

She turned back to Liam. 'Does that bother you?'

'Not really. Your previous relationships are not my concern. It's the current one I don't like.'

Alannah sighed as she stared into her drink before sculling a large mouthful. 'What do you have against Austin? I mean aside from jealousy over me.'

'Well to begin with, there's the fact that he's a vampire and owes his loyalty to a Queen who wants to curse or kill you. But it's mostly his past behaviour that worries me. I don't know all the details, but Austin and Brendan used to have a rep for tag-teaming girls. I suspect they employed hypnotic coercion in some cases, but Brendan never admitted that much and there was no proof. What I do know is Austin became addicted to feeding on the girls and took it too far on a couple of occasions.'

Alannah's jaw kept dropping as Liam shed light on her boyfriend's past. She did not want to believe it, but Brendan had already alluded to his dark times. 'What do you mean "too far?"'

'Two of the girls went to hospital on the brink of death and needed blood transfusions. Austin's dad covered it up with all his money and powerful connections, so it never got out to the wider mage community, but Brendan confessed to me. The whole mess distressed him. A lot.'

'Shit. I guess that's why Austin was so reluctant to bite me when I first asked. He was afraid of putting me in hospital.'

Liam frowned. 'I can't believe you asked him to feed on you, Lana. Why the hell would you do that?'

'I figured it would be hot. I didn't know there was such a risk, at least not at first. If I'm honest, I had a bit of a vampire fetish even before I knew they were real. I'm a big fan of Anne Rice and Joss Whedon. When I learned what bites could feel like—'

'So what? You ignored the warnings in the training books?' He shook his head in bewilderment.

'I don't need to justify my actions to you, Liam. I'm a pleasure seeker and I refuse to feel ashamed about it. Some risks are worth the reward.'

'You've changed a lot in the last nine years. You were such a sweet girl back then.' There was no bitterness in his tone, merely resigned acceptance.

'No, Liam. I've always had these tendencies. Obviously, they flourished more when I hit puberty, but your princess was never all that innocent. You simply refused to see me for what I was.' Alannah looked over at Brendan as she cast her mind back to their childhood. They were only five when the two of them discovered her mum's copy of the *Kama Sutra*. They had giggled a lot on their first read through, but it soon became their mission to learn as much as they could about sex. A year later, their game of Sleazy Chicken began.

'What's that supposed to mean?' Liam asked.

'Let's just say, my sex education started about five years before my hymen broke.'

'Christ!' Liam must have followed her line of sight because when Alannah returned her attention to Liam, she saw his blanched face glaring at Brendan.

Chapter Fourteen

The rest of the week passed with little incident, mostly thanks to the amount of schoolwork everyone needed to finish before the end of term. Even Liam seemed content to sit back and supervise Alannah without getting pushy or personal and she began to wonder if he had given up on the idea of dating her. Deciding to test the waters during the first week of the mid-semester break, she walked into the living room and addressed Liam: 'Austin and I are going to the movies tonight.'

Shifting his focus away from the television, he glared at her. 'Not happening.'

'What, why? Do you have other plans, because you were meant to tell me what nights you were busy?'

'I refuse to be the third wheel on one of your dates, Lana. Sorry, but I can't deal with the sight of you making out with him, or anyone else for that matter. If you must see him, keep it to the bedroom.' He turned back to the TV. 'And try to keep his teeth out of your neck, for the love of the Gods.'

'What the hell is your problem, Liam?'

He grabbed the remote to pause his crime show. Tossing it aside, he gave her a penetrating stare. 'I've already told you how I feel about you. What do *you* think my problem is?'

'You've been distant for the last week, so I thought you'd gotten over me.'

Liam shot up from the couch in a flash and pulled her into his arms, pressing her head against his hard chest. His heart was racing. 'Is this a better proximity for you? Because I wish I could keep you this close all day, every day. What I feel for you is not a passing crush, Lana. I've been in love with you for as long as I can remember. Not something I can "get over" that easily.' After loosening his grip on her, he gently lifted her chin to look into her eyes. 'Now tell me how you feel.'

She gazed up into his big blues and years of feelings came crashing into her heart. *Shit!* It would have been all too easy to give in to him there, but she knew it would not be fair on either him or Austin. 'I do want you and I don't even have to dig that deep to find those feelings, but things are complicated now.'

'Because of Austin? Or is there someone else too?'

'Yes, because of Austin. Who else would there be?'

'I don't know Lana, you tell me.' This time his tone was bitter.

'Is this about my relationship history? You said that didn't bother you. Look, I've only ever been in love with three guys in my life and I assure you I've moved on from my ex.'

There was a flicker of emotion in his eyes. 'And the other two?'

'Are you and Austin.' She heard the slightest gasp slip through his teeth. 'Please give me time to sort my head out.'

Liam released his hold on her and slumped back onto the sofa. 'I can give you time, but don't expect me to chaperone any dates.'

When the first week of October ended, Alannah was chomping at the bit to get out of the house. After her heart to heart with Liam, she did not feel like dragging him out of the house much.

The night before their camping trip, Alannah tossed and turned in bed. Sleep was eluding her overactive mind as she thought back to the previous night:

It was her only date-night with Austin that week, and they had spent it in her room. Austin scrutinised her with narrow, unwavering eyes. 'You're unusually quiet, Alannah. What's wrong?'

She did not want to worry him when she was still working through her feelings, so she told a partial lie. 'I'm annoyed we can't go out on proper dates because Liam has to shadow me.'

'I know how you feel. This is trying, but I know a good way to channel our frustrations.' He grinned as he pulled her onto the bed.

Even their lovemaking lacked the usual passion. Is that because I put a stop to his attempt to bite me? He didn't even hide his disappointment when I told him I was not feeling well.

It was early the next morning when Liam drove Alannah and Brendan to the camping grounds in his blue Audi Q7. Brendan had chosen to travel with them, claiming the music on his brother's radio was more tolerable than his mother's Enya CDs. His presence was a welcome buffer for the tension between her and Liam and she suspected he knew as much.

As soon as 'Wonderful Life' by Bring Me the Horizon started playing on the radio, Alannah cranked the volume.

'Fuck yeah!' Brendan cried from the backseat. He joined her in screaming along with the song.

The sight of Alannah's head banging and 'singing' to rock music kept drawing Liam's attention as well as a few laughs and smiles. It did wonders for thawing the ice between them.

The next song was one of those Aussie hip hop tunes none of them liked, so Alannah connected a streaming service on her smartphone to the stereo. Something heavy and progressive started playing.

'Who's this?' Liam asked.

'A band known as TOOL. Apparently, they were big in the nineties.'

After driving through some scrubland, they arrived at their destination: sixteen campsites nestled among tall gum trees that Alannah figured were stringybarks from the signage. The mages had booked the whole place.

'Wow!' she exclaimed. 'It feels like we're in the middle of nowhere.'

'That's the point,' Liam explained. 'Gives us the privacy we need for ritual magic and training exercises. Can't have regular humans seeing what we do.'

The remoteness of Gaeilge Shores made sense. Supposedly, their small country town was the magic capital of the state because it was the seat of the High Magus. She had once thought it odd that the mages chose not to live in the city.

'I've only ever camped in caravan parks before. Are there toilets here?' She started to look around.

'City girl!' Brendan mocked with jest. 'The toilets are over there. Hot showers too.' He pointed to a rustic wooden shack in the centre of the ring road providing access to each campsite. The facilities were about one hundred metres from their site.

Ross approached Alannah and the guys. 'Liam and Brendan, I want you to keep a close eye on Alannah all weekend.' He dumped a large blue canvas bag in front of Liam. 'The three of you are sharing this tent. Your mum's filling up the airbeds at the car.' He returned to his own camp site on the other side of his four-wheel drive.

A huge grin appeared on Brendan's face as he helped position the tent base. 'Looks like I get to sleep with you again, Lana.'

She laughed. 'Just don't poke me in the arse when spooning.'

Brendan let out a pantomime sigh. 'Fine. I guess I can make do with *poking* your front.' He added emphasis to the word by inserting one of the poles into the tent.

Alannah leaned a little closer to lower the volume of her voice. 'Am I to gather you prefer anal?'

Dropping the bag of pegs, Brendan stepped up to her and whispered, 'I would happily take you every which way, Lana.'

That won him a bright flush of red in Alannah's cheeks.

He slapped her left butt cheek. 'Looks like I'm back at the top of my game.' Backing away slowly, he added, 'The champ returns.' Spinning on his heels, he strode away.

Liam called out after him, 'Where are you going, Brendan? We haven't finished here.'

Brendan shouted his reply as he continued walking, 'Gotta see a man about a horse.'

Alannah silently helped Liam stake the tent into the ground for several minutes.

As she caught the rain fly Liam threw across the top, he stopped what he was doing to look at her. 'Lana?'

'Yes, Liam?'

'That night after we found your family tree…' He seemed apprehensive.

'What about it?'

'Did you, uh… sleep with Brendan that night?'

'Yeah, I did.' She tried to hide her amusement as Liam's face turned crimson.

'I'm gonna kill that pipsqueak….' He started towards the toilet block.

The laugh finally escaped her. 'We only slept though.'

Liam spun back around. 'Wait, so you didn't have sex? What about on other occasions?'

'No, I haven't done *that* with him.' She was still struggling to contain her hysterics.

'It's not funny, Lana. The thought of you with Brendan pains me far more than what you have going with Austin. And you know how much it kills me to see you with that vampire.'

She calmed herself with a few deep breaths. 'Sorry, but the two of you really do take sibling rivalry to the extreme. Didn't your parents ever teach you to share?' She winked at him and when he blushed, she considered introducing him to Sleazy Chicken. It might be the only way to get any wins. But it was probably too cruel, considering his feelings for her. 'You don't need to worry about Brendan and me. We enjoy flirting, but it means nothing.'

He gave her a sidelong glance but dropped the subject.

Focus, Brendan! The silent mantra did little to help shift Brendan's concentration back to the ritual High Magus Kieran was leading them in. Alannah was standing next to him and awareness of her presence was all-consuming. Looking that good in ceremonial robes should be a crime. *Shit! This isn't good.* His hormones had never interfered with his magic before. Alannah was going to be his undoing.

The circle had been cast and the High Magus was inviting them to join. The man stepped in front of Brendan. 'How do you enter the circle?'

After stumbling at first, he got the words out. 'W… with love and peace.'

Kieran eyed him with concern before responding, 'Blessed be.'

With the first stage of the ritual complete, Kieran blessed some oil. He approached each member of the circle to anoint them. 'May the Gods watch over you and keep you safe from harm.'

The smear of oil applied to Brendan's forehead pulsed, and warmth spread from it throughout his body. He knew the effect would be temporary, but it was still a welcome shield from the threat his grandmother posed.

Once the protective ritual had concluded, the campers settled in for a relaxed night around a few fires. The Council members convened at one end of the campgrounds, while the initiates were at the other end.

Brendan sat with Connor and Bailey across from Alannah, who sat with Liam and Cara. But it was not long before Bailey moved to the other side of the fire to join Cara. Brendan shook his head. 'That man's a lost cause. Cara will never yield to his advances.'

'Pessimism doesn't suit you, Brendo,' Connor observed.

He laughed. 'Just calling it as I see it. That girl's in love with someone else.'

'Are we still talking about Cara?'

When he looked at Connor, his friend was smirking. 'Come on man, out with it,' Brendan demanded.

'Why do you sit back and let your best mate and brother do all the chasing?'

'Because I've read enough of her feelings to know she's not receptive to me.'

'Bah! You haven't tried hard enough to open her eyes.' He rose in his seat. 'I'm grabbing another drink. Be right back.' Connor left Brendan alone with his thoughts for a moment.

If there was one thing he understood about Alannah: aggression was not the right approach with her. But it was possible Brendan's attempts had been too subtle. He had caught the occasional glimpse of desire on her part, but she was always so quick to shut herself off from those thoughts and emotions.

A set of female hands gripped his shoulders. 'Hey there, little brother. Why the glum face?' Monique appeared beside him.

He intensified his frown. Brendan always hated it when she faked familiarity with him. 'I'm not your brother, Monique.'

'No, but you were practically my brother-in-law for years.' She sighed as she sat next to him. 'I think I made a big mistake and went after the wrong brother.' Her hand began rubbing his thigh.

Trying to ignore the insane girl's flirting, he kept his gaze fixed on Alannah and Liam as he sipped his beer. The two of them were sitting much closer than necessary and Alannah was laughing at something Liam told her. *What the hell? She never laughed at Liam.* His lame attempts at humour usually fell flat with her.

'You know, I've always wondered what sex would be like with an enchanter,' Monique continued her attempt at seduction. It was almost laughable. She was attractive, sure, but Brendan detested everything else about the girl.

He looked at her. 'What are you doing, Monique? If you're hoping to get laid, I'm sure Blake would be obliging.'

'But he's only an illusionist and you're the best enchanter around.' She was giving him the lewdest bedroom eyes he had ever seen on a girl.

Brendan sighed and returned his attention to Alannah, who was leaning in to whisper something in Liam's ear. Whatever she said made him smile.

'You want her too, don't you?' A quick glance at Monique told him her eyes had followed Brendan's. 'Apparently all the guys do. Personally, I don't see what's so good about her.'

'You don't even know her!' Brendan snapped.

Monique laughed. 'Yep, you've got it bad. I could help you forget about her for a while. We could have some real fun.'

Forget? What would I give to forget the pain of envy and unrequited love, even for a few hours? He realised he had not had sex in months; not since his feelings for Alannah had rekindled. Brendan looked at Monique and saw the flicker of flames reflected in her eyes. 'Screw it.' He jumped up and dragged Monique beyond the tree line.

She giggled as they made their mad dash for the cover of the forest.

Once among the dense foliage, Brendan pushed Monique up against a large tree and savagely kissed her. He switched to full channelling mode, reading her every thought and feeling as he heightened her senses. This was how he had become so good at what he did. He focussed on what the girl really wanted and pressed every single button that sent her into a fit of ecstasy.

Monique's triggers were all quite vanilla, which meant he did not need much magic to please her. *Easy, yes—but not exciting.* Brendan much preferred the girls who had at least some inclination for kink.

Having rocked Monique's world, he dressed in silence and walked back to camp without a word.

Liam noticed Alannah yawning. As much as he hated the idea of their night ending, he was getting tired too. Talking to her about anything and everything had felt so good, so right. But there was always the chance they would get some time alone in their tent. The idea made him smile. 'I think it's bedtime.'

'I think you might be right,' Alannah agreed as she stood. She turned to Cara and Bailey. 'Night guys.'

Liam followed her back to their tent, glancing around the place as they walked. Even with the protection spell in place, he would not shake the habit of remaining alert of their surroundings.

As soon as they reached their little dome shelter, Alannah slid into her sleeping bag and started removing her clothes.

Liam fought the impulse to avert his eyes. She covered herself anyway, so he should not feel so damn modest.

Brendan stepped into the tent as Alannah removed her bra and dropped it on her backpack. He whistled and clapped Liam on the shoulder. 'I wouldn't normally include my brother in a threesome, but I guess these are extenuating circumstances.'

Alannah laughed.

But Liam glared at him. 'You are truly disgusting, Brendan.'

'Why thank you, Liam. I aim to please… or offend. Either works for me.'

He pulled Brendan outside the tent. 'By the way, I saw you disappear with Monique tonight.'

'And what of it? Don't tell me you're jealous?' Brendan grinned.

'Hardly. I dumped her, remember? But I know how her mind works. She's probably using you to get back at me.'

'I'm not an idiot, bro. You may be the superior mage, but when it comes to girls, I'm leagues ahead of you. I know the game she's playing, and I don't really care.' Brendan shrugged himself out of Liam's hold and moved back into the tent. 'Nice bra by the way, Lana. Black lace and satin lingerie will never go out of style.'

Liam sighed, stepping back inside.

Alannah had slipped into a black satin nightgown and the cover of her sleeping-bag dropped into her lap. 'Just as well since it's all I ever wear.'

Overcome with some strong urges, Liam ducked for the cover of his own sleeping-bag. After stripping down to his boxer shorts, he lay back to look at the blue canvas ceiling.

Brendan sniggered. 'Hey Lana, I think you made Liam blush.'

'Well that makes one of you.'

'Don't worry, Lana, you turn me red too, just not in the face.'

Alannah laughed. 'Doesn't count if I can't see it.'

Brendan's voice lowered. 'Are you saying you wanna see my cock, Lana?'

Liam groaned as he covered his ears. 'Christ, would you two give it a rest!'

They both burst into a fit of laughter, but when Alannah calmed down, she placed a hand on Liam's arm. 'I'm sorry.'

He turned and locked her eyes with his. Her gaze was unwavering as she chewed on her bottom lip. Liam took a deep breath and relaxed. Alannah's hand was still on his bicep, so he grabbed it and pressed his lips to the soft skin on the inside of her wrist. 'Good night, Lana.'

She gasped, but did not pull her hand back, not even when she settled down for sleep. 'Good night, Liam.'

Having her fingers intertwined with his, Liam fell into the 'sweetest' of dreams.

Wildflowers and grass trees lined the track Alannah hiked along with her fellow mages. It was a sunny spring day, too sunny for her liking. Alannah hoped the sunblock she had applied that morning held out long enough.

Liam was certainly in his element and even Brendan was enjoying himself. They both kept behind her, watching out for danger.

Alannah tried to keep a little distance in front of the guys as she walked alongside Cara. Starting out at a casual pace allowed for some chatting.

Leaning closer, Cara spoke in a hushed voice. 'It looked like you were getting pretty close to Liam last night. Anything you wanna share? Like what happened when the two of you went to bed together?'

'Nothing happened. Brendan joined us soon after we got to our tent.'

'Oh? I thought he spent the night with Monique?'

Alannah screwed up her face. 'Where'd you get that impression?'

'Didn't you hear, the two of them hooked up last night? Brendan as good as confirmed the rumour this morning.'

Shaking her head, Alannah dismissed the odd pang of jealousy she felt. She figured it was probably more disgust at Brendan's poor taste in sexual partner. 'Of all girls, why the hell would he go for her?'

'Probably because she was all over him last night. Monique was easy prey. I doubt he cares for her if that's what you're worried about.'

'I'm not worried, just surprised and grossed out.'

Cara stopped walking for a moment and drew Alannah's attention to her face. 'If you're not worried, I'll eat my hat. I know you care about Brendan and don't want to see him get hurt any more than I do.'

They resumed their stroll before the guys were able to catch up with them. 'Brendan's a big boy, I'm sure he can handle Monique. I thought he had better standards though.'

'Oh my God! You're jealous!' Cara cried.

'No, I'm not! I told you I don't like him that way.'

'Sure, whatever. It's a pity Liam and Brendan don't get along well, because that'd be a pretty hot threesome otherwise.' Cara giggled.

Alannah entertained the idea a moment before punching Cara in the arm for putting the thought in her head.

'Ouch! Gods, Alannah. What was that for?'

'I didn't need that mental image.'

The Council members at the front of the group began to pick up the pace and talking became too difficult. Alannah needed to focus on her breathing and where she was treading.

About three hours into the hike, the group stopped in a clearing where they set up a picnic lunch. After their meal, High Magus Kieran instructed the initiates to sit in a circle and provide a demonstration of their current powers.

Monique was up first. After a minute of meditation, she started with a simple summoning spell from which an old Cabbage Patch Kid appeared. The doll had blonde hair and a purple dress and as Monique worked her magic, the doll began to walk. It was the stuff of nightmares and Don Mancini movies. Directing the doll to return to her, she placed a letter opener in its hands. She sent it walking across the circle to her friend Jessica who handed the doll an envelope. The little plastic construct deftly sliced open the envelope and handed it back to Jessica. Monique clicked her fingers and the doll disappeared, along with the small blade it carried.

A few people gasped and most joined in a round of applause. Alannah remained silent, in awe of the girl's powers.

Brendan, who had chosen to sit next to Monique, was next. The sight of them together was infuriating.

The High Magus scoffed. 'Brendan Winters. Do you have any useful powers to show us yet?'

Monique giggled, along with her friends. 'The demonstration he gave me last night was *quite* useful.'

'*Monique!*' Kieran chided her.

The girls grew quiet.

Unfazed by Monique's behaviour, Brendan grinned at Kieran. 'Sure, I do, Your Honour.' He closed his eyes and commenced meditating.

A few minutes later, Alannah heard Brendan's voice in her head, a power he had mastered in their last training session. *'Hi Lana. You wanna tell me why you're feeling jealous?'*

She felt her cheeks flush.

'I can sense you blushing. I'll take that as your answer.' Opening his eyes, Brendan puffed his chest out at all the wide eyes and gaping mouths staring at him.

Alannah wondered what he had said to everyone else.

Several other mages displayed their abilities, such as Connor healing Bailey who intentionally electrocuted himself with a lightning bolt, and Cara making a nearby sapling grow at an accelerated pace.

Alannah's turn followed. She took a few deep breaths to calm her nerves, but they did not seem to help.

Brendan's voice was in her mind again. *'It's okay, Lana. Treat it like one of our training sessions. Here, I'll help.'*

A sudden sense of calm washed through her. Closing her eyes, she cleared her mind and began to channel the mana in her matter ring. She focussed the energy on conjuring up the practice sword she had commenced training with. When she opened her eyes, the wooden weapon was firmly in her grip. She smiled with relief. *It worked!* Closing her eyes again, she visualised the shelf the sword belonged on and willed it to return there. A second later it vanished.

The group clapped their praise.

As she looked up, she found Liam staring at her. He was sitting with Ross and Nora and all three of them were beaming with their heads held high. But Liam's gaze was different: focused and intense. It sent a rush of blood through Alannah's body. When she averted her gaze, she caught Brendan's eyes, but he was not betraying any of his thoughts or feelings. She smiled and mouthed 'thank you' to him.

'You're welcome, Lana. Oh, and don't look now, but your display of power gave every straight guy here a hard-on.'

She narrowed her eyes on him, sensing exaggeration in his words. What she had done was hardly impressive. It did not compare to Monique's demonstration.

'I speak the truth. You were only initiated a couple of months ago and you've achieved more than any other mage could in that time. Plus, you're a Winters babe.' He grinned lasciviously at her.

Thanks to the telepathic exchange with Brendan, Alannah was only vaguely aware that the magical show and tell had continued. Once concluded, they packed up and hiked back to camp.

❉

Following dinner, Alannah dragged her aching legs over to the campfire.

The moment she yawned; Liam gave her a reassuring smile. 'It's okay, I can see the tent from here. Go get some rest.'

'Thanks.' Not having him follow her straight away was a little disappointing. She was secretly hoping for some alone time with Liam. When Alannah reached the tent, she was surprised to find Brendan already in bed, reading by lamplight. 'Hey.'

Peeking over his novel, he grinned. 'Hi, Lana. Calling it a night already, huh?'

'Yeah. That walk almost killed me.' Glancing at his reading material, she recognised Stephen King's *It*. 'Good book, that one, although a bit slow to start. I loved the movies too.' Sitting on her mattress, she removed her shoes and slipped into her sleeping bag.

'I haven't watched them yet. I prefer to start with the books.' Brendan closed his novel and put it aside.

'Me too, actually.'

The moment he turned back to face her; Brendan's bare chest came into full view. His abs reminded her of Liam. When her eyes ventured back to his, they gave her a smirk.

'Don't you get cold sleeping out here without a shirt?' she asked.

'Not at all. If anything, I overheat in this sleeping-bag.'

Her eyes wandered back to his muscles and lingered there a moment.

'Lana, you wanna tell me why you're fucking me with your eyes right now?'

Alannah almost blushed but clamped down on her emotions. She was not letting him get to her that easily. 'It occurred to me, I've haven't ever touched a guy's six pack. I've never dated guys with that sort of muscle tone.'

Brendan's visage began to smoulder. 'Well, go on.'

Letting curiosity get the better of her, she pressed her right hand against his pecs and let it slide down over the ridges and valleys forming the terrain of his well-sculpted body. 'Christ, your abdominal muscles feel rock hard.'

'They're not alone. I dare you to keep travelling south and find out how hard I can get.' His unblinking eyes leered at her.

Not one to back down from a challenge like that, Alannah slowly moved her hand lower, keeping her gaze locked with Brendan's. He did not falter once as she inched closer to his waist. Brendan did not even flinch as her fingertips lightly brushed over the soft skin beneath his belly button.

Reaching the top of his boxer shorts, she paused. She took a deep breath and continued, choosing to stay above the silky fabric to avoid getting tangled in his hairs. Her fingers walked hesitantly onto the top of his pubic region, yet he kept a straight face. *By the Gods, how far is he willing to let me go?* Another step and he licked his lips. *Shit!* Losing her nerve at the last, she pulled her hand back.

'Yet another win for me.'

'Hey, that doesn't count. I didn't blush,' she protested.

'No, but you did chicken out, and that, my dear, is the name of the game.'

She sighed and settled back into bed. 'Fine, whatever.'

'So, now you've mastered summoning, what's next on your magic agenda?'

'Constructs, I suppose. Although I think I'll stick to golems rather than Chucky dolls.'

He laughed. 'That was pretty freaky.'

'What's next for you?' Alannah turned to face him.

Brendan was staring at the ceiling as he replied, 'The big one.' He looked at her. 'Mental manipulation.'

The implications sent a shiver down Alannah's spine.

They spent much of Sunday on combat training. Alannah felt a flutter in her stomach when Liam insisted on being her partner for the whole day.

Kieran frowned. 'Alannah would benefit from facing more opponents to learn how other combatants fight differently.'

'With all due respect, Your Honour, Alannah has only started her weapon training. She's not ready to face other opponents.'

'Very well. But don't let your own skills slip. Be sure to get in some practice with at least one experienced fighter this afternoon.'

'Yes, sir.' Liam grabbed a couple of wooden swords and led Alannah to a clear spot. He handed her one and dropped the other on the ground. 'Do you remember the grip and stance I showed you?'

'I think so.' She held the sword in front of her.

'Close.' Liam stepped behind her, encircling her in his arms to correct her grip and posture. 'Try to relax your arms and legs more.' His breath tickled her ear as he spoke.

Intoxicated by his presence, Alannah melted into his hold.

She heard his sharp intake of breath. 'Not that I'm complaining, but that's not exactly what I meant.'

'I know. I guess I got a little caught up in the moment.'

Pressing his body hard against her back, Liam's fingers stroked her left arm as he whispered, 'Save that thought for later.'

Alannah laughed. 'If you insist.' Flirting with Liam was almost as fun as it was with Brendan and it had the added element of meaning.

'I must insist, otherwise neither of us will get any sword practice in today.' His voice was an even deeper pitch than normal. 'Now try that starting stance again.' Liam stepped back enough to give her the room she needed.

She adjusted her weight and kept her limbs relaxed.

'Good.' Liam released his hold and grabbed his own sword. After stepping her through various positions slowly a few times, he taught her how to parry.

Alannah was thankful for the much-needed lunch break when it finally arrived. Every part of her body was aching, and she was perspiring profusely. When she saw that none of the other mages showed any signs of tiring, she wanted to crawl under a rock and hide.

Liam sat on the ground beside her with his own sandwich and smiled sympathetically. 'I guess we'll have to work on your endurance.'

'And how do you suggest we do that?' Her voice came out gruffer than usual, likely due to the warm tingles developing between her thighs.

His eyes darkened. 'Increasing the duration of our combat training sessions, of course. Or did you have something else in mind?'

'Ha! When did you become such a shameless flirt?'

'I dunno. You must be rubbing off on me.' He grinned.

Taking a bite from her salad roll, Alannah tried to hide the extent of her amusement at his choice of words.

'I was thinking you should sit out and watch for the rest of the afternoon. I don't want to break you; plus, I need to duel some of the others.'

'Suits me fine.'

Alannah settled into one of the deckchairs and enjoyed the show. Liam faced off against Blake to start with. It was a good fight, if a little one sided, with Liam clearly more skilled.

After a few more duels in which Liam wiped the floor with his opponents, Brendan approached him. 'Bring it bro. First to draw blood wins.'

'Fine, but it's your funeral.'

Brendan grinned. 'We'll see about that.'

They both tossed their wooden weapons aside and reached for real blades.

Alannah watched intently. She had no idea what Brendan's fighting skills were like, at least not these days. She only ever trained with Liam and the last time she had seen them fight was nine years ago.

The sound of metal clinging against metal filled the air and before long, the Winters boys had drawn a decent crowd. They were both excellent swordsmen and from what Alannah could tell, equally matched.

'Impressive, ain't it?' Cara commented as she pulled up a chair next to Alannah, offering some chips from the bag she had opened.

'Very,' Alannah agreed. She grabbed a handful of the potato crisps. *Ooh, barbecue flavour, nice.*

'Brendan once told me Ross started training them when the boys were five and six. Most of us don't start combat training until after we're initiated.'

Riveted by the display of speed and skill, among other things, she kept her eyes glued on the fight. 'I guess he predicted the need for it.'

The guys were finally starting to break a sweat and showing the first signs of fatigue. Neither of them had struck the other when they both stepped back for a quick breather. Brendan took the opportunity to tear his shirt off and wipe his brow with it. Cheers and wolf whistles coming from Monique's direction rewarded him. As if not wanting to disappoint his own captive audience, Liam followed suit. The cheers continued.

Moving to the edge of her seat, Alannah had become enthralled and aroused by the spectacle. She noticed Brendan was gaining the upper hand as he pushed Liam back. *Shit! Didn't see that coming.* A moment later, he nicked Liam's right arm.

Liam jumped back. His left hand clamped over his bleeding gash as he scowled at the scene before him. Brendan's cheer squad were surrounding him, and Monique showered him in kisses as he revelled in his victory.

Alannah flew to Liam and wrapped her arms around him. 'Are you okay?'

He tore his eyes away from Brendan and looked down at her with a slight smile. 'Yeah. My pride's hurting more than my arm.' Pulling his hand away, he inspected the wound.

Chancing a glance herself, Alannah almost fainted. *So much blood!* 'You better get your dad to fix that, pronto.'

He sighed. 'I guess.' Liam grinned at her. 'One problem with that plan though.'

'What?'

'You'd have to let go of me first and I think I'd rather bleed to death.'

Frowning, she released him. 'Please don't joke about that right now.'

'Seriously Lana, it's not that bad. But I'll get it seen to now, if it makes you feel better.'

'Please do.' After watching Liam walk over to Ross, Alannah directed her gaze toward Brendan.

His fan club continued fawning over him, but his attention was on Alannah. When their eyes met, he shrugged his way out of the hands that were groping him and joined her. 'Is Liam okay? I didn't think I cut him that deep.'

'He claims to be fine, but there was a lot of blood. I insisted on having your dad patch him up.'

'Sorry, Lana, I didn't mean to scare you.'

'It's okay.' She smiled. 'I enjoyed the show.'

He gave her an impish grin. 'Really? Was it the sight of me, or Liam shirtless? Or the fact that I put Liam in his place?'

'All of the above. But shh, don't tell your brother.' She winked at him. Spinning on her heels, she walked over to Liam, the sound of Brendan's laughter trailing away behind her. Looking at Liam's arm again, she found the wound had healed over completely.

Liam smiled at her. 'See, nothing to worry about. Right Dad?'

'Right. It looked worse than it was,' Ross agreed as he packed away his first aid kit. 'That said, you did lose a bit of blood, so you'd better take it easy and get an early night.'

They were walking back to their campsite when Alannah turned to Liam and spoke seriously. 'Will you follow your doctor's orders and rest tonight?'

'Will you be my nurse if I do?' His tone was incredibly suggestive.

'If that's what it takes to make you behave.'

'Who said anything about behaving?' There was a mischievous glint in his eye.

Pausing at the entrance to their tent, Alannah narrowed her eyes and chided him firmly. 'Liam.'

His hands went up in surrender. 'Okay, fine. I'll be good.' They moved inside so Liam could lie down before dinner. 'I'm gonna change my trackies.'

Sitting on her bed, Alannah tried and failed to avert her eyes while he changed out of his blood-stained, sweaty trackpants. The lack of t-shirt did not help matters either. There was also the fact that Liam's boy-leg shorts gave her a perfect view of his shapely backside.

The whistle slipping through Alannah's teeth alerted Liam to her watchful eye. Glancing over his shoulder, Liam smirked. 'And you call *me* shameless!'

'Well, you're the one changing in full view of me.'

'You didn't have to watch.' He finished getting into a pair of clean, grey pants that hung a short distance below the line of his boxers. Still no shirt.

'How could I look away when you gave me such a good show?'

Liam unzipped his sleeping bag to recline on it rather than in it. He shifted onto his side to face Alannah.

She decided to settle down next to him. 'Shove over.'

His face lit up as he made room for her on his mattress. After enfolding her in his arms and staring into her eyes a moment, he whispered, 'Lana? What's going through that beautiful head of yours right now?'

'I'm thinking about how much I want to kiss you.'

Liam gasped. 'Does that mean you've made your choice? You're done with Austin?'

She smiled. 'Yeah. I'll break it off with him as soon as we get home.'

Sliding his hand behind her neck, he pulled her closer. His lips devoured hers with a fierce hunger.

Alannah responded with equal fervour. *By the Gods!* Her lips locked with Liam's and it was every bit as wonderful as she had imagined, if not better. His fresh scent and salty lips filled her olfactory senses.

Rolling Alannah onto her back, he deepened the kiss from above. With his body against hers, the extent of his arousal became evident. His lips travelled along her neck and back to her mouth.

She noticed he was still supporting some of his own weight. *Probably just as well.* Liam was ninety kilos of solid muscle and could easily crush her. It was a passing thought, lasting all of one second before she lost herself to the passion. At some point, her top and bra came off and Alannah moaned in response to the feel of skin-to-skin contact.

'Shit!'

Alannah and Liam both turned toward the entrance of their tent.

Brendan stood frozen in place, mouth aghast, and eyes popping from their sockets. 'I thought Liam was supposed to be resting.' He spat bitterly before taking off, leaving the tent flap slightly open.

Letting out an exasperated sigh, Alannah tried to free herself of Liam's hold, but he still had her pinned down.

Liam narrowed his eyes. 'Lana? What's wrong?'

'Brendan's right. You're meant to be resting. We shouldn't let things go any further yet.' She fixed her stern, unwavering eyes upon him. 'You promised to behave, remember?'

He laughed, shifting onto his back. 'Sorry, Nurse Winters.'

After throwing her top back on, Alannah glanced at the time. 'Dinner's probably ready by now. I'll get some and bring it back for us to eat here.'

'Thanks. One last kiss before you go?'

She yielded to his request by pressing her lips chastely to his.

But Liam grabbed a chunk of her hair and gazed upon her intensely. 'I love you, Lana.'

'I love you too, Liam.'

Chapter Fifteen

Alannah needed to act. For all the bliss she felt with Liam, a great big chasm had opened between herself and Brendan and she hated it. The guy had avoided her for the remainder of their camping trip and even chose to ride with Ross and Nora for the drive home. Apparently, Enya is preferable to 'being Liam's third wheel'. He did not even come down to dinner that night.

She barged through his bedroom door. 'Talk to me, Brendan! What the fuck is wrong?'

'Christ, Lana! Ever heard of knocking?' He had emerged from his bathroom, wearing nothing but a towel around his waist, wet hair still dripping water down his face and torso.

A multitude of emotions inundated Alannah in that moment. Initially, her core grew moist and tingled. A racing pulse and burning cheeks followed. Finally, she found herself wishing she had knocked. Yet she stood firm. 'As if you would have answered.'

'Right. And I have my reasons for that.'

'Which is why I'm here. Why are you avoiding me?'

'I'm surprised you even noticed.' His bitter tone, full of vitriol, staggered her. 'I figured the two of you would want some privacy.'

She narrowed her eyes. 'Cut the bullshit. It doesn't take aura reading skills to know you're upset. I want to know why.'

'When did you break up with Austin?'

Taken aback by his question, she stumbled with her answer. 'I… I haven't yet. I plan to do that tomorrow.'

'So, not only are you about to dump my best mate, but you're cheating on him too.'

'Is that what this is all about?' She rubbed the side of her face with her palm. 'I had only sorted through the mess in my heart. I wasn't even sure I'd choose Liam over Austin until last night. You knew I was trying to work through these feelings.'

'I didn't think things would progress so quickly. You should have ended things with Austin first.'

'All we did was kiss, geez. Since when do *you* take the moral high ground over shit like this?'

'Since it involves the people I love. And that was a pretty heated kiss.' Brendan sat on the edge of his bed.

'But still just a kiss.' She perched beside him. 'Sorry about Austin. This hasn't been easy for me either. I'm not looking forward to breaking his heart.'

Brendan sighed. 'Austin's not the only best friend I'm worried about. More time spent with Liam means less time with me.'

Alannah fixed upon his gaze. 'So that's what this is *really* about, huh? We can still hang. You'll probably need to become more tolerant of Liam, though.'

'Bah! He's the intolerant one. The rest of our friends will freak out though.'

'They already did when Liam became my bodyguard.'

'That was nothing. When they see the two of you together, you're looking at social murder. Just warning you.' Humour had returned to his eyes, much to Alannah's relief. 'There are two things I'll miss when you're with Liam.'

'Oh?'

He gave her a wicked grin. 'No more waking up in the middle of the night when you're having kinky vampire sex.'

She blushed and thumped his solid bicep with her fist.

He laughed. 'But this is what I'll miss most of all.'

'This?'

'Our games of Sleazy Chicken.'

'Who said that has to end?' Alannah felt a pang of grief at the thought of no more Sleazy Chicken.

'Are you kidding? Liam would kick my arse!'

'I saw the way you handled yourself in that fight. I don't think you have anything to worry about. Besides, I'll make him aware it's part of how we relate. He will learn that Alannah and Brendan are a package deal.' She smiled at him.

'Damn straight we are.' He stretched out his arms, inviting a hug. 'Bring it, Cuz.'

'But you're wet and naked!' she complained.

'So? Get over here before I make *you* wet and naked.'

Alannah laughed. 'I'd like to see you try!'

His eyes flashed with evil intent. A moment later, Brendan had Alannah pinned down on his bed.

She squealed at first, an automatic response to the sudden movement. As she took stock of her situation, Alannah realised he was straddling her. Brendan's face was mere inches away from hers, water dripping from his hair. Her cheeks burned.

'Be careful what you wish for, Lana.' He remained still a moment, searching her eyes for something. Pulling back, he stood, the towel dropping to the floor as he did so.

Eyes bulging at the sight of what he was packing, Alannah swore under her breath at first. 'By the Gods.'

Even when limp, Brendan was obviously hung like a horse. He tittered. 'See something you like?' When she met his eyes, he gave her an impish grin. He reached for a pair of black satin boxers and turned around to slip them on. After drying his hair briefly, he threw his towel in the bathroom. 'Now bring it!' His arms opened wide for her again.

Alannah rose from the bed and stepped into Brendan's arms. 'You know I love you right?'

He squeezed her tighter. 'Yup, but it doesn't hurt to hear you say it every so often.'

'I love you, Brendan.'

He drew a deep breath, and exhaled the words, 'I love you, Lana.'

Austin was waiting for Alannah at her locker. She spotted him first and took the opportunity to whisper her warning to Liam. 'Remember I haven't spoken to him yet. He doesn't know what's going on.'

Liam grumbled his response. 'I know. The sooner you talk to him, the better. This waiting is torture.'

It had taken Alannah a week to find the courage to face Austin and break the news to him. When he asked to meet during the second week of school holidays, she gave him the excuse training had exhausted her. It was not a complete lie.

Austin's eyes lit up the hallway when he saw her. As soon as she reached him, he had her pinned up against her locker. 'Gods, I've missed you.' His mouth was on hers in a flash.

Alannah hesitated at first. She did not want to upset Liam, but she did not have time to talk to Austin before classes started.

As she began to yield to Austin's demanding lips, Liam pulled Austin away by his shirt collar. 'That's quite enough of a show for now, thank you.'

Austin growled at him. 'What's your problem, man?'

'You are. I don't like you and I hate seeing your filthy claws and fangs on Lana.'

'You're just jealous. I've seen the way you look at her. Pity she's not pure, huh?'

Liam pushed Austin against the lockers, pinning him by the throat as he raised his fist.

'Liam! Stop it!' Alannah cried. Glancing through the assembled audience, she could see a couple of teachers headed their way.

He lowered his fist but maintained his hold on Austin's throat. 'Don't push me, Pearce.' A second later he released his grip.

'Everything okay here?' asked Mr. Dougherty.

'Just fine,' Austin replied as he glared at Liam.

'Liam?' the teacher asked doubtfully.

'It's okay, Mr. Dougherty. Austin and I were simply voicing our difference of opinion. I'll be going to class now.' He smiled at Alannah. 'See you later.'

'Yeah. See ya.' After watching Liam walk away, she turned to Austin. 'Will you come to my window tonight?'

'Gods, yes.'

'Great. I'll see you then.' She forced a smile, but Austin's goodbye kiss engulfed her lips before she finished the attempt.

Most of Alannah's first day back at school passed with little further incident. That was until final period when her Ancient Studies class spent their lesson on research in the library.

She was sitting next to Cara at one of the group tables, when an unwelcome face appeared. An icy chill seized Alannah as she watched the woman take the seat across from her. 'Grandmother?' Her question was barely more than a whisper.

'Hello, dear child.'

'Alannah? What's wrong?' Cara's voice seemed a distant echo.

Glancing around, she noticed that no one paid any heed to the strange woman in her red cape. Even Cara was looking at Alannah rather than the evil Queen. She returned her attention to Tara.

'They cannot see or hear me. Handy illusion spell, that one. They can, of course, hear you; so, if you continue talking to me, they will assume you are talking to yourself. I suggest keeping your words in your head. I can read your thoughts anyway.'

What a terrifying thought.

'Exactly.' She gave Alannah a wicked grin.

What do you want?

'You know what I want, Alannah. The clock is ticking. If you do not have that handsome vampire man of yours turn you soon, I will send one of my less desirable cursed subjects to do the job.'

Why curse me? I don't understand.

'To put it simply, your very existence as a mage is a threat to my power. I have dominion over all the cursed. When you become one of us, you will swear your loyalty to me.'

Alannah laughed. *I don't see how I'm such a threat. I'm not even a pure a mage.*

Tara's eyes narrowed. 'Has no one told you that your mother conceived you at Beltane?'

What's that supposed to mean?

'I am sure one of your cousins would be happy to explain. Dennis was not your real father. Sorry about his death, by the way. An unfortunate case of collateral.'

That was you? You broke into my house?

'Technically one of my ghouls. I have many cursed servants willing to do my bidding, dear child.' Tara vanished, speaking her final words in Alannah's mind as she left. *'Tick, tick, tick.'*

Trembling with fear, Alannah stood up abruptly. *Gotta find Liam.*

'*Alannah Winters!*' Cara screamed at her. That got Alannah's attention. 'What's wrong?'

Everyone in the library was staring at them. Alannah replied in a hushed voice, 'I need to find Liam.' She started to run out of the library.

Cara hurried to keep up with her. 'We're in the middle of class, Alannah. Now's not the time for a make-out session.'

Stopping dead in her tracks, Alannah realised she had no idea where to look for Liam. She turned to Cara. 'This isn't about that. Tara showed up and threatened me again. I need to tell him.'

Cara gave her a sidelong glance. 'Have you finally lost the plot? I was sitting with you. There was no sign of Tara.'

Alannah decided to head for her locker so she could retrieve her phone. 'That's because she used illusion magic to hide herself from everyone else's view.'

Cara walked beside her. 'Seriously?'

'Honest to the Gods.'

'*Shit!* That must be some powerful magic if she could hide from another mage.'

'That's not even the scariest thing she did. She read my mind, Cara. She was in my fucking head.'

Cara shivered. 'That's so creepy.'

When they reached her locker, Alannah grabbed her phone and wrote a quick text: TARA CONFRONTED ME AT SCHOOL. I'M KINDA FREAKED AND WANNA GO HOME. She knew Liam would not have his phone with him, so she sent the SOS to her Uncle and Aunt.

Nora sent a prompt reply: OH GODS! ARE YOU OKAY? I'LL BE THERE SHORTLY.

Alannah typed a quick response: I'M FINE, JUST SCARED. She proceeded toward the front office. 'Hi Miss O'Leary. I'm not feeling well. I've contacted my Aunt and she's gonna pick me up soon. Can I wait here with Cara?'

Miss O'Leary smiled warmly. 'Of course, dear.'

They both sat in the waiting area.

At first sight of Alannah, Nora rushed to embrace her. 'Oh sweetheart, you're still shaking.' She pulled Alannah up to the front desk. 'Hi Patsy. There's been a family emergency, can you please call my sons over the PA?'

Miss O'Leary's visage filled with concern. 'Of course.' She spoke into the microphone: *'Liam Winters and Brendan Winters, please come to the front office. Liam Winters and Brendan Winters, to the front office, please.'*

Panic and dread shook Brendan to the core. Two names, not three. Two members of the Winters family, not three. Brendan jumped up and hot footed it to the front office.

Every metre he covered on the approach was one too many and he cursed his legs for not moving faster. He ignored the teachers yelling out to him to stop running in the hall. Consequences be damned. *If anything has happened….* He could not even finish the thought: that train was too fucking painful. Rounding a corner, he fled the Maths and Science building and dashed across the yard toward the 'Administration' sign.

As soon as he entered the office, he released the breath he had been holding. Alannah was there and she was still standing. 'Oh, thank fuck! You're okay, Lana.'

Mum, who was holding Alannah's trembling form, looked up and frowned.

Alannah turned her head to him. The tears in her eyes combined with her trembling lip floored him.

'Gods, what happened?' He pulled Alannah into his arms.

She whispered two words in his ear, 'Tara happened.'

That was enough to make the blood drain from his face. Icicles stabbed at his spine. A flash of movement in the corner of his eye drew Brendan's attention.

Cara rose from one of the chairs. 'I should go. I'll talk to you guys later.' She placed a hand on Alannah's shoulder. 'Take care, okay?'

She nodded. 'Thanks, Cara.'

Brendan heard a commotion outside which sounded like Cara and Liam arguing. His brother burst through the doors a moment later. '*Lana?*'

She shifted out of Brendan's hold and rushed into Liam's embrace. It felt like she had ripped away another chunk of his heart in the process.

'Come on, get your stuff. We'll talk in the car,' Mum declared.

'Right. Come on Lana, let's get my bag.' Liam led her away towards the Seniors building.

'Brendan?' Mum's voice brought his attention back from the sight of Alannah walking away with Liam holding her hand.

'Sorry, Mum. Just a sec.' He sprinted to his locker and grabbed his bag.

The rest of them were waiting in the carpark. Alannah and Liam took the back seat, so Brendan jumped in the front. 'What happened, Lana?' he asked as soon as they were all strapped in.

He heard her take a deep breath. 'Tara showed up in the library during my Ancient Studies research lesson. She cloaked herself with some form of illusion magic, so not even Cara could see or hear her.'

Brendan let a whistle escape through his teeth. 'Damn, that's hard core.'

'She reminded me time is running out. If I don't choose to become cursed soon, she will send one of her subjects to do the job.'

'Don't worry, I won't let anyone hurt you Lana,' Liam reassured her.

'There's more,' Alannah's voice shook. 'I think she had my dad killed.' She paused as Liam comforted her. 'And she wants Austin to curse me. She said something about getting my vampire boyfriend to turn me.'

Liam released her. 'Christ! I told you he's trouble. When are you going to dump his arse?' His tone was one of bitter hatred.

Even Brendan had to admit Liam was right. If Austin were not already acting under direct orders, Tara could still compel him to hurt Alannah. The cursed were physically incapable of disobeying their sovereign.

'Tonight. I planned to talk to him alone, but now I'm afraid of how he'll react.'

'No way am I letting you spend any more time alone with that creep. I'll be there when you talk to him.'

'Thanks, Liam.' Alannah fell quiet for the rest of the drive.

A cursory glance told Brendan she was silently sobbing against Liam's chest. He sat back in his seat and sighed. As much as he hated seeing them together, Alannah needed both her cousins if she was going to get through this.

'Just a minute, Brendan.' His mum's voice stopped him from following Alannah and Liam into the house as soon as they got home.

He turned back to see her leaning against the side of the car, so he stepped up to her. 'What is it, Mum?'

'I know you're hurting, but remember, all good things come to those who wait.'

'What's that supposed to mean?'

She pushed the hair aside from his right eye. 'It means you shouldn't give up on love. I remember what it felt like at your age. All matters of the heart were urgent, and unrequited love was the end of the world. Alannah may not be receptive to you now, but that doesn't mean her feelings won't change. And even if they don't, the odds of finding love elsewhere are stacked highly in your favour.'

It was easy to forget his mother could read people's emotions when she spent most of her days caring for animals. 'Thanks, Mum.' He hugged her before heading inside.

Sitting on the edge of her bed, Alannah waited anxiously for her midnight visitor. With her tendency to avoid conflict wherever possible, breakups were not something she was fond of instigating. Cole was the only guy she had dumped, and the circumstances that had driven her to end that relationship had been beyond her control.

Knowing Liam was hiding in her wardrobe was some comfort, but only as far as her fear extended to the possibility of Austin attacking her. Oddly, that was the least of her worries. He may be a vampire, but she was confident he genuinely cared about her and that was what had her stomach doing somersaults.

Tap, tap, tap. Tap, tap, tap.

Crap! It was time. She took a deep breath and made her way to the window.

'Hey, beautiful.' Austin gracefully climbed through and landed with ease on the floor. He swept her up into his arms and kissed her fervently.

Gods, she was gonna miss these kisses, among other things. Drawing on her newfound courage and the knowledge of Liam watching, she pushed him back gently. 'We need to talk.'

'Oh-oh. That's never a good precursor to a conversation.' Stern eyes bore down on her.

Tugging on his hand, she led him across the room to sit on her bed. 'Were you ever planning to tell me about your past?'

Austin exhaled sharply. 'So, Brendan finally told you, huh?'

'Brendan only hinted at it, but I learned more from another source.'

His eyes popped. 'Who?'

'Does it matter? I want to know why I didn't hear it from you.'

Dropping his head into his hands, he ran his fingers through his long, black hair. A minute later he frowned at her. 'I'm sorry, Alannah. I would have told you eventually, but those were dark times for me. I find it hard to talk about them. I almost killed two girls.'

'Don't you think that's exactly why you should have told me?' She rose and paced the room. 'Christ, Austin! I let you feed on me. You could've killed me!'

Tears pooled in his eyes. 'I tried to warn you in the beginning. It's also why I've only ever done so with Brendan nearby.'

She blinked at him, trying to make sense of his words.

'If you ever started to feel faint or scared, he would have felt your emotional state and come to your aid.'

Alannah shook her head. 'He would have to be actively reading me at the time.' She remembered what Brendan had told her. Her eyes widened on him. '*Shit!* You knew he was reading me the whole time?'

'Of course. It was the only way I felt safe doing what we did.'

'Didn't help those other girls though, did it?'

He hung his head low. 'Things were different then.'

'Different how?'

'Brendan was… preoccupied. Safety wasn't our first concern.'

Closing her eyes, she braced herself for the difficult question. She held his gaze a moment before asking, 'Did you ever use hypnotic coercion on those girls?'

Austin winced. 'A few times, yes.'

Sprinting into her bathroom, Alannah barely reached the toilet in time to bring up her dinner.

She felt a hand on her shoulder. 'Alannah?'

'Get the fuck away from me!'

Austin recoiled. 'Alannah, please. I told you they were dark times. I'm not proud of what I did. I hated who I was back then.'

Leaning back against the cold, hard tiles on the wall, she squinted up at him with pursed lips. 'Have you tried hypnotism on me at all?'

'Gods, no! I love you, Alannah, I would never…' kneeling in front of her, he attempted to reach out and comfort her.

But Alannah put up a hand in protest. 'Have you been working under direct orders from my grandmother or one of her representatives?'

He was gobsmacked. 'What? No! Alannah, please trust that I would never want to hurt you.'

'It matters little now. Tara knows about us. She can use you against me.'

Sinking back against the shower screen, Austin blanched, an impressive feat for someone so pale. 'What are you saying?'

'I'm saying we're done. You and I are finished, Austin.'

His eyes teared up again. 'Alannah, please don't do this. Surely we can find a way to work things out. I won't let Tara use me.'

'From what I understand, you might not have a choice.'

'What if we spoke to your Uncle? He's a very skilled abjurer. He could craft protective charms for me.'

Damn it! He is not making this easy for me. She was hoping to avoid letting the cat out the bag. 'Austin, please don't fight this.'

'Why not? I'll fight the world for a chance to be with you. I swear to the Gods, I'll find a way to block the Queen's—'

'*Austin!*' she screamed. When he fell quiet, Alannah whispered, 'There's someone else.'

His face shifted into a grotesque grimace. 'Who?'

She remained silent.

'Is he one of your cousins?'

Alannah slowly nodded.

'*Fuck!*' Austin rose and punched a fist into the wall beside the basin, shattering one of the tiles. He turned back toward her with a wicked grin. 'You know if it's Brendan…'

Horrified, she shook her head. 'No, Austin. It's Liam.'

He left a second later.

Reclining against the wall, she closed her eyes and tried to settle her heart rate with some deep breathing.

'Hey.' Her eyes opened to find Liam in front of her, one hand resting on her knee, the other offering her a breath mint.

'Thanks.' Taking the mint, she relished the shock of the strong peppermint burst in her mouth. She took the hand he extended to help her up.

As they walked back into her room, Brendan burst through the door. 'Well that was quite the rollercoaster. You okay now, Lana?'

She perched on her bed and leaned against Liam before replying. 'I think so. What sort of a read did you get on Austin?'

'Let's see, from the top, there was love, lust, anxiety, fear, remorse, sorrow, guilt, anxiety, fear, desperation, envy, anger, anguish, and sorrow. I should spend more time around couples breaking up: they'd give me an endless mana source.'

Alannah narrowed her eyes at Brendan. 'But was he lying about hypnotising me or working for Tara?'

He sighed. 'No. As far as I could tell, he was completely honest with you.'

'Right. Thanks, Brendan. Now get the fuck out of my sight.' She pierced him with a frown.

Frozen at first, Brendan took a moment to register what she meant. With hunched shoulders and moist eyes, he nodded his resignation before leaving the room.

Austin sprinted through the scrub at supernatural speed, swearing to himself the whole time. When he reached the roadside, he collapsed against his car and screamed. 'Curse you, Winters!' He slammed his fist into the roof of his Lexus.

'I am already cursed, but I assume you mean one of my descendants.'

Spinning around on his heels, Austin found himself face-to-face with his Queen. He quickly kneeled before her. 'I'm sorry, Your Majesty, but I have failed you. Alannah wants nothing more to do with me.' He made no attempt to hide the anguish in his tone, or the tears in his eyes when she commanded him to rise.

'This is grave news indeed. What reason did she give you?'

'She's with Liam now… and she doesn't trust me anymore.'

Tara's eyes widened as her head jerked back. 'My mental and emotional barrier spells are first rate. No one should be able to sense your deception.'

Austin frowned. 'It's not that, Your Majesty. She knows you are aware of our relationship and fears you will use me against her despite my best intentions.'

A rictus grin formed on the Queen's face. 'She is a smart girl.'

He sighed. 'Intelligence runs in the family, Your Majesty.'

'Flattery gets you everywhere, my pet. Come along. You can sink your teeth into some pretty young thing at my haven. Then we will formulate a new plan.'

Fuck! The news announcer on the radio alarm told Brendan it was already seven in the morning and he still had not caught a wink of sleep. Insomnia had never been a problem for him before. Even during his more stressful times, Brendan usually slept like a log. But that look on Alannah's face haunted him all night. He needed to find a way to apologise for his past sins. Being on Alannah's shit-list was worse than losing her heart to Liam.

Slamming his fist on the 'Off' button silenced the alarm. *Oops! That was a little permanent.* He needed to calm his shit, so he dragged his sorry arse out of bed and jumped under the shower. With the water set to scorching, he closed his eyes and began to meditate. The process grounded him and he felt ready to face the day. At least that was what he told himself.

After completing the rest of his morning routine in a daze, Brendan joined his mates on the bus, bumping fists on his way to the back seat.

'Hey man.' Jacob slapped his palm and bumped his fist before their fingers shimmied away. 'Is Alannah okay?'

Cara inched forward in the seat beside him with her ears pricking up.

He sighed as he slumped down next to Jacob. 'She's safe for now, but not in the best emotional state. She broke up with Austin last night.'

Jacob shook his head. 'Shit! She won't be the only one in a foul mood today.'

Closing his eyes, Brendan recalled the turmoil his best mate had felt when Alannah broke the news to him. He wondered if Austin would even show up to school that day. 'No kidding, especially since she told him she's with Liam now.' When his eyes shot open, he found everyone on the bus gawping at him. Ignoring the rest of the crowd, he focussed on his friends. 'Come on, as if you didn't all see it coming.'

When everyone else turned away, Jacob spoke to him in a hushed voice. 'So, are you hurting for Austin or yourself?'

Brendan glared at him. 'Don't even go there, *friend.*'

Jacob threw his hands up defensively. 'Woah there, easy tiger.' He laughed nervously. When they alighted on campus, Jacob hung back with Brendan and watched as Bailey chased after Cara. 'Gods, that man is relentless.'

Tired and fed up, Brendan threw morality to the wind and turned to Jacob. 'Listen, man, you should go for her. She wants to bang your brains anyway. To hell with Bailey.' He slapped Jacob hard on the shoulder and stormed off toward his locker.

Dread started to fill the pit of his stomach as he approached homeroom. *What sort of reception is Alannah going to give me this morning?* When he reached the door, his heart stopped at the sight of her. Head face down, she was resting on her table, cushioned by her folded arms. She appeared to be sleeping. Cautiously, Brendan approached his seat, which was right next to hers. He stared at her, desperately wanting to say something, but afraid of the response she would give him. So, he sat and waited like a coward.

The bell rang and their teacher commenced the roll call, yet all the while Alannah kept her forehead glued to her arms. When her name breached the chasm, she lifted her face briefly, responding with a simple 'Here' before dropping her head again. This was how she sat through the morning's announcements. As the bell sounded for first period, she stood and left the room without even acknowledging Brendan's presence. *Shit! Not good.* He rose from his chair and started for the door.

Connor stepped beside Brendan, clapping a hand on his shoulder. 'You weren't kidding about her mood. I can still see the icicles around her table. Why do I get the feeling there's more to this than her breakup with Pearce?'

He looked into Connor's unwavering eyes. 'Because Austin confessed the full truth of our past antics.'

'Shit! No wonder she's pissed at you.' Connor was the only person who had known the extent of Brendan and Austin's shared past. He was the one to pull them out of their dark times, after all. He shook his head as they walked along the hall. 'Sorry, Brendo. Maybe give her some time. I'm sure she'll come 'round.'

'I hope you're right.' After a quick fist bump, Brendan parted ways with Connor and headed towards his Maths class. A flash of red in the corner of his eye drew Brendan's attention to the fence surrounding the school. A woman in a red-hooded raincoat and long black dress was walking along the outer perimeter. Her face was not visible, but instinctively he knew who she was. He froze as his heart beat quickened. An idea took hold. *If I can save Lana…*

Resolute in his decision, Brendan put up his mental and emotional walls. He cast a quick glance around the yard to ensure no one was watching before jumping the fence. Ducking behind trees and building corners, he shadowed the woman along Rafferty Street and on to High Gate.

She walked north a few more metres and stopped to allow a figure in a long, black-hooded coat to open the door of a limousine for her. The man in black, presumably a ghoul or vampire, sat in the driver's seat.

Crap! I can't lose her now. Looking around quickly for options, Brendan spotted a young woman stepping out of her car, so he seized the opportunity. He put on all his charms and used his powers to manipulate her. 'Excuse me miss, may I please borrow your car?'

The anxious blonde—who was probably about twenty— hesitated at first, so he placed his hand on her arm and poured all his powers of seduction into it. 'If you tell me your address, I promise to return it tonight.' He gave her a mischievous grin. 'And I'll even pay you a visit if you like.' He had no intention of doing any such thing, especially since this qualified as coercion, but he desperately needed wheels.

'O-of course.' She dropped the key in his hands.

'Do you have a pen and paper?' he asked, cursing himself for the habit of leaving his phone in his locker 'I still need your address.'

'Oh, right.' She smiled. Reaching into her bag, she produced a small notepad and pen which she scrawled on.

As soon as the note was in his hand, Brendan pushed past her into the driver's seat and took off without another word. Thankfully, he could make out the black Bentley ahead. It took all his self-control not to floor it, but he was still in the middle of town and drawing any unwanted attention, especially from the cops, would mess with his plans. The limo turned right at the end of the road. When Brendan followed, he saw them heading up the hill and out of the populated area.

Thirty minutes and a few dirt tracks later, Brendan pulled into the driveway of an old, ruined farmstead. He parked the car behind a copse of trees and walked the rest of the way down the gravel path. Once the main house was in view, he found a sturdy old plum tree promising a good vantage point. Reaching the upper branches was simple enough for a master tree climber like Brendan. Finding a relatively comfortable nook, he settled in for the stakeout.

'Hi, Lana.' Liam drew her into his arms the moment she stepped out of English. He gestured with a nod over her shoulder toward the classroom. 'Did Brendan wag?'

She frowned, still distressed by Brendan's past behaviour. 'Yeah, seems he's up to his old tricks.'

Liam stiffened.

'What?' she asked, studying his narrow eyes.

'Austin skipped class too.'

Alannah shook her head disapprovingly. 'Come on, let's get some lunch.' She took his hand and they walked along the corridor toward her locker. It felt good to show the rest of the school they were a couple, but she still feared what would happen when Uncle Ross found out. When they reached her locker, she dumped her books inside and grabbed her purse.

The moment she locked the door, Liam pressed her against it and kissed her deeply. When they came up for air, he was smiling. 'Gods, I've wanted to do that for so long.'

'What, kiss me? I recall doing that several times throughout the night and this morning.'

'I meant pushing you up against your locker to kiss you.'

'Mm. Anywhere else on campus you want to make out?'

Pressing against her, Liam twirled a strand of her hair between his fingers. 'The list is so long I don't even know where to start.'

She gave him a wicked grin. 'Why don't we find one of those more isolated spots and hide out there for our lunch break?'

Apparently, she did not need to ask twice since Liam grabbed her hand and pulled her towards the building's exit.

'Just a sec though.' Alannah stopped him. 'I need the bathroom first.'

He sighed. 'Fine, but hurry. I'm hungry, but not for food.' Liam winked at her as she disappeared into the ladies' room.

Having completed her business, Alannah was washing her hands when she became aware of the unnatural silence. Not even the sound of footsteps and chatter from the hall permeated the space. *What the hell?* She looked up at the mirror, but did not see anything, so she glanced over her shoulder. Still nothing. The back of her neck prickled. *Is someone watching me?* Shrugging it off as paranoia, she grabbed a handful of paper towels.

Suddenly, a pair of arms pulled her up into the ceiling space. Alannah tried to scream, but a strong male hand shoved a gag in her mouth. She kicked and struggled to free herself, but it was no use: her attacker's grip was too strong. She could not see him, but the smell of rotting flesh suggested he was a ghoul. The cursed man dragged her through the ceiling briefly before dropping her into a dark, empty classroom.

Disoriented, she attempted to run in the direction she hoped was the exit, but another set of arms grabbed her before she got far. This man was taller and stronger, with a less abhorrent odour. As soon as he carried her into a tunnel that had opened in the brick wall, Alannah knew she was in serious trouble.

Several minutes later, someone removed her gag and threw her onto the floor of the vampire common room. Glancing around, she noticed flickering and she was lying inside a pentagram of blood on the floor.

A handsome vampire with short blond hair and glowing blue eyes stood above her, grinning. 'Hello Miss Winters. My name is Anthony. It is such a pleasure to meet you at last.' His accent sounded British, with a gravity suggesting he was much older than his apparent age of twenty.

'The pleasure's all yours, I'm sure.'

Kneeling, he straddled her. 'Not for long.' Pinning her arms, he bared his fangs.

A second later a sharp pain pierced her jugular and Alannah screamed, but it was not long before a familiar ecstasy turned her protests into more pleasant groans. *Christ! I didn't know a vampire's bite could still feel this good without involving sex.* In the back of her mind, she knew she should try to fight back, but it was difficult to find the motivation, so she resigned herself to whatever fate awaited her.

She started to feel faint and a moment of panic seized her mind. It was enough to break the spell and Alannah drew on the mana in her matter ring. *Stupid vampire didn't think to remove my ring first!* She concentrated on a summoning more advanced than any she had attempted and prayed to the Gods it would work.

'*Lana! Oh Gods!*' Liam's voice filled the room a moment before everything went black.

Chapter Sixteen

iam sat propped up against the headboard of Alannah's bed with her sleeping deeply beside him. Dad had already performed her blood transfusion in the hospital and arranged for her immediate release so he could monitor her at home. He had promised she would be okay after some rest.

But Liam would not believe his father until he saw her eyes open. So, he sat alone with his Lana, waiting anxiously for some reassurance she would be okay. It was terrifying to think how close he had come to losing her. *If she hadn't….*

Alannah's eyes fluttered and opened. 'Thank you for rescuing me, Sir Liam.' She strained her voice.

He smiled. 'You're welcome, Princess. You did well to summon me in time.'

She coughed, so he handed her some water. After draining the glass, she lay back. 'I remembered something. What does it mean to be conceived at Beltane?' she asked.

Liam thought that was an odd question, given the circumstances. 'Why do you ask?'

'Because apparently Mum conceived me at Beltane. That was the other thing Tara mentioned.'

Liam's heart jumped at the news. 'Seriously? If that's true, you would have to be a pure mage. Not only that; it means you are blessed by the Gods.'

'But how?' Alannah's blinking eyes searched his own for several seconds. With a yawn, her lids began to droop.

'Shh, it's okay, we can discuss it later. You need to rest more.' He gently stroked her face to reassure her. Pressing his lips to hers, he kissed her chastely. Her eyes beamed with love for a second before fatigue pulled their lids shut and she drifted off.

Reassured she would be okay; Liam took the opportunity to grab a bite of food. It was almost midnight and he realised he had not eaten since recess. After raiding the fridge for some leftovers, he threw a plate of curry in the microwave.

When he sat down to eat, he heard the front door slam, followed by footsteps in the hall.

Brendan appeared in the kitchen a few seconds later, looking dishevelled with his messy hair, wrinkled clothes, and rotten stench.

'Where have you been?' Liam demanded.

'Out.'

Liam rolled his eyes, assuming his brother had been sleeping around again, or worse. 'Well while you were "out," I was busy saving Lana's arse. One of the cursed attacked her at school today.'

Brendan's brows shot up from his bulging eyes. '*Shit!* Is she okay?'

'It was a vampire attack, so she needed a blood transfusion. She's resting now. Still a little sore, but she's fine. Oh, and apparently she's a pure mage.'

'Hm.'

He eyed Brendan suspiciously. 'What's that supposed to mean? This is good news, right?'

'For you, maybe. But it would give Grandmother dearest more cause for concern.' His voice trailed off as he appeared lost in thought.

'Come on man… if you know something, spill it,' Liam demanded.

Brendan sighed as he collapsed on a chair across from Liam. 'I spent the day tracking Tara. I found one of her hideouts at an old farmstead up in the hills and a horde of vampires live or work there.'

'So, you think Tara sent this vampire to attack Lana?' Liam asked. Brendan's initiative impressed and surprised him.

'That's what I'm worried about. I know it's not Beltane yet, but she may have grown impatient, especially since Alannah broke up with Austin,' Brendan replied, struggling to keep his eyes open.

Liam knew he should let Brendan go to bed, but he needed to know more. 'Was Austin at Tara's?'

'No.' He yawned. 'I still don't have any evidence to suggest he's been working for her directly.'

'I guess I'll have to find out for myself. I'm going to do some of my own digging. Can you give me the directions to Tara's hideout?'

'Fine.' Brendan rose and grabbed a pen from the cup by the phone and wrote instructions on the message pad. Tearing off the page, he handed it to Liam. 'I'm going to bed now.' He started for the door.

'Hold up.'

Brendan spun around and glared at him. 'What?'

'I might be gone a few days. Watch over Lana for me, would you?'

'Liam, dear brother, I will keep an eye on Lana for her sake and my own, but not for yours.' The brief hint of a wicked grin crossed his face before he turned back and walked upstairs.

Sighing, Liam finished his meal, dropped his plate in the sink, and dashed to his room to pack some supplies. On his way out, he decided to check on Alannah once more, so he doubled back to her room. At first, he was startled to find Brendan curled up beside her, but Liam had asked Brendan to watch her. He stepped closer to the bed and looked down at the two of them. Their sleeping faces were angelic, and it took him back to their childhood when the three of them would often share the one bed. They were so innocent back then, or so he thought. But he remembered what Alannah had told him about her sex education and he shuddered. Dismissing the thought as quickly as possible, Liam pressed a kiss to her forehead and whispered softly, 'Goodbye my love. See you again soon.'

Stirring in bed, Alannah snuggled up against the back of the warm body beside her. She slipped a hand across his side and pressed it against his hard stomach muscles. *Gods I love those abs!* But as she became more conscious, she took in the scent of her bed companion and realised she was not holding Liam. She bolted upright. *'What the fuck?'*

Brendan rolled over and grinned at her. 'Morning, Lana. Good to see you're feeling better.'

'Why are you in my bed?'

'Have you forgotten last night?' He feigned offence. 'I'm so hurt. Girls never forget a night with Brendan Winters.'

Alannah glared at him.

But her evil eye did not deter him. 'It must be denial. You couldn't believe how good it was. How else could you go back to Liam otherwise?'

Losing control of her rage, Alannah slapped him hard across the face, leaving a bright red handprint on his cheek.

Grinning wickedly, his own hand covered the mark. 'Damn Lana, that was hot. I didn't think you would be in the mood for foreplay again already.'

Clenching her fists, she screamed, *'you're infuriating, Brendan.* Quit the act and tell me why the hell you are here.'

He sighed. 'Fine. Liam made me your temporary bodyguard. And after yesterday—I'm not taking any chances.'

Alannah shook her head to clear the fog from her mind. 'So, where's Liam?'

'Had some business to take care of out of town. He'll probably be a few days.'

Liam's lack of communication hurt Alannah. He did not even say goodbye.

'He didn't have time for a proper farewell, but he did give you a kiss while you were sleeping.' It was uncanny how Brendan knew what she needed to hear.

She narrowed her eyes on him. 'Are you reading me?'

'Sorry, Lana. I have to while I'm your bodyguard.'

'I'm still really pissed at you. What you did back then...' Closing her eyes, she tried to search for the right words. 'It was so wrong.'

Brendan's forehead creased as his head hung low. 'I know.'

'Do you know how serious a crime you committed? I know the human legal system would have a hard time proving supernatural coercion, but don't mage laws prohibit rape too?'

He cringed at her use of the 'R' word. 'The Council forbid enchanters from using powers of manipulation for such purposes, but it's a lot harder to police vampires. I never used my own powers...'

'It doesn't matter, Brendan! I dunno, but it might be worse. You took the coward's way out by using your best friend to get what you wanted.'

'No, Lana! It wasn't like that. Austin used his hypnotic powers when he was desperate for a feed. I never asked him to do it. Yes, I was party to the act—and I feel like shit for my part in it all—but you've gotta believe I was never the instigator.'

'But you knew you would get laid.'

Brendan's gaze was downcast for several long seconds. Looking up, he replied, 'Not the first time.'

'What happened? How did you get caught up in Austin's mess?'

Brendan hated thinking about those times, let alone talking about them. But if anyone had a right to draw this story out of him, it was Alannah. Closing his eyes and taking a deep breath, he travelled two years back in time. 'Austin and I had been best mates since… well since you left in Year Two. Dad tried to warn me to stay away from him, but I was hurting from losing you, so began my rebellious phase. But at that age, we didn't do much. We were just defiant brats, really.'

Alannah sat with her hands and chin resting on her knees, watching him intently.

'I knew Austin was a vampire back then. A mage normally starts learning about the magic world at a very young age, but Mum and Dad warned us not to talk to you about it. They didn't explain why. But I digress. Following my initiation at the age of twelve, my attunements came to me easily. I kept Austin updated with my progress, and when it was obvious I would become an enchanter, he joked about using my powers to score chicks together. At least, I thought he was joking.'

'Your voice broke at twelve?' she asked.

'Eleven, actually, but the folks thought I was too young for initiation, so they put it off until Liam was also ready.'

Her eyes bulged briefly. 'Go on.'

Brendan nodded and continued his story. 'I was nearly fifteen when it started, and I already had a rep for sleeping around.

I had been wandering around town with Austin for the better part of two hours since eating dinner at the pub. It was a warm summer night, and we were getting bored. The human bouncer had kicked our underage arses out of the bar, but not before I charmed that lovely bartender enough to score a few drinks. She even slipped us a bottle on our way out.

We started along the esplanade when I peered into the neck of the whiskey bottle. 'Damn.'

Austin spun around to face me. 'What?'

'Empty.' I threw the bottle towards the beach and heard it smash against the rocks. 'What da ya wanna do now?'

A wicked grin took over Austin's pale visage. 'I'm feeling thirsty for something warmer than Jameson's.'

'Hells no! You're on your own there, man. The sight of blood turns my stomach.'

'You're such a pussy, Brendo. Come on, it'll be fun. We'll find a couple of pretty girls. One for me, one for you.'

Come to think of it, I was in the mood for some action. 'Fine. But keep the feeding out of my face.'

Austin laughed. 'You'll be too balls deep in vag to even notice me.'

The thought alone had my cock stirring. We continued walking along the shoreline. Most of the hotties hung around this area on summer nights. We spotted one solitary girl sitting on a bench in the park across the road. It looked like she was texting or something on her phone.

'Forget it, Austin. Only one babe there. I'm not fighting you for her.'

The vampire was sniffing the air. 'But she smells so sweet. We could talk her into calling a friend.' Austin began to cross the road.

I rolled my eyes. Once the guy set his mind to something, there was no stopping him. I trailed slowly behind.

Austin waited for me on the opposite footpath before stepping onto the lush green lawn. 'Let me do the talking,' he insisted in a hushed tone.

I shrugged, not about to argue. Austin had plenty of experience with hunting, although he usually did so alone. When we were a mere three metres away, the girl looked up at them. I had switched on my active reading powers, but even my passive abilities would have picked up the fear emanating from this girl.

Austin's nose twitched. He must have smelled it too. But he wasn't concerned. His eyes began to glow brighter as he approached her. 'Hey there, beautiful.'

'Leave me alone!' she cried. 'My boyfriend will arrive any minute.'

'Boyfriend, huh? I bet we can show you a better time.'

The nervous brunette—who appeared to be about sixteen—was shaking her head frantically.

'Come on, bro, she's clearly not interested.' The intensity of her fear was overwhelming me and a huge turn-off.

But the bright red aura surrounding Austin suggested it had the opposite effect on him. Austin glared at me. 'Shut up, man.' He sat beside the girl and smiled at her. He motioned for me to take a seat on her other side.

I hesitated at first, but Austin pouted and fluttered his lashes. With a sigh, I slumped down beside the girl.

Austin's arm enclosed her shoulders, and he pulled her eyes into his gaze as he began to sweet-talk her. Slowly, the trepidation in the girl's aura dissolved into lust. 'You wanna get out of here? I live close by.'

The girl giggled. 'Yes, please.'

The pair of them rose and started walking toward Austin's house. When he realised I wasn't following, he turned and yelled to me. 'Don't wimp out on me now, bro.'

After sending a silent prayer to the Gods, I stood up and followed them. The walk took longer than usual because we kept stopping for the frisky couple to pash. When we finally reached the door to Austin's house, I moved close behind the girl and tapped her on the shoulder. 'Hey, you gotta friend you can invite to join us?'

She shook her head. 'I'm new in town, so I don't really have any friends here yet.'

Crap! No way was I gonna sit around and watch Austin feed. I turned to leave.

'Don't worry, Brendan. I'm sure Bethany here would be happy to have fun with both of us, wouldn't you beautiful?' Austin's glowing eyes fixed her own.

She giggled. 'Oh yes.' Her hand gripped my arm, and she fluttered her eyelids. 'Please stay, Brendan.'

Those big brown eyes, with thick lashes that went forever, did me in. There was something in the depths of that look suggesting she wasn't asking me to stay for sex. Even her aura showed me she was still afraid. 'Of course.' I trod across the threshold to Austin's home and before long we were in his room.

Sinking into the desk chair, I turned away from the sight of them undressing. The mood hadn't struck me, even with waves of the girl's own desire lapping at my senses, so I turned off my active reading, closed my eyes and tried to relax.

The girl's shock pierced my passive awareness, and the most intense orgasm I'd ever known a girl to have promptly followed. The sensation was enough to make my dick hard in an instant. When I looked toward the bed, Austin was feeding from the girl's neck as he fucked her. In that moment, I was surprised to learn the sight of blood trickling down the girl's neck did not disgust me.

Mesmerised by the strangely erotic scene, I drew closer to the bed.

The movement must have caught Austin's attention because he glanced up, blood dripping from his fangs. He grinned. 'You wanna go?'

I couldn't speak, so I nodded as I stripped out of my clothes. I chose to lie on my back so Bethany could straddle me. A moment later, I was slipping inside the girl, loving every minute of her riding me, as Austin took her from behind and continued to feed on her.

'I'm feeling a little faint,' Bethany said a moment after another amazing orgasm.

'Sorry, beautiful,' Austin replied. 'I'll stop biting you. Have you had enough sex?'

She giggled and smiled sweetly at me. 'No way. God it feels so good.'

I grinned up at her. 'You ain't seen nothing yet.' I switched my active powers back on at that point and gave Bethany a night to remember.

Opening his eyes, Brendan looked at Alannah. 'It wasn't until I sobered up the next morning, that I realised what I'd done… what Austin had done. I felt like shit, but at the same time, I wanted to feel those sensations again. Joining Austin on his hunts became an addiction for me, just as blood straight from the vein became Austin's. On most occasions, we found willing girls at parties, but there were a couple of other nights like the first, when we approached strangers on the street.'

Alannah stared at him with wide eyes but remained silent.

'After the second girl went to hospital… I sank into a pretty deep depression. I hated myself for my part in the whole sordid affair. I was skipping a lot of school and drinking myself into oblivion: anything to wipe away the memories of those girls lying on the bed unconscious and pale as corpses. I stopped going out with Austin, ceased going to parties. Connor was the one to pull me out of my funk. He also put Austin on the straight and narrow.'

'I'm sorry, Brendan.' Alannah leaned back against the headboard and placed her hand gently on his shoulder. 'I can see that was a painful memory to relive but thank you for explaining everything.'

He rested his own hand on hers and looked into her eyes. 'Does that mean I'm forgiven?'

'Have you ever used your own powers of coercion to get sex?'

'Gods no!'

She smiled. 'Then yeah, I forgive you. I'm curious about something though.'

'Oh?'

'How old were you when you had sex for the first time?'

Brendan let out a sigh of relief. The interrogation was over, and things were back to normal with Alannah. 'Eleven.'

Her mouth curved into a big grin.

It was enough to give him stirrings. 'What?'

Alannah slapped him on the thigh before getting out of bed. She was at the bathroom door before she turned back to him. 'Yet another thing we have in common.'

Brendan laughed as she vanished behind the door.

The Queen perched herself on the edge of the large four-poster bed taking up most of the guestroom she had given Austin. She ran a long fingernail along the spine of the naked succubus corpse lying face down beside him. 'Tsk, tsk, tsk. Did you have to drain this one too? You are wasting some of my best girls. I will have to teach you a thing or two about restraint.'

Austin grinned as he tugged on the ropes binding the dead girl's limbs to the bed posts. 'I know plenty about restraint.' He still felt drunk on the succubus' blood. It was almost as magically potent as Alannah's.

Tara smiled. 'Yes, I suppose you do. You may well be my new favourite pet. Especially since Anthony failed me.' She rose and strode over to Austin's side of the bed. Her hand slipped over his shoulder and began to caress his bare chest. 'How would you like to become my new paramour?'

'I'm flattered, Your Majesty, but surely I don't deserve such a privileged position.' Austin knew most vampires would literally kill for such an honour and many had. There was no denying the Queen's beauty. She was a Winters, after all. Hair and eye colour aside, he could see the strong resemblance to

Alannah. Tara often wore green contact lenses when in public, but never bothered hiding her true self from her subjects.

'True, you have not yet earned access to my bed, but I am going to give you the chance to do so.'

'I will do anything, Your Majesty.'

She sniggered. 'Of course you will. I would like you to convince Alannah to become a vampire.'

Austin sighed. 'You forget she doesn't want me anymore. She's in love with Liam.'

'You have given up too easily. I think you should be more persistent. Here—' she handed him a red potion— 'a few drops of this in her drink will turn her to putty in your hands.'

Austin shook his head. 'She's a mage; surely she'll have active resistance spells.'

The Queen grinned. 'You forget she is still a novice. I doubt she has even learned enchantment resistance yet.'

'Okay. I'll give it a go, but no promises.'

Having called in sick for the rest of the week, Alannah and Brendan spent a few days on magic training with renewed vigour. Alannah strove to master as many powers as possible before confronting her grandmother. She had finally succeeded in constructing and animating a clay golem the day before and was biting at the bit to try something new.

But Brendan was the focus of today's session. As much as she hated the idea of letting anyone into her head, she trusted Brendan and there were few volunteers lining up and offering to become his puppets. So, she agreed to help him.

They sat in the ritual circle facing each other and holding hands. His touch and the fact she was about to let him inside her mind felt strangely intimate and Alannah's skin became hot as her heartbeat increased.

'Relax, Lana.' Brendan spoke with a calm, soothing voice.

She obeyed him even though he was not in her head yet. After a few deep breaths, she whispered to him, 'I'm ready.'

He replied telepathically, *'Good, I'm in and I have control of the mainframe.'* His eyes flicked open and he smiled.

Alannah laughed. 'Now what?'

'A simple test to start with. Touch your nose with the tip of your right hand.'

Her hand moved as instructed, even without her giving any thought to the action. It was an odd sensation.

'A good start. Now pat your head and rub your tummy.'

Alannah groaned. She sucked at doing this, but her hands complied. It was uncanny. Seeing Brendan succeed made her smile. 'You're doing it, Brendan,' she whispered.

'Yup. But this is child's play. It's not like I'm making you do anything you don't really want to do. You're not going to like my next order… at least not entirely.' He winked at her.

She stiffened. *Gods, what is he planning?*

'Do you trust me, Lana?' His thumb was gently caressing her hand.

After gulping, she pushed away her fears and nodded. 'Yeah, I trust you.'

'Good, now take off your robe.'

'What?' Surely, he knew she had nothing but underwear on beneath her robe.

He grinned. *'Would you rather remove* my *robe?'*

Alannah blushed. 'Ah, no. I don't want to remove either garment. I'm not wearing much beneath mine.'

'*That's the point, Lana. I'm not going to do anything to you. But I won't know if I have the hang of this power unless I can get you to do something you don't want to do. Do you still trust me?*'

She nodded.

'*You know you want to remove your robe for me, Lana.*'

The voice in her head sounded so convincing. Reluctantly, she released Brendan's hands and stood. Lifting the hem of her robe, she brought it up her thighs, past her belly button, above her breasts. Once it was over her head, she looked at Brendan, breathing easier when she saw his closed eyes. 'My robe is off.'

'*Good. Now, you know you want to throw it to me.*'

Almost without a second thought, she obeyed him.

Brendan caught it with one hand and smiled, still with his eyes shut. 'I'm not gonna lie to you Lana. I would love to see what you look like right now, but I'm not going to peek without your permission.' He was talking aloud again.

And she no longer felt his presence in her head. 'Thanks for being honourable.' Standing there in front of Brendan wearing nothing but her bra and panties, she wondered what the big deal was. She was not naked. Maybe she could have fun with this too. 'You can look at me if you *really* want to.'

He laughed. 'You don't think I want to see your *almost* naked body?'

'Well, you *are* keeping your eyes closed even though I gave you permission to open them.'

A second later, Brendan's gaze was upon her, scanning her up and down. He whistled through his teeth. 'Hot damn! Liam's one lucky bastard.'

She tried not to blush as she kneeled on the floor in front of Brendan. A twinkling of light on the altar caught her attention. Bringing her hand to rest on one of the mana rings in the open case, a cold shiver ran through her body. She took the sparkling opal ring and put it on her left hand.

'Lana?' Brendan's voice was distant.

But she was not afraid. Not even as the white mist in front of her shifted and resolved into an apparition of her mother. 'Mum?'

The ghost's voice was in her mind. *'Hello darling child. I'm so proud of you.'*

'Mum, is it really you?' She wanted to hug the woman, but the ghostly apparition appeared too insubstantial.

'Yes, Alannah, it's me. I've been keeping an eye on you ever since I ascended.'

A tear came to Alannah's eye. The ethereal glow surrounding her mother made her even more beautiful in spirit form.

'You have accomplished so much in so little time. It has been a joy to watch you train. Your grandmother is a formidable opponent and I'm sorry I didn't prepare you for this world, but I have faith you can defeat her.'

'But how?'

Her mother smiled warmly. *'Keep this ring with you at all times. It was mine once and it will connect you to the spirit world. You have many friends on this plane and in your own mage community. And at the end of the day, do not be afraid to seek help from unlikely allies.'* Her mother turned to mist.

Alannah blinked and the room was normal again. She turned to Brendan who was utterly gobsmacked. 'Are you okay, Brendan?'

'W… what happened?'

'Mum's spirit paid me a visit.'

'Wait, what? Aunt Aileen was here?' Trepidation struck his features.

'Yeah, she's been watching all of my training apparently.'

'*Fuck!*'

'What's wrong?'

Brendan held up her robe and gestured to her nearly naked body. 'I'm in for such a spiritual arse-whooping.'

She laughed. 'I don't think Mum worried about that. She had some encouraging words for me regarding Tara.'

He breathed out heavily. 'I hope you're right.' Brendan appeared to relax. '*Shit!* Lana, do you realise what you did?'

'What?'

'You channelled Aether, the celestial element. It could be your third attunement and I'm impressed! There are only three other mages in town who can do that.'

'Really?'

'Really,' Brendan beamed. 'This is fucking awesome!' He drew her up into a strong embrace. 'We're totally gonna kick Grandma's arse! This calls for a celebration.'

'Damn straight! And you pulled off the mind tricks. That's a pretty big deal.' Realising Brendan was wrapping his arms around her barely clad body, she blushed. 'Speaking of which, can I have my robe back now?'

'I dunno. This…' he held it up in one hand, still gripping her with his other arm, 'is proof of my success. I'm tempted to keep it as a trophy.'

'But I will need to consecrate a new practice robe,' she complained.

'Worth it, though.' His hand came down and held the robe behind his back.

Alannah reached around Brendan's waist, but he lifted it high in the air again.

'Please, Lana?' His eyes pleaded with her.

'Are you for real?'

'Yup.'

'You are so weird. But fine, if you really want to keep it.'

He grinned widely and threw his other arm around her to pull her tight against him. 'Thanks, Lana. You know, I have an idea for how we could celebrate,' he whispered seductively into her ear.

She decided to play along for a bit. 'Oh? What did you have in mind?'

'Well, after three days without Liam, I figure you must be feeling… restless. I could show you a good time. You know I got mad skills, right?'

Alannah rolled her eyes and snorted. 'You don't believe in modesty, do you?'

Brendan still held her close but pulled back enough to look into her eyes. ''Course not. Modesty is for chumps.' He grabbed her hips, the fingers of his right hand started to trail up from her left hip along her side. As he reached her bra strap, Alannah felt herself blush, but he did not stop. His fingertips started to trace the outline of her bra towards her breast, all the while keeping his gaze locked with hers.

'Why aren't you stopping? I'm sure my face is bright red already.'

'Because you haven't told me to stop.' His eyes remained steady.

She gulped. 'Since when was that part of the rules?'

'Since now,' Brendan grinned. 'Don't you want to see how far I'll go?'

'I'm beginning to think you have no shame.' Alannah suspected he might not even be playing. It was a scary thought. Arousing, but still scary. Liam would never forgive her. 'Let's stick to the original rules. Game ends as soon as one of us blushes.'

He pouted as he released her from his grip. 'Fine, but if you won't have a private party with me, let's go to Connor's.'

Alannah shook her head. 'I don't know about leaving the house without Liam.'

He tapped her forehead lightly. 'Excuse me, who are you and what have you done with my Lana?'

She laughed.

'Seriously, since when do you obey all orders? I'm your bodyguard now. I'll keep an eye on you and there'll be a bunch of other mages there to watch your back.'

Alannah sighed. *A party sounds grand.* She smiled. 'Okay, let's do it.'

Chapter Seventeen

Liam had spent the better part of three days camping out in the Adelaide Hills where he would frequently spy on Tara's hideout. He had seen plenty of vampires and ghouls come and go, and the evil woman herself made the occasional appearance, but still no sign of Austin.

He perched atop a plum tree out the front of the house on a Friday evening. His legs hurt, his back ached, and he was growing weary of the whole mission. Perhaps he was wrong about Alannah's ex. Giving up on the idea, he dropped down from the tree and began to move back towards the road when he heard the front door open. Ducking for cover behind the tree, he glimpsed the creep he had been looking for.

Austin walked across the yard to a black sportscar. Liam could not see what make it was, but judging by the shape, he suspected a Porsche. When Austin took off in the vehicle, Liam raced back to his own car and followed. Thirty minutes later, they were in the outskirts of their hometown and from a distance, he observed Austin turning into Connor's driveway.

Several more cars followed the Porsche, and as Liam entered the driveway, it became obvious Connor was hosting the Friday night party.

'Wait here,' Brendan instructed. 'I'm gonna make sure the coast is clear.' He left her standing in the hallway. Alannah saw him talking to Bailey before disappearing outside.

She sighed as she leaned against the wall.

'Hi Alannah.' Turning her head to the right, she found Austin approaching her from inside the house. 'Can we talk?'

'What's there to talk about, Austin?'

'I was hoping we could still be friends. Will you at least come and have a drink with me?' Those luminescent blue eyes were pleading with her.

'I s'pose.' She followed him into the living room.

'Grab a seat. I'll get us some beers.'

Alannah chose one of the armchairs rather than a sofa.

A cup appeared in front of her face a minute later. 'I wanted to apologise.' Austin sat down. 'For not being upfront about my past.'

'It's okay, Austin. I understand why you didn't want to divulge those details. If I'm completely honest, what you did back then hasn't really changed my opinion of you. Both you and Brendan tried to warn me about your feeding addiction early on and I didn't care.' Alannah sipped her beer. *By the Gods it tastes so good!* She sculled the rest of it down in one mouthful.

Leaning forward, he placed a hand on her knee. 'So why did you break up with me?'

Looking into his gorgeous eyes, Alannah realised how much she still loved Austin. 'I… I'm not really sure. I guess I overreacted. I'm sorry, Austin.' She smiled sheepishly. 'Will you have me back?'

Scooping her up into his arms with supernatural speed, Austin whispered, 'Absolutely.' He kissed Alannah passionately as they moved through the house.

Next thing she knew, Alannah was making out with Austin in one of the spare bedrooms.

Stepping out of his car, Liam hit the lock button on the remote as he walked through the crowds of arriving guests. He could no longer see Austin. 'Damn it.' Pushing past a group of smokers, he moved closer to the house. He spotted Brendan and began to feel anxious. Rushing forward, he grabbed Brendan's t-shirt and spun the guy around to face him. 'Hey, where's Lana?'

Brendan gave him a stunned expression. 'Chill bro! She's safe inside. I asked Bailey to watch her while I did a sweep of the perimeter.'

Liam shook his head. '*You* were supposed to watch her.'

'I am. I've only been out here for a few minutes. What's got you in such a tizzy?'

'I tracked Austin here. I followed him from Tara's hideout, but lost him outside of this place somewhere.'

'*Shit!*' Brendan rushed inside. '*Fuck!* She's gone.' Liam detected panic in Brendan's tone. 'Okay, you try upstairs, I'll look around down here.'

Liam took off with bullet speed, not caring what normal humans saw. When he reached the second floor, he searched each room, ignoring the protests from irate couples. His heart was pounding as he began to fear the worst. *What if Austin has already killed her?*

But the sight he beheld behind door number five sent his blood boiling.

Alannah sat on the bed giggling as Austin began to light candles around the room. 'Why are you being so romantic? We didn't even do this for our first time together.'

'I want things to be just right for our reunion.'

'Oh, but they are. There's you and me and a big-ass bed. What more could we want? I mean, aside from the obvious.' She grinned at him as he approached her.

But he did not come to her; he stepped up to another candle beside the bed, which he was whispering to as he lit it. She could not understand him, but it sounded like Gaelic.

'Are you doing some kind of magic?'

He turned to her and smiled. 'I'm sending a prayer of thanks to the Gods for bringing you back to me.' A moment later he was kissing her amidst a frenzy of flying clothes. Pinning her to the bed with his strong arms, Austin gave her a wicked grin. 'Did you miss me?'

Alannah gasped as he entered her. 'Hell yeah.' She began moaning as Austin moved inside her. On the verge of climax, she heard a familiar voice.

'What the fuck?'

Looking over Austin's shoulder, Alannah saw Liam standing in the doorway, mouth agape. His visage reddened as it transformed into a grimace.

When Austin turned his head, he growled at Liam, pressing his weight possessively against Alannah.

The force of him thrusting took her over the edge. The orgasm rippled through her and a deep, guttural sound escaped her throat. She heard the door slam, but Liam's intrusion and sudden exodus did not bother her in that moment.

The next sensation that had her attention was a sharp, piercing pain in her neck, but it was fleeting as a new wave of pleasure started crashing through her.

Brendan was about to step outside to continue his search for Alannah, when a familiar sensation struck him. *Shit! That can't be good!* As he approached the stairs, he spotted Liam running down them. 'Don't tell me you left her up there?'

Startled, Liam spun to face Brendan. The emotions erupting from him almost knocked Brendan to the floor. 'If she wants him that bad, she can have him. I'm done!' Liam bolted through the front door.

Shit! Brendan leaped up the stairs, taking them two at a time. Stalking along the wood-panelled floor, he tried the first bedroom.

Jacob gaped at him. 'What the hell?'

'Sorry, man. I'm looking for Bailey or Connor.'

Cara stuck her head around Jacob's shoulders, her face flushed, and hair ruffled. 'Why, what's wrong?'

Brendan stifled the smile he felt creeping onto his face when he discovered Jacob's companion. The congratulations would have to wait. 'Austin's got Alannah, and he's gone rogue again.'

Jacob threw his legs over the edge of the bed and ran his hand through his hair. 'Crappers.' He stood up and gave Brendan an eyeful. 'You want backup?'

'Sure, but put some pants on first, man.' Brendan left the room and made his way down the hall. Flinging open the fifth door, he gaped at the erotic scene unfolding before him. It was enough to stir his dick. But it did not. Concern for Alannah took priority. He understood Liam's reaction. From this angle their heaving bodies worked together in perfect synchronisation and her moaning was the hottest sound he had ever heard. One could easily assume she was consenting.

But the hairs prickled on the back of Brendan's neck. Stepping closer, he tuned into what the couple before him were feeling. Austin was salivating as the metallic taste of blood washed over his tongue and a surge of power was rushing through his own blood stream. *Shit! Austin's blood lust is more prominent than his sexual appetite.* Focusing on Alannah, he could feel her growing faint. *The arsehole is sucking her dry.* He drew closer. *'Get away from her!'*

Blood trickled down Austin's chin when he looked up, his fangs still extended. The sick bastard grinned at him. 'Hey man, why don't you join us. You can fuck her while I feed. Just like old times.'

Something snapped in Brendan. *No one treats Lana with such contempt!* He rushed forward and slogged the vampire in the side of the head. The blow knocked Austin back, leaving him unconscious. Brendan pulled Austin's limp form away from Alannah and threw the guy to the floor.

By the Gods, she looks divine! The sight of her naked body sprawled out on the bed made his blood surge. He smacked himself in the face to regain his composure before shaking her shoulder. 'Lana?'

Her eyes opened slightly, and she gazed at him from beneath heavy eyelids. 'Hey, sexy. Have you come to rock my world?'

Brendan was still empathically aware of Alannah's emotions and he could feel hot, liquid lust gushing from her like torrential rain. *Fuck! It is going to take all my willpower to resist her. Austin must have drugged her or given her a potion to bring on such intense levels of desire.* He scanned the floor and found her clothes. Returning to the bed, he started dressing her.

Alannah giggled. 'You've got it all wrong. You should be taking your clothes off, not putting mine back on.'

Oh hell. Just keep focused. Brendan kept chanting the mantra to himself.

She began pouting. 'Don't you want to fuck me?' Her hand slid between his thighs and groped him. His semi-stiff cock hardened completely at her touch. 'It feels like you want me.'

He kept reminding himself that her feelings were not real. 'Not here, gorgeous. Come on, let's get you home.'

'Christ!' Jacob's voice came from the doorway.

Brendan wrapped himself around Alannah to shield her from Jacob's eyes. 'Can you get Austin out of here?'

Jacob moved in and inspected Austin's unmoving body. 'You got him good.' He dragged Austin out of the room.

Cara shut the door and came forward. 'Did you need help dressing Alannah?' A lopsided grin was tugging at her lips.

The spectacle Alannah was making was probably hilarious to onlookers. Her hands were all over him and she was desperately begging him to fuck her.

'I'll manage,' he insisted. 'Can you find someone sober enough to drive?'

'Sure.' Cara's brow arched. 'You're relishing this too much. Don't do anything stupid.'

Brendan laughed. *I am definitely enjoying this more than I should.* 'Don't worry about me.'

She hesitated a moment before leaving the room.

He continued dressing Alannah despite her verbal protests. Her weakness made the task easier because she was too weak to fight him physically. Brendan wondered how much blood she had lost, especially when he lifted her to her feet, and she fainted on him. His pulse quickened and it took considerable effort to maintain his grip with such clammy hands.

Rushing downstairs, he found Connor. 'Hey man, I need your help. She's lost a lot of blood.'

'What happened to her?'

'*Austin* got carried away feeding.' He practically spat the vampire's name.

Connor frowned. 'You're a terrible liar. This was intentional, wasn't it? Put her on the couch.'

'Yes. Austin was either trying to kill her, or…' *Shit!* Brendan had not thought about it at the time, but in hindsight he realised Austin had filled the room with ritual candles. Brendan gently placed Alannah on the sofa.

His friend started working his healing spells. Relief washed over him when he heard Alannah's breathing deepen and even out. 'Can you detect the effects of any potions or drugs in her system?'

'Yeah. She's taken a strong love potion. It'd take a more skilled mage than me to remove it from her system though.'

Brendan sighed. *Figures. Why else would she come on to me?* 'I'll get Dad to do it. Thanks for your help, man.' Lifting her back up, he carried her as he went in search of Cara.

'There you are.' Cara rushed forward. 'Shit. Is she okay?'

'Yup. Connor healed her. Did you find us a driver?'

Cara nodded. 'Nick's still sober. He's waiting out the front for you.'

'Thanks, Cars.' He moved to the door, pausing to turn and smile at her. 'Congrats to you and Jacob, by the way.'

She beamed. 'Thanks, Brendan.'

He hurried outside to find Nick. The drive home was torturous. Even in her sleep, Alannah was all over him and her hand would not leave his dick alone.

Nick kept laughing every time he caught a glimpse of them in his rear-view mirror. 'You're a better man than me for resisting those moves.'

'Yeah, but you don't have to live with the consequences. *Ah, Christ.*' Alannah had managed to unzip his fly and slipped her hand inside to get a proper grip. Having reached the limits of his self-control, he resolved to let her have her fun as he sat back to enjoy the ride. At least she remained dressed and too out of it to jump him.

When Alannah stirred the next morning, her head throbbed, and she felt foggy. Groaning as she rolled over, she found Brendan sleeping next to her. This was no cause for alarm. He had been doing this every night since Liam left. But something felt wrong. She tried to piece together her memories of the previous night but kept drawing a blank. *How did I get to bed and*—she glanced at herself under the quilt—*how did I end up wearing only panties and a singlet?* And Brendan was only wearing boxers. *Surely not?*

Sitting back, Alannah tried some deep breathing and mindfulness. As she did so, a few images flashed through her mind. The training session, Sleazy Chicken, arriving at the party, drinking a beer with Austin. But then nothing. *Did I really drink that much?*

As soon as Brendan woke, he sat upright and focused his unblinking eyes on her. 'Are you feeling okay, Lana?'

'Um, I think so. I've got a killer hangover, but otherwise okay. How much did I drink last night? I can't remember anything.'

Brendan frowned. 'Dad warned me this might happen.'

'What might happen?'

'A side effect of the treatment he gave you. Probably just as well. I don't think you want to recall what you did last night.'

She clapped her hands to her mouth. A moment later, she curled her fingers down enough to talk. 'Oh Gods! Did we?'

'Have sex? No, *we* didn't. But you did. I had to drag you out of a dangerous situation.'

Alannah's eyes widened as dread set in. 'W-what did I do?'

A grimace took over Brendan's visage. 'It wasn't your fault, Lana. You gotta believe me. Someone drugged you with a powerful potion. It took all Dad's strength to cleanse it from your system.'

Dread turned to fear. 'Who drugged me?'

'Austin.'

'*Shit!* Then what?'

'Then… he took advantage of you.' Brendan closed his eyes. 'He… he was about to turn you, Lana. I'm sorry, I never should have taken my eyes off you.'

'Wait. So, he…' Alannah couldn't bring herself to use the 'R' word. It was too painful to fathom. 'Did Austin drug me and have sex with me?'

When Brendan's eyes opened, they were full of sorrow. 'Yes.'

She began to shiver, so Brendan pulled her into his arms. 'Why didn't the other guys notice Austin dragging my drugged body upstairs?'

He spoke softly against her ear. 'Because you appeared to be enjoying yourself. They thought you got back together with him. It was a love potion, Lana. It made you believe you wanted whoever was touching you.'

Alannah pressed her head against Brendan's chest and began to sob. Something dawned on her. 'Oh Gods! Did you say I believed I wanted whoever was touching me? So, when you pulled me out of that mess?'

'Shoosh, Lana. Please don't go there'

She flushed, but she had to know. Her voice became firm. 'What did I do?'

'It wasn't you — not really. And I didn't let you take things too far.'

Sitting back, Alannah narrowed her eyes on him. 'Brendan, what did I do?'

He sighed. 'You mostly just said stuff. Very provocative stuff.'

'Mostly, huh? What else?'

He squeezed his eye lids closed. The memory was clearly painful for him. 'You also groped me… like a lot.'

She sprung out of the bed. '*Fuck!* I'm so sorry, Brendan.'

Brendan rose from the bed and drew her back into his embrace, despite her protests. '*Shoosh, Lana!* It's okay, seriously. I knew it was the potion, not you. It wasn't that bad. Not for me. I mean, what guy wouldn't want a hot girl grabbing him, right? I'm more worried about you right now. What Austin did to you was inexcusable.'

'What happened to him in the end?'

'I knocked him out cold. Jacob and Connor sent him packing.'

'Good. That creep better not show his face in town again. Any word from Liam yet? When will he get home?'

Alannah felt the muscles in his arms and torso tighten, but he didn't reply.

'Oh Gods! Don't tell me Liam got hurt!' She stepped back to look him in the eyes.

'No, Liam is unharmed. Physically anyway. Not that I've seen him since he took off last night.'

'What? Liam was there last night? Why didn't he…' A horrible realisation hit. 'He saw me fucking Austin, didn't he?'

Brendan nodded.

'Did he know about the potion?'

Brendan shook his head.

'Fuuuuck!' She stormed across the room and grabbed her phone. The call rang out at first, so she dialled him again.

This time, a spiteful female voice answered. 'Liam doesn't want to talk to you, *Alannah.'*

'Monique?'

'Yes, that's right. Liam came crawling back to my arms after the stunt you pulled. You screwed up, as I predicted. Have fun with your vampire lover, bitch!' The phone line went dead.

Alannah threw her phone at the wall. She collapsed to the floor in hysterics.

Brendan did not say anything. He simply picked her up and put her back in bed. Sitting beside her, he wrapped her in his arms.

The last of the sun's rays peeked through the bottom slits of the blinds in a last-ditch effort to illuminate Alannah's room. They scattered among the dust particles dancing around the window. As they disappeared, she decided it was okay to move again, because the gloomy ambience matched what she felt in her heart. She shifted her weight and looked at the plate of sandwiches Aunt Nora had left on the desk for her and Brendan. 'I think I'm ready to eat.'

Brendan grinned. 'Thank the Gods! I'm starving.' He reached across to her bedside table and turned on the lamp. Retrieving the food platter and two bottles of water, he brought them back to Alannah's bed.

After eating in silence, Alannah found her legs and stood for the first time in hours. She grabbed a pair of yoga pants from her wardrobe and slipped into them. Thankfully, Brendan had had the decency to put his jeans and t-shirt back on before tucking her into bed earlier that day. She turned to face him and noticed his attentive gaze. She blushed a little before shrugging it off as concern. 'You know what I really need right now?'

'I'm guessing it's not ice-cream or chocolate.'

A slight grin pulled at her lips. 'You know me too well.'

Brendan laughed. 'Well enough to know we're probably going to get shit faced tonight.'

'Can you smuggle a couple of bottles in here?'

'Is my name Brendan Winters?'

The smile was complete. 'Thanks.'

'Anything for my Lana.' He winked a moment before vanishing beyond the door.

In the meantime, she walked into the bathroom to freshen up. A glimpse of herself in the mirror was terrifying. Her eyes were red and swollen, skin blotchy, hair messy. Attempting to tame her locks with a brush achieved partial success. Not much she could do about her face though.

'I got us some snacks too,' Brendan declared as he walked back into her room.

When she returned from the bathroom, Alannah laughed at the mountain of chips and biscuits in the middle of her floor, surrounding two bottles of whiskey and two glasses. 'All my favourite treats. Good work.'

'You know me. I aim to please.' He gave her a wicked grin before dropping a couple of large cushions next to the drinks and collapsing onto one of them.

'Or offend,' Alannah finished for him. 'But in this case, I am pleased.' She locked her door and joined him on the floor. After cracking the seal on the first bottle, she poured them each a shot. They clinked their glasses and drank up. She savoured the burn in her throat for a full minute before pouring the second round. After the third drink, she began to feel the blanket of numbing comfort settle into place. Sighing, she leaned against Brendan. 'At least you didn't give up on me.'

He placed an arm across her shoulder. 'Lana, I will never give up on you.'

She looked into his eyes. 'Promise?'

Holding her gaze, he tucked a strand of hair behind her ear. 'I promise.'

Alannah smiled. 'Thanks. Next round?'

'Sure.' He grabbed the bottle and served the shots.

Several rounds later, Alannah's thoughts shifted from the whole Liam and Austin drama to her success with magic. She smiled to herself and started laughing.

Brendan's eyes squinted. 'What's so funny?'

'I realised I'm a kick-arse mage.'

'Of course you are. But how did you only just realise? I've been telling you all along.'

She shrugged. 'It only just sank in.' Stuffing her mouth with a handful of chips, she revelled in the salty goodness. 'So, what's the big deal with channelling Aether?'

'Are you kidding me? It's like a direct link to the Gods. Only three types of mages attune to the celestial element.'

'Tell me Brendan, what type of mages attune to the cest... celest...ial element?'

He laughed. 'You're drunk.'

Grinning, she bumped his shoulder with her own. 'Kinda the point. Now pour me another drink and answer my querest... quest*ion*.'

Brendan refilled the glasses and drank his before clearing his throat. 'Right, so as I was saying, three types of mages channel Aether. Council leaders, spiritual leaders, and necromancers. Leaders use it to connect to the spirit world and communicate with the Gods. Necromancers use it to talk to *dead people.*' He emphasised the last two words with his best Cole Sear voice.

Alannah shivered. 'Does that mean I may end up becoming a necromancer?' *Talking to Mum was one thing, but other ghosts? No thanks.*

'It's possible, but I wouldn't worry about it. While your attunements choose you to some extent, you do have some agency of choice when it comes to selecting your magus path.'

An analogy occurred to Alannah. 'Kinda like the sorting hat at Hogwarts?'

Brendan laughed loudly. 'Yup, or like how the penis—I mean wand—chooses the wizard.'

She glared at him. 'You spend too much time in the cesspools of social media.'

'But they're the best parts of the internet. Very entertaining.'

Alannah shook her head as she held her glass out for another shot. He happily obliged.

After slamming his own glass back on the floor, Brendan grinned. 'The fact that you can channel Aether also confirms something Liam mentioned.'

'Oh?'

'Only pure magic races can access the celestial element. It's one of the reasons our ancestors were so particular about our bloodline.' He leaned in closer. 'Is there something you're not telling me, Lana?'

'Oh right. I'd almost forgotten about that. Tara mentioned something when she confronted me at school. She said Mum conceived me at Beltane.'

His eyes widened. 'That's fucking awesome, Lana! Do you realise what that means?'

She sighed. 'That Dad wasn't really my dad?'

He curbed his enthusiasm a little. 'Well aside from that. The courtship and fertility rites of Beltane are sacred, so any children conceived at the festival are a literal blessing. They are generally also more powerful than other mages.'

'So how does it… how does that mean Dad wasn't my bio father?'

'Because the High Magus hosts the official Beltane festivals and he only allows pure mages to attend. There are other unsanctioned events in the wider mage community, but Grandmother dearest wouldn't make a big deal about your conception if Aunt Aileen got knocked up at one of those.'

'So how do I find my biological father?'

Laughing, he handed her another shot. 'Here, I don't think you're drunk enough. You can still pronounce bio…logical. Short answer, you can't.'

She arched her brows, waiting for his explanation.

'Thing is, Beltane is a little like Vegas.' He paused for effect. 'For those who participate in the official rites, the Gods choose their partner or *partners* (plural). It's One. Big. Sacred. Orgy.' After flashing a smouldering grin, he downed another shot before continuing. 'No one talks about it after. If a married woman conceives during the official rites of Beltane, it's accepted that the child is a blessing and her husband accepts the child as his own, even if there's a good chance he's not the daddy. I can't wait for my first Beltane.'

Alannah laughed. 'Sounds like your sorta party.'

Those bedroom eyes returned. 'Come on, Lana—as if it doesn't sound like fun to you.'

'Maybe. I'm not sure about the whole blind-date aspect though.'

'All part of the charm really. It's not like you have to fuck everyone you're paired with.'

'Well in that case, sign me up.'

'Would if I could. We gotta wait 'til we're eighteen. For obvious legal reasons, they can't have minors attend.'

Alannah sank into quiet contemplation for a moment. 'Hey, Brendan?'

'Yes, Lana?'

'What if we hosted our own unsanctioned event for the young magic population?'

The widest grin she had ever seen spread across Brendan's face. 'Genius. Pure genius. See, this… is why *you* are a woman after my own heart.' Slapping his chest with force; he fell backwards.

Alannah burst out laughing and collapsed next to him. Before long they were both rolling around on the floor, laughing together. She carried on until her ribs hurt too much to continue and even then, she needed to take several deep breaths to calm down. By this point, Brendan had settled, and he lay on his back with his eyes closed. Sidling up next to him, she peered down into his face. 'Brendan?'

His eyes shot open to lock with hers. 'Lana?'

'Thanks for today.' She reclined her head against his armpit and threw an arm across his chest.

Brendan's arm pulled her in tight and he exhaled sharply. 'You're welcome.'

They remained in this position for the rest of the night, or at least until Alannah fell asleep.

Chapter Eighteen

Alannah was alone in her bed when she awoke and hurried to the bathroom, to rid herself of the toxins she had imbibed the night before. When the urge to retch subsided, she slowly ventured downstairs. The house was unusually quiet for a Sunday morning, and her pulse quickened as she drew closer to the kitchen.

Normally the bustling sounds of crockery clanking, and the aroma of fried food filled the air. But she remembered it was usually Liam who cooked breakfast, or occasionally Aunt Nora. She knew her Aunt and Uncle were busy with the Council all day, and a quick glance of the clock told her midday neared.

Upon entering the kitchen, she was relieved to see Brendan at the table. But she took note of how rugged his appearance was. Slumped over the table, he was nursing a coffee mug, not even looking up as she approached. He simply pushed the green bottle of hangover begone towards her.

She downed a shot of the goop and put the potion back in the fridge before turning on the coffee machine. Taking the seat across from her cousin, she studied him for a minute. 'You're unusually quiet, even with a hangover. Something on your mind?'

He looked up into her eyes and held her gaze for several seconds before returning his attention to the cup in his hands. 'Just a bit.'

'You wanna talk about it?'

After sculling the last of his brew, he pushed his chair back and left his dishes on the sink. 'No, Lana. I don't want to talk about it. For one thing, you need to focus on your magic training right now. I'm gonna shower. I'll meet you in the cellar.' He turned and left the room.

What was up with him? Oh well, there is no use speculating. He is right: I need to concentrate on training if I am going to beat Tara. She went for another mouthful of her drink and cursed, realising her cup was empty. A glimpse of the bench reminded her of the effort required to work the coffee machine. So, Alannah gazed longingly into her empty coffee mug, hoping it would refill itself. Maybe if she focused hard enough, she could summon a cup of the divine drink. It was probably wrong, but she was desperate for more and really did not feel up to the effort of grinding more beans, et cetera. Visualising the coffee machine at her favourite café, she imagined it dispensing a shot of espresso, willing the substance to appear in her cup. When she opened her eyes, she was pleasantly surprised to find it had worked. 'Damn, I'm good.'

With the second shot of caffeine coursing through her body and a sense of accomplishment, she was able to stomach some breakfast and face the day.

As steaming hot water cascaded over him, Brendan thought about his predicament. He had a huge fucking dilemma on his hands. *What the hell am I going to do about Lana?* Even without intentionally reading her, he had caught a glimpse of those feelings last night, yet he could not bring himself to take advantage of the situation. If he played his cards right, he knew he could have her in weeks, if not days. But he also knew it was only a matter of time before Liam discovered the truth about Austin. And as much as he hated to admit it, Alannah needed Liam's protection. She needed as many damn allies as she could get for the impending war.

Shit! The honourable thing would be to kick his brother up the arse and make him face the truth. Of course, that meant Liam would take Alannah back in a heartbeat. But Brendan's inner rogue was telling him to say *'Fuck that! Get the girl, consequences be damned.'* Nothing would piss Liam off more than learning the truth about Austin, only to find Alannah had moved on to his little brother. *Will he still fight alongside us in that case? Will he still protect Lana?*

'Fuuuck!' He punched the tiled wall of the shower, shattering one of the ceramic squares and sending several hairline fractures radiating from the epicentre. When he drew his fist back, Brendan observed rather than felt the cuts on his knuckles. Placing his hand under the stream of the shower, he watched the water wash away his blood in a state of catharsis. With that momentary distraction, he knew what he would do.

Finishing in the shower, Brendan dressed for training. As he pulled out one of his practice robes, he caught sight of the one he had won from Alannah and smiled. But as he finished getting ready, he adopted a more solemn expression. Shit was getting serious.

He found Alannah in the ritual circle, consecrating a new practice robe, so he sat back and watched her.

Once finished, she turned to him and smiled. 'I finally replaced the one you absconded with.'

'Hey, I won that fair and square.' Brendan waggled his brows.

'That was anything but fair. Even so, I conceded willingly, and I'd give up all my robes and train in my underwear if it helps us win this fight.'

'Christ, Lana. You're killing me here.'

She gave him a smouldering grin. 'Sorry Brendan, you're the last person I want to be dealing lethal force to right now.'

Fuck! He could feel his resolve crumbling away and needed to change the subject, pronto. 'So, what's next on your magic agenda?'

'Well, I was thinking about what you told me last night. About channelling Aether. I want to see if I can attune to other mana sources.'

'What? Already? You haven't even mastered all the powers of conjuration yet. You've only imbued one item and that was a fluke. And what about learning to travel by ley lines? That could prove very handy.'

Alannah sighed. 'Call me overconfident, but I feel as though I could probably do those things in a pinch if I needed to. I never told you this, but when that vampire attacked me at school, I was able to summon Liam to help me. I'd never summoned a living being before, but somehow, I knew how to do it.'

He stared at her in amazement. There were few conjurers in the world who could do that. 'Right, well you know the drill. Did you want my help?'

'I'm feeling a little anxious, so I could use some of your calming magic.'

So could I, to be quite frank. 'Great. Let's get to it.'

Alannah recast the circle to bring Brendan into it. They knelt side by side.

He placed a hand on Alannah's shoulder, and channelled the sensation of touch, giving him the power to will her into a state of calm. As her nerves settled, he tapped into her serenity and let it wash over him.

She picked up the silver band with the green peridot crystal and eased it onto her right index finger. Closing her eyes, she began the arduous process of connecting to a new mana source.

Brendan kept his hand on her shoulder, continuing to soothe her and create the feedback loop he so desperately needed.

Finally, after what felt like hours, she opened her eyes and sighed. 'Nothing.' Her shoulders slumped.

'I'm sorry, Lana. Maybe next time?'

'Maybe. Right now, though, I'm famished. Let's get something to eat.' After dropping the ring back in the box on the altar, she rose and broke the circle.

Following her upstairs, Brendan watched as she slipped into her room. He stepped into his own bedroom and changed out of his robe. With this setback in mind, he collapsed on his bed and picked up his phone. He hesitated a moment before dialling.

'Hi Brendan. Is everything okay?'

'Hi Dad. I need you to contact Liam for me.'

Liam was on the phone. A moment after answering the call, he looked up at Monique and told her, 'It's Dad with Council business, might take a while. Can I use your study?'

She simply nodded. Knowing he would be occupied for some time, she wandered out into the garden. The sun was out and only a few white, wispy clouds were in the otherwise perfectly coloured sky. With the weather this good, she decided to go for a run.

Turning onto the gravel driveway, she increased her pace from brisk walking to jogging. As soon as she reached the road, her feet pounded the bitumen at a sprint. She was only a few kilometres down the road when she observed the limousine parked on the verge. *Odd spot for a limo. Is the occupant lost?* Slowing down to a jog, she approached the vehicle cautiously, rubbing her thumbs against her mana rings.

When she reached the driver's door, she knocked, but the passenger window behind the driver lowered. 'Can I help you?' she asked as she approached the back. But when the woman's face came into view, she froze as instant recognition filled her with fear.

'Yes, Monique Lane, I am hoping you can help me. I have a business proposition for you. Something of mutual benefit to the two of us.'

'Why would I help you?' she spat with bitter contempt.

'Because I know how much you despise my granddaughter.'

'Almost as much as you, which brings me back to my question.'

The Queen of the Cursed smiled viciously. 'If you help me, both Alannah and I will leave you and this town alone.'

'A tempting prospect, but what's the cost?'

'A simple favour is all I ask. Alannah and her cousins have something of mine in their possession and I want it back. Will you retrieve it for me?'

'You have the powers of a conjurer, why can't you summon it yourself?'

'Oh, I have tried, believe me. But my daughter kept it sealed away and hidden from me for years. Even now, my son has placed magical wards around his property, blocking all my magic. I even sent one of my pets to obtain it from Alannah's

Melbourne home, but that ended badly. I lost one of my favourite ghouls and my daughter's husband wound up dead.'

Monique shook her head in disgust. 'Ross is a smart man and a skilful mage. What do you expect me to do if *you* can't bypass his wards?'

'You have Liam's trust and confidence, do you not?'

'Yes, but—'

'Use that to your advantage. Find out where they have it hidden and take it. Simple. Will you do it?'

'On one condition.'

'Name it.'

'I don't just want you to leave town. I want you out of Australia, permanently.'

Tara grinned. 'Shall not be a problem. I was planning to return to my husband in Romania anyway.'

'It's a deal.'

Returning to Monique's bedroom, Liam spotted her phone, but did not see her, so he searched the house. Considering the enormity of the Lane family manor, it was no easy task. On the verge of giving up, he left the library when the front door slammed shut. He hurried up the hallway. 'There you are!' His voice was breathless.

She lowered her gaze and looked at him from beneath long lashes with a demure smile. 'Sorry babe, I went for a run.'

'I need to get home. Turns out I made a complete arse of myself over the business with Alannah and Austin. He drugged her with a powerful love potion.' Running his fingers through his hair, Liam braced himself as he processed the news. '*Shit!* That creep raped her, and I walked away from the situation. I let him do it.' He collapsed against the wall, sliding down to the floor. It felt like tears were threatening to break the dam.

Monique knelt beside him and placed a comforting hand on his arm. 'It's not like you knew about the potion. You can't blame yourself.'

He shook his head. 'No. I should have known. I should have trusted her. I knew Austin had come from Tara's. I swear to the Gods if I see that bastard again, I will kill him on sight.' As he said the words, he felt his phone vibrate with a text message.

BY ORDER OF THE COUNCIL OF MAGES, I WISH TO ADVISE ALL MAGI THAT THE VAMPIRE AUSTIN PEARCE IS A PUBLIC ENEMY. YOU ARE PERMITTED TO KILL OR CAPTURE HIM ON SIGHT. ANYONE HARBOURING THIS FUGITIVE WILL BE CHARGED WITH TREASON. It was from High Magus Kieran.

Laughing drily, Liam showed Monique the message. 'Looks like your dad shares my sentiments.' It was one thing to target a bunch of human nobodies, but Austin harmed a pure mage this time and no amount of money or influence on his father's part would help him. 'I should go.' Liam rose, but as he moved toward the front door Monique pressed up against him.

'Wait. I want to come with you.'

'I don't think that's a good idea, Monique. Lana will freak out.'

She stood her ground. 'Alannah's gonna need all the assistance she can get. I will help protect her.'

Liam was gobsmacked. 'You would do that?'

Monique smiled. 'Of course. But I need to shower first. Give me a sec.' She sprinted up the stairs.

Leaning back against the wall, Liam thought about how Alannah must have felt when he abandoned her at such a critical time. *Christ! If Brendan hadn't gotten her out of there when he did…*

The implications were too painful to consider. Liam had fucked up big time, and he prayed Alannah would forgive him.

'Okay, let's go.' Monique came racing down the hall in one of her brightly coloured spring dresses: one that had been a favourite of his, and he had told her as much when they were a couple. She wrapped her arms around him, planting a kiss on his cheek. Grabbing his hand, she pulled him out the door.

Everyone was talking in the living room when he got home. Alannah diverted her attention from the discussion to take in the sight of Liam and Monique arriving together. Tears instantly brimmed in her eyes and she quickly turned away. He noticed how close she was sitting to Brendan. Their legs were touching, and he had an arm stretched out behind her, across the back of the couch. Liam's eyes narrowed, meeting at the creased bridge of his nose. Brendan was not paying Liam any attention, however.

Dad was talking about the Council's orders to treat all cursed with suspicion. 'After the reports Liam and Brendan gave me concerning Tara's hideout, it is fair to assume she is exercising her powers as puppet master. You should alert all your friends.'

'What direct actions are the Council taking against Grandmother dearest?' Brendan asked.

Their father visibly cringed at Brendan's use of Tara's familial title, even though the tone was bitter and sarcastic. 'A number of soldiers are investigating the hideout, and Austin's family are under house arrest. Kieran issued every magus in the state with a kill or capture on sight command for Austin.'

Alannah's eyes widened. 'That seems pretty extreme. What if he was acting under the Queen's influence rather than his own accord?'

Liam could not believe what he was hearing. 'Are you seriously gonna defend that arsehole after what he did to you?'

She glared at him. 'Why not? He might not have had free will, unlike you when you chose to leave me there.' The venom in her voice pierced his heart, causing it to constrict painfully.

So that's it—Alannah hates me. Liam's eyes darted around the room as he hung his head low. 'I'm sorry, Lana. I didn't know.'

When his gaze rose, her eyes penetrated him with burning intensity. 'You ought to know me better.'

'He apologised already. What else do you want?' Monique piped up.

Alannah placed her hands on her hips as she scowled at Monique. 'What the fuck are you doing here anyway?'

'I came to offer you my help and to provide my boyfriend with emotional support.' Monique drew close to Liam and placed her hand on the small of his back.

Fuck! This was not going well.

'So, it's official again, huh?' Alannah narrowed her eyes on Liam.

Liam wanted to correct Monique and clear up the whole misunderstanding, but his dad stepped in first. 'Girls, please. This is not the time for bickering. We need to be a united front against the Queen and her army of cursed. Now go and call all your mage friends. It's time to muster the troops. We have plenty of spare rooms in the house, plus there's the guesthouse. The rest of the district Council agree that with my wards up, this is the safest house for initiates to take refuge in, while the rest of us prepare for battle.' He turned to leave the room but paused at the door. 'Liam, as soon as you've made your phone calls, please join me in my office.'

'Yes, sir.'

The assembled group began to disband. Monique kissed his cheek before stepping outside to make her round of calls. Alannah gave him a scowl before leaving the room.

Brendan remained seated and Liam observed the way his brother's eyes trailed Alannah intently.

Clenching his fists, his blood was boiling when he returned his attention to Brendan. 'You wanna tell me what's going on between you and Lana?'

The twerp gave him a smug grin. 'No, not really.'

Liam stepped closer. 'So, something happened?'

'It was bound to, leaving her with me for so long, abandoning her in her hour of need.'

He could feel a fireball forming in his hand. 'What did you do, Brendan? Did you touch her?'

'It's none of your business, bro. You're the one who ran into Monique's loving arms. Alannah's really fucking pissed with you. You can't blame her for seeking comfort elsewhere.'

Opening his fist, he let Brendan see the fire blazing in his palm. 'I don't blame her for anything. But I warned *you* to keep your filthy hands off her. Now tell me, little brother… Did. You. Touch. Her?'

With wide eyes focused on Liam's hand, Brendan shook his head. 'No. Despite what you may think of me, I wasn't prepared to take advantage of her vulnerability. This is Lana we're talking about. I don't want to hurt her.' As Liam lowered his hand and extinguished the flame, Brendan stood up and confronted him. 'You're not the only one in love with her. I also happen to have her best interests in mind, which is why I conceded to you this time. But the next time you fuck up… let's just say I won't hesitate again.' Brendan turned and stormed out the room.

Slumping onto the sofa, Liam heaved a huge sigh. He pulled his phone out of his pocket and dialled Blake's number.

'What are you doing?' Alannah asked when she found Monique snooping about in the cellar.

The girl did not even bother facing her to reply. 'Taking stock of your tools and weapons. We need to arm everyone, which means imbuing a bunch of gear.' Monique looked up at her. 'How many weapons have you imbued since the Solstice?'

Alannah bit her lip.

Monique was holding one of the ancient swords Alannah had found in her mother's collection. 'As I figured. Most of these will prove useless against an army of ghouls and vampires. Only blessed weapons will kill them.' She dropped the sword down onto its display stand. 'Face it Winters, you need my help. For all the guys harping on about your immense power and gift with magic, they seem to overlook your faults.'

'Why do you want to help me when you clearly dislike me?' she asked warily.

'You're right. I don't like you. I'm willing to help you yes; but I'm doing it for the street cred and because it helps Liam. The benefits you reap are of no consequence to me—unless of course you try to worm your way back into Liam's bed.' She began walking alongside a shelf covered in crystals, running her fingers along them as she went. 'But if I'm reading things right, it looks like that won't be a problem. You appear to have moved on to your next victim already.'

Alannah furrowed her brow. 'What are you talking about?'

Monique stopped and looked at her. 'Don't play stupid with me, Alannah. I saw how close you and Brendan have become.'

'That's how we are. You're reading too much into it.'

She raised an eyebrow. 'Am I? Are you sure that's how Brendan sees it? You should ask him how he feels about you.'

Is she for real? Alannah began to reflect on recent time spent with Brendan and things began to add up. '*Shit!*'

Monique grinned. 'Has it only just occurred to you? Maybe I gave you too much credit for your smarts.'

Alannah flew from the room, Monique's laughter behind her. She found Brendan sitting on his bed, talking on the phone. She closed the door and marched up to him, challenging him with her stare.

He cocked his pierced brow as he finished his conversation: 'I gotta go, man. See you tonight, yeah?' Brendan dropped his phone on the bed covers. 'Lana?'

'Is it true?'

'Is what true?' His visage became an expressionless mask, completely unreadable.

'Are you in love with me?'

His eyes grew wide for a split-second before the wall went back up. 'Who the hell told you that?'

'Monique suggested it, so I got to thinking about your recent behaviour. Is it true?'

He gave her an impish smile. 'Do you want it to be true?'

Oh hell, I hadn't even thought about it. Do I? 'Honestly, I don't know. Maybe. But you haven't answered my question.'

'Maybe, huh?' His eyes narrowed. 'Have you considered Monique is trying to stir trouble for you and Liam?'

'Right now, there is no me and Liam.'

Brendan leaned back on his bed, propped up by his elbows. 'But there could be. If you forgave him, I mean. He isn't really back with Monique.'

This was news to her. She stood at the foot of the bed, towering over Brendan's prone body. It was almost as if he was inviting her to join him, which reminded her she was still waiting for an answer. 'You're deflecting, Brendan.'

He sighed. 'Sit down, Lana.'

She perched on the edge of his bed, stretched out beside him, and lay on her side to face him.

'Or you could do that too. It seems like that maybe's leaning toward a yes.' He winked at her.

She glared at him.

He rolled onto his side to face her properly, his nose a hair's breadth from her own. Brendan's eyes searched hers during an incredibly tense moment of silence. 'You know I love you, Lana, but am I *in* love with you? I don't know, but I don't think we should entertain the idea.'

'Why not?'

'You're still in love with Liam, for one thing. And he'd kick my arse if I so much as touch you.'

She studied him for a few seconds, but he was not betraying any of his feelings. 'Is Liam the only reason?'

'No. He'd be right to kick my arse if I touched you, because he knows what I'm like. I don't want to hurt you, Lana. Even you know what I'm like with girls: I'm not boyfriend material.'

'Why is that?'

He shrugged. 'I dunno. I guess I like variety.'

'Either that, or you've never really found someone you want to settle down with.'

'The thought of me wifed up is like trying to imagine an Oscar nomination for a porno.'

'It's a shame.'

'Yup. There are some damn good pornos out there that deserve better recognition.'

Alannah laughed. 'I was talking about you not wanting to commit to someone.'

His expression began to smoulder. 'Why is that a shame, Lana?'

'Oh, you know, for all those girls out there who happen to fall in love with you.'

'Right. I'm such a heartbreaker and all. But are you really concerned about those nameless girls you don't even know?'

'No.' She tried reading him again, but still got nothing from his intensely focused eyes as they studied her. Their gazes locked together, and Alannah wondered if she really did want Brendan to be in love with her. *If so, does that mean I'm in love with him?*

There was a knock on the door. Brendan rose and answered it.

'Dinner's ready. Is Lana in here?' It was Liam's voice.

'Yeah, I'm here.'

Popping his head around the corner, he saw her on the bed and frowned. *Great! Now he probably thinks something is happening with me and Brendan.*

Alannah stood up and followed the guys downstairs.

Chapter Nineteen

The town's initiates assembled in the living-room as they arrived after dinner. Alannah was anxious to see Cara and ran to her the moment she appeared.

Cara embraced her. 'How are you holding up?'

'I'm surprised I'm standing to be honest. I feel like shit.'

'I can imagine.' Cara pulled her aside, out of earshot from Liam and his friends. She continued in a hushed voice, 'I can't believe Liam dumped you over this! At least Austin's gonna get what's coming to him.'

Alannah sighed. 'I think the Council is overreacting. Yeah, I'm pissed with Austin, but I don't want people killing him for what he did. What if he wasn't acting with free will?'

'Alannah, honey, you're the one who told me he used to rape girls with his powers of hypnotism. Even if he drugged you against his will, don't those other girls deserve some justice?'

'I s'pose. But the death sentence without a trial? It's so barbaric.'

'The magic legal system may seem archaic, but it's necessary and it works. Austin had his trial; we just weren't there. The Gods judged and sentenced him.'

'Oh.' Alannah recalled some of her recent reading on mage law, how Council leaders can communicate directly with the Gods to seek advice where a case is not black and white.

Uncle Ross entered the room and cleared his throat. The din ceased, and all eyes focussed on him. 'Right, now that everyone's here, I have a few housekeeping matters to discuss. Firstly, I'd like to thank Brock Sheridan and Charlotte Rowan for volunteering your services. Since you've both recently graduated to full magus status, you don't have to be here, but I appreciate your help.'

The pair simply nodded their acknowledgement.

'Now, there ought to be enough beds, but some of you will need to share rooms. While it should go without saying, I will have to insist on no gender mixing in shared rooms.' An audible groan of disappointment travelled through the group. He turned to Alannah. 'With that in mind, Alannah, I am going to insist you choose a roommate for added protection.'

'Cara can share with me.'

Her uncle nodded his approval. 'I will arrange a foldup bed for her. Now, on to kitchen and dining matters…'

Alannah tuned out as he harped on about the chores roster and cleanliness expectations. Her attention was on Liam, who was looking at her. Aura reading would have been useful in that moment because his expression was blank. *Am I prepared to forgive him?* Seeing Liam again brought a lot of suppressed feelings to the surface. *Brendan was right: I am still in love with Liam.*

'Alannah?' Ross' voice drew her back to the present issue.

'Sorry?'

He sighed angrily. 'I asked if you could imbue the weapons in our armoury?'

'Um, I can try.'

'Get Monique to help you. I want everyone armed with a blessed weapon. While I can guarantee that my wards will keep you safe from Tara and her spells, there is a chance her cursed minions could attack. Guards are stationed around the perimeter, but it is best to prepare. As for school hours, I don't want any of you to travel alone. Even when going to the bathroom, always have a friend with you. Well, that's it. You may get yourselves settled now.' Ross left and the noisy chatter returned.

Alannah looked at Cara. 'Come on, grab your gear and follow me.' She headed for her room, where they found a spare bed.

'This'll be fun. It reminds me of having slumber parties,' Cara said.

Rolling her eyes, Alannah snorted. 'Yeah, only this time instead of watching the horror movies, we are in lead roles of our own.'

'Hey, I'm sure everything will be fine.' Cara began unpacking her bags. She put her toiletries away in Alannah's bathroom. Looking around the room, she beelined for the wardrobe. 'Is it okay if I hang some stuff in here?'

'Knock yourself out.'

Cara opened the closet and her jaw dropped. 'By the Gods, don't you own anything that isn't black?'

'I have that green dress I wore to the spring equinox.'

'Is that it? Geez woman. I gotta take you shopping for some more threads. Being Goth doesn't preclude other colours, you know. You'd look hot in reds and purples too.' She began hanging up her own clothing. 'So… what's up with you and Liam now?'

Alannah sank onto her bed. 'I dunno. I'm confused about my feelings.'

'Confused how?'

'On one hand I'm pissed at him for leaving me and running back to Monique. But I still love him and want him.'

'Are you able to forgive him?'

'Yeah, I think so.'

Cara sat beside her. 'What's the problem?'

'Something Monique said earlier today got me thinking.'

Cara groaned. 'You're not gonna listen to a word outta that bitch's mouth, are you? She's a troublemaker.'

'Brendan said as much too, but that's beside the point. What she said got me thinking about my own feelings. This is what has me perplexed.'

'Go on.'

'In addition to Liam, I think I might be in love with someone else.'

Her eyes lit up. 'Who?'

Alannah felt herself blushing. 'Brendan.'

Cara smiled. 'Called it. Remember what I said on that camping trip? So, what are you going to do?'

'I don't know. As I said, I'm confused. I might be mistaking my strong familial affections for him as something more than they are. Or it could be lust. It's not like this is the first time I've thought about jumping his bones, but I don't know if I could see myself in a relationship with him.'

'Wow, the two Winters brothers,' Cara chuckled. 'Could make for a hot threesome.'

She punched Cara lightly in the arm. 'What's with the Liam and Brendan threesome obsession?'

'Just think about it a moment and tell me you don't agree. Objectively speaking, they are the two sexiest guys in school for one thing.'

Alannah closed her eyes and visualised it. Cara was right. The thought of both guys pleasuring her at the same time… *fuck!* 'Gods damn you, Cara. I'm gonna start having wet dreams about it now.'

She giggled. 'I told you. Do you know how Brendan feels about you?'

'Yes and no. I asked him outright if he was in love with me, but he wouldn't give me a straight answer. He told me he didn't know, but he wasn't prepared to go there.'

'Hm.'

'What?'

'It's probably for the best. If you are still in love with Liam, he is the more sensible choice. Brendan's love could be dangerous. He does break a lot of hearts. That's why I made a point of resisting his charms.'

'You're probably right, and he said as much himself, but that adds to his appeal. I'm not afraid to admit I have a bad-boy complex.'

Cara shook her head. 'If your relationship with Austin was anything to go by, I can believe that. Just be careful, okay? And please try to keep your head in the game. This is a very dangerous time for distractions.'

'I know.' She took a deep breath to clear her mind before changing the subject. 'So, you and Jacob, huh?'

The biggest grin Alannah had ever seen spread across Cara's face. 'Yeah. He is amazing!'

There was a knock at the door and Brendan peered into the room. 'You girls wanna join us for Kelly Pool in the games room?'

'Sure.' Alannah stood and made her way to the door.

'Sounds great,' Cara agreed.

As soon as Blake knocked Alannah out of the game, she stood back against the wall beside Connor. 'Is this the misery wall where we losers come to lick our wounds?'

Connor smiled. 'Not so miserable now that you're here.'

'Right, 'cause I'm such a ray of sunshine.'

'That's exactly what you are. Your smile lights up any room you are in.' He winked at her.

Alannah laughed. 'Is that your best pickup line? No wonder you're still single.'

He clasped his chest above the location of his heart. 'Ouch, woman. You have shattered me.' A sly, lopsided grin graced his features. 'We don't all have the looks and charms of the Winters clan, but I get by.'

She was mid eyeroll when a hand slipped into hers and Liam's voice whispered in her ear, 'Can we talk?'

Alannah turned to see Liam standing in the doorway. She nodded and followed him upstairs.

Liam pulled her into his room and closed the door. 'I'm really fucking sorry, Lana. I know I should have trusted you, but it was like a short-circuit in my brain when I saw you with him. It did not occur to me he could have drugged or even hypnotised you.' His expression was full of shame and remorse as he closed in on her and pressed her against his door. 'I hate myself almost as much as that creep and I know I don't deserve your absolution, but I'm begging you to forgive me.'

His plea for mercy softened her heart and left her skin tingling. 'I forgive you, Liam.' With those words out, Liam's mouth covered her lips. She hesitated a moment before yielding to him. The kiss was even more passionate than their first, filled with a hunger brought on by days of separation. When Alannah came up for air, she pressed her hands to his chest and challenged him with a furrowed brow. 'What about Monique?'

'There's nothing there. I spent one night seeking comfort in her bed.'

'She seems to think you are back together.'

Liam shook his head. 'I never promised her anything. I'm in love with you, Lana.'

She replied with another kiss. Within a few minutes, Liam carried her across the room and laid her down on his bed. Their tops came off, followed by everything else Alannah was wearing. Only Liam's boxer shorts remained as they explored each other's bodies. The moment his fingers plunged inside her, she arched her back and moaned loudly.

Liam attempted to muffle the sound she made by kissing her again. 'Shh, my dear. We don't want anyone else to hear us.'

She grinned at him wickedly. 'You'll have to gag me if you keep this up. Oh Gods. Mm.' He added a third finger and began rubbing her clit with his thumb. Intense pleasure surged through her.

But he covered her mouth with his again and continued thrusting his fingers, bringing her to a strong climax and shaking her to the core.

Alannah could feel Liam's arousal pressing into her leg. Gripping his erection firmly in her hand, she whispered, 'I want you, Liam. All of you.'

Smiling, he tried to stifle a groan. 'Are you sure?' It was not only a question of sex. She knew Liam was asking if she was ready to take the next step in their relationship.

She nodded. 'Yes, I'm sure.'

Sucking in an audible breath, his eyes lit up. Liam stood and walked across to his chest of drawers to retrieve a condom. Their eyes remained locked in a searing gaze as he began to tear the packet open with his teeth.

A sudden movement at the door drew their attention. Monique burst through, jabbering as she entered the room. 'There you are. Surely your dad's rules don't really…' Pausing, she took in the sight of him standing there in his underwear. The foil packet must have caught her attention because she shot a look toward the bed. When her eyes fell upon Alannah, she screamed. *'You fucking bitch! How dare you!'* She charged.

Alannah sat up and promptly covered her breasts with her hands.

Liam acted quickly, grabbing Monique before she could do any damage. 'What the hell, Monique.'

The Queen Bee squirmed in his arms. She turned to face Liam, tears streaming down her cheeks. 'You don't really want to sleep with that whore, do you? Not when you've got me. What about us?'

'Monique, I'm sorry if you got the wrong idea, but there is no us. I'm in love with Lana.'

She flipped, flailing about and beating her fists against his chest. *'What? You can't be serious?* You slept with me. You never have meaningless sex.'

Alannah sat there gobsmacked by Monique's display.

'Look at me, Monique.' Liam tugged her chin, raising her eyes to his. 'I'm sorry. I came to you for solace and I was weak. I never should have let things go that far.'

Monique went rigid. 'Screw you all.' Her tone became ice cold. 'You can fight this damn war without me.' She broke free of Liam's hold and fled through the open door.

'Christ! Monique, where are you going?' he shouted from the doorway.

'Anywhere but here! It's not like you care.' It sounded as though she was on the stairs.

Shit! I can't afford to lose Monique's help. Alannah brought her knees to her chest and sighed as she dropped her head to rest on them.

Liam dashed after Monique. 'You can't leave the house. It's not safe.'

'What's all the commotion, bro?' Brendan's voice came from down the hall. 'Lover's spat?'

'*Shut up, Brendan.*' Liam's voice trailed off.

'Lana?'

Looking up, she found Brendan standing in front of her. Her nudity did not escape his attentive eye as it scanned her up and down. She flushed.

'What's going on, Lana?'

'Monique walked in on Liam with me. It tipped her over the edge.'

He nodded.

'Can you, uh, pass me my clothes?'

Letting out an exaggerated sigh, he bent down and scooped up the clothing pile on the floor. 'I suppose.' He dumped them on the bed beside her.

She plucked her black lace panties out of the pile and looked at Brendan again. 'You gonna turn around so I can dress?'

Leaning casually against the bedpost, he grinned at her. 'No. You've seen me naked, so it's only fair.'

Alannah glared at him. 'I'm not in the mood for games right now.'

'Who said I was playing?'

'Brendan, please.'

'Fine.' He turned, crossing the room to pick up the half-open condom wrapper from the floor. 'I guess she caught you guys at an inopportune moment.'

'Yeah. Talk about cockblocking. It would have been the first time with Liam.'

Brendan spun around as she retrieved her bra. 'Seriously? You guys haven't done it yet?' His eyes dropped to her breasts.

Blushing, she attempted to cover them with her bra, but fumbled and dropped it.

He exhaled sharply; his eyes pinned on her chest.

'Brendan! I told you to turn around.'

'Sorry,' he whispered, unwilling or unable to avert his eyes.

Giving up, Alannah threw her clothes on in front of his heated gaze. She advanced toward the door.

As she reached him, Brendan blinked a couple of times, and grabbed her arm. 'Shit. I'm sorry, Lana. I forgot myself for a moment there.'

She looked from where his hand gripped her wrist to his eyes. His unwavering gaze focused on her. She smiled. 'It's okay. I guess we're even now.'

Releasing her, Brendan grinned. He continued talking as he followed her out of Liam's room. 'So, you guys really haven't had sex yet?'

Alannah strode toward her own room. 'Not yet. He wanted me to be sure I was ready for a serious relationship.'

Seizing her hand, Brendan stopped her. He stepped closer and stared. 'It's the real deal with Liam, isn't it?'

'Yeah.'

There was a flicker of emotion in his eyes before Brendan's expression went blank.

'Does that bother you?' Alannah tried to read him, but his wall was too high.

'Of course not. Why would it?' His visage gave nothing away, but his thumb was gently stroking her knuckles.

'Because of what we discussed earlier today.'

Dropping her hand, he sighed. 'I don't feel that way about you, Lana. I'm sorry if I gave you the wrong impression.'

'So, you're not in love with me?'

'No.'

His admission stabbed her in the gut and knocked the air from her lungs. It was a ludicrous reaction, considering she had Liam, and was not even sure of her feelings for Brendan. *Does that mean…?* She dismissed the idea before letting it surface. 'Well, if you're sure. You had me wondering back there when you kept staring at my boobs.'

He laughed. 'I'm still a hot-blooded guy, Lana. Those amazing tits on anyone would captivate me.'

She smirked at him. 'So, you liked what you saw?'

Brendan pinned her against the wall with his hands pressed against her wrists. 'You're lucky I value our friendship and my own life so much. If I didn't, I would have shown you how much I liked what I saw right there on my brother's bed.'

The thought gave her a mental image that sent sparks shooting through every nerve in her body. Alannah looked to his lips and wanted to kiss him. *I'm done denying Brendan's sex appeal.*

He gave her a devilish grin and stepped closer.

Fuck! Every part of her body was humming, and her core was throbbing. She should have pushed him away, but instead she looked at him with lidded bedroom eyes.

A step closer and Brendan pressed his body against hers. He probably thought they were playing. 'Nice aura, Lana.'

'I told you not to read me.' She spoke with a hushed voice.

'I can't help it when your emotions are this strong. Be careful what you wish for, Lana. I only have so much self-control.'

'I thought you said you didn't want me.'

His eyes narrowed on hers. 'I didn't say that. I'm not in love with you, but that doesn't mean I don't want to fuck you.' Brendan's hands travelled up her arms and down her sides, pausing on her hips.

Alannah breathed in deeply as she revelled in the sensation of his hands on her body.

He pressed his forehead to hers and clenched his eyes shut.

Just kiss me, damn it!

His eyes shot open, penetrating her with their ferocity.

'Get away from her!' Liam growled as he pulled Brendan back and flung him into the opposite wall. He followed up by punching Brendan in the eye, knocking his face sideways.

Brendan turned back to look Liam square on with a smug grin. 'Sorry, bro, I didn't realise Lana was off-limits when you went running after Monique.'

Liam—still in only boxers—clasped the collar of Brendan's t-shirt. 'You promised you wouldn't touch her.' He raised his fist again.

Alannah screamed in panic. *'Stop it, Liam! Nothing happened.'*

He turned to stare at her, releasing Brendan. 'That didn't look like nothing.' Liam stepped closer to her. 'The two of you were about to kiss, weren't you?'

Tears began to trickle down her face.

'Weren't you?'

What can I say? It's probably true. She wanted it to happen and that alone made her feel guilty. She bit her lower lip and lowered her gaze.

'Christ! I need some air.' He stormed off to his room and slammed the door.

Alannah felt stunned. *What have I done?* Liam emerged from his room several minutes later, fully dressed. She ran after him as he darted down the stairs and out the front door. 'Listen to me, Liam.'

Reaching the carport, Liam pulled a set of keys from his pocket. 'I don't want to hear it. Not right now. I have to find Monique before she gets herself killed.' He was in his car and gone in a flash.

She turned back to the house, freezing as Brendan stepped outside.

'I'm so fucking sorry, Lana. I never meant to hurt your chances with Liam.'

'It's not your fault. I should've stopped things progressing that far. I don't know what came over me.'

'I do. It starts with L and makes your aura bright red.' Brendan smiled.

She rolled her eyes. 'I didn't—'

A pair of strong arms pulled Alannah off the ground, hoisting her onto the roof of the carport. A man held her back against his body and a knife at her throat. 'This has been a very entertaining piece of family drama to watch, but all good shows must come to an end.'

'Austin?' Alannah croaked the name, overwhelmed by the rising terror she felt with the cold steel against her skin.

'Hello again, beautiful.' His tone was full of bitterness. 'Looks like you've got yourself mixed up in an interesting love triangle. Let me see if I have this right. Liam and Alannah are in love, but that's not enough for our kinky Alannah is it? She's gotta have more, so she seduces Brendan, who is fed up with holding back from months of pent-up sexual frustration… and bam! It happens, but Liam finds out and loses his shit. This leaves Alannah without the man she loves and wishing she had behaved herself because she knows it'll never be more than sex with Brendan. Or will it? Does that sum it up?'

'What the fuck do you want, Austin?' Brendan roared from the ground.

'The same as you and Liam: I want Alannah. Only I'm not afraid to take her. Here's how this is going to work. I'm going to leave with Alannah, and nobody will get hurt. But if anyone tries to stop me, I will use this knife.' He pressed the tip of the blade into her throat, producing a droplet of blood.

'Please, Austin, this isn't you. Tara must be pulling your puppet strings,' Alannah pleaded.

'That's where you are wrong, my dear. I serve my Queen freely.'

'Then kill me already. I'd rather die than become a vampire.'

'*No, Lana!* Don't!' Brendan cried.

'His love for you is touching, really. But I feared you might say something like that. Thing is, my Queen really wants me to bring you back alive; so, I brought a backup plan. *Advance!*' he called out. A large mob of vampires and ghouls stepped out of the trees and slowly moved towards Brendan. 'I wonder if you love Brendan as much as he loves you. Give yourself over to me and my friends will back down. Otherwise, we will stand here and watch them tear your cousin limb from limb and feast on his flesh and blood.'

Alannah swallowed a lump in her throat. 'Fine. You win. Just don't hurt him.'

'*Lana, no!*' Brendan screamed as he moved closer to them.

'Naw, so sweet. Makes me speculate on how much the two of you really feel for each other. I guess you'll never know. Men, stand down and return to base.' Austin pulled Alannah into a firm hold and rose into the air.

She could no longer see Brendan, but she heard him crying after her as Austin floated down towards the road.

'*Lana!*' Brendan screamed as though at a lost limb, anguished and real as death.

Chapter Twenty

Liam pulled into his driveway and killed the engine. He threw his head back against the seat and closed his eyes. *Could my love-life get any more twisted and complicated?* After driving around for about an hour to check Monique's usual haunts two or three times, he had returned unsuccessful. He hoped she had found somewhere safe to hide out.

It was time to confront Alannah and Brendan. *Why can't my douchebag brother keep his hands to himself?* Liam got out of the car and stormed into the house. Feeling parched, he beelined for the kitchen to grab a bottle of water.

'You can't simply waltz into her hideout, Brendan. It would be suicide.' Dad's stern voice drifted in from the direction of the dining room. 'I know you're hurting, but you need to think rationally. Let the Council handle this.'

Curiosity got the better of him, so Liam popped his head around the corner and saw Brendan and his friends sitting at the table with Dad. No sign of Alannah though. This was probably his chance to catch her alone before kicking his brother's arse again. He was about to make his way upstairs when Brendan looked up and caught his eye. *Shit! Had he been crying?* His eyes were red and puffy in addition to the bruising around his left eye from Liam's punch.

Ducking out of view, Liam headed to the stairs. He was not ready to deal with Brendan's drama. But he only made it up the first three steps before a voice stopped him.

'Where are you going?'

Turning, he met the scowl on Brendan's face. 'To talk to Lana. She is *my* girlfriend, after all.'

'She won't be *yours* much longer.'

'Fuck you, arsehole.' Liam resumed his climb.

'You won't find her up there.'

Liam sighed. He was not in the mood for Brendan's games. 'Where, pray tell, is she?'

'I don't know for certain, but if I were to hazard a guess, I'd say Tara's hideout in the Hills.'

His heart stopped for a moment as he spun around to face Brendan again. 'What the fuck?'

'Austin took her after you left. Sound familiar? Liam abandons Lana, leaving her at Austin's mercy.'

It felt as though he was flying when he charged at Brendan and knocked him back into the wall. 'I left her with *you*, you little shit! Don't pin this on me.'

'Why not? If you hadn't run away like a pansy, she wouldn't have gone after you and Austin wouldn't have grabbed her.'

'And if you weren't about to shove your tongue down her throat and Gods know what else, I wouldn't have left in such a fury.' Liam practically spat his retort in Brendan's face.

Brendan cast his gaze downward. 'I was trying really fucking hard to resist her.' His voice had dropped to a whisper.

'What was really going on with you and Lana?'

'In short? Nothing.'

Liam shook his head. 'Bullshit. I saw what almost transpired between you. I want the truth.'

'I'm telling you the truth, bro. Nothing like that has ever happened before. Monique's intrusion probably left her frustrated. Her aura was flashing "come fuck me signals" all over the place and she was literally begging me to kiss her.'

'She asked you to kiss her?' *How could Lana betray me like that? And so soon after being intimate with me.*

'Well, not verbally. I read it in her thoughts.'

Liam felt his jaw drop. 'You can read minds now?'

Brendan nodded. 'Surprise! Just keep that little detail between us though, hey?'

'Since when?'

'A few months now. Whatever almost happened, it was nothing. She's in love with you Liam, not me.'

'You must take me for a fool because I saw the way she was looking at you. That wasn't nothing.' Sick of his brother's face, Liam marched away and shut himself in his room. Collapsing on his bed, he kicked off his shoes and stripped back to his boxers. He felt a wave of nausea when he thought of how close he had come to making love to a girl who would happily jump from his bed into Brendan's. Thinking back, he realised he had been an idiot to believe Alannah when she told him the flirting with Brendan meant nothing. He should have seen this coming, especially after what he had overhead Alannah telling her friend Emma all those years ago.

'You wanna tell me what's going on with Liam?' Dad's voice startled Brendan as he watched Liam walking off in another huff.

'Not really.'

'That wasn't a question, son. I'm guessing that shiner was his doing?'

Brendan sighed. 'Fine. But you'd better sit down.' They walked into the living room and took their usual seats. 'Firstly, did you know Liam and Alannah were a couple?'

Dad's wide eyes answered even before he spoke. 'Ah, no. I assume this must be a recent development since she recently ended her relationship with Austin.'

'Officially, they hooked up on the second day of term. Alannah dumped Austin because of Liam. But it's been a long time coming. They have always been in love with each other.'

'I see. Is that why Monique left abruptly? She was jealous?' It was almost possible to see the gears turning in his father's brain as he put the pieces together.

'Yup. But there's more.' He took a deep breath. 'I also happen to have some strong feelings for Alannah and Liam knows this. He warned me to keep my hands off her.' Brendan paused to gather his courage. His old man was not going to like the next part.

Dad narrowed his eyes. 'You didn't heed his warning, did you?'

'I tried, believe me I tried. Technically I didn't do anything. But there was an incident earlier tonight…'

'Go on,' Dad prompted him after a moment of silence.

'After Liam ran off after Monique, Lana and I had a… uh… heated moment in the hallway. We were on the verge of kissing when Liam caught us. Hence the black eye.'

Dad was shaking his head in disbelief. 'You couldn't leave well enough alone, could you? You were always jealous and coveted what your brother had.'

His words cut deep. 'We're not kids anymore. This isn't like fighting over toys.'

'I know that, Brendan. This is much more serious. You made a move on his girl. You're lucky to have escaped with one black eye.'

'You sound so misogynistic. We are talking about Alannah here. She is not just "Liam's girl."'

'Watch your tone, young man. I'm perfectly aware of whom we are speaking and frankly, I'm appalled by both of you for betraying Liam.'

Brendan was furious. He rose from his chair and towered over his dad. 'Don't my feelings count for anything here? Wait—no—of course they wouldn't! Not when compared with those of your fucking golden boy. *Well, fuck you Dad!*' He was fed up with the lot of them. Had they all forgotten what happened to Alannah? It was time for someone to act. He raced into the cellar and grabbed Alannah's athame.

'What are you doing?' Dad called from the doorway.

'I'm getting her back.'

'You will do no such thing. It's too dangerous.'

After collecting a few other weapons and crystals, Brendan stood face to face with his father. Sometime in the last couple of years he had managed to outgrow the man in height and muscle tone. 'Get out of my way.'

'Don't be stupid, Brendan. You'll get yourself killed.'

'Why do you care? I've only ever been one huge disappointment in your eyes.' He used his superior strength to push past. Bolting up the stairs, he burst into Liam's room.

Liam sat up in bed and glared at him. 'What the—'

'*Shut up!* I'm only gonna say this once, so you'd better listen carefully. I don't give a shit what you think of me or how you feel about that almost-kiss. Austin kidnapped the woman we love tonight and here you are moping about like a sad-sack. I, for one, am not gonna sit back and wait for the Council's members to get off their lazy arses and do something. I'm gonna get her out of there, even if it kills me, which it probably will. But I'd stand a higher chance of success with your help. So, why don't you stop being a pussy! Lana needs you now more than ever. What do ya say?'

Liam's outer aura resembled the Aurora Australis as waves of different emotions washed over him while Brendan spoke. When he concluded his tirade, the colours surrounding Liam settled to a courageous orange. 'Fine. Let me get dressed.'

He leaned against the doorframe and waited with his arms crossed.

Black jeans, black t-shirt, black hoodie. It was the same outfit Brendan had changed into. Liam was a dolt in many respects, but when it came to matters of war, he knew exactly what he was doing. They both made their way out to Liam's Audi in silence.

Brendan had not banked on the farewell party waiting for them by the car. As much as he loved his friends, he was not keen for any more delays.

'We're going with you,' Connor announced.

He raised his brow in surprise. 'You guys know this is certain death, right?'

'Yeah, but this is Alannah we're talking about. You guys aren't the only ones who love her.'

Brendan looked around at the assembled group. Bailey and Cara were there of course, but they had also recruited the help of Locky, Ben, Nick, and Caleb. Even a few of Liam's mates joined the party. 'I guess she has that effect on people. Come on, time's a-wasting.' They all loaded into various vehicles. To avoid the tension with Liam, Brendan chose to ride with Nick. It was heartening to see how many mages and other magical folk rallied around him and Liam.

Grandmother dearest is in for one hell of a rude shock.

After opening her eyes, Monique gasped as she realised she was chained up against some dusty old stone wall. The last thing she remembered was running down Liam's driveway, then nothing but blackness. *Someone must have knocked me unconscious, but why?*

Shivering, Monique looked down and found all but her bra and panties missing. When she noticed her fingers were bare, she panicked. *They took my channelling rings!* Whoever captured her either thought they held some monetary value or knew what they were really for. The latter prospect terrified her.

She took in her surroundings. Judging by the old barrels, the room must have been a wine-cellar at some point. But the various anchor points bolted into the walls, along with the stainless-steel tray of surgical tools sitting beyond her reach, suggested the space had been repurposed for more nefarious use. It was a dimly lit area, with one small filament globe in the stone ceiling.

The sound of a bolt shifting out of its lock drew her attention to the door. 'Ah, I see you are awake at last.' Tara Winters stepped into the room.

Her blood froze. 'Wha… what do you want from me? I th… thought we had a deal?'

'That is right, we had a deal. But you are yet to fulfil your end of the bargain despite having the time and opportunity to do so. Where is it, Monique?'

'I… I don't know. I tried looking, b… but couldn't find it.'

'You are lying. I know, because I can still read your surface thoughts and I sense you are trying to hide something. Now tell me, where is it?'

Shit! Her mental block was not strong enough. Closing her eyes, she took a deep breath and focused more. She visualised the tendrils of Tara's power creeping into her mind and pushed them out. One by one, she pried them away and warded herself. 'There's a mystic chest in their ritual room. It was the only place I didn't look, so I assume it was in there. I couldn't get the chest open.'

Tara picked up a scalpel and stepped closer. 'Couldn't… or wouldn't?'

Her eyes widened at the sight of the blade.

'You have two options, Monique. You can either let me into that precious little head of yours, or you can slowly bleed out from the hundreds—or possibly thousands—of tiny cuts I will inflict upon you. What will it be?'

'Your Majesty, sorry to interrupt, but we have her.' The familiar man's voice came from upstairs.

The distraction was a welcome relief. At least she would not have to endure any torture yet. But her heart sank when she watched Austin enter the cellar and chain Alannah's unconscious body to the opposite wall. *The war is as good as over before it has really begun.*

'You have done well, my pet. Come, let me reward you a little. My granddaughter will not wake for a while.' Tara pulled Austin out of the room.

They bolted the door shut, leaving Monique alone with her thoughts and Liam's unconscious cousin.

Chapter Twenty-One

When Alannah came to, the first thing she noticed was an intense, throbbing headache. She was afraid to open her eyes and accept defeat. Perhaps if she went back to sleep, she thought, her dreams could become her reality. Her subconscious returned to that moment in Liam's bedroom, only this time there was no intrusion. *After pulling on the rubber, he mounted her gently. He penetrated her, driving himself deep inside and bringing her to climax over and over, all while telling her how much he loved her.*

A strange rattling noise brought her back to the real world and her eyes flicked open.

'About time you woke up. I was starting to get bored.'

'Monique? What are you doing here?' *And why is she only wearing underwear?* That was when Alannah noticed her own state of undress matched the girl on the opposite wall. *Did my dreams take a turn for the worse?*

'Waiting to be tortured. Apparently, it doesn't pay to get on your grandmother's bad side. But you probably knew that, huh?'

Fuck! So, this was it. She was Tara's prisoner and would soon become another of her vampire servants. 'What did you do to piss her off?'

'It's what I didn't do. She wanted me to steal a trinket from you. But there was no way in hell I was doing anything to help that bitch. I lied and told her I'd do it so she would leave me alone. Probably not my brightest moment.'

Who would have thought Monique Lane would ever earn my respect? Alannah laughed. 'I bet she was furious.'

Monique smiled. 'Yeah, that's putting it mildly. Look, I'm sorry for how I acted with Liam. I know how much he loves you. I couldn't handle losing him again. But if I'm honest with myself, I never really had him in the first place. Even during the years I dated him, I knew his heart belonged to you.'

Alannah's chest tightened. It hurt to think about what she had lost. Even if by some miracle she escaped this hellhole, Liam would never forgive her. 'Thanks. Not that it matters now, but I think I blew it with Liam.'

'What? How?' Monique perked up and spoke with more volume.

She sighed. 'It happened after you left. What started out as some innocent flirting with Brendan rapidly escalated into a heated moment. Liam caught us in what felt like an almost-kiss. That's what it looked like to him, anyway. I don't know what Brendan's intentions were.'

'I knew it! You totally want Brendan too. Did you ask him about his feelings?'

'Yeah. He said he's not in love with me.'

Monique shook her head and laughed. 'And you believed him? That guy has had a boner for you since you returned.'

'If anything, it's probably only physical attraction. To be honest, I don't really know how I feel about Brendan, but I know I love Liam, and the thought of losing him is heart-breaking.'

'That's something I can relate to.' Monique gave her a wicked grin. 'But come on, you can't tell me you're not at least curious about what it would feel like to have sex with Brendan.'

'Maybe a little.'

Monique arched an eyebrow and gazed at her sceptically.

'Okay, fine. More than a little. You know, you're probably the only girl who's slept with both those guys. If either of us should be jealous, it's me.'

A satisfied grin took over Monique's visage. 'I never thought of it that way, but you're right.'

'So… who was better?'

Monique giggled. 'You aren't serious! You don't really want to know, do you?'

'Sure, I do. It's not like I'm gonna get a chance to find out for myself.'

Frowning, Monique's tone turned serious. 'Have you resigned already?'

Have I? 'I dunno. I guess so. Aren't you?'

'No. There's gotta be some way out of here. What if we both try to channel the surrounding matter together?'

'I s'pose that might work, but then what?'

'We could summon a pair of big ass bolt-cutters. I know my dad has a pair in his shed that could break these chains.'

'I never thought I'd say this, but you're a fucking genius Monique. Let's give it a try.' They both closed their eyes and Alannah began to slow her breathing down. After a few minutes of meditation, she pressed her hands against the stone wall and drew on the mana within the atoms making up the rocks. As she felt the buzz of power collect in her hands, she directed the flow of energy in Monique's direction.

'You can stop now.'

When Alannah opened her eyes, Monique was holding the bolt-cutters. She could almost taste her freedom.

After cutting her own chains, Monique stepped forward and got to work on Alannah's. As soon as Monique finished,

Alannah stretched her limbs and basked in their moment of victory.

'That was the easy part. Now to get out of wherever the hell we are. Any ideas?'

'What about magiportation?' Alannah suggested.

Monique sighed. 'I already thought of that, but I can't sense any ley lines within range.'

'If you can lend me your powers, I could create a golem from the clay beneath the cellar floor. We could imbue it with the strength to break down the door and smash a few vampire heads.'

'Sounds like a plan.'

Everything was dark and quiet on the approach to Tara's hideout. Brendan looked across to Liam and waited. He was listening to his brother's thoughts for the signal he needed.

'Okay, Brendan. Go.'

As soon as his brother gave him the command, he stealthily led his taskforce around the back of the house.

Their strategy was simple enough. Liam's team would create a diversion with an outright assault, while Brendan located Alannah and got her out. He brought Connor with him in case any healing became necessary, and Bailey could provide covering fire. But if things went according to plan, he would not need either of them.

He found a hiding spot in the back garden and waited. Liam's next signal should be obvious enough. But the sudden tremor beneath his feet, followed by shouting inside the house, were not what Brendan expected. Connor and Bailey both shot him concerned glances. *Is that magic, or an earthquake?*

The ground shook more violently, and the guards posted at the back door ran inside. Liam must have taken advantage of the confusion within to make his move, because the sky lit up with the biggest fork of lightning Brendan had ever seen, and it appeared to strike somewhere in the front yard.

Brendan's heart was racing, and he was eager to move, but he forced himself to wait and count a full minute before doing so. Stepping up to the windows, he peered inside, but it was too dark to make out any details. He closed his eyes and tried to get a read on Alannah.

A few minutes later, he breathed a sigh of relief. She was still a mage, and by the feel of it, she was performing some powerful magic. He waved the guys over and stepped inside. It was necessary to heighten his vision to see, so he spoke telepathically, '*Stick behind me and stay close.*'

The minute Brendan stepped inside, a strong arm grabbed him around his throat and reeled him up against a man's body. A hand clasped his mouth, so he could not even cry out a warning to his friends.

'I should kill you now,' a familiar voice hissed in his ear in a hushed tone.

Brendan felt a chill down his spine as the guy who had once been his best friend showed his true colours. Some part of him had been holding on to the hope Tara had been pulling Austin's puppet strings all this time.

'But I think I'll have too much fun hurting you.' Austin ran a sharp blade along Brendan's cheek, causing him to flinch from the sting of the shallow cut.

Their physical contact allowed Brendan to get a solid read on Austin and his heart sank at the realisation there was no cloud of mental compulsion in the traitor's mind. Oddly, there were no surface thoughts available for him to read either, but that was not surprising. The Lich Bitch had probably provided all her goons with protection charms, which would have been how Austin slipped through Brendan's radar in the beginning.

All attempts to wriggle free of Austin's grip were futile. The jerk was unnaturally strong, too powerful even for a mage well-trained in the art of combat. As Austin dragged him further into the house, he heard a couple of muffled cries behind him.

Austin sniggered as Brendan tried to turn his head back to see what was happening. 'Looks like the ghoul guards have caught our other mates. I guess it's just us for now.'

Austin freed Brendan's mouth, allowing his bitter retort to spring forth: 'You will pay for raping Lana, you fucking arsehole.'

Stopping before a solid wood door, Austin laughed. 'Such a pity you turned into a pussy-whipped coward. Tell you what, I'll give you a chance to redeem yourself. Help me with Alannah's transformation ritual and I'll let you live. Not only that, but I'll even share her with you.'

The implications of Austin's offer hit him straight away. Involvement in such a ritual would send him down the path of a dark mage, if not result in an outright curse of his own. *Is it worth it for a chance to save my own life and be with Alannah?*

They both staggered as the ground shook violently beneath them. 'Fuck,' Austin cussed. The hint of fear in his voice suggested whatever was happening was not part of Tara's plan. 'Hurry up and decide, bro. I'm growing impatient.'

The heavily bolted door across the hall collapsed in front of them, forcing Austin to jump back, but his reflexes were not quick enough to avoid a blow to the head which sent him flying and losing his grip of Brendan.

As he dropped to the floor, Brendan rolled out through the doorway in time to see two figures step through it, followed by a big fuck-off golem. Once the dust had settled, he copped an eyeful of Alannah and Monique's scantily clad bodies, complete with manacles around their wrists and ankles.

Jumping up, he brushed himself off and grinned. 'Hot damn, I feel like I've walked onto the set of an award-winning porno.' He kept his voice hushed as he directed his comment toward Alannah.

She grinned. 'But not an Oscar award.'

'No, that would be inconceivable.' A glance in Austin's direction told him the vampire was out cold. He sent off a quick mental message to Liam: *I found Alannah and Monique.*

'Good, get them out of here.'

He gestured for the girls to follow. 'Come on. I know a quick way outta here.'

'Wait, what about Fluffy?'

'Fluffy?'

'My golem. I named him after my first cat.'

Brendan laughed. 'You are full of surprises. I don't think he should come with us though. He'd draw too much attention. Can you instruct him to move through to the front of the house, crushing all the vampires and ghouls he encounters? Could be a helpful distraction.'

Alannah nodded. 'Right.' She placed a hand on the golem's arm, closed her eyes and softly chanted a new set of instructions.

Fluffy took off a moment later and the girls followed Brendan outside.

Connor's eyes practically bulged from their sockets when he saw Alannah. 'Um, hi. Are you hurting anywhere?'

'Nah, I'm good.' Alannah slapped Connor on the shoulder. 'But thanks for asking.'

With a sigh, Connor slumped his shoulders and averted his gaze.

It had not ever occurred to Brendan before that night how much his mates also fancied Alannah. *I wonder if Liam has noticed the extent of his competition.*

'Ahem.' Monique grabbed everyone's attention. 'Can we go now, please?'

Brendan retrieved a couple of citrine crystals from his backpack and handed them to Alannah and Monique. 'Did you girls wanna summon some clothing first? Not that I'm complaining, but it's pretty cold out here and I don't want you dying of exposure.'

'Ah, thanks.' Alannah took the crystal and promptly produced an outfit much like Brendan's. He kept his eyes glued to her. *It's amazing how she even makes getting dressed look erotic.* As she tied the last of her boot laces, she looked up at him and held his gaze for a few seconds, searching his expression. She stood, breaking their eye contact. 'Well, I'm ready.'

'Me too,' Monique chimed in. 'Let's go.'

Brendan was scanning the grounds. 'Where's Bailey?'

'He took off after a couple of ghouls through those trees. You go, I'll wait here for him.'

'But…' Brendan began to protest. He hated the idea of leaving his friends behind.

Connor cut him off. 'We all signed up for this. Get the girls to safety.'

Nodding silently, Brendan gave Connor a sideways hug and pat on the back before leading Alannah and Monique around to the front yard. He made a point of keeping behind the cover of trees along the fence-line.

Brendan caught his first glimpse of Nick's car when he heard Alannah gasp behind him. Spinning around, he saw her frozen in place by something catching her attention. When he followed her sightline, he cursed under his breath. Tara was advancing on Liam. She had him suspended in the air by some invisible hand that was choking him. 'No Lana, don't!' Brendan hissed as he grabbed her arm. He had come this far—he could not lose her now.

Ignoring him, she shrugged free of his grasp and charged into the fray. *'Liam!'*

The moment the ground began to rumble, several vampire guards burst forth from the front door to join their comrades on the front porch. Their clustered formation was too good for Liam to resist, so without any further ado, he brought a shitload of lightning strikes down on their cursed arses. Their bodies crumpled to the ground, sending the distinct odour of burnt flesh wafting in his direction.

That was too easy, Liam thought.

A cliché evil laugh emerged through the front door, followed by a cloaked figure. 'Do you honestly think I would station so few guards out here? That I was unaware of you breaching my perimeter tonight, or on those previous occasions?'

Liam had little patience for discourse with his horrid grandmother. Without hesitation, he sent a lightning bolt in her direction.

But Tara was one step ahead of him, deflecting the attack and redirecting it at Blake's real form, not one of his many illusory images. His best mate screamed in agony as he dropped to the ground.

Shit! This woman is powerful and brutal.

She laughed. 'Have you only come to realise that now, dear boy? Your father has not told you much about me, clearly.'

And an expert mind reader who can bypass our mental defence spells! Great.

'Let me introduce you to my pets.' Tara's arm extended in a sweeping gesture.

A second later, a swarm of ghouls and vampires stepped out from behind the trees and shrubs surrounding the large front lawn area.

'I'm going to give you a choice, Liam. Send your friends home and join me or die here tonight.'

'That is no choice. I'd rather die than further your sickening cause.'

She grinned viciously. 'So, you would not even consider it to save your brother?'

'Are you okay Brendan?' He frowned at the radio silence.

'I guess Brendan is a little preoccupied with my new favourite. I do wonder how long Austin will keep up that torture.'

Shit! So much for that plan.

'Sorry, Liam dear, but no one gets the better of me, not even my own family.' There was no hint of remorse in her tone, only pure malice. 'This is your last chance. Stand down and join me and I will spare your brother from further harm. Just think — following your precious Lana's path will make life much easier.'

'I still refuse to sink to your level,' Liam spat.

The tremor he had felt earlier intensified and Tara's smile vanished. 'That troublesome girl,' she hissed. 'I thought Austin used cold iron to restrain them. You lot,' she pointed to a group of ghouls, 'get in there and stop my granddaughter. The rest of you, engage the enemy, but leave my grandson to me.' She returned her attention to Liam. 'I am going to enjoy watching the life drain from your worthless body, you piece of Council scum.'

The sounds of blades clashing, teeth gnashing, and claws slashing filled the night air. Drawing his sword, Liam charged Tara, but she pushed him back with a strong gust of wind, knocking him to the ground.

'*I found Alannah and Monique.*' Brendan's thoughts pierced Liam's mind.

He let out a quick sigh of relief. At least this fight would not be for naught. '*Good, get them out of here.*' The moment he replied to his brother, Tara's lips curved upward again, and he reprimanded himself for forgetting she could read his mind. *We are all fucked!* There was no way to outwit or overpower this woman. Well, he would still die trying. Rising to his feet, he attempted to move toward her.

But Tara's arms jutted forward and lifted as Liam felt his feet leaving the ground. Her hands appeared to grip something as an invisible force tightened around his throat. He struggled at first, but there was no use fighting anymore. The vice around his neck was crushing his windpipe, depriving him of air. His vision began to blur as his imminent death approached.

Chapter Twenty-Two

When Tara spied Alannah approaching, she dropped Liam and laughed maniacally. 'It never ceases to amaze me how stupid people will act for the sake of love. You could have been well on your way by now, dear child.'

Clutching the citrine tightly, Alannah raced forward, empowered by her love for Liam and hatred for Tara. With a mere thought, she summoned a sword from the family armoury. Gripping the hilt as she continued to advance, she prayed in a whisper, 'I call upon The Dagda. Please bless this weapon with your strength and magic.'

'*Lana, no! Get out of here!*' Liam's strained voice shouted.

The sword began to glow when she reached him. 'I'm not leaving you. Here, take my sword and give me yours.'

After rising to his feet, he swapped swords with her in time to run the blade into a vampire who ran at them.

She blessed the sword she took from him and struck out at a ghoul who tried to sneak up on her. Power was surging through her and it felt incredible. Movement in her peripheral vision caught her attention and she grinned as Brendan closed ranks with her on the left. She noticed he held a small dagger. 'Give me your weapon to bless.'

'Nah, I'm good. You did this one already.' Opening his hand more, he revealed her athame.

'Oh, what a lovely surprise.' Tara's bitter voice drew their gazes. 'A family reunion. Such a pity Ross couldn't join us too.'

Alannah's heart began to sink as she observed the swarm of cursed encircling them, shuffling slowly forward with teeth and claws bared. But something sparkled on Tara's finger, catching her eye. In a flash, Alannah lunged forward and clasped her grandmother's hand. She glared straight into the startled woman's eyes as she spoke. 'If a reunion is what you're after, I can do you one better.' She looked to the sky. 'Come forth Aileen Winters and all spirits who call themselves my ally.'

Hundreds of white, swirling shapes circled above them, slowly descending as each spirit manifested into a recognisable form. Landing, they surrounded the army of cursed and charged them. It was quite a sight to behold, as these beings of pure, heavenly light tore the vampires and ghouls limb from limb.

Alannah spotted a warm, friendly face. Stepping forward, Mum smiled briefly before turning to face Tara with a scowl. 'Hello mother. Up to your old tricks, I see. I thought I told you to leave Alannah alone.'

'That was on the condition she remained uninitiated. She is very much an active initiate now, so no more deal.'

Alannah gasped as realisation dawned. Her hand was still gripping Tara's when the woman whirled on the spot and threw her at Austin, who stepped out of the swarm of cursed.

'Grab her, quick, and disarm her.'

Austin pulled her into his arms, holding her firmly with her back against his chest. He yanked the sword from her hand and slipped it into his belt.

Tara grinned, turning back to face Aileen, Liam and Brendan, who all froze. 'Now if any of you make a move against me, Austin will kill your precious Alannah. I suggest you all drop your weapons and stand down.'

Everyone who held a weapon obeyed her instruction.

Using his bodyweight, Austin pushed Alannah forward slightly. They stood directly behind Tara. He spoke softly in her ear: 'Whatever happens, I want you to know I will always love you and I'm sorry for all the pain I caused you.' His tone was genuine and caring, without any of the bitterness she had come to expect from him of late. A second later, he returned the sword to her hand and released his grip as he whispered, 'Now!'

Alannah did not hesitate to plunge the blade deep into Tara's heart. Her grandmother went rigid and let out a strange gurgling sound before collapsing.

At the sight of their dead Queen sprawled out and bleeding on the ground, most of the cursed fled the scene. The few who remained were either injured or bowing in submission. Austin was the only one who remained standing. He smiled at her, slowly dropping to his knees like the others.

She returned the smile and mouthed a 'thank you' before turning back to face her friends.

Brendan rushed forward and scooped her up into his arms, lifting her off the ground as he swung her around. *'You were fucking amazing!'*

Alannah laughed. 'Put me down, I'm getting dizzy.'

'Oh right. Sorry.' He set her down and grinned widely.

Glancing at Liam, Alannah noticed his beetroot-red visage, and the veins pulsing in his temples. Everything seemed to slip into slow motion as she watched him grab a blessed sword from the ground and charge toward Austin. By the time she realised what he was doing, it was too late. But she still screamed at him: *'Liam, no!'* She sank to her knees as the blade pierced the vampire's heart.

Austin gave her one last look as his life slipped away. Not an expression of surprise or pain, but of love.

Liam glanced back at her briefly to see tears streaming down her face. He picked up Blake's lifeless body and walked away, leaving her at a complete loss.

What the hell happened? One minute, Brendan was revelling in victory with Alannah. The next minute, Liam lost his shit and killed Austin. He drove his thoughts into Liam's brain, *'Seriously, what the fuck, bro? Sure, the guy had it coming; but still, there are ladies present.'*

He watched as Liam turned a cursory glance toward Alannah. There was still battle rage in his expression, but his aura told Brendan something different.

Liam's thoughts filled his mind. *'Tell her I did it to protect her; because I love her.'*

Brendan shook his head. Even though he understood Liam's motives, the guy was a Class A moron who would be lucky if Alannah ever forgave him.

Liam gathered up Blake's scorched body and walked away. *Shit!* Brendan did not even notice Blake had fallen. A quick scan of the battlefield revealed he was not the only one. A few others were sitting up nursing wounds, but the shot of green hair atop the motionless head of a goblin drew his attention.

'Locky!' he cried as he rushed over. 'Oh Christ, dude!' Tears began to trickle down Brendan's face at the sight of his mate's limp body. There were several ghoul bites, including one that had torn a large gash in the side of Lachlan's neck. Judging by the red stain on the grass, the guy must have died from blood loss.

'It's okay, man. I'll take his body home. Go comfort Alannah.' Brendan looked up into Caleb's teary eyes.

Rising to his feet, he nodded and patted Caleb on the shoulder. Approaching Alannah, the tears in her eyes broke his heart. Kneeling beside her, he put his arm across her shoulders. 'Hey, let's get out of here. I don't know about you, but this place gives me the creeps.'

She looked at him and nodded. With Brendan's assistance, she rose to her feet and let him lead her to the car.

When he reached Nick's station wagon, one glimpse of Bailey's unconscious body on the back seat had his heart rate galloping and his palms perspiring.

Holding their friend in his lap, Connor looked at Brendan with an ashen face. 'I'm trying everything I can, but he needs your dad ASAP.'

'What happened to him?' Brendan asked.

'Ghoul bite.' Connor shifted slightly to show him the large chunk of flesh missing from Bailey's side. It was deep enough to see the muscle tissue.

'*Fuck!*' It was depressing how few of them were returning unscathed. Images of Locky's dead body flashed in his mind and clawed at his heart. Losing Blake was a huge blow too. He may have been Liam's best mate, but their older cousin was still a decent bloke.

The sight must have been too much for Alannah because she buried her face against Brendan's chest.

'You guys can ride up front,' Nick called from the driver's seat.

He let Alannah climb in first, pulling her onto his lap to make room for Monique.

When they got home, Nick and Connor carried Bailey inside, where Dad was waiting for them. They placed him on the bed Bailey had been using so Dad could begin his work.

Liam and most of his friends had retired for the night, but Brendan and his mates gathered in the living room and waited anxiously for news on Bailey's condition. Alannah clung to Brendan the whole time.

While the guys were debriefing on the fight, Brendan pressed his mouth to Alannah's ear. 'Hey, Liam still loves you. That's why he did it.'

'He has a funny way of showing it. Was it out of jealousy because he saw Austin as a threat again? Does that mean you're his next target?' Her tone was intensely bitter.

Brendan sighed. 'No, Lana. He did it to protect you. If I were in his shoes, I would have killed Austin too, although I wouldn't have done it in front of you. The guy was a scumbag and the Council had already sentenced him to death.'

She flashed him a glare. 'Do you know what he said to me before I killed Tara?'

Brendan shook his head.

'He told me he was sorry, and that he would always love me. He was the one who enabled me to take Tara down.'

'Christ! You sound like a domestic abuse victim, Lana. That jerk date raped you and almost turned you into a vampire. If I hadn't pulled you out of there, you'd have much sharper teeth by now.'

'I know. You're right. Still, I can't help but wonder if he did all that to win Tara's trust and give me that opportunity.' She had an interesting point.

'I guess we'll never know.' He wondered about that mind shield of his. 'So… you did an amazing job out there tonight. How did it feel to kick arse like that?'

She grinned. 'Yeah, it felt exhilarating.'

It was so good to see her smile in the face of everything. 'You know I got a major hard-on when I saw you go all badass.'

She snorted. 'Trust you to have sex on the brain in the middle of a serious skirmish.'

He gave her his biggest smoulder. 'You ought to know sex is *always* on my mind.'

'No doubt,' she sighed. 'I know we did well to defeat Tara and most of her army, but I can't fight this nagging feeling in my chest that something's wrong.'

'We did lose a couple of friends tonight, and we still don't know if Bailey will survive.'

'True. I guess that must be why.'

As if on cue, Dad entered the room, and everyone stopped talking. 'Bailey is in a stable condition. He will recover well after some rest.' They all let out a chorus of relieved breaths. 'What you did last night was reckless and stupid. All of you could have been maimed or killed. You should have let the Council handle Alannah's rescue.'

The other guys lowered their heads submissively, but Brendan glared defiantly at his father.

'That said, I want to thank you all for saving my niece.'

Their heads rose.

'What you kids did took strength and courage. It proves your loyalty to this family. Which is why you are always welcome in my house from this day forth.' There were a few murmurs in the group. He smiled. 'Yes, even those of you who are not mages. But only you lot. I don't want...'

The din of chatter in the group made it impossible to hear him continue. Brendan rose and clapped his dad on the shoulder. 'I hope you realise you essentially declared this house party central. You should probably stock up on ingredients for that hangover cure.'

Dad shook his head walking away mumbling something about being a masochist.

Alannah felt exhausted, so she turned in despite her friends protests and Locky's vigil. She was making her way to the stairs when Monique stopped her in the kitchen.

'You got a minute?'

'I guess. What's up?'

Monique fidgeted uncomfortably with her head lowered. 'I uh… I wanted to apologise for the trouble I've caused you.'

Alannah's eyes widened. Even after their bonding session in Tara's cellar, she found it hard to fathom such remorse from Monique. 'Um, thanks.'

Raising her head, Monique focused on Alannah with serious, unblinking eyes. 'I promise I won't try anything more with Liam. I know things are well and truly over for us, and I respect that the two of you are in love with each other.'

'I appreciate that. Thank you.'

Monique walked across the room. Pausing at the door, she turned back and grinned. 'It was Brendan, by the way.'

Alannah squinted. 'What was Brendan?'

'Remember that question you asked me in the cellar?'

Casting her mind back, Alannah recalled their discussion and snorted. 'Figures.'

'I don't know if that knowledge will influence your decision concerning which brother you want to be with, but in either case, I'm still done with Liam. I can't promise to stay away from Brendan though.' She winked and left the room.

Alannah sighed and headed upstairs. As she passed Brendan's room, she noticed his light illuminating the gap beneath the door. Pressing her forehead to the wood panelling, she took a few deep breaths before knocking.

'Come in, Lana.'

After closing the door behind her, she took in the sight of Brendan, who sat above the covers of his bed. He wore a pair of grey trackpants, but no shirt. *It's fortunate he's holding his legs to his chest.* 'How did you know it was me?'

He shrugged without looking at her. 'Call it a hunch.' Lifting a glass Alannah only noticed in that moment, he took a sip of the amber liquid within.

She took a seat beside him and placed a comforting arm around his waist. 'How're you holding up?'

'I've been better.' After grabbing the whiskey bottle beside him, he turned and offered it to her. 'Want some?'

The Jameson's was practically begging for her to drink it, so she took the bottle. 'Thanks. Got a spare glass?'

'No, sorry. If it makes you feel better, I'll stop using mine and we can both slum it.' He downed the rest of his glass and threw the empty vessel aside, where it landed on a pile of dirty laundry.

Alannah took a few swigs from the bottle before returning it to Brendan. 'Wanna talk about it?'

He looked into her eyes for a moment. 'I'm a huge fucking mess of emotions right now. I'd like to focus on my grief for Locky, along with the other guys downstairs; but I'm also conflicted over Austin.' He sighed. 'That dude was my best mate for nine years. How do you turn your back on all those years of friendship? He hurt me, Lana. And I'm not only talking about the cuts he inflicted tonight.' He pointed to the fading scar on his cheek where the five-centimetre gash had almost vanished thanks to Connor's handiwork.

'I get that, Brendan. I really do. He hurt me too. Don't forget I was in love with the guy not so long ago.'

A sardonic laugh slipped from Brendan's lips. 'Trust me, I'll never forget what he did to you. That pain he caused you is what hurts me the most.' He chugged on the whiskey for a bit, piercing her eyes with an intense focus as he handed it to her. 'But it's not as simple as feeling hurt and betrayed, either. Something Austin said got me thinking that if I were in his shoes, I'd likely succumb to temptation too. I'm not angelic like Liam. I am full of darkness, Lana.'

'We all have darkness inside, even Liam. It's what we do to keep it in check that matters.'

'Trust me, gorgeous, my inner demons are much bigger than Liam's.'

Her chest tightened to see him like this. She wished she could reach into him and mend the damage. But she needed to know where she stood first. After drawing on some liquid courage, she gave him the bottle and took a deep breath. 'Brendan?' She gazed directly at him.

'Yessm?'

'About what happened in the hallway earlier…'

His breath hitched. 'I guess I took our game a little far. I'm sorry, Lana. I didn't mean to cause any trouble between you and Liam.'

Alannah's level of disappointment surprised her, but she buried her feelings. 'Apology accepted. It might pay to ease up on the game for a while, especially when Liam's around.'

'Of course.' His face betrayed a hint of a scowl before he gave her an impish grin. 'But not for too long.'

Laughing, she fell back into the bed. 'That's like no time.'

'I told you I'm wicked.' His eyes scanned her body. 'Christ, I need to get laid. Unless you want to do the honours, Lana, I suggest you remove your sexy arse from my bed right now.'

She folded her arms behind her head. 'Is that your way of propositioning me?'

He swiftly moved to straddle her, his face mere inches from her own. 'Is this your way of consenting to my proposition?' The heat between them was sweltering. Brendan did not usually press the weight of his body into her when they played this game, but he was not holding back this time. Alannah could even feel the growing bulge in his pants.

Is he really playing, or is this for real? The raging fire in her core tugged at her resolve. *I'm done fighting this. If he does want me, he can fucking have me.*

Their eyes remained locked in a contest of wills for several long minutes.

Brendan leaped from the bed, grabbed a box of condoms from his drawers and headed for the door.

The moment Alannah realised he was not sticking around, the disappointment returned tenfold. 'Chicken,' she goaded him, trying to mask the anguish in her tone.

Stopping at the door, he refused to face her as he replied, 'I'll give you this round.'

When he walked out of the room, Alannah decided she would never allow herself to entertain sexual thoughts or feelings for Brendan ever again. *He does not want me, so garnering any hope will only frustrate me. If he only wants to play games, that is exactly what I'll do.*

There must be some truth to the adage 'time heals all wounds,' Alannah thought, because after two weeks she felt she had mourned Austin enough and was ready to forgive Liam. The two of them had been avoiding each other since the night at Tara's hideout and, on those occasions where they needed to be in the same room, the tension between them was palpable.

When he returned home from his morning surf, Alannah ambushed Liam on the back porch. 'We should talk.'

Liam jumped, spinning around to face her. '*Christ, Lana!* You scared the shit outta me.' He still wore his wetsuit through which Alannah could see every ridge and valley of his delicious eight-pack.

She tried to remind herself they still had unresolved issues to discuss. But when he ran a hand through his wet hair to pull the longer strands out of his eyes, she practically melted in a puddle of her own juices.

He hung up his surfboard, slumped into one of the patio chairs and sighed. 'So, talk.'

'Why did you kill Austin only minutes after he helped me defeat Tara?'

'Why did you want my brother to kiss you only minutes after we were about to make love?'

She stared at him intently. 'Answer my question first.'

'He hurt you, Lana. There was no excusing what he did. I could not risk him doing anything to you again. I'm not sorry for what I did, but I am sorry you had to see it.'

'Did you worry I still harboured feelings for him? Did you act out of jealousy at all?'

He frowned. 'No. Should I have worried? You took his death harder than I expected.'

'I was sad because I lost an ally and friend, but I wasn't in love with him anymore.'

Liam shook his head, spraying water about and sending a few drops in her direction. 'I don't understand how you could call that man a friend after what he did to you.'

'I don't expect you to understand. But thank you for your apology.' She breathed deeply. 'As for what happened with Brendan—' Liam stiffened and narrowed his eyes. 'Our encounter left me aroused and frustrated after Monique's interruption. When he instigated a round of our little game… things got carried away.'

'Game? What game?'

'We call it Sleazy Chicken. It's something we've been playing since we were six. We flirt and do sleazy shit. The first one of us to blush or chicken out loses the round. It was usually harmless fun.'

'Usually. Except when you almost kissed?'

She bit her bottom lip as she nodded.

He sat back and crossed his arms. 'Are you in love with Brendan?'

'No.' She did not hesitate. After two weeks of shutting those feelings away, she had almost convinced herself.

'You should be careful playing that game with him. I doubt his intentions are as innocent as yours.'

'We have spoken at length about our feelings and intentions since that night, and I can assure you there is nothing to worry about.'

He eyed her sceptically. 'You should still be careful. Despite what Brendan says, he is a hot-blooded guy, and I wouldn't put it past him to take things too far again. I don't want to see you get hurt.'

'I promise to be more careful.'

'Good. I'm glad that's settled.' He rose from his seat and headed for the door.

Alannah stood quickly. She wasn't finished with him. 'Liam, are you still in love with me?'

Turning back to face her, his expression softened. 'Always. And you?'

'Yes.'

He moved swiftly, pulling her into his arms and pressing his lips to hers. Gods, how she had missed his kisses. His mouth tasted extra tangy as their tongues found each other. Sweet and salty: such an addictive combination. When they finally came up for air, they were both panting.

'We should probably try to take things slow, though. After everything that's happened,' Alannah suggested.

She caught a flicker of disappointment in his eyes, but he smiled. 'Yeah, we should.'

'Why don't you go shower and change, then meet me in the living room and we can hang out.'

'I'd love to, but I've got a biology exam tomorrow, plus two other exams this week. I need to study.'

'Oh right. Sorry.' This time Alannah tried to hide her own disappointment. She had forgotten Year Twelve exams were much earlier than her own.

'But I'm sure I'll need a break tonight. Let's watch a movie after dinner.'

Alannah beamed. 'It's a date.'

Chapter Twenty-Three

Nine Months Later

The sound of the front-door closing had Alannah jumping to her feet and racing through the kitchen, to accost her boyfriend. Anticipation for the night ahead fuelled her, but glimpsing Liam in his work gear sent tingles coursing through her bloodstream. She had never figured herself the type to go weak at the knees for the boys in blue, but Liam in a police cadet uniform definitely did things for her. 'How are you? How was your day?'

Liam laughed as she jumped into his arms and swung her legs around his waist. 'I'm great and I could get used to greetings like this.' His mouth clamped down onto hers, kissing her deeply.

They had been going steady for nine months and Alannah doubted she would ever tire of Liam's strong, passionate kisses, or the feel of his rock-hard body pressing against her.

'Unless you're gonna invite me to join you, would you guys get a room?' Brendan called out as his footfalls approached from the hallway.

Snorting as she lowered herself to the ground, Alannah swung around to look at him. She kept her arm around Liam's waist as she gave Brendan her best attempt at bedroom eyes. 'Well come on.' Liam's body tensed, even though she had told him countless times the flirting was meaningless fun.

Brendan laughed as he drew closer to her. 'You know I would in a heartbeat, Lana, but I'd like to live long enough to see you graduate and Liam's eyes alone are killing me.' He slapped Liam on the shoulder and walked into the kitchen.

Alannah followed him with Liam close behind her. 'So how was school?'

Brendan had plans to finish high school so he could study a bachelor's degree and become a youth counsellor. It was a job he was going to be amazing at, and not only because of his powers as an enchanter. 'Good. How was TAFE?'

'So far so good. I'm especially loving pattern drafting and design work.' After discovering Nora's sewing machine eight months ago, Alannah had fallen in love with sewing and dressmaking. It was her ambition to run her own business as a designer and dressmaker of alternative fashions. She figured it would tie in well for her conjuring work, because she would be able to make robes and battle gear imbued with magic upon request. And her vision had driven her to explore the vocational education system in her senior year of high school.

'Sweet,' Brendan replied. 'Well, I'm gonna get ready for tonight.'

As soon as they had the room to themselves, Liam pulled her back into his arms and pressed his face into her neck. 'Gods, you smell so good. I should go shower. I probably stink after the physical training we had today.'

She inhaled his manly scent mingled with ocean fresh cologne. 'You smell pretty damn hot to me, but I might be biased.'

Liam smiled and shook his head. 'It still amazes me how you could get so turned on by my sweat.' He pressed a kiss to her forehead. 'I'll see you in a few minutes.'

Alannah had spent the last two hours getting ready for her big night, so she returned to the living room and picked up the fashion magazine she had been reading. Life had been relatively peaceful since the showdown with Tara. While there had been the odd run in with the town's ogres and other undesirables, most of the surviving vampires in the state kept to themselves and magic crime was at an all-time low. That was not to say Liam was in for an easy ride with his future career. Mundane crime kept the local police busy, but it was nothing they could not handle.

Even so, Alannah was still unable to shake the doubts that had lodged themselves in her subconscious after the night she had killed Tara Winters. The fact that the Council had been unable to locate the Queen's body during their clean-up operation, did not help to ease her mind either.

But this night was not a time to worry. When she looked up from her magazine at the two handsome men who stood before her, both dressed in tailored suits, she beamed with joy. Having the love and support of them both made her feel like the luckiest woman alive. The brothers stepped forward and linked arms with her as they escorted her from the house, down the garden path, towards the ceremonial grounds in her Uncle's backyard.

It was time to celebrate her eighteenth birthday by becoming a full magus and registered conjurer. The ceremony marked an important milestone on her magic path, possibly more important than her initiation. This ritual was not a secret, unsanctioned event: Alannah was done hiding. This was the night she stepped into the public eye and joined the wider mage community—one weighed down by archaic laws. But if she got her way, that was all about to change. *The Council of Mages will not know what hit them.*

To be continued…

What's Next?

Thank you for reading *Winter's Maiden 1* Reviews are the lifeblood of authors, and they make a huge difference to the success of a book. Could you please post a review to one or more of the following sites?

Goodreads
BookBub
Amazon
Other Bookstores

Keep reading because Alannah's story will continue in *Part 2: Winter's Maiden 2.*

Bonus Content

What happens when Liam and Alannah take a second chance at love? This bonus chapter will fill in some gaps with all the juicy details of their first official date:

Winter's Maiden 1: Second Chances

You can find this and more exclusive content on the FREEBIES page of my website: www.starlaarts.com.

Winter's Maiden 2

Winter's Magic Part 2

L. STARLA

Dedication

— In loving memory of Joan Elizabeth. Your legacy is the love you inspired in the lives you touched.

Epigraph

"Equality is not a concept. It's not something we should be striving for. It's a necessity. Equality is like gravity. We need it to stand on this earth as men and women, and the misogyny that is in every culture is not a true part of the human condition. It is life out of balance, and that imbalance is sucking something out of the soul of every man and woman who's confronted with it. We need equality. Kinda now."
— Joss Whedon

Book 2 Playlist

"Stronger" by The Score
"Rush" by The Score
"The Dark Side" by Muse
"Mischief Maker" by All Systems Know
"Now or Never" by Metric
"Danger to Myself" by The Unlikely Candidates
"Pure Morning" by Placebo
"Play with Fire" by Sam Tinnesz & Yacht Money
"I'm So Sorry" by Imagine Dragons
"Oh My Dear Lord" by The Unlikely Candidates
"Hellfire" by Barns Courtney
"Evil Night Together" by Jill Tracey
"No Harm" by Editors
"Stay Around" by American Authors
"Mad About You" by Hooverphonic
"Bloodsport" by Sneaker Pimps
"Legendary" by Welshy Arms
"Yellow Sea" by Landroid
"Touched" by Vast

Playlist available on Spotify.

The Cast of Characters

<u>**The Council of Mages, Fleurieu District**</u>
High Magus: Kieran Lane, Monique's father (Mayor)
Seat of Aether Mana: Alannah Winters (Conjurer, Dress Maker)
Seat of Elemental Mana: Liam Winters (Warlock, Police Officer)
Seat of Organic Mana: Ross Winters (Abjurer, Doctor), Liam & Brendan's father
Seat of Emotional Mana: Nora Winters, née Maher (Shaman, Vet), Liam & Brendan's mother
Seat of Energy Mana: Steve Maher (Alchemist, Pharmacist), Liam's cousin & best mate
Seat of Names Mana: Monique Lane (Alchemist, Council's Secretary), Liam's ex-girlfriend
Seat of Cosmic Mana: Lucas Ó Máille (Clairvoyant, Lawyer), Liam's friend
Seat of Physical Forces Mana: Clayton Rowan (Warlock, Police Officer)
Seat of Matter Mana: Mr. Duncan Sheridan (Alchemist, Pharmacist)
Seat of Senses Mana: Mr. James Maher (Illusionist), Steve's Father & Nora's brother

Pure Blood Mages

Brendan Winters, (Pure-mage Enchanter, School Counsellor), Liam's brother

Jessica Ó Máille (Clairvoyant), Lucas' younger sister & Monique's friend

Claudia Rowan (Shaman, Dancer), Clayton's twin sister

Chester Rowan (Conjurer), Clayton's younger brother

Danielle Sheridan (Abjurer), Monique's friend

Reginald (Abjurer), Eyre Peninsula district

Wendy (Shaman), Eyre Peninsula district

Richard Lane (The Inquisitor), Kieran's brother

Other Magicals

Cara Hughes (Half-mage Shaman, Conservationist), Alannah's best friend

Jacob Bennett (Boggart, Gangster), Brendan's best mate

Nick Patterson (Orc, Orchardist)

Ben Sanders (Weredingo, Vet Assistant)

Caleb Hawthorn (Fae- Endarkened, Unemployed)

Bridey Hawthorn (Fae- Endarkened), Caleb's older sister

Connor Foley (Half-mage Abjurer, Marine Biologist)

Bailey Dougherty (Half-mage Warlock, Bartender)

Bianca Oakley (Fae- Wood Nymph, Cabaret Singer)

Amy Smith (Dwarf, Metallurgist & Council Blacksmith)

Prologue

Three Years and One Month Since Alannah's Eighteenth Birthday

Returning to her office, the woman settled in behind the solid oak desk and turned on the Waterford crystal lamp. She withdrew a pad and fountain pen from the drawer to her right and commenced:

> *Alannah,*
>
> *While I understand it is not customary for a mage conceived at Beltane to concern themselves with the identity of their biological father, it has come to my attention you are pursuing such knowledge. If this is indeed the case, I have some insights of great value to offer.*

Rising from her desk, she deliberated over the wording of her next paragraph while peering out through the tempered glass of her window. The street below buzzed with the city nightlife one would expect from Sydney on a Saturday night. She looked forward to joining them, but she needed to finish the letter. *Time to stop procrastinating.* Returning to her seat, she resumed writing:

> *Sharing this information puts me at risk, so it will not come free. If you are willing to meet at a secure location, I am sure we can strike a suitable deal. Rest assured I mean*

you no harm and I guarantee a safe rendezvous. It is of no consequence to me should you choose to disregard this letter and decline my offer. However, accepting my invitation would be of much benefit to you.

If you decide to seek me out, please contact Patrick, my agent, to arrange a time and place. I have enclosed his business card.

Regards,

Scarlett.

She allowed the ink to dry, detached the top sheet from the pad and neatly folded the page. Her deft hands slipped it into the envelope addressed to Alannah Winters of Gaeilge Shores, South Australia. She tucked the letter into her handbag and grabbed her coat. After riding the elevator down ten floors, she left the office building and stepped out into the cool, early September air. She stopped at the red post box a few metres down the street and dropped the letter inside before ducking into her favourite cocktail bar.

Chapter One

Five Days later

High Magus Kieran was the epitome of pompous ass. 'Thank you, Councillor Rowan. Councillor Alannah Winters, do you have anything to report?' He stared at her with a stern eye. Her appointment to the Fleurieu District Council of Mages still displeased him, and it continued to show in his open hostility at every meeting.

'There has not been much activity involving the use of Aether, Your Honour, and none of it has caused any negative energy.' As the representative for all mages attuned to Aether in her district, one of Alannah's responsibilities was to remain open to this mana source to detect any misuse and investigate the issue. Given how few mages were even capable of channelling the divine element, she had an easy time of it.

Being one of a handful of mages in the state with this attunement had its benefits. There was no competition when she applied to fill the seat vacated by the late Shaun Ó Máille in August of the previous year, a few days after her twentieth birthday. But even with the community endorsements she received following her epic showdown with Tara all those years ago, the High Magus was not happy about having a Winters woman on the Council.

'Are you certain of this?' Kieran did not second guess the other Council members.

He is such a chauvinistic bastard. Clenching her fists in her lap beneath the table, she bit back the sarcastic retort on the tip of her tongue. 'Yes, Your Honour.'

'Very well. On to our next matter of business…'

Most mages regarded the seat of Aether with reverence because the mage in that role has a direct link to the Gods. Alannah recently learned the High Magus treated her predecessor with far more respect. Kieran had always insisted Shaun Ó Máille present his report first rather than last. Still seething, she tuned out while Kieran harped on about some bureaucratic nonsense, catching the odd buzzword here and there like commendation, sanctioning, and authority. Using mindfulness meditation, she calmed herself.

This is so damn boring. Alannah had expected more focus on hunting magic criminals when she signed up for the Mages Council. It made her mourn the days of fighting her grandmother's threats. Gaeilge Shores may have been a dangerous place with Tara Winters around, but it was a hell of a lot more exciting.

A sudden nudge in her side brought Alannah's attention back to the room. She looked at Liam, the owner of the offending elbow, and met his frown as he gestured in Kieran's direction.

'Huh?'

The High Magus gave her a death glare. 'I asked, if you had an opinion on the matter, Councillor.'

'Oh. Sorry Your Honour. No, I have nothing to add.'

'I look forward to the day when you have anything at all to contribute to these meetings, Miss *Winters*.' His cronies sniggered.

Aunt Nora, representative for emotions, smiled at her with pursed lips. As one of three women on the Council, along with Monique Lane, she understood the difficulties Alannah faced in such a patriarchal system.

Kieran glanced at his watch, and turned to face his daughter, Monique, who took the minutes. 'I would like to call the meeting closed at seven fifty.' He stood up and the room filled with the sound of chairs scraping against wooden floorboards as everyone else rose. Standing whenever the High Magus was on his feet in the Council Chambers was important etiquette.

They all waited for him to exit the room before collecting their belongings and leaving.

After saying goodbye to Ross and Nora, Liam spoke in a hushed tone as he followed Alannah outside. 'You shouldn't take your place for granted Lana. Kieran could easily step down into your seat if you keep pissing him off.'

She huffed. 'I doubt he'd be willing to give up his position of power. That said, it's not like I'm actively trying for top spot on his shit list. He's never liked me and my being on the Council is enough to make him hate me. Besides, it's not my fault bugger-all mages practice necromancy in this area.'

Pausing when they reached the car, Liam sighed. 'I know. But you could at least try to pay attention to the rest of the business.' He unlocked the car but waited for her.

'Why? It's pointless paper pushing. Where's the real action?' She slumped into the passenger seat.

He dropped into the driver's side and shook his head. 'I warned you it wouldn't be all fun and games. I get as much admin work as a police officer, if not more sometimes.'

'The whole bloody system needs reforming. When I become High Magus, my first order of business will be to liven up those damn meetings.'

'I hate to burst your bubble, yet again, but you know that'll never happen. They would never allow a woman to head up the Council.'

'Never say never, sweetheart. I will get there or die trying. Once I get my fourth and fifth attunements, it's game on.'

They rode the remaining two blocks from the Town Hall to their seaside terrace house in silence. Council meetings were long and draining, and neither of them felt up to walking on such nights. Getting home to eat and sleep was the priority.

Shortly after earning his badge on the force, Liam had asked Alannah if she wanted to buy a house in town with him. They had been in a solid relationship for years by that point, so it made sense and she had been keen to move into her own place. While Alannah had drawn up an extensive list of requirements, Liam only voiced two criteria: a place in town close to work and easy access to the ocean. Even with all his responsibilities to the Council and the police force, her boyfriend lived and breathed the surf. It took them a while to find somewhere suitable, so it was like a dream come true when this place became available almost a year ago.

Liam groaned at the sight of his brother's Jag as they pulled into the driveway. She could not blame him. Alannah understood Liam's moods and anyone's company, other than her own, was the last thing he wanted to deal with when exhausted. But she did not mind. Spending time with her best friend and cousin, Brendan, was exactly what she needed to lift her spirits.

'Dagnammit!' Brendan jumped at the sound of the front door slamming, cursing as he dropped a serving spoon on his foot. He had almost finished laying everything out on the dining table for dinner. *At least I wasn't holding a plate!*

Liam stormed into the open-plan living area and threw his keys at the kitchen bench. 'Don't you have a home of your own?'

'Well hello to you too, bro.' Brendan still lived with his parents on their country estate, and while the privacy of the guest house was great for taking chicks home, on school nights he much preferred the convenience of a place to crash in town, especially one Alannah lived in. Pushing past the grumpy sack, he placed the rogue piece of cutlery in the dishwasher and grabbed a replacement from the drawer. 'And is that any way to talk to your chef?'

After casting a cursory glance at the plastic containers on the table, Liam turned his scowling face back to Brendan. 'Unless you're now moonlighting as a Chinese chef at the local take-away, I doubt you can claim any credit.'

He smacked Liam hard on the shoulder blade. 'Well, you're welcome.' Turning aside from his ungrateful brother, he grinned at Alannah and drew her into a hug. 'Hey, gorgeous, how's life?'

When they stepped out of the embrace, she gave him one of her award-winning smiles. 'Mostly good. Although I came close to dying of boredom and frustration in that meeting. I need a drink. You guys want one?' She approached the bar fridge.

'I can't. I have an early start tomorrow,' Liam complained.

Brendan returned to the table and took a seat. 'I'll have a pale ale, thanks, Lana.' He also had work the next day, but a couple of beers wouldn't be a problem for his job as school counsellor.

Alannah handed Brendan the drink in a stubby holder and sat across from him. Reaching forward, she clinked the tip of her own bottle with his. 'Cheers.' Tilting her chin and lifting her gaze skyward, she took a huge swig of her drink.

Damn, that woman makes drinking beer look sexy.

Returning her attention to him, she smiled again. 'So, how's work and stuff treating you?'

'Same old, same old. Work's not bad, but the ol' social life could use some more excitement.' He took the opportunity to check her out while she filled her plate. He liked Alannah's new habit of wearing her long black hair in a half ponytail. It reminded him of Katie McGrath as Morgana.

Sitting back, she gave him an impish grin. 'Social life, or sex life?'

'Both, but you're right, I do need to get laid soon. How's tomorrow night looking for you?'

She snorted before turning on the smoulder. 'I'll check my calendar.'

Liam growled as he pointed his chopsticks at Brendan. 'I know the flirting is part of your stupid game, but please spare me. I'm not in the mood to put up with your bullshit.'

Brendan had gone to serious lengths to assure his brother there was nothing going on with him and Alannah, after messing up and almost kissing her four years ago. He even managed to convince Alannah he was not interested in a relationship with her. As much as it pained him, especially when Alannah first expressed interest, it was for the best. He reasoned he would end up hurting her. Not to mention getting a major arse whooping from Liam—almost one-hundred kilos of pure muscle with perfect aim when rapid firing lightning bolts—not someone whose bad books you wanted to be in.

He narrowed his eyes at Liam. 'Right, 'cause your mood is the only one that matters. I was trying to cheer up Lana.' As an enchanter attuned to emotions, Brendan could tell Alannah felt miserable. He could sense it through his empathic link.

Rising from his chair, Liam pressed a kiss to the crown of Alannah's head before grabbing his plate. 'I'm sorry, gorgeous, but I'm exhausted. I'll take this to bed and see you there later.'

'Okay, night.' She stood to peck him on the lips, and he deepened the kiss in a possessive display obviously intended for Brendan's benefit.

The tension in the room lifted and Alannah heaved a huge sigh as though breathing freely for the first time in hours.

'What got up his arse and died?' Brendan asked.

'Well aside from his mundane work being relentless, High Magus Kieran got snarky with me tonight. I know these things get to him. And I didn't help matters when I zoned out again.'

He laughed. 'I don't envy you, Lana. Those meetings sound like a big waste of time.'

She went quiet for a few minutes and toyed with her food. Biting her lip, she gazed up at him. 'Maybe you should look at renting a place in town. As much as I love having you here, the frequency of your visits is wearing at Liam's patience. He can't relax when you're here this often.'

'That man can't relax properly full stop.' He sucked a noodle into his mouth and sighed. 'But you're right. I'll start searching this weekend.'

Stretching her arm across the table, she placed a hand over his. The warmth of her touch sent a jolt of pleasure through his nerves. 'Hey, you are still welcome here and I'll drop in to see you. If you have your own place, we could both escape Liam's moods.'

'I know. I guess it's time I grew up and cut the apron strings.'

Humour returned to Alannah's visage. 'Just don't grow up too much. I love your carefree attitude.'

A hearty laugh escaped his throat. 'Trust me, that'll never happen. I'm a playboy for life, remember?'

'Right.' Her fingers were still resting on the back of his hand, and he perceived their rough pads brushing against his skin. Hours of sewing every week for years had produced callouses on the tips of her otherwise soft hands. The sensation was strangely erotic.

Flipping his wrist, he grabbed her hand as he stared into her eyes and probed her mind. Brendan knew he should not invade her private thoughts, not only for the immorality of it, but because knowing the truth would be futile either way. But he could not help himself.

She grinned, but there were no thoughts suggesting she wanted him. Only the usual *'I'm not gonna let him win.'* Over the past few years Alannah had become a lot better at Sleazy Chicken, a flirtatious game they started playing at the age of six, although he still won most times.

Rising to his feet, Brendan pulled her up against his chest and planted soft kisses along her arm, running from her hand towards her neck. He watched her face for signs of blushing. There was no hint of colour in her cheeks as she gave him bedroom eyes that made his blood rush. It was just as well he was able to magically control his erections; else he might give away his true feelings.

Closing in on her shoulder, he could no longer see her face when she drew an audible breath. 'Stop. You win.'

A wicked grin formed on his face when he stepped back to look at her. 'The reigning champion keeps his crown.'

'You will have to give it up to me one day.'

'Oh, I promise I'll give it to you one day, Lana. I'll give it to you real hard.' He winked at her, seized his beer, and chugged down the rest of the bottle.

After tiptoeing across the bedroom floor, avoiding the squeaky floorboards, Alannah slipped into bed alongside Liam's sleeping form. He looked handsome beyond compare when asleep, the stress and fatigue gone from around his eyes.

Liam must have sensed her presence, despite her best efforts to avoid disturbing his sleep, because he snuggled in closer to her. He groaned the moment their bodies connected, and his eyes flittered open. The bright moon peeking through a slit in the curtains was the only light illuminating the room, but it was enough to reveal the features of his face. He smiled. 'Hey gorgeous.'

'Sorry for waking you.' Although Alannah was secretly glad she had, still feeling horny after the game of Sleazy Chicken.

'You're the one person who doesn't ever need to apologise for that.' His deep voice was raspy from sleep, and it heightened her arousal. 'I love you, Lana. You are the most incredible woman to walk this earth and I feel blessed to call you mine.'

Her heart melted at his words. Rendered speechless, she inhaled sharply and claimed his mouth with a heated kiss. Before long she straddled Liam's naked body, grinding against his pelvis. Her hands skated along his muscular arms as she immersed herself in the addictive sweet and salty taste of his mouth.

After making out for ten minutes, Liam rolled them sideways and fell back asleep. Alannah sighed - another typical weeknight, with Liam exhausted after work and mage commitments. She would be calling on her rabbit again soon.

Brendan beelined through the front bar of Doyle Dougherty's, the only pub in Gaeilge Shores, and found his mates in a booth. It was Friday, the night following his dinner at Alannah's. Ben and Nick were arm wrestling, giving the girls around them a show of bulging tatted muscles. Connor had an arm wrapped around Amy, whispering sweet nothings in her ear. Bailey and Caleb were showing each other memes and sharing metalcore music on their smartphones. And Cara sat in Jacob's lap, sucking his face off. *Yup, business as usual. Except someone was missing.*

Bailey looked up as Brendan approached. 'Hey, Brendo. How ya doin', man?' He extended his hand out for a fist bump.

'Okay, I guess. What's up with you all? And where's Bianca?' He slid down next to Caleb, an endarkened fae and the only member of their group to have more piercings than Brendan. Caleb gave him a silent nod before vaping some sweet-smelling herbal stuff.

Jacob came up for air a moment later, giving Brendan an impish grin. 'Didn't you hear? Bianca has a dark cabaret band now. They're rehearsing tonight.' The red-headed boggart had become his best mate in the years following the death of Lachlan Munroe. The goofy goblin had been Jacob's closest friend at school and losing him in their battle with Tara Winters had been heartbreaking for all his crew. The passing of Austin Pearce, Brendan's previous bestie, also contributed to their growing bond. Although Austin was dead to Brendan when he date-raped Alannah.

'Yeah, they are gearing up for a regular spot at some cabaret lounge in Adelaide,' added Bailey.

'Oh? This is all news to me.' *How am I the last to hear about all this?*

Nick, the punkish orc, tittered. 'I guess you guys are always too busy boning to talk about her side hustle.'

While true to some extent, it was not like they *never* talked. But it had been a few months since he had invited Bianca to his bed. He did not want to give her the wrong impression, even if she was the best lay he could get in town. Commitment was a dirty word to Brendan in most cases. Leaning back into the seat, he sighed. 'I guess I'll have to hook up with a human tonight.' Brendan did not mind human girls, but they did lack the magical talents of a nymph like Bianca.

'Well Chelsea's had her eye on you since you arrived.' Ben directed his head of long, caramel coloured hair towards the table of girls a few metres away. The weredingo's attention shifting to that group of girls did not surprise Brendan. Ben's reputation as a man-whore was almost as notorious as Brendan's.

Brendan shook his head. 'Been there, done that too many times. I need a challenge. I want more excitement in my life.'

'What about her?' Ben's gaze travelled to the door where a stunning woman with long black hair entered. Legs reaching the sky were on display beneath a short black skirt. She completed her outfit with a purple brocade corset and silver necklace. Her curvaceous figure alone took Brendan's breath away. The moment he looked up at her face, he found himself drawn into her eyes. As dark as night and outlined with purple makeup, they scanned the room. Peering through the veil of her glamour, he glimpsed pointy ears lined with silver studs from lobe to tip. *Most likely fae and her dark colouring suggests unseelie.*

'Son of a gun!' Caleb's eyes widened, as though he had seen a ghost.

As if hearing Caleb's muttered curse, the woman turned her attention to their group and grinned, eyes darting to each of them before settling on Caleb. She advanced and Brendan felt Caleb trembling beside him. Reaching the booth, she scrutinised Caleb as she spoke in a deep, rich voice, 'Hello, Brother dearest.'

Chapter Two

'And done.' Having sewn on some black lace as the finishing touch to her latest dress, Alannah sat back to admire her work. *It is damn sexy, if I do say so myself— and I can't wait to wear it out.* Modelling her designs was an important marketing strategy for her business. She cracked her knuckles and stood for a few stretches.

A cursory glance at the old grandfather clock on the wall told her the afternoon was ending. *Liam will get home soon. I ought to think about cooking dinner.* Needing some fresh air first, she strolled out to the letter box to collect the mail.

After sifting through the advertising, which went straight in the recycling bin, and the bills she threw on the buffet in the hall, Alannah found one item of interest: A letter addressed to her in a neat cursive script without any sender details, but the postmark was from Sydney. She walked into the loungeroom to get comfortable and opened it. The business card of a Mr. Patrick Douglas dropped into her lap as she unfolded the letter.

> *Alannah,*
> *While I understand it is not customary for a mage conceived at Beltane to concern themselves with the identity of their biological father, it has come to my attention you are pursuing such knowledge…*

She inhaled deeply and took a moment to process the contents of the letter. *My bio dad?* Alannah's mind buzzed. *Could he be alive?* Her heart thrummed, playing a rhythm of hope on her ribs like a xylophone, but she put a stop to it by calming her breathing. Nothing about Scarlett's words suggested anything of the sort. Only a fool would entertain such fantasies. Yet she could not deny wanting to know who her real father was.

The sound of keys jingling at the front door broke her reverie. Alannah jumped to her feet and tucked the letter and Patrick's card into her handbag. She needed to talk to someone about this letter, but Liam would not understand, so it would have to wait.

Liam met her in the kitchen, where they embraced. He beamed, blue eyes bright and full of life. 'Hi, gorgeous. I hope you haven't started cooking yet. I want to take you out for dinner.'

Alannah's whole face lit up and she kissed his full lips, running her fingers through his mid-length brown hair before replying. 'As it happens, I haven't yet. I'm keen to eat out.' Pausing, she gazed upon him. 'So, what has you in a marvellous mood?'

'It's Friday night and I have a full weekend off work. I want to make the most of my time with you.'

'Gods, I love you. Give me a few minutes to get ready.' She was still wearing her usual work attire: trackpants and an old, tattered t-shirt.

He followed her into the bedroom. 'I want to change too. And I need a shower. Care to join me?'

When she turned to look at him, the unbuttoned shirt displayed his eight-pack. Heat coursed through her blood at the sight. 'How can I refuse an invitation like that?' *There is no urgency to get to dinner. It's not like I'm hungry… for food anyway.*

The strong fragrance of violets assaulted Brendan's nose.

'Bridey? W…what are you doing here?' Caleb frowned at his sister.

So, this is Bridey Hawthorn, Brendan thought. He had never met the girl, but Caleb had told him a lot about her. Like the fact she grew up with their dark mage (read: rogue) father in the city while their elven mother raised Caleb in the country. They originally lived in the Adelaide Hills where their parents' marriage declined when their dad's eye turned from his wife to his teenage daughter. Unfortunately, Bridey had no qualms pandering to daddy's desires. She was every bit as perverted as he was and even put the moves on an unwilling Caleb when he first hit puberty. This was the final straw for their mother, who packed up and fled with Caleb to Gaeilge Shores to hide. It was smart. Few dark mages would chance a run-in with the High Magus and the Council.

No wonder poor Caleb trembled. Brendan placed a supportive hand on the guy's shoulder as he spoke up. 'Well, well, well. The wayward sister returns.' He pierced Bridey with a glare.

Bridey shrugged off Brendan's hostile vibes. 'And you are?'

As he read her aura, he saw curiosity at first. As her gaze intensified, the tell-tale bright red flicker of lust pulsed around her. She licked her lips seductively and his cock instantly hardened. *Gods! Have I met my match? Get a grip, dude.* He took a deep breath and refocussed his mind. 'Brendan Winters. Perhaps you've heard of me?'

A wicked grin lit up her features. 'Oh, indeed. The infamous enchanter of Gaeilge Shores. I didn't realise my brother had such interesting friends. Mother did such a stellar job of hiding him from me.' She looked at Caleb and smiled. 'Relax, darling. I'm not going to hurt you. I'm here on business and I'd like your help connecting with the magic community in town.'

'Just business?' Caleb narrowed his eyes.

'Yes sweetheart, *just* business; unless you want more.' She gave him a lewd grin and he shivered. Bridey's head fell back as she cackled. 'Oh, Caleb, you are precious. And far too much like our sweet Mother. But your friends?' Her eyes travelled around the group before settling on Brendan. 'I think your friends will be a blast. And I'm all for mixing business with pleasure.'

It took all of Brendan's willpower to hold back the groan threatening to escape his lips as his dick stirred. She arched her right brow at him. *Hell! Is she an enchanter too?*

'May I sit?' She directed her question at Brendan.

He shrugged. 'It's a free country.'

There was no room for her on his side of the booth, so she perched herself in Brendan's lap, leaving him to splutter as she ground into his erection.

Caleb stared aghast at their display.

Scowling, Bailey rose. 'I'm getting another round of drinks. Who's in?'

Everyone pushed their glasses forward. Brendan doubted lowering inhibitions around Bridey was wise, but he needed some alcohol to take the edge off.

'I'll have a Purple Haze, thank you darling,' Bridey demanded.

Bailey frowned at her. 'A what?'

'*Pur-ple Haze.* It's a cocktail. Don't tell me this backwater doesn't know about cocktails!'

'Sure, we know about cocktails,' Bailey retorted. 'We're just not pretentious enough to care.'

'Oh dear. I see I'm going to have my work cut out for me with you. What's your name, handsome?'

After a moment of hesitation, he replied. 'Bailey. Bailey Dougherty.'

She gasped with delight. 'As in *the* Doughertys? Owners of this fine establishment?'

'Exactly. So, I suggest you show this *backwater* more respect if you don't want piss in your fancy-schmancy drink.' Bailey turned on his heels and strode off to the bar.

'Wow. What a gem.' Bridey's tone oozed sarcasm. 'So, Caleb, who else do we have here?'

Caleb reluctantly introduced everyone. Ben and Nick were both drooling when Bridey cast her eyes over them. She even distracted Jacob, who was oblivious to the stink eye his girlfriend, Cara, sent Bridey's way.

At least I'm not alone. This woman is trouble with a capital Oh Hell!

Bursting into Brendan's room in the Cailleach Estate guesthouse on a Saturday morning always came with risks, Alannah knew that. But she figured she had seen it all, multiple times in fact. And the girls? She had seen them all too. Most of them had grown accustomed to Alannah, but a few still freaked out or got irritable when she intruded.

Yet nothing could have prepared her for the scene greeting her that morning. They were *still* at it. All four of them. Grunting and groaning filled the room and Alannah wondered if she had accidently stumbled onto the set of a porno film. She had no idea who the fae girl was, but she recognised the inked skin of Ben and Nick.

While Alannah thought three men taking one woman at the same time was outrageous, none of it compared to seeing Brendan in action. The thing she knew he was most reputed for was the one thing she had never see him do. Pressing her back to the wall, she covered the gasp slipping from her mouth. Ben may have been the weredingo and Nick was the orc with staghorns, but Brendan was the one who fucked like an animal: biting, clawing, and slapping as he thrust into the fae chick. *So damn hot!* Brendan's transformation into a ruggedly handsome man only enhanced the hotness factor. His face had filled out more over the years, transforming his gaunt appearance into a strong, well-defined jawline covered in designer stubble. He had also cut his fringe back, so it no longer slipped down over his right eye, but the choppy strands were still long enough to cover most of his forehead.

She should have left, but she could not tear her eyes away. She should have announced her presence, but she could not bring herself to stop them. She wanted to touch herself as she watched them but did not dare. Explaining *that* to Brendan would be difficult. So, instead she stood there, frozen.

Several minutes later, Brendan turned his head and glimpsed her. He did not stop. His full lips curled into a lascivious grin and his green eyes pinned her in place as he continued pounding into the back of the fae chick. *Oh Gods!* She squirmed and felt her cheeks flush but did not break the eye contact.

Alannah had worked hard to shut down any feelings of lust around Brendan in the last four years. She did not want to risk him reading such feelings in her. But in the heat of the moment, she let her guard down and she was so busted. *Right— time to deflect*. She shifted her attention to the other guys, hoping

Brendan would think it was the sight of them turning her on. She even contrived to bite her lip.

Brendan spoke in her mind, *'I guess I should tell Liam to get some tats on his buff bod.'*

There was no need to feign the blushing.

'Don't worry, I won't tell Liam, or these guys. But to save yourself anymore discomfort, I suggest stepping out before they see you. We'll finish soon.'

She took his advice, waiting beyond the door. About ten minutes later, the porno party emerged.

'Oh, hi, Alannah,' Nick greeted her on his way past.

Ben followed with his arm around the fae woman. 'Hey, girl.' He winked at her as he passed.

Catching a proper glimpse of the woman, Alannah startled at her striking looks.

'Who was that?' Alannah heard the woman's deep voice ask as they left the guest house.

The sound of Brendan clearing his throat drew her attention back to his bedroom doorway. He stood there in nothing but a pair of red satin boxers. The scent of sex mingled with his musky cologne—*or is it his natural odour?* 'I had no idea you were into voyeurism, Lana.'

Forcing her eyes to focus on his face, she exhaled sharply. 'Neither did I. First time for everything, right?'

His eyes narrowed on her. 'Right. So, to what do I owe the pleasure? With you, that is. My previous pleasure was obvious enough.'

Alannah snorted. 'Who was that girl anyway? I've never seen her around before.'

'Caleb's sister.'

'Caleb has a sister?'

Brendan frowned. 'Yup. They grew up apart, with separated parents. He doesn't like her much, so please don't tell him about what happened.'

'I guess we both have some new secrets to keep.'

Humour returned to Brendan's visage. 'I still can't believe…'

'Can we drop it, please? I need to talk to you about something.'

'Okay. Give me a sec to clean up.' Brendan moved to the bathroom. When he came back, he joined Alannah on the couch in the living area, smelling cleaner. 'What's up?'

'I received this strange letter yesterday. I want your opinion.' She handed him the offer from Scarlett.

Brendan read in silence, folded the letter and returned it. The right side of his face lifted for a moment. 'Have you shown this to Liam?'

'No, only you. Liam won't understand my need. He's an old-fashioned sort, big on tradition and whatnot.'

He nodded. 'True. How did the letter come to you?'

'Through the post. It came from Sydney, but there was no return address.'

Brendan put his feet up on the coffee table and reclined into the couch. 'I don't like it. The letter reeks of suspicion and evil agendas. It's a pity we aren't friends with a non-Council affiliated clairvoyant.'

'I know, right. I really want this info, but I don't trust this Scarlett. What should I do?'

'I dunno. The letter doesn't stipulate meeting alone, but her agent might insist on it. If you contact him, ask about taking a bodyguard. Don't agree to going alone.'

'Fair point. But who would be a suitable bodyguard? Most warlocks we know are loyal to the Council. Even Bailey.'

'So, don't take a mage. What about Nick?' Brendan winked. She began to object when he stopped her, pressing a finger to her lips. 'Think about it. The guy can kick some serious butt. And he can channel the elements almost as well as a warlock.'

She sighed. 'I suppose.' Alannah considered her options. 'Okay, I'm gonna do this. I'll start by asking Nick, then see what I can arrange with this Patrick dude. Thanks for your help.'

'Anytime, Lana. Just be careful, okay?' Brendan's forehead creased.

'Yeah, of course.'

'Can you keep me updated, too?'

With a plan in place, Alannah smiled. 'Sure thing. Well, we better head into the house. Your mum is cooking brunch and Liam will come drag our arses out there soon.'

Brendan collapsed into one of the hammocks on the front porch and sighed as he watched Liam's SUV carry Alannah away.

'Quite the minx, isn't she? If I didn't know better, I'd think she was a succubus.'

Startled by the unfamiliar man's voice appearing out of nowhere, Brendan jumped to his feet. When his eyes fell upon the red glowing eyes of a demon, his skin prickled. Noticing the blue courier uniform, he exhaled. Demons copped a bad rap thanks to humans and mages alike. While the Gods did curse the evil doers and banish them to the Underworld, most of these poor souls inherited their fate. When summoners beckoned them to the mortal plane, they entered a pact requiring full obedience. Their bosses were the ones to worry about.

'Lovely day, isn't it?' The demon courier smiled, withdrawing some paperwork from his satchel. 'One package for a Brendan Winters of Cailleach Estate, Gaeilge Shores. Are you the Brendan in question?'

'Yup, that's me.'

'I'm so glad. Now you need to sign for it. In blood, please.' The courier's skeletal hand extended, offering him a clipboard.

Brendan took it and inspected the delivery documents. *No mention of the sender's name. Makes sense, given the use of forbidden blood magic.* He pricked his finger using the quill pen tied to the binder and signed the parchment. As soon as he returned the clipboard, a large book-shaped parcel wrapped in brown paper materialised in his hands.

'Right then. Have a great day.' The demon vanished.

No way I'm showing my parents an item delivered by a demon courier using blood magic. He walked around the side and headed into the guesthouse.

Sitting on the couch, he tore away the brown paper to reveal a black leather-bound book. The cover was blank, devoid of any symbols suggesting the content. Not sensing any nefarious magic at work, he opened the tome.

'Ho-ly shit!' He drew a deep breath before flicking through the rest of it. After scanning the bulk of the pages, he leaned back to process the significance of what he was holding. The more he thought about it, the more he realised he possessed the proverbial goldmine of potion craft: the most extensive collection of magic tinctures, elixirs, tonics, and poisons known to the magic world. There were potions for every attunement, with multiple recipes for every spell effect. The best part? It was all in English, so he would not need to spend time translating anything. This volume would even put the recipe section of Alannah's Book of Shadows to shame.

Who sent this book and why? What do they expect me to do with it?

A tapping noise on the guesthouse door broke his train of thought, so he shoved the compendium inside the ottoman.

His best mate, Jacob, waited at the door, a wide grin revealing his sharp boggart teeth. They fist bumped as Brendan let him in. 'Hey, man.'

'Hey. You wanna drink?' Brendan made his way to the bar.

'I'll have a coldie. Thanks.' Jacob took a seat on the couch.

Once they were both settled with their beers, Brendan withdrew the leather volume from its hiding spot. 'Check this out. A demon courier dropped it off.'

Taking the large book, Jacob's brows drew together. He whistled through his chompers as he perused the content. 'Who was your benefactor?'

'No idea.'

Jacob read out some of the potion titles in the Emotions section. 'Love potions, narcotics, and stimulants. Curious. There's a recipe for a tincture that's pretty much the magical equivalent of ecstasy. You could make a fortune by making and selling this stuff.'

'It could be interesting to try some of these potions. You wanna help me?'

Jacob's eyes lit up. 'Hell yeah.'

'But this stays between us, alright. I don't want too many people knowing about this book, or what we are cooking up.'

Chapter Three

'Ugh. This place is way too modern for my liking. It lacks warmth and old-world charm.' Alannah followed Brendan into the apartment's master bedroom. His invitation to attend an open inspection on Monday afternoon had excited her until she discovered all his taste was in his mouth.

After glancing around the space, he gazed at her in the floor to ceiling mirror on the built-in wardrobe. 'Modern is exactly what I'm after. Old places are often in disrepair.' He grinned. 'And they don't usually have as many mirrors in the bedroom.'

The eyeroll was instinctive. 'I bet we could find an old place in shipshape condition.' After a pause she added, 'And you can always add your own mirrors.'

'I like modern places, okay. They are more efficient with energy use and space.'

Alannah shook her head. 'Gawd, it feels like we're on an episode of *House Hunters*.'

Brendan blinked as he cocked his head.

'It's a show where couples with different tastes look for their dream home.'

He leaned in close to her with a mischievous glint in his eye. 'Are you implying we are like a couple, Lana?'

She snorted. 'In your dreams, buddy.'

An eyebrow shot up. 'How did you know about those dreams? Have you been training as a clairvoyant?'

Without thinking, she smacked his arm, hitting a hard bicep. 'Even if I had, I wouldn't want to know about your filthy dreams.'

Grabbing her arm by the wrist, he drew her close, bringing their chests together. 'I bet you would though, given your recent propensity for voyeurism.'

Damn. I can't deny I would love front row seats to a viewing of his wet dreams. They remained locked in a stare down until the real estate agent cleared her voice from the doorway.

'Would you like to complete a rental application, Mr. Winters?' Sylvia Green eyed them askance. The tall, blonde woman of mixed-mage-blood was a few years older than Alannah. She was also a notorious bigmouth.

Brendan gave her a big smile. 'Yes, this place is great.'

Sylvia beamed, gesturing with a manicured hand for them to follow her down the hall.

Alannah pulled herself free of Brendan's grip and whispered in his ear. 'Just as well we aren't a couple. You don't need to take my preferences into account.'

He looked at her and all humour faded from his visage.

When they reached the living area, Sylvia directed her attention to Brendan. 'Is Miss Winters signing the lease as well?'

'No—' Alannah began.

But Brendan threw his arm over her shoulder and cut in. 'What my dear cousin was about to say is she won't be living here. But I'm sure we will have plenty of sleepovers, so let's put her on the lease. Just in case, you know?'

Alannah stiffened in his hold under the sidelong gaze of the agent. *Gods! What must Sylvia think?* Gossip travelled fast in a small town like Gaeilge Shores, especially if the news involved the founding families.

'Well, here's the form. You can either email or fax it through to me.' The agent handed Brendan the paperwork. 'And here's my card. Don't hesitate to call if you have any questions.'

Brendan took the business card, giving her the smile that inspired half the female population to drop their panties. 'Thank you, Ms. Green.'

'Please, call me Sylvia.' She reached out for a handshake.

When he took the offered hand, he drew it up to his lips and kissed it. 'Then you can call me Brendan.'

The woman's eyes darkened, and Alannah knew they would end up calling each other all sorts of inappropriate names.

Outside, Alannah stopped Brendan on the curb beside his Jag with a firm hand on his shoulder. 'If I get word of any nasty rumours after the stunt you pulled, I will strangle you.'

He spun around to face her with a lascivious expression. 'Kinky. I love a bit of breath play.'

She shook her head. 'Is there any form of kink you don't like?'

Narrowing his eyes, Brendan licked his lips. 'Do you really want to go there?'

Hell yes, she thought. 'No. It was a rhetorical question.'

Brendan hitched his eyebrows.

Oh crap! Am I projecting my aura? Alannah had spent years suppressing all inappropriate thoughts and feelings for Brendan after he rejected her. Not to mention her love for Liam and the guilt she felt over harbouring desires for his brother. 'Can we go now?'

'Yeah. I gotta get to one more inspection.'

Alannah felt like a fish out of water in the sailing club. When she told Liam about forming a women's group, he suggested using the clubrooms for meetings. The idea was rational at the time, but the splendour of the place gave her doubts, as did the glances she got from some of the elite as they peered down their toffee-stuffed noses. *Perhaps I should dress up more next time.* On this occasion, she wore jeans and her favourite t-shirt: the black one with an Irish whiskey logo.

As the last of the ladies entered, she closed the door and stood at the head of the boardroom table. 'Thank you all for taking time out of your Tuesday evening to attend.' She glanced at Cara, beyond grateful her best friend had magiported in from work for this meeting. Cara offered her an encouraging smile, giving her the strength she needed to continue. 'I have a confession to make. I haven't invited you all here for the sole purpose of chatting over Devonshire tea. I have some important issues to discuss with you all.'

A few murmurs and the general sound of discontentment filled the air.

She projected her voice. 'That said, I have still provided tea and scones for you to enjoy at the end of my speech. Please hear me out first. If you decide you are not interested in my cause, you are still welcome to enjoy the refreshments before you take your leave.'

The din settled and all eyes were on her.

'It is time the women of the magic world push for change on the political front. Our society is behind the times when it comes to women's rights in the Western world. The country we live in has already had a female prime minister. Other countries have had women in leadership roles, yet we have still never seen a female High Magus, let alone adequate representation on most district Councils.

Stunned silence.

'But this isn't only about seats of power. How many of you would like the opportunity to register as warlocks?' Alannah directed her gaze at Claudia, a woman she knew to have the attunements of a warlock, forced to become a shaman simply because she lacked a Y-chromosome.

Claudia nodded for her to continue.

'Or to choose your own field rather than having the men in your family dictate what you can register as?' This time she glanced at Monique, who would have made an excellent conjurer, but her father insisted she be an alchemist because he did not want to risk her going to war if the summons came.

'I am proposing we form a lobby group to campaign for change in the Mages Council, to push for equal rights. If enough of us get our voices out there, the momentum will grow across the country, then across the world. Together, we can fight for what we deserve. Who's with me?'

Every single woman in the room rose and applauded her.

Monique approached Alannah when the group had broken for tea. 'Compelling speech. I can see you making a great High Magus one day.'

'Thanks, but doesn't it bother you I might oust your dad from his position?'

'Dad's resilient. He will probably use the opportunity to advance in the mage ranks. Or to gain a sideways promotion. So, what do you plan to focus on first?'

Looking around the room at the assortment of female mages—both pure and of mixed-blood—she considered her next course of action. 'We should push for a gender quota on the Council in every district. Once we achieve that, we can form a women's faction, making it easier to pass the rest of the bills.'

Monique smiled. 'For someone who falls asleep at most Council meetings, you have a lot more political nous than I gave you credit for.'

'Those meetings are rarely about real politics or even magic. There's also something to be said for growing up in the human world.'

'So how are we gonna do this?' Jacob sat in an armchair, turning his gaze upon the potion book on the coffee table.

Brendan handed Jacob one of the beers he carried and slumped onto the couch. After chugging down a large mouthful, he put the bottle aside and picked up the book. Casting his eyes over the recipe, he made a mental note of the ingredients they needed. *Essence of joy, essence of excitement, essence of lust, 30% ethanol.* He flicked to the section of essences. 'Hmm. Some of these recipes are quite vague in their instructions. I guess that's why they call potion craft more of an art than a science.

'Yeah, I guess. How can I help?' Jacob sat on the edge of his seat; anticipation painted all over his face.

The professional counsellor part of Brendan reared its concerned head at Jacob's enthusiasm for making what was essentially a recreational drug. But the more dominant hedonistic side of him was keen. 'I'll have to make the essences because they involve emotion-based mana channelling. How about you get us the ethanol? We could either source it pre-diluted or prepare it ourselves with the concentrated stuff and some purified water. We also need an imbuement funnel.'

'A what?'

'It's an enchanted funnel that allows the magical properties of the essences to transfer into the end product.' Brendan paused to consider their options. 'I'd ask Alannah to make one for me, but I don't want her getting mixed up in this. It might put her seat on the Council at risk. Can you ask Amy?' Most dwarves were skilled conjurers, and it was likely their dwarven friend could craft what they required.

'Yeah, sure. Is there anything else we need?'

'Just some standard laboratory glassware, although we need to consecrate it. Is that something you can manage, or should I do that?'

'How about I get the glassware and you consecrate it? I'm not into all that ritual mumbo jumbo. Never needed to be since I started life with my one and only attunement.'

'Sounds like a plan. Please don't tell me how you acquire the stuff.' Brendan knew boggarts were notorious for theft (an easy feat when they were skilled illusionists) and Jacob was no exception.

'Okay fine. Just don't tell me how you go about preparing them essences.'

Brendan chuckled as he reached for his beer. 'By the way, I plan to move into town soon. I accepted an offer for a small rental house near the school.'

'Sweet. That'll make mornings easier for you.'

'And my brother less crabby with me.'

Jacob's brows rose. 'You've been overstaying your welcome there, haven't you?'

He sighed. 'You might say. Getting my own flat was Alannah's suggestion. That girl has been giving me all sorts of mixed messages lately.'

'Oh?'

'After she shut me out of her thoughts and feelings for years, I caught glimpses of her mind again recently.' Brendan thought back to their previous night of house hunting. 'Her head is a mess, let me tell you.'

Jacob gave him an impish grin. 'Read any interesting thoughts?'

Letting his own devil horns show, Brendan smirked. 'Yup.'

The moment Liam left for work on Wednesday morning, Alannah jumped in her blue hatchback. She had contacted Nick on Sunday to arrange a meeting, and this was the earliest suitable time. With what she was about to ask him, she did not want to use an unsecure phoneline.

When she reached the end of her street, she took the road leading to the southern exit out of Gaeilge Shores. Passing through the outskirts of town, she braked as something caught her attention: the tell-tale shimmering of a glamour spell. And it came from the old ruins which had once been the heart of a large farmstead before they crumbled into disrepair.

Alannah killed the engine and concentrated on peering through the veil. It was the most powerful illusion she had ever encountered, clearly meant for hiding something from mages as well as humans. Luckily, Alannah was gifted with exceptional magic sight.

A few minutes later, the veil faded, and her eyes widened at the sight of a warehouse within the ruins. *Odd.* Questions of who, what, when, and why flooded her mind, but she pushed them aside and made a mental note to investigate this place later. She had somewhere to be.

Driving straight to Nick's house took fifteen minutes, crawling along the bumpy dirt track forming his driveway for five of those. Alannah did not mind though, because the Pattersons' orchard was a stunning place, the entrance lined with blossoming almond trees.

Nick waited on the front porch for her, leaning against the stone veneer wall with his arms crossed. His orcish muscles bulged from beneath a tight black t-shirt, showing heavily inked arms that reminded her of his naked body merging with a fae chick in Brendan's bed. He shaved most of his head, leaving medium length strands of pink and black streaked hair to cover the right side. That was the colour he broadcast with his glamour. She knew his hair was in fact dark brown, his olive-coloured skin leathery, and he had stag horns and pointed ears. Alannah considered herself a tad shallow, because when it came to her magical friends who were not mages, she preferred to look at their projected image.

Once she parked, Nick pushed off from the wall and reached her in a few long strides. The moment she emerged from the car; he squeezed her tight in an embrace. 'Hey, little lady.' He was the only guy she did not reprimand for calling her little. Like most orcs, Nick's stature was mammoth, both in height and width, dwarfing almost everyone. Yet despite his build and punk image, Nick was a big softie.

'Hey Nick,' Alannah replied as soon as he released her, returning air to her lungs.

He gave her a playful grin. 'So, what's with the secret rendezvous? Have you come to your senses and decided to ditch those cousins? If we leave now, we might hit the state border by nightfall.'

'Ha! Why drive when I can use ley lines?' She made a show of wiping away the imaginary drool from Nick's chin. 'Seriously though, you know Liam's the only cousin I'm involved with, right?'

'Yeah, but we all see the sexual chemistry between you and Brendo. It's out of this world. Just a matter of time, sweet.'

He put his arm across her shoulders to lead her inside. 'Come on then.'

Alannah rolled her eyes. 'You know the flirting is fake, right? It's part of the game we play.'

'If you say so. Here, take a seat.' He gestured to the Victorian settee that matched the rest of the antique furniture but did not fit with the rugged appearance of the farmhouse's occupants. 'Can I get you a drink? Tea, coffee… something cold?'

'A coffee, thanks.' *It is still morning after all.*

When Nick returned, he set the drinks down on a coffee table and sat in one of the sturdier armchairs. 'So, what's up?'

'I need a bodyguard.'

Nick's eyes narrowed, but he remained silent, allowing her to explain.

'This is something I don't want Liam to know about.' She gave Nick the letter from Scarlett.

'I can see why,' he agreed as he returned it. 'I'm in. What's the plan, sweet?'

Alannah smiled. 'Thanks, Nick. The next step is to call this Patrick dude and make the arrangements. Mind if I use your phone?'

He pushed his iPhone across the table.

'Thanks.' Taking a deep breath, she dialled the number.

The call connected after three rings. 'Patrick Douglas speaking.'

'Uh, hi Mr. Douglas. My name is Alannah and I'd like to arrange a meeting with Scarlett.'

'Certainly. What is your location, please?' He sounded formal and proper.

'Gaeilge Shores.'

'That's in South Australia, yes?'

'Yeah.'

'Just a moment, please.' Putting her on hold, he subjected her to some horrendous easy-listening music. She was thankful when Patrick returned a couple of minutes later. 'Scarlett can meet you in Adelaide on Friday night. Will this time suit you?'

'Yeah, that's fine.' Pausing, she glanced at Nick, who gave her an encouraging smile. 'Is it okay if I bring my bodyguard?'

'Scarlett will permit one escort, but she would like to know their name before granting approval.'

Being able to take someone surprised her. 'His name is Nick Patterson.'

'Very well. I will contact her and send you a message to confirm the details. Can I text you on this number?'

'Yes, please.'

'Great. Thank you for your call, Alannah.'

Well, that was odd.

Nick's brows rose. 'So, how'd it go?'

'Fine, I think. Patrick needs to check if Scarlett will allow you to accompany me, but apparently, I can take one person with me. He will text your phone with the details. We are meeting on Friday night; I hope that's alright?'

'All good. I'm sure the lads won't mind if I skip pub night to help you.'

'Excellent.' Alannah sculled her tepid coffee.

'So, uh, how much did you hear going on in Brendan's room on Saturday morning?'

Her heart fluttered as memories of four sweaty bodies colliding together flashed before her. She bit her lip.

His eyes narrowed. 'That much, huh? You know, I'm not usually like that. I don't know what came over me on Friday night. I...'

Alannah raised a hand to stop him going on. 'It's okay, Nick. You don't need to explain. What you guys do behind closed doors is none of my business and I don't think any less of you for it.'

'You're such a sweetheart. I sure hope I can find a woman like you one day. Liam's such a lucky bugger and I bet he doesn't fully appreciate what he's got with you.'

Does Nick have a thing for me? 'Uh, thanks.'

A text came through on Nick's phone. 'It's Patrick. He says Scarlett will permit me to attend as your bodyguard and we should meet at some place called The Magic Martini at ten. You know the place at all?'

'Yeah. It's a fae cocktail lounge in the East End. Bianca took a few of us there once.'

Nick frowned. 'Hmm. Sounds swanky. I s'pose I'll have to buy a suit.'

'Not a bad idea.' She reached into her purse and retrieved a wad of cash. 'This should cover most of it.'

He pushed her hand away. 'Don't be silly. I can buy it myself. I'm doing this to help out a friend and I don't expect any money.'

'Ah, okay. Thanks, Nick.' She smiled. 'You're a legend.'

'No biggie.'

Alannah rose. 'Well, I should get going. I've got work to get back to. Let's meet here at half-past eight on Friday night.'

'Righto.' Nick followed her outside, giving her another bear hug before letting her leave.

Alannah stopped outside the old ruins on her way back into town and rang Liam.

'Hey, gorgeous. How are you?'

She grinned into the phone, feeling all warm and fuzzy from his greeting. 'I'm fine. Listen, I spotted something strange as I was driving past the old ruins. Can you meet me there?'

'Yeah, of course. Give me ten.'

'Okay, great. See ya soon.'

'Will do. Love you.'

Alannah never tired of hearing him say it. 'Love you too.' After hanging up, she got out of the car and took a short stroll down the road to South Seas Café, figuring there was enough time for a coffee. Assuming Liam was in town, she would be able to see his patrol car passing by.

Brigette, the human barista—who was around a year younger than Alannah—greeted her with a warm smile. 'Hi hun. Will it be the usual today?'

'Yes please. Oh, and an extra muffin to go, thanks.' Alannah was addicted to their white choc and raspberry muffins. She took her usual seat by the window, where she watched the world go by. It humbled her to think much of humanity went about their business oblivious to mages and magic.

Once Brigette had delivered her order, Alannah's eyes swept the room. Catching the gaze of one of the older ladies sitting up the back, she offered a polite smile. But the woman frowned and shook her head, whispering something to her fellow cronies. The rest of them sneered at Alannah.

'What the?' she whispered to herself. Those ladies had never been rude to her before, despite the way she dressed. Turning back to face the street, Alannah tried to ignore the hostile vibes emanating from the rear of the coffee shop and focussed on her morning tea. As she downed the last of her latte, she spotted Liam driving past.

He walked towards the café when she stepped out. 'Figured you'd be waiting in there.' Pulling her into a warm embrace, Liam kissed her passionately. 'This is a pleasant surprise.' His grin ran from ear to ear.

'As tempting as it is to pull you into the back of your car and waste the morning, I need to show you something.'

Liam laughed. 'I wouldn't complain, but what did you want to show me?'

Alannah tugged on his hand, leading him back to the old ruins. She pointed toward the warehouse. 'Can you see through the glamour spell?'

Narrowing his eyes, Liam focussed on the spot in question. 'Hmm… not unaided.' He pulled out a potion vial from a small pouch on his belt and swallowed it. A moment later his eyes widened with alarm. 'Doesn't bode well. Whoever uses that warehouse must be up to foul play if they are hiding from mages.'

'That's what I figured.'

He glanced around the street, then at Alannah. 'Let's take a closer look. I wanna scout the place out. Do you have any invisibility potions?'

She shook her head. 'I wasn't expecting to need any when I left home this morning.'

'Here, take mine.' He retrieved another vial from his pouch and gave it to her.

'But what about you?' she protested.

'Your safety comes first. Please, Lana,' he pleaded. 'Besides, I can defend myself more readily.'

She sighed. 'Fine.' After drinking the bitter tincture, Alannah grabbed both of Liam's hands, allowing him to see her, and put her phone on silent. They had worked enough stealth missions—both real and in training drills—to be able to fall into an effective routine. Trailing Liam with silent footfalls, she kept her eyes and ears peeled.

They both needed to moderate their pace when they reached a section of ground covered in rubble from a busted stone wall: one wrong step would not only risk a fall, but it would give them away. Reaching clear, level ground, Alannah let out a breath she did not know she held.

When they reached the warehouse, Liam tried every door to no avail. Not even his lock picks worked. 'They must be magically warded'. After a full perimeter sweep, they returned to the roadside. 'What are your thoughts, Lana?'

'I'm worried about the lack of windows. Could it be a nest of fugitive vamps or ghouls?'

'Unlikely. They wouldn't have access to such strong wards and glamour magic, not without a lich. And as you saw with our grandmother, liches prefer more luxurious quarters. Whoever is using the facility wants to keep prying eyes out of their business. It could be a dark mage or unseelie operation. Possibly even dark elves, but we haven't seen them around this state for decades.'

'Hmm. Should we report this to the Council?'

'Yes. I'll ask Kieran if we can assemble a special taskforce to get inside. For now, I need to get back to work. Will you be all right to get home, or did you want a lift?'

'I'll be fine. My car's over there.' Alannah pointed to where she parked across the road. 'See you tonight.'

They kissed with a fervour to rival their greeting until Liam took his leave.

Alannah gave the mysterious warehouse one last glance before making her way home.

Chapter Four

aving finished in the Sailing Club's showers, Liam made his way over to the bar to join his cousin, Steve Maher, for a quick drink. While the rascal had always run with Liam's crew, the death of Blake, Liam's best mate and Steve's big brother, had solidified their friendship. Liam felt he owed it to Blake to watch out for Steve, especially when Blake had sacrificed his life to save Alannah.

Steve leaned on the bar with his left arm while his right hand raked a few tangles out of his wavy blond hair. 'Hey man, awesome swell you conjured for us out there.'

When it came to surfing, Liam's talent for elemental magic was often sought-after. He grinned. 'I'm glad you could handle it. Lucas was such a Barney out there. Did you see him wiping out?'

'Hey, I heard that. Not cool bro!' Lucas chided from down the bar, but there was humour in his tone.

As he glanced in his mate's direction, Liam noticed a group of middle-aged men at a nearby table staring at him as they whispered and laughed. *What the hell?* The moment he considered confronting them, the sound of Aqua's 'Barbie Girl' chiming from his pocket interrupted his thoughts. 'That little shit!' He knew who was ringing even before seeing Brendan's name on the caller I.D. His brother had developed a nasty habit of hacking Liam's phone over the last few years and pulling stunts like changing the personalised ringtones for certain contacts. He always set the most irritating tunes for his own entry so Liam would get annoyed and even embarrassed when the twerp rang him. 'What is it, Barbie?'

Brendan laughed. 'Did you only just discover that one? Or did you keep it because you secretly love the song?'

'Is there a point to your call, other than tormenting me?'

More laughter. 'Mum wants to know what time to serve dinner. Oh, and Lana is already here. I gave her a lift on my way out of town.'

He glanced at his Omega watch. *I must have lost track of time.* 'I'll be there in fifteen minutes.'

'Super. We're all famished here, so don't keep us waiting any longer. You know how lethal Lana gets when she's hangry.' Alannah giggled in the background and Brendan groaned. 'Ouch! Hell, woman. You're just proving my point.'

Liam tensed his jaw at the sound of them flirting. 'I'll see you soon.' He hung up, not waiting for Brendan's response. Looking up from his call, he noticed everyone in the club fixed their eyes on him. He leaned in close to Steve, adopting a hushed tone. 'Do you know why everyone is gawking at me and whispering?'

Steve's eyebrows rose. 'You haven't heard the rumours yet? You're normally one of the first to catch wind of gossip.'

He frowned. 'What rumours and why am I only hearing about them now?'

Gulping, Steve's Adam's apple bobbed as he combed his fingers through his hair. 'Um, I'm sure they're bollocks, that's why I didn't bring it up with you.'

Liam's clenched his fists. 'What. Damn. Rumours?'

'About Alannah and Brendan hooking up.'

Liam's heart skipped a beat, his blood froze, and he saw red. Without further hesitation, he stormed out of the Sailing

Club and dived into his SUV, paying no heed to Steve calling after him. He did not care about speed limits as he gunned it all the way to Cailleach Estate. A single thought occupied his mind on the torturous drive: *If Brendan has touched Lana, I will spill his blood.*

Upon arrival, he burst through the door, ignoring his mother's greeting as he stalked down the hall. He found the two of them laughing in the living room, sitting much too close. Rage coursed through his blood and the moment Brendan looked up, he paled at the sight of Liam's advance. To avoid a show in front of their mother, he grabbed his brother up from the sofa and dragged him out the back where Liam shoved Brendan up against the double-brick wall of the house.

Alannah rushed outside after them, shouting, *'What the hell, Liam?'*

Liam focussed his seething eyes on the rogue before him. 'Did you touch her?'

Brendan smirked. 'Who? You mean Lana? Of course I touched her. I touch her all the time.'

His fist collided with Brendan's jaw.

'Liam! Stop it!' Alannah's screams barely registered.

'Did you screw her?' He hissed the question.

'What? No!' Alannah cried in protest. 'What's gotten into you?'

Turning his head to the side, Brendan spat blood on the ground before casting his insolent scowl back on Liam. 'Why don't you ask Lana? Or is your relationship so insubstantial you don't trust her?'

Ross emerged from the house. 'Liam? What's going on here?'

Maintaining his grip on Brendan's shoulders, Liam turned to his father. 'That's what I'd like to know, Dad. Would anyone here like to tell me why all of Gaeilge Shores are under the assumption my brother is sleeping with my girl?'

'I'm sure it's only a vicious rumour, Son.'

Snapping his attention back to Brendan, Liam glowered. 'Is this because of your stupid flirting game?'

'Maybe.' Brendan smirked, tempting Liam to wipe the expression away with his fist.

'I warned you about pulling shit in public. As Council members, Lana and I both have reputations to uphold. This doesn't only hurt me.'

All trace of impudence left Brendan's visage as he hung his head. 'I'm sorry, Lana.'

When Liam released his hold of Brendan, he turned to Alannah and his heart sank at her red-faced, wide-eyed visage.

'Ross and Liam, can you please go back inside. I'd like a word with Brendan.' Alannah's mouth set in a hard line.

Liam hesitated as he watched his dad walk inside.

She pierced him with a glare. 'Liam, please.'

Alannah watched Liam stride through the door with deflated shoulders, back into the house where the mouth-watering smell of Nora's cooking called to her. First, she needed to confront Brendan about the stunt he had pulled. Shaking her head, she turned back to him. 'Why did you do it, Brendan? You haven't started a game out in public since I got back with Liam. Why now? Was it to get a rise out of him?'

'Pretty much,' he deadpanned.

'And what of the backlash I'm gonna have to deal with?'

Brendan lowered his gaze. 'I didn't think things through.' He sought her eyes again. 'I'm sorry, Lana. I didn't want to hurt you.' Stepping closer, he drew her into his arms. 'Hurting you is the last thing I've ever wanted.'

'Yet you keep doing it,' she mumbled under her breath.

His body stiffened. 'What?'

As she pulled back out of his grasp, Alannah noticed how wide his eyes had grown. 'Nothing. Don't worry about it.'

'How do I keep hurting you, Lana?'

She feigned a smile. 'Damn your magic hearing.'

Brendan's gaze narrowed on her. 'Stop deflecting. How do I keep hurting you?'

A vice gripped her heart. 'Can we forget I said anything?'

He shook his head and grabbed her shoulders. 'There's no way I'm letting this slide. Tell me, Lana.'

And there's no way I'm telling you about the wound inflicted by your rejection and how every time we play Sleazy Chicken, I'm reminded of that pain. Tears threatened to escape her eyes as she attempted to suppress her thoughts and feelings. Breaking free of his hold, she moved toward the house. 'Come on, dinner's going cold.'

The air of tension at the dining table was thick enough to plunge a fork into. The Winters family's dysfunctional dynamics had always added some discomfort to their fortnightly dinner. Brendan's resentment over Ross favouring Liam was a big part of it, along with several other sibling rivalries between the boys. *And now I'm one such dispute.*

Liam alternated between puppy dog eyes directed at Alannah and death stares pointed at his brother. Brendan, with his attention focussed on Alannah, failed to notice Liam's glare. Meanwhile, Alannah welcomed the distraction of tasty roast pork and veggies.

Nora broke the excruciating silence: 'So Alannah, have you got any new dresses to show me tonight?' The woman's beaming smile and loving blue eyes warmed Alannah's heart.

'Yes, actually. I'm planning to show it off in the City on Friday when I go out for a girls' night.'

Liam cleared his throat. 'You never mentioned anything about this girls' night.'

'I just did. Consider yourself notified,' she clipped at him, still pissed he did not come to her about his concerns first. *Does he not trust me?*

A snicker slipped from Brendan's mouth. 'Damn that was hot.'

Along with the rest of the group, Alannah turned her own evil eye on Brendan.

His heated gaze remained fixed on her as he crunched through a piece of crackling.

'*Get out!*' Ross roared at him.

'To hell with you, old man.' Brendan spoke with a mouthful of food.

'Brendan, please leave the table,' Nora begged.

After an exaggerated sigh, he rose, pushing his chair back with enough force it clattered as it struck the floor. Grabbing his meal, he stormed off toward the guesthouse.

'I wanna throttle the jerk,' Liam mumbled.

'Liam, please,' Nora pleaded. 'Enough is enough.' She placed a comforting hand on Alannah's arm. 'I'm sorry, sweetheart. I don't know what's up with my boys at the moment.'

Liam made a guttural noise akin to a growl. 'Don't feign ignorance, Mother; it's not very becoming. You know exactly what's going on.'

After shooting Liam another scowl, Alannah turned her attention back to Nora.

Nora sighed. 'You know I can't share the insights I gain from my attunement to emotions. It's not my business.'

After finishing their meal in silence, Alannah and Liam made a quick escape. As soon as they got home, Liam beelined for their home gym and slammed the door.

Alannah sank onto the couch and let it all out with a gut-wrenching cry. Once her sobbing had subsided, she found Liam punishing a punching bag with the angry screams of the Dropkick Murphys blaring through the stereo. She lowered the volume, prompting him to look at her. Crossing her arms, she tried to remain calm when she addressed him. 'Why didn't you ask me? Why did you go straight to Brendan?'

He dropped his boxing gloves and took a reluctant step toward her. 'I was furious when I heard the rumours.'

'But how could you even believe a word of that gossip? Don't you trust me?'

'The thought of him touching you flicked a switch in my brain. I wasn't thinking rationally. I'm sorry, Lana.'

'There must be some aspect of mistrust for that switch to even exist. How many times do we have to reassure you neither of us harbour any of those feelings?'

'Don't be so damn naïve, Lana. Brendan's always had designs on you. And don't take me for a fool. The fact he hasn't tried anything further until recently also tells me you must have done something to encourage him.' He drew closer, a fierce expression in his eyes. 'I'd like to know what you did.'

After gaping at him, she frowned. 'I haven't *done* anything. I can't believe how little faith you have in me or in us.' The wound in Alannah's heart wept and her eyes were not far from joining it. Liam was not ready to resolve matters, so she left him to his own devices and collapsed on the bed in the guestroom.

Brendan stood upon Jacob's threshold and listened to footfalls scurrying toward him.

Jacob threw open the door. 'You got the stuff?'

'Yup. Here's the secret sauce.' He handed over the vial containing the combined essences.

After glancing at the white contents, Jacob raised a brow. 'Do I want to know what's in here?'

Brendan grinned. 'Probably not.' Gaining a precious glimpse at Alannah's thoughts the previous night had renewed his hope. It provided him with all the inspiration he needed to feel joy, excitement, and lust. He simply had to bottle those feelings while channelling their power.

Jacob screwed up his nose. 'Well, it's comforting to know we are working with a homeopathic potency and you're a pure mage.'

'Oh, why's that?'

'Because you guys don't get any of those nasty human infections.'

Laughing, he slapped Jacob on the back. 'Come on, let's get on with it.'

'Right. The equipment is all in the kitchen.'

Brendan followed him down the hall of his cottage. The kitchen blinded him, with its lemon yellow Laminex bench tops, powder blue cupboards, and black and white checkerboard linoleum floor. The most hideous feature was the wallpaper depicting ice-creams and doughnuts in pastel shades of pink, yellow, and blue.

After throwing up in his mouth, Brendan focussed on the dining table, covered in potion vials, glass beakers, volumetric flasks, measuring cylinders, and pipettes. The first step was consecrating the glassware, so he got to work with setting up a ritual circle. Jacob helped him move the table to the middle of the room. Brendan checked the cardinal points with his compass and drew a pentagram on the floor around the table in thick white chalk. He placed a candle at each point; red to the North, yellow to the East; green to the South, blue to the West, and silver at the apex. Symbols for each of the elements joined the candles.

Jacob watched casually from one of the dining chairs at the edge of the room. With everything in place, Brendan glanced at him. 'Once I start this, you can't enter the pentagram under any circumstances. Doing so will break the circle and screw up the whole ritual. Do you understand?'

'Yeah, got it.'

'Good.' Brendan cast the circle, calling upon each of the elements as he lit the candles. He picked up a beaker in each hand and took them to the red candle and passed them a safe distance above the flame. 'I call upon the Guardians of the North to consecrate these beakers and charge them with emotional energies. I purify them this night and make them sacred.'

Brendan moved through each point, finishing at the apex. 'I call upon Cailleach, mother of mages, to consecrate these beakers and charge them with your energies. I purify them this night and make them sacred.'

He repeated this process for all the potion making equipment. By the time Brendan drew his athame across the chalk line to break the circle, Jacob was snoring in his chair. Laughing, he poked his friend in the ribs.

Jacob startled as he awoke. 'Gods! I'm glad I don't have to share a bed with you. So not cool, man.'

Brendan grinned. 'Don't worry. I treat any lady lucky enough to share a bed with me to a more pleasurable wakeup call. I finished consecrating everything. It's time to mix the potion.'

'About time. That ritual rubbish took hours.'

'What do you expect with so much equipment? Now pass me the box containing the imbuement funnel, and whatever you do, don't directly touch it.'

'O-kay. Why can't I touch it? Is it dangerous?' Jacob stared at it with wide eyes.

'Relax bro, it's not dangerous.'

'Yeah but Amy enchanted it with some magic voodoo stuff. I don't know these things.'

A roaring laugh escaped Brendan's belly. 'You crack me up man. I've known humans less ignorant of magic than you.'

Jacob frowned. 'I'm glad you find me amusing. Here's your damn funnel.' He thrust a white cardboard box at Brendan's chest.

'The reason you can't touch the funnel is I've consecrated it for personal use. If you touch it, we will lose some of the power within it. The same goes for the rest of this glassware.'

'Well bugger. What can I do to help now, seeing as I can't touch anything?'

'You can pass me the ingredients as I ask for them. You should be able to touch the potion vials too since they will hold the finished product. They have been specially made to protect the magical energies within.'

Jacob nodded his understanding. 'Right. Let's do this.'

Brendan grabbed a one-hundred millilitre volumetric flask, a measuring cylinder, and a couple of different beakers. 'I need the water and the ethanol first.'

'Here.' Jacob handed him two glass flagons each holding about two litres. One contained '95% ETHANOL', while purified water filled the other.

After decanting an approximate amount of both liquids in separate beakers, Brendan poured the ethanol into the measuring cylinder until he obtained the desired volume. Given he had failed high school chemistry, it was fortunate Brendan got roped into helping his father prepare healing potions during his teenage years. He tipped it into the flask and topped it up with water to the graduated mark. With the stopper in place, he gave the mixture a gentle shake. 'That's our alcohol made. Now I need the mother tincture.'

Jacob blinked. 'The what?'

'The secret sauce. Its technical name is mother tincture.'

'Oh right. Here.' Again, he grimaced as he held the mixture out for Brendan.

Brendan used a pipette to measure the essence mixture into a second flask, making up the volume with diluted ethanol. He repeated the process until they had used all the mother tincture, at which point he decanted the potions into vials. 'Now my man, we are done.'

Jacob beamed. 'Sweet! It's time to party!'

Nick sighed. 'As much as it kills me to say this, I'm with Liam on this one.'

'What?' Alannah glanced at Nick, her bodyguard for the night. His massive bulk barely fit within the confines of her hatchback. She had confided in him about the family drama, hoping for a sympathetic ear. Normally, Cara would have been her go-to on matters like this, but her fiery haired shaman friend worked a fly-in fly-out job which involved revegetation around the state, and she was only home on weekends.

Brendan still had not spoken to Alannah since that dinner and the few words she had had with Liam in the last two days were bitter and distant. Before leaving in the morning, he had demanded she stop playing the Sleazy Chicken game with Brendan.

Returning her attention to the road in time for the expressway entrance, she huffed. 'I thought you had my back?'

'In most things, I do. But if you were my girl, there's no way I'd tolerate your flirting game with Brendo. It wouldn't matter if there were feels on either side, or neither. It would make me uncomfortable, and it obviously gives some people the wrong idea about you two.'

'Does it give *you* the wrong idea?'

'Depends on how you and Brendo honestly feel. The impression I get is you are both hot as hell for each other. If not, I guess I have the wrong idea. I'm not attuned to emotions, so I don't have an accurate read on things by any means. But the only valid opinion here is Liam's since he's your actual boyfriend. How would you feel if Liam continually flirted with one of his female friends? If you're still in love with him, you need to shut that shit down.'

Alannah took a deep breath. 'You're right. Brendan and I have been playing this game for so long, I stopped thinking about how others perceive it. It all started out as innocent fun, you know?'

'That's where an outside perspective can help.'

'Yeah, I guess.' Her voice trailed off as she let her thoughts enter dangerous territory.

'Are you okay, sweet?'

'What?' She glanced at him.

'You were lost in your thoughts. I'm wondering if you're okay?'

Alannah bobbed her head. 'Ah, yeah. I was contemplating something you said about getting an accurate read on things. Do you know much about Sylvia Green?'

'The real estate chick?'

'Yeah, her.'

'Not much, why?'

'She probably started the rumour after I went to an open inspection with Brendan. What if she is attuned to emotions?'

'Why would that matter? It was only a rumour, right?'

'Because I want to know if she got an accurate read on either of us.'

'Holy cow!' Nick bellowed. 'You *are* lusting after Brendo!'

Alannah sucked on her lip. 'Promise me you won't tell a soul. Especially not Brendan.'

'You have my word, but you know there's no hiding your feels from that man.'

'Well, I've made him promise he won't intentionally read me. I've also worked hard to shut off my emotions around him, so I don't project my aura.'

'This may be a stupid question, but if you've got the hots for Brendan, why are you wasting time with that asshat boyfriend of yours?'

Alannah stifled a laugh. 'I happen to be in love with that asshat of mine. Besides, Brendan turned me down four years ago when I was good and ready for it. To put it simply, Liam's a sure thing, while Brendan is not.'

When stopped at a red light, she observed the gobsmacked expression on his face. After a minute of silence, Nick spoke up. 'I had no idea. I'm sorry, sweet.'

She shrugged. 'It is what it is.'

After finding a street park a few blocks away, they walked among the Friday party crowd hopping in and out of bars, cafes, and night-clubs. While not as busy as Melbourne, it was one of Adelaide's more vibrant evenings.

Their destination, The Magic Martini, was in the basement of a human bar, disguised as a private function space. At first glance, the doorman resembled the typical burly bouncer, but after piercing the glamour, Alannah saw a lizard-like humanoid known as a kobold. They were a species of fae resulting from elves mating with dragons or wyverns who act as knights and vassals for the Seelie Court.

This kobold had golden scales instead of skin and when he cast his eyes on Alannah, he looked her up and down, offering an appreciative grin before opening the door for them.

She muttered 'pervert' under her breath as they entered.

'Well you do look sexy as sin in that dress,' Nick pointed out.

Alannah shook her head as she continued down the stairs. 'Why do so many of my friends have magic hearing?'

'I'm gonna assume that's a rhetorical question.'

'Good call.' She scanned the room upon entry, taking in the sensual ambience, complete with café jazz playing in the background. The colour scheme was deep reds, dark browns, and warm metallics. Antique-style filament globes hung at various heights throughout the room and the interesting patterns on the floor and ceiling, combining straight lines and curves, reminded Alannah of Art Deco.

Nick ordered their drinks, a mocktail for her and a Coke for himself, and followed Alannah to a table near the back of the room. 'What's the plan?'

'Now we wait. I presume she will recognise me and approach us. I have no idea what she looks like.' Alannah checked the time on her phone. 'We're a few minutes early.'

'Hmm. You nervous?

'Hell yeah. You?'

'A bit, but only because I don't know who we're dealing with. I figure the whole bio dad thing is adding to your anxiety.'

She sighed. 'It's weird you—'

'*Hello, dear child.*' The familiar voice inside her head was like a knife twisting in her heart.

'Are you okay sweet?' Nick's brow puckered. 'You look like you've seen a ghost.' He glanced around the room searching for the hidden face in the crowd.

'*Before I reveal myself, I want to assure you I mean you no harm.*'

Alannah jumped to her feet. 'Let's get out of here.'

He stood with her. 'Why, what's wrong?'

She started walking toward the door.

'*Wait child! Please, give me a chance. I can tell you all about your father.*'

Something deep in her subconscious stopped Alannah in her tracks. Strangely, she felt she could trust those words.

'Alannah? What's going on?' Nick's tone was urgent.

Returning to her seat, Alannah beckoned Nick to sit next to her. 'Fine. I will listen if you show yourself.'

Nick's eyes squinted as he sank beside her.

A second later, a woman in a scarlet-red cocktail dress appeared on the seat across from them. She had dyed her once white hair black and styled it a French knot. Coloured contacts gave her white eyes their brown tint. The name change and disguise would have fooled most people, but there was no hiding her identity from her granddaughter.

'I thought I killed you. How are you alive?' Alannah hissed in a hushed tone.

Nick glanced at her, then in the direction she faced. 'Who are you talking to, Alannah?'

Alannah narrowed her eyes on Scarlett. 'Show yourself to my friend here, or I will leave and report you to the Council.'

Scarlett sighed. 'Very well. But you have to ensure he will not scream bloody murder.'

She turned to Nick. 'Scarlett is here, but she is currently hiding from you. I need you to promise you won't do anything to give her away unless she threatens me.'

'I promise.' Nick nodded. When he turned back to face Scarlett, he gasped. 'You!'

'Please, Nick. You promised.'

His Adam's apple bobbed as he gulped. 'I know. Give me a sec.' He took a moment to calm his breathing. 'Okay.'

Scarlett smiled. 'Splendid. Now, to answer your question Alannah, I am a lich. You cannot kill me by the same means as other cursed. I am truly immortal.'

Alannah's eyes widened. *How is this not known to other mages?* 'Do you still want to curse and control me?'

Her grandmother's head shook daintily. 'No dear. I am no longer the Queen of the Cursed; I do not hold such power. I simply seek your forgiveness and an opportunity to get to know you better.'

She eyed the woman suspiciously. 'Why?'

'Because you are my granddaughter, and you have a great aptitude for magic. It would be my honour to help you realise your potential.'

'How can I trust you not to kill me, or those whom I love?'

Scarlett grinned. 'Because if I wanted to kill you or your loved ones, you would already be dead.'

Alannah rolled her eyes. 'Still as arrogant as ever, I see. So, what's the deal? What do you want in return for info on my dad?'

'I would like the opportunity to teach you. I know you are seeking to further your position on the Council, and I want to help. Train with me and you will have your five attunements in no time. Once you have those attunements, I will tell you all you want to know about your father.'

'Is that it? I don't see what you get out of the deal. What's the catch?'

'Tsk, tsk. Such a cynic. As I said before, I want to spend time with you and help you achieve your goals. Call it vicarious living if you like.'

Alannah considered the terms for a few minutes. The deal was too remarkable to be real, warranting a cautious approach. Scarlett likely wanted to manipulate her and use her as a puppet if she became High Magus, but her natural scepticism ought to guard her. 'Fine, but how are we going to meet? We can't train at my house—Liam would go ape if he found out.'

'An astute observation. I will prepare a space and contact you when it is ready. May I have your direct contact details?'

The fact her grandmother knew Alannah had given someone else's number did not surprise her. She withdrew a pen and scrap of paper from her clutch. After scribbling down her number she pushed the slip of paper forward. 'Here.'

'Thank you. Expect to hear from me within a week.' Scarlett disappeared.

The sound of Nick's throat clearing brought Alannah's thoughts back to the room. 'Well, that was… uh… interesting.'

'Indeed.' She looked at him and smiled. 'Thanks for backing me up. I'm sure it goes without saying you won't breathe a word of this to anyone.'

Nick arched a brow. 'Not even Brendan, who knew you were meeting Scarlett tonight?'

'Especially not Brendan. He would freak. That woman took a lot from him. Besides, I'm consorting with a fugitive, so the Council could name anyone who knows an accessory to my crime.'

He frowned. 'I don't like it, but I get it. Although, if anything happens to you, I won't be keeping my lips sealed any longer.'

'Fair call. Now, the night is still young. Wanna party?' She batted her lashes.

Exhaling, he smiled. 'Okay. But first I need to shoot Brendan a text to let him know the meeting is over and you are safe and well.'

She retrieved her own phone to message Cara: MEETING FINISHED. I'M THINKING OF SEEING SOME BANDS. WANNA COME INTO THE CITY?

Cara replied straightaway: ALREADY IN THE CITY. AT A NIGHTCLUB. COME JOIN US.

Alannah winced. A NIGHTCLUB? REALLY?

REALLY. IT'S NOT HALF BAD. LOTS OF EYE CANDY.

Even though Cara could not see it, Alannah rolled her eyes. She knew Cara and Jacob had an open relationship, but the whole thing was strange to her.

DID YOU JUST ROLL YOUR EYES? Cara's text made her laugh. The girl knew Alannah too well. GET YOUR SEXY LITTLE ARSE OVER HERE.

Glancing up, Alannah planted a stupid grin on her face. 'The other guys are in the city tonight. Cara invited us to join them. You wanna?'

He nodded. 'Let's go.'

Chapter Five

When Jacob first proposed a nightclub, Brendan hesitated because the music usually sucked balls. But after stepping through the doors of The Vault, Brendan admitted the club impressed him. A smoky haze filled the air, intensifying the coloured light beams radiating from the stage and ceiling, and scantily clad chicks danced in cages dotted around the perimeter. The official dancers were not the only ones showing a lot of skin. One glimpse of the writhing bodies on the dancefloor and Brendan understood why Jacob had suggested the place.

Ben stepped up close beside him. 'Gods, man. Look at all that tail.'

An arm fell across Brendan's shoulders, and Jacob's head jutted in between his and Ben's. 'Gentlemen, this is the ultimate candy store. Now let's go treat ourselves.'

Brendan handed them both a potion vial and popped the lid from his own. 'Here's to a wild night.' After tapping their vials as though they were drinks, he threw the tincture down his throat.

'How long before this takes effect?' Ben asked. He was the only other friend Brendan felt comfortable sharing their test batch with. Not only was the weredingo a bigger party animal than either of them, but he also possessed an insanely strong constitution.

Brendan shrugged his shoulders. 'I dunno. This is the first time any of us are trying it. Come on, I'm buying the first round.' He made his way to the bar, his mates following close behind.

With beers in hand, the group clustered around a table overlooking the dancefloor. Brendan was taking it all in when Cara placed a hand on his shoulder, speaking in his ear: 'What was that potion I saw you guys taking?'

Brendan laughed. 'You don't miss a thing, do you? It was a magical pick-me-up.'

'Figures. Where's mine?'

'I only had three. Sorry.'

She slapped his arm. 'Sharing's caring, jerkwad. Why didn't you get one for me?'

When he turned to face her, his heart almost melted for the pleading puppy dog eyes. 'We don't know if this stuff is safe. Jacob didn't want you taking the risk.' His lip curled into a lewd grin. 'But hey, I'm sure you'll reap the benefits from him later.'

Cara huffed as their phones beeped.

He had a message from Nick. MEETING WITH SCARLETT FINISHED. IT WENT WELL AND ALANNAH IS SAFE.

Brendan let out a sigh, releasing the knots of stress Alannah had planted in his shoulders. THANKS MAN. YOU'RE A CHAMP. With that business over, he was truly free to let loose. Seeing Cara still busy texting, he made his escape. He downed the rest of his drink and pushed his way through the crowds and onto the dancefloor.

Ben was already putting the moves on a group of bleach-blonde girls who appeared close to their age. Catching sight of Brendan, he smiled. 'Hey man, come meet my new friends!' he shouted over the thumping bass. 'Ladies, this is my mate, Brendan. Let's see if I have this: Tina, Simone, Chloe, and Madison. Am I right?'

The girls all nodded and giggled. 'Are you single too?' inquired the one closest to Brendan. She wore a short red dress with a plunging neckline showcasing her ample assets.

He gave her his most charming smile. 'Madison, was it?'

She nodded with vigour.

Brendan moved closer, leaning toward her. 'Tonight, I can be whatever you want me to be.' He heard her suck in a breath before he drew back to peer into her sparkling eyes.

'So, in essence, you're available right?'

He gave her his seductive laugh. 'Yup. That's what I meant.'

Madison's huge smile was more radiant than the sun. Before he knew it, she was bumping and grinding up against him. He was clueless when it came to dancing to this electronic noise, so he scanned his surrounds to see how other guys were moving. A few were getting right into it, but most swayed on the spot, letting the chicks do most of the work. He chose the latter approach.

A few minutes later, his heartbeat quickened as a rush of endorphins coursed through his system. *This must be the potion kicking in.* He groaned as light beams brimmed beneath the surface of his skin and bokeh bubbles flashed in his field of vision. Without thinking, he slid his arms around Madison's waist, prompting her to giggle. Within seconds, his body was magically in tune with hers and the rhythm she danced. It occurred to him he was passively channelling emotional mana. *Is this a side-effect?* It felt sensational to have magical power flowing through him without the need to concentrate. Closing his eyes, he lost himself in the experience.

Minutes passed—or it might have been hours. Time ceased to mean anything to Brendan until a sudden awareness yanked his attention back into the room. Something or someone was amplifying the emotional wave he was riding. His eyes flickered open, and he looked at Madison, wondering: *is she doing something new?* But she was only dancing. He glanced around to see how his mates were doing.

Ben was beaming with two of the girls flanking him, while Jacob was making out with the fourth blonde. He scanned the room further to check Cara and Bianca were safe. The moment he spotted them; he saw the reason for his surging hormones. *By the Gods! She is so damn sexy.* His dick jumped to attention and Brendan wanted nothing more than to ravish her.

Alannah's eyes pierced him from where she stood on the edge of the mezzanine level balcony. She sipped her drink casually as her heated gaze locked onto him with her lust-filled aura on display for the whole magic world to see.

Oh hell!

While the music the DJ pumped out was not to Alannah's usual taste, it was alright. Heavy and full of energy, there was a level of complexity to it unlike what she had come to expect from most dance music.

Heading for the bar, it did not take long to find the girls. Cara dived at her, pulling her into a bear hug. 'Gods, I missed you!'

'I missed you too. Sorry about last weekend. Liam had time off so—'

'So, he monopolised all of your time. I get it. Liam doesn't like to share you. At least not with us.'

As she pulled back from their embrace, Alannah gave Cara an exaggerated eyeroll. 'Well, we're fighting at the moment, so you will get me for most of this weekend. I might even need to crash at your house.'

Cara's eyebrows rose sky high. 'Sounds serious. Wanna talk about it?'

Alannah nodded. 'Line up at the bar with me and I'll fill you in.'

They left Nick and Bianca immersed in a conversation of their own.

'I love that dress, by the way. Is it your latest work?'

'Yeah'. Alannah wore a skater style dress of layered black lace, incredibly short with a V-neckline of scandalous dimensions.

'Nice. I might have to order one of those. So, what was this fight about?'

'Brendan.'

'Ah, what now?'

Alannah sighed. 'A rumour has circulated through town about me hooking up with Brendan. It started because he initiated a round of Sleazy Chicken when we were house hunting. Long story short, Liam lost it, punched Brendan, accused the two of us of cheating on him, and got pissy with me for provoking Brendan. Liam wants me to stop playing the game now.'

Cara's jaw dropped. 'I'm away for a week and I miss all that. I'm gonna have to find a new job closer to home. Did anything happen between you and Brendan?'

'Of course not. I would have rung you during the week otherwise. But there was an incident last weekend and things have changed between us.'

'Oh my Gods, what?'

A bartender approached Alannah, putting their conversation on hold. She ordered a beer, moving to the edge of the balcony to resume their chat. 'I walked in on him having sex. Let's just say I enjoyed the show a bit too much.'

A hearty laugh broke free from Cara's lungs. 'Holy shizza, woman! Did he see you watching?'

'Uh huh.'

'Damn. So, what are you going to do about Liam?'

'I dunno…' her voice trailed off the moment her eyes landed on Brendan, ambushed by a surge of desire. He danced with a blonde who made Barbie dolls look real. His movements were incredibly erotic, and she imagined herself replacing the bimbo. She was vaguely aware of Cara laughing and moving away. But Alannah focussed on the man stirring emotions which, until a week ago, she had kept dormant for years.

When Brendan's gaze locked with hers, her instincts initially told her to look away, but a devilish idea occurred to her. *Perhaps this is my opportunity to test Liam's theory.* Letting all those pent-up feelings out, she narrowed her eyes in a lust-filled stare and broadcast her aura to ensure there was no mistaking what she wanted.

His gaze raked her up and down before returning to her eyes. He filled her mind with his voice, *'You're playing with fire, Lana.'*

If she had been able to reply telepathically, her retort would have been, *'Who says I'm playing?'* But instead, she settled for a lascivious grin.

Plastic girl drew his attention away. A moment later, they were kissing and feeling each other up.

Alannah sighed. *So much for that theory.*

'I know I'm a simple guy, but if you want him, you should tell him,' Nick whispered in her ear.

She snorted. 'Were you watching?'

'We all were. You weren't exactly subtle.'

Glancing at her friends, Alannah caught Cara and Bianca looking at her with raised brows. *Crap!* She forgot Bianca—a wood nymph attuned to emotions—was standing nearby. If the nymph did not know how Alannah felt about Brendan before, she sure as hell knew then. It was time for some damage control. She stepped closer to the girls, addressing them both. 'Promise me you won't tell a soul about what you saw.'

'You know I'd never talk shit about you behind your back,' Cara reassured her.

Alannah turned her attention to Bianca. 'I know you saw my aura.'

Bianca grinned. 'Yeah, I did. And I'm beginning to wonder if the rumours are true.'

Alannah crossed her arms and glared. 'I haven't cheated on Liam if that's what you're insinuating.'

'Not yet, but I can see you want to.'

She shook her head. 'I don't want to cheat. I—'

'It matters naught to me which of those brothers you bone, nor whether you make a clean break from one before bedding the other. You know I'm not a gossiper, Alannah.'

Her shoulders relaxed as she breathed easier. 'I know. I'm sorry for doubting you.'

Bianca smiled. 'All good. Now let's go dance.' She dragged Alannah and Cara down onto the dancefloor. The three of them had a blast dirty dancing together through several songs.

Leaving her alone with Bianca, Cara exposed Alannah's back, providing the perfect opening for male attention. A solid chest pressed up against her back and a hand slid around her waist, prompting Bianca's eyes to widen. Alannah almost broke out of the hold, but a familiar musky scent filled her nose. Instead, she spun around to face him. 'What happened to your Barbie doll?'

Brendan's eyes glazed over, and she wondered if he was high. 'She had to leave with her friends.' Their bodies swayed together of their own accord.

'Oh. I'm sorry.' Alannah laced her tone with sarcasm. 'She would have been an easy lay.'

With his best attempt at bedroom eyes, he reeled her in closer. 'I'm not worried. There's still plenty of time to get lucky tonight.'

'Why are you dancing with me? You should be making your next move.'

A wicked glint lit up his eyes. 'What if I want to get lucky with you?'

Her breath hitched. 'This game has to stop, Brendan.'

'Who says I'm playing, Lana?' he replied, throwing back the retort she had thought of earlier.

Gods damn, is he a mind reader now? 'I'm serious, Brendan. No more Sleazy Chicken. It makes Liam too uncomfortable.'

Brendan scowled. 'I don't give a rat's arse about Liam's comfort. Besides, he's not here right now.' His hand found its way to her thigh and his fingers travelled beneath her hemline.

Alannah almost jumped out of her skin from the contact. 'Brendan, please.'

Leaning in, he brushed his lips against her ear as he spoke in a gruff voice. 'Mm. I love hearing a woman beg.' His fingers had reached the edge of her panties. Any closer and he would feel how wet she was.

'Brendan, please stop.' She knew her plea lacked conviction.

'Stop what? Do you mean these?' His fingers tickled her bikini line. 'If you wanted them gone, I'm sure you would have swatted my hand away by now.'

The emotional tornado spinning around inside her came to head as Alannah burst free of his grip. '*Stop all of it!*' she screamed; 'the flirting, the touching… all of it. I can't deal with the games anymore.' She turned and fled toward the door, only stopping once she was outside and able to breathe in the fresh air.

The sight of Jacob's bare arse greeted Brendan when he stumbled out of his guesthouse bedroom on Saturday morning and threw a blanket over him. 'Bloody hell, man! You could at least wear some undies when sleeping on my sofa bed.'

Rolling onto his back, Jacob groaned, rubbing his eyes. 'Old habits, sorry. What time is it?'

'Nine something.'

'How and why are you awake so damn early?'

'I didn't sleep well after what happened with Lana.'

Jacob's brow creased. 'Ugh. Sorry bro.'

He strode across the loungeroom, toward the door. 'I'm grabbing some coffee from the main house. You want one?'

'I thought you'd never ask. And how about some of you dad's hangover cure?'

'Sure.' When he found the main house empty, Brendan breathed easy, glad he would not have to face his parents. It felt like someone had spent the better part of the night going at his head with a jackhammer while pouring caustic soda down his throat. He grabbed the magic green elixir and poured two shots, downing one himself. After giving it a few minutes to kick in, he ran the other out to Jacob before making the coffees.

Jacob had dressed, and the sofa bed folded up when Brendan returned to the guesthouse. Slumping onto the couch, he heaved a heavy sigh.

After sipping on his brew in silence for a minute, Jacob smiled. 'So, that potion was the best juice I've ever taken, I gotta say.'

'Same here. Pity my own high was short lived. I was hoping to see what it did for me in the bedroom. Maybe I should give Madison a call and see what she's up to tonight.'

'You mean the blonde with the boob job? She looked lively.'

Brendan snorted. 'That's one way of putting it.'

'Didn't strike me as your usual type though.'

He arched an eyebrow. 'I didn't realise I had a type.'

Jacob laughed. 'Of course you do. Except for Monique and now this Madison bird, I've never seen you hook up with blondes. You usually go for the dark-haired beauties. Can't think why.'

He glared at Jacob. 'You're treading on thin ice, man.' The wound of Alannah's rejection had re-opened and it still felt raw. Trying to shake it off, he stretched his neck. 'Maybe I just need to shake things up.'

Jacob slapped a hand on Brendan's shoulder. 'Be sure to include me and some of her friends in your plans. I need some action too after the stunt you pulled with Alannah got me exiled from my own bed.'

Brendan rubbed his palm against his forehead. 'Even with all my experience, I still don't get women. Why the hell did Cara kick you out for my stupidity?'

'Because Alannah is staying at our place and Cara didn't want to put her up on the couch. I could have used it, but I figured you'd need the company.' Jacob grinned. 'Besides, your sofa bed is much more comfortable than my crappy couch.'

His ears pricked up at the news of Alannah. 'Why is she staying at your house?'

Jacob shrugged. 'I dunno, something about relationship problems with Liam. Cara wouldn't give me any details.'

'Hell! I had no idea their relationship got so rocky. No wonder she freaked out last night.'

'Does this have anything to do with the latest news on the rumour mill?'

'Yeah, but you know that's all bull. It all started when I flirted with Lana in front of Sylvia Green. I guess she read something in my aura and jumped to conclusions.' Recalling the previous night, Brendan's mind drifted away for a while.

When Brendan's attention returned to his friend, Jacob drained the last of his coffee, and frowned at the empty cup. 'Is there more?'

Brendan laughed. 'There's still plenty in the pot. Help yourself.'

'Cheers man. Back in sec.'

As Jacob returned, Brendan decided to air his thoughts. 'You know, after last night, I'm wondering if my aura wasn't the only one Sylvia saw something in.'

One of Jacob's brows shot up. 'Oh?'

'Before Alannah stepped onto the dancefloor last night, she was watching me from the balcony. Her eyes were dark with lust, and she was broadcasting her aura as clear as day. I thought she wanted me. That's why I came on strong with her later.' Brendan sighed. 'I dunno what she wants. I'm so damn confused.'

'Hmm.'

Narrowing his eyes, he pinned Jacob with a serious stare. 'What?'

'Has it occurred to you that Alannah's struggling with feelings for you because she's in a serious relationship with your brother?'

'Damn. When did you get all wise and whatnot?'

Grinning, Jacob took a leisurely, reflective sip from his cup. 'From now on you will address me as Sensei, *young Grasshopper*.' His Mr. Miyagi impersonation cracked Brendan up.

'Too funny, man.' Brendan let out a belly laugh.

'What has you amused, *young Grasshopper*?'

After laughing until he struggled to breathe, Brendan punched Jacob playfully in the arm. 'Killer. Just killer.'

'So, getting back to this potion. I'm convinced we could make a fortune selling this on the Unseelie Market.' He referred to the magic world's black market, controlled by various criminal syndicates of unseelie origin.

Brendan's expression turned grave. 'I dunno, man. Sounds a bit too hardcore. Some of those thugs are lethal.'

Jacob narrowed his eyes on Brendan. 'You know I'm one of those thugs, right?'

'Sorry bro, I didn't mean any offence. But unlike you, I wasn't born into that world and the stories I've heard about unseelie gangs are terrifying. I can't reconcile that stuff with the Jacob I know.'

Leaning back, Jacob sighed. 'It's not all bad you know. There is such a thing as honour among thieves. If you handle the production side, you could let me take care of the business transactions. And we split the profits down the middle. What do ya say?'

Brendan reclined his head and closed his eyes to mull over Jacob's proposal. On the one hand, he knew there were risks dealing with Jacob's associates; and if The Council of Mages caught him dealing unsanctioned potions on the Unseelie Market, he would be up shit creek. On the other hand, this opportunity might provide the excitement he had been seeking. He turned to

Jacob with a wicked grin. 'Okay, but we need a suitable street name for this stuff.'

Tapping his chin, Jacob stared into space. 'What do you think of Rapture?'

Arching a brow, Brendan laughed. 'Isn't that the drug in *Spider Man*?'

'Good point. What are some other ecstasy synonyms? Bliss, elation, euphoria, delight…'

Brendan roared with laughter. '*Delight?* Do you honestly want to market a drug with the name Delight? Sounds more like a brand of herbal tea for grannies. We may as well go with Glee.'

Jacob frowned. 'That's a TV show, dude. Besides, I'm just throwing words out there until something sticks.' A lightbulb turned on inside his brain. 'How about Rhapsody?'

Chapter Six

Four days had passed since Alannah's outburst in the nightclub, and life was returning to normal.

Brendan rang on Saturday afternoon to apologise for 'acting like a dick,' as he put it. Turns out he *was* high on Friday night, explaining how he had not been thinking straight when he came on to her. He even smoothed things over with Liam, reassuring him there would be no more Sleazy Chicken. It certainly made interactions more civil for them all when they helped Brendan move into his apartment on Sunday.

But life could never be truly normal for Alannah Winters: living the life of a pure blood mage had seen to that. And even though her mother had tried her darndest to protect Alannah from the magic world, to hide her from the most powerful woman in the world, there was no keeping Alannah from her calling. The magic in her blood would never allow her to continue her old mundane existence.

By all appearances, Alannah was enjoying a cup of the best coffee in Gaeilge Shores, sitting in her favourite seat by the window where she could watch the normal world go by. But in a world where magic was real, appearances were always deceptive. This was especially true on that fine spring day because no one else could see or hear the woman in a red dress sitting across from Alannah.

Her grandmother had called in the morning, instructing Alannah to meet her at the South Seas Café at one o'clock.

'*Surely you have a less conspicuous location arranged for my training?*' Alannah did not voice the question, she merely thought it.

'There have been some complications with the location I had procured. The local unseelie had promised a strongly glamoured warehouse down the road, but their magic was not strong enough to hide it from the Council. Warlocks ransacked the place on the weekend. I will need to set up new training grounds. I will choose a place further out of town this time.'

Alannah's eyes widened. '*The place in the old ruins was yours?*'

Tara—who had been going by the pseudonym of Scarlett—huffed out a laugh. 'I am guessing I have you to thank for the Council discovering the place? Figures. At least that restores my faith in unseelie magic.'

Alannah smiled, happy to resolve the mystery of the warehouse, at least for herself. '*So, what's the plan for today. I guess my training will have to wait.*'

Her grandmother sighed. 'You look like your mother when you smile.'

The comment wiped the smile right off her dial. '*The same mother who died at your hands.*'

'My son has clearly filled your mind with half-truths about our history.' Scarlett's eyes glistened with the faint threat of tears. 'I loved Aileen and I never wanted her to die. I did not even raise my own hand against her. The Council poisoned her against me and my sister. So, when she confronted us, she took us by surprise. Had she known the secret to killing a lich, she would have succeeded but she wasted her energies trying in vain.'

If Alannah's jaw could have dropped any further, it would have struck the table. She regained her composure, not wanting to arouse suspicion. *'Why would the Council send Mum against you?'*

'Aileen was their best hope of taking me down. My power threatens them—power I obtained by forbidden means according to their laws. They were not content to label me an outcast for my supposed sins. If you are to survive in their world, dear child, you will need to learn about the true nature of your precious Council. This is the premise of your first lesson, which starts right now. Theory should always come before practice, after all.'

Brigette approached the table. As she picked up Alannah's empty cup, she smiled sweetly. 'Is business slow this week?'

'Yeah, it is quiet, but I need the break.'

'I hear ya. Can I get you another coffee?

'Yes please.' Alannah retrieved the coin for her drink and dropped it in the girl's free hand.

'Thanks, hun. I'll bring it right over.'

She looked back at Scarlett. *'Go on.'*

'We are all taught there is only one way to find our attunements, but that is the Council's way of controlling us. By focusing on specific mana sources, we close ourselves off to the ultimate source.'

Alannah gasped and inclined her head to her phone to give the impression of reading something interesting. *'You're talking about the primordial?'*

'Yes, dear. That is exactly what I am referring to. It is the power of the universe. Not only does it open us to all mana sources, but it is also the key to instinctive spell casting.'

'Why would they not share the power with all registered mages? It would make our job of policing the magic world a lot easier.'

'I like the way you think, Alannah. Now you are beginning to see the tip of the corrupt iceberg we call the Mages Council. They argue such power should not be going around unchecked. But who is watching the watchers?'

Brigette returned with Alannah's cappuccino. 'Here you go, hun. Let me know if you would like anything else.'

'Thank you so much.' After taking a sip of the cocoa-coated foam, she cast her gaze back to Scarlett.

The woman shifted in her seat, crossing her left leg over her right. 'Have you ever heard of the Secret of the Beltane Blessing?'

She nodded. *'I've heard rumours of such, but I have no idea what it is about.'*

'What the big wigs of the Council do not want to tell the general population is blessed children, such as you and me, possess innate gifts.'

'Makes sense. It explains why I could perform magic before my initiation.'

'Here is the real kicker. The reason we have these natural abilities stems from our inherent attunement to the primordial. We just need to learn how to channel it effectively.'

Alannah was gobsmacked and utterly lost for words.

'If we are to continue training, you need to decide if this is something you want to learn.'

A golf-ball sized lump formed in her throat when she considered the consequences for dabbling with such magic. *'Will my use of the primordial be traceable, like the other major sources are?'*

'No, dear. The Council can only detect spell effects related to a specific source. If you cast an illusion spell while channelling the primordial, it will show up as use of senses mana. I will ask you again: do you want to channel the primordial?'

'Yes, I absolutely want to channel the ultimate source.'

Standing in a dark alleyway reeking of piss, Brendan's stomach felt like knotted Shibari ropes. It was a Monday night, so the west end of the city was dead, with only the occasional thumping bass of a car stereo or police siren to break the silence. He tried to shut off his emotions as he looked at Jacob. 'Remind me why I'm needed at this meeting. You were meant to handle all the business dealings.'

Jacob, clearly in his element, was the very image of composure. 'Apparently the new Underboss wants to meet the mastermind behind our operations. And when such a figure of authority requests a meeting, you don't decline.'

Brendan shook his head. 'Have you met this new Underboss?'

'Not yet. But Violet's reputation precedes her, so I feel like I already know her.'

He narrowed his eyes on Jacob. 'What sort of reputation?'

'Well… apparently she's sexy as fuck.'

'And?'

'And… uh… ruthless. Quite the femme fatale and all that.'

Brendan snorted. 'Great. I hope we can at least raise enough to cover our funeral expenses.'

Jacob waved his hand dismissively. 'Oh, ye of little faith.'

Movement at the northern end of the lane drew their attention to where three figures approached. Shadows masked their faces, but their body-shapes suggested a tall, curvaceous woman and two bulky men. Brendan gulped, wishing he had brought Nick and Ben as backup.

'Relax man,' Jacob hissed.

As soon as the party of three stepped beneath the soft, pink neon light of an adult emporium sign, Brendan sucked in a breath as recognition hit. 'You.'

The woman gave him a wicked grin. 'Oh, this is too good. I should have known those potions were the work of the infamous enchanter of Gaeilge Shores. I *have* experienced your work firsthand, after all.'

Jacob spun to face Brendan. 'Wait. You slept with her? Thornsy's gonna be pissed if he finds out.'

'Shut it, Associate. You will not speak until I address you directly,' Bridey snapped.

'Sorry, Madam.'

The endarkened woman returned her gaze to Brendan and licked her lips. 'Another member of the Winters clan turns dark. This will please the Boss.' She drew closer, bringing her hands up to Brendan's chest. 'Mm, your heart is beating fast for me again.' Bridey wore another purple corset emphasising the cleavage of her D cups.

Sweat poured from every follicle on Brendan's body despite the cool night air. 'What do you want, Br—'

'Uh, uh. When it comes to Syndicate business matters such as these, you will address me as Madam or Lady Violet.' Leaning in close to his ear, she whispered, 'But you can call me whatever you like in bed.'

Brendan felt his dick twitch. *Oh hell! Not again.* 'Sorry, *Madam.* Why is it you wanted to meet me tonight?'

She slid a finger along his cheek. 'You mean aside from putting this delectable face to the potion known as Rhapsody, a tincture so potent it took the magic underbelly by storm in one weekend?'

A sharp breath escaped through Brendan's teeth. He knew they had been successful in selling the first full batch of vials over the course of the previous weekend, but he had no idea how much popularity the magic drug had gained. Memories of all the wild sex he'd had during his own high brought a smile to his face.

'Quite the ego boost, isn't it Mr. Winters? But getting to the point, I have a proposition for you.'

'Go on.'

'The Boss wants to spread Rhapsody throughout the country. And I have an offer you can't refuse.' Leering at him, she winked. 'You do your bit with making that secret sauce and sell us the method for turning it into happy juice. When this stuff hits the streets, I promise your cut will make you a rich man.'

Brendan's lips curved into a slight grin. 'How much mother tincture will you need to start with, and when?'

'As much as you can manage. At least ten vials to start us off would be great.'

He was in the middle of setting up his new apartment, but ten lots of the stuff should still be achievable in a week. 'Okay, fine. I'll let Jacob haggle the price.'

Bridey grinned as she traced a fingernail along the throbbing artery in his neck. 'Terrific. It has been an *absolute pleasure* doing business with you, Mr. Winters.'

When Alannah walked out to the parking lot of the sailing club, Monique approached her. 'Alannah, you got a minute?'

'Sure. What's up?'

'Another great meeting tonight. I'm excited to get some more of the girls onto the Council. I was thinking about approaching some of the guys who might be willing to support our campaign. What do you reckon?'

'Did you have anyone in mind?'

'Well, I assume Liam's on board, right?'

Alannah grinned. 'Yeah, of course he is. He knows better than to oppose me on this stuff.'

'Right. We can use some other family and friends ties to garner support. Like getting Claudia to win Clayton over, and it wouldn't take much for Jessica to talk Lucas around. Could Liam talk Steve into voting our way?'

She gave it some thought. 'Possibly. Getting the majority vote in our own district won't be hard. Thing is, we need to get the other districts following suit if we are going to bring about constitutional change, which is why reaching out to women everywhere else in the state is an important first step. But I like your idea. When we do make contact, we can ask the other women to take a similar approach. Can you get into your dad's files to dig up some info on who's who in the other districts? This might allow us to go with a more targeted approach.'

Monique beamed. 'Totally on it. I'll email you the deets.'

'Thanks.'

'No probs. See ya round.'

'See ya.' Alannah waved as Monique got into her silver SUV, watching as the vehicle disappeared around the corner.

'I never thought I would see the day when you and Miss Lane got along well.' Scarlett's voice came from close behind her.

Alannah jumped. 'Gods, woman! You scared the hell out of me. Don't sneak up on me.' She paused to catch her breath before retorting in a bitter tone, 'You know, we have you to thank for our friendship. Nothing like bonding in a dungeon cell.'

Her grandmother smiled. 'Come, we must hurry if we are going to achieve anything.'

One eyeroll and a huff later, Alannah stepped into the back of the red Mercedes, alongside Scarlett. She glanced at the driver, doing a double take at the demon behind the wheel. But she remembered her grandmother no longer had power over the living cursed. 'You employ demons now?'

'Of course. They are useful and do not demand a salary.'

'But they are evil. Not to mention the risks of channelling nether.'

Scarlett laughed. 'You have much to learn, dear child.'

Alannah feared asking, so she continued the rest of the journey in silence. They reached their destination twenty minutes later, pulling up to an old wooden shack in the middle of dense scrubland. The hut resembled the sort campers used, but it had fallen into disrepair. KEEP OUT signs warned visitors of danger and as they walked past, and Alannah noticed half the roof was missing, breathing easier when she realised the dilapidated structure was not going to be her training room.

Rounding the corner, a large, galvanised steel shed came into view. It looked a lot like the warehouse she had shown Liam at the old ruins. The Federation green building sparkled and shone, at odds with the natural environment. When they stepped inside, Alannah welcomed the cool air. She had expected the metal to act as a heat trap, but there was a split system air conditioner moderating the temperature. Aside from modern office furniture, Scarlett had arranged the space much like the cellar at Cailleach Estate, complete with a large pentagram painted in the middle.

'This place is yours, Alannah. Your own personal training grounds. The property title and deeds are in those drawers, along with forged identification documents pertaining to your own pseudonym.' She pointed toward a large filing cabinet beside a bookshelf. 'And these are yours.'

Speechless, Alannah stared down at the set of keys in Scarlett's outstretched hand. It took her a whole minute to come to her senses and accept the offer. 'Uh, thanks.'

'From now on, when we communicate, you are Ebony, and you will address me as Lady Scarlett or Madam. Is that clear?'

Looking at Scarlett, she nodded.

'Now let us commence. I want to see you cast the ritual circle.'

Calling upon the guardians of the elements had become second nature to her over the years. As a matriarch in training, it was one of many duties expected of her. With the candles lit and the circle drawn, both women knelt on the floor.

Scarlett gave her a silver ring with a pearlescent blue stone. Upon closer inspection, the gem also had a black streaky pattern. 'This is labradorite, a volcanic rock as old as the world. I want you to meditate on this ring and open yourself to the mana surrounding us.'

Alannah placed the ring on her finger, closed her eyes and breathed deeply. *In, one-two-three, hold one-two-three, out one-two-three.*

Her grandmother's voice was soft and soothing as she continued her instructions: 'As you reach out to a mana source, do not try to focus on one. Free your mind of all limitations and seek out the underlying power in all things.'

The soft white glow of celestial clouds had been her usual visual since opening a permanent connection to the Celestial element. But she reached beyond and saw various molecular structures woven together, transferring from one state to another. She felt the power of matter drawing her in but resisted the pull and tried to find the link between it and Aether. But she could not see it. 'I can't.'

'Do not worry. It is rare for a mage to succeed on their first attempt,' Scarlett reassured her. 'Even when we are blessed.'

Feeling deflated, Alannah opened her eyes and looked at her grandmother. 'Did you?'

'No, I did not. But I know what might help. Sunstone crystals provide a stronger connection to the primordial. The one I used to use is in your uncle's cellar. If you bring it to our next session, along with some other quartz crystals, you might get some results sooner rather than later.'

Alannah sighed. 'I dunno.' She hated the idea of stealing from her uncle.

'It is not theft, dear. Remember, you are now the matriarch of the Winters family. Everything in that ritual room belongs to you.'

She eyed Scarlett, searching for signs of deceit in her features. After a moment, Alannah forced a smile. 'Okay. I'll get the crystals.'

The moment Brendan stepped into the family home; his father called him into the study.

'What's up, Dad?'

'Take a seat.' He pointed to one of the two leather armchairs situated in front of the fireplace. The old country house was often chilly at night, even on a warm spring day such as they had, so he welcomed the heat of the gas fire.

He slumped down into the seat. Dad only ever summoned him for private chats when there was bad news or to lecture him—neither had occurred since he left high school.

Ross sat down, placing one leg across the other knee. 'It's time you stopped messing around with all the riff-raff. You are twenty-one now and it is time to start thinking about the future, which means finding a suitable woman.'

Taken aback by his father's sudden interest in his life, Brendan's blood boiled. 'Are you for real?'

'I couldn't be more serious, which is why I took the liberty to invite someone to dinner.'

'What the actual fuck?'

'You would also do well to tone down your language and start acting like a gentleman. I honestly thought you'd grow out of your infantile behaviour by now. I was married and a proud father by your age.'

'Well times have changed, pops.'

'Not in our world, they haven't. As pure mages, we have obligations—you've always known that. Why is it a constant struggle with you? Your brother accepted his fate long ago.'

Brendan let out a derisive laugh. 'Your golden boy can do no wrong, but he's always had it easy.'

Dad scowled at him. 'Liam has worked extremely hard to get where he is. He also gave up on the love he once harboured for Cara because he knew it could never go anywhere.'

'Yeah, and now he has the only decent pure blood woman out there.'

'Is that what this is about? For everyone's sake, Son, you need to get over your pointless obsession with Alannah and move on. Starting right now. Get out there and be nice to our guest.'

He rose. 'Whatever.' Brendan made his way down the hall.

The smiling face of Jessica Ó Máille greeted him when he entered the living room. 'Hi Brendan.' The girl was pretty enough, with long, wavy, auburn hair and bright green eyes; but she was still a townie, one of Liam's crew, all of whom he had made a point of avoiding. Well, except for that one time with Monique.

'Uh, hi, Jessica.'

His mother entered, holding a couple of glasses and a bottle of chardonnay. 'Oh, hi sweetheart.' She smiled as she put the wine down, crossing the room to embrace him.

'Hi Mum.' Stepping back, he decided he needed something stronger to get through the evening. 'I'm gonna grab a drink. Be right back.'

When he returned with his whiskey on ice, he found Jessica laughing with his mum. 'Thanks for the wine, Mrs. Winters.'

'Oh sweetie, please call me Nora.'

Jessica beamed.

His mum signalled for Brendan to join them. 'Come and sit with us, Brendan.'

As he moved toward an armchair, Jessica giggled. 'I won't bite, Brendan. Please sit next to me.'

Hell! I should have grabbed the whole bottle. After hesitating a moment, he eased himself carefully onto the couch.

'How are you, Brendan? Gosh, how long has it been since I saw you last?'

'I've been fine. The last time would have been high school.'

'Wow. I guess so. Why don't I ever see you at the Spring Equinox?' She lowered her voice, attempting to sound seductive. 'Or at Beltane?'

'I prefer to celebrate with the wider magic community.'

'But…' she began, stopping herself and settling for a meek 'Oh.'

Distant voices sounded from the direction of the front door, followed by footsteps.

'Sounds like the rest of the family are here.' Mum smiled, standing to leave the room.

A hand clamped onto Brendan's thigh, and Jessica whispered in his ear, 'Tonight doesn't have to be awkward for us,

Brendan. Let's enjoy each other's company. From what I hear, you're the fun-loving type.'

When he looked at her, he glimpsed a red flash of lust in her aura.

Movement in the doorway caught his attention. Alannah walked into the room, the neck of a beer bottle halfway down her throat. She gazed at the pair of them. 'Uh, hi Jessica. What are you doing here?'

Lowering the glass of wine she had been daintily sipping, Jessica smiled warmly. 'I'm Brendan's date this evening.'

Alannah's eyes bugged out as beer sprayed from her mouth. '*What the?* Can I have a word with you, Brendan?' She glanced at Jessica. 'Excuse us a moment.'

He sighed and rose from the couch.

After exiting through the back door and walking as far as the guesthouse, Alannah spun around to face him. 'Since when have you been dating her?'

Brendan could not read Alannah, yet her petulant tone aroused his suspicions. 'For the most awkwardly contrived half-hour of my life. Why? Are you jealous, Lana?'

Her face turned an intoxicating shade of pink.

Gods I love making her blush.

'What? No.'

Drawing closer, he let his breath tickle her neck. 'Prove it. Let me read your aura.'

She stepped back and narrowed her eyes. 'Brendan, please don't.'

'Don't what? See your true feelings for once? You call me your best friend, yet you constantly shut me out. Why is that Lana?'

'Please don't do this, Brendan.'

'I'm serious. I want to see those pretty emotions of yours. You do still have those, right? Or has your heart turned to stone?'

Alannah gaped, and her expression darkened like storm clouds. 'Why do you even care?'

Groaning, he threw his hands in the air. 'Oh, I dunno. How about the fact you're my cousin and used to be my best friend? We were close once, Lana. What happened? Is it because of Liam?'

She sighed. 'I guess so. You know how he can be. He gets paranoid about the nature of our relationship.'

'But he doesn't have anything to worry about, does he?' Then it dawned on him. Grabbing her shoulders, he reeled her in close enough to hear his hushed words. 'Or is that why you close yourself off from me, Lana? Do you worry I'll read feelings you shouldn't have?'

Pushing him back, she rolled her eyes. 'Get over yourself, Brendan. Not every woman in town is in love with you.'

She's deflecting. She is so *deflecting!* 'I don't give a damn about most women, but I do care how you feel.' He smirked. 'And if you don't start showing me your colours, I'm gonna assume you're in love with me.'

'Ugh, you're so full of it.'

The sound of snapping twigs ended their conversation. Looking up, Brendan saw Liam approaching with a glare. 'Dinner's ready.' He reached for Alannah's hand.

As the three of them walked together, Alannah jabbed Brendan in the arm. 'So, what are you going to do about *your date*?'

He shrugged. 'No point wasting an opportunity to get lucky.'

Liam growled in that alpha wolf way of his. 'You better not mess with Jessica if you know what's good for you. Her brother will kick your arse so hard you won't be sitting for days.'

Raising his hands in supplication, he grinned. 'Not my fault if she can't keep her hands off me.'

Richard smiled warmly as he stepped out of his rental car and cast his eyes upon the beaming face of his niece. He had not seen her for a few years and her elegance and maturity impressed him. With his line of work, he had never managed to settle down and have kids of his own, so Monique had always been a daughter to his heart.

She flew into his arms and squeezed him tight. 'Hey, Uncle Ricki.'

'Hey, Pumpkin. Have you missed me?'

'Damn straight, I've missed you. We all have.'

He laughed. 'Your dad stopped missing me when I became the better mage.'

'That's still debatable.' Kieran's voice drew Richard's attention to where the man stood on the porch with a rare glint of humour in his eyes. 'Hello, little brother.'

Richard released Monique and took a few long strides toward his brother. 'Hello, Kieran.' They exchanged a firm handshake. 'Good to see you again.' Aside from some minor sibling rivalry when it came to magic, the Lane brothers respected each other and got along well enough.

His sister-in-law drew him into her arms. 'Welcome home, Ricki.'

'Thank you, Janice.' They shared a polite, formal hug befitting the founding families.

Kieran followed him when Richard returned to the car to grab his luggage. 'Why didn't you magiport?'

After shutting the boot and locking the vehicle, he handed one suitcase to his brother. 'I like to fly under the radar when on official business. Channelling risks alerting the rest of the Council, and word travels fast around here. I can't afford to lose the element of surprise.'

'Hmm. Smart move. Come and get yourself settled, then I'll brief you on the issue.'

They always kept his old room for him and as such, the décor represented his minimalist taste. The only personal touches were the trophies and ribbons from his youth, when archery and guns had been his biggest passions. He might have joined the army if The Council of Mages allowed it, but they forbade pure mages from engaging in human warfare. So, he did the next best thing, and became a federal agent. The job was perfect for granting him access to high-level government intel and the networking opportunities were invaluable. But it was all a cover for his real role in the magic world. After tossing his jacket on a chair, he removed his tie, put his clothes away and made his way back downstairs.

Kieran was in his office. 'Please, come in and shut the door.'

Richard complied with the request, taking a seat across from his brother. 'So, why do you have need of the Inquisitor?'

'It has come to my attention we have a rogue mage problem I need you to investigate.'

Chapter Seven

The doorbell announced the first of Brendan's party guests. He fastened the last of his shirt buttons and gave himself a quick spritz of his favourite musky cologne before answering.

Alannah stood upon the threshold, beaming. 'Happy housewarming!' She leapt into his arms for a bear hug.

Liam—who stood back in awkward silence holding a potted plant—glanced at Brendan's hands on the small of her back, giving him the old stink eye.

Brendan averted his eyes to focus on Alannah. 'Thanks, gorgeous.'

Liam's predictable growl followed. The dickwad hated it when Brendan used that term of endearment for Alannah. To be fair, Brendan had been calling her gorgeous long before she started dating the tosser.

As Brendan ushered them into the hallway, Liam handed him the plant. 'This is for you.'

After glancing at the herb, he squinted at Liam.

'It's lemon balm,' Liam replied flatly.

'I know what it is. I did learn some things during our herbology lessons. I'm wondering why you are giving it to me.'

Liam shrugged. 'It was Lana's idea.'

The sound of a hairdryer starting up in the ensuite bathroom reminded Brendan of his other houseguest.

Alannah cast an inquisitive eye in the direction of the noise before returning her attention to him. 'Plants are a traditional housewarming gift. I figured you'd find this one useful.'

He studied her and smirked. 'I appreciate the gift, but you know I don't need to use herbal aphrodisiacs with my mad skills.'

A hint of pink flushed her delicate cheeks. 'I read this stuff is useful in several different enchanter's potions. I'm sure you'll find a use for it.'

Brendan led them down the hall and put the lemon balm by the large window filling his modern kitchen with lots of natural light.

A moment later, his latest hook-up appeared in the open plan living area. 'Oh, hi.' She smiled at Liam and Alannah, who sat on one of the couches before turning to Brendan. 'I didn't realise you had guests.'

'We are early for the party, but being family means we have certain privileges, right Brendan?' Alannah's teased. 'I hope we weren't interrupting anything.'

'Not at all, Madison was just leaving.'

The blonde ignored him, making her way further into the lounge area. 'Did you say party? What's the occasion?'

A wicked gleam shone in Alannah's eyes. 'Brendan's housewarming.'

She spun to face him. 'Oh wow, that essentially means you just moved into this place, right?'

'Right,' he replied with an exasperated breath.

'So, Madison, was it? I'm Alannah, Brendan's cousin.' She rose to shake the girl's hand. 'And this is my boyfriend, Liam.'

'Hi.' Liam remained seated and inclined his head in her direction.

Madison's eyes bounced back and forth from Alannah to Brendan. 'I can see the resemblance. You essentially look like twins, right?'

Alannah laughed as she dropped back to her seat. 'Ironic, when Liam and Brendan are the only siblings here.'

Brendan nodded. 'It's true. Liam's my older brother.'

Madison's brow furrowed as she processed the information in her tiny little brain. Several seconds later she gasped. 'Wait, that *essentially* means Alannah and Liam are related right?'

Crossing his arms, Brendan casually leaned against the breakfast bar. 'Yup.'

'That's *essentially* incest, right?'

Alannah squirmed as Liam stiffened. The magic community did not have a problem with their relationship because it was common for first cousins to marry for the sake of maintaining bloodlines. But the human world viewed these things differently, and they had copped a bit of flack for it over the years. 'No, Madison,' Alannah explained, 'the term incest only relates to closer relatives, like siblings or a parent and child. It is legal and safe for cousins to become intimately involved.'

'Oh, okay.' Madison accepted Alannah's explanation without question.

As the tense atmosphere dissipated, Alannah smiled. 'What are you up to tonight, Madison?'

The question made Brendan stand up straight. He glowered at Alannah as he projected his thoughts into her mind: *'Don't you dare!'*

She winked before turning back to Madison.

'Oh, not much. I'm essentially free.'

'Why don't you stay for the party? Madison's *essentially* welcome, *right*?' Alannah directed the last question at Brendan with a big grin.

Oh hell! 'Yeah, whatever.' Brendan shrugged with resignation. 'The more the merrier, *right*?' He glared at Alannah for a second. She knew who else was coming to his party. *'I will get you back for this, Lana.'*

Alannah snorted. 'Right.'

With the music cranked and the arrival of more friends, Brendan was able to avoid Madison's grating voice and unwind. He even snickered to himself when 'Mischief Maker' by All Systems Know played through his stereo.

Arms wrapped around Brendan's torso and a warm body moulded to his back when he retrieved a beer from the fridge. 'There you are. Happy housewarming, darling.'

He turned within Jessica's grip. 'Uh, hi.' Before he could do or say much more, she devoured him. Brendan took his fill of her, loving the pressure of her full lips and the way her tongue probed his mouth. 'Quite the greeting.'

'What can I say? I missed you last night.' She was glowing, thanks in part to the bright orange dress giving the sun a run for its money.

'We spent both Wednesday and Friday night together and you're still not sick of me huh?' He tried to keep his tone light-hearted even though he felt tense, silently cursing himself for taking things as far as he had. Not that he knew how clingy she would be when Dad set them up earlier in the week.

After trailing her tongue along the pulse point in his neck, she giggled. 'I'd never grow sick of you, Brendan. The things you can do to my body… let's just say I've never known such pleasure before.'

He should have put a stop to her antics then and there, but he was a sucker for flattery coming from a hottie like Jessica. That and the way she was touching him was… *Mm*. Turning on the bedroom eyes, he gazed at her. 'Well, you know what they say.'

'Maybe, but tell me, what do they say?'

'Enchanters do it better.'

She giggled. 'So true. Well, at least with you. You're the only enchanter I've been with.'

A flash of movement near the French doors caught Brendan's attention and spying Madison made his pulse erratic. He leaned in close to Jessica's ear. 'Hey, why don't we go have our own private party?'

More God damn giggling. 'I like your thinking, but I want to catch up with a few people first.'

Oh hell! Madison walked directly toward them. *Six steps… five steps…*

'How about a quickie first?' He pouted.

Four… three.

'I appreciate your enthusiasm, sweetheart, but I know you could never be quick.'

Two… one.

'Oh, hey Brendan. Your friends are essentially hilarious, right? Thanks for letting me stay.'

And boom!

Jessica glanced down her nose at the blonde. 'Who are you?'

'Hi, I'm Madison. And you?' She reached out her hand.

But Jessica ignored the invitation to be civil. 'I'm Jessica, Brendan's girlfriend.'

Madison paled. 'Oh.' She shot a dagger at Brendan. 'You told me you were single.'

Jessica spun to confront him. 'Wait, don't tell me you cheated on me with this slut?' Her hand thrust out toward Madison and waved furiously.

'*Excuse me, you bitch*! I am *not* a slut.' Madison moved up close to them and poked Brendan in the chest with her index finger. 'Don't call me again. I will not be a part of your cheating, not even for sex that awesome.' She stormed out in a huff.

'If I knew it'd be so easy to get rid of her, I'd…' *Slap!* Brendan's face stung from the impact of Jessica's hand.

'You bastard! How could you?'

His friends were gathering around to watch the drama unfold. Recovering his composure, Brendan grabbed Jessica's arm and pulled her down the hall and into the spare room. 'We've seen each other what, twice this week? Just 'cause we slept together both times; doesn't mean we are a couple. Did you ever hear me define our relationship as anything other than casual sex?'

Her lip trembled. 'But I thought…'

Clenching his fists, Brendan's tone turned bitter. 'Well you thought wrong. You know my reputation, so you have no excuse for misreading things.'

Jessica scowled. 'I'm telling your father and my brother about this.' She marched out of the room, out of his house, and with any luck, out of his life.

Alannah found Brendan hiding out in his room. 'Well, that was *essentially* an entertaining shitshow, *right?*'

Brendan sat up on his bed, cradling a glass of stiff amber liquid. He snorted. 'You love to watch the trouble my dick gets me in, don't you?' A lewd grin took over his face. 'Among other—'

She marched up to him and placed a silencing finger over his mouth. The contact sent tingles dancing across her skin, almost forgetting herself as she gazed upon his lips. Brendan's whole body stiffened at her touch and his eyes blazed. The air between them was more electric than a thunderstorm. Breathing in sharply, Alannah took a much-needed step back. 'So, uh, your dad's gonna shit bricks when he hears about Jessica.'

He laughed. 'Screw him. Besides, he'll just invite the daughter of another founding family to our next dinner.'

'You could at least try to be monogamous for a bit.'

'Nah. I'm good.'

Rolling her eyes, she sat beside him. 'Why do you live like this?'

'Just because my life isn't perfect like yours, doesn't mean I can't have my pleasures. It's not like I can love any of those women, so I may as well enjoy sowing my wild oats.'

'Why can't you love any of them? I've gotten to know most of those girls, and they aren't too bad.'

He polished off his drink, reclining against the headboard. 'I can't love anyone else because a girl took my heart years ago and never gave it back.'

This is news. 'Who?' she whispered.

'Na uh, I'm not going into it now.' He squeezed his eyes closed for a few long minutes.

Alannah felt a lump in her throat. *Is that why he didn't take a chance with me all those years ago? He still loved this other girl, whoever she was.* 'My life isn't perfect, you know.'

Brendan's eyes shot open and narrowed on her. 'Oh really? You've got your dream job, a seat on the Council, and the requited love of a suitable partner who will probably marry you one day and give you lots of pure mage babies to carry on your legacy. You've had it pretty easy compared to me, Lana. You haven't lived in your sibling's shadow, struggling to gain the approval of your father and the rest of the mage community. And… you won't be forced to marry someone you don't love.'

'It's not all rainbows and unicorns for me, Brendan. For one thing, my parents are dead; it's not like I've got any expectations to live up to. As for my seat on the Council, it's a constant struggle for me to get anywhere because I'm a woman. Then there's this whole business of trying to find out who my bio dad is. You don't even know the extent of my predicament.' She felt a single tear slide down her cheek.

'Oh, Lana. I'm sorry. I didn't mean to upset you. Come 'ere.' He reached out and drew her into his arms. 'You know I'm here for you, always. Talk to me. Tell me what's going on with your father.'

Alannah clung to his familiar warmth. 'I still don't know anything. Scarlett struck a deal with me, and it could be months, or even years before I can uphold my end of the bargain.'

Brendan's body tensed, but he kept her tucked against his chest. His heart beat rapidly. 'What sort of deal?'

'She wants to train me to channel my next two attunements.'

'So, Scarlett's a mage?'

She braced herself for the lie she needed to tell. 'Of sorts.'

He shifted their position so he could peer into her eyes. 'Hold up. What do you mean "of sorts?" She's not a dark mage, is she?'

Biting her lip, she hoped averting her eyes would deflect from the truth.

'Ah hell, Lana! What have you gotten yourself into?'

'It's not as bad as it sounds. I'm not doing anything wrong.'

He shook his head. 'You mean other than consorting with an outlaw?'

Alannah cringed. 'It's not like I'm helping her with anything illegal.'

Brendan pulled her back against his chest and stroked her back. 'I get that, gorgeous, but do you realise you're risking your seat on the Council by working with her?'

'I know. That's why she set up a secret training site and forged a fake ID for me.' She scoffed. 'I even have a codename. She calls me Ebony now. Apparently, people in her organisation have some sort of colour themed name.'

She heard Brendan's breath hitch.

'What?'

'This woman sounds dangerous, Lana. I'm worried about you.'

'I know she's dangerous, Brendan. I'm not naïve, nor defenceless. I can handle her. I'm just not sure if I've got what it takes to achieve what she's trying to teach me.'

He tugged on her chin, forcing eye contact. 'Hey, you're Alannah Fucking Winters. If there's anything I've learnt about you in the last five years, it's you are a kickass mage. I know you'll get those attunements in no time.'

Alannah felt herself getting pulled into his enchanting green eyes. Brendan's hand remained on her chin, and the awareness of their skin contact sent a surge of desire down to her core. Drawing her bottom lip between her teeth, Alannah's eyes fell to his mouth for a split second. When she released her lip, she looked up again to see Brendan's attention focussed on her mouth. His thumb glided along her bottom lip. 'Brendan?' she whispered.

'Hmm?' He continued to stare at her mouth.

Her heart skipped a beat. She would have given anything to know what he was thinking. *Does he want to kiss me? Please, Gods, let the answer be yes.* Some of the walls she had carefully constructed around her heart over the last few years began to crumble away. 'I told you, no more games.' She spoke in a hushed, but firm tone.

His eyes flicked up to hers, but his hand remained on her chin. 'I'm not playing any games, Lana.'

In an instant the rest of her walls crashed down as their eyes locked together. Brendan smirked and Alannah knew she was in trouble.

A loud knock at the door broke whatever was going on between them. Brendan released his hold of her as Liam entered. 'Ah, there you are.' He cast them a sidelong glance when he observed Alannah's proximity to Brendan. 'What's going on?'

Alannah jolted upright, spurting her explanation in rapid fire, 'We were just discussing Brendan's Jessica predicament.'

Liam sniggered. 'You are boned. She already posted the news online. You might want to see the comment from Lucas. I feel pretty justified with an *I told you so*.'

'Meh. I'm not scared of that clairvoyant pussy. What's he gonna do? Hit me with predictions of my future?'

'How about his raw strength?'

Brendan cocked a brow. 'Have you seen me fight recently?'

Liam grinned. 'Actually, no. We haven't had a decent sparring session in months. Perhaps we should remedy that.'

'You're on, bro. But not tonight. I'm too plastered already.'

Alannah's thighs quivered at the thought of Liam and Brendan brawling, both shirtless of course.

Brendan leered at her as his voice entered her mind. *'Looking forward to the show, are you gorgeous?'*

Yep, so much trouble.

Thanks to Liam having the public holiday off, the rest of Alannah's October long weekend passed with plenty of reasons to stay away from Brendan. After their *moment* at his housewarming party, she did not trust herself alone with him. But avoidance would be more difficult with school holidays spelling the start of Brendan's leave. When he rang Tuesday morning to ask if they could meet, she told him she had an urgent order for a set of ritual robes. It was not a complete lie: she only fibbed about the urgency.

As she embroidered the last of the details, she put the velvet garment aside and checked the time. Six o'clock. *Phew, one day filled*. Liam was working late, as he did most Tuesdays, so she fixed herself a quick dinner with some left-over pasta.

The doorbell broke the trance she had entered when her she finished her meal. Clearing her mind of all thoughts pertaining to Brendan, she snatched the bag she had filled with various crystals and made her way to the door.

Scarlett greeted her with a passive expression. 'Are you ready?'

'Yes, Madam.' Alannah locked up and followed her. It was a different car this time. When they reached the black Tesla, Alannah drooled over her dream car: sexy and ecofriendly.

'I want you to drive us there this time. It will help you remember the way.'

Alannah gazed upon her grandmother with the grateful eyes of a child who had received her most desired Christmas present until reality sank in. 'How am I going to explain this to Liam and my friends?'

'I am sure you will think of something.'

Sighing, she let the gears spin wildly in her mind as she tried to come up with a valid lie. 'I'll need the keys.'

'You already have them on the keyring I gave you. This car is yours too and the registration papers are in the glovebox.'

She was gobsmacked. 'Um, thanks.' Alannah noticed the custom numberplate: EBONY02. 'Why the two on the end? Am I the second Ebony?'

'No. It relates to your birth year.'

Once they were in the vehicle, Scarlett gave directions. The Tesla was a smooth ride and Alannah was in love with it by the time they arrived at the hidden training sanctuary.

'Now, set up the crystals on the altar, and cast the circle.'

Alannah placed the sunstone front and centre, surrounding it with a variety of quartz crystals—amethyst, rose, smoky, citrine, and clear—along with one she could not identify, resembling a clear quartz with a strange red glow.

Scarlett stepped forward and showed her how to construct a crystal grid using a mandala template on parchment paper. With the geometric pattern complete and the circle cast, Alannah began meditating. But as much as she tried to focus, her mind kept returning to her moment with Brendan. *Crap!* She felt defective. She had never had trouble concentrating on magic because of guys before, not even when she was a teenager. Denying Brendan was getting under her skin was getting harder. He was seeping into the empty cracks in her heart and soul.

She could almost feel Brendan's thumb on her lip as well as the heat of his gaze. The memory sent scorching waves coursing through her blood. *Oh Gods! Such intense arousal!* The feeling became amplified, and she almost climaxed right there on the floor with Scarlett in the room. 'What the hell?' she muttered.

'You are channelling emotions.' Scarlett's voice sounded distant. 'Or rather, you are channelling one specific emotion. A rare gift. Most mages attuned to emotions are unable to filter out all the different emotions surrounding them when channelling. I want you to create your visualisation for this mana source. Make it your new attunement.'

An easy request. Alannah already possessed the perfect inspiration for her visualisation. She pictured Brendan again, but this time he was naked, and she could see his warm yellow aura surrounded by shades of bright pink and red. The intensity of the emotional power source flowed through her.

'Now I want you to find the underlying cause of this feeling. Use a visual focus if you have to.'

Isn't Brendan the underlying cause?

'No, he is the inspiration.'

Oops of course Scarlett is reading everything going on in my filthy mind.

'The cause is fundamental to all life.'

Focussing on the mana doing all sorts of naughty things to her body, she realised it would be an effective form of masturbation. *Did Brendan jerk off when channelling like this? Gods! Did I just think that? Focus, woman!* After a few deep breaths, she pictured people having sex around the Beltane fertility fires. It hit her: babies are born from these feelings—we have these feelings because we are born—the cycle of life is tied to our emotions.

'Now dig deeper and think back to a time before people; before animals.'

Tracing the origin of species backwards in time, she could see each precursor in the human evolutionary line. She pictured the formation of the Earth at the hands of the creator Gods. *Were the Gods the cause?*

'No. The primordial came before the Gods.'

Of course! The Earth was relatively young compared to the age of the Universe. Supposedly, it all started with the big bang.

She visualised the creation of the Universe and the formation of stars which produce hydrogen. *Matter and energy.* But before they even existed, there was something: *Primordial power.* She could see a red-hot glow from which everything originated. She felt it! *Holy hell!* The surge of power was unreal. It felt like she caught fire. Her body pulsed between euphoria and agony; unlike anything she had ever experienced.

'Excellent. Now solidify your visualisation. Become attuned to the almighty power source.'

Imagining what the birth of the Universe was like became her visual focus. When she opened her eyes, she grinned, feeling high from the power flowing through her.

'You have done well. Next week I will show you how to use the primordial to tap into other mana.'

Chapter Eight

Alannah sat alone at the boardroom table of the Council chambers when she really wanted to just curl up in Liam's arms and sleep. Thoughts of Brendan kept haunting her, distracting, exhausting, and plaguing her with guilt. Every time she woke from one of those wet dreams, she glanced at the man sleeping beside her—the man who loved her—and dread settled into the pit of her stomach. It became impossible to get back to sleep.

So, as she waited for the rest of the Council to arrive, she rested her head on her arms and tried to get some shut eye.

'Oh look, Alannah's already nodding off and Kieran's droning hasn't even commenced.' The voice of Liam's cousin, Steve, cut through her slumber.

A warm hand rested on her shoulder blades. 'Are you okay, Lana?'

She gazed into Liam's bright, cobalt eyes. 'Yeah, I just haven't been sleeping well.'

His brows furrowed as he sat down beside her. 'That's normally my problem, not yours. Has something been bothering you?'

'Yeah, but I don't want to talk about it here.' *Or at all with you.*

'Okay. Maybe you should ask to present your report first so you can take your leave and get some rest.' Liam's caring warmth made her smile.

'Not a bad idea. You won't mind?'

'Of course not, gorgeous. Your wellbeing will always come first.'

She kissed his lips chastely. 'I love you so much.'

'I love you too, babe.'

'Naw, you guys are adorable.' The booming voice of Lucas announced his arrival. The man's larger-than-life presence and muscular bulk even made the likes of Nick and his Orc clan appear scrawny. What Lucas lacked in magical power, he made up for in physical strength *and* intellect. 'Yo Liam, just a heads up—I plan to pummel your brother into the dirt.'

Liam laughed. 'I did warn him.'

'Maybe someone should cut his dick off,' Steve suggested.

Oh Gods, what a horrifying thought. Alannah's stomach turn. Brendan might be a cad, but that dick of his had been a source of immense pleasure for a lot of women. Along with those hands, and those lips…

'Whose dick are we cutting off?' Clayton asked as he entered the room.

Lucas glared at him with his fists clenched. 'Whose do you reckon?'

Clayton laughed. 'Oh right. I'm guessing you mean our resident enchanter. I say power to him. If I had half his magical talents, I know I'd be wanting to share them with the lady folk.'

Alannah snorted. She had always liked Clayton. He was less uptight than most pure-bloods and she would never forget the first time she saw him and his twin sister, Claudia: their fire dancing at the Spring Equinox gala had been spectacular.

Lucas' left eye twitched. 'I doubt you would feel that way if he'd done the dirty on *your* sister.'

Clayton shrugged. 'Wouldn't bother me. Claudia's a big girl—she can take care of herself.'

'Evening all.' Ross walked in, putting an end to all talk of Brendan.

'Hello boys and Alannah.' When Nora saw Alannah's eyes, her smile disappeared. 'Oh sweetheart, are you okay? You look terrible.'

She forced her lips to curve into a smile as Nora sat next to her. 'Just sleep-deprived.'

'So, I gotta know,' interrupted Clayton. 'Who owns that shiny black Tesla in the carpark? That thing's a real beauty.'

Alannah beamed. 'That'd be mine.'

Liam whipped his head around to gape at her, while the other guys stared. 'Since when?'

'Since I bought it today,' she lied. She had hidden the car at her hideout for as long as it took to sell her old rust bucket.

'Why didn't you consult me first? Are you sure we can afford the finance?'

'I bought it outright, with my own money, so I don't see why I needed your permission first.' She spoke with more defensive bitterness in her tone than intended and hoped it did not give away her secret.

Liam narrowed his eyes. 'How the hell did you afford it? Those things cost a fortune.'

'I've been saving.' It was an absolute crock of shit and Liam probably figured as much, but they had kept their finances separate so he had no idea what her bank account looked like.

He shook his head as a couple of the older Council members took their seats quietly and turned to his mates to talk about surfing.

Nora continued to study Alannah. 'You're not hiding your aura anymore.' She spoke in a whisper: 'I can see something's eating at your conscience. If you need to talk about it, you can always come to me. You know that, right?'

This time, Alannah's smile was genuine. 'Thanks, Nora.'

Monique rushed in and stood behind her chair. 'All rise for the Honourable Richard Lane and High Magus Kieran Lane.'

What is the Inquisitor doing here? Alannah stood with the rest of the Council as the two powerful men strode into the room with smug confidence. They both wore charcoal business suits, pressed to perfection. The only difference in their attire was their choice of tie: Kieran's was blue and gold, while Richard's was black.

'Thank you, Lady Monique.' Richard scanned the mages assembled around the table. 'Please be seated.' When everyone settled, Richard prompted Kieran to speak.

'I am opening the meeting at four minutes past seven. We have an important matter taking precedence over all other Council business this evening. I know many of you are wondering why the Inquisitor is with us tonight.'

Alannah nodded along with several other members at the table.

'I have evidence to suggest we have a rogue mage in our midst, so I have called upon the services of the Honourable Richard Lane to help flush them out.'

Oh crap! Does he mean…

The piercing stare of Richard's frosty, dark eyes of steel cut Alannah's thought short. He cocked his head as his brows arched.

Not good!

Kieran continued speaking. 'After Lady Nora's last report on the spike in emotional mana channelling, I did some digging of my own and came across this.' He placed a potion vial on the table.

Breath returned to Alannah's lungs. Richard was not here for her.

'This is an unsanctioned potion that found its way onto the Unseelie Market and into the hands of magical people who frequent urban clubs.'

Alannah inspected the potion. It was almost clear, with a milky white tint. It was a tincture of some kind.

'According to my sources, it goes by the street name Rhapsody, and it elicits a high much like the human drug ecstasy. However, the side effects are quite different. Being mystical in nature, this potion does not harm the physical body of a magic person. This stuff is dangerous because it opens a user to emotional mana, causing them to passively channel the power source and giving them access to magic abilities beyond the understanding of those untrained in the area.'

Oh wow, that's some potent magic.

'It is also highly addictive. The demand has been high enough to prompt mass production around the country.'

Ross raised his hand.

'Yes Councillor?'

'If this potion is all over the country, why is the Inquisitor *here*?'

'An excellent question, Lord Ross,' Richard replied. 'I have been in contact with all of the districts in this state as well as across the Nation. The spikes in emotion channelling reported elsewhere have only recently begun. They originated from the Adelaide area prior to the spread.'

Ross nodded. 'Thank you, Your Honour.'

Richard continued to address the room. 'My investigation will begin with the routine questioning of all Council members, followed by the registered mage community. This is standard protocol and nothing for upstanding citizens to fear.' His attention focussed on Alannah, sending a chill down her spine. 'Please make yourselves available upon my request.'

'It's a good thing I love you so damn much, Lana. Seeing your smile makes sacrifices like this worthwhile.' Liam gave Alannah an impish grin as he linked his arm with hers and escorted her into Doyle Dougherty's. The bar was nothing special: a typical country pub with nondescript wooden furniture and a floor covered in beer-stained carpet that might have been red once. But this place was always buzzing on a Friday night.

'Oh come on! My friends aren't *that* bad.'

'I guess most of them are okay. But I still don't like seeing you hang out with unseelies.'

Alannah shook her head. 'Jacob and Caleb are harmless. You should know. In all your time as a cop, have you ever had cause to arrest them?'

He sighed, conceding she had a point. 'No. But I still don't trust them.'

An arm fell across his shoulder, and a second later Brendan's head poked in between Liam and Alannah. 'Hey there fam. Who don't you trust, bro?'

'You and your sleazy arse for one,' he retorted, tensing at the sight of Brendan's other hand on Alannah's shoulder.

Brendan recoiled and clutched his heart in an exaggerated manner. 'I feel so wounded, Brother. My arse is the least sleazy part of my body.' The twerp winked at Alannah, grabbing her hand and pulling her over to their booth.

Liam watched Alannah greet the rest of her friends with hugs as he ambled his way over. By the time he got there, she was deep in conversation with Cara, so he slipped into the seat next to her. Her hand naturally gravitated toward his thigh, where he clasped it in his own. He smiled, thinking he would never grow tired of the small gestures of love in their relationship.

After a few minutes, Alannah straightened and smacked the table to get everyone's attention. 'So, did you guys hear the Inquisitor is in town?'

Cara waved a hand dismissively. 'Bah. He's probably visiting his family.'

It was no secret the Inquisitor was High Magus Kieran Lane's brother.

Liam shook his head. 'This time he's on official business. We arrested a couple of unseelie folk for dealing unsanctioned potions in the city last weekend, so Richard's here to shut down the whole operation.' He directed an accusing eye at Jacob. 'You wouldn't happen to know anything about this drug ring?'

Alannah punched his bicep in the adorable way that hurt her fist more than his arm. 'Liam! Don't be rude to my friends.' She shot Jacob a smile. 'I'm sorry.'

Jacob shrugged. 'It's okay. And to answer Liam's question: no, I don't know a damn thing. My ties to the family business are "tenuous" at best.' He even used air quotes.

'Any idea where these potions might be coming from?' Brendan directed his question at Liam.

'If I were to guess, I'd say a dark mage is the source. Most unseelie fae aren't known for their potion making skills and we don't have many endarkened in this district. Richard explained he is going to systematically question every registered mage in town to rule us all out before he moves on to flushing out any outlaws living in our midst.'

A snicker came from across the table and all eyes landed on Caleb.

Liam glared at him. 'What's amusing, freak?'

Caleb scowled. 'You guys have no idea what you're in for. I've seen that man at work and it ain't pretty. His methods are barbaric. Think full-fledged effin witch-hunt. Your so-called pure blood won't help any of you because he don't discriminate. Every little secret you mages are keepin' will be brought to light and if you try to keep him out of your heads, he'll torture you until you let him in.'

Connor, Bailey, and Brendan all stared at him with wide eyes. When Liam glanced at Alannah, he saw the same expression on her face, so he squeezed her hand. 'It's okay, babe. We don't have anything to hide. We'll be fine.' When her eyes connected with his, she bit her bottom lip, sending a heavy lump down his throat and into the pit of his stomach. *What is she hiding?*

Brendan could hardly breathe. Having the Inquisitor in town would have been bad enough but knowing the most powerful Council member in Australia was investigating his racket sent him into palpitations. He exchanged a look with Jacob and spoke to him telepathically. *'We need to shut down our operations. I can't have Richard Lane finding all the gear in my shed.'*

Without reacting, Jacob mentally replied, *'Keep your calm, bro. Acting this suspicious will give the game away.'*

'How can you expect me to be calm? You heard what Caleb said.'

'If you pull out of this deal, Violet will skin you alive. We'll move the lab and I'll get you a mind shield so Richard can't read your thoughts.'

Brendan drained the last of his beer, already feeling the need for something stronger. '*Thanks for the reassurance, I feel so much better knowing I have to worry about that psycho bitch as well as the sociopathic Inquisitor. Oh and—*' A glance at Alannah broke his concentration.

She was in a silent stare-down with Liam, her eyes wide while Liam's gaze narrowed upon her.

'You're not hiding anything, are you Lana?' he queried.

Oh hell! Brendan remembered what she told him about Scarlett.

She hesitated. 'No.' Her eyes shifted to Brendan, pleading with him.

Liam glanced at each of them and paled.

Brendan maintained a neutral expression.

'Is this why you haven't been sleeping, Lana?' Liam sneered. 'Have you been sneaking off to meet Brendan in the middle of the night?'

'What? No!'

'Or is it when I'm at work?'

'There's nothing going on between Brendan and me.' She kept eye contact with Liam.

'Then what's going on? I know something is bothering you and it's been keeping you awake at night.'

Deciding it was time to step in and help, Brendan spoke into both their minds. '*Lana has been receiving magic training from someone of dubious repute. She's concerned the Inquisitor will find out.*'

'Dubious how?' Liam's eyes narrowed on Brendan.

'*Unregistered, but not dark. Right, Lana?*'

'Right.'

'Damnit! Do you realise the trouble this could bring down on us?' Liam snapped.

'I know. I'm sorry.' Alannah was on the verge of tears. 'I'll fix it, I promise.'

Brendan looked at Jacob. *'Can you get us some selective mind shields?'*

He gave a single nod. *'Given enough time and money, I'm sure I could.'*

'Brilliant. Get one for Lana too.'

'Okay, but who's paying?'

He could see Liam and Alannah were still arguing. *'I'll front the bill for all of them. And make sure they are quality.'*

When Liam rose and stormed off in a huff, Brendan moved around to take the vacated seat. 'Don't worry, Lana. I've got a plan to help protect you from the Inquisitor.'

She smiled at him. 'Thank you. And thanks for defusing the situation with Liam.'

'No probs.' Brendan knew he had Alannah trapped in the booth, with Cara and Jacob flanking her. Grinning, he grasped the golden opportunity. 'Now, Lana, how about telling me why you've been avoiding me all week. Does it have anything to do with those sleeping difficulties Liam mentioned?'

Her face lit up like a brothel light. 'No, of course not.'

'You're a terrible liar, Lana. Something you will have to work on.'

She frowned. 'Why do you assume I'm lying?'

'For one thing, you avoid eye contact. Also, the pitch of your voice rises.' He lowered his voice and gave her a suggestive grin. 'Why don't you come back to my place tonight and I'll give you a lesson in effective bluffing?'

'That's unwise. Liam's already in a pissy mood. I should get home and sort things out with him.'

'You know as well as I do Liam will need a few hours to calm down before he sees reason. Stop making excuses, Lana.

What's the real reason you don't want to spend time alone with me?'

Creasing her forehead, she stared at him. 'You seem to know, so why don't you tell me?'

He arched a brow. 'Are you giving me permission to read you?'

'You may as well. I'm sure you've caught enough glimpses lately anyway.'

She had let her guard down again last weekend, allowing Brendan to see the extent of her arousal. He leaned in to whisper in her ear: 'I think you're afraid of your feelings for me, Lana. Some inappropriate feelings, given your situation. Am I right?'

Alannah bit her lip. 'I'm in love with Liam and I'm not going to cheat on him.'

Bloody Liam! What did she see in the asshat? Brendan leaned back and crossed his arms. 'You needn't worry though. It's not like I'd try anything.'

She clenched her eyes.

Dagnammit! Lana must have mistaken my meaning.

But before he could explain, Jacob tugged on his sleeve. 'Hey bro, we gotta clear outta here *now*.'

'*What*?' he clipped, annoyed by the interruption.

'Richard's here. We should go lay low for now.'

Brendan glimpsed the entrance and observed both Richard and Kieran making their way to the bar. *Oh hell! What were they doing here?* That sort usually went to the sailing club to socialise.

As if sensing their apprehension, Bailey piped up. 'I'll show you out through the staff exit.'

He grabbed Alannah's arm as he rose. 'Come on, you better get out of here too.'

She nodded and followed them.

Once outside, Brendan turned to Alannah, but before he could say anything, she magiported away. 'Gods damnit woman!'

Alannah lay in bed hours after Liam got up for work on Saturday morning, curled in a ball and staring blankly at the closed window. She knew pining over Brendan's constant rejection was illogical. *It's not like I can act on my feelings anyway.* Her love for Liam was real and requited, affirming her determination to remain faithful. But she could not help indulging in a pity party, especially since Liam was still in a foul mood when he left.

The first two times the doorbell rang, she ignored it. But the sound of someone bashing at her door roused her. Throwing on a plush dressing gown and matching pink slippers, she shuffled down the hall. Glancing through the peephole, she froze.

'Open up, Councillor Winters. I know you are home,' the Inquisitor's deep voice demanded.

She took a deep breath and opened the door. 'Sorry, Your Honour. I was still in bed.'

Richard took in her dishevelled state and simpered. 'Rough night?'

'Something like that. What can I do for you?'

'I have a few routine questions to ask you. May I come in?'

'Certainly.' She opened the security screen and stepped aside. They moved into the front sitting room. 'Please give me a minute to get dressed.'

'Of course.'

She returned to her room to change, before shooting Brendan a text. INQUISITOR AT MY HOUSE NOW! WHAT WAS THAT PLAN OF YOURS?

His reply came promptly: DAMN! … I WAS GOING TO GET YOU A SELECTIVE MIND SHIELD. … TRY TO FOCUS ON ANYTHING OTHER THAN SCARLETT. … EVEN IF YOU HAVE TO IMAGINE ME NAKED :P

Alannah rolled her eyes as she deleted their message history. She took another deep breath and walked back to the front room. 'Sorry for the wait, Your Honour. Can I get you a drink?'

He gave her a warm smile. 'Just a glass of water, thank you.'

She got them both a glass and brought a jug of chilled water out from the fridge. Having poured their drinks, she sat on the edge of her seat. 'What would you like to know?'

'To start with, can you please tell me your full name and date of birth?' He withdrew a notepad and pen.

'Alannah Kayleigh Winters, born thirty first of July, two-thousand and two.'

After jotting something down, he regarded her a moment.

Is this a scare tactic? Alannah tried to redirect her surface thoughts. Images of Brendan's naked body were the first things to enter her mind. *Damn him!*

Richard sipped from his glass and smiled. 'Tell me what you know about the potion called Rhapsody.'

'I only know what you and High Magus Kieran told us at the Council meeting.'

'And when was the first time you learnt of this potion?'

'At said Council meeting.'

Richard dabbed his pen against the notepad as he studied her. 'Have you heard of the Dark Syndicate, Lady Alannah?'

'No, Your Honour.'

He stopped tapping his pen and crossed his legs. 'What about the Unseelie Market?'

'I have heard of it. Its existence is common knowledge to the Mages Council.'

'Of course it is. Do you know anyone within the Unseelie Market?'

'Not directly, no.'

Richard leaned forward in his seat. 'Please explain your use of the word *directly*.'

'I have a couple of unseelie friends. While they are not part of any criminal organisations, I assume they have relatives who are. But I don't know their families, nor have I heard of anything to support my assumptions.'

'Indeed. Who are these unseelie friends?'

'Jacob Bennett and Caleb Hawthorn. I went to school with them, Your Honour.'

'You have some interesting friends, Councillor. Most mages of your status would not associate with the magic underclass.'

What an insufferable snob! 'I was friends with them before I knew what they were, or what I was for that matter.'

The hint of a frown touched his features before his poker face returned. 'What do you mean, before you knew what you were?'

'My parents raised me ignorant of my heritage to protect me from my grandmother. I did not know anything about the magic world until I returned to Gaeilge Shores at the age of sixteen. Even then, it was some time before my cousins told me anything.'

'Ah yes. The infamous Tara Winters. She tried to curse you, did she not?'

'Yes, Your Honour.'

'Strange how she disappeared after you killed her. Do you know what happened to her body?'

Her thoughts wandered to the memory of Brendan's thumb on her lip and the desire to kiss him. 'Uh, sorry Your Honour… what was your question?'

Richard smirked. 'Something is distracting you, Lady Alannah. I wonder, how would Lord Liam react if he knew of the feelings you're harbouring for his brother?'

Alannah gasped and her chest constricted.

'Don't worry, I won't tell him.' He winked at her. 'That concludes my questioning for now. Thank you for your time.' He rose from the chair.

'No worries.' After standing, Alannah walked him to the door.

Stepping outside, he turned to her. 'Oh, did you know Tara's sister, Dana, now sits on the Cursed Throne?'

What? This is news! 'No, Your Honour, I had no idea.'

'It is a little-known fact. Have a great day, Councillor.' He turned and left.

Chapter Nine

Pacing the living area, Brendan mulled over Alannah's message about her visitor. 'Dagnammit!' When she did not reply to his last text after a few minutes, he scrolled through his contacts. Finding Jacob, he hit the call button.

'Hey bro, what's up?'

'I need those mind shields *now*!'

'Gods, Brendo! I told you these things take time.'

'We don't have time. The Inquisitor is at Alannah's house right now.'

Silence.

'Jacob? You still there?'

'Yeah, I'm here. I thought we agreed not to tell her about the potion making.'

'I haven't told her jack. This isn't about that. But she has her own secrets and I promised to protect her from the Inquisitor.'

Jacob's exhaled breath almost deafened Brendan. 'Heck, bro. You had me pissing myself for a minute there. I'll see what I can do. But if the Inquisitor is there now, it might be too late for her.'

Brendan slumped into an armchair and tossed his head back against the backrest. 'Just see what you can do, okay?' He hung up, sending Alannah another message: Call me when Richard leaves. Better yet, get your sexy arse over here.

As soon as he sent the message, his doorbell chimed. 'Thank the Gods!' He ran to the door and flung it open, expecting to see Alannah; but she was not the Winters woman standing on his doorstep. His already pale complexion must have turned as white as the ghost before him.

'Hello Brendan, dear. Miss me?' Tara Winters was there in the flesh, wearing a red dress and appearing different to the last time he saw her corpse lying cold on the ground.

'Not on your life, or unlife. How are you here, and what do you want?'

'You have lots of questions, I am sure, but time is of the essence. I want to help you and Alannah with your Inquisitor predicament.'

'How do you know about that?'

'Did I not say we do not have time for all of your questions? Word on the Syndicate grapevine is you need these.' She held up three silver amulets, each engraved with the shield Celtic knot.

'You're in the Dark Syndicate?'

'Oh, sweetheart, I *am* the Dark Syndicate. Now, are you going to take these or what?' She thrust her hand toward the security door.

'How much do I owe you?'

'Nothing.'

He eyed her askance. 'What's the catch?'

'No catch. I am protecting my investments. I am glad you found my book useful, by the way.'

'That came from you?'

Tara smiled. 'Oh yes. Alannah cannot be the only one with a Winters family heirloom, after all.' She swung the amulets like pendulums. 'Take them or leave them. I will not stand here all day.'

'Okay, fine.' He opened the screen door and snatched them from her bony fingers. 'Now get the hell out of my face.'

'As you wish. Oh, and send my regards to Alannah.' She turned and strode toward a red Mercedes.

Brendan watched Tara leave. When she climbed into the car parked in his driveway, he glanced at the number plate. As SCARLETT64 took off down the street, he collapsed to his knees and screamed, '*Fuuuuck!*'

Well, that could have gone much worse, Alannah thought as she watched Richard leave. After having her morning coffee, she returned to her room to collect her phone and noticed the text from Brendan. Smiling at his reference to her arse, she grabbed her purse and keys and made her way outside. Feeling the need for fresh air, Alannah travelled the short distance to Brendan's house on foot.

When Brendan opened his door, he yanked her inside and threw his arms around her. 'Thank the Gods you're okay.'

Alannah clung to him as if he were a life raft on a stormy sea. In some ways, his hugs had always comforted her regardless of whatever was going on between them. He was still her best friend. 'Brendan—'

'Shoosh. Let me hold you.'

She had no idea how long they remained locked in each other's arms, but it was easily the longest embrace of her life; yet when he pulled back from her, it was too soon.

'Come on.' He led her down the hall. 'Jacob will arrive in a minute, then we need to talk.'

'Maybe we should talk before he gets here.'

There was an expressionless mask on his face as he shook his head.

'I need to tell you about my chat with Richard.'

'Wait for Jacob.'

'But Brendan—'

'No, Lana. Things are more complicated than you realise.'

She wanted to protest more, but the doorbell cut her off, so she made herself comfortable in an armchair.

Jacob entered the room a moment later. 'Oh, hey Alannah.' He shot Brendan a look. 'What's she doing here? I thought we—'

'Sit down,' Brendan snapped.

Jacob threw his hands up in supplication. 'Whoa man. What crawled—'

'Sit. The. Hell. Down.'

Gods! Alannah could not remember the last time she had seen Brendan in such a state, if ever.

After picking his jaw up from the floor, Jacob sat on the couch.

Brendan paced the room, stopping in front of her. 'We have a serious problem. Lana, remember the letter you received from Scarlett?'

She nodded.

'You weren't the only one to get some mysterious mail.' He retrieved a book from inside the ottoman and dropped it on the coffee table. It landed with a loud thump, startling Alannah. 'Inspect it thoroughly.'

It was a large volume, requiring two hands to pick up. She noticed the cover was black leather, much like her Book of Shadows. But there were no markings on the front of this one.

'Turn to page two-hundred and fifty-three.'

Opening the book, she found a recipe for an enchanter's tincture. As she read about its effects, the penny dropped. 'Oh crap! This is Rhapsody. Does this mean you're the source?'

'Yu*p*.' He popped the P. 'And Jacob here. He's my partner in crime.'

'What the hell, Brendan?'

'Oh, it gets better. You see, I learnt who sent me the book. None other than your friend Scarlett.'

Dread took root in the pit of her stomach.

'Alannah knows Lady Scarlett?' Jacob blinked, eyes bouncing from Brendan to Alannah and back again.

'Oh yeah, they go way back. Don't you Lana?'

Crap! Does he know?

'What I'd like to know, Jacob, is how well you know the Boss lady?'

'Never met her, why?'

Brendan studied Jacob for a few seconds. 'Scarlett paid me a visit today. She wanted to deliver these in person.' He pulled three amulets from his pocket and thrust them on the table.

Jacob grabbed one. 'Heck yeah! You got the mind shields.'

But Brendan paid him no heed. He stared at Alannah. 'And she sends her regards to you, Lana.'

'Oh crap!' she mumbled.

His gaze became challenging. 'When were you going to tell me? I'm at least hoping for before she stabs us all in the back. Or are you Team Scarlett now?'

'I'm sorry, Brendan. I was trying to keep her away from you and Liam.'

'Don't you mean keep us from her? Because after what she did to us all, I feel pretty justified in ripping her heart out and feeding it to her.'

'Wait, what am I missing here?' Jacob wrinkled his forehead.

They both ignored him as Brendan's hands came to rest on the arms of her chair, caging her in as he towered over her. His eyes glowered. 'How much do you know about the Dark Syndicate, Lana?'

Second time today someone asked me about the nefarious gang. 'Nothing.'

'That's interesting, considering you're a high-ranking member.' He snorted. 'I can't believe it didn't occur to me before.'

'Wait, Alannah's in the Syndicate?' Jacob took a deep breath and eased it out.

'Oh right, I believe introductions are in order.' He stood upright. 'Jacob, meet Lady Ebony; Lady Ebony, meet Associate Jacob.'

When she looked at Jacob, his eyes widened. 'That's where you got the new car from?'

Alannah squinted. 'What are you talking about, Brendan?'

'The Dark Syndicate is a powerful criminal organisation comprising of dark mages and unseelie. They like to give their top-ranking members colour themed codenames to protect their identities. What's your rank, Lana? Captain? Underboss?'

The blood simmering away beneath Alannah's skin overboiled. 'I told you, I don't have a damn clue! Today is the first time I heard mention of this Syndicate. Besides, it's not like you can talk. You're selling them unsanctioned potions.'

Brendan took a deep breath. 'I guess she's playing all of us and we're goners if we don't work out her endgame soon.'

'Hold up. Who's playing us?' Jacob inquired.

'Lady Scarlett.' Brendan turned to face Jacob. 'Or should I say, Tara Winters?'

'Bloody hell! Scarlett is Tara? As in *the* Tara?' Jacob was pale, panting, and trembling.

Brendan might have felt sorry for him if the rascal had not gotten them into this mess in the first place. Tara must have known Jacob's family were Syndicate members and manipulated the situation to bring Brendan into the fold. He turned back to Alannah. 'What has she been teaching you?'

'We've only had a couple of training sessions thus far and she's focussed on getting me to channel the primordial.'

He shook his head. 'That takes an Arch Mage apprentice years to master. How the hell can she expect you to do it? Or is that her plan: to drag the training out and not give you the information you want?'

Alannah sighed. 'I had my first breakthrough on Tuesday night. It won't take me long to become fully attuned.'

His eyes were bugging out. 'Are you for real?'

She nodded. 'Apparently, I was born attuned. Something about the secret of the Beltane Blessing.'

'By the Gods!' he whispered.

'Did I hear right? Is Lady Scarlett—I mean Tara—training Alannah?'

'Yes, Jacob,' they replied in unison.

'I told you she had her secrets,' Brendan added with a sly grin directed at Alannah.

'Her endgame is pretty obvious.'

Brendan turned to face Jacob. 'Oh?'

Jacob nodded. 'She's going Palpatine on your arses.'

They both wrinkled their brows.

'You know, Emperor Palpatine from *Star Wars*?'

He glared at Jacob. 'I know who he is, asshat. But what do you mean?'

'Tara wants to bring you both over to the dark side.'

Brendan contemplated Jacob's theory. 'But what does she stand to gain from turning us dark?'

'She wants us to be allies, not enemies,' Alannah replied. 'It's been my theory all along. She is preparing me for a seat of power in the Council. I figure she's trying to manipulate me so I can be her puppet when I gain said position.'

Brendan dropped into an armchair and grinned at Alannah. 'See, I always knew you were much more than just a pretty face.'

Her eyes smouldered, and Brendan caught another glimpse of her lusty aura. She crossed her legs, bringing attention to her thighs as her short black skirt rose.

When Brendan lifted his gaze, her gleaming eyes narrowed on him, and her lips puckered.

Jacob cleared his throat, breaking the hold of Alannah's emerald eyes on Brendan. 'So, what's the plan?'

'I say we continue business as usual and use our positions to search for Tara's weakness.' Alannah suggested.

Brendan arched a brow at her. 'What weakness?'

'A way to bring about her true death. We can't kill liches by conventional means. That's why she didn't stay down when I killed her the first time.'

Damn, she is sexy when strategising. 'Okay, but we will have to be extra cautious. We should use these around the Syndicate, as well as Richard.' He held up one of the mind shields. 'Speaking of Richard, how did things go with him this morning?'

After picking up her own amulet, Alannah smiled. 'Better than expected. Your deflection technique worked. Although...'

'Although what?'

'Your visualisation suggestion worked too well.'

Brendan's eyes widened. 'You didn't?'

Those sweet cheeks turned pink as she bit her bottom lip.

Hot damn! His mind ran through all the dirty things he wanted to do to her right then and there. Thankfully, Jacob was present, else Brendan's resolution to keep his hands off her might have crumbled.

Alannah blinked, humour vanishing from her visage. 'Richard also told me something potentially useful. Apparently, Tara's sister, Dana, is now Queen of the Cursed. I don't know what their relationship is like, but we should investigate it.'

'Stupendous idea,' Jacob agreed.

'On that note: I'm gonna head over to Cailleach Estate and do some research.'

As soon as Alannah was on her feet, Brendan drew her into his arms. 'Please be careful, Lana. I can't bear the thought of losing you.'

'Likewise, Brendan.' Her head dropped into the crook of his neck, and he felt her inhale deeply. Pulling free, she glanced at Jacob. 'See ya.'

Jacob saluted her. 'Laters.'

Sighing, Brendan slumped back into his chair.

'Bro, it's as clear as my mum's obsessively cleaned windows how much Alannah wants you.'

'You don't need to tell me, or are you forgetting who's the enchanter here?'

Jacob shook his head. 'Sometimes I wonder if you're blind when it comes to her. But if you know how she feels, what's holding you back?'

'She's still with Liam.'

'So? What has he ever done to earn your loyalty?' Jacob retorted. 'Alannah is ripe for the picking and if you don't act soon, you might lose your only chance to get the girl.'

Brendan sat up in his chair, his heart thrashing erratically. 'You're right.'

Jacob grinned. 'Of course I'm right, *young Grasshopper*. Now let's get the lab moved. I got us a glamoured warehouse in Lonsdale.'

Most of the women had assembled in the Sailing Club meeting room. Alannah listened to Jessica Ó Máille and Danielle Sheridan gossiping about the girls their brothers were dating. On occasions like this, she missed Cara immensely. Even though the girls had warmed up to Alannah, she still felt like an outsider.

Unable to concentrate, she turned her attention to the window to watch the springtime drizzle trickling down the glass. Mesmerised by the view, she slipped into a meditative state. The familiar tingle of mana flowed through her, although she did not recognise the source.

A flurry of movement at the door drew everyone's attention and Alannah lost the connection. Monique strode into the room, flanked by Claudia and Charlotte Rowan. Alannah began to rise, but Monique pinned her in place with a deadly glare. 'Sit down.'

'Um, o…kay.' Alannah's heart thumped wildly. *What is going on?*

Monique moved to the head of the table. 'Ladies, it has come to my attention Alannah here is no longer a suitable leader for our group.'

'What? Why?' several voices queried.

'As you would all know by now, my uncle, the Inquisitor is in town.'

Oh Gods!

'And he has officially declared Alannah a *person of interest*. He won't say why, but it doesn't matter. His suspicions are enough to taint her reputation.'

A chorus of gasps shot through the room, including Alannah's. *Why am I hearing this from Monique rather than Richard or Kieran?* All eyes fell on her. 'I swear to the Gods I have no idea why he suspects me of anything. I haven't done anything wrong.'

'Monique's right, it doesn't matter. Your reputation will hurt our campaign,' Jessica retorted. Several others concurred with nods and muttered words.

Charlotte stepped forward. 'I nominate Monique to head up this lobby.'

'I second that,' Jessica agreed.

'No!' Alannah whispered, her heart racing as she felt her life spiralling out of control.

Danielle stood. 'All in favour of Monique Lane taking Alannah's Winters' place as our campaign leader?'

All but Alannah thrust a hand in the air. They may as well have plunged knives into her heart. At least she would not live to feel the sting of betrayal for long. Her stomach swam as she drifted toward the door.

Monique grabbed Alannah's arm as she passed and glowered. 'I told you I don't tolerate rogues.'

Yanking her arm free, Alannah returned the evil eye, and stormed out of the room.

When she got home, Alannah let the tears flow and her first thoughts turned to Brendan and his comforting hugs. Without thinking, she rang him.

'Hey, Lana.'

'Can you come over?'

'Hell! It sounds like you're crying. What's wrong?'

She choked back the lump forming in her throat. 'I need you here, Brendan. Please.'

'I'll be right there.'

A few minutes later Brendan burst through her front door without knocking. Panting heavily and imitating a drowned rat, he approached her in the front sitting room.

Alannah spoke through her sobs. 'Did you… run here?'

'Of course I did.' He tugged his wet t-shirt over his head and threw it over the bar heater. The sight of his bare chest sent a sudden jolt of heat to her core. Brendan had bulked out since high school, sporting an eight pack to rival Liam's. A twinkling of light caught her attention, highlighting the silver sleeper piercing his left nipple.

He dropped beside her on the antique divan, grabbed the soft fleece blanket she huddled under and wrapped it around them both as he pulled her into his arms. 'What happened, Lana?'

'You know the women's group I started?'

'Yeah.'

'Monique stole my position and ousted me from it tonight.'

'*What?* That bitch!' Brendan's tone was seething. 'Why did she betray you?'

'Apparently I am a *person of interest* in Richard's investigation.'

'Oh hell!' He squeezed her tighter. 'I'm sorry, Lana. This all my fault.'

'Brendan, don't. Please just hold me, okay?'

He sucked in a deep breath. 'Okay.'

With the sound of rain pelting against the roof, Alannah was lulled to sleep in Brendan's warm embrace.

Chapter Ten

Brendan did not whistle often. It usually took an incredibly wild night in the sack to elevate his mood enough, but all he needed this time was the memory of Alannah's warm body sleeping in his arms. Even visions of the murderous blaze in Liam's eyes—when he had come home from work—to find them curled up together could not kill Brendan's current buzz.

Placebo's song 'Pure Morning' played as he drove to his parents' place for the fortnightly family dinner. The lyrics resonated with him all day, and he whistled the tune as he stepped out of the car and walked toward the house.

'You sound cheerful this evening.' Nora, glancing up from salad preparation, smiled at him as he entered the kitchen.

He leaned over and planted a big wet one on her cheek. 'That's 'cause I am.'

Laughing, she wiped her cheek dry with the back of her hand. She stood upright and studied him a moment. 'Hmm. You're swooning. Just don't tell your dad. He's already angry with you after the stunt you pulled with Jessica. There's another girl here tonight. Her name's Wendy and she's from the Eyre Peninsula.'

Brendan grabbed a beer from the fridge, leaning against the pantry. 'Well, this Wendy form the Eyre Peninsula should go home because I'm not interested.'

Mum rolled her eyes. 'You haven't even met her yet. She is very pretty.'

'I don't care if she is Australia's next top model. Dad has to learn he can't dictate my love life.'

'You know he will keep trying until you settle on a pure mage.'

'Then he can stop trying because I've already settled on a bloodline babe.'

Her eyes widened, and she smacked his arm. 'Why didn't you say so before? Now don't keep me in suspense. Who is she?'

Raised voices sounded at the front door. 'Ah, that'd be her now. But shoosh; don't tell Dad.' He winked.

As soon as Nora recognised Alannah's voice, she frowned. 'Your joke is in poor taste.'

Hell! Are Liam and Lana arguing out there? 'It's not a joke. You'll see.'

Liam entered first. 'Hi Mum.' He embraced her briefly, glimpsed Brendan and gave him a death glare. 'What are you looking so smug about?'

'I don't know what you're talking about.' Brendan gave Alannah his best panty-dropping smile as she walked in. 'Hi gorgeous. How'd you sleep last night?'

Slamming the fridge after grabbing his drink, Liam growled and left the room.

'Brendan, must you…' Mum began, but she looked at Alannah and froze. Because of her Council position, Nora Winters was always open to emotions mana. There was no doubt she saw it too.

'Hey,' Alannah replied to Brendan as though he were the only person in the room. Crossing the floor, she squeezed him in a bear hug. All the while, her aura was broadcasting not only bright red, but bright pink too: the tell-tale mix of lust and love.

He glanced over Alannah's shoulder at his mother and gave her a satisfied grin.

Shaking her head, Nora mouthed *'Be Careful.'* She did not need to tell him. He knew he was playing with fire—quite literally in Liam's case—but Brendan had gained new determination to win Alannah fair and square.

When Brendan entered the living room, he did a double take at the sight of their two guests. *Woah! Aboriginal mages.* You did not see many of them around anymore. White settlement wiped most of them out, resulting in the migration of European mages to Australia during the Eighteen-Hundreds. His mum was right: the girl was attractive, but she was not his Lana.

Dad stepped forward. 'Brendan, I'd like to introduce you to Reginald and his daughter Wendy. They are from the Eyre Peninsula district.'

'Hi.' He shook their hands.

Following the remaining introductions, they all sat in the lounge area for their aperitif.

'So, Alannah… I heard you are leading a women's lobby group,' prompted Wendy.

Alannah's shoulders slumped. 'I was, but they kicked me out.'

'What?' Liam and Nora formed a chorus.

She focussed her attention on Liam. 'That's what upset me last night. According to Monique, Richard has declared me a *person of interest* and the rest of the group voted me out because of it.'

'Oh Gods, that sounds awful.' Wendy was trying to retreat into the depths of her chair. She was such a contrast to fire-cracker Jessica, the first of Dad's failed matchmaking attempts.

'Wait, why would Richard have reason to suspect you of anything?' Liam gave her a sidelong glance.

Alannah sighed. 'He interviewed me on Saturday. I didn't think he read anything to arouse suspicion, but I guess I was wrong.'

'And you failed to mention the Inquisitor came to visit? I'm sick of all the secrets, Lana.' Liam folded his arms and flared his nostrils.

'I wouldn't need to keep them from you if you were more tolerant and understanding.'

'Is that why you go crying on Brendan's shoulder instead of mine?'

'I've had enough of this.' She vaulted from her seat and escaped out the back door.

Brendan rose to follow her.

But Liam jumped in front of him. 'Where the hell do you think you're going?'

He glanced into the blue storm clouds staring back at him and smirked. 'To give her a shoulder to cry on.'

'Stay. The. Hell. Away. From. Her.' Drawing up to his full height, Liam towered over Brendan.

'Screw you, bro.' Brendan shoulder checked Liam as he strode toward the door, pausing to smile at Wendy. 'I'm sorry you had to see our family drama.' Without further ado, he took off.

After trudging along the side of the house, Alannah settled into one of the wicker hammocks on the front porch. She was taking stock of the epic clusterfuck she called her life when she heard footsteps approaching. Tensing at first, she released her breath as Brendan rounded the corner.

'Come on, Lana, let's get outta here.'

'I can't just leave.'

He smiled. 'Sure you can.'

'But Liam—'

'Is a douche canoe who needs to get over himself.' He reached out a hand to help her up. 'Now come on. It's time to pay our friend Jameson a visit.'

The hint of a smile crept onto her face. 'How do you always know what I need?'

His left brow, the one with the piercing, arched in the sexy way it does. 'Is that a rhetorical question, 'cause you know what my attunements are, right?'

She grabbed his hand and pushed herself out of the hammock. 'Yeah, but I reckon it's more than that.'

'Oh, you do, do you?'

'Yeah, I do.'

When they reached his Jag, Brendan opened the passenger door for her. After getting into the driver's seat, he looked at her. 'What do you think it is?'

'Hmm… I'm not telling.'

'I bet I can get you to tell me after a few drinks.'

Alannah sank into the comfortable upholstery and closed her eyes. The scent of leather blended with Brendan's cologne: an intoxicating mix. 'We'll see.' She loved his playlist too.

They stopped at the bottle shop in town before driving down to the beach front where Brendan found a secluded spot to park. He killed the engine, but kept the music going. 'Mind passing the two shot cups from the glovebox?'

She gave him a sidelong glance. 'Is drinking in your car a frequent occurrence?'

'Frequent enough. Are you gonna pass them over, or make me come and get them?'

Hmm, now there's an idea. She grabbed the two small plastic cups and examined them. 'Do you drink with all those girls you bone? I'm not gonna catch anything from using these am I?'

He chuckled. 'Firstly, you're a pure mage so you can't get human STIs. Secondly, I don't have the second cup for my hook-ups.'

'Then who do you drink with?'

'Jacob mostly. Sometimes one of the other guys.'

Relieved she was not about to share a shot glass with half the town's female population, she held them out for Brendan to pour their drinks. Alannah welcomed the burn of the whiskey going down. 'Gods, that feels awesome.' A moment later, she was reaching her hand out for more.

Brendan was smiling at her with amusement in his eyes.

'What?'

'You've always been my favourite drinking buddy.'

Alannah felt her heart swelling. 'Why?'

There was an impish grin on his face as he poured another round. 'That information will cost you.'

She laughed. 'Name your price.'

'An exchange of intel.'

'Nice try, but you won't get it out of me so easily.'

Brendan's pout was adorable. And too damn sexy. 'Shame. I guess I'll keep my secrets too, then.'

Sam Tinnesz and Yacht Money were singing 'Play with Fire', so Alannah closed her eyes and immersed herself in the strong, sensual beat. 'I love this song. You have much better taste in music than Liam.' Wondering why he did not make a smartass retort, she peeked at Brendan and sucked in a sharp breath.

His eyes were blazing. 'You're pretty pissed with him right now, aren't you?'

She nodded.

'I have an idea.' Brendan continued. 'How about you tell me all the ways I'm better than Liam and I'll tell you all the reasons you're my favourite drinking buddy.'

Alannah snorted. 'Can your over-inflated ego handle it?'

'When it comes to how I compare to Liam, I will take all the ego boosting I can get.' Given their history, Brendan was telling the painful truth.

'Okay, it's a deal. We'll go piece for piece. Since I began, you need to tell me something now.'

Grinning, Brendan poured more drinks, and settled back into his seat. 'For one, you hold your liquor better than most, Jacob included.'

'Wow, okay. Well, you are more tolerant and understanding than Liam.'

'I'll drink to that.' He downed his shot. 'You laugh a lot when drunk and I love your laugh.'

'You're a better fighter than Liam, both armed and unarmed.'

He gasped. 'Damn it's gratifying to hear it. You're more attractive than the others.'

'Hmph, the others are blokes and you're straight, so that's not hard.'

'Hey. I'm including Cara, Amy, and Bianca here.'

Her heartbeat sped up. 'You think I'm prettier than Bianca?'

Brendan smiled. 'Much.'

Considering Bianca was the girl he slept with the most, Alannah felt flattered. 'You have a better sense of humour than Liam. His jokes always make me cringe.'

'Ooh, damn, that's quite the burn. Which brings me to my next point. You throw shade better than anyone I know.'

'I don't need alcohol for that,' she scoffed.

'True, but it doesn't hurt. Speaking of which.' He held the bottle out and poured her another.

After throwing it back, she looked at Brendan and whispered. 'You give the best hugs.'

'Oh, Gods! You melted my heart, Lana.' He leaned back and closed his eyes a moment. Brendan's lids remained closed as he spoke. 'We click more than I do with the others. It feels like we have this deep understanding of each other. Being with you is more exciting and more… meaningful.'

Woah! Talk about heart-melting. 'That's why…' she whispered.

His eyes flicked open. 'What did you say?'

Alannah found herself leaning toward him to keep her voice hushed. 'That's why you always know what I need. You know me better than anyone else.'

'Better than Liam?'

She nodded. 'Yeah, even better than Liam.'

Brendan bit his lip and winced. 'Damn that bastard. There's still one way he knows you better.' When his penetrating gaze turned on her, Alannah's cheeks flushed. His eyes flashed and he brought his fingers up to her face, brushing his knuckles along her burning skin.

Power surged through Alannah and an acute headache struck, forcing her eyes closed. In her mind she saw Brendan bending her over a bed and fucking and spanking her hard while her screams of pain induced ecstasy rang through the air. Suddenly, Liam barged in and shot Brendan with a lightning bolt. She opened her eyes again as the vision ended.

'Are you okay, Lana?' Brendan's voice trembled.

While short, the vision packed one hell of a punch. And she knew it was a cosmic warning.

'Lana?' His hand cupped her chin.

As the pain eased, she looked at him. 'I'm okay. It was just a headache. I think I've had enough to drink.'

Brendan screwed up his face but held his tongue. Something on her nose drew his attention. 'Okay.' He tapped her diamond stud. 'I have an idea.'

'Oh-oh. Sounds dangerous.'

'You know I live for danger.' He winked and started the car. Five minutes later he parked the car. 'How about we get some new body bling?' Brendan gestured toward a shop with a small white neon sign: *Brocade Spider, Body Art and Piercings*. 'My treat.'

When they stepped back out of the salon, Alannah no longer felt tension in her shoulders. Meredith, the lady who pierced her belly button, was a hoot.

Brendan linked her arm with his. 'Where to now, my lady?'

Not wanting to tempt fate, she sighed. 'I should go home.'

His brows furrowed. 'Are you sure?'

'Yeah.'

'Okay.' They walked to the car in silence. Music filled the short drive, lessening the tension in the air.

Liam's car was absent from the driveway when they arrived, alleviating the knots in Alannah's shoulders. She hated dealing with his moods. Brendan followed her inside and down the hall. When they reached the kitchen, she glanced at him. 'Coffee?'

'Sure. Thanks.'

While Brendan sipped his drink, she studied him.

He glanced up from his cup and cocked his left brow. 'What?'

'I'm wondering what you had pierced tonight.'

Brendan smouldered. 'I'll show you mine if you show me yours.'

'Fine.' Alannah put her coffee down and unbuttoned her jeans. She gasped when he did the same. She was expecting him to lift his t-shirt to show her a second nipple piercing since she could not see anything new on his face or ears.

His eyes widened. 'Now I'm intrigued.'

'So am I.' *Where exactly did Brendan get his bling?* All sorts of images filled her mind, none of them wholesome.

'How intrigued?' He nudged his waistband down while his mouth twisted into a lewd grin.

'Did you seriously get a cock piercing?'

'Yup. Now tell me if you *want* to see it.'

'This feels like a game of Sleazy Chicken.'

'Once more, for old time's sake?' His eyes pleaded with her.

'Okay, I'll bite. Besides, it's not like I haven't seen you naked before. But I doubt you'll show me. Willingly baring yourself to me is different to incidental exposure.'

'This isn't a question of how far *I'll* go; it rarely is. The issue here is whether you truly want to see it. Do you want to feast your eyes upon my dick, Lana?'

Alannah's cheeks flamed as lust pooled at her core.

Brendan rushed her, pinning her against the wall. 'Do you know why I usually win Sleazy Chicken?'

Swallowing hard against the tension mounting in her throat, Alannah held his gaze. 'Because you're a bigger sleaze than me.'

He inched closer. 'Wrong answer.'

'Okay, then why?'

'Because I'm never bluffing.' Brendan pushed his weight against her and hissed telepathically in her mind. *'I. Want. You. Lana. I've wanted you for as long as I can remember. When I said I wasn't in love with you; I lied. And right now, all I want to do is kiss you senseless, throw you down, and bang your brains out.'*

Another of her instinctive powers manifested, showing her Brendan's aura. The bright red flickering of lust within the bright pink colour of love confirmed the truth. Not to mention the bulge in his pants. *'Fuck!'* she whispered through clenched teeth.

'Exactly.' His expression turned wild and wicked.

The sound of keys unlocking the front door, followed by approaching footsteps resounding off the wooden floorboards of the hall sent Brendan darting across the room. He fastened his jeans with expert deftness, as though he had been in similar situations countless times. *Then again, he probably had.*

Her own jittery fingers fumbled with her button fly, scarcely getting the last one as Liam entered the room. Bracing herself for his rage, she bit her bottom lip to stop it trembling.

But when he slumped against the kitchen bench there was no spark left in him. 'I didn't think you would come home tonight.'

Alannah's heart broke. Stepping up to Liam, she wrapped her arms around him. 'I'm sorry,' she whispered.

Bringing his own arms up to encircle her, Liam peered into her eyes with barely constrained tears. 'It feels like I'm losing you, Lana.'

'I'll see myself out.' Brendan's bitter tone cut through the air and into Alannah's already aching heart.

She wanted to go after him, but Liam needed her too. *When did it all become so complicated?* Pressing her forehead to Liam's, she felt a tear slide down her cheek. 'You haven't lost me. I'm right here.'

He claimed her mouth in a hungry kiss. She could not remember the last time they had kissed with such raw passion. The taste of choc-mint on his breath mingled with her own coffee and whiskey aftertaste, fuelling the fire of desire in her core. Alannah wrapped her legs around Liam's waist, clinging to his body like a monkey. They continued kissing as he walked them through the hallway and into the bedroom.

After he took his sweet time making love to her, Liam enfolded her in his arms. 'I'm sorry, Lana. I haven't been here enough for you. I'm taking some time off work to spend with you.' He tucked a strand of hair behind her ear. 'If you still want me?'

Tears were streaming from her eyes as she nodded.

'Hey, we've just had a hiccup, but we'll get past it. And I promise to support you more. I love you so much, Lana.'

'I love you, too,' she sobbed. *And my heart tears in two.*

Chapter Eleven

The next morning, Liam needed to head into the police station to finish some paperwork and tie up a few loose ends before taking leave. So, Alannah took the opportunity to confront Brendan. After ringing his bell twice, she beat down his door.

He eventually answered, yawning as he opened the door. 'What the hell, Lana? Do you know how early it is?' Brendan's jet-black hair was more dishevelled than usual, and his only clothing was a pair of low-hanging baggy grey track pants. Under different circumstances the sight might have been a serious distraction for Alannah.

'Stop your whingeing. You'd be at work by now if you weren't on holidays. Can I come in?'

Crossing his arms, he narrowed his eyes. 'Depends.'

'On what?' She could feel her patience slipping away.

'Are you here because you dumped my lunkhead brother and want to spend the day trying every position of the *Kama Sutra* with me?'

'What? No! Brendan—'

'Then my answer is no.' He slammed the door in her face.

Crap! What a disaster. Grabbing her keys, Alannah let herself in. *'Brendan!'*

He was halfway down the hall. 'Why did you bother asking if you were gonna barge your way in?'

'I was trying to be polite. Now stop being a dick and listen to me.'

When they reached his living room, he sprawled out on the couch and scowled at her. 'I'm all ears.'

Letting out a sigh, Alannah pushed his feet off the sofa and sat next to him. 'Are you seriously sulking because I won't screw you?'

'You also woke me up. And you know I'm not a morning person at the best of times, let alone when hungover.'

She shook her head. 'You only had four shots last night. I drank more than you.'

He pulled an empty whiskey bottle from under the couch. 'Finished it when I got home. I'll give you three guesses why.'

Alannah blinked at him.

'What? Not even one guess? Fine, I'll tell you why. Only minutes after I bared my heart to you, Lana, you went running back into Liam's arms. I honestly thought I was getting somewhere with you last night, but once again the golden boy comes in and sweeps you up.'

Speechless. She was utterly speechless for several long minutes while staring at him. Averting her eyes, she inhaled deeply. 'Why did you have to wait until now to make your move? Now things are serious for Liam and me? You had plenty of opportunities in the past.'

'You truly want to know?'

She turned back to face him. 'Yes, Brendan. It's about time you were open and honest with me.'

He sniggered. 'Like you're one to talk.'

'What's that supposed to mean?'

'You're the one who's been shutting me out these last four years.'

'I've had my reasons.'

Tucking his thighs up to his chest, Brendan dropped his chin to his knees. 'Just as I had reasons for keeping my feelings under wraps. There has never been a right time with you, Lana. When we were kids, you were always like "Liam this, Liam that." I'll never forget the night following your mum's funeral. That day was doubly painful for me: not only did I lose Aunt Aileen, but I felt like I lost you too.'

Alannah's brow creased. 'What are you talking about?'

'Liam and I came to check on you that night. When we stopped outside your door, we overheard you talking to your Melbourne friend, Emma.'

She gaped at him, recalling the personal chat.

He continued, 'You remember it, don't you? Sometimes the conversation replays in my mind:

Emma started it. 'So, those cousins of yours are way hot.'

You giggled before responding, 'Yeah, they are.'

Liam and I exchanged glances and he almost went to leave, clearly feeling guilt over eavesdropping. But I grabbed his arm and gestured for him to stay quiet and remain listening with me.

'So, you're down with kissing cousins?' Emma queried.

'Hell yeah. I would totally let one of the guys comfort me in bed tonight.'

I got painfully hard hearing your admission. Then I saw the surprise in Liam's eyes and almost laughed out loud. He was so innocent for a fourteen-year-old guy; something that was an endless source of amusement for me.

Emma asked the question Liam and I were both dying to hear you answer: 'Who would you choose?'

The time you took to consider your answer was a nerve-racking moment for the two of us. We stood there staring at each other, waiting with bated breath.

You cleaved my heart in two when you replied, 'Well, I've had the biggest crush on Liam for as long as I can remember, so it would feel divine to have him kiss my tears away.'

The biggest grin I've ever seen formed on the mofo's face, and he stared at me with smug satisfaction. Not wanting to cause a scene on such a sombre occasion, I flipped him off and hightailed it out of there.

Heaving a huge sigh, Brendan leaned back and pressed his head against the back of the couch. He shut his eyes for a second. Still reclined, he turned his face to her. 'When you returned to us, I kept trying to read you, to see if your feelings had changed; but aside from the odd flash of lust, you didn't give me hope of mutual affections.'

'So, what's changed? Why now? I'm more in love with Liam than ever.'

'I know, and it scares me, Lana. I figured I had to act before I lost my chance entirely.' Moving closer to her, Brendan grabbed the nape of her neck and gazed down upon her. 'The morning you walked in on me with Thornsy's sister, you let your guard down, just as you have a few times since. Not to mention the nightclub.'

She closed her eyes to suppress the threatening tears brought on by the painful memory of that night.

'Open your damn eyes, Lana.'

'I can't.'

'Why do you keep shutting me out?'

It was no use. The tears broke free as she pushed out of Brendan's grip and jumped to her feet. She glared at him as she screamed, *'Because it hurts to let you in.* Every time I opened myself to you, and to the possibility of intimacy with you, you rejected me. I don't know what twisted game you are playing with my emotions, but if your goal is to inflict maximum pain, you won. Congratulations for breaking my heart.' Unable to take anymore, Alannah fled from Brendan's apartment.

'Oh hell.' Brendan raced after Alannah but stopped at the door, remembering he was half-naked.

After a quick shower, he threw on the first clothes he could find in the washing basket, jumped in the Jag and gunned it until he reached Alannah's house. But when he saw Liam getting out of his SUV, Brendan refrained from leaving his own car. *What the hell is he doing home already?*

The arsehole turned toward Brendan with a smug grin.

'Damnit!' He smacked the steering wheel and took off.

One roadhouse coffee and steak sandwich later, he found himself driving aimlessly around the countryside. *How did I botch things so much with Lana? I am meant to be the expert when it comes to reading people.* He floored it as soon as he hit the highway. Brendan needed a rush—any rush to numb the pain! And he did not even care when a speed camera flashed behind him. But even the thrill of riding his second-favourite girl was not enough to get his mind off the first.

His subconscious drove him to Bianca's estate, not surprising him at all. The nymph waited for him on the porch as usual because she could always sense him coming. 'Well hey there, stranger. It's been a while.' She styled her long black hair in the usual pigtails and wore a short black mesh dress that left nothing to the imagination.

He grabbed her arms in a vice grip. 'Quit with the pleasantries and screw me already.'

Bianca giggled and the green vine pattern all over her tanned skin glowed as she channelled mana. 'Your rotten mood tells me this is gonna be some angry sex. I can't wait!'

'Then why are you still talking?' Brendan growled as he pulled her into his arms and devoured her mouth.

Clothes flew to her bedroom floor in a frenzy and only his satin boxers remained as they crashed onto her bed. Their lips and tongues duelled for several minutes until Brendan drew back to grab a foil packet from his wallet.

With the distance between them, Bianca gasped; her eyes wide as she stared at him.

He flinched. 'What? Do I have a nasty bruise or something?'

She shook her head gradually as she whispered, 'Your aura.'

'Tell me sweetheart, what do your nymph eyes see? Aside from the healthy red glow telling you I'm about to rock your world.'

Her eyes sought his, killing the mood when he saw tears swelling in them. Dropping back on the bed, Brendan reached out to place a comforting hand on her shoulder, but she backed away. 'You're freaking me out now, B. What's wrong?'

'What have you done, Brendan?'

His brow creased as he approached her, prompting her to retreat further. 'What do you mean, what have I done?'

'Your inner aura. It's tainted with shades of grey. You've been practising dark magic.'

He recoiled. 'Damn! I didn't realise how nasty things were. Promise me you won't tell anyone?'

The tears slid down Bianca's cheeks. 'I'm not gonna tell anyone, but whatever you've been doing is wrong Brendan, and it's damaging your soul. You need to stop as soon as possible. If you don't, you're gonna do permanent damage. Once your inner aura goes completely dark, there's no coming back.'

He rubbed the side of his face. Brendan did not know the potion making was dark enough to corrupt his soul. He understood Bianca's warning though. The fall of the dark warrior was among the parables Dad had read to him as a bedtime story. It was a lesson taught to all young mages meant to keep them in line:

> 'Stick to the right-hand path, Son, and your soul will never darken. Mages who defile their souls by performing unsanctioned magic become dark mages.'
>
> 'What is a dark mage, Dad?'
>
> 'Outlaw mages who lose their way—like Donovan, the dark warrior. He became so obsessed with power for its own sake his soul darkened over time until it turned black. Once that happened, he could no longer seek redemption. Upon his death, Donovan's soul joined the cursed in the Underworld. And he fathered children with tainted souls too.'

Tara's plan is working. 'Thanks for the warning, B. I'll try to stop, but it won't be easy to get out of the mess I'm in.'

'Does this have anything to do with the Inquisitor investigating Alannah?'

Hearing Alannah's name was like having the knife in his heart twisted. 'You know about that?'

Bianca nodded. 'Yeah. Cara told me.'

Leaning back against the headboard, Brendan sighed heavily. 'Everything's complicated right now. It's best if I don't tell you anything, for your own sake.'

'Oh, sweetheart, I'm sorry. I can see how much you're hurting. Come here.'

And so, Brendan lost himself in Bianca's arms, forgetting his grief for a few sweet hours.

Alannah had survived the start of pub night by confining herself to the corner of their booth with Cara for quality girl chat. But when her bestie headed for the bathrooms, Jacob stalked after her, giving Brendan an opening.

He slid across the seat and leaned in. 'Are you still avoiding me, Lana?'

She eyed his beer. 'Depends.'

'On what?'

'If you're buying the next two rounds.'

Brendan slapped some money down in front of Bailey. 'Be a pal and get us two more jugs, will you?'

Bailey frowned at him. 'I'm not your damn beer wench, bro.'

'Please, pretty please?' Brendan gave him a pouty face complete with batting lashes.

'Fine, but I'm keeping the change.'

With Bailey gone, Caleb was the only person left at their table and he was busy scrolling through memes on his phone. Ben and Nick were playing pool, and Connor and Amy had taken off early for some couple-time.

Moving in close enough for their thighs and shoulders to touch, Brendan whispered in her ear, 'I've been trying to catch you at home since yesterday morning, but Liam's been hanging around you like a bad smell.'

'He took leave from work to spend time with me.' Alannah stole Brendan's drink and chugged it down in one go.

'Bloody hell, woman, you're killing me.' He grinned. 'So, where is that bad smell tonight?'

'The Council summoned him for business. The Inquisitor has his pet warlocks on the prowl trying to sniff out anyone using or dealing Rhapsody.'

A wicked gleam appeared in his eyes. 'Did you call Liam a dog?'

'What? No!'

'You totally did. You said, and I quote, "A pet on the prowl trying to sniff people out." Sounds like a dog to me.'

'Hmph! Liam's more like an alpha wolf.'

'Touché.' He waggled his brows. 'Don't tell me you have a thing for weres now, Lana?'

Alannah snorted. 'No way!'

'*Sure...* Tell me, did this furry fetish come on before or after you saw Ben in action?'

She punched his arm. 'Will you ever let me live that down?'

'Hell no!' He laughed.

Bailey delivered their jugs of ale and resumed his conversation with Caleb.

After taking a decent mouthful of her drink, Alannah giggled as the alcohol buzz kicked in. She pressed her mouth to Brendan's ear. 'You know the only reason I looked at Ben and Nick that time was so you wouldn't see who initially drew my attention.'

'Hmm, is that so?'

She nodded.

'So, you weren't getting aroused by the sight of so much inky muscle?'

Alannah let out a hearty laugh. 'Nope. Tats don't do it for me as much as piercings.'

Brendan shot the other guys a cursory glance before whispering, 'Hell! I better not let you see Thornsy naked.'

'You are treb… turb… terrible.'

He grinned at her. 'And you're drunk.'

'No shit, Sherblock.'

Brendan burst out laughing and Alannah joined him. When he was able to catch a breath, he gazed at her and nodded. 'Yup, still my favourite drinking buddy.' But then his expression turned serious. 'I'm sorry, Lana.'

Her brow furrowed. 'For what?'

'For messing everything up between us.' Reclining against the backrest, he closed his eyes. 'I thought I was doing the right thing when I gave Liam a second chance with you.'

She inhaled sharply. 'What do you mean?'

Brendan looked at her with glistening eyes. 'Remember the time he left you and hooked up with Monique because he misread the situation with Austin?'

Wincing at the memory, she sobered. 'Yeah.'

'Our drinking session that night was the first time I sensed you wanted me. It took every ounce of willpower in my depraved brain to keep my hands off you.'

Alannah's eyes widened. 'Why *did* you… (swallow)… keep your hands off me?'

'Because we needed Liam on our side in the war against Tara.' He took a deep breath. 'And if I'm honest with myself, it's 'cause I'm a damn coward for heeding Liam's threats.'

Biting her lip, Alannah found her mind churning through a bunch of what-ifs.

'What are you thinking about, Lana?'

'I wonder how different things might have been if you'd stuck around to hear the rest of that conversation with Emma.'

'Why?'

'Because if you had stayed, you would have heard me tell Emma I wanted you.'

Brendan stared at her in silence.

'After I told her about my crush on Liam, she retorted:

'But Brendan looks so fuckable.'

'Ah huh. Which is why he'd be my choice for the night. That guy is like a wet dream walking, and I'm sure he'll feature in mine for years to come.'

Emma snorted, 'Ha! Come! I get it.'

I gave her one of my eyerolls before continuing. 'There's nothing I wouldn't let him do to me. With the bad boy look he's got going, he's like all my wildest fantasies come to life.'

'Wait, does that mean you want them both?'

'Yeah, I suppose it does.' I shrugged with a devilish grin.

'Gods damn, woman, I am so hard for you right now.' Brendan paused for a deep breath. 'Explains why Liam didn't comfort you in bed that night. He must've been fuming.'

'Crap! Was he still listening after you left?'

Brendan nodded. 'Probably wanted to hear you go on about him some more.'

'No wonder he always worries about the two of us.'

Pinning her with a scorching gaze, Brendan rested his hand on Alannah's thigh as he addressed the elephant in the room with a deep, toe curling voice, 'Question is, should we give him a real reason to worry?'

Chapter Twelve

After sealing the last of the mother tincture vials, Brendan glanced up from his work to see Jacob entering their industrial hideout. 'Hey, man.'

Jacob stepped up for a fist bump, casting his eyes over the stainless-steel bench. 'Woah, bro, is that a double batch?'

Flopping down on a couch in their make-shift lounge area, Brendan stretched his arms victoriously, and placed them behind his neck. 'Yup. Let's just say inspiration struck.'

'Good work. This should keep Violet off our backs for a while.' Jacob joined him on the sofa. 'Does this inspiration have anything to do with a certain goth beauty?'

'Maybe.'

'Ah, come on, man. I saw how cosy the two of you were last night. Did anything happen after I left?'

Brendan drew a deep breath, easing into the backrest. 'Nothing physical, but I made a breakthrough with her. Lana admitted she wants me.'

Jacob's face lit up. 'That's great, Brendo.' Contorting his face, he leaned forward. 'So, why aren't you spending your weekend making sweet, sweet love to her?'

'Because she won't cheat on Liam. She also needs time to think before making her decision because of some misguided affection for the wanker.' Brendan had had a lot of wicked thoughts since parting ways with Alannah at the pub and a new one was forming. 'I have to keep proving to Lana I'm her best option. Liam's bound to slip up eventually.'

'That's the spirit.' After rising to his feet, Jacob returned to the bench and grabbed half the vials of potion concentrate. 'I better get one of these batches in Syndicate hands before they send the collectors after me.'

'Collectors?'

'They're the brutes who get sent to collect on late shipments; with interest, mind you.'

The idea made Brendan's skin crawl. 'Would I be right in guessing the interest isn't anything with monetary value?'

'All depends how generous their boss is feeling on any given day. Besides, most things carry monetary value on the Unseelie Market.'

A shiver travelled down Brendan's spine. 'That's dark, bro.'

Jacob shrugged. 'Welcome to my world.'

'I'd rather stay as far away from your world as possible, thanks. Once we work out a way to deal with Tara, I want out of this potion business.'

'For real?' Jacob's lips pressed tight together as his forehead creased.

'I'm sorry, man, but this venture is destroying my soul, literally. It's been fun and all, but I won't turn dark for it.'

Jacob sighed. 'Fine. Speaking of fun, have we got any spare Rhapsody of our own? I'm planning on hitting the clubs with Cara tonight.

'There's plenty in the fridge.'

'Sweet.' After grabbing a few vials, he held one up in Brendan's direction. 'You wanna come with?'

He shook his head. 'Liam's busy tonight, so I'm gonna work my magic on Lana some more.'

Jacob arched his brow. 'You sly devil. Good luck.' As he approached the exit, he turned around with an impish grin. 'Just don't do anything I wouldn't do.'

Brendan laughed. 'Sounds like free reign to me.'

He snorted as he reached for the doorhandle.

'Oh, and Jacob?' Brendan called after him.

Jacob glanced over his shoulder. 'Hmm?'

'Be careful out there. The Inquisitor has every warlock in the state on the hunt tonight.'

'Thanks for the heads up,' Jacob nodded before leaving.

With Liam on annual leave, Alannah did not know when she would get another opportunity to see Scarlett for a while. She decided to kill two birds with one stone and emphasise the platonic condition of meeting Brendan.

As soon as Brendan answered his door, Alannah hugged him, savouring the feel of his body pressed against hers. Reluctantly releasing him, she strode toward her Tesla. 'Come on, we'll take my car.'

'Wait up a minute. Shouldn't *I* be taking *you* out?' He waggled his brow.

After suppressing her traitorous hormones with a deep breath, Alannah simpered. 'Not a date, remember?'

He let out an exaggerated sigh. 'So you keep reminding me.' Sitting in the car, Brendan connected his phone to the stereo. 'But I still get to choose the music.'

Alannah shrugged as she started the engine. 'Fine by me. We like all the same tunes anyway.' When he did not reply, she glanced at him and caught the biggest grin she had ever seen on his face. 'What?'

'I was remembering all the ways *you* think I'm better than Liam.'

She giggled. 'You're relentless.'

Brendan leaned in close to speak in her ear. 'And you're gorgeous.'

Exhaling sharply, Alannah tried to ignore the flutters in her stomach and focussed on the road. His first song choice — 'Play with Fire' — had not escaped her attention. *Figures Brendan is playing dirty now the cards are all on the table.* Liam's ignorance of the situation gave Brendan an unfair advantage and she needed to keep reminding herself of that at times like this.

As soon as they left town, Brendan shifted in his seat, turning to gaze upon her. 'So, where are we going?'

'You'll see.'

'Hmm, colour me intrigued.' His voice was deep and sexy. 'What are we going to do when we get to this *mystery* location?'

'You'll see.'

'If you don't give me any clues, I'm gonna start imagining all manner of erotic things.'

Alannah snorted. 'You can imagine what you like; it won't change the reality.'

'True, but it will get my cock hard, and when you see the effect you have on me, your thoughts will go there too.'

Her mind was already there thanks to his filthy mouth.

'And there he goes,' Brendan remarked.

Unable to help herself, Alannah glimpsed the tent in his jeans. As her eyes rose, Brendan's gaze caught her. The distraction was enough to make her swerve onto the other side of the road. 'Crap!' *Thank the Gods there was no oncoming traffic.*

'Eyes on the road while driving, Lana. But if you want a better view, you could always pull over.'

She rolled her eyes. 'Nice try.'

'I'm just getting started, gorgeous.'

Something occurred to Alannah. 'If you did not bluff when playing Sleazy Chicken, how is this only the second time I've seen your arousal?'

'I'm sure there have been more times when you didn't notice, but as a rule I used magic to control my own emotions.'

'I suspected as much.' Glancing at Brendan, she gestured to his erection with a flick of her eyes. 'You might want to do something about *that* before we arrive because we will have company when we get there.'

'Would you like to help me?' Again, with the voice.

'I'm not touching your dick tonight, Brendan.'

He sighed. 'Shame.' The sound of a zipper opening hit Alannah's ears.

She willed herself not to peek. 'What are you doing?'

'Do you want a detailed description? Firstly, I've lowered my fly, so now my hand…'

Alannah felt her cheeks flush. '*Brendan*! Don't you dare jerk off in my car!'

'Hey, you told me to take care of it.'

'I meant by using your emotion controlling powers.'

'Then you should've specified.'

She shook her head. 'You're incorrigible.'

'Only when it comes to you.'

Alannah felt sceptical. Brendan's history with girls and his self-professed need for variety were the main factors weighing against him and they were biggies. But she did not know how to approach the issue with him.

Brendan fell silent, focussing on his breathing, until they reached the old wooden hut. 'Mm.' His tone was suggestive.

'Mm, what?'

'A secret rendezvous in the woods. This seems less like a date and more like skipping straight to the part where we rip each other's clothes off and…'

When they rounded the corner, Scarlett's Mercedes came into view, shutting him up. Alannah parked alongside the red car and turned to face a gaping Brendan. 'You were saying?'

'Hell, woman! You could have warned me!'

'I thought you might not agree to come with me,' Alannah admitted as she grabbed her mind shield and put it around her neck. Holding the silver charm, she focussed on blocking all thoughts about Scarlett and the Syndicate. She activated the illusion spell by pressing the blue lace agate in the centre, rendering it invisible against her chest.

Brendan did the same, narrowing his eyes on her. 'For the record, I'd rather walk into the pits of the Underworld with you than enter the Celestial realm without you. I just want to be with you Lana, regardless where.'

Her breath hitched at his words.

After a pregnant pause, Brendan broke the silence by clearing his throat. 'So, what's the plan here?'

'Tell her you're here to make sure I'm safe because you still don't trust her. Then watch the training session and suss out the situation. We will debrief afterwards.'

His brow rose. 'Is that it? Won't Tara alter her approach with me present?'

'It's possible, but I suspect she trusts you because of your ties to the Syndicate.'

Brendan sighed. 'Okay, let's get on with it.'

Scarlett smiled as they entered the sanctuary. 'Hello Brendan. What a pleasant surprise.'

He scowled at her. 'I'm here to make sure Lana's safe.'

Their grandmother nodded. 'Of course. I would not expect any less from you, given the depth of your love for her.'

Hearing Scarlett confirm Brendan's feelings knocked the air out of Alannah's lungs. When she glanced at him, his eyes fixed on her.

He spoke in her mind. *'It's true, Lana.'*

Scarlett stepped closer. 'Well Brendan, do you want to enter the circle, or watch from the lounge?'

'I'll take my chances *in* the circle, thanks,' he replied.

'Very well. You know what to do, Ebony.'

Alannah commenced casting the circle. When they sat, she placed her athame between herself and Brendan. This would allow either of them to cut their connection to the circle.

Scarlett looked at her. 'I want you to attempt the channelling exercise I talked you through last week, only without my guidance this time.'

She sank into a meditative state. Before long, the familiar rush of primordial power flowed through her.

'Excellent, dear child. Have you been practising?'

'Yes,' Alannah admitted.

'Keep it up. Once it becomes second nature, you should be able to keep the channel open in much the same way as you do with Aether. This will allow you to access any other mana source you want.' Scarlett leaned forward and retrieved a large white crystal cluster from the altar. 'Do you know what this?'

'No.'

'This is apophyllite, often used in healing magic—but it has a hidden property few mages know.' She looked from Alannah to Brendan, and back again. 'It provides a safe way to channel the stygian element.'

'*What?*' Brendan interjected. 'There's no way you're teaching Lana that shit.'

'Brendan, please.' Alannah's eyes pleaded with him, and his jaw stiffened as he stopped himself from talking. She returned her attention to Scarlett. 'I don't like the idea of messing with nether.'

'Just hear me out, please. I will not force you to do anything you do not want. In fact, I only planned to give you a demonstration tonight. It is true working with nether has its dangers, the least of which being the use of the highly toxic cinnabar crystal. Apophyllite does not only negate the need for a mercury compound, but it also protects the mind, body, and soul from the necrotic effects of nether.'

'What about the moral and legal repercussions of channelling such an evil power source?' Brendan glared at her.

Scarlett laughed. 'Your concern surprises me, considering your recent activities. But to answer your question, there is nothing innately evil with channelling nether; how you choose to use the power matters. But because the Council is stubborn with rules, it is illegal to even access it, which is why there is no representative for it. The flipside is the Council cannot detect use of the stygian element.'

Alannah leaned in. 'Aside from summoning demons, what use is there in channelling nether?'

'It can also be used to negate the effects of other spells, which is what makes it useful, but also dangerous in the Council's opinion. They reserve such knowledge for Arch Mages.'

'Yet more secrets,' Alannah mused.

Scarlett grinned. 'Exactly. Now, can I show you how?'

Alannah nodded. 'Yeah, okay. Just don't summon any demons.'

The drive back to Brendan's place was silent and tense, with Alannah losing herself in thought. Gods knew what was going through his mind. Intending to drop him off and go straight home, she pulled up along the curb.

Brendan sucked in a breath and stared at her. 'You coming in?'

'I don't think I should.'

'We still need to debrief. And Liam doesn't get home for hours yet.'

Alannah sighed. 'Fine.' She followed him through the small cottage garden leading to his apartment.

When they reached his open plan living area, Brendan grabbed a bottle of expensive whiskey and two glasses. 'I don't know about you, but I need something to take the edge off.'

'Thanks.' Settling on the lounge, Alannah turned her whole body to face Brendan. 'So, what do you make of everything?'

After draining his glass in one mouthful, he gazed at her. 'Your theory about her grooming you to be a puppet is pretty accurate. The woman's manipulations are subtle and effective. And the worst part? She let me read her the whole time, so I know she wasn't lying.'

'What if she's a convincing liar?'

He shook his head. 'With the way I read her, there's no way she could have been. That's not to say she wasn't lying by omission, but the words she spoke were true. Every single one of them.'

'Damn. So, why is she manipulating me?'

'Am I right in guessing she's been drip feeding you high level Council secrets each time you meet?'

Alannah took a moment to think back over their previous meetings, finishing her drink as she did. 'Pretty much, yeah.'

Brendan nodded. 'She wants to turn you against the Council so you'll challenge their authority and push her agenda. And it's already working. I could see how pissed you were about all the secrets they keep from us.'

Rage flared through her blood. 'Aren't you? They have no right to keep this crap from us.'

A lascivious grin formed on his face. 'You are so damn hot when you get fired up like this. I'd love to translate your anger into passionate sex.'

Her jaw dropped to the floor, and she punched his bicep.

Brendan grabbed her wrist upon impact. 'Do you have any idea how much your small outbursts of violence turn me on?'

Speechless, Alannah shook her head.

His eyes lit up with wicked intent a second before he pulled her onto his lap such that she straddled him. Her skirt rode up, exposing her most intimate parts to the sensation of Brendan's arousal grinding against her through his jeans.

Alannah's core flooded with desire.

His eyes darkened with pure lust. 'Oh hell! You are so damn wet, Lana.'

A small moan escaped her mouth when his deep voice uttered her name, and again as both his hands tightened their grip on her wrists.

'You are so horny I bet I could take you over the edge with friction alone.' He bucked his pelvis a couple more times.

Alannah let her head fall back as her throat released a guttural sound. Brendan was right; her climax was imminent.

'If you don't stop me now, Lana, I will do it. I will make you come all over me.' His tone was low and threatening in the sexiest way possible.

A distant part of her brain screamed at her to stop, but she could not hear it over her groans. She was putty in Brendan's hands and resistance was useless. His movements became harder and faster, tipping her over the edge. '*Aaah!*' He ripped the scream from her, along with her orgasm.

'Wowsers!' Brendan mumbled as she collapsed against him. He encircled her with his arms, and whispered in her ear, 'Was that possible because I turn you on like no one else can, or because Liam hasn't been taking care of your needs?'

'Could you shut up for a minute?' she mumbled against his hard chest. Guilt and shame mixed with the sweet pleasure of her afterglow. When Brendan caressed her head, Alannah trembled. It was too much to process. She clambered free of his hold and curled up on the opposite side of the sofa.

He regarded her with darting eyes, as though she was a wild animal.

After a few deep breaths, she relaxed her muscles. A glimpse of the wet patch on Brendan's jeans set her cheeks on fire. 'You… uh… might want to change those.'

'Nah, I'm good. In fact, I doubt I'll ever wash them again.'

She screwed up her nose. 'That's disgusting.'

'There's nothing gross about your sexual juices, Lana. I didn't have you pegged for the type to be self-conscious about them either.'

'I'm not, but those jeans will turn rank after a while.'

He grinned. 'I'll cross that bridge when I come to it.'

Alannah sighed. 'I still haven't made my decision, Brendan.'

After jumping to his feet, Brendan spun to face her. 'What else is there to think about? You've already listed about six ways in which I'm better than Liam, some of which are a pretty big deal in my opinion. And the chemistry between us is *so* off the charts you just sprayed the evidence all over me. What more do you need?'

Rising, she faced him head on. 'I need commitment—something I can't trust a playboy like you to give me.' She escaped down his hallway as tears burst forth, cascading down her enflamed cheeks like the rains of a summer storm breaking a heat wave.

When she reached her car, Alannah pressed her forehead against the cool metal roof and tried to catch her breath. But she did not get to draw in the much-needed air because her head filled with immense pain, turning everything black as her legs gave way.

'Hot damn, Lana! They look like real handcuffs.'

Alannah smirked at Brendan as she cuffed his naked body to the bed. 'I stole them from Liam. Now I have you, there's no way I'm letting you escape.'

He felt his already hard cock twitch in response. 'I've already promised to never leave you, but if this is what it takes to convince you, I won't complain.'

Squeezing his dick in her dainty hands, she smirked. 'I don't see any complaints here either.' She ran her calloused fingers along his shaft, drawing a loud groan from his diaphragm. A moment later, she eased herself onto him, wrapping him in her tight, wet folds.

'Gods, you feel incredible, Lana.' The sight of her long black hair falling across her bare breasts as she mounted him was the most erotic thing Brendan had ever seen. She rode him. Hard. So hard, the sound of the bed banging against the wall deafened him.

'Oh Gods! Slow down, gorgeous, or I'm not gonna last.'

But she did not listen to him. Her own climax came within seconds, curtailing Brendan's guilt when his own release poured into her seconds later.

Oddly, the sound of the bed banging against the wall continued even as she collapsed in his arms. *And why is the strawberry scent in her hair fading?*

Brendan jack-knifed into a sitting position on his bed. The vivid dream left his face dripping with sweat and his legs sticky from his own release. And the damn knocking on his front door persisted. He was tempted to ignore it, *but what if it's Lana?* After cleaning himself with a tissue, he slipped into his track pants and dragged his sluggish body to the door.

Instead of bright green eyes, glacial blue ones burning like dry ice greeted him. 'Where is she?' Liam demanded.

'What?' he blinked his bleary eyes, wiping away some sleep.

'I swear to the Gods you're as good as dead if she slept with you.'

'Hold up bro, what the hell's your problem?' Not wanting to air their dirty laundry outside any longer, Brendan opened the screen door to let Liam inside. He stalked down the hall in search of much needed coffee.

'Alannah! Get your arse out here,' Liam screamed as he barged into Brendan's room.

Wow! He never uses her full first name. Did she tell him what happened last night? Brendan opened a jar of instant coffee. It was inferior to the real stuff, but it did the trick when he was desperate for a quick fix. 'Lana's not here.'

'I call bullshit! Why is her car still parked out the front after she didn't come home last night?'

The jar slipped from his fingers and smashed on the floor as Brendan's jaw dropped. 'What?'

Liam grabbed Brendan by his throat. 'You heard me. Now where is she hiding?'

A snarl escaped Brendan's lips. 'I told you, she's not here. Lana didn't stay here last night. If she didn't go home, something happened to her.'

'Shit!' Liam dropped Brendan and moved into the lounge area where he paced across the floor.

Brendan swept the broken glass to the edge of the room, too frantic to bother picking it up. 'You should have more faith in her, *Brother*. You never deserved Lana.'

'And what makes you think a perverted player like you has any right to her either?'

'Fuck you.' He was not in the mood to argue. Alannah was missing. 'We have bigger things to worry about right now.'

'Do you have any idea where she might be?' Liam begged.

'No, but I could use my emotional connection with Lana to track her magically.'

Liam scowled at him and sighed. 'Fine. I'll put a call in at the station to see if I can get a unit deployed to help.' He approached the front door and paused. 'Call me as soon as you get a read on her.'

'Trust me, Brother, if I get a read on her, I'm not gonna wait for you before tearing into the arsehole who is doing Gods know what to her.'

Liam winced. 'Just call me, okay!' He stormed out of the house.

As soon as Brendan finished dressing, he rang Nick.

'Hey man, what's up?'

'I need your help. We have a serious problem.'

Pain was the first thing Alannah noticed when she awoke. Agony. Her head throbbed with the intensity of a hundred hangovers, and the skin of her wrists and ankles was raw from chaffing against the metal cuffs shackling her against the bumpy metal wall. But despite the aching and stinging, she found the strength to meditate.

A deep laugh cut through the dark room. 'Good luck escaping those restraints, Miss Winters. They are pure, cold iron: the only material known to block the flow of magic.'

Why is his voice familiar? Alannah's skin prickled as she took stock of her physical state. Her clothes remained, except for the boots, and she sensed the amulet against her chest. *Thank the Gods!*

'The feel of your fear flowing through me is quite intoxicating, Alannah. More so than the naughty orgasm you shared with your lover's brother.' Her captor's voice drew closer.

'W…what do you w…want?' Her lips trembled. A match came to life in her face and she squinted at the sudden brightness.

When his face came into focus, he leered at her. 'The truth. It's all I've ever wanted. But I should know better than to expect it from a woman. You're all filthy, lying whores, the lot of you.' He extinguished the match against Alannah's inner arm, bringing forth her gut-wrenching scream. 'Do you know what they did to whores like you in the witch-hunts of old?' The Inquisitor lit another match.

Alannah glared at Richard with tears welling in her eyes.

'They burned them alive.'

He doused the flame on the exact same patch of skin and she screamed louder still.

'Tell me, Alannah, what do you know about channelling nether?'

She gasped, failing to draw in enough oxygen. 'It's dangerous and against the law. Use of the stygian element is the only known way to summon demons.'

'How very textbook of you.' He lit another match. 'Now tell me who has channelled it recently.'

'I don't know anyone who messes with nether.'

'I think you do.' He blew the match out in her face, the smoke stinging her eyes as it filled her nostrils.

When he stepped away, she breathed again. The flicker of another flame brought the room into view and Alannah realised he was lighting a few candles on a small table a metre away. But her eyes fell on the torture instruments beside the candles and her heart sank into the pits of the Underworld.

'Here's what we're going to do, Alannah. You're going to tell me everything you know about the practice of dark magic in this state. I want names and locations. Including anything involving the production of Rhapsody. And in turn, I won't satisfy this strong desire I have to break your mind, body, and soul.'

'I don't know anything.'

A rictus grin formed on his face. 'I'd hoped you'd resist for a bit because I am going to enjoy this.' Richard stepped up to her with a scalpel in his hand. He cut her shirt down the middle and ran the blade across her bare stomach.

It stung like nobody's business and a small line of blood trickled down her front.

'Do you have anything to tell me now?' he demanded.

'I honestly don't know anything or anyone.'

Another cut, this time along her chest. 'How about now?'

'No,' she spat out.

The Inquisitor continued to inflict small cuts upon her body until the torment became unbearable and she passed out, praying the Gods would take her soul.

Chapter Thirteen

'Is this Scarlett's doing?'

Brendan shook his head. 'No. I got a pretty clear read on her last night. She doesn't want to hurt Lana.'

Nick sighed. 'So, I guess you know who Scarlett is?'

'Yeah. And thanks for the heads up, bro.'

'Hey, Alannah swore me to secrecy. I can't go breaking her trust.'

'I know. I'm sorry.' Brendan closed his eyes to focus on the link. 'Turn left at the end of this street.'

'How do you know her captor wants to hurt her?'

After taking a deep breath, Brendan opened his eyes. 'Because I can feel her pain.' *And it hurts beyond the Celestial Realm.* After their intimate moment the previous night, Brendan was more in tune with Alannah than ever. She was almost a complete mana source on her own.

'Oh. Sorry man.' Nick fell silent.

Brendan did not complain. The quiet helped him concentrate on the connection. As much as it pained him, it also drew him closer to finding her; to freeing her. Holding on to that scrap of hope kept him going. He refused to entertain the possibility of being too late.

Ten minutes later they drove along an unfamiliar dirt track and Brendan was thankful for the four-wheel drive feature in Nick's car. 'Stop here.'

'But there ain't nothin' here.' Nick was half right: they had reached a desolate paddock without so much as a single cow in sight.

'I can feel her close. There has to be something hidden here.'

'Okay, I'm trusting you on this.' He parked along the embankment and jumped out.

Brendan followed him, closing his eyes after a moment to tune into Alannah again. 'This way.' He took off at a run.

'Wait up, man!' Nick's feet came pounding after him.

They were sprinting at break-neck speed when Brendan slipped and fell down a set of concrete steps recessed in the ground. *'Ah, bugger!'*

Nick squatted beside him. 'You okay?'

'I twisted my ankle. Who leaves a damn hole in the ground like this unguarded?'

'Whoever it was didn't expect company. Look,' Nick pointed.

Peering further into the depths of the pothole, Brendan's eyes landed on a door. Alannah's signal was weak, but he was sure she was beyond the door.

'Here, let me help you up.'

He accepted Nick's hand, leaning on him as he limped down the steps. The corrugated iron structure buried in the ground put Brendan in mind of the old Anderson-style bomb shelters from World War II. The dishevelled nature of the materials suggested that very purpose.

The lock on the bunker did not deter Nick. The orc made quick work of the door with the old hip and shoulders.

As soon as they entered, Brendan gagged at the smell of burnt flesh. The room was gloomy, with only a hint of light coming in through the door. It took a moment for his eyes to adjust, but when they did, his heart sank. 'Oh hell.'

Alannah slumped, unconscious in her chains. He limped up to her and checked her for signs of life. His own breathing resumed when he felt the faint tickle of air escaping her parted lips. As soon as he noticed the tattered scraps of fabric failing to cover her, Brendan swallowed the bile pushing its way up. 'What kind of sick bastard did this to her?!'

Nick, who had remained near the door, sauntered over. 'By the Gods. Are they burn marks?'

'Looks like it, along with a million shallow cuts.' Brendan was hard pressed to find an unharmed patch of skin on the front of her body. It took all his strength to fight back the threat of tears. It was not time to let them out; Alannah needed him. 'Give me a hand with these manacles.'

With another display of raw strength, Nick ripped the chains from the wall, releasing Alannah's limp form into Brendan's hold. He stumbled under her miniscule weight, forgetting his injury.

'Why don't you let me carry her? You shouldn't put too much pressure on your ankle.'

'Don't. I need to do this.' There was no way in hell he was letting her go until she woke up, even then he might not. Reminding himself the discomfort he felt was nothing compared to what Alannah had gone through, he ignored the pain.

'The arsehole who did this is pretty lucky we didn't catch him.' Nick mused as they walked up the steps. 'I wouldn't be able to stop myself from killing the prick if he were here right now.'

'I know how you feel.' Brendan conceded to Nick's supporting him as they crossed the paddock. Once he had settled into the back seat with Alannah resting against him, he got on the phone.

'Yes, Brendan?' Ross answered with the sounds of a social gathering in the background.

'Drop whatever you're doing and meet me at your place.'

'Brendan I won't—'

'Lana is unconscious and injured. I pulled her out of some nightmarish torture dungeon, so don't give me your damn excuses.'

'Okay, calm down son. I'll be there. Maybe open with that next time.'

'Whatever, just be there.' He hung up and considered ringing Liam. But when he gazed down at Alannah, the tears threatened again. Liam could wait. It did not even matter if Nick was witness to his breakdown. It was happening. One loud sob after another resounded through the vehicle's cabin. Brendan did not cry often, but when he did it was always because of Alannah: she was the only woman who got under his skin and tugged on his heart strings.

Even Ross paled at the sight of Alannah when he greeted them. 'Bring her into the first guestroom.'

Brendan hobbled in through the front door with Nick's help. 'Thanks man, I'll take it from here. I'll call you when she's awake.'

'No worries.' Nick slapped him on the back and left.

'Looks like you're injured too,' Ross observed.

'I'll be fine. Focus on Lana.'

'Oh Gods!' Mum gasped as soon as she approached. 'The poor, sweet girl.'

With Alannah settled on the bed, Brendan sat beside her and removed what was left of her clothes. He rested a hand on her arm.

'I need room to work, son.'

'You'll have to work around me, 'cause I'm not moving from her side until she's better.'

Ross started to argue but sighed and got to work. He set up her drip, before cleaning and dressing her wounds with healing ointments. When he reached her pubic region, he looked at Brendan. 'Do you know if…'

Fresh tears sprang to Brendan's eyes. 'No idea.'

After a deep breath, Ross Winters adopted a professional mask to perform the internal examination. 'There is no sign of tearing or discharge in either opening.'

Brendan let out the breath he had been holding. 'Thank the Gods.'

Once her visible injuries were tended to, Ross used his attunements to assess the extent of her head injuries. 'She has a severe concussion. I'll give her a magical boost; the healing tincture in her drip should do the rest.' Laying his hands upon her forehead, Dad closed his eyes and performed his magic. Rising, he handed a potion to Brendan. 'She'll be okay. Take that for your injury.'

Brendan nodded and skulled the tonic. 'Thanks.'

'Does Liam know?'

'Not yet. I'll contact him in a minute.'

'Okay. Call me if either of you need anything.' His father left the room, closing the door behind him.

Being careful not to dislodge the drip, Brendan turned Alannah onto her side to snuggle up behind her. Not wanting to risk touching any of the wounds on her front, he kept his free hand on her shoulder blade. He drew the blanket up to cover them both, letting the rest of his tears flow free.

About an hour later, Alannah stirred and moaned. 'Urghm.'

'Are you okay, Lana?'

'Brendan?'

'Yes, Lana?'

'Did you save me?'

'With Nick's help, yeah I got you out of there.'

'Thank you.' She sucked in a deep breath. 'Everything hurts and I'm tired.'

'I know. I'm sorry, gorgeous.' He kissed her shoulder. 'Go back to sleep. We can talk later.'

'Please hold me.' She spoke with a faint whisper.

'I am holding you.'

'I mean properly.' She reached back for his hand and pulled it forward.

'Are you sure? I don't want to hurt you.'

'This is fine.' She let his hand rest on her bare stomach.

Brendan felt the new piercing in her belly button and half a smile tugged at his lips. It was a bittersweet feeling to have Alannah sleeping in his arms given the circumstances.

Liam was on the verge of conniptions when he got off the phone to his dad. *That little punk didn't call!* He had spent the better part of the day driving around in a daze searching for Alannah when Brendan had rescued her over two hours ago.

As soon as he got to his parent's place, he flew through the door and into the first guestroom. The sight of Brendan spooning Alannah brought his blood bubbling to the surface. 'What the hell do you think you're doing?'

Brendan glanced up at him and Liam was taken aback by the red, puffy appearance of his eyes. 'Shoosh. She's sleeping.'

It had been years since he had seen evidence of Brendan crying. Liam sat on the edge of the bed and peered down at her. She appeared peaceful. 'What happened?' he whispered.

'I don't know. She was out cold when I found her.' Brendan sucked in an audible breath. When he continued speaking, his voice shook with emotion. 'Her condition was nasty, Liam. Covered in millions of cuts and burns.'

'Gods!' Liam ran his fingers along the side of Alannah's face.

Her eyes flickered open. 'Liam?'

'I'm here, gorgeous.' He leaned down to press a kiss on her lips.

'Please hold me.'

Liam smiled. 'Of course, baby.' He glared at Brendan. 'You can go now.'

'No, please. I need both of you.' She batted her lashes atop her brilliant green orbs.

When he glanced at Brendan, Liam half expected a smirk, but there was no trace of levity in his brother's expression.

Liam sighed as he removed his boots. 'Okay, gorgeous.'

She was asleep again when he returned. Lifting the blanket, Liam was greeted by another infuriating sight and he glared at Brendan. 'The hell? She's naked. Get your filthy hands off her, you pervert.'

'Calm your crazy, bro. Lana's injured. There's nothing suss going on.' Brendan slid his hand across her stomach, along her hip, and up to her shoulder.

'Looks pretty damn suss to me.' Liam slipped under the blanket and nestled up to Alannah's front.

'Get over yourself, Snowflake, and be a good boyfriend for once,' Brendan deadpanned.

Liam felt a growl slip from his throat, but he bit his lip to hold back from arguing.

Alannah felt safe, warm, and loved as she lay there cocooned in the arms of her two favourite men. It was a shame her blissful bubble would have to burst once she recovered. *Can I pretend for a while? It sucks that I needed to be injured to get both Liam and Brendan in bed with me at once.* Visions of a threesome consumed her, sending a rush of blood through her veins.

Brendan chuckled in her mind. *'Are you having sexy thoughts, Lana? Are they about me or Liam?'*

Alannah blushed. With payback in mind, she nudged her backside against Brendan.

But he reciprocated by pressing his hardon against her, sending more signals through her bloodstream and straight to her core.

She should have known better, after all their years of playing Sleazy Chicken. *He was never bluffing.* Nonetheless, Alannah loved pushing Brendan's boundaries, or lack thereof.

After another small thrust from Alannah, Brendan's hand moved from her shoulder down to her arse and swatted it. *'Careful, Lana, or I'll bang you right here, in front of Liam.'*

A small moan slipped out as arousal pooled between her legs.

'Or is that what you want?' Brendan's hand slid down her arse until his fingertips brushed against her clit. *'Mm. I love how wet you get for me, gorgeous.'*

Clenching her teeth did not stop the hissed curse escaping: *'Jesus!'*

Liam's eyes shot open with concern. 'Shit! Are you okay, Lana? I didn't hurt you, did I?'

When Brendan's hand moved back to her shoulder, she sucked in a deep breath. 'No. I'm okay.'

His countenance relaxed. 'How are you feeling?'

'Much better.'

'That's reassuring.' Liam touched the cannula on her hand. 'You probably don't need this anymore. Are you awake, Brendan?'

'Yeah.' Brendan's breath tickled Alannah's neck as he spoke.

'Why don't you go get Dad?'

'Okay.' But Brendan did not budge.

Liam growled. 'Now would be good.'

'Relax, bro, I'm sending him a telepathic message.'

Tension formed in the set of Liam's jaw, but he let the issue slide and focussed on Alannah. 'Do you know who did this to you?'

Alannah had tried to recall the source of her injuries a few times as she drifted in and out of sleep but kept drawing a blank. 'I don't remember.'

Liam's hand, which had been resting on her waist, came up to her face. 'Fair enough. It must have been too traumatic.'

'What happened to me? What were my injuries?'

Glancing over her shoulder, Liam looked to Brendan. 'Should I tell her?'

Brendan took a deep breath as he rubbed her arm. 'Yeah. Lana's ready.'

When Liam peered into her eyes, tears welled in his own. 'You must have been abducted when leaving Brendan's place last night. Your car was still out front this morning. I'm sorry, Lana, but I assumed the worst of you when you didn't come home. I knew you were at Brendan's because I saw your Tesla there on my way home. I spent the night waiting up for you and… But if I'd gone to confront you earlier…' A tear slipped from his eye.

She brushed it away with her thumb. 'It's okay. Go on.'

'Brendan found you in an old bomb shelter. You were chained to the wall with cold iron and…' His Adam's apple bobbed. 'Your clothes were ripped to shreds and you were covered in cuts and burns.'

They burned them alive. Alannah remembered the smell of burning flesh, her flesh. And the pain. 'Oh Gods, I'm gonna spew.' She sat up.

Liam seized a bucket from the floor. 'Here.'

As she leaned forward to empty her stomach, Brendan pulled her hair back—a simple yet touching gesture. He topped it off by stroking her back with his other hand.

Ross entered as she finished retching. 'Hmm. It might be too early to remove your drip.' He pressed his hand to her forehead and frowned. 'You're still concussed, Alannah. Can I see the rest of your wounds?'

Alannah bobbed her head as she handed her sick bowl to Liam. It felt awkward having her Uncle see her naked, even if he was a doctor. She lowered the blanket.

'Look away now, Brother,' Liam demanded.

'Are you forgetting how I found her?'

'Don't make me poke your eyes out.'

Alannah sighed. 'And the truce ends.' She had removed the blanket by this stage and looked down at herself. Aside from a lot of ointment residue, there were no signs of the cuts and burns that had covered her skin.

'They have healed well,' Ross observed. 'You can put a night gown on now.'

Liam let out a sigh of relief as he grabbed a white cotton slip from the bedside table. He disconnected the tubing from Alannah's hand and helped her into the nightie.

She watched as Ross replaced the empty IV bag with another pouch of clear fluid. He refitted the tube to her cannula and studied her with knitted brows. 'How's your stomach feeling? Are you ready for food?'

Her stomach growled as if on cue. 'I think that's a yes.'

Ross smiled. 'I'll see if Nora can fix you a sandwich.'

'Thanks.' When he left, Alannah sat back against the headboard and closed her eyes. The rest of her memories hit her, and she winced. *The Inquisitor*.

Brendan stiffened beside her as if he had read her mind.

'Liam, could you please get me a clean change of clothes from home?'

'I'm sure Mum has something you can wear when the time comes,' Liam suggested.

She sighed. 'I need to talk to Brendan. Alone.'

Liam's eyes flashed through a symphony of emotions. But rather than voice his thoughts, he leaned forward and kissed her lips before leaving the room.

'Caleb wasn't wrong about Richard's love of torture.'

'Oh hell! What was he trying to extract from you?'

'Everything I know about dark magic in the state, including the production of Rhapsody.'

Tears shimmered in Brendan's eyes, which were red and puffy. 'I'm so damn sorry, Lana.'

'Hey, don't you dare blame yourself. Besides, the potion business wasn't his main reason for capturing me. Richard's primary concern was the recent channelling of nether.'

Brendan's eyes burst wide open. 'But Scarlett said it couldn't be detected.'

'I guess there are some Council secrets she doesn't know. I'm going to arrange to meet her tomorrow and put a hold on the training sessions for now. We all need to lay low while the Inquisitor is in town.'

Brendan gnawed at his lip a moment. 'Did he, uh, get anything from you?'

'No. The shield was still active until I passed out the first time. By the time he found and removed it, I was too weak to think about much at all. He mentioned something about bringing in an abjurer to heal me and start the process all over again. I guess you found me while he was out.'

'Yeah, not a minute too soon either. You were barely holding on when I got there.' A few tears slid down Brendan's cheek. 'I thought I was going to lose you, Lana.'

She pulled him in for a hug. 'Hey, it's okay. I'm fine, thanks to you.' Alannah let him sob in her arms for a few minutes.

A knock sounded at the door before Nora entered with two plates of sandwiches. 'I thought you might be hungry too, Brendan.'

Still clinging to Alannah, Brendan turned to face Nora. 'Thanks Mum.'

'I'll leave them here.' She put the plates on the dressing table and dashed out the door.

'I reckon Nora knows something's going on between us.'

Brendan wiped his face with his sleeve and smiled. 'She's always known how we feel about each other.' He rose and grabbed their food.

Alannah nibbled at her sandwich, not wanting to risk a relapse of the upchucks. Brendan, on the other hand, scoffed his. As she watched him eat, a question formed in Alannah's mind that she could not hold back any longer. 'How did you find me?'

He looked up from his meal and swallowed his last bite. 'I could feel you.'

She gasped. 'What do you mean?'

After placing the empty plate on his bedside table, Brendan shuffled closer to her and placed his hand on her bare thigh. 'I have a strong empathic link to you, Lana. Since you returned five years ago, I've been able to feel what you feel, even with a bit of distance between us. It's not always active and I can switch it on at will if I need or want to.'

She stared at him. 'Do you have the link with anyone else?'

'No. I need to be actively channelling to feel other people's emotions; and even then, I can't pinpoint who is who unless I can see their auras.'

The air around her felt like a sauna. 'What does it, uh, feel like?'

'I imagine I feel whatever you do. The same emotions, identical sensations.' He trailed a finger up her leg. 'Just like I can feel this on my own leg as well as the pleasure response it evokes. The main difference—' his hand reached her apex—'is when you feel something on or in your *feminine* parts.'

Alannah whimpered as he flicked her swollen bud, almost dropping her sandwich.

'In that case,' Brendan continued toying with her as he spoke in his deep bedroom voice, 'my body translates the feeling into something more *masculine*.'

She flung the rest of her food aside and arched her back as the intensity of her arousal increased. *Holy heck! He isn't even inside me, but Gods do I want him to be!*

'Do you want more, Lana?'

Biting her lip, she nodded.

Grinning with wicked delight, Brendan plunged two fingers deep inside, pulling an orgasm straight out of her. 'I'd love to do much more to you, gorgeous, but you are still recovering from head trauma. Best if we go easy on you, yeah?'

'Thanks,' she rasped.

'For the orgasm or the reprieve?'

Alannah smiled. 'Both.'

'My pleasure, *as you know.*'

Chapter Fourteen

The woman in red used powerful illusionary magic, which most mages would not detect, to hide herself. But Richard's secret attunement allowed him to pierce the veil. Sitting in a dark corner of the café, he watched as she took her usual seat by the window. *Strange how she chooses to sit facing in rather than make the most of what her seaside vista has to offer. Perhaps it is to avoid an unsuspecting human sitting in her lap.*

Grabbing his tablet, he opened the file he had been compiling with what he knew about her thus far. After rereading his last entry: *Powerful magic user, but not a registered mage. Possible dark mage or cursed?* He glanced at her again, adding: *Also appears familiar, but from where?*

Richard almost called for another coffee refill when a new arrival caught his attention.

'Hi hun. Will it be the usual today?'

'Yeah, thanks Brigette.' Alannah Winters stood at the counter looking as healthy as ever. She had been laying low since her escape from his custody a few days ago, only stepping out in public with one of her devoted cousins. But this time she had an orc with her. *Curious.*

His interest piqued further when she sat at the red woman's table. Richard used a far-sighted spell to get a better view of the two women together. *Holy realms! No wonder Red is familiar!* The family resemblance was striking.

Red smiled at Alannah. 'Hello, dear child.' She glanced at the orc. 'Hello, Nick.'

'Hello, Madam,' Alannah's replied telepathically.

The orc remained silent.

Thinking quick, Richard grabbed an amethyst chip from his satchel and inserted it into the SD slot of his smartphone. The magic tech would allow him to record telepathic communication. He took a quick photograph of them together and opened a voice recording app.

'Do you wish to schedule another training session?'

'No, Lady Scarlett. We need to put those on hold for a while. At least until the Inquisitor leaves town.'

Scarlett, huh? Fitting name. Why didn't I think of it? It is better than Red.

'Oh?' Scarlett inquired.

'Don't ask me how, but he detected your channelling the other day.'

Bingo! Richard's intuition never led him astray.

Scarlett laughed. 'The shady fellow must have some unsanctioned tricks of his own. He sounds like a worthy opponent.'

'Please be careful of him. He's cruel and sadistic; something I barely lived to tell you about. If Brendan hadn't...'

Scarlett's eyes widened. 'He caught you? What did you tell him?'

'Nothing. And I'm fine now, Grandmother, thanks for asking.'

Wait? Did she address Scarlett as her grandmother? Richard grinned. *Oh, this is too good.*

'I told you to address me formally, you silly girl.'

'It's not like anyone is listening right now.'

'That we know of.'

Alannah paled, scanning the café.

Richard pretended to read the paper as he sipped from his empty cup. He was confident his own glamour spell would hold up, so mages would only see an old human man sitting there.

'*There are no magic auras here,*' Alannah observed.

Having enough evidence, Richard folded the paper, ceased the recording and snuck out of the café, not sparing either of the women or the orc another glance.

With Liam and Brendan both back at work, Alannah had spent the days following her abduction hanging out at Nick's orchard. She refused to go out in public without one of the guys with her, and Liam agreed she needed the protection. Liam still did not know who had kidnapped her, but he knew Alannah was keeping secrets again and he did not hide his displeasure from her. She might have felt guilty if he had not been such an aloof ass about it.

Brendan, on the other hand, had been vigilant, checking in on her every chance he got. He also toned down the flirting and intimate contact after telling Alannah the ball was in her court. It was odd. He was almost the perfect gentleman. Almost. Brendan would always be mischievous and cheeky to some extent, but she would not have him any other way.

Following the afternoon meeting with Scarlett, Nick dropped Alannah off at Brendan's apartment.

The door flew open, and Brendan pulled her inside for a massive bear hug. 'Hey, gorgeous. Miss me?'

Alannah tried to laugh with the small amount of air left in her lungs, but it came out as a wheeze.

'You're squashing her,' Nick remarked.

Brendan released her and bumped Nick's fist. 'Hey, bro, thanks for looking after my girl.'

She gave Brendan an exaggerated eye-roll before turning to Nick. 'Thanks again. Same time tomorrow?'

'No worries, sweet.'

As soon as Nick left, Alannah walked down the hall. 'Got any movies in mind for tonight?'

'No. I was gonna let you pick.' Brendan followed close behind her.

'Do I still get to pick the pizza toppings?'

'Of course.' When they reached the living area, he grabbed her arm, spinning her around to face him. 'Hey, how'd the meeting go?'

'Fine. Scarlett agreed to postpone further training.'

'That's a relief.' He pulled out his phone, loaded the food delivery app and handed it to her. 'Here, go wild.'

She arched her brow. 'You should be careful about giving me such open invitations.'

He laughed, pushing himself up to sit on the kitchen bench. 'Why? There isn't anything I wouldn't let you do to me.'

Alannah sucked in an audible breath. 'Anything?'

Brendan nodded. 'Yup.'

A wicked grin tugged at her lips. 'Even spinach pizza?'

'Oh hell. Are you trying to kill me, woman?'

She huffed. 'Fine. We'll go with the usual unhealthy crap.'

'I'm glad we have an understanding, gorgeous.'

After submitting the pizza order, Alannah slumped on the plush suede couch and slipped her shoes off. She started flicking through movie options on a streaming app when the doorbell startled her. 'That was quick.'

Brendan rose. 'I'll get it. You keep searching.'

Alannah heard voices at the door, followed by two sets of footsteps approaching. Her eyes grew wide when Liam appeared. 'Oh, hey. I thought you had a Council Meeting tonight.'

'I do. And so do you.'

She frowned. 'Liam, we talked about this. I don't feel comfortable about going after what Monique did.'

He sighed. 'I know, but High Magus Kieran specifically requested your presence tonight.'

Alarm bells rang in her head. 'Why?'

'I don't know. He just asked me to make sure you show up.'

'And if I don't?'

'I'm not going to force you, Lana. But I can't imagine you'll still have your seat if you refuse an official summons.'

'Fine.' She put her shoes back on and dragged herself up. 'Sorry, Brendan; looks like you'll have to eat my share of the pizza tonight.'

Brendan shrugged. 'I can take one for the team.' During their farewell embrace, he whispered to her, 'Good luck, gorgeous.'

Liam clutched her hand and led her out to the car.

Bat sized butterflies held a party in Alannah's chest as she sat in the Council meeting room. The other councillors' glares did not help either. At least Liam kept a supportive hold of her hand.

Monique entered to announce both Kieran and Richard's arrival and Alannah's heart did backflips as she rose with everyone else.

'Please be seated,' Kieran ordered. 'Now, before we commence our usual business, Inquisitor Lane has an important matter to bring to the table.'

'Thank you, High Magus.' Richard grinned at Alannah. *Crapola!*

He pulled a phone out of his pocket. 'While I know the main purpose of my visit has been to find the source of that accursed potion, Rhapsody, another dark magic problem has come to my attention—one I can't ignore. I present my first piece of evidence.'

After hitting a button on the touch screen, a voice recording commenced: *'Do you wish to schedule another training session?'*

Dread settled in the pit of Alannah's stomach when she heard Scarlett's voice. *Surely Richard didn't get the other side of the conversation?*

Her own voice came through clear as day.

'No, Lady Scarlett. We need to put those on hold for a while. At least until the Inquisitor leaves town.'

Every eye in the room was on her. With a trembling lip, she turned to Liam for help. His mouth drew a hard line as he leaned in and whispered, 'Is this about the unsanctioned training?'

She nodded.

Liam's eyes widened. *'Damnit!'* He squeezed Alannah's hand and held her gaze in a show of support. At the mention of Richard's torture, compassionate tears hovered in his eyes. But they vanished as he dropped her hand and gaped the moment the recording revealed Scarlett's identity.

When the recording ended, Richard stood, and his malicious voice boomed across the table. 'Warlocks, seize Councillor Alannah.'

Clayton jumped to obey, but Liam moved in slow motion.

Tears streamed down her face as they pulled her from the chair.

'Alannah Winters, by the authority of The Council of Mages, I am placing you under arrest.'

Cold iron cuffs clamped her wrists behind her back.

'You are charged of treason and under suspicion of practising dark magic.'

Liam stood gobsmacked and frozen in front of her while Clayton frisked her for weapons and magic tools. She winced when he groped her between the legs.

'You are not obliged to say anything, however anything you do say can be used in evidence against you.'

Clayton led Alannah out of the room, with Liam close beside her. The holding cells were in the Council chamber's basement, sparing her the humiliation of walking outside in public view.

They stopped in a stuffy storage room where Clayton shoved her into Liam's arms. 'Out of respect for you, Liam, I'll let you do the strip search, but I will have to watch to make sure you don't miss anything.' He grabbed two empty plastic tubs from the shelves and placed them on a nearby bench. The yellow one for *Personal Effects*, while the red one was for *Evidence*.

Liam turned her around and looked down at her with arctic eyes as Clayton removed her cuffs. 'Remove all of your clothes slowly and hand each item to me.' None of the usual tenderness or excitement laced his request. As she removed her panties, Alannah heard Liam growl. 'Stop enjoying yourself, Clay.'

'I'm sorry, man, but it's not every day we get to apprehend such a fine piece of arse.'

Her cheeks burned.

Liam glared at Clayton, his eyes turning from arctic ice to molten lava. 'Shut your trap before I do it for you.'

Clayton raised his hands in supplication. 'Okay, chill out, bro. Please, continue.'

Liam grimaced when his attention returned to Alannah's naked body. 'You have to squat and cough now.'

She blanched, slipping into stunned silence. *I can't believe the Council uses such an intrusive procedure.*

'Alannah, please don't make this any harder than it needs to be.' His eyes pleaded with her.

She gulped, sinking to the floor in a squatting position. After coughing, she opened her mouth for Liam to peer inside with a small torch. *It is absurd. What the hell am I going to hide in my throat or mouth?*

'It's a routine precaution, Alannah,' Liam explained. 'If I don't go through the motions they could accuse me of nepotism, or worse.'

Alannah gave a silent nod, closing her eyes as Liam's hands continued searching the rest of her cavities. *At least it is Liam's hands,* she reminded herself.

'You can stand up now.'

Releasing the breath she had been holding, Alannah rose.

Liam handed her a set of teal pants and t-shirt reminiscent of surgical scrubs, along with clean white cotton underpants. 'Put these on.'

Once she finished dressing, the men logged her belongings and put them away before taking her into the bowels of the building. When the cage-like door of her cell closed her in, Clayton left. Liam remained with a sneer on his face. 'I have to return to the meeting, but I will return to talk to you as soon as it finishes.'

Probably for the best. Alannah felt too choked up to talk to him. Nodding, she took stock of her dimly lit surroundings. The first thing she noticed was the single bed, followed by a drinking fountain to her right, along with a toilet and wash basin sat in the left corner. The walls were some type of granite judging by the grey and white colouring. They were all lined with metal bars extending across the ceiling and floor. Collapsing on the bed, she discovered a lumpy mattress full of broken springs, and groaned. Evidently, her comfort was not a concern for the Council. She sighed and breathed deeply, to calm the storm of emotions brewing within.

A few hours later, Alannah sprang to her feet when she heard people approaching. Clayton and Liam both wore sombre expressions when they stepped up to her prison.

'Stand back from the door,' Clayton ordered. As she did so, he unlocked the cell, letting Liam in before locking it again. 'I'll give you fifteen minutes. Buzz me if you want out earlier.'

'Thanks, man,' Liam replied.

When Clayton left, Alannah ran toward Liam, but he put a hand up to stop her. She gasped. 'Liam?'

'Don't touch me, Alannah. I'm here to clear a few things up because my head is spinning right now.' He crossed his arms and leaned against the stone wall.

Her heart sank. 'Is this an official interrogation?'

Liam sighed. 'No. They wouldn't put me in charge of your case even if I wanted them to. You and I are going to have a personal chat.'

She nodded, and sat on the bed, avoiding the worst of the springs that were hell bent on giving her a proctocolectomy.

'I don't even know where to start.' He paced the floor. A minute later, he stopped in front of her. 'Was Tara training you?'

'Yes.'

'Why *the hell* were you training with her?'

'It was a condition of obtaining the information I wanted. She promised to tell me who my bio dad was if she could help me obtain two attunements.'

Liam shook his head. 'Which attunement have you gained so far?'

'I'm not sure if it counts, but she reconnected me to an innate source I have because of the Beltane Blessing.'

'What—was it—Alannah?'

She shivered at the impersonal way he used her full first name. 'The primordial.'

His eyes bugged out. 'What the…?'

'I know, that's what I thought at first. But it's true, Liam. I can now channel any mana source I want because of it.'

'Does the Inquisitor know this? Is this why he kidnapped you?'

'No. He was more concerned about the channelling of nether.'

'*What?*' Liam's voice rose several decibels.

'She only showed me how to do it safely. I haven't attempted it myself. I swear to the Gods I have not practised any dark magic.'

He collapsed on the bed next to her and slumped into his raised knees. 'And here I thought your big secret was an affair with Brendan.'

'Liam—'

'But this is much worse.' He glared at her. 'How could you do something so dark and dangerous, with our arch nemesis, no less?'

'I—'

'And don't give me the bio dad bollocks. I'm not buying that excuse as enough to warrant the risks you took.'

'It was about my father at first. But I became invested in what Tara taught me about the primordial. For the record, I didn't know Scarlett was Tara's pseudonym when she first wrote me.'

'When did she make initial contact?'

'Early September.'

He went silent for a few minutes. 'Is Brendan part of this?'

'Not directly. He didn't even know about Tara at first, but when the Inquisitor showed up, I went to him for help.'

'Why do you always run to him, Alannah? Why didn't you come to me for help?'

She searched her heart for the truth. 'Because Brendan has always been there for me. And I was afraid you would react like this. What would you have done if I'd told you about Tara back then?'

'I would have put a stop to it and gone after the bitch.'

'It wouldn't have helped me, Liam. I needed protection from the Inquisitor, not Tara. Even when she had me locked in a dungeon cell; Tara never tortured me like Richard did. Sure, she did some messed up things, but at the end of the day, Tara didn't *want* to hurt me or my mum.'

Liam looked at the ceiling as if it could provide some insight. 'I can't believe I'm hearing this. Tara is poisoning your mind.'

'No, Liam. The Council is poisoning our minds… like hiding the truth of the Beltane Blessing.'

'I've heard enough of this rubbish.' Jumping up, he grabbed the bars of the door, pressing his forehead against them. He turned to glare at her. 'Now tell me the damn truth. Have you been screwing Brendan?'

'No, Liam. How many times do I have to tell you?' *Those two unexpected orgasms didn't count, right?*

'But you've wanted to, haven't you?'

She bit her lip, unable to deny it, especially knowing Liam heard the conversation with Emma all those years ago. 'That doesn't make me a cheater, Liam.'

'No, but it might be emotional infidelity. Are you in love with him?'

'Liam—'

'It's a simple question, Alannah. Are. You. In love with Brendan?'

She exhaled sharply. 'Yes, but—'

'Then you can call him to bail you out. We are done.' Liam pressed the intercom button, standing in silence as he stared out into the hallway.

'Liam, please listen to me.'

'No.' He continued facing away from her.

'I'm still in love with you too, Liam.'

'Doesn't matter anymore.'

'Why?'

Liam spun around to face her. 'Because you're a traitorous whore.' Pure hatred dripped from every pore. His words stabbed Alannah in the chest like a hot poker, knocking the wind from her.

Clayton appeared a moment later.

After leaving her cell, Liam paused to glance at her one last time. 'Dad was right about the women in our bloodline: you're all a damned disgrace.' He turned and left, leaving Alannah to grieve more than the loss of her freedom.

Hours passed. Alannah could not surmise more without a clock or window to the outside world. Having cried herself dry, she clambered up to the drinking fountain, savouring the feel of the cool water on her parched lips. Alannah's hands were no longer cuffed, but all attempts to connect with her attunements proved useless. She figured the bars must be cold iron, acting like a Faraday cage to block magic. She returned to the bed and attempted to rest. Sleep was futile, so she did the next best thing and slipped into a meditative trance.

The sound of a door slamming broke her reverie and she jumped to attention. Clayton appeared at her door wearing different clothes, and he was alone. 'Morning, Alannah.'

'Gee, is it morning already? How time flies.'

'That's a hilarious mouth you got there. If you weren't expected upstairs right now, I'd be tempted to learn its other talents.'

'You're a creep, Clayton,' Alannah spat in a seething tone.

He grinned wickedly. 'Don't taunt the alligator, *sweetheart*.' His pearly whites flashed at her as he leered and snapped them. He pulled a set of keys from his pocket and dangled them in front of his face. 'Now turn around and bend over the bed like a good whore.'

She stood there defiantly.

Sparks formed on his fingertips. 'Do you want me to hurt you?'

Swallowing bile, she turned and placed her hands on the bed.

The sound of the door opening and clicking shut reverberated through the room. She felt Clayton's body ram against her backside. 'Liam's not gonna defend you now, *sweetheart*.' He thrust his pelvis against her and pinched her arse. 'Mm. I bet he was too much of a prude to take you back here.' His hand slipped inside her pants and rubbed against her bare cheeks. 'Question is, have you let anyone else in this tight little hole? Like your vampire ex, perhaps?'

Alannah's eyes brimmed with tears as she shook her head.

'No? What about Brendan? I doubt he would hesitate to claim your arse, given the chance.'

She continued shaking her head.

'Hmm, this is a virgin arse? Lucky me.' His finger pressed against her puckered opening. 'You know, I've been dreaming about this ever since your striptease last night.' He removed the offending limb with a sigh. 'But my gratification will have to wait.' Tugging her arms back, he cuffed her wrists and pulled her upright. 'Come on. The High Magus wants to see you.'

Alannah squinted when they entered the ground floor corridor. Too much sunlight poured in through the windows after she had become accustomed to the gloom of her prison. She blinked with relief when they entered the lift taking her up to Kieran's office.

The High Magus did not even look at Alannah's face when she arrived. 'Please remove her restraints and leave us, Warlock Clayton.'

'Yes, Your Honour.' Clayton released her hands, slapping her on the arse before making his exit.

Kieran did not bat an eyelid at the obvious sexual harassment. 'This is your official notice of dismissal from the Council.' He handed her an envelope. 'Seraphina will finish the booking process with you, after which you will have the opportunity to post for bail.' Already appearing bored, he returned to his desk and resumed working on his computer.

His brunette half-mage secretary escorted her into an adjacent office. 'Please be seated, Miss Winters.'

Alannah sat in one of the gas-lift chairs, welcoming the relative comfort of a soft seat.

'I need you to complete this paperwork confirming your registration details.'

She reviewed the form. As a registered mage, the Council had all her vital information, including mug shot, fingerprints, blood group, and DNA samples. After Alannah signed a declaration, Seraphina handed her the *Application for Bail* form.

'Please read the conditions of bail carefully, especially the part about remaining within this Council district and making yourself available for a court appearance.'

When Alannah returned the completed papers, Seraphina signed as a witness and looked at her. 'Is there someone willing to act as your guarantor?'

Alannah's first thoughts went to Liam's hurtful dismissal, and she had to choke back the lump forming in her throat. 'I'd like to ask Brendan Winters.'

A faint smile broke the woman's otherwise neutral expression.

Oh hell, had Brendan slept with her too?

Seraphina handed her a desk phone and directory. 'Very well. Call him.'

Alannah grabbed the phone and dialled without need for the listing. Brendan's number was one of three she had memorised.

Three rings. 'Hello, Brendan Winters speaking.'

'Hey, it's me.'

'Oh, Gods, Lana, are you okay? When Mum told me what happened, I was frantic. I couldn't even sleep.'

She inhaled deeply as his deep voice flowed through her, calming every nerve. 'Yeah, I'm okay. They are letting me out on bail, but I need a guarantor. I was kinda hoping—'

'Of course, I'll do it. I'll be right over.'

Alannah smiled. 'Thanks, Brendan.'

'Anything for you, gorgeous.'

Chapter Fifteen

The memory of Alannah's ordeal kept Brendan grounded like sandbags on a hot air balloon. Without those weights, he would have floated away. *She rang me, not Liam!* He knew he should not have jumped past the conclusion and straight into epilogue territory, but neither his heart nor cock were listening to that part of his brain when he hit the pedal to the metal.

After flying across town, he parked right in front of the Council chambers, ignoring the No Standing sign, and burst through the glass doors.

'Oh, hey handsome,' the receptionist greeted him. The redhead was familiar, but he could not remember her name. She fluttered her lashes at him. 'Can I help you?'

'I have business in Kieran Lane's office.'

Her face drooped before she put her emotions in check. 'No worries, hun. I'll buzz you up. Do you know where to go?'

'Yup.' Brendan had never been in this building, but he didn't need a map. He beelined for the lift, hating every second it took to climb the five floors separating him from Alannah. He could feel her racing heart and wanted to squeeze every ounce of that worry and fear out of her, filling her with nothing but positive emotions.

The door opened on the top floor. He strode up to an office with the name plaque, *SERAPHINA BLACK*. *Oh joy, another one-night stand.* He knocked on the door.

The moment he caught sight of Alannah; their gazes locked. He pushed past the other woman and scooped Alannah up in his arms. 'Everything will be okay, gorgeous.'

Seraphina cleared her throat. 'Excuse me, Mr. Winters, but I need you to sign for Alannah's bail.'

He reluctantly let Alannah go. 'Right, of course.'

After pushing through the tedium of bureaucracy, he turned to Alannah and noticed her attire: the awful prison uniform. *Poor Lana.* 'I should have thought to bring you a change of clothes.'

'You can have these back now, Miss Winters.' Seraphina placed a yellow tray on the desk that including last night's dress. 'There's a bathroom down the hall you can change in.'

When Alannah was ready, she marched straight up to Brendan, grabbed his hand, and kept walking. 'Please get me out of this Gods forsaken place.'

Trying to keep things light, he saluted her. 'Yes, ma'am.' Truth be told, he could not wait to get out of the stuffy place either. There was a stench in the air that was far worse than defecation: it reeked of affectation.

Once seated in the Jag, Brendan smiled at Alannah. 'Let's get you home.'

Alannah took a deep breath, stopping Brendan from releasing the park brake with her hand on his. 'No. Please take me to your house.'

He tried to ignore all the cells in his body as they high-fived one another. 'Not that I'm complaining, but why my house? Have you—'

'Liam dumped me.' She spoke with a voice void of all emotion, looking at him with hollow eyes. But Brendan knew it was a mask. He could feel the pain she suppressed.

'Oh, hell! I'm sorry, Lana.'

'Why? It's what you've wanted isn't it?'

Brendan had indeed dreamt of the day that Alannah broke up with Liam, but he never wished for it to be at her expense. He had imagined her being the one to kick Liam's sorry arse out on the street. And in his fantasy, it was because she had chosen him. 'Not like this, Lana. Not with you hurting.'

She flinched.

Squeezing her hand, he gave her a reassuring smile. 'My place it is.'

The fridge was Alannah's first port of call when they got home. Brendan's new place had become a second home for her after all. She glanced over the door and grinned. 'Is that my pizza?'

'Yup. I worried about you too much to eat last night.'

It did not take her long to devour the food and wash it down with a beer, all while standing in the kitchen.

Brendan watched, his dick at half-mast while he half-frowned. 'Are you okay?'

She grabbed a couple more beers and bumped the fridge door closed with her arse. 'I feel a hell of a lot better now I've eaten. I give the hospitality in that place minus five stars.'

'Wow, okay.'

Alannah handed him one of the beers and moved to the couch.

He sat beside Alannah, pulling her into his arms. 'You don't have to hide your emotions from me anymore, Lana.'

She sighed. 'I'm not hiding them, I'm processing. And… trying not to fall apart. I feel like I've already cried enough for two lifetimes lately. I don't know if there are any tears left.' She took a few deep breaths. 'I feel so damn angry.'

'Angry with who?'

'The lot of 'em.' Alannah closed her eyes. 'But mostly Richard. And Clayton—that creep needs to burn.'

The hairs on the back of Brendan's neck prickled and violence churned deep in his gut. He sat up and gazed deep into her eyes. 'Did that bastard touch you?'

Alannah bit her lip.

'Oh hell!'

Before he could say anything more, she shook her head. 'Not like that. He couldn't keep his hands to himself; but no, he didn't take it far. Although I wouldn't put it past him, given the opportunity. I'm glad I didn't have to spend another night locked up there.'

'So am I. And I swear to the Gods next time I see the wanker I'm gonna teach him a lesson in respect.'

'Don't, Brendan. Please don't go caveman on his arse.'

'Are you kidding me? He needs to pay.'

'I agree, but Clayton's a powerful warlock and he's protected by the Council. We need to fight smarter, not stronger. The same goes for taking Richard down.'

'Why does it sound like you're cooking up a plan?'

Something mischievous gleamed in her eyes as she gave him a lopsided grin. 'Because I am.'

After picking up a few things from home, Alannah collapsed on Brendan's couch with another beer.

He cocked a brow at the sight of her sprawled out. 'You wanna skip the pub and stay in tonight?'

She gave him two thumbs up. 'Once again with the knowing what I need.'

Brendan smiled. 'I bet I know what else you need.' He chuckled at her side-eye. 'You assume I'm going to say something dirty, don't you?'

'Well you usually do.'

'Touché. But not this time. Despite popular belief, I don't always think with my dick.' He moved her legs to sit on the sofa, but instead of letting her feet drop to the floor, he pulled them into his lap, and massaged one.

Alannah threw her head back as the pleasure of his touch shot through her. 'Oh, Gods, that feels unreal. Are you sure this has nothing to do with sex?'

'Only if you want it to.'

Pulling her other foot back, she aimed a kick at his chest, but Brendan caught the offending foot.

'Careful now, Lana. A degenerate like me might mistake your actions for foreplay.'

She glared at him. 'You expect me to believe your intentions are honourable when you say stuff like that?'

He gasped. 'Hell, Lana. You think I'd pressure you? Your side of Liam's bed hasn't even grown cold yet and I know your heart still aches for him. Please, give me more credit. I was only trying to lighten the mood with some flirting.' Sighing, he pushed her feet from his lap and grabbed his own beer.

'I'm sorry, Brendan. I didn't mean to imply you would.'

Humour returned to his eyes as he gave her a big grin. 'I bet the sex with Liam was lousy.'

Alannah did not say anything, she simply rolled her eyes.

'What? Too soon? Isn't it a best friend's job to throw shade on your ex when they break your heart?'

'Yeah, but that's more Cara's domain. Things are more… complicated between us.'

'But you gotta satisfy my curiosity because you know how competitive I get with my brother. Was he any good in the bedroom?'

She sighed. On the one hand, it felt wrong to divulge this stuff with the one person that would never let Liam live it down, but on the other hand…*screw him*. 'You're right. The bedroom chemistry was way off. He wasn't into anything kinky, and he left me unsatisfied most nights of the week because he was too tired.'

'Hell! I'd never leave a woman wanting, no matter how tiring my day was. I figured he was dull, but that's unforgivable.'

Shaking her head, she tittered. 'Not everyone has your insatiable appetite for sex, Brendan. People are entitled to a rest. Besides, priorities change over time in long-term relationships.'

'Not that a playboy like myself would know much about that, though huh?' A hint of acrimony laced his tone.

Alannah snorted. 'Will you settle down if you find the right woman?'

His right eyebrow almost lifted off his face. 'That's a loaded question.'

'How so?'

His left brow joined its friend, and his eyes bored into her. 'The question assumes I haven't already found the right woman.'

She forgot to breathe for a split second. 'Have you?'

'I don't know, Lana. You tell me.'

She struggled to breath in that moment. 'So much for giving me time.'

'You asked. I'll give you all the time you need. But know this, gorgeous: none of those other girls were you. That's why I didn't commit to any of them.' Brendan leaned in close, his breath tickling the sensitive spot on her neck as he spoke into her ear. 'And as soon as you give me the green light, I will bang you six ways from Sunday.' He sat back with a twinkle in his eyes. 'I haven't forgotten your comment about kink either. I bet you like it rough.'

Alannah's lips curved into a half-smile. 'Maybe.'

'Do you like to dish out the pain, or receive it?'

She paused a moment to consider her answer, but also to read Brendan's aura. There it was: his emotions pulsed bright pink and red, confirming how much he loved and desired her. 'Receive it, mostly.' She observed the lust intensify and felt her skin tingle all over.

Puffing his breath through pursed lips, he shifted in his seat. 'That sweet mix of pleasure and pain makes for some of the steamiest sex. Just thinking about doing that stuff with you is turning me on.' His eyes narrowed: 'As you can see in my aura.'

A gasp escaped her mouth. 'I'm sorry.' She attempted a coy smile. 'But how did you know?'

'It's okay. I don't mind having you read me like a book. As for the *how*…' Brendan smirked. 'You're not the only one with a secret power or two.'

'Tell me, Brendan. How did you know?'

'I read your thoughts.'

Alannah's jaw dropped. 'When did you start reading minds?'

'When we were sixteen.'

Her skin was heating, and it began to prickle.

Brendan swept in close and seized her hands. 'Now before you get mad, hear me out. I don't always read your mind, and even then, I only get the surface thoughts.'

'But you still read me. Why?'

'Come on, Lana. Stop pretending you don't get me. When you asked me to stop reading your aura, I wanted to respect your request, but I needed a way to gauge your feelings for me.'

Glaring, Alannah shook her head. 'My thoughts are a lot more personal than my aura.'

'I know, which is why I only caught the occasional glimpse when I needed to know if things were still unrequited. And you did an effective job of shutting me out of your mind over the last few years anyway.'

Sighing, Alannah reclined into the couch. 'Before tonight, what was the last of my thoughts that you heard?'

'You were asking me about my empathic link as my finger trailed up your leg.'

She bit her lip as the memory of their sensual moment stirred the same heat and moisture between her thighs.

'You remember what was on your mind then, hmm? I wasn't planning to take things further, but it was hard to resist your mental plea to plunge that finger deep inside you.'

Withdrawing her hands from his grip, Alannah closed her eyes and focussed on a quick breathing exercise. She needed to get her hormones in check. Tempting as it was to jump Brendan's bones then and there, she needed a full night of rest after her tribulations.

'I won't read your mind again if you don't want me to.'

She opened her eyes and smiled at him. 'It's okay, Brendan. I kinda like having you in tune with me. I wish I could read *your* mind.'

He laughed. 'You sure you want in there? It's a pretty filthy place.'

Alannah grinned. 'It could be fascinating. And I am capable now with my primordial attunement.'

Brendan smirked. 'Be my guest, gorgeous. Just don't expect me to pay for your therapy bills.'

As Alannah drained the last of her beer, a huge yawn escaped. She dropped the empty bottle on the coffee table and snuggled into Brendan's side. 'Don't worry Brendan, you're the only therapist I need.' She closed her eyes.

'Gods, I love you, Lana.' Brendan's arms tightened around her as she drifted off to sleep.

Alannah inspected the crystal grid she had made with apophyllite at the centre. The gems took up all the space on the small wooden altar in Brendan's cramped training room. She stood up and faced him. 'It's ready.'

'Are you sure about this, Lana?' Brendan surveyed the altar before eyeing her.

'Yeah, I am. Smarter not stronger, remember? This is the best option.'

He sighed. 'I understand your plan, I do, but I still hate it. There must be another way. I don't like risking you. What if I do it?'

She shook her head. 'You will get in a lot more trouble if they catch you. Besides, there is still the Clayton issue to deal with.'

Grimacing, he stepped closer and pulled Alannah into his arms. 'I dislike that part of your plan the most.'

After swallowing against the lump in her throat, she squeezed both his biceps. 'I appreciate you willing to make the sacrifice, but time is not on our side. It could take you months to gain access to the stygian element. My trial date is just over two weeks away. I have a better chance of learning how to harness the power in time.'

'What if we run away and hide?'

'No. I have to do this.'

Brendan dropped his forehead to hers and sucked in a deep breath. A couple of tears fell from his eyes, dripping onto her lips. 'You are the bravest person I know.'

Her tongue darted out to taste the salty residue of Brendan's pain. The motion drew his eyes to her mouth, transfixing his gaze. She did not need to read his mind to know what he was thinking. Alannah thought it too. Her resolve teetered on the edge but giving in to the primal need would distract her too much from the bigger picture. She pushed back from him. 'I'll be okay Brendan, I promise.'

'How can you promise when dealing with such unpredictable, sadistic arseholes?'

'Because I have something they don't.'

'What?'

She smiled at him. 'Someone worth fighting for.'

He exhaled through pursed lips. 'You're pushing the limits of my restraint here.'

Yours and mine both.

Brendan's eyes flashed as he took a step toward her.

'Crap, did you hear that?'

Nodding, he took another step. One more would bring them toe to toe.

'I need to focus on the task at hand, Brendan. But if I succeed with the channelling today, we can celebrate tonight.'

The left side of his lip curled into a lopsided grin. 'Celebrate how, Lana?'

'Like a date.'

His brows launched into outer space. 'For real?'

'Yes, for real.'

'Fuck!' He beamed from ear to ear.

'Later,' she offered with a mischievous grin.

Brendan's eyes were ablaze as he leapt at her. Alannah squealed as she ducked out of the way, but he still managed to grab her by the arm and whirl her around, pinning her against the closed door. 'That better be a promise, Lana, because it's some vicious teasing if not.'

'Damn it, Brendan, you're making things hard.'

'No, Lana. *You're* making things hard.' He thrust his pelvis into her to prove his point. Do you have any idea how close I am to bending you over the altar and defiling both you and this sacred space?'

'Okay, point taken.'

Brendan gave her a lewd grin. 'Not yet, it's not. You know, I'm wondering if it might be better to screw all this sexual tension between us away before attempting to practise the dark arts.'

The fires of the Underworld would have been cooler than Alannah's skin. Biting her lip, she considered telling him.

'Tell me what, Lana?'

'Crap. That mind reading is getting frustrating.'

His right hand moved to her left breast and pinched her hard, aching nipple. 'Do you need me to redefine frustration? *Tell me.*'

Squirming from his continued torture, she let out an exasperated sigh. 'I need the sexual tension for my channelling exercise.'

Brendan's mouth fell agape, and his right hand dropped to his side. But he kept her trapped against the door with his left arm and body weight. 'Since when? Tara never mentioned anything of the sort.'

'I read about it in my book of shadows. When channelling nether, pent up sexual energy helps a newbie achieve results quicker.'

After staring at her in stunned silence for nigh on a minute, his gaze turned fierce. 'Did you just play me, Lana?'

'What? No, of course not. You should be able to feel how much I want you with your empathic link. We just need to hold out a tad longer.'

Still caging her in, he drew his bottom lip between his teeth and sucked on it. Her skin dripped with perspiration and if he did not move soon, Alannah knew she would cave.

'Please,' she pleaded in a whisper.

He drew a deep breath, stepping back. 'Fine.'

Alannah dashed across the room and snatched up the gas lighter to start the ritual before it was too late.

Brendan let out a low, sexy laugh. 'I love your enthusiasm, gorgeous.'

She would have chastised him, but he dropped to his knees on the edge of the pentagram and fell quiet. After casting the circle, Alannah channelled the primordial. Only this time, she hardwired the images in her mind to keep the channel open. 'Phew. Step one complete.' She looked at Brendan. 'Now the tricky bit. You know what to do if things get hairy?'

He nodded. 'Cut the circle and drag your sexy arse out of here.'

'Right.' Closing her eyes, she slipped back into a mindful state and visualised the Underworld, starting with the upper layer—a large, barren desert—and working her way down through the freezing tundras and glaciers, putrid swamps, and finally the Volcanic Pits that were the source of nether.

She made use of her carnal desires in those pits, picturing herself chained up as a demonic form of Brendan ravished her. The heat was sweltering, and she could feel the power start to flow through her. *By the Gods!* She thought it was pleasurable channelling lust and the primordial, but this was something else.

It was like comparing the light rush of blood following a minute of hanging upside down with the adrenaline high of abseiling.

Alannah had a decision to make. She could either stop the exercise and sever her link to the most erotic power source of all, or she could keep the gateway open. Her body cried out for a release; so, she moved her hand between her legs to bring on the climax she yearned for. As the release came, Alannah made her connection to the forbidden mana permanent, thus sealing her fate.

Opening her eyes, she glanced at Brendan's gobsmacked expression and grinned. 'It's date time.'

Brendan licked his lips. 'Can I bang you first?'

She laughed. 'That's not how dates work, Brendan. The sex usually comes at the end of the night *if* you're lucky.'

He scoffed. '*If I'm lucky*? I was right there in in your head during those visions. I know what you want, and I intend to make every one of your wild fantasies come true.'

She arched a brow. 'Is that a threat or a promise?'

'To satisfy *your* kinks, Lana, it will have to be both.'

Alannah rose. 'Well then, time's-a-wastin'.'

'The city, huh?' Alannah queried as the Jag turned onto the highway.

Brendan glanced at her; an infectious grin plastered on his face. 'I'm hardly gonna take you to the local pub on our first official date, gorgeous. I've dreamt of this night for at least a decade. It's gonna be special.'

Alannah's heart performed acrobatics again. It had become such a habit of late, that she was thinking of giving the organ a stage name. 'Wow. And here I thought your idea of a dream date would be tying me to the bed and drinking shots from my navel between rounds of coital bliss. Who knew you could be romantic too?'

He laughed. 'There you go spoiling my surprise for the second date.' After parking in a secure garage, Brendan turned to her. 'Wait there a second.'

She could only manage a nod while calming her breath.

Brendan got out of the car and circled around to open her door. 'My Lady?'

Gods! This was almost too much. But Alannah loved every second of it. She gave Brendan her hand, letting him help her up as she smoothed down her short, red cocktail dress. Not a colour she had worn before, but she felt like a change.

Her date wore a black suit. From what she understood, Brendan hated formalwear, but he had gone all out for her.

Once out of the car, Alannah took a moment to admire the vision in front of her. 'Damn you look hot in a suit, Brendan. You should wear them more often.'

Linking his arm in hers, he leaned in and pressed his lips against her ear. 'Anything for you, gorgeous.' His voice was deep and erotic, eliciting a rush of hormones through her bloodstream.

They walked in comfortable silence for a block until they reached a dimly lit, non-descript door. It led them down a dingy staircase into a narrow corridor toward a red glow. Alannah gave him the side eye. 'If we weren't dressed to the nines, I'd be thinking sex dungeon right about now.'

Brendan replied with a deep, throaty laugh. He pulled her to a stop in front of a kobold bouncer who stood in front of a black door beneath a red lightbulb.

The draconic man gave them a polite nod. 'Good evening, sir, Madam.' He stepped aside to let them pass.

As soon as they stepped beyond the black door, Alannah froze, stunned by the beauty before her. 'Wow, what is this place?' Warm, sparkling light glittered from crystal chandeliers and bounced from the reflective walls which contained specks of quartz. A stage at one end of the room drew her attention. She watched a seelie ensemble performing sensual, jazzy music. A nymph in a long, sleek, black dress covered in sequins fronted the band. Upon closer inspection, Alannah recognised Bianca.

'The Crystal Cabaret. It's a popular hangout for magicals and a refuge from pure mages. They only let me in because I'm friends with a bunch of fae and they know I won't cause trouble.'

'And me?'

'Well, they know you're not exactly in the Council's good books right now.'

Alannah snorted. 'Putting it mildly.'

'*Wowsers!*' Brendan muttered as he gazed at her.

'What?'

'Your eyes. They burned red for a split second. Must be a side effect. Do you feel okay?'

She grinned. 'Better than okay. I guess I should have mentioned I kept the channel open. I guess there's a little demon in me.'

Brendan exhaled sharply, leaning in close to speak in her ear. 'I wish I was that demon right now.' Grabbing her hand, he led her through the club.

Alannah turned to him as they reached the bar. 'You wanna be a demon, huh?'

'I told you, Lana, if you go to hell, I'm following you there.' He focussed his attention on her, sending her heart down the road in a series of cartwheels.

Hmm, how about The Magnificent Flipping Felicity?

'What can I get you to drink?' a soft voice asked.

Alannah faced the bartender, but the gem encrusted counter bedazzled her, sparkling in every colour imaginable. The bartender himself was a clurichaun. Serving drinks was a fitting job for fae born of alcohol-induced debauchery.

She returned the man's smile. 'I'll have a single malt whiskey, thanks. Whatever you recommend.'

'Make that two.' Brendan handed over a wad of cash.

With drinks in hand, they settled into a booth where Brendan's left arm rested across Alannah's shoulders. She took a moment to study their surrounds. 'No one's using glamour in here.'

'This club is off limits to humans. It is one of the few public places where magicals can be themselves. Most find it liberating.'

She nodded. 'I guess it would be exhausting to keep up those illusions all the time. We are lucky we appear human.'

'I guess. But it's not why I'm feeling lucky tonight.' Brendan's eyes fixed on her as he spoke in that bedroom voice of his.

Blushing, she bit her lip and turned her attention to the stage. 'Bianca's got some pipes.'

'I suppose she has.'

Alannah sipped her drink, enthralled by the music when Brendan grabbed her and pulled her onto the dancefloor.

His arms held her close, and they swayed to Bianca's deep, sensual voice singing about spending an 'Evil Night Together.'

'You know, I don't normally dance to jazz music.'

'This isn't jazz, it's dark cabaret. Also, shoosh.' He wrapped his arms around her, dancing with their bodies pressed close.

Alannah's blood still hummed with the effects of nether flowing through her, although the intensity had waned since first connecting with the power source. But another sensation slid across her skin and seeped into her pores and Brendan's hands—clamped on her backside—were the source. Resting her head against his chest, she inhaled his rich, musky fragrance. 'Are you trying to enchant me, Brendan Winters?'

'Not intentionally. Holding you like this feels incredible and I'm instinctively channelling your touch.'

Looking up at him, she found Brendan staring at her, his eyes blazing with passion. Alannah glanced at his lips, full and kissable, drawing her in.

Brendan licked those luscious lips, tilting his head down. His mouth was a hair's breadth from hers when his head jolted upright, glimpsing something over her shoulder. *'Damnit!'* He swung Alannah around, and stood in front of her like a shield.

When she peeked out from behind his broad frame, Alannah felt the blood drain from her face as two warlocks approached.

'I see you waste no time, *Brother*,' Liam hissed.

Brendan tried to block their access to her, but Clayton dodged around him and grabbed her. 'Keep your damn hands off her!' Brendan seethed.

As the cuffs clamped around her wrists, Liam grimaced. 'Alannah Winters, you are under arrest for the crime of channelling the stygian element.'

Damnit! She did not think they would come for her this soon.

'You will be held in custody until your trial without the option of bail,' Liam continued.

'No!' Brendan cried as he moved toward them, but Liam pinned him against the wall with a forceful gust of wind. Brendan's eyes filled with tears that streamed across his cheeks like a waterfall. His voice entered Alannah's mind. *'I love you, Lana. Stay strong for me, gorgeous.'*

She caught a final glimpse of Brendan as Clayton ripped her away from the warmth and safety of his presence. She hoped he heard her parting thought. *I love you too, Brendan.*

Chapter Sixteen

There were some days when Liam detested being a warlock and this was one of them. Even after everything that happened, and all the pain Alannah had caused him, it killed him to arrest her. Seeing how she had rushed into Brendan's arms, and most likely his bed, did not help Liam's mood either.

It was late when he got home. He threw his keys at the buffet, kicked his boots off in the hall, and beelined for his bedroom. As he flicked on the light, he jumped out of his skin. *'Holy shit!'* When he recognised Brendan slumped over the edge of his bed, Liam's pale face turned red. 'I knew I should have changed the locks. Why the hell are you lurking in the dark like a creeper?'

When Brendan looked up, the raw emotion on display floored Liam. 'Oh good, you're home. I need your help, bro.'

'I might be your brother, but I'm not your damn bro. That ship sailed long ago when you started putting the moves on my girl.'

Brendan sighed. 'Be honest, Liam: that ship didn't even dock in the first place. Lana was never your girl; you just hated seeing how close she was to me and drove yourself between us like a wedge over and over. But I'm not here to debate the finer points of our age-old rivalry. I need your help; or rather, Lana needs your help.'

He tensed. 'There's nothing I can do to help her now; she dug her own grave.'

Brendan shook his head. 'I can't believe you dumped Lana over this business with Tara. Did you even get her side of the story, or was your head stuffed too far up Richard's arse to hear it? You should know her heart and soul are too pure to turn to dark magic without decent reasons.'

Liam heaved the air from his lungs and collapsed on the edge of the bed beside Brendan. 'I was angry about the Tara stuff, but it's not why I broke things off with her.'

'Then why?'

'Are you dense, Brendan? Why do you think she went running to you?'

'Because you left her in a time of need, yet again.'

'But why *you*, Brendan? Why not Cara, or Mum? She always went to you, even when I *was* there for her.'

Brendan gulped as he stared at Liam. Seconds later, a smug grin developed.

'Congratulations Brendan, you got the girl. Pity she's in prison. Now get out of my house before I throw you out.'

His expression sobered. 'Wait! Do you still care about Lana at all?'

'Of course, but—'

'Then I'm guessing you don't want her to get hurt by sadistic arseholes while in prison.'

Holding his breath for a second, Liam processed Brendan's meaning before exhaling. 'It's okay, Richard doesn't have access to her in there and no one can bribe the elven guards.'

'Richard might not be able to get to her, but his buddy Clayton can, and that man's torture methods are lot more sexual in nature.'

White hot rage boiled his blood. '*The hell?* What. Did. He do?'

'So far? Only a bit of handsy harassment, but I worry he will make good on his threats over the next two weeks.'

Liam rocketed off the bed. 'I'm gonna kill him.'

'*Liam*! Wait!'

He paused at the door.

'Lana has a plan. A super sucky plan, but I promised her I'd stick to it. Sit down and hear me out.'

Turning, he returned to the bed. 'Fine.'

Over a week had passed. Eleven days by Alannah's count, but she based her assumption on the regularity of her twice-daily meals. The guards never spoke to her when they delivered the food, even when she asked them questions. At least they were feeding her this time.

The only regular visitor who talked to her was Liam, but she did not want to talk to him. His previous hurtful words and abandonment still stung. When he had come the morning after her arrest, he had apologised:

> '*I'm sorry, Lana. Brendan told me everything.*'
> *She looked up from her seat on the bed. 'Will you help with my plan?'*
> *Liam winced as he nodded. 'Yes. I get what you're doing with regards to Richard, but I hate the risk you are taking with Clayton.' He slipped a phone beneath her mattress. 'I've set the voice recording app to start, and I'll swap it out daily with a freshly charged burner.'*
> *'Good.' She turned around to face the wall.*

'I really am sorry. I said all those things because I was hurting, but I didn't mean any of it. Please, you have to forgive me.'

'I don't have to do anything for you, Liam. Please leave me alone.'

She heard him sigh, but he did not press the issue.

Memories of Brendan kept her going through the agonising loneliness and stifling silence. The feel of his strong arms wrapped around her; the sound of his deep, erotic voice saying dirty things; those inviting lips almost kissing her and the desire in his eyes promising much more. Their almost-kiss drove her wild at night when she tried to sleep. *When I get my freedom back, kissing the hell out of those lips is the first thing I will do.* She prayed her chance would be sooner rather than later.

On the verge of sleep, Alannah woke with sudden awareness chilling her to the bone. Her eyes flicked open, and she tried to scream.

But his strong, rough hand clamped over her mouth. 'Did you think I would forget about that fine arse of yours, *sweetheart*? I've been waiting for the right opportunity to come and claim it,' the horribly familiar voice growled.

She tried to fight him off, even biting his hand, but nothing deterred him. The bastard was naked, and the more she struggled, the more obvious his arousal became.

'Guess what, *sweetheart?* These walls are soundproof, so you can scream all you like. It will only make me harder.' He pulled his hand from her mouth and flipped her over.

'You'll burn in hell for this, arsehole!' she cried out.

He sniggered as he cuffed her hands to the bars at the head of the bed. 'And you'll burn right alongside me, you filthy dark mage whore. Mm, I guess I'll get an eternity of fucking this arse in the afterlife. Lucky me.'

Alannah's legs flailed as he tore her pants from them. She hoped to kick him in the nuts but being on her front made it impossible to aim. When his solid body pushed her down against the bed, she swallowed hard. She knew resistance was futile at this point, but her fighting spirit would not let go. '*No!* Get off me you creep!'

Clayton's putrid breath oozed across her neck as he spoke in her ear. 'Not gonna happen, *sweetheart.*' Pulling her hips up, he forced her to kneel. He ran the tip of his cock along her back passage. 'Can you feel how big I am, Alannah? I won't lie: this is going to hurt.' He drove himself inside her with lethal force.

She screamed bloody murder. While she had never tried anal with a partner before, she had read about it and knew it took a lot of foreplay and lubrication to prepare for an enjoyable experience. Clayton tearing her open was the least pleasurable experience of her life. Her eyes watered as she cried out.

When it became unbearable, her breathing slowed, and she prayed. *Oh Gods, please make the pain stop.* Then it did. She could not feel the physical ache, or the grief. In fact, she could not feel anything except a wonderful sense of peace.

Opening her eyes, Alannah gasped at her surrounds. No longer kneeling on the wretched bed of broken springs, she stood in an open field full of purple wildflowers as far as the eye could see. *Stunning.*

An oddly familiar stranger in blue velvet robes approached her. White wispy clouds surrounded him, and his aura was strong and pure. 'Hello, dear child.'

'W-where am I?' she stammered, not quite sure how to address the powerful man.

'The Celestial Realm.'

She blinked a few times. *Yep, still here.* Peeking down at herself, Alannah observed her own white and wispy form. 'A-am I... dead?'

He gave her a sympathetic smile. 'No, Lana, your soul just needed a holiday from your body.'

'How did I get here?'

'Through your Aether connection.'

'I thought the cage prevented my access to mana.'

This time his smile broadened. 'Some magic is more powerful than anything earthly... like love, or the bonds of family.'

A few of the words the man had spoken dropped into place for her. Child. Love. Family. Unable to suppress her hope, Alannah wagered her heart on a hunch. 'Dad? You're my real dad?'

'Yes, I am. It is lovely to finally meet you, Lana. I've been keeping an eye on you over the years and you have done much to make me proud.'

A sobering thought occurred. 'Wait, if you're up here, that means you are dead.'

'Please don't mourn for me, dear child. While I do not live in your realm, I am happy living here. And one day, when your time does come, you will join me.'

If she could cry, she would have. 'But with all I have done, I might not get the chance to return.'

'You will, I promise. All the Gods know your intentions are honourable. You are a strong and brave woman, Lana. The strongest of Cailleach's daughters yet. I hope you can take heart in my words and the knowledge that you are on the right path.'

The feeling of peace returned, and she felt herself smile. 'Thanks.'

'I must go now, and it is time for you to return home. Remember what I have told you, okay?'

'Okay.'

'Goodbye for now, dear child.' He turned and walked away.

'Wait! I didn't get your name.'

But her dad had already vanished, and she felt her body tugging at her soul.

When consciousness returned, Clayton had gone, but the burning sensation remained. Whimpering, she turned to face the wall, away from the security camera, and reached under the bed for the phone Liam had smuggled in. After sending a quick SOS text, she curled up in a ball under the blanket and sobbed with the last of her energy reserves.

Alannah must have fallen asleep because the next thing she knew, Liam shook her. 'Hey Lana, I'm here. Everything will be okay now.'

But she was too tired and weak to move.

He pulled the blanket away, sending bitter chills dancing across her bare skin. '*Oh Gods!* You're bleeding, Lana. Dad! There's so much blood! You've gotta help her.'

'Give me space, Son,' Ross commanded in a calm tone.

Liam stepped back, and Alannah felt her uncle's hands on her head. His hand shifted to inspect the damage.

'Why is she bleeding?' Liam gulped.

'She has a large anal fissure.'

'*Shit!* That bastard is going to pay for this.'

'Alannah, honey.' Ross' voice was warm and soothing. 'I don't know if you can hear me, but I need to take some samples now. I will try to be gentle, but some of this might hurt.' The first few swabs were external, brushing her thighs and buttocks with a tickle, but she did not flinch. The first of the internal swabs was vaginal—uncomfortable, but not painful. But the anal swab was a different story. Her eyes shot open wide as her leg jolted, but Liam caught it before she could move far.

'It's okay, Lana, everything will be okay,' Liam's voice trembled. 'The bastard won't ever touch you again, I promise.'

Ross moved into her field of view. 'I have all the samples I need, Lana.' He handed her a potion vial. 'Here, drink this. It will help with the pain.'

Alannah gaped at him.

'*Oh Gods!* She's in catatonic shock, Dad.'

'I know.' Ross sat on the edge of the bed and pulled her into his arms, wrapping the blanket around her. After opening the vial, he tilted her head back and encouraged her to drink the potion.

Liam growled. 'She needs a therapist and to get out of this hell-hole.'

Ross sighed. 'I agree, but you and I both know Richard won't allow it. The best we can do for her now is process the evidence so we can put Clayton away.' He stroked the side of her face. 'I'm sorry this happened to you, sweetheart.'

Boom!

Alannah turned manic, pushing away at the hands holding her. '*No! Get off me you creep!*' she screamed.

'Get back Dad!' Liam knelt in front of her. 'Lana, it's okay. No one here wants to hurt you. You are safe now.'

This time she blinked through the tears. 'Liam?'

'Yes, princess, I'm here. You're safe now. Dad has the samples, and we are going to destroy the man who did this to you.'

Alannah nodded. 'Good.' She reached for the phone. 'Here. There's an audio file on it to prove my lack of consent.'

Liam took the phone, reaching out to touch her face but she recoiled from him. 'Lana?'

'I'm still pissed with you.'

Shoulders sagging, tears swelled in his eyes. 'I'm so sorry, Lana.'

'Please leave me be. Both of you. I'm tired.'

'Yes, of course. You've need to rest and heal,' Ross agreed. 'If you still have pain tomorrow, get one of the guards to call me, okay?'

She nodded, curling up under the blanket again.

Liam hesitated.

'Come on, Son. Give her time.'

Alannah drifted off to sleep as the cage door locked.

Alannah glanced around the courtroom: smaller than she had expected from watching television and movies. Scanning the room confirmed Clayton's absence, which eased the tension in her shoulders. Liam was the warlock to escort her into court, under Monique's supervision. He sat beside her, while Monique stared daggers at her from the Clerk's desk.

Her eyes lit up the moment Brendan entered the room, walking straight up to her. His voice entered her mind on approach. *'Hi gorgeous, miss me?'*

She scoffed. *'Understatement of the year.'*

As Brendan reached her, she moved in for a hug, but he shook his head and whispered, 'Not here. We have to show decorum and whatnot.'

Alannah nodded. 'How did you score front row seats?'

He grinned. 'I convinced the Council to let me represent you.'

'For real? You're not even a lawyer.'

'Doesn't matter. A lot of the best magic lawyers are enchanters. And I did a crash course in legal studies during your confinement. I'm considering a career change now.'

She gaped at him.

'Plus, it beats doing this by yourself. You've been through enough lately.' He frowned.

'All rise for the honourable Kieran Lane.'

The High Magus entered and took his place at the judge's bench. Once everyone returned to their seats, he addressed the room. 'Good morning, ladies and gentlemen. Calling the case of Alannah Winters versus the magic State of South Australia. Are both sides ready?'

Lucas Ó Máille stood up and Alannah heard Brendan curse under his breath. 'Ready for the State, Your Honour.'

Brendan rose. 'Ready for the defence, Your Honour.'

Kieran instructed Monique to swear in the jury, a diverse cross section of the magical community. Alannah did not recognise any of them from town. Kieran turned his attention to Lucas. 'I call the prosecution forward for an opening statement.'

Lucas stepped up. 'Thank you, Your Honour.' He turned to face the jury, reading from his notes. 'Ladies and gentlemen, the defendant has been charged with the crimes of treason and for practising dark magic. A witness will testify the defendant met with Tara Winters on the nineteenth of October to discuss unsanctioned training. This will be supported by audio and visual evidence. Following bail, the same witness discovered the defendant channelling the stygian element on the twenty-first of October. The evidence I present to you will prove without doubt the defendant is guilty as charged.' The room fell quiet as he returned to his table.

'I call the defence forward for an opening statement.'

Brendan winked at Alannah and rose to face the jury. 'Greetings, Your Honour and ladies and gentlemen of the jury. Please recall that according to law, my client is innocent until proven guilty. I will show you there is no case against my client. Firstly, Alannah Winters worked to undermine Tara Winters and secondly, there is no evidence to suggest she ever used her channelling for nefarious purposes. Therefore, my client is not guilty.'

When he returned to the seat beside Alannah, she smiled at him, thinking: *You seriously rocked that speech.*

He grinned. *'Thanks, gorgeous. When this is all over, I will rock the rest of your world.'*

She clamped her legs together. *Damn.*

'The prosecution may call its first witness.'

Their heads snapped forward as Lucas called Richard to the witness stand. After running through all the evidence of Alannah's meeting with Tara, Lucas moved onto the more pertinent question. 'Please describe the dark magic you witnessed the defendant practising on the twenty-first of October.'

'Certainly. I monitored her following her bail. On the day in question, I saw her use a ritual circle to open a connection to the nether. As you know, magic law strictly forbids this mana source because of its connection to demonic forces.'

Lucas nodded, pausing for dramatic effect. 'How did you know she channelled nether?'

Alannah and Brendan both edged forward on their seats.

Richard stared straight at her, his lips curling into a smirk. 'Because I could read her mind when she performed the visualisation exercise.'

She paled at the thought of Richard being party to such an intimate experience.

'Can you describe the visualisation?'

'I will spare you all the explicit details, but the gist of it is Alannah performed sexual acts in the volcanic pits of the Underworld.'

There were a few gasps from the jury and a couple of sniggers.

Brendan placed a reassuring hand over hers as he spoke telepathically. *'Don't let him get to you, Lana.'*

Lucas shook his head. *'Tsk, tsk.* Thank you, Inquisitor. No further questions.'

Kieran looked at Brendan. 'Does the defence have any questions?'

He stood. 'Yes, Your Honour.'

'You may approach the stand.'

'Your Honour, I seek permission to use the Cuffs of Truth.'

Kieran's eyes narrowed on him. 'The witness has already sworn an oath, Mr. Winters. What grounds do you have to require such an archaic method?'

'I have evidence to support a possible mistrial, Your Honour.'

The High Magus arched a brow. 'What type of evidence?'

'Testimony by means of cross-examination to prove the prosecution's witness is guilty of misconduct and obtaining evidence by wrongful means, Your Honour.'

Kieran frowned. 'Very well. Warlock Winters, please deploy the Cuffs of Truth.'

Brendan and Liam exchanged nods and glances before Liam stepped up to the bar to present an old wooden box. He withdrew an old set of cold iron manacles from the chest.

Monique inspected them before announcing, 'I confirm the deployment of authentic Cuffs of Truth, Your Honour.'

Liam took the cuffs up to a disgruntled Richard and fastened them to the Inquisitor's wrists before returning to

Alannah's side. Aside from humiliation, the cuffs themselves were not designed to hurt. They did, however, prevent Richard from using his own magic to hide the truth. Their worth came from what an enchanter could do to their wearer.

Alannah's pulse became manic. This was the moment she had been eagerly anticipating. She had planned to have Brendan present, working his magic in the background; but having him right there to challenge Richard was even better.

Brendan stepped up to the witness stand. 'Tell me, Inquisitor, are you certain Alannah Winters channelled nether? Perhaps her vision was part of some wild sexual fantasy.' He glanced over his shoulder and winked at Alannah.

More titters from the jury.

'Yes, I am certain.'

'What makes you certain?'

Richard glowered at Brendan with a twitch in his eye. 'I detected the channelling.'

'Hmm, interesting. How, pray tell, was that possible?' The two men became locked in a contest of wills as Brendan attempted to pull the truth out of him.

'B-because I have an open nether channel.'

The intake of breath drawn by every single jury member was more predictable than a Skrillex bass drop.

'Are you admitting to the same magic practice for which Alannah has been charged?'

'Objection, Your Honour,' Lucas cried out. 'The witness is not on trial.'

Kieran shot Brendan an annoyed glance. 'Sustained. Keep to the facts, Mr. Winters.'

'Fine. What do you use the stygian element for?'

'Detecting other users, obviously.'

'Obviously. Anything else? Such as the summoning of demonic sex slaves perhaps?'

Richard gasped. 'What? No! I've never summoned demons. That is true dark magic. I also use it to block the effects of other people's spells.'

The jury murmured.

'Silence!' Kieran demanded.

'Interesting. So, you don't think channelling nether is true dark magic?'

'I know it isn't. Dark magic taints the soul, but the simple act of channelling nether doesn't.'

Brendan turned and grinned at Alannah for a second before turning back to Richard. 'Had you suspected my client of channelling nether on a previous occasion, Inquisitor?'

'Yes.'

'Was this because of your own nether channel?'

'Yes. But also because I sensed she was hiding something when I conducted my first interview.'

'Indeed. How did you go about questioning her the second time?'

Richard's brow furrowed. 'Please clarify the question.'

Brendan drew closer to the stand. 'Fine. I'll spell it out for you then, shall I? Did you abduct and torture Alannah Winters in an abandoned bomb shelter?'

The eye twitch returned. 'N-yes.'

'And did your torture involve chaining her to a corrugated iron wall with cold iron manacles so you could cut into her with a scalpel and burn her flesh with a cigarette lighter?' Brendan's voice rose with each accusatory word.

'Yes.'

He glanced at the jury's wide eyes and slack jaws before returning his attention to Richard. 'Did you know such methods of extracting information from a suspect have been illegal in the magic world for over a century now?'

Richard sighed. 'Yes.'

'Why did you do it?'

This time a wicked grin formed on Richard's face. 'Because I enjoyed it.'

Alannah's stomach churned.

Brendan oozed disapproval. 'Did you enjoy watching the surveillance footage of your friend Clayton raping Alannah in prison?'

Lucas jumped up. 'Objection Your Honour, that is not relevant to this case.'

Kieran sighed. 'Are you going somewhere with this line of questioning, Mr. Winters?'

'Of course, Your Honour,' Brendan replied.

'Then carry on.'

Brendan nodded. 'Thank you, Your Honour. Please answer my question, Inquisitor.'

'Yes. I enjoyed the show.'

The bile climbed up her throat.

'Did you know Clayton was going to do it? *Did you let the arsehole brutalise her*?'

'*Mr. Winters!*' Kieran cried out. 'Watch your language and temper in my courtroom or I will have you removed.'

'Sorry, Your Honour.' Brendan took a deep breath and paced. 'Inquisitor Lane, were you complicit in Clayton's plan?'

'No. I didn't know he would violate her.'

'But you didn't stop him or reprimand him when you saw the live video feed?'

'I didn't stop him, no, but I chastised him for potentially compromising this case.'

Brendan stopped pacing and scowled. 'Rather than arresting him for such a violent crime, you gave him a smack for putting your own work in jeopardy. Was that before or after shaking his hand and thanking him for the unsolicited porn?' Lucas rose to object, but Brendan put his hands up in supplication. 'Rhetorical question. So, to summarise, Inquisitor, have you practised magic deemed illegal unnecessarily because it is not dark, and mistreated my client to gain the evidence for this trial?'

Richard growled. 'Yes.'

'No further questions, Your Honour.' Brendan returned to his seat with a victorious smile Alannah felt compelled to return.

'Warlock Winters, please take Inquisitor Richard Lane into custody.' Kieran's words were sweet, sweet music to her ears.

'With pleasure, Your Honour,' Liam replied as he moved toward the witness stand.

Alannah fixed her gaze on Brendan, who spoke in her mind. *'Telepathic high five, gorgeous.'*

Heck yeah!

'I'd like to call a short recess. Monique, will you escort Miss Winters into the defendant's waiting room?'

'Yes, Your Honour.'

Chapter Seventeen

The stuffy air was full of tension, owing in part to the cold iron lining the walls, but mostly to Monique's glowering presence.

'What?' Alannah snapped.

'You will pay for what you did to Uncle Ricki.'

'Oh, I'm sorry, Monique. Did you have a close relationship with the sadistic arsehole? Remind me to be more mindful of your feelings next time I consider retribution for torture.'

Monique went to open her mouth, but there was a knock at the door, so she rose to answer. 'Get lost, Brendan. The defendant is not permitted visitors during recess.'

'She has a right to speak with her legal representative though.'

Huffing, Monique stepped aside to let him in, and slammed the door.

'*Gods!* Someone's turned into a serious grumplestiltskin.'

If looks could kill, Brendan would have been travelling express to meet his maker.

Brendan turned his attention to Alannah and pulled her into a bear hug. 'Gods, I've missed you. How are you holding up?'

'Better now after your kick-arse performance. But I'm still pissing kittens about the verdict.'

Still holding her close, he sighed. 'I know what you mean. I had hoped Kieran would throw the case out of court after all the crap Richard pulled, but I guess nepotism and corruption run deep in the Council.'

'Shut up, Brendan,' Monique hissed.

'Hey, Lana? Can you hear an annoying buzzing sound?'

She snorted. 'See, this is why you're the only therapist I need. Between the hugs and laughs, you've got it covered.'

'We haven't even gotten to the sex bit yet, gorgeous,' he whispered.

Every nerve in her body tingled. 'I can't wait.'

'Fuck, I'm gonna need a cool shower before returning to the courtroom. My usual magic tricks aren't working.'

Alannah chuckled. 'That's because we're in a cold iron room, jackass.'

She could feel his chest rumble against hers as he stroked her head. 'I totally knew that.'

'Are you guys gonna stand there grinding against each other the whole time? It's making me nauseous.'

'Hmm, there's that buzz again,' Brendan retorted.

'Don't mind Monique, she's just jealous. You should hear what she told me about your mad skills.'

'*Alannah!* You are such a bitch!'

A loud knock sounded at the door, followed by one of the court officials popping their head in. 'Recess is over.'

Brendan released her. 'Go on. I'll join you in a moment.'

Alannah studied him with uncertainty until his eye movements gestured to the tent situation in his pants. She bit her lip to suppress the grin threatening a global invasion of her face. 'Okay.'

When everyone settled back in their places, Kieran addressed the room with is his eyes focussed on Alannah. 'After some deliberation I have decided to exclude all existing evidence pertaining to the charges of dark magic. In the absence of permissible evidence, I am dropping these charges.'

Alannah beamed.

'However, there is still the matter of treason, for which the existing evidence remains legitimate. The remainder of this case will focus on such charges.'

Her heart sank again.

'Does the prosecution wish to call any further witnesses?'

Lucas rose. 'No, Your Honour.'

'The defence may call its first witness.'

After a quick squeeze of her hand, Brendan stood. 'I wish to skip straight to the defendant's own testimony, You Honour.'

'Very well.'

Liam led her up to the witness stand. After swearing a sacred oath to the Gods and stating her name for the record, Brendan approached.

'Is the audio recording in question an accurate record of a conversation had by you on the nineteenth of October?'

'Yes.'

'In this conversation, you referred to the other woman as Scarlett, except at one stage, when you addressed her as Grandmother. Is this woman really your grandmother?' Brendan turned toward the jury for a moment.

'Yes. Scarlett is her nickname, but her real name is Tara Winters.'

He spun on his heels. 'But didn't you kill Tara Winters four years ago?'

Amused by his antics, she tried hard to suppress a smile. 'I thought I did, but being a lich, she was able to come back to life. She told me this the first time we met following the incident. Apparently, there is only one way to bring true death to a lich.'

'And how does one bring about this true death?'

Alannah sighed. 'I don't know. I was hoping to learn this by meeting with her.'

Brendan shot her a grin. 'Can you please explain the true purpose of your meetings with Tara Winters?'

'Certainly. As far as she knew, they were training sessions in which she tried to turn me against the Council. But I saw them as an opportunity to gain her confidence and learn her secrets so I could put a stop to her once and for all.'

'So, does that mean you were working against Tara, not with her?'

'Yes, that's right.'

Brendan gave the jury one of his charming smiles before continuing. 'Why didn't you bring this matter to the Council?'

'Because I knew it would compromise my situation and potentially endanger the people I care about.'

'Thank you, Alannah. I have no further questions, Your Honour.' He returned to his seat and winked at her.

'Does the prosecution have any questions?' Kieran asked.

'Yes, Your Honour.' Lucas approached her. 'Miss Winters, what was the nature of the training Tara facilitated?'

'She was teaching me to reconnect to an innate power source I have because of my Beltane Blessing.'

Lucas raised his brows as if intrigued. 'What mana source?'

'The primordial. She explained all blessed children have this gift and we can access all other mana via this power source.'

The entire courtroom erupted in chatter.

'*Silence!*' Kieran cried. But no one paid attention and he needed to use the gavel to bring order back.

'Did you succeed in channelling the primordial, Alannah?'

'Yes. And I now have a permanent connection.'

The room fired up again but fell silent as soon as Kieran shot a lightning bolt at the roof.

'Why didn't you register your new attunement, Miss Winters?'

'Firstly, it isn't new—I was born with it. Secondly, I was arrested shortly after confirming the connection.'

'I have no further questions, Your Honour.' Lucas slumped into his seat.

Kieran looked at her. 'The witness is excused.' When she sat down, he focussed on Brendan. 'Does the defence rest?'

Brendan bobbed up to reply, 'Yes, Your Honour.'

After issuing instructions to the jury, Kieran asked if the final arguments were ready.

Both representatives rose. 'Yes, Your Honour.' Lucas stepped up to the jury as Brendan returned to his seat. 'Ladies and gentlemen of the jury, the High Magus has asked for proof of three criteria. Two of these are simple. Firstly, as a registered mage of South Australia, the defendant has sworn allegiance to the State. Secondly, the defendant has admitted to engagement with Tara Winters, a known enemy of the State. Therefore, all we must prove is the intent to assist the enemy. The defendant admitted Tara was using their training sessions to gain influence. Knowing this, the defendant still complied with the enemy's wishes by going along with the training. Training, which, I might add, opened an incredibly powerful mana channel she could use against the State. This shows the defendant *intended* to assist the enemy. The evidence proves the defendant is guilty of treason.'

Brendan approached the jury as Lucas retired. 'Ladies and gentlemen of the jury: remember my client is innocent until *proven* guilty. Alannah Winters has explained she had no intent to assist Tara Winters in any plots against the State. She said, and I quote, the training sessions were "an opportunity to gain (Tara's) confidence and learn her secrets in order to put a stop to her once and for all." Does this sound like intent to assist the enemy? It is the prosecution's job to prove beyond reasonable doubt they satisfy all three criteria. Has the prosecution *proven* Alanna Winters assisted Tara by agreeing to training sessions? It sounds more like Tara assisted Alannah. Perhaps Tara should be the one on trial for treason.' That earned him a few laughs. 'Seriously though folks, there is reasonable doubt here. Alannah Winters is clearly not guilty. I rest my case.' He took a melodramatic bow and returned to his seat.

Alannah was struggling to contain her own laughter as the jury stepped out to deliberate.

'True calling, just saying,' Brendan whispered.

She snorted. 'Gods! Kieran would have a coronary if he had to deal with you on the regular.'

A few minutes later, the jury returned.

'Has the jury reached a unanimous verdict?' Kieran queried.

The jury's foreperson stood. 'Yes.'

Alannah took a deep breath and held it.

Monique collected a sheet of paper from the foreperson and took it to Kieran.

The High Magus glanced at the page, looking up to announce, 'The jury finds the defendant not guilty. Alannah Winters may continue meeting Tara Winters to gather intel, but must report back to me with everything she learns.' He concluded the hearing by striking his gavel against the sound block.

She heaved out that breath with the force of a tornado.

'*Yes!*' Brendan cheered, high fiving her for real.

'Now get the hell out of my courtroom.' Kieran smirked at them.

As soon as Liam unlocked Alannah's handcuffs, Brendan grabbed her hand and dragged her outside at breakneck speed. He scooped her up in a whirlwind embrace and she hooked her legs around his waist, laughing and crying with joy. The moment Alannah caught her breath, she crashed her lips against his in an all-consuming kiss.

Kissing Brendan was everything Alannah had imagined and more. His intoxicating musky scent filled her senses as her skin tingled from the contact. Hungry lips devoured her as though she was their first and last meal. His stubble grazed her chin, a foreign yet exhilarating sensation.

'Mm. I've been dreaming of this moment.' His husky voice spoke against her lips.

Alannah pressed her forehead to his. 'I've been craving this since the Council stole the moment from our first date.' She smacked her lips to his again. Cheers and wolf-whistles summoned her awareness of the crowd gathering around them. Alannah tittered, feeling the heat rise in her cheeks.

'There I go making you blush again. Gods, I love seeing these turn pink.' He brushed his nose against her right cheekbone. 'Knowing only *I* have this effect on you has always given me such a thrill.'

She drew her bottom lip between her teeth, savouring the residual salty taste of Brendan's kiss.

'Hey, Brendo, stop monopolising all the Alannah hugs,' Nick's voice boomed as he approached from the courthouse.

When she glanced over Brendan's shoulder, still with her arms and legs gripping him tight, she saw Jacob elbow Nick in the ribs. 'Shut the hell up, bro,' Jacob chastised. 'They just had their first kiss.'

'Ah bugger! I take a whizz and miss all the action.' He grinned and turned to Ben with an outstretched hand. 'Pay up, man.'

Scanning the crowd around the courthouse doors, Alannah realised most of her friends were there watching them. Liam was sulking in the shadows, arms crossed as he leaned against one of the pillars. She averted her gaze.

Jacob's eyes widened. 'Wait! You guys bet money on them hooking up?'

Nick shrugged. 'What? It always seemed inevitable to me. Ben's the one who lacked faith.'

Squirming, she hid her face in the crook of Brendan's neck.

Brendan's laugh vibrated against her and he pressed his mouth to her ear. 'You wanna get out of here?'

'Yeah.'

He started walking her away.

'Oi, dipshit!' Cara cried out. 'Don't even think about stealing her from me yet. We've got some serious celebrating to do!'

'O.M.G. Cara!' Alannah squealed as she slipped out of Brendan's hold and ran into Cara's arms. 'You came to see my trial?'

'Of course, hun. There's no way I'd miss something so important. Not that the Council allowed us inside the courtroom. Are you okay, sweetheart?'

Boom!

'No! Get off me you creep!' Alannah pushed away from the hands holding her.

Brendan pulled her into his arms, calming her with his magic touch. 'Hey, gorgeous, it's okay. I've got you.'

Alannah noticed Jacob helping a startled Cara up from the ground and turned in Brendan's arms to get a better view. 'What happened? Cara, are you okay?'

Cara brushed off her knees. 'Yeah, I'm fine, but what the hell was that? You decked me.'

Glancing at Brendan, Alannah's brow knitted together. 'I did?'

His eyes were wide as he nodded. 'I don't know what happened, but you freaked out and pushed Cara away.'

'It was a PTSD episode,' Liam explained as he drew closer. 'The same thing happened when Dad held her in gaol. Cara must have said or done something to trigger her.'

Cara's mouth dropped open. 'What did I do?'

Sighing, Liam shook his head. 'I don't know, I wasn't close enough to tell.' He pulled a memory card from his pocket and handed it to Brendan. 'I know you didn't want to see this before, but you should watch it to better understand her potential triggers. I synced the video and audio.'

Alannah gasped. 'Is that what I think it is?'

Liam gave her a solemn nod. 'I also have news that might help your recovery. Kieran announced the declaration of two divine verdicts.'

Brendan took the SD card and pulled her in closer to his side.

'Two?' Alannah queried.

'Yes. The Gods have sentenced Richard to exile from the mage community, officially stripping him of all his titles and property. He won't be allowed to set foot in the State again and if he does, we have been ordered to execute him.'

Alannah exhaled.

'And the other arsehole?' Brendan demanded.

'Life in maximum security magic prison,' Liam replied.

She huffed. 'Is *that* all? Austin got the death sentence and he only *date* raped me. At least that was pleasurable as far as I can remember.'

Liam cringed as Brendan tensed beside her. 'You know his attempts to curse you played a role in his punishment. The main thing is the bastard can't hurt you ever again.'

'Hopefully some ogre will make Jerkface his bitch and give him a taste of his own medicine,' Brendan seethed.

'One can only hope,' Liam agreed. Alannah's jaw hit the floor. Liam was usually more concerned with justice than vengeance. 'Commendable job in there, by the way.' He directed his comment to Brendan.

Brendan's eyebrows launched up. 'Um, thanks.'

'I'd best hit the road. See you both later.' Liam shook Brendan's hand before jogging down the steps and up the sidewalk.

Alannah was gobsmacked. 'What the? Did he compliment you and shake your hand?'

'Yup. I wonder if someone has kidnapped my real brother and sent an illusionist in his stead.'

She shrugged. 'Suits me. I could get used to this reasonable imposter.'

'Not too used to him I hope.' His tone was light and jovial, but Alannah could see the anxiety in his aura.

'Please don't worry about me and Liam. That relationship is well and truly over.'

'Are you sure?' He scrutinised every inch of her face.

'Yes, I promise you I'm done with Liam.'

Brendan released the breath he held and leaned in to kiss her.

He got as far a peck on the lips when Nick's hand clamped him on the shoulder. 'Come on guys, we're going to the pub to celebrate.'

Brendan smacked Nick upside on the head. 'You and Cara are seriously cramping my style, you damn cockblockers.'

Laughing, Nick nudged him in the arm and took off down the street.

Turning back to Alannah, Brendan smiled with pursed lips. 'They're being persistent. Are you okay to go to the pub for a bit?'

Alannah nodded. 'Yeah. It'll be a nice way to unwind.'

Returning to the familiarity of her old watering hole, Alannah felt as though she was seeking comfort by a friend's roaring fire in the middle of a storm. Cara bought them a round of drinks and squeezed into the booth to flank Alannah, with Brendan on her other side. The fiery redhead held up her beer. 'Let's toast to Alannah's crushing victory over those self-entitled wankers who tried to put her down and keep her down.'

There was a resounding chorus of 'Cheers!'

Beaming, she clinked her bottle with each of her friends. Even Bianca was there and not the least bit bothered by the way things had developed between Alannah and Brendan.

Cara gripped Alannah's arm. 'So, chickadee, how does it feel to be free again?'

Alannah grinned. 'Fantastic.'

'Just in time for Beltane tomorrow, too.' Jacob waggled his brows.

'Oh my Gods yes!' Cara clapped her hands. 'You should come to the festival with us, now you've cut old Stiffneck loose.'

Alannah tensed. She had not had a chance to talk to Brendan about her plans yet.

Brendan groaned. 'You're the worst, Hughes. First you stop me from taking Lana straight home, and now you're inviting her to an orgy? Have you considered the poor girl might want a bit of peace and quiet after her ordeal?'

Caleb sniggered.

Brendan glanced at Caleb. 'Something funny, Thornsy?'

'We all know why you want time alone with Alannah. Don't sugar coat it, man.'

'What's your problem, bro?' Brendan gritted his teeth.

'Oh, you think boning my sister gives you the right to call me your bro?'

Brendan paled. 'Where did you hear that?'

'Bridey told me.' Caleb narrowed his eyes at Alannah. 'I'd watch my sister if I were you. She's a real prickly one.' Rising, he left the group as a shiver ran down Alannah's spine.

Cara's eyes popped out of her skull. 'When did you sleep with Bridey?'

Brendan sighed. 'First night she arrived in town.'

'You're a moron, Winters. I can't blame Caleb for being pissed.' Cara's complexion turned a shade of red matching the roots of her dye job.

He winced. 'Can we please drop this now? It's killing the buzz for Alannah.'

Truth! Alannah had not realised how difficult it would be to deal with Brendan's past. *Will I keep looking at the women in town wondering if they were one of his many conquests? If they still have designs to get in his pants?*

Brendan's hand grasped her leg as he spoke in her ear. 'Hey, just remember they meant nothing. You're everything to me, gorgeous.' His words and calming touch did a lot to settle her thoughts, but not to remove the seed of doubt taking root deep inside.

Conversation shifted to lighter topics and the general mood improved.

When most of their group had scattered around the bar, Brendan squeezed her thigh again. 'Hey, what did you want to do for Beltane? I could set up something special at home if you like.'

She smiled at him. 'I appreciate the gesture, but I had something else in mind.'

His brows rose. 'Oh? Is it kinky, 'cause you know I'm down, right?'

Alannah bit her lip. 'Please don't hate me for this, but I'd like to try the full Beltane maiden experience at the official festival. I never got to do it when I was with Liam and if things become serious with us, I don't know if I'll get another chance.'

'Oh hell! Are you sure that's smart? The mage community haven't exactly warmed up to you again yet. What if you're partnered with an arsehole?'

'I trust the Gods will do right by me.'

He shook his head. 'You're putting a lot of faith in the Gods, Lana.'

'I have legit reason to do so.'

His left brow arched. 'What reason?'

'It's a long and difficult story I'll explain later.'

Realisation dawned on Brendan's face. 'Damnit! If you do this, you know you can't have sex for five days either side of Beltane. I wanted to ravish you tonight.'

Alannah snorted. 'Sorry to burst your bubble, babe, but I'm looking forward to a long bath followed by an early night. I have a lot of sleep to catch up on.'

After heaving a huge sigh, Brendan nodded. 'Of course. I'm sorry.'

'I want to do the Beltane thing, but I'll only go if you do it too.'

Brendan gaped at her. 'Earlier you were freaking out about the notches on my bed post and now you want to send me into a situation where I could end up screwing any number of random women?'

'This is different. Beltane is a sacred festival. Besides, there's a chance we get paired.'

'You know, a great way to increase those odds is to stay home and have our own private celebration.'

'You're missing the point, Brendan. I see this as an exciting opportunity.'

He studied her eyes for a tense moment. 'Are you sure this is what you want?'

Alannah nodded. 'Yes.'

'Then I'll do it.'

Having parked his Jag, Brendan turned to her. 'Are you still sure about this, Lana? It's not too late to go home.' He gave her an impish grin. 'We could still have our own private Beltane celebration.'

As tempting as it sounded, with the butterflies multiplying in her gut and spreading through her bloodstream, she needed to do this. 'I'm sure.'

Exhaling sharply, Brendan got out, rounding the car to open her door. As soon as she stepped out, he hugged her tight. 'Just know I'm gonna be praying something fierce to get paired with you.'

She grinned. 'Thank you.'

He squinted. 'For what?'

'Praying for me.' Alannah kissed his lips chastely before pulling out of his arms. 'Good luck in there.' She winked at him, turned, and walked through the estate gates. Parting ways with Brendan pinched at her heart. But Alannah felt the need to embrace what may be her only night as a single woman for a long time—or hopefully ever, if things went well with Brendan.

When she queued at the registration desk there were a few locals peering down their noses at her. Ignoring them, she turned her attention to the nearby display of old farm equipment. Rusted chunks of metal had never fascinated her so much. Her body began to thrum as the iron in her blood resonated with the ancient machinery's, opening her matter attunement for a second before the crowd pushed her forward.

An unfamiliar middle-aged blonde woman greeted her from behind the trestle table. 'Good evening miss. Blessed be.'

'Blessed be.' She submitted her finger to the pinprick test to prove the purity of her blood.

The woman dropped Alannah's blood in a potion vial and watched it turn the green substance clear. 'Thank you miss. Have you abstained from sexual intercourse in the last five days?'

Alannah giggled. 'It's been weeks actually.' She glimpsed the woman's gaping mouth. 'Sorry, you didn't need to know that.'

'You are cleared for entry, miss. Are you here alone?'

Alannah took a deep breath. 'Yes.'

'Maiden or mother?'

'Maiden.'

'You seem nervous. First time?'

Alannah nodded. 'First time alone, yes.'

The woman offered a sympathetic smile. 'You'll be fine, doll. I remember my first time. It was delightful. The maidens are gathering to the far East.' She pointed in the direction Alannah needed to go.

'Thank you.' As she moved through the warded barrier, she caught sight of a familiar face stopping her dead in her tracks. Liam lined up alone at the registration desk and he stared straight at her. *Crap!* She did not anticipate seeing him there. *Did he know I was coming? It will be beyond awkward if we get paired.* Blinking, she turned away from his penetrating gaze and continued to her destination.

After passing through a thicket of scrub populated by red gums, grass trees, and wattles, Alannah reached a large, fenced-off clearing. Her own boots joined the hoof prints spotting the paddock, reminding her of the first time she attended Beltane with Liam. She had made an off-hand remark: 'I hope the cows don't interrupt us. Might kill the mood, somewhat.'

Liam had grinned. 'Don't worry, Kieran has all the cattle shifted to other pastures to enjoy their own form of Beltane.'

With a sigh, she dismissed the memory and made her way to the Easternmost bonfire, joining a group of women for the disrobing ritual. This stage of the courtship and fertility rites of Beltane was new to her. She had spent previous Beltane festivals with Liam at the central fire where other committed couples worshipped the Gods without undressing. They had then found their own private spot to make love. Not that all couples spent Beltane this way—only those who were uncomfortable sharing their partners.

An acolyte priestess—one of the devout crones of the mage community—cast a large circle. Alannah watched with wide, attentive eyes as the powerful woman called upon each of the fertility Gods and Goddesses.

The priestess invited Alannah forward. 'How do you enter the circle?'

'With love and peace.' Alannah removed her white velvet robes and handed them to the crone.

'Blessed be.' The priestess turned and threw the robes in the sacred fire.

Alannah had researched the Beltane rites, so she expected this part of the ritual sewing special robes for the event.

Once everyone was in the circle, the priestess prayed, 'These maidens surrender themselves to you, oh Great Ones. Watch over them and bless them with the gifts of love, happiness, and fertility. And bless their children with the gifts of your magic.'

Alannah stepped up to the earthenware urn painted with gold Celtic knots that would decide her fate. She dipped her hand inside and retrieved a small slip of paper with the number three written on it. This told her which of the small campfires she needed to make her way to. The Gods would choose her partner. But she still stopped to pick up one of the staghorn crowns as insurance. This was her way of giving consent. Even though mages put their faith in the Gods to choose a suitable match, they could make the final call on who to mate with.

Approaching the site sign-posted with a large number three, Alannah marvelled at the vast estate with at least two-hundred other small fires dotted about the place. She gave thanks for the warmer weather because being naked on a crisper night would have been uncomfortable, despite the warmth of the fires.

Sitting on the wooden bench in front of the fire, she put the crown aside and examined the contents of the cauldron bubbling away. The fragrance of the mulled wine washed over her, easing her jitters, so she returned to her seat and waited. A few minutes later, she heard footsteps behind her. She remained frozen in place. Something touched her head and she realised it was a wreath of flowers. The man had not even seen her face before declaring his intentions.

A second later, a pair of warm hands rested on her shoulders and a familiar voice spoke, 'Remind me to send the Gods a thank you note.'

Brendan could not believe his luck when he found Alannah at his campfire. He stood in front of her and grinned, taking in the glorious view. She wore nothing but the floral crown upon her head. The vision sent signals straight to his dick. *By the Gods, he'd never seen such a perfect body*! Her skin was flawless, and her breasts were firm and perky. A twinkling of light drew his attention to her navel: the diamond adorning her midriff— beautiful and sexy. It was a superb match for the dainty stud piercing her nose. 'Nice body piercing.'

'I could say the same for you.' Her eyes darted south a moment before returning to lock with his.

It did not take his mind-reading skills to know she referred to his Prince Albert rather than the silver sleeper in his left nipple. 'Can I get you a drink?'

She rewarded him with the most precious smile known to man- or mage-kind. 'Please.'

Brendan ladled the warm, spiced wine into a pair of ceramic goblets, and handed her one. After casting an eager glance at the golden stag horns remaining on the edge of the bench next to Alannah, he took his seat beside her.

Alannah drank a few mouthfuls of the wine before turning to Brendan. 'Do you remember when we used to play those pretend games as kids and Liam was always the hero who rescued me from you?'

The memories made him smile. 'I'll never forget those days. Even when I complained about being the rogue, I loved every minute of it. Chasing you around the garden was exciting.' He winked at her.

She gave him an impish grin. 'Something about those times occurred to me recently. There was a reason I preferred having you play the villain.'

'Oh?' His heart raced as his mind considered the possibilities.

'Because of the thrill I got from having you catch me and press kisses on my lips.'

Brendan gasped. 'Lana?' he whispered.

'Shh.' Alannah placed a finger on his lips. A second later, she put the staghorn crown upon his head.

He was already hard, but even more blood surged south. The rest of him rose and pulled Alannah up with him. Their arms clung to each other as Brendan's mouth claimed hers. When he hoisted her feet off the ground, her legs wrapped around his waist. *Gods!* Her strong thigh muscles felt like vice clamps. *She is divine!*

Like most of her skin, Alannah's lips were soft and smooth, yet she writhed and moaned, kissing him with an unbridled passion telling him she was anything but fragile. Brendan carried Alannah to a patch of grass near the brazier and laid her down, breathing in the scent of her hair as he did so. Strawberries mingled with the smell of smoke from the woodfire. *Gods! How is it possible to get more aroused?* He brushed his lips across her ear. 'Is it okay if I use my powers tonight? To enhance the experience?'

'If you promise me one thing.' Her voice was deep and breathy.

Brendan gazed deep into her eyes, running his fingers through her long black locks. 'What's that?'

Alannah's gaze darkened. 'Promise me a mind-altering experience.'

He grinned. 'I promise[3].'

---

[3] For more juicy details, check out this bonus scene: *The Heat of the Beltane Fires*. Available at www.starlaarts.com > Freebies.

Chapter Eighteen

atching Alannah sleep in his arms after the night they shared was surreal. Brendan did not even care if it made him a creeper. She was the sexiest, most beautiful woman he had ever seen, and she was finally his. Her peaceful expression, the way her luscious lips parted, and the frame created by her long black hair all added to the picture of perfection he could not get enough of.

He felt wrecked because they had gone until dawn before returning home, yet he was still too hyped to get any sleep. His dick did not want rest either. If Alannah had not insisted on honouring the sacred customs, he would have given into temptation, waking her up for another round. But the sun had risen to herald the end of Beltane, marking day one of five. He understood the reasoning was to ensure any child conceived in this period was the result of the Beltane rites.

Brendan placed his hand on Alannah's abdomen, wondering if he had put a baby in there. The thought would have terrified him if she were anyone else, but the idea of starting a family with the woman he loved thrilled him. And it amazed him because he had never considered himself dad material, but as he lay there holding Alannah, he thought anything was possible.

The doorbell startled him out of his reverie. Glancing at the clock on his bedside, Brendan saw it was almost two in the afternoon. *Wowsers!* He had spent the last six hours watching

Alannah sleep. Being careful not to disturb the angel in his bed, he crawled out from under the quilt and slipped into his trackpants. As the door swung open, he froze mid yawn.

'Hello, handsome. Looks like you had quite the Beltane.' Bridey drawled in a deep voice.

'What the hell do you want?'

She narrowed her gaze. 'Are you going to let me in, or do you want the neighbours to hear us discussing business?'

Grumbling, Brendan opened the door for her, and led her down the hall to the living area. He leaned against the breakfast bar with his arms crossed. 'Well?'

Bridey stepped close to him and trailed a fingernail along his bicep. 'Your latest shipment is late.'

He gulped. 'Don't you normally send your goons for jobs like this?'

A wicked grin formed on her face. 'Normally, yes. But we have a special arrangement in place.' Her hand moved from his arm to grope his junk.

Brendan flinched as he glared at her. 'Not gonna happen.'

'Shame. I guess I'll send the Collectors to Jacob.'

He grimaced at the thought of his friend suffering.

Her eyes flashed with delight. 'Hmm. I thought that might make you reconsider.'

Grinding his teeth, Brendan thought about Alannah sleeping soundly only a few metres away. *Sorry Jacob, but there is no real choice here.* 'Still not happening.'

Bridey's brow arched. 'Wow, and here I thought you cared for the scamp. You must be turning dark, after all.'

'Brendan? I hope you're making coffee,' Alannah's voice approached, sending his heart into palpations.

Lady Violet cocked her head. 'Or could it be the infamous Brendan Winters has actually fallen in love. Oh, this is priceless.'

She began to bring her arms up around him, but Brendan pushed her back across the room.

Alannah entered the room wearing only a silk dressing gown and he could feel her heart beating fast as she looked from Brendan to their visitor. Bridey turned to Alannah, taking in her dishevelled appearance, one side of her mouth curling up. 'Seems like you also had a delightful Beltane. Tell me hun, did Brendan keep you up all night too? His endurance is exceptional, isn't it?'

Alannah blinked her bleary eyes and glowered at Bridey. 'Who the hell are you?'

'Lana, this is Lady Violet, and she was just leaving.'

'Lady ...' Alannah's jaw hit the floor.

Bridey clicked her fingers. 'Of course, that's where I recognised you from. You're the cousin who barged in on my four-way with Brendan. I've heard so much about you, *Lady Ebony.*'

Alannah eyes widened. 'You're Caleb's sister?'

'Yes dear, why? Has he mentioned me? Caleb is such a sweet boy.'

Her eyes pierced Brendan. 'Why didn't you tell me Bridey is your Syndicate contact?'

'Because she isn't. Jacob is my contact. Lady Violet is *his* boss, not mine.'

Alannah crossed her arms, her face turning red. 'A minor technicality, I'm sure. You should have told me.'

'Lana, can we please deal with Lady Violet first? We can discuss all the things I should and shouldn't have done once she leaves.'

She huffed. 'Fine. Lady Violet, is it?'

Bridey nodded.

'What do you want from Brendan?'

'Lana,' Brendan warned.

Bridey's face lit up with a mischievous glint in her eyes. 'Would you like the comprehensive list?'

'Just the business particulars, thank you,' Alannah clipped.

'Brendan is late on his shipment of mother tincture. I came to collect, with interest.' She added the last detail with a lewd smirk in his direction.

Alannah turned to Brendan. 'Do you have the potions?'

'No. I've been a bit preoccupied lately. Kind of hard to prepare essence of joy when the woman I love is locked in prison at the mercy of sadist pricks.'

Her expression softened. 'I'm sorry.'

'This is touching and all, but I have a business to run. Handsome here should be able to channel other people's emotions if he can't evoke the feelings in himself, although now you're here, Lady Ebony, I'm sure he'll have all the inspiration he needs. You have until tomorrow to pay up. Including the interest.'

Taking one step closer to Brendan, Alannah unfolded her arms. 'What's the interest?'

He gritted his teeth. 'You don't want to know.' Brendan turned toward Bridey. 'I want out of the business, Violet. I'm done making your damn potion.'

'Sorry, handsome, but you're under contractual obligation for a full year.'

Brendan gasped, feeling the air grow too heavy. 'What? Since when?'

'Since you put your signature to this piece of paper.' She pulled a copy of their contract from her purse and handed it to him.

He snatched it from her. Sure enough, it was the deal he had signed. This time he read the full terms and conditions more thoroughly, feeling the blood drain from his face. Violet had even spelled out the nature of interest payments for late shipments: *Sexual favours of Lady Violet's choosing to be provided by the aforementioned primary producer.* His jaw dropped. *'Oh hell!'*

'Did you fail to read the fine print before signing, Mr. Winters?' Bridey grinned. 'Tsk, tsk.'

Alannah grabbed the contract and tensed as she read it. 'Oh Gods, I think I'm gonna be sick.'

'As you can see, the only way *you* can break the contract is by dying. Payment tomorrow, Mr. Winters. And I will have my interest, with or without your consent.' Bridey kissed him on the cheek and walked out of the house.

Alannah flew to Brendan as he collapsed to the floor. He drew his knees close to his chest and looked at her from beneath his heavy brow. Her heart ached for him.

'I'm sorry, Lana. I messed up big time. It was stupid of me to sign that thing. I should have read it properly. I didn't know…'

Kneeling before him, she wrapped her arms around his and kissed his lips. 'Shh. It's okay, we'll sort this out. Perhaps we could use your recent crash course in legal studies to search for loopholes in the contract. And I could try calling in a favour with Scarlett.'

'No! Don't take any more risks with her. I don't want you getting wrapped up in my mess. You've been through too much lately.'

She pulled his hands into hers, placing one over her heart as she did the same on his chest. 'Feel that? Our hearts are beating as one now. We are in this together, no matter what. This is what it means to be in love.'

He sucked in a breath. 'Gods!' Dropping his legs, he pulled Alannah into his lap to kiss her deeply. When he broke the lip contact, he smiled. 'How do I deserve you, Lana?'

'By being awesome.'

He cocked his left brow. 'More awesome than Liam?'

'Way better than Liam.' Alannah bit her lip a moment, wondering if she should tell him.

Brendan gave her a sidelong glance. 'Tell me what, Lana?'

Her cheeks flushed. 'Let's just say after last night, there are several more items for that list.'

His entire face broke out in a victorious grin, and he squeezed her tight. 'Tell me all of them.'

Alannah laughed. 'Seriously? Isn't it enough to know you're better overall?'

'Nah, uh. I'm not letting you go until you tell me all.'

She flashed him a devilish grin. 'What if I don't want you to let go?'

Brendan groaned. Rising to his feet, he pulled her with him. She wrapped her arms and legs around him, hanging on tight as he walked her down the hall, eyeing her with ravenous need.

Alannah squealed as her dressing gown fell to the floor. 'What are you doing, Brendan? You know we can't have sex yet, right?'

His lustful eyes narrowed on her. 'Doesn't exclude all forms of pleasure, gorgeous. I've been hungry for another taste of you since last night.'

She felt a rush of desire and tingles all over her bare skin. 'But we still need to sort out your contract dilemma.'

'Hmm. Dilemma you say. Should I eat you now, or after hours of studying contract law? That is a dilemma.'

Alannah laughed as he laid her down on the bed. 'How about before *and* after?'

Brendan licked his lips. 'Brilliant suggestion, my love.'

…

When they cuddled together after, Brendan's eyes twinkled as he played with a strand of her hair. 'You're incredible, Lana. Best I've ever had.'

She beamed. 'Awesome. I'm glad I compare well to all those other girls.'

Brendan straddled her, pinning her arms to the bed as his mouth moved to her ear. 'You are infinitely better than those other girls. Please stop worrying about my past, gorgeous.' His lips trailed kisses along her jawline until he reached her mouth and claimed it passionately. But he jerked back when his dick grew hard again. 'I'm gonna take a cold shower before I do something sacrilegious.'

She snorted as he disappeared into the bathroom. Getting up, she threw some clothes on before returning to the living room. After brewing some coffee and fixing herself a quick afternoon brunch, she sat down to study the copy of the contract Bridey had left. There had to be a way for Brendan to get out of the interest payments in the very least. *I will not let that endarkened bitch touch my man!*

'So, I'm your man now, huh?' Brendan clamped his hands down on her shoulders.

Alannah jumped out of her skin. 'Jesus, fuck! You scared me.'

Brendan moved around to the chair beside her and sat down, smelling of fresh shower gel, hair still damp and dripping. 'Sorry, gorgeous.' He gave her an impish grin. 'For the record, I've always been yours. You just took all this time to stake your claim.'

Breathing in deeply, she leaped into his lap, and kissed him fervently. 'Gods, I can't get enough of your lips.'

'Mm. I know exactly how you feel. I can't get enough of you in general, but especially these.' He brushed his thumb over her lips and groped between her legs. 'And these lips.'

When Alannah felt the bulge in his pants grow, she rolled her eyes and moved back to her chair. 'You are insatiable.'

'Yup.' He grinned. Sighing, he grabbed the contract and studied it. After reading over it several times, Brendan grabbed a textbook on contract law and got comfortable on the couch.

Alannah took the agreement and sat next to Brendan as she kept reading over the clauses.

After about an hour, Brendan threw the book across the room. 'This is useless. There's no point turning to the law on this when dealing with criminal activity. The contract is illegal anyway, so it's not like Violet will use legitimate channels to enforce it.'

She sighed. 'True. That's why we need to focus on the wording of these terms and conditions. I can't believe she put a sexual favours clause in here. The woman is repulsive. I can see why Caleb doesn't like her.'

'You don't know the half of it,' Brendan replied.

Bile churned in her gut. 'What do you mean?'

'Let's just say not even her brother was safe from her coercive charms.'

'Ick!' Shivering, she returned to reading. '*Of course!* It's right here. Reference is made to you as the primary producer, a term Violet defined as "the mage who produces the mother tincture for the potion known as Rhapsody". What if you aren't the only primary producer?'

Brendan beamed. 'Lana, you're a genius!'

'I hope you're right about this.' Jacob paced across their warehouse. 'What if Violet still insists on the last shipment with interest?'

Brendan offered Alannah a reassuring smile. He had asked Jacob to arrange for the meeting to occur at their place of business to save Alannah from seeing Bridey again. But she had insisted on coming with him, promising to floor the bitch if she tried anything. 'That's why I'm making it a condition of the deal,' Brendan explained. 'She'd be stupid to refuse my offer and Violet is a lot of things, but she's not stupid.'

'No, but she is a sick, twisted bitch and she's not touching my man,' Alannah added.

Jacob laughed. 'Gods, I still can't get my head around you two being a couple now.'

The buzzer sounded at the front door. Brendan glimpsed Bridey with two of her goons on the security monitor.

'Here goes.' Jacob got up and answered, creating an awful grating sound as he pulled the metal beast of a door open, then closed again.

'Thank you, Associate.'

'Madam.' He bowed his head.

Bridey cast an inquisitive eye at Alannah before focussing on Brendan. 'Do you have my potions Mr. Winters?' She drew close to him—too close.

Brendan gulped. 'I have something better.'

Her brows furrowed. 'You'd better not be—'

'Shoosh.' He put a finger up to silence her, flinching when he accidentally touched her lips in the process. 'It is apparent demand for Rhapsody is high, yes?'

Still gobsmacked by his brazen move, she nodded.

'So, it makes savvy business sense to have more than one primary producer, right? I'm willing to sell you the full recipe for the mother tincture, complete with explicit instructions for essence making, along with this warehouse, on the condition you find me a replacement and allow me to exit our contract unharmed and unmolested.'

'How do I know you won't set up a competitive operation elsewhere?'

'I'm willing to sign a non-compete and non-disclosure agreement.'

'Hmm.' She went silent for a few tense minutes. 'What about Jacob?'

'He remains in the Syndicate. This is his world, not mine.'

Sighing, she circled around him, trailing a finger along his shoulders. 'Pity. You had such potential as a dark mage, and we could have had so much fun. Lady Scarlett clearly misplaced her faith in you and Lady Ebony.'

Brendan could feel his traitorous dick responding to Bridey's mild attempts at coercion. Alannah advanced on them, but he shot her a warning glance as he spoke in her mind. *Wait, Lana. She's only toying with me.*

'I will expect a discount considering you have not fulfilled your last shipment,' Bridey continued.

'Of course. Jacob will negotiate the particulars. Do we have a deal?'

She grinned. 'Yes, Mr. Winters. We have a deal.'

He let all the air gush out his lungs.

Bridey clasped the erection through his pants and leered at him. 'If you ever need a real woman to take care of your darkest desires, you know where to find me.'

Alannah sucked in a sharp breath between clenched teeth.

'I already have a real woman,' Brendan hissed, pushing her away.

'See you later, Mr. Winters.' Bridey winked at him and left.

'Thank the Gods!' He collapsed onto the couch and watched as Jacob pulled the heavy sliding door closed, filling the air with the screeching sound of metal parts grinding together.

Jacob grabbed them each a beer from the small bar fridge. 'Congrats, bro. You're a free man.'

Brendan clinked his bottle with Jacob's, followed by Alannah's, before pulling her into his lap. 'Cheers to that. If I never see Violet again, it will be too soon.'

Chapter Nineteen

The front door slammed, startling Alannah and making her botch the stitches in her latest sewing project. She cursed under her breath, pushing her work to one side of Brendan's dining table. Odd how she still did not think of the place as hers. They had not yet talked about her moving in officially. She still had a lot of her stuff at Liam's and moving would mean an awkward confrontation she was not ready for.

As soon as Brendan appeared, holding a black leather collar with attached lead, she knew she was in trouble. He gave her a wicked grin. 'The wait is over, gorgeous. Beltane was six days ago.'

Yep, sweet, sweet trouble. She bit her lip and simpered. But she felt the stygian channel stir through her blood and instinctively knew her eyes appeared more demonic than angelic.

He stalked toward her, holding up the collar. 'Do you know what this is, Lana?'

'It's a bondage collar.' She knew enough lifestyle kinksters to recognise it.

Brendan smiled. 'Do you know what it means to wear one of these?'

'The collared person submits to their dominant partner.'

When he reached her, Brendan circled his arms around her waist, letting the collar hang from his elbow. 'I see you've been talking to Cara and Amy about this stuff.' His fingers trailed along her arm, bringing goosebumps to the surface and she wondered how far he wanted to take things. 'Don't worry, gorgeous. I'm not interested in the full lifestyle. Let's focus on exploring those dark fantasies of yours, plus a few of my own. Sound good to you?'

Heart pounding, Alannah bounced on her heels. 'Uh, huh.' Her voice dropped low, becoming breathy.

He followed up his lascivious grin with a passionate kiss. 'First, we'll need a safe word. Something not associated with sex and the more repugnant the better.'

'How about Richard?'

'Love it. Richard it is.' Brendan twirled a strand of her hair in his hand. 'I know you've had some traumatic experiences with restraints lately, so we can forget the bondage if you prefer.'

Gods, I love this man! 'No, I trust you, Brendan. And bondage is an important part of my fantasy. Just don't use handcuffs or anything cold iron and we'll be fine.'

'Are you sure, Lana?'

'Yes, I'm sure.'

Brendan inhaled deeply. 'Any other limits?'

'No. I meant it all those years ago when I told Emma there's nothing I wouldn't let you do to me. That's still true.'

Brendan's breathing became heavy. 'Even after what that creep did to you? I will understand if any form of anal is off the cards.'

She brought her hand up to cup his cheek. 'Everything you do to me is going to feel spectacular. I'd like to have more pleasurable associations with all of it, and I know you can give me those. So, try anything and if it gets too much, I'll use the safe word.'

'Ah heck!' He kissed her again. Straightening, he ogled her. 'Are you ready for me to collar you?'

'Yes.'

He smirked. 'You don't look ready.'

Without further ado, Alannah stripped herself naked and knelt beside Brendan. Instinctively falling into her role, she bowed her head.

'Gods, Lana! I'm already hard and we just started.' The moment the collar attached to her neck, the air between them became superheated.

Crawling on all fours, she followed his lead towards the bedroom.

Brendan positioned Alannah face down, tying her to his bed in record time. After placing a red satin blindfold over her eyes, he straddled her back and rasped in her ear. 'I'd like to try something magical tonight. And I mean in every sense of the word, Lana. I reckon with what we're about to do, we can establish a two-way empathic link. Would you like that?'

'Yes, sir.'

'Mm, you are such a good girl. Although I do hope you will give me some reason to punish you tonight.'

She grinned. 'You don't need a reason, sir.'

'True. So, getting back to this idea of mine. I'd like for you to try and channel my emotions and my senses simultaneously. Can you manage that?'

'Yes, sir.'

'I'm going to have my empathic link active, which means I will feel everything you do. This will have an amplifying effect when you channel my touch, enhancing all the pleasure and pain I subject you to. Will you be able to handle it?'

Desire coiled around every nerve ending, like elastic bands winding up. 'Mm, yes sir.'

'Excellent. I'm going to start by massaging you. Once you have the channels open, let me know and I'll start to ramp things up, okay?'

'Okay, sir.' As Brendan's hands rubbed her back, Alannah focussed on his emotions first, being the more familiar power source. She felt a jolt of tingling pleasure the moment she connected, followed by a strong rush of arousal flowing through her. Senses mana was a new one, though, and she needed a visualisation. Given what they were doing, sex with Brendan was the obvious option. So, she cast her thoughts back to Beltane, bringing to mind the sight of his naked body, the sound of his husky voice, the smell of his musky cologne, the taste of his salty lips mixed with the mulled wine, and the feel of his big, strong hands all over her body. Recalling the full sensory experience, she became hyperaware of his hands on her skin. 'I'm ready, sir.'

'What's the safe word, Lana?'

'Richard.'

'Good girl.'

The impact play came next, and Brendan worked his way up through spanking, flogging, whipping, and caning. She had never experienced anything so exhilarating. The hot wax followed. For this, he drove himself inside her first, making love to her as the droplets of heat seared into her skin. It was a true test of her pain threshold, and without the added pleasure, it might have been too much. But instead, it took her over the edge, releasing the wound tension in those elastic bands around her nerves. The moment Alannah surrendered herself to Brendan, they came together.

'Gods! That was extraordinary.' Brendan removed her bonds and collar before collapsing beside her. He drew the quilt up to cover them both and hugged her. 'How are you doing there, gorgeous?'

Alannah turned to face him and smiled. 'Overwhelmed, in a rapturous way.' She brushed her lips against his and closed her eyes.

He held her for a few minutes before moving. 'I'm gonna run us a bath; be right back.'

When Brendan left the room, Alannah felt a strange sense of loss, like part of her soul was missing. A moment later, her hand felt wet. 'What the hell?' she muttered to herself. But then it dawned on her. 'Brendan?'

He returned to the bed. 'Yes, gorgeous?'

She reached forward and pinched his arm.

'Ow, what was that for?'

Alannah grinned. 'It worked. I can feel everything you do.'

Beaming, Brendan moved in to embrace her. 'You have no idea how happy that makes me, Lana.'

'Actually, now I do.'

The moment Alannah opened her eyes the next morning, she found Brendan staring at her. 'Hey.'

'Morning, gorgeous.'

'How long have you been watching me?' Her voice was still gruff from the dryness in her mouth. Sitting up, she grabbed the water bottle beside the bed and gulped down two large mouthfuls before snuggling into Brendan's arms.

'Only a few minutes this time. I slept like a rock after last night.'

Memories of their night flooded Alannah's mind: after a bath and take-away dinner, they had spent several more hours going at it, although they eased up on the more painful stuff. She felt warm and tingly from the recollection. 'Mm. Beltane was special, but last night was easily the best sex of my life.'

Brendan rolled her onto her back and straddled her as he peered into her eyes. 'Do you mean that?'

'Yeah. It was even better than kinky vampire sex.'

'I love you so much, Lana.' Before giving her a chance to reply, he crashed his lips to hers and kissed her ardently. Within minutes, Brendan plunged deep inside her.

'Wait, Brendan. I'm still not covered by birth control after Beltane.'

He pressed himself deep inside her and gazed lovingly into her eyes. 'Does it matter? Whether I impregnated you at Beltane, or if it happens now, I'll still be with you to raise our child.'

Her eyes bugged out. 'You've thought about this?'

'Yes, Lana. I promised you once, I'll never leave you, and I mean it. You're stuck with me now.' He thrust into her and before long they were writhing together.

An hour later, they collapsed alongside each other, still panting. Regaining control of her breathing, Alannah glanced at the clock: 9AM. 'Oops! You're late for work.'

'I called in a sickie. I want to spend the whole day with you.'

She arched a brow. 'Are you sure that's wise after all the time you took off recently?'

Brendan shrugged. 'Those kids are a lost cause anyway.'

Playfully shrieking, Alannah slapped his arm. 'How could you say that!'

'Because it's true. I'm better off becoming a lawyer to defend their delinquent arses in court.'

'Are you honestly considering such a career change?'

'Yup. What do you think?'

Alannah contemplated the idea. 'You'd be a great lawyer. And if you defend dark mages, you'd be like the Devil's Advocate.'

His eyes widened, grabbing and pinning her to the bed. 'Are you comparing me to Keanu Reeves?'

She giggled. 'No. I meant the Neiderman book character. Aside from the black hair, you don't look anything like Keanu.'

'No?'

Alannah shook her head. 'Nuh, uh. You're way hotter. More like Ian Somerhalder.'

'Oh? Still have a thing for vampires, do you?' He dived for her neck and nibbled the skin.

It tickled at first, but before long the intensity of his bites increased. She arched her back as moans escaped her and their foreplay escalated into another hour-long lovemaking session.

When they finished, Alannah heard something growl. 'Is that my stomach or yours?'

Brendan smiled. 'Both. Come on, let's eat.'

As he moved away, Alannah felt the same aching feeling of loss, so she rushed after him. Sticking close to his side, she helped Brendan cook up a full Irish breakfast. They were halfway through the meal before she broached the topic. 'Thank you for staying with me today. I don't know how I'd deal with the pain of separation so soon.'

Brendan peered up over the slice of toast he'd bitten into with raised brows. 'What do you mean?'

'You know, with the empathic link? When you walk away from me, it hurts. I guess I need to work on switching it off.'

'Oh wow. I'd forgotten about the pain after acclimating to it long ago. I can still feel the distance between us when the link is active, but it doesn't hurt per se. It's more like a homing signal drawing me to you.'

She huffed. 'Great! I'm the one who gets stuck with the separation anxiety and you get the stalker power.'

'Hey, you might still be able to track me. We haven't tried yet. I have an idea. Why don't we spend some time in town testing it out?'

Alannah frowned. 'Didn't you hear me say it hurts?'

He gave her a wicked grin. 'Incentive to find me sooner.'

She punched his arm. 'You are such a sadist!'

A lopsided grin formed on his face. 'Well duh. But I didn't see you complaining last night.' Rubbing the red mark on his bicep, he gazed at her lustfully. 'Don't forget I'm also a masochist.'

After gaping at him a moment, she made the connection. 'That's why you were able to keep the link open when you were caning my arse last night.'

'Bingo, babe. Are you going to finish eating those?' He pointed his fork at her plate.

Huddling around her food, she glared at him. 'Don't touch my hash browns buddy.' She made a show of scoffing them down as quick as possible and licking her lips.

Brendan's eyes darkened. 'Damn that was hot.'

Alannah used to think he was teasing her when he said such things, but this time she could feel the extent of truth in his words. She rolled her eyes. 'Is there anything I do that doesn't turn you on?'

He paused for thought. 'Hmm. Only one thing comes to mind, and you better not do it anymore.'

'What?'

'Boning my brother. He's the one man I would never consider sharing you with, so you can forget *those* threesome fantasies.'

She should not have taken her final sip of coffee because she sprayed it all over Brendan. Words failed her.

He wiped the coffee from his face. 'On that note, it's time for a shower.'

'So, what's the plan?' Alannah glanced at Brendan as he drove north along the Esplanade.

'How far do you feel like walking?'

'What do you mean?'

'I'll drop you off somewhere, then I'll go hide. You will need to walk to find me, so how far are you willing to travel?'

The thought of parting ways with Brendan, even for a short time, was like pilers pinching at her heart. *Weird*. She hated the idea of dependence on any man, even if he was the love of her life. 'I dunno. Maybe three k's.'

He sniggered. 'You *do* have it bad for me.'

She glared at him. 'Do you want me to hit you again?' As the grin formed, she added, 'Wait! Don't answer that.'

'I'm sorry, Lana, but I love teasing you. Always have, always will.'

Always will. Two simple words became music to her ears. Alannah's expression softened and she knew in her heart Brendan was hers forever.

'Right, here we are.' They had stopped outside the boatshed, north of the bridge leading across to the small island housing the Sailing and Lifesaving clubs. 'I'll text you when I reach my destination. If you can't pinpoint my direction within thirty minutes, call me and I'll come get you, okay?'

'Okay.' She leaned across the car to peck his lips and hopped out.

The Jag sped through the middle of town a moment later.

Alannah doubled over from the pain once he disappeared. 'Crapola!'

Footsteps came running toward her, and strong arms caught her before she hit the ground. 'Gods! Are you okay, Alannah?'

She smiled at Connor's concern. 'Yeah, I'm okay. Just a strong muscle cramp.'

'Do you want me to look at it?'

'No, I'll be fine. But thank you.' She noticed his hair was wet. 'Have you been diving today?'

'Yeah, just finished collecting and processing some aquatic plant samples. I'm heading into town for an early lunch. What are you up to?'

'I'm looking for Brendan.'

'Ah, well I saw him—'

'No! Don't tell me. I'm trying to use magic to locate him. It's a training exercise.'

Connor eyed her askance. 'O-kay.'

Alannah sighed because Connor was not stupid. Magical tracking was rare and usually involved a clairvoyant using scrying crystals on a map. 'We have created an empathic link. Well, my side of the link is new; Brendan's felt me for years.' She grimaced. 'That sounded dirty. Anyway, I'm testing whether or not I can use the link to find him, like he can with me.'

Connor cracked up laughing. 'You guys are adorable. I'm glad you finally hooked up. Would you like some company on your hunt? In case you have another muscle cramp?'

Figuring some conversation could distract her from the pain, she nodded. 'Yeah, sure. Give me a minute.' Alannah checked the message she received from Brendan.

READY AND WAITING FOR YOU, GORGEOUS.

Closing her eyes, she focused on the part of her soul linked to Brendan's. *He feels excited.* She sensed it, the strong pull. Opening her eyes, she headed for the centre of town. 'This way.'

Gobsmacked, Connor followed her. 'So, if you have this link, does that mean you are attuned to emotions and senses as well?'

'Yeah, I suppose it does.'

'So, how many attunements do you have now?'

She counted them in her head. 'Seven.'

'Woah! That's more than the High Magus.'

Alannah smirked. 'Good point.' They walked in silence for a few minutes, giving her a chance to confirm the direction they headed. 'Connor, can I ask you a personal question?'

He cocked a brow. 'You can ask, but I can't promise I'll answer.'

'Do you and Amy ever swap roles, or is she always the Dom?'

'No. We aren't switches like Jacob and Cara. I like being Amy's sub. Why do you ask?'

'Just curious.'

Connor's eyes narrowed. 'Does Brendan know you're interested in kink?'

Alannah laughed. 'You should know there's no hiding this stuff from Brendan. Of course he knows. We even dabbled last night.'

'Is that so? Did you establish roles, because I'm having a hard time placing who would be the Dom in your relationship?'

'I subbed to Brendan.'

'Wow. I can't imagine you subbing to anyone.'

Alannah sighed. 'I guess the bedroom is the one place where I feel I can let go. It's nice to give up all sense of control sometimes, you know?'

'Yeah, I know exactly what you mean. So, are we gonna start seeing you and Brendo at the dungeon?'

'No. At least not anytime soon. We aren't planning to take things beyond the bedroom.'

Connor shrugged. 'Shame though. It'd be fun to have you guys visit on occasion.'

'Does the club allow visitors?'

'There are nights when we can invite friends.'

Curiosity got the better of her. 'Has Brendan ever gone on these nights?'

He bit his lip. 'Maybe you should ask *him*.'

'He totally has!' She sniggered. 'No wonder he knew what he was doing last night.' Alannah felt Brendan's presence close by. She tuned in to the sensation and glanced in the direction she expected to see him. When her gaze fell upon the Veterinary Surgeon sign, her heart almost ruptured from all the love she felt. She had been thinking about how much she missed Nora that morning. Ross had cancelled the last family dinner due to Beltane, and Alannah had been in prison the fortnight prior. When she thought about it, the last proper chat she had with Nora was seven weeks ago. She turned to Connor. 'Well, thanks for the talk. This is my stop.'

'No worries, Alannah. See you round.'

As soon as she stepped into the waiting room, Brendan jumped up and ran to her, pulling her into his arms. 'I guess it worked.'

Smiling, Alannah pushed up on tippy toes and kissed him. 'Yeah, it worked.'

Brendan tightened his hold and deepened the kiss.

'Naw, you guys are such a cute couple.' Ben's voice drew Alannah's attention. She noticed he was wearing scrubs, with his long hair tied back.

'Aren't they just?' Nora agreed. 'I haven't seen the two of them this happy since… well, ever. Hi, honey.' She opened her arms and Alannah flew into them.

'Hi Nora.' After their hug, Alannah turned to the man in scrubs. 'Hi Ben. I didn't know you work here.'

Ben smiled. 'Yeah. I started a couple of months ago after finishing my studies.'

'Ben is my assistant. He has exceptional rapport with the patients here,' Nora explained.

'The discount medical bills are a bonus too.' Ben gave them a toothy grin.

'I just have to keep him away from these little ones.' Nora walked over to a large cage holding a few playful kittens, all with plastic cones around their necks.

Alannah heard Ben's inner dingo growl as she approached the cats. 'Aww, they're adorable.' Brendan moved in close to her side as she put her finger through the bars. She addressed them with a cutesy voice, 'Why are you here to see Dr. Winters, hmm?'

'The local animal shelter brought them in for de-sexing and shots as part of their adoption program,' explained Nora.

Brendan gasped. 'You mean to tell me these poor critters will never know the joys of sex? I'm horrified, mother.'

Alannah laughed and elbowed him in the ribs.

Ben snarled. 'We don't need more of those filthy things breeding.'

A pure white kitten pounced at Alannah's finger, reminding her of another white cat she had once met. 'Oh Gods, my heart just melted. This one is too cute.'

'Would you like to hold her?' Nora stepped up beside her.

Alannah's eyes widened. 'Could I, please?'

'Of course.' She opened the cage and retrieved the white fluffball. 'Here. Be careful of these stiches.'

As Alannah cuddled the kitten, it stared at her with wide blue eyes.

Brendan's arm circled Alannah's waist as his other hand joined hers in patting the kitten. 'You wanna adopt a fur baby together?'

She shot him a look. 'Can we? I mean the place is a rental.'

'Won't be a problem.'

'Then yes, I'd love to take this precious girl home. How much does the adoption cost?'

'Don't worry about it, hun. I've got it covered.' Her aunt smiled.

'Really?'

Nora nodded.

'Thank you, so, so much.'

'What do you want to name her?' Brendan asked.

'I have the perfect name. I want to call her Luna.'

Chapter Twenty

Later that afternoon, Alannah curled up on Brendan's couch to read from her book of shadows with a kitten snuggled in the crook of her neck. It was the sweetest, most heart-warming sight he had ever beheld. He moved behind her to pet the sleeping fluffball. 'I'm going to die from cuteness overload here, Lana. You know, I still can't believe you called her Luna.'

'What's wrong with Luna?'

'Don't you think it sounds a lot like Lana?'

She shrugged her free shoulder. 'I suppose it does. I named her after another white cat I'd met in foster care after Dad died.'

Brendan sat beside her. 'That's all well and good, gorgeous, but don't get mad at me if I mix up your names.'

She snorted. 'So long as you don't call out for the cat during sex, I'll deal.'

Laughing, he glanced at the book in her lap. 'How are you going? Find anything yet?'

Alannah was searching for a spell or ritual to help her control the empathic link so Brendan could do stuff like run to the shops and go to work without subjecting her to excruciating pain. 'Nothing helpful yet. From what I've gathered, these empathic links generally require a strong spiritual connection.'

'I always thought we were soulmates.' He gave her a big dumb grin.

She arched her brow. 'Corny much?'

'Yup. But I know you love it.'

'Not as much as I love you.' She leaned in and planted a sloppy kiss on his lips.

The movement disturbed Luna, who scurried off Alannah's shoulder and skidded across the room where she hid under the entertainment unit. They both laughed at the kitten's antics before returning their attention to the book.

Alannah flicked through a few pages when a few Gaelic words stood out to Brendan. 'Wait. What about this one? "Ceangal Anamacha" means the connecting or binding of souls. Didn't you say the pain feels like having part of your soul torn away?'

'Hmm. Valid point.' She pulled out a translator and continued reading.

Brendan would have read along with her, but Luna decided to attack his leg, so he scooped her up and cuddled her. He had never thought of himself as much of a cat person before, but this kitten stole his heart, much like Alannah had. Perhaps it was the experience of caring for another being together. As Luna curled up and drifted off to sleep on his lap, he became distracted by thoughts of raising a child with Alannah.

'Oh my Gods! This is it!' Alannah's outburst sent the kitten running again.

He focussed on the book. 'Fantastic. Let's get started. What do we need?'

She pursed her lips. 'Oh. Sorry, this isn't about the empathic link. But it is the secret of the lich. It has to be. Look here.' Alannah pointed to a passage of the ritual. 'It talks about preventing true death by binding the soul to a crystal.'

Brendan's eyes widened as he read the passage. 'You're right! What sort of crystal?' He scanned the rest of the page, finding it and tapping the word. 'Clear quartz.'

'For real? The stuff is like way too common for such powerful magic.'

'Rarity has nothing to do with it. The magic powers of crystals come from their chemical composition and origins. Clear quartz has strong psychic and spiritual properties. Mages also know quartz for its stability and longevity, with some crystals being billions of years old—so it makes sense.'

She gaped at him. 'How do you know all this stuff?'

'I've been studying magic theory since I could read, Lana. Crystals always fascinated me.'

'Hmm. Fair enough.' She returned her attention to the book. 'Apparently the crystal glows once the mage binds their soul to it.' Her mouth gaped open. 'I remember seeing a crystal like it in Mum's mystic chest. I kept it with the others in your parents' training room until…' Alannah jumped from the sofa.

Brendan sprung to his feet. 'What is it? What's wrong, Lana?'

'I took the crystal to my sanctuary with a bunch of others because Scarlett—I mean Tara—suggested they would be useful for my training.' She ran to the door and put her shoes on.

He rushed after her. 'What are you doing, Lana?'

'I need to go and check if the crystal is still there. What if she took it? Or, better still, what if she didn't? We could have the means to destroy her once and for all.'

A light switched on in Brendan's mind. 'Do you think destroying the crystal would bring about her true death?'

'That's exactly what I'm thinking. It makes perfect sense. Maybe this is why she trained me all along. She wanted me to bring the crystal to her.'

He sighed. 'If so, I doubt she left it there.'

'Only one way to find out. Come on, let's go.'

Brendan insisted on driving, knowing how many thoughts distracted Alannah's mind.

The moment they arrived, she bolted into the glamoured shed and rummaged through her stash of crystals. 'Damnit! It's gone.' Alannah dropped to the floor.

He sat next to her and pulled her into his arms. 'On the plus side, we can be even more certain the crystal is the key to Tara's true death. She is less likely to leave something so important lying around in the hands of the enemy. Maybe we need to find her current hideout.'

Alannah sighed. 'You're right. I guess it's time to see if I can meet her again.'

Tara examined Alannah and Brendan when first entering the sanctuary an hour later. 'This is a curious development. I suppose congratulations are in order.' She directed her gaze at Alannah. 'You have made an excellent soulmate choice, dear child. Brendan is a more suitable match for you than Liam. That boy is too much of a Council pet, like his father.'

Alannah could feel Brendan's chest swelling. She turned and smiled at him, before returning her attention to Tara. 'What are you talking about, Madam?'

'Please tell me your soul link connection is an intentional choice.'

'You mean the empathic link we have? It was Brendan's idea, but I was delighted to make it a two-way link. But how did you know about it?'

Tara laughed haughtily. 'Have you seen your auras lately?'

Alannah's attention shot to Brendan. 'Have you?'

'No. I don't need to see your aura when I can feel your emotions strongly now. Give me a sec.' He took a few steps back to study her.

She read his aura too. Knowing what to expect from his outer colours, she focused on the main aura. 'Wowsers… that's different.' The right side was still his usual yellow, although murky from the dark magic he had been mixed up in. But the left side of his aura was orange.

Tara drew up close behind Alannah. 'I assume you are both aware your auras are a visual representation of your soul. Brendan is now seeing a mirror image of what you can see, dear child. Soul linking is the ultimate commitment mages can make to each other. No one has performed it in these parts for decades. Couples often accompanied the private ritual with a public declaration involving a handfasting ceremony. They chose ribbons based on the colours of the joining souls. Am I going out on a limb here to assume your ignorance on these matters means you did not know what you were getting yourselves into?'

'Not entirely,' Alannah agreed. 'Did you know, Brendan?'

He shook his head.

Alannah tilted her head. 'But why did Brendan already feel the link before we, uh, joined.'

'You do not need to act coy on my account, dear child. I am aware of what soul linking entails. Besides, I have indulged in acts of debauchery that would make your head spin.'

Ew, too much information Grandmother!

Ignoring Alannah's thoughts, Tara went on, 'If Brendan felt the connection before, it meant he already devoted himself to you. So much so his soul instinctively chose yours.'

Brendan grinned at her, conveying a telepathic message, *'Told you.'*

'So, it had nothing to do with Brendan's attunements?'

'Actually, being an enchanter has a lot to do with Brendan's inclination towards the link. The traditional joining ritual requires both partners to channel emotions and senses during the act of intimacy. It took some mages years to master the arts necessary, making the commitment even more meaningful.'

Brendan chuckled. 'So, what you're saying is Alannah and I had the magical equivalent of a Vegas wedding?'

Tara smiled warmly. *Such an odd sight.* 'That is one way of putting it.'

Alannah decided to leap on the opportunity. 'Why does it hurt me every time Brendan leaves my side?'

'You are suffering a symptom of the honeymoon phase. It should wear off after a month.'

'Honeymoon phase?' Alannah and Brendan chimed in unison.

'Newly linked soulmates are supposed to spend their first month focussed on each other as way of kickstarting their family.'

'How do I switch my side of the link off and on like Brendan can?'

'With practice, you should be able to push thoughts and feelings for Brendan from your mind using mindfulness, bringing them back in much the same way. This will help modify the physical aspects of the soul connection.' Looking at Brendan, she pursed her lips. 'I guess years of unrequited love gave you plenty of opportunities to hone this skill?'

He nodded, eliciting a sharp pain in Alannah's gut. Squeezing her hand, he spoke in her mind. *'Don't worry about it, gorgeous. All water under the bridge now.'*

She gazed into his eyes, feeling lost in them a moment.

Tara cleared her throat. 'Was there another reason you called me here, or have we finished?'

Blinking, Alannah sighed. 'Yes, actually. I noticed one of my crystals have gone missing, a white quartz. You took it, didn't you?'

'Hmm. I see you have discovered the secret of the lich. Yes, I took my soul crystal back, and I have hidden it safely. I know you still don't trust me, and it would be foolish to leave the instrument of my undoing in your hands.'

Alannah gasped at Tara's candid response. 'If you are aware of my intentions, why are you meeting with me?'

'Because I am not your enemy, Alannah. I had hoped our training sessions and everything I have done for both of you would have proven this.'

Brendan snorted. 'What have you done for me other than send me a potion book that landed me in a world of trouble, then given me a mind shield to protect me from the legal consequences?'

Tara huffed. 'Show some respect, boy. What you did with my book was your own choice, Brendan. When I saw you had aligned yourself with the Syndicate, I stepped in to mediate matters for you. Without me, you would be at Lady Violet's mercy. And why do you think you were able to absorb so much knowledge during your crash-course in legal studies? I have been looking out for the two of you in more ways than you realise.'

They were both gobsmacked. Brendan dropped to his knees in front of her, adopting a playful tone, 'Please Lady Scarlett, I beg you to share your magic wisdom with me. Like the trick of yours for quick learning.'

Tara laughed as Alannah rolled her eyes. 'Brendan, please stop grovelling; you look ridiculous.'

Casting his gaze her way, he poked his tongue out at Alannah, before pulling himself up to his feet. 'Seriously though, I'm keen to learn.'

'I would be happy to teach you both everything I know.' Tara moved across the room and sat at the table.

Alannah watched with a frown as Brendan followed Tara like a faithful puppy. Before joining them, she needed the truth. 'Lady Scarlett?'

'Yes, dear child?'

'Has your goal been to turn me and Brendan dark?'

Tara's brows rose. 'Did you not meet your father?'

Brendan's head snapped in Alannah's direction; his brow creased.

'Yeah, I did. But how did you know?'

Her grandmother smiled again. 'Because I arranged the meeting. What did he tell you, Alannah?'

'Wait a minute,' Brendan interrupted. 'When did you meet your old man and why am I only hearing about it now?'

Alannah sat down next to him. 'Because it is difficult to talk about that time. I met him in the Celestial realm when I was… defiled.'

'Oh, hell!' Brendan gasped, jumping to his feet. '*You died? That bastard killed you?*'

She shook her head. 'No! Please calm down, Brendan. It was more like… astral projection.' When he returned to his seat, she continued, 'When I met my father, he told me he was proud of me and I was on the right path; he guaranteed my place in the realm if I stay on this path.'

Tara nodded. 'What does that tell you about the nature of my influence?'

Alannah scratched her head. 'But you are cursed and tried to curse me. You tried to damn my soul!'

Tara sighed. 'You have much to learn, dear child. It was never my intention to hurt you. Cursing was a means to an end. I needed your allegiance and as Queen at the time, I saw an opportunity to bring you in line when you became close to Austin. It was a short-sighted approach and I am sorry for what transpired.'

'Why didn't you ask me directly?'

'To protect you from the Council. They cannot see you working willingly with me. Surely you gathered as much from your time on trial?'

'I still don't understand.'

'Because you still have much to learn and revealing too much too soon will put you in extreme danger.'

'Danger from whom?' Brendan demanded.

'It is best you do not know yet. Knowledge can be a dangerous asset to possess in a world full of mind readers. Richard may be gone, but they will appoint another Inquisitor soon enough.' She placed another mind shield on the table and pushed it toward Alannah. 'This should help in the meantime, but both of you need to study the art of deception and perfect your skills before I tell you much more.'

Alannah hated the idea of becoming a deceiver, but she had suffered enough at the hands of the Council to appreciate the need. 'Okay then, guru. Teach us how to become liars.'

Catching her breath, Alannah moaned pleasurably. 'I'm loving this honeymoon phase concept.' It was late afternoon and they had spent the day making love. In fact, it was day seven and counting of their staycation and she was more than thankful Brendan had chosen to spend the full month by her side, to prevent the pain of separation. At least she had learnt to switch off the link when she needed to focus on other tasks.

Brendan's fingers trailed along her bare stomach. 'Mm, yes. Best idea ever. Pity it only lasts a month, 'cause I could spend all day, every day like this with you, Lana.'

As if sensing another break in carnal activities, Luna jumped onto the bed and rubbed up along Alannah's side, purring profusely as she did.

Alannah giggled from the sensation. 'Hey kitty, that tickles.' The cat pounced. 'Ow, Fuck! Luna, you bad kitty!'

Brendan jack-knifed, wearing a huge grin, and clutching his nipple. 'Did she bite your boob?' When she replied by biting her lip and blushing, he rolled onto his side and roared with laughter. 'Too. Damn. Funny.'

With their empathic link still open, she could feel his mirth and let it infect her as she joined the hysterics.

The sound of Timberlake singing 'Sexy Back' through Brendan's phone ended their fit of amusement. Naturally, he had to answer with a well-timed, 'Yeah… Hang on Cara, slow down. I'm gonna put you on loudspeaker so Alannah can hear you, okay?'

With the phone held in front of her, Alannah leaned in. 'Hi hun, what's going on?'

'Hi Alannah. I'm freaking out because I can't get hold of Jacob. When was the last time either of you saw or spoke to him?'

'At the pub, three nights ago.' Brendan exchanged a glance with Alannah.

'I haven't been able to contact him since flying out Sunday night. It's not like him to miss my calls and not return them. I'm worried. Can you please check in on him at home?'

'Okay. Do you want us to stay on the line while we head over there?' Brendan asked.

'Yes, please.'

'Just give us a minute to get ready, okay?' Alannah added.

'Okay.'

When they got there, they found Jacob and Cara's door locked, so Brendan thumped it with his fist. No response. He hammered against it.

Alannah held the phone. 'The door's locked and he's not answering, Cara.'

'Can you use your matter attunement to pick the lock?'

'Alright. Hang on a minute.' She handed the phone back to Brendan and placed her hands over the door and the lock while she connected with the material mana source. When the familiar power source flowed through her, she visualised the locking mechanism and liquified the pins. 'Done. Sorry, hun, but you'll need a new lock.'

'Least of my worries right now,' Cara replied.

Brendan and Alannah both withdrew combat knives from their belts and made a stealthy entrance. It did not take them long to scout the place and confirm all was in order, except for the complete lack of Jacob.

Brendan retrieved the phone from his pocket. 'There's no sign of him, Cara. Place is locked up tight, no sign of a struggle or anything out of the ordinary.'

'Shit! Where the hell is he?' Cara's voice increased in pitch and volume.

'I can think of one likely avenue to explore, but I'll need to sign off and call you back later tonight,' Brendan explained.

'Okay, please don't be too long.'

'I'll do my best. I promise.'

'Thanks, Brendan.'

He signed off and looked at Alannah. 'You know I wouldn't do this if I didn't absolutely have to, right?'

Her heart sank because she realised what Brendan had in mind. 'I know. This is for Cara and Jacob's sake. At least let me come with you.'

Brendan smiled. 'I wouldn't expect otherwise, gorgeous. Come on. We better hurry.'

An hour later, they were walking into the underground lair of Bridey Hawthorn, aka Lady Violet. It was everything Alannah would have expected of the endarkened enchantress: opium den meets brothel, with Victorian boudoir furnishings of purple velvet and black leather.

Her leather-clad guard, Aiden, stopped them in the hallway beyond the main chamber to announce their arrival.

'Let them in,' Violet's voice called out in response from beyond the velvet curtain.

When Aiden pulled the curtain aside, Alannah stared aghast at Bridey sprawled out on a chaise longue, wearing nothing but a corset and smoking something herbal with a cigarette holder, while a guy with long black hair continued to eat her out. Several other men in various states of undress surrounded her. *This woman has no shame.*

Alannah also sensed Brendan's discomfort as he dragged his feet forward.

Bridey tapped her current lover on the head. 'Oh look sweety, your friends are here.'

When the endarked man turned his head to face them, Alannah's stomach churned from the recognition. But Caleb maintained a passive expression as he leaned back against his sister's naked thigh.

'The hell?' Brendan thundered. 'Violet, let him go—right now!'

'Why, handsome? Did you want to take his place?'
Caleb snarled at Brendan.

'Hell no. Enthralling your brother is twisted and wrong.'

Bridey tittered. 'You seem to be of the mistaken impression Caleb doesn't want to be here. Tell them, sweety.'

'It's true. I love my sister and want nothing more than to please her.'

Brendan shook his head. 'Unbelievable.'

Alannah glared at her. 'Would you mind covering up?'

'Aw, what's wrong petal? Are you afraid your new soulmate won't be able to resist my feminine wiles?'

Alannah's eyes widened.

'Oh yes, I can see the link. Brother dearest, did you know we have a pair of newlyweds to congratulate?'

'What?' Caleb squinted.

'Brendan and Alannah made the *ultimate commitment* and linked their souls. Isn't that sweet? I wonder how long it will last before one of them *begs* me to sever the connection.' Bridey sat up and closed her legs, forcing Caleb to rise and join the rest of her (reverse) harem. 'You know, severing soul links is one of the many services I offer in this fine establishment. Is this what brings you here tonight?'

'No. We are content with our link, thank you,' Brendan hissed. 'We are here because Jacob is missing, and I want to know what you have done with him.'

Bridey burst into laughter. 'Oh, you are precious, Brendan. You ought to know better than most how the sneakthief can get himself in plenty of trouble without my help. Why would you assume I have anything to do with his disappearance?'

'Because you're his boss, for one. And I have firsthand experience with the underhanded ways of the Syndicate.'

'Well I have no idea what happened to him. But do let me know when the scamp shows up. He owes me an interest payment.' Bridey winked at Brendan.

It took all of Alannah's self-restraint to hold back from clawing the bitch's eyes out.

'If you want my advice, I'd start by checking all the warlock holding cells around the state. There was a big potion bust on the weekend. Failing that, try the local drug dens. Now, unless you want to join the merriment, Aiden will show you out.'

They both spun on their heels and strode out of the cesspit of sin.

Chapter Twenty-One

ilence prevailed on the drive to Cailleach Estate. Breaking the news of their soul link to the family would be awkward, but it did not weigh as heavily on their minds as their missing friend. They had spent the last twenty-four hours searching for Jacob to no avail and Cara was beside herself. Alannah wanted to be with her, but Cara had insisted on bringing Liam into the search, which meant resolution time.

As the Jag came to a stop, she turned to Brendan. 'Are you okay?' It was a stupid question. Alannah could feel his mood was not pretty.

'I should be out there searching for him, not enjoying a family meal.'

Alannah sighed. 'I know, but we promised Cara we would try this her way.'

'Well, let's get this over and done with.' Brendan made his exit from the car and Alannah followed close behind.

Nora squealed with delight when they entered the kitchen. 'There's the happy couple.' She pulled up short of hugging them when she noticed the clouds hanging over them both. 'What's wrong?'

'Jacob's missing,' Brendan replied.

'Oh sweety, I'm sorry. I know you are close to him. I'm gonna have to insist on that hug now.' She pulled Brendan into her arms and opened the embrace to Alannah.

'What's with the group hug?' Ross crossed the room.

Nora stepped back and smiled at him. 'They have good and bad news to share tonight.'

'Best get the bad news out the way so we can have the good news over dinner,' Ross advised.

'What bad news?' Liam entered the cramped room.

'Alright, everyone out of my kitchen. Take it into the dining room while I finish up in here.' Nora pushed them all out the door.

Once they sat, Brendan turned to Liam. 'Jacob Bennett is missing. I know you're not a big fan of his, but I'm hoping for your help in tracking him down. We could use police and Council resources on this.'

'You're right, I'm not a fan. He's an unseelie, Brendan. The Council won't spare him a second thought and I don't owe him anything.'

'No, but the police ought to. He is still a citizen,' Alannah added. 'And we are asking you to do this for us and for Cara. I know you still care about her, despite your complicated past.'

Liam sighed. 'Fine. What do I need to know?'

Alannah smiled at him. 'Thank you, Liam.'

Brendan filled him in on the details, avoiding any mention of the potion business.

'If he is as dodgy as he sounds, I can't promise I won't be locking him up when I find him.'

Anticipating Brendan's hostile response, Alannah intervened. 'At least we know the Council will keep him safe, right Brendan?' She placed a reassuring hand on his thigh.

'Right.'

Nora's timing with dinner was perfect for a change in conversation. And topics were much lighter while they ate.

Alannah breathed easier knowing she had succeeded in winning Liam over for the help they needed.

When dessert came out, Nora also brought out a bottle of expensive champagne and winked at Alannah. *Oh Gods!* It was the moment she had been dreading. This time, Brendan gave her the reassuring hand squeeze.

Liam's eyes narrowed on the glass flute Nora poured sparkling wine into. 'What's with the bubbles, Mum?'

Brendan smirked. 'This is the good news bit—although you might want a stronger drink, Brother.'

Liam's eyes flicked from Brendan to Alannah, and he paled.

'Dad, you can stop trying to set me up with pure mages, because I have the perfect woman right here.'

'I figured something was going on between the two of you. So, are you an official couple now? Is that what we are celebrating?' Ross asked.

Liam locked Alannah in a stare as Brendan's words spilled out.

'Yup. Alannah and I have made the ultimate commitment.'

'*What?*' Liam's attention snapped toward Brendan.

'Have you heard of soul linking, Liam?'

Liam's face turned red. 'Is this some kind of joke?'

Dropping his guard briefly, Brendan let his colours show. 'No joke. Just ask Mum. She can see our mirror image auras *right now.*'

Liam turned to Nora, who nodded while squirming in her seat. 'Shit!' Liam leaped out of his chair and stormed out the back door.

'I'm sorry.' Nora hunched over her place at the table. 'I didn't think he'd take the news so disagreeably. I thought he knew the two of you were together and he'd had time to deal with it.'

'I'll go talk to him. We still have a lot of unresolved issues.' When Alannah stood up, Brendan made to follow her. 'No. I have to do this alone. I'll be able to deal with the short distance.'

'Okay.' He pecked her on the lips and sat down.

Alannah found Liam on the swinging loveseat hanging from the Moreton Bay Fig and sat beside him. 'Talk to me, Liam. What's going on?'

'Not much. My life has been pretty uneventful since you left it; oh, except for the bit where you ripped my heart out.'

'That's hardly fair, Liam. You left me, remember? You even pushed me into Brendan's arms, so don't tell me you're surprised by how things turned out.'

'Biggest regret of my life. I thought if you got him out of your system, you'd eventually find your way back to me when he messed up and did the dirty on you like he does with every other girl. And when I saw you alone at Beltane, I allowed myself to hope. I didn't expect things to escalate this fast… so honestly, I am extremely surprised.'

She stared aghast at him. 'That's stupid logic, Liam. And what you did by dumping me in prison was wretched.'

Tears fell from his eyes. 'I know and I am so damn sorry, Lana. I still can't forgive myself when you won't even forgive me.'

Seeing how much he was suffering melted her heart. Without thinking, she moved a hand to his face to wipe away his tears. 'I forgive you, okay.'

Liam grabbed her hand and pulled her into his lap to kiss her savagely.

His attack on her senses blindsided Alannah and it took her several seconds to realise what was happening. She pushed back out of his arms. 'Liam! What the hell?'

Kicking off from the swing, he rose. 'I'm sorry, Lana. I've had a harrowing time living without you.'

'Well, you're gonna have to get over me because I'm with Brendan now. And what I have with him isn't a passing phase. He and I are forever.' A moment later, Alannah collapsed to the ground as the familiar agony winded her.

'What's wrong, Lana?' Liam rushed to her and scooped her up from the dirt.

The pain she felt could only mean one thing. 'Brendan crossed the threshold. He must have left already.' When he squinted, she summarised the honeymoon phase symptom.

'Why would he run off?' Liam's brow furrowed.

'I don't know. Maybe he got word of Jacob? Let's go find out.' Thanks to the crippling pain, she hobbled back to the house with Liam's help. When they got back, Alannah directed her question to Nora: 'What happened to Brendan?'

'He was on the phone, then rushed back inside to tell me something urgent came up before he drove off.'

'Sounds Jacob-related to me,' Liam agreed.

Alannah tried ringing him, but the phone went straight to voicemail. 'Hey. Just wondering what's going on. Call me as soon as you can. Love you.' She looked at Liam. 'Can you please give me a lift home?'

'Yeah, okay.'

The air was thick with tension even after Liam and Alannah had left the room. Brendan averted his gaze from his father's cold glare. 'I'm gonna check in with Cara.' Pulling his phone out of his pocket, he stepped out onto the back porch.

'Hi Brendan. Please tell me you have good news.'

'Sort of. Liam has agreed to help.'

'What a relief. Thank you so much.'

He sighed. 'Don't thank me. Lana talked him around.'

'I knew she would. Please pass on my gratitude.'

'Will do. I'll keep you posted.'

'Okay, bye Brendan.'

He had not even realised he had been walking into the garden until he hung up, but it made sense. Alannah's pull on him had been much stronger since completing the soul link. As soon as they came into view, he stopped himself from advancing. Brendan did not want to eavesdrop on their conversation, contented to gaze upon the beautiful woman he loved. The woman who was finally his—mind, body, and soul.

Her hand touched Liam's face, and Brendan froze. When she leaped into Liam's lap and kissed him, something deep inside Brendan broke, along with all the promises they had ever made each other. Unable to watch anymore, he turned and fled.

Rushing back through the house, he cried out, 'Something urgent came up.' Jumping into his Jag, he gunned it out of there. 'Fuuuuuuck! Fuck! Fuck! Fuck!' He banged his hand against the steering wheel. *How could I have been so stupid? Of course she would still have feelings for Liam.* Brendan never even gave them a chance to resolve their issues before besieging her with his own love.

Tears streamed down his face as he reached the expressway. In addition to the grief, he felt the tearing of his soul—something he had not experienced for years.

Brendan only knew one way to deal with what he felt. When he got there, he barged in and dropped to his knees before her. 'Please make the pain go away.'

'Well, that didn't take long now, did it handsome?' Bridey smirked.

'Please. You said you could sever the link. I want it gone. *Now.*'

'It'll cost you.'

'Name your price.'

'Mm. You are precious. I want a year of your sexual servitude.'

'Done. Now make it stop.'

When Alannah got home, curling up in bed was all she could manage. The pain became unbearable. 'Please, Brendan, come home to me soon,' she whispered to the empty room.

Luna jumped onto the bed and batted at her nose. 'Meow.'

'Hey kitty. Are you hungry? Let's get you some dinner.' Hauling herself out of bed, she clung to the walls as she walked down the hall. She struggled with the ring pull on the cat food tin. 'Fucker!' The bastard snapped. She flung the can across the room and poured some biscuits in Luna's bowl instead. Sinking to the floor, she watched the cat eat. At least it took her mind off the pain.

A few minutes later, she began to nod off as the pain eased. *Are you on your way home now, my love?* Alannah crawled down the hall to the bedroom, remembering with fondness the first time she had done so; only Brendan had been by her side then. She stripped herself bare in anticipation of his return and climbed back under the quilt. Try as she might, she could not hold sleep off any longer. *Brendan will have to wake me when he gets back.*

Alannah woke with a start. The room was dark, and Brendan's side of the bed was empty. She moved her hand into the vacant space. 'Still cold.' Her separation pain had subsided. *Odd*. She got up. 'Brendan?' Searching every room of the apartment to no avail only served to intensify her heartbeat. Grabbing her phone, Alannah checked for messages. Nothing. She rang him again.

'Hi this is the voicemail of Brendan Winters. I'm currently bringing sexy back, so you'll need to leave a message after the tone…'

She sighed as the beep sounded. 'Hey baby, I'm getting worried now. Please call me; or better still, bring your sexy arse back to bed. I love you.' She typed out the same message in a text and sent it to his phone and every one of his social media accounts.

After a few deep breaths, Alannah tried to focus on their spiritual connection to see if she could track him. But she felt nothing. 'Crap, that's scary.' Normally she could at least gauge his mood and feel what his hands were doing. When she failed to get a read on Brendan, the jitters set in.

Finding Cara in her contacts, she hit CALL.

'Hey hun, please tell me you have good news.'

'Have you heard from Brendan tonight?'

'Not since he rang to tell me you got Liam on board. Thanks, by the way.'

'You're welcome. But listen Cars, Brendan's still not home and I'm freaking out.'

'What do you mean he's not home?'

The tears chose that moment to start. 'I think he went to follow up on a lead regarding Jacob and I can't get hold of him.'

'Hang on, can't you track him with your soul link?'

'I tried,' Alannah sobbed. 'But I can't get a read on him. I can't feel him at all, Cara. Oh Gods, what if he's unconscious in a ditch somewhere. Or worse?'

'Hang on hun, I'm coming over.' The line went dead, followed a few minutes later with knocking on the door.

Still naked, Alannah threw on one of Brendan's rock band t-shirts that was long enough to be a nightie. Cara assaulted her with a massive bear hug.

'Come on, let's start the ring around.' Cara attempted to smile but grimaced instead.

Alannah pulled up her friends contact list. Most of them were clueless on Brendan's whereabouts and a couple of the guys did not pick up, which was fair enough considering the early hour.

Cara pursed her lips when they exhausted the friends. 'It's time to bring in the big guns.'

She nodded through her tears and rang Liam. It took a couple of tries to reach him.

'Hey Lana, it's 3AM. Is something wrong?'

'I can't find Brendan,' she cried into the phone.

'Can't you use your link?' He spoke with a hint of acrimony in his tone.

Alannah choked back a sob. 'I can't feel him at all, Liam. I'm terrified something awful has happened.'

'Okay, I'll alert the Council and petition a search party. Have you called my parents?'

'No. I don't know if I should yet.'

'You should. Ask them to come over. Mum can calm you down and Dad might give you a potion to help you sleep.'

She lost all control of her emotions and screamed at him, '*I don't want to sleep, damn it. The love of my life is missing and possibly dead! I can't lie back and do nothing.*'

The line went silent.

Alannah realised what she had said. 'Oh, crap! Liam, I'm sorry.'

He sucked in a sharp breath. 'Just call them, okay. You won't be able to help much in your hysterical state. Get some rest and let the Council handle things for a bit. You can join us when you have calmed down.' He hung up.

When Alannah put the phone down, Cara gazed at her with raised brows. 'Well?'

'He will get the Council on the case. Hmph, at least this way they will have to look for Jacob as well, presuming Brendan went after him.'

'I'm sorry, hun.' Cara embraced her.

Pulling free a few minutes later, Alannah picked up her phone again. 'I need to call Nora and Ross.'

Telling them their son was missing and possibly dead was one of the most difficult things Alannah had ever done and calling on their aid made it much worse. But she was thankful they both came to her, doing exactly what Liam had suggested they would.

Cara provided some comfort, snuggling with Alannah in bed as Brendan's scent surrounded her. It was not much, but it allowed the sleeping potion to take effect and Alannah drifted off with dreams of Brendan holding her.

The irritating sounds of Europe singing 'The Final Countdown' startled Liam. He searched the room, wondering where the hell the awful music was coming from. Spotting the illumination on his phone, he groaned at the name on the screen, but picked up the call with haste. 'Where the hell have you been?'

'Chill, bro. What's got your knickers in a twist?' Brendan shouted over the thumping bass line of the music in the background.

Liam growled. 'Are you serious right now? You disappeared for over a week without telling anyone. I half expected to find you dead in a ditch somewhere. Now I'm thinking I'll be the one to put your corpse in said ditch.'

The background music stopped. 'Woah bro, that's pretty harsh, especially coming from you right now.' There was a hint of malice in his brother's voice.

'I warned you to keep your hands off her.'

'Relax, man. It was just a fun tumble in the hay. I doubt it meant much to her considering she has you again now.' Liam attempted to cut him off, but the stubborn twerp paid him no heed. 'And you can tell our princess it meant about as much to me too. Oh, and if she doesn't believe you, let her know I severed the link and I'm now whiling away the hours in the arms of a real woman—one who takes care of all my darkest desires.'

The sickening laugh of a woman's deep voice sounded through Brendan's phone, confirming part of the bollocks he spewed forth.

'If you're content in your newfound *happiness*, why call me? What the hell do you want?' He spat the words into the phone.

'I wanted to say goodbye now I've settled into my new home beyond the state borders. Plus, I had those messages for you to deliver to Lana.'

Liam shook his head. Brendan's behaviour was off the charts, even for the rogue he knew his brother to be. 'I'm glad you left town, Brendan, because you've saved me a homicide charge.' His tone went grave. 'And I mean it when I say, if I see you again, I will kill you for what you did to Lana. Good riddance, *Brother*!'

Brendan laughed as he hung up the phone.

'What are you doing here?' Alannah opened the door for Liam. 'Don't you have a Council meeting?'

He beelined for the lounge area. 'Sit down, Lana.'

'What? Why?' It had been eight days since Brendan's disappearance and, along with Cara, Alannah had begun to accept the possibility that her man was not coming back. They had even turned into a pair of old widows together; at least that was their ongoing dark joke on those few occasions when humour became possible.

'I have news of Brendan.' He frowned, a disconcerting sign.

She sagged to the floor, but Liam caught her and helped her to the couch. 'Is he dead?' Her voice squeaked.

'No. This is much worse.'

'What could be worse than death?' Alannah imagined all sorts of horrid things.

Liam paced. 'See, this is why I warned him not to touch you. I knew he would pull this shit.' He muttered to himself more than telling her.

'Liam, stop wearing a hole in the damn rug and tell me!'

He halted in front of Alannah and faced her with a grimace. 'He's gone, Lana. I'm sorry.'

'What do you mean, *gone*?'

Liam clenched his jaw. 'He left you.'

'*No!* He promised he wouldn't ever leave me. Brendan loves me and he told me I was his everything. His forever.'

'You wouldn't be the first girl he promised to world to, Lana. He told me to tell you the sex was meaningless, just a bit of fun,' Liam spat.

Shaking her head, she screamed at him, '*Did he want to impregnate those other girls too?*'

'What?' Liam was gobsmacked.

'If the sex was meaningless, why did he tell me he wanted to raise a family with me?'

All the blood drained from Liam's face. 'Did you stop using all forms of contraception?'

She nodded.

'*I'm gonna murder that perverted bastard!*' He clenched his fists.

'Liam, please. I'm freaking out here. What's going on?'

He sighed and collapsed on the sofa beside her. 'Brendan must have figured you wouldn't believe me, hence the message.'

Alannah's eyes widened. 'You spoke to him? Is he okay?'

'More than okay, by the sounds of it. I don't want to tell you this, but he has a message for you.'

Her heart beat double time. 'Go on.'

'He said that he severed the link and that he's now wiling away the hours with a real woman. One who takes care of his darkest desires.'

A sliver of hope returned. 'Bridey! She must have enthralled him.' Alannah plucked up her phone, thinking for a moment.

'Who's Bridey?' Liam asked.

'Caleb's sister. Can I borrow your phone? Caleb won't recognise your number.'

He nodded and handed it to her.

'Hello?' Caleb spoke with caution.

'Caleb, it's Alannah.'

'Son of a mother!' He mumbled. 'I'm not getting involved.'

'Wait! Tell me one thing: Did she enchant him?'

He sniggered. 'No. Brendan came willingly. And I can't say I'm surprised.'

Alannah's heart stopped. For one split second, it forgot to beat. 'You don't have to be such a jerk about it.'

'Hey, I just call things as I see 'em. Shall I send Brendan your regards?'

'Whatever.' Alannah ended the call as she doubled over from the excruciating pain of her soul shattering into tiny shards.

Liam pulled her into his arms as she howled the house down. When her throat was too hoarse to vocalise her pain, she continued with sobs until her eyes dried out.

'Come on, Lana. You shouldn't be alone tonight. Let me take you home.'

She nodded numbly.

Liam helped Alannah to her feet as Luna rubbed up against his legs. 'Hey you. Do you want to come too?'

The kitten meowed, triggering a new stream of Alannah's tears. She reached down and picked up Luna, leaning into Liam as he carried her outside.

When they got to Liam's place, he went to put her in the spare room, but it still smelled like Brendan. 'This won't do. The place reeks of him even after all these months.' Instead, Liam tucked her into his bed and stood back. 'I'll be on the couch if you need me.'

'No, wait! Please hold me.'

Liam hesitated a moment before sitting on the edge of the bed to slip out of his shoes and stripped down to his boxer shorts. He climbed under the quilt and eased himself up to her side, where he gingerly pulled her into his embrace. 'I'm sorry, Lana.'

Sniffling, she gazed into Liam's big blues and remembered the caring man she fell in love with years ago. Alannah did something she thought she would never do again. She leaned in and kissed Liam's lips. Tentative at first, but when he returned the kiss, she climbed into his lap and deepened it.

Awareness of Liam's arousal knocked the air from her lungs, and she jerked back. 'Shit! Too soon. I'm not ready...'

Liam closed his eyes and drew a deep breath. He forced a smile and tucked a strand of hair behind her ear. 'It's okay Lana, I shouldn't have taken advantage of your vulnerability. I'm the one who should be sorry. If you decide you want me back, I swear I'll never leave you again.'

'I wish you guys would stop making empty promises,' she choked out between sobs.

Liam pulled her into a bear hug. 'I mean it this time. You will have to kick me out if you want me gone, because I am not making the mistake of letting you slip from my arms again.'

She let him tuck her into bed where he spooned her. As Liam drifted off to sleep with his arms around her, Alannah accepted the harsh reality that Brendan had left, and he was not coming back.

Chapter Twenty-Two

The harsh reality of another day dawned, and Alannah groaned.

Liam snuggled into her side. 'What is it, Lana?'

'I hardly slept a wink.'

'I'm sorry, gorgeous. I wish I could make the heartache go away.' He kissed her forehead. 'You should stay here and rest as long as you need.' His lips caressed her left cheek, then her right before hovering above her lips.

Alannah felt numb as she returned the gentle kiss Liam pressed to her lips. Uncertainty plagued her mind, so she inched back from him. 'Shouldn't you be getting ready for work?'

'Yeah,' he sighed. 'I wish I could spend the day with you though. Will you be okay on your own today?'

'I'll be fine.'

Liam jumped out of bed and headed for the bathroom. He returned ten minutes later wearing a towel around his waist. 'Shower's all yours.' Not even the sight of water trickling down his naked chest did much for her anymore.

Taking her time getting ready, she did not hear the commotion at the front door until she opened the bedroom door.

'What do you want?' Liam fumed.

'Tell me where Alannah and your brother are, and I'll leave you alone.' The horribly familiar voice of the ex-Inquisitor acidified her blood and gripped her spine with ice. She ducked back behind the bedroom door.

'I'm not telling you anything. By rights, I should be blasting you and sweeping up your remains with a broom.'

'Do that and you'll be taking an innocent life right along with me,' Richard smirked. 'Not that he's exactly innocent. The boggart and I had an interesting chat, didn't we Jacob? You should hear the mischief he's been making.'

Jacob? Alannah had to know he was okay. Peeking around the corner, she noticed there were three silhouettes at the end of the hall, but she could not make out Jacob's features thanks to the glare of the morning sun through the window. She tip-toed a few steps closer, freezing when one of the floorboards creaked beneath her feet. *Crap! That's a new one.* Alannah used to know all the panels to avoid when sneaking through the house at night.

Liam's head jerked towards her. 'No! Get out of here, Lana!'

Too late. Richard glared at her with malicious intent. 'Hello, Alannah. I must admit, I'm surprised to see you here. I thought you were living with Brendan. Is he with you, or are the brothers sharing you now?'

A low growl crept out of Liam's throat.

She registered Richard's words, but Alannah focussed on the sorry sight of Jacob's battered face. Bound in cold iron cuffs, his shoulders hunched, and he stared at Alannah with wide eyes while Richard used him as a shield. The last Jacob knew, she was celebrating her honeymoon with Brendan. But the duct tape on Jacob's mouth prevented him from voicing his thoughts. 'I guess you didn't hear.' Alannah kept her attention on Jacob. 'Brendan left me for Bridey.'

Jacob's eyes bugged out.

Richard sniggered. 'An interesting turn of events. I guess he went darker than I thought he would. Never mind, I'll catch up with him later. The four of us are going for a drive now.'

'I'll pass, but thanks for the invite,' Alannah deadpanned.

Sparks lit up Richard's hand. 'You seem to be under the misconception that you have a choice in the matter, Miss Winters. If you value this boggart's life, you will come with me. *Now.* Both of you.' He opened the door for them and pointed to the black SUV with darkly tinted windows in the driveway.

Alannah stepped beside Liam. 'Your dispute is with me. Leave Liam out of it.'

Shaking his head, Liam grabbed her arm. 'I'm not letting you go without me, Lana.'

'How touching,' Richard grinned. 'Liam will join us whether you like it or not. I need to be certain he won't go to the Council. Now get moving.'

Jacob shook his head furiously, but Alannah refused to leave him at Richard's mercy. She could not live with herself if she let him die and Cara would never forgive her. Alannah strode out to the car, with Liam following close behind.

Once they settled in the back, handcuffs appeared out of nowhere and fastened themselves around their wrists. Alannah studied Richard, who took the front passenger seat, and saw him close his eyes as he mouthed a spell. He pulled their phones from their pockets and took possession of them. A glance of the demonic driver was all Alannah needed to confirm her suspicions without the need to read Richard's aura. 'Looks like you've turned dark too.'

Once the SUV had turned onto Main Street, Richard turned toward them. 'I do what I must to survive as an outlaw. Oh, and speaking of dark mages, Liam—did Alannah tell you about Brendan's extracurricular activities?'

She paled as Liam eyed her.

'What is he talking about, Lana?'

Alannah opened her mouth, but no words came out.

'Oh, now you go quiet.' Richard laughed. 'Jacob was much more open to sharing Brendan's secrets than you, Alannah. Does that mean he was more susceptible to torture, or just less loyal to Brendan than you were?'

'Lana, please tell me. I promise not to freak out on you.' Liam's eyes drilled into her.

She sighed. 'Brendan was the source of Rhapsody.'

'*What?*' He was gobsmacked.

'And Jacob was his business partner for dealing on the Unseelie Market,' Richard added.

Liam appeared furious as he turned toward Jacob. 'You bastard! I knew there was something fishy about you.'

Alannah was glad she sat between them; else Liam may have used his elbows to add to Jacob's injuries.

After a few deep breaths, Liam regained his composure. 'I can understand your need to protect Brendan, Lana. You don't need to explain. But I can't pretend I'm not disappointed you kept this knowledge to yourself, especially after what he did to you.'

'It wasn't relevant anymore. By the time I found out, he was in the process of pulling out of the business and last I knew, he *was* out.'

Liam frowned. 'At least that's what he led you to believe. Gods know what actually transpired, given his current choice of lover.'

Tears trickled down Alannah's face.

'I'm sorry, Lana.' Liam lifted his bound hands and attempted to caress her face and wipe her tears away. 'Just knowing what he did to you… and now this potion business; it all makes me angry and disgusted with him.'

Jacob mumbled something from behind his gag, so Richard telekinetically tore the tape away. 'Ow, bloody heck!' Jacob rubbed the raw patch of skin around his mouth gingerly. 'I don't know what the hell Brendan was thinking when he left you Alannah, but I know he loved you and he definitely left the potion business when he sold the mother tincture recipe to Lady Violet. Maybe she enchanted him to pull him back into it?'

Liam squinted. 'What am I missing here? Who's Lady Violet?'

'Lady Violet is Bridey's pseudonym, and she is an underboss in the Dark Syndicate,' Alannah replied. 'And I already thought of that, Jacob, so I rang Caleb. He confirmed Brendan went to her willingly.'

'Let me get this straight,' Liam interrupted. 'Brendan made Rhapsody with Jacob and sold it to Caleb's sister, who is actually a crime boss for the unseelie Dark Syndicate? And now he is shacking up with this same whore?'

'Yes. That about sums it up,' replied Alannah. 'Except the Dark Syndicate isn't just an unseelie organisation. It includes dark mages and Lady Scarlett runs it—aka Tara Winters.'

'Oh hell!' Liam stared at her wide-eyed.

'An interesting titbit you left out, Jacob,' admonished Richard.

Jacob scowled at him. 'Must have slipped my mind.'

Alannah peered past Liam and out the window. 'Where are we going?'

'The middle of nowhere, about nine hours northeast of here. I'm hardly going to seek my revenge on the notorious Alannah Winters in the middle of her own territory, am I?'

She exchanged furrowed brow looks with Liam, who twisted in his seat to accommodate her in his lap. Curling up against him, Alannah tried to make the most of what could be her last hours with Liam—*or any man for that matter.*

'Hey, are you awake Lana?' Liam's hushed voice spoke in her ear.

Alannah's eyes fluttered open, and she sat up to stretch her stiff neck. After yawning, she chanced a glance at the passing scenery: mostly open plains with a sparse scattering of trees. 'Where are we?'

'We crossed the New South Wales border. We'll be passing through Broken Hill soon,' he whispered.

She had never travelled so far north, and the countryside became barren. 'Hmph. Pity my first time in this state isn't under more favourable circumstances.'

'Tell me about it,' Liam agreed.

She looked deep into his blue eyes. 'If we survive this, Liam, I want to give *us* another chance.'

He grinned. 'Something to look forward to.'

They huddled together in silence as the car journeyed on, and every so often, Liam would kiss the crown of her head. After passing through the township of Broken Hill—where they took a quick rest stop—the driver headed due north. A large reserve to their right signposted as THE LIVING DESERT intrigued Alannah.

The rocking motion of the vehicle eventually lulled her back to sleep when they hit a dirt track. But a sudden stop startled her awake. An old stone farmhouse sat amid a desolate field. Richard had not been kidding about the middle of nowhere.

Their captor opened the back door for them. 'Right. Everyone out.'

Liam stumbled as he tried to exit the car with his hands still bound.

'Jacob, you can lead the way to the cellar.'

Filing in after him, with Richard on their rear flank, they entered what would have once been a wine cellar, or possibly even food storage. The place was easily two hundred years old, if not more. Alannah froze the moment her eyes fell upon a wooden structure fitted with leather restraints. Thanks to her recent foray into BDSM, she knew exactly what it was and trembled at the thought of Richard's intentions.

A pair of strong, rough hands gripped her shoulders. 'How do you like my St. Andrew's Cross, Alannah? I see you recognise what it is, but after what you and Brendan got up to, I'm not surprised.' Pushing her forward into the dungeon, he closed the door. He tied Liam and Jacob to wooden chairs cemented to the floor and gagged them both.

Dread found its home in the depths of her soul as Alannah drew some nasty conclusions.

With the guys fixed firmly in place, Richard grabbed her and pulled her over to the cross. 'I wonder Alannah, does Liam know you let Brendan tie you up and beat you?'

She could see his eyes bulging out of their sockets as she shook her head.

'Or how you enjoyed every minute of the punishment? It's no wonder I didn't get far with my torture. You enjoy pain a bit too much. But I was going easy on you back then. I won't make that mistake this time.' Producing a pair of scissors, he cut away her clothes, leaving her exposed to all three sets of eyes in the room.

Alannah's stomach twisted, shooting acid up her throat.

Richard released her cold iron cuffs and threw them aside. In the split second she had, Alannah tried to summon a weapon to hand. But Richard laughed when she felt an oppressive weight blocking her mind. 'I figured you might try a conjuring spell. Are you forgetting my attunement to the nether? I can easily block any of your attempts to use magic against me.'

She narrowed her eyes on him. 'But not my attempts to escape.'

'Oh, I know you won't escape, because if you do, I'll kill your friends over there.' He directed her attention to Liam and Jacob, who both sat wide eyed.

'You weren't wrong to refer to me as a sadist, Alannah,' Richard continued as he pressed her front to the cross and strapped her in. 'Perhaps more than you realise. What I'm about to do to you will bring me pleasure, not only for the pain I deal you, but because the sight of your suffering is going to torture one if not both of our onlookers.'

'You're not only a sadist, Richard—you're a psycho!'

'Perhaps.' Once he finished tying her in place, he pressed his body into her back. 'I thought we could start with a full re-enactment of the first time you indulged your fantasies with Brendan. Let's show Liam what a deviant whore you are.'

Alannah's mouth fell open. 'How would you know?'

'I got the whole thing on video thanks to the cameras I hid about the place when the Council released you on bail. Kieran must have forgotten I had surveillance on you when he booted me out of the state. I connected those nifty devices to my phone, and they proved quite the source of entertainment.'

'Fuck!'

'Indeed, Alannah. Now, let's skip the massage and get straight to the spanking, shall we?' The intensity of his blows started stronger than Brendan ever had, and he did not bother to rub her arse in between each one. Nor did the assault bring her any of the pleasure she had felt with Brendan.

But she managed to keep quiet, not wanting to give him the satisfaction. Her strategy worked right up until he brought the cane down across her thighs, at which point she let out a gut-wrenching scream. Alannah hated how Richard was poisoning the memory of her most intimate and erotic time with the man she loved; not even Brendan's betrayal had done so.

The smell of burning wax filled her nose with smoke and her throat with bile as she heard the zipper of his fly. Alannah gulped, unable to bear the thought of another man raping her, especially in front of Liam. She remembered what her father had told her: *Some magic is more powerful than anything earthly.* Nether was not exactly earthly, but it was still inferior to Aether. *Worth a try.* Alannah prayed for divine strength.

A second later she felt the power flowing through her as she burst out of her bonds. Richard was halfway through undressing when she spun around and sent a shockwave from her body into his.

He fell on his backside and stared at her with his mouth agape. 'What the hell?'

'More like heaven.' Alannah stood over Richard and kicked him in the head with as much force as she could muster. It was not much, but it did knock him unconscious. She tried to focus on conjuring a sword, but something continued blocking her connection. 'Crap! I still can't channel matter near him. His nullification spell must still be active even while he's unconscious.' She crossed the room to free Liam of his bonds, starting with the ball gag.

'What are you doing, Lana? Get out of here while you still can.'

'Are you kidding me? There's no way I'm leaving either of you here. I could never live with myself if I let you guys die.

Besides, I've already lost Brendan—I can't lose you too.' As soon as he rose free of the bindings, she helped Jacob.

Liam ran across to Richard and attempted his own magic to no avail. 'I guess I'll have to rely on brute force to deal with him.'

Releasing the last of Jacob's tethers, Alannah noticed Liam grab Richard in a choke hold. Everything sank into slow motion as the arsehole opened his eyes and sent Liam flying with a kinetic blast.

She watched in horror as Richard's fingers sparked. 'Liam! Watch out.'

He ducked in time to avoid the lightning bolt. *'Get out of here, Lana!'*

'I'm not leaving you, Liam!'

Dodge-rolling got Liam out of the path of another attack, then another. 'I'll hold him off while you go get help.'

Tears sprung forth. 'I can't.'

Liam managed to get close enough to punch Richard in the jaw, staggering him for a moment. *'Lana, please get help!'*

Seeing Liam hold his own, Alannah conceded. 'Promise you won't die on me, Liam.'

'I promise. Now go!'

Sensing a ley line beneath them, Alannah grabbed Jacob and magiported the hell out of there.

Liam was royally screwed and the rictus grin on Richard's face confirmed his opponent knew it too. His best bet was to remain on the defensive and try and tire the man out, both physically and magically, hoping his own stamina was beyond Richard's. With the adrenaline pumping through his blood, Liam felt like he could go for days, although he knew the rush would only be short-lived.

Ducking and weaving Richard's attacks put Liam in mind of training sessions with Brendan. Thanks to his brother, Liam had spent years learning to hide his true intentions and mask them with bluff tactics to fool even the most skilled mind reader. This was one of those rare occasions when he was grateful for something the twerp had done.

As a fireball grew in his opponent's hands, Liam let Richard think he would dodge to the right, when in fact he went left. *Perfect! That damned wooden cross is ablaze.* He still could not believe how close he had come to witnessing Alannah's defilement *again*. Only this would have been right in front of him, and he would have been helpless to save her. Nothing had made him feel so impotent and useless before.

'I see you have developed some effective deflection skills. Am I right in guessing your dark mage brother helped you with those?'

Liam growled at him. 'You don't know jack about my brother.'

'On the contrary, I believe I know more than you. Did you enjoy my re-enactment? There was much more I could have shown you. Based on what I saw him do to you precious Alannah, I suspect he might be even more sadistic than me.'

Damnit! Liam had not banked on this strategy. Richard knew exactly how to poke the grizzly bear inside Liam that begged to come out and play.

Another fireball came hurtling towards him, so he dropped and rolled out the way, kicking out as he did so, which brought Richard to the floor. Liam grabbed the opportunity to jump on the guy and deal another blow to his face, this time clocking him in the left eye.

Richard sniggered. 'Tell me Liam, what was it like spending all those nights alone knowing Brendan was banging the woman you love.'

'Screw you, arsehole!' He landed a blow on Richard's right eye.

'No thanks. I'll wait for Alannah to get back. Clayton was right, she is a fine piece of arse.'

When Liam brought his hand down again, Richard grabbed it and sent a powerful bolt of electricity through his body, throwing Liam back and giving his opponent the advantage.

Richard's tall, muscular frame towered over Liam's prone body and fire flicked between his fingers. 'This time, when Alannah returns to me, she won't have you or your delinquent brother to save her.'

In her weakened state, Alannah was not exactly fit for travelling by ley line, so the moment they reached the first junction, she stumbled and collapsed into the dirt. But something—or rather someone—soft broke her fall.

'It's okay, Alannah, I gotcha,' Jacob's soft voice reassured her.

Resting her head against his chest for a moment, Alannah allowed herself a few seconds to catch her breath. But she felt something hard pressing against her stomach. Her skin prickled and she scowled at Jacob. 'What the hell, dude? How can you get aroused at a time like this?'

'Ah, hello? Extremely attractive naked woman? I am the hot-blooded man you have your bare breasts pressed against, among other parts. But you can call me Jacob, or whatever you want, since you're on top right now.'

Crap! She had forgotten about her nudity. Glancing up, Alannah thanked the Gods for landing in a deserted field, or whatever the large patch of dirt was. Standing, she took stock of their surroundings. Nothing in sight for miles except for the stunning sight of the setting sun.

Jacob drew up close beside her. 'Not that I'm complaining about the view, but you might want to conjure up some clothes before heading into town.'

She glared at him a moment before doing what he suggested. 'We should try to get back to Broken Hill and call on help from the local mage community.'

He shook his head. 'Correction: we go back, and you call on help. I doubt the local mages will help you if I'm in tow.'

Alannah sighed because he was right. 'Fine. But you should ask the local fae to get you back home ASAP, then send us some reinforcements. Oh, and can you please feed my cat when you get home?'

Jacob nodded. 'Sure thing. Come on, let's go.'

She grabbed his wrist, but he pulled her in closer with an arm around her waist as he winked at her. Rolling her eyes, she tuned into the ley lines and focussed on getting them to their destination. A few minutes later, they were standing on the outskirts of town.

'I'd better lickety-split. But first...' Jacob held his arms open.

Knowing this could be the last time she saw the cheeky boggart she had come to adore, Alannah obliged and squeezed him. 'Tell Cara I love her like the sister I never had.'

'Gods, woman! You're making this sound like a final goodbye.'

'It might be.' A rogue tear and its friend escaped her eyes.

'Nuh, uh. You and Liam are going to kick arse as usual, and you'll come home heroes once again.'

'Thanks for having faith in us, Jacob. I do hope you're right.' They parted ways before one of the town's warlocks greeted Alannah.

The tall man pierced her with eyes to match the blue of his police uniform. 'Miriam was right about someone magiporting into town. Who might you be, and what brings you to this neck of the woods, miss?'

'Hi there. I'm Alannah Winters of the Adelaide district. I seek aid because the exiled Inquisitor kidnapped me and my… boyfriend.' She gulped as the word tumbled out, but there was no time to explain the complexity of her relationship with Liam. ' I only just got out with my life, but Liam's still stuck back there trying to fend Richard off *without* the use of his magic. Please, I don't know what else to do. He took our phones, so I can't even call home.'

'Hold up there, miss. Did you say Winters? As in *the* Winters clan?'

'Yeah, that's right.'

'Ah, hell. And you said this man of yours is Liam? As in Liam Winters?'

She nodded.

'Well, we best be getting my buddies out there to help. I'm Jaxon Hayes, by the way.'

'Thanks, Jaxon.' She offered half a smile.

He pulled out his phone and made a quick call to someone named Shane. Turning back to her, he smiled when the call ended. 'From what I hear, Liam is a great Councillor and warlock to boot. But did you say he doesn't have use of his magic?'

Alannah sighed. 'Yeah. Richard is channelling nether and using a nullification spell. We are going to need weapons and fighting skills to take him down.'

'Hmm. We don't have much of an arsenal out here. I can phone in for some backup from Sydney and Adelaide, though.'

'Backup's prudent. I can conjure up some weapons from home if I know what training you and your men have.'

'Nice. Follow me and I'll introduce you to the lads.'

Chapter Twenty-Three

Liam rolled to the left, narrowly avoiding a fiery death. He pushed himself back to his feet and scowled at Richard. 'Is that the best you've got? No wonder you needed us warlocks to do your dirty work as Inquisitor.'

'Oh, I'm just warming up.'

'Well, come on.' Liam was not sure if it was wise to taunt him, but he was tired of Richard's ramblings.

A long rope flew across the room and wound around Liam's legs. A moment later, Richard dropped Liam to the floor and dragged him closer. 'Try dodging my attacks now.' Liam channelled enough energy mana to break free of the ropes as another lightning bolt struck the floor millimetres away from his head. *His power is waning.*

Rolling on to his front, Liam got up on his knees in time to see the next fireball coming straight for him. 'Shit!' he muttered as he jumped to the right too late to avoid getting his left hand singed. '*Mothercranker!*' Burns were nothing new to him, having trained with elemental fire magic for much of his life, but they still hurt like a bitch.

Richard grinned. 'Is the great Liam Winters dragging his feet?'

'Why don't you turn off your pussy arse nullification spell and fight like a real man?' Liam spat.

'Now why would I do something so stupid? I know you wouldn't hesitate to kill me, as per your orders. You are the Council's golden boy, after all. Tell me, have you enjoyed living up my brother's arse all these years?'

'I don't have any qualms with Kieran. He's a respectable man and it would seem we have more in common than I thought.'

'Oh?' Flames danced on Richard's fingertips. 'Let me guess, you've taken up stamp collecting.'

What the…? 'Uh, no-o. I was referring to the fact we both have piece-of-filth brothers.' Those flames flared and flickered toward him. But Liam slammed into Richard before the bastard even saw it coming. Next thing, they were wrestling on the floor. Liam pinned him, one hand securing Richard's wrists, while the other pressed down firmly on his throat.

A kinetic blast threw Liam back against the stone wall with enough force to wind him. Liam slumped to the floor, trying to catch his breath as he waited for his diaphragm to settle.

Stalking across the room with a sneer, Richard did not give Liam any time to recover as he shot sparks. The shock carried more charge this time, burning Liam's shoulder at the point of entry.

Liam hissed as blistering agony charred his flesh. He tried to get to his feet again, but Richard grabbed his hair and shoved him back against the wall. Kneeling in front, Richard pressed a heated finger into the fresh wound, causing Liam to howl. Cornered and weakened, Liam failed to resist the pull of Richard's brutal hands as they tore at his scalp, or the cold iron cuffs clamping around his wrists and ankles, fixing him against the wall. He barely even had the puff to vocalise his distress from the constant onslaught of electric shocks. All he managed was praying for unconsciousness or even death to take him.

His prayers were on the verge of being answered when an explosion blew the door in. Something red flashed through the room, throwing Richard away from Liam.

'What the hell?' Richard yelled, as the woman ambushing him pressed a heeled boot into his chest.

The woman grinned down at him. 'We meet at last, Mr. Lane.'

Richard's eyes widened. 'Tara Winters?'

'In the flesh.' She emphasised her double meaning by driving her stiletto into his sternum, forcing out a distorted yelp. 'I have been looking forward to paying you back for all the pain you have inflicted upon my grandchildren.'

Liam blinked in disbelief, possibly more astonished than Richard.

'*Oh Gods, Liam!*' Alannah shrieked as she ran through the cellar opening a second later. Her warm body pressed against him as her arms tried to embrace him.

Taking in the sweet smell of her strawberry-scented hair, Liam felt his aches and pains soothed by her loving presence. He brought his mouth close to her ear. 'Why is Tara helping us?'

Her gaze focussed on him. 'I told you, she doesn't want to hurt me.'

'By rights I should kill her.'

Tears formed in Alannah's eyes. 'I know, which is why I can't let you out of these cuffs yet. We need her help. Please promise you won't reveal her identity to the others.'

'Others?'

The trio of armed warlocks who entered the room a moment later answered his question. 'Thank the Gods.' Liam had never been so happy to see sword-wielding mages before. 'Lana, please get me out of these restraints.'

She shook her head. 'Not yet. Besides, you're not fit to fight right now.' Alannah pecked him on the lips, drew a sword from her belt and spun around to join the fray.

The battle appeared tense when Alannah turned back to face Richard. Kinetic blasts foiled most of the guys attempts to approach him, sending them flying and falling unconscious when their heads hit the ground. Only Tara had any luck drawing close, appearing immune to his attacks.

Tara must be using her own nullification spell. She made a mental note of asking her grandmother to teach her the spell the next time they met for training, along with asking her how the hell she had known Alannah was out there and in need of help.

Seeing her chance while Tara distracted Richard, Alannah switched her sword for a dagger and snuck up behind him. She was a hair's breadth from stabbing Richard in the back when he spun around and grabbed the blade, flinging it into Tara's heart a second later.

Crumpling to the floor, Tara sniggered as she bled out. 'You are a fool, Mr. Lane. I am no ordinary cursed being. Not even a blessed blade will bring about my true death.'

Richard grinned. 'No, but what if I destroy this?' He retrieved a glowing quartz crystal from his pocket, leaving Alannah gobsmacked as he approached the prone lich.

Tara's humour vanished as her mouth gaped open. 'Where did you get that?' She garbled the words as blood pooled in her mouth and dripped from her lips.

'Oh, Tara dear, didn't you know demons can have more than one master? They are not the most honest and loyal of servants.' He sent the crystal spinning across the room with enough force to smash on impact against the wall.

'*No!*' Alannah cried.

A white wispy cloud broke free from the crystal and merged with Tara's body, making it jolt and convulse.

Alannah ran to Tara. 'Don't you dare die on me, Grandma.'

The woman smiled warmly. 'This is the first time you called me that.' She spoke in a low, hoarse voice between shallow breaths.

Pressing her hands firmly around the knife, Alannah tried to staunch the bleeding.

'*Lana! Watch out!*' Liam bellowed.

The moment she looked up; Alannah saw Richard launch a fireball in her direction.

Using her body as a shield to protect Tara, Alannah's instincts kicked in as she screamed, '*Damn you to hell, Richard Lane!*' A protective bubble formed around her as the flaming projectile hit it, causing it to rebound with equal force and swallow Richard in the blast.

He ran screaming from the room as fire engulfed his clothes.

Alannah returned her attention to Tara, whose life continued to slip away. 'Gods, I wish I knew healing magic right now.'

An old, frail hand reached for Alannah as Tara's face wrinkled and her eyes drooped. The crone's voice sounded in Alannah's mind. '*It is too late for me, dear child. The blade has pierced my heart. Just know I was never the real enemy. One day you will discover the truth and succeed where I have failed.*'

Alannah ran to her. *What do you mean? What truth?*

'*You will find it if you keep striving for greatness. It is your destiny.*' Tara's arm fell limp beside her and the last of her glamour faded, revealing the lich who had hidden behind the Scarlett persona.

One of the other guys groaned and stirred as Alannah pulled the knife from her grandmother's chest. It was Jaxon. 'Hole-ee heck! Did you take out Tara Winters?' Before Alannah could correct him, his eyes widened. 'Where's Richard?'

'Lana set him on fire, and he ran away crying like a baby. You might want to stop him escaping,' Liam replied for her.

Jaxon glanced at each of them with wide eyes, grabbing his sword, he bolted after Richard.

'I'm sorry, Lana. I didn't realise how close you'd become to her.'

'Thank you, Liam.' Looking at him, Alannah noticed cuffs still restrained his limbs. She dashed over to him, keeping her eyes averted from his as she used her primordial attunement to channel the kinetic forces needed to break the iron free from the wall. When he fell forward, it took all of Alannah's strength to remain upright as she helped him to one of the chairs. 'Bloody hell! You've taken a nasty beating, Liam. We need to get you home so Ross can patch you up.'

'Don't worry about me right now. Just get out there and make sure the arsehole is dead.' When she hesitated, he added, 'I'll be fine. I promise.'

After a quick peck on the lips, she took off after Jaxon.

When she found him in the front yard, Jaxon stood alone scratching his head. 'I'm sorry Alannah, we lost him. I searched all through the house and there's no sign of him.'

'Damnit! Why won't the bastard die?' She scanned the grounds as best she could in the darkness. *It must be around three or four in the morning by now.*

Jaxon pulled out his phone. 'Do you want me to call HQ and see if we can track him?'

'Yeah, okay. I guess it's worth a try, although his nullification spell will probably block scrying magic.'

'Sure, but it won't stop us tracing his phone's GPS signal.'

'Hmph. With how much magic rules my life, I forgot satellite tracking was even a thing we could do.'

Jaxon smiled. 'My old man had a saying: "Save your magic for when human technology can't do the job. One day you might find that same technology will work where magic doesn't." Wise words from a wise man. Just give me a sec.' He stepped away to make the call.

Alannah went back inside to check on Liam. He was talking to the other two who had woken up from their blunt-force trauma-induced sleep. Shane and Tyler gazed up at her, along with Liam. 'Hey, Lana, what's going on?'

She sighed. 'Richard got away. Jaxon's trying to get a trace on him.' She looked at the other two warlocks. 'Are you guys okay? You both took some pretty nasty blows to the head.'

Shane rubbed the back of his skull. 'Yeah, just a slight bump. I'll be fine.'

'Me too,' added Tyler as he sat up and gazed lasciviously in her direction.

She returned the grin instinctively, either despite or because of Tyler's uncanny resemblance to the jerk who had ghosted her. 'There's no point sticking around here anymore. I assume you have a healer back in town?'

'Yeah, we got a couple.' Tyler's attention remained fixed on her.

'Great.' She broke the eye contact and helped Liam up from the chair. 'Let's get you fixed up before you jump back into the action, soldier.'

He laughed. 'Yes, ma'am.' But before she could take him much further, he pulled her in for a deep, possessive kiss. This time she yielded without hesitation.

Liam could see Alannah fidgeting as she watched Tanya, the town's best abjurer, perform her healing spells.

Once Tanya finished, she turned to Alannah. 'Liam will be fine after a full day and night of rest.'

'What if we don't have a full day and night?' Liam asked. 'We should get back out there as soon as they find Richard. It's better to strike before he fully heals and restores his energy levels.'

'They have to find him first,' Alannah reminded him. 'But if they do find him before the night is through, I will go without you.'

'What? No!'

'Liam, you took a metric fuck tonne of electric shocks and burns. Your body needs time to heal.'

'I can't sit back here while you are out there fighting the biggest jerk known to mage-kind. I need to be in there, helping you.' Liam clenched his fists.

Alannah sighed. 'I appreciate you wanting to help, but knowing you are at greater risk because of your existing injuries will distract me from the fight. You will compromise my safety as well as your own.'

Tanya cleared her throat. 'Your girl is smart, Liam, you should listen to her.'

Laughing, Alannah put her hand on the healer's shoulder. 'I like you, Tanya. Let's stay in touch after this.'

'Sure thing, hun.'

Liam groaned. 'Uh, Tanya? Mind if I have some time alone with Alannah?'

'So long as you don't get up to anything too strenuous.' She winked at them and left the room.

Alannah snuggled up to Liam's side. 'How are you feeling?'

'Okay, I guess. A bit tired, but more frustrated than anything.' The burns still ached like hell, but he did not want to cause her undue concern with everything else going on.

'I don't want to fight over this, Liam.'

With a sigh, he conceded. 'Don't worry. I get it, Lana. If our predicaments reversed, there's no way I'd want you out there in my state.' With his arm, he reached across her waist and pulled her in closer for a kiss. He peered into her eyes and sighed. 'I've been thinking about Tara's death. You should roll with Jaxon's misread of the situation. It would help you regain favour in the Council.'

Her eyes bugged out at his suggestion. 'I can't do that. It would dishonour Tara's memory.'

'I don't think it would. She must have had reasons for making us believe she was the enemy, right?'

Alannah's jaw dropped. 'How did you know?'

'Call it a hunch. I'm not gonna pry into the secrets she shared with you. It's best if I don't know. Much safer to maintain the pretence and I'm sure that's what she would want.'

'You're right. I guess I'm not the only smart one here.'

Liam poked his tongue out and Alannah nipped it between her teeth before drawing it into her mouth and consuming him with a kiss reminiscent of their prior love and passion. Perhaps there was hope for them again after all.

The two of them drifted off to sleep in each other's arms, only to wake a couple of hours later when Jaxon stirred her.

'Sorry, Alannah, but we found Richard and we should launch an assault now while he is still licking his wounds.'

Alannah sighed, looking at Liam. 'I'm sorry babe, but I need to go.'

'It's okay. I'll follow the doc's orders and rest up on one condition.'

'What's that?'

'You kick Richard's arse extra hard for me.'

Smiling, she leant in and planted a sloppy kiss on his lips. 'I love you.'

He sucked in a sharp breath. It felt wonderful to hear her say those words again. 'I love you too. So. Damn. Much. Now go show him who's boss.'

Alannah stepped out of Liam's room. 'Where is the prick hiding?'

Jaxon bit his lip, exchanging a look with Shane, who waited in the corridor.

She narrowed her eyes on Jaxon. 'What?'

Jaxon shuffled on his feet. 'He has presented us with quite the challenge.'

'How so? Is it a hard-to-reach location, or something?'

'No, but we are going to have to be extremely careful about how we approach him,' Shane explained.

'Why?' Alannah did not like how cagey they were acting.

'Because he is in a large population centre,' replied Tyler as he walked out of Tanya's living room.

'Crap! That's unfortunate. Where are we talking?'

This time Jaxon pulled up his big boy panties. 'Right in the heart of Sydney's Kings Cross. He knew we'd be after him, knowing we can't stage an all-out war in such a public place, full of so many non-magicals.'

'Oh hell.'

'Yep, it's like everything's gone to crap and we're all out of bog roll,' Tyler remarked with a smirk.

Alannah grunted as she tried to stifle her laugh. *Just when I thought the toilet paper jokes had gone out of fashion.* 'How are we going to get to him in one of the most commercial and busiest districts of the nation?' She considered their predicament for a few minutes as the guys fell silent. 'We can't use magic anyway, right? So, maybe we need to treat him like a regular criminal—a fucking dangerous one at that. I say we tag him as a terrorist and use our contacts in the feds to help bring him down. We can all get uniforms and cordon off the area. This will get the non-magical community out of our way so we won't expose them to any magic.'

Tyler grinned. 'Hell, I think I'm falling in love with you, Alannah. You can talk strategy to me all night, baby.'

Jaxon laughed. 'Stop mistaking love for lust, bro.' He turned his attention to Alannah. 'The plan is pretty solid, but what do we do about the non-magical cops?'

'Keep them posted around the perimeter where they can't see Richard and make sure they don't have any loaded guns in case we can't contain the bastard and he goes full Carrie White on them.'

'Carrie who?' Jaxon asked, earning a snigger from Tyler.

Alannah rolled her eyes. 'Never mind. Let's get moving.'

As soon as they stepped outside, Tyler flung his arm across her shoulder. 'So, you're a horror fan too, huh?'

Jaxon laughed behind them. 'Give it up bro, she's got a boyfriend already—a powerful warlock at that. You don't want to be crossing my man, Liam.'

As they continued along the gravel driveway, she glanced at Tyler. His green eyes showed an impish glint as they scanned her body up and down before connecting with hers. 'I'm flattered Tyler, but Jaxon's right: you don't want to get on Liam's bad side. He gets protective of me.'

He leaned in to whisper in her ear, 'Why aren't you pulling out of my arms, beautiful?'

A damn good question. But as soon as she thought about it, the painful realisation struck. 'Because you remind me of someone I should be trying to forget.' Increasing her pace allowed her to slip free of his hold and hide the escaping tear.

'Alannah, wait! I'm sorry.' Tyler jogged up behind her. 'I didn't mean to upset you. I thought we had some kind of… connection. But I was out of line, and I'm sorry.'

Wiping her eyes, she smiled at him. 'It's okay.'

When they reached the end of the path, Alannah tuned into the ley lines and mapped a route to Sydney in her mind. She held hands with Jaxon and an over-eager Tyler, leaving Shane to take Jaxon's other hand, and the four of them magiported across the state.

Half an hour later, they had reached a riverside suburb known as Parramatta on the northwest side of the city. Jaxon took in their surrounds. 'We should contact the feds before we get much closer.'

Alannah nodded. 'Okay. You know this city better than I do, so I'll follow your lead on this.'

When he stepped aside to make some calls, Alannah noticed Shane appearing pale and clammy. 'Are you okay?'

Shane waved dismissively. 'Just motion sickness.'

'He always gets like this from magiporting,' Tyler explained.

They both watched on as Shane ran into the bushes lining the road. 'Welp. There he goes. You okay there, buddy?' Tyler followed his friend.

Jaxon returned a moment later. 'Right, we're all set. We just have to rendezvous with the feds and our backup support.' When he observed Shane returning from his upchucking, he sighed. 'I guess we find a car and drive from here.'

Alannah's plan was falling into place. They surrounded Richard's Kings Cross apartment block, and a few non-magical police had gone in to stealthily evacuate the innocent civilians. She hid in the early morning shadows along with her three new friends, hoping to avoid detection. They had figured it would be better to keep all mages back until the humans were safe; less chance of crossing any detection wards and alerting the bastard.

Richard's voice sounded in her mind, and judging by how the other guys jumped, she was not the only one to receive the communication. *'Hello again, Alannah. Apparently, you can't get enough of me. Have you come for another spanking? You can't deny how much it turned you on.'*

The other guys looked at her with wide eyes, although Tyler also tilted his head and arched his left brow.

'It's not what you think. I never enjoyed any of *his* torture,' she explained in a hushed voice.

'Perhaps I should film us this time and send it to Brendan as way of returning the favour. I know where he is hiding out, by the way.'

Her face burned hotter than the volcanic pits as she instinctively moved toward him.

But Jaxon held her back and whispered, 'Don't let him taunt you. We gotta stick together for this to work.'

Alannah stopped in her tracks and nodded.

A voice came through Jaxon's radio. 'We're all clear.'

Jaxon gestured to their backup team huddled on the other side of the entrance, letting them know it was time. He led Alannah and the other two guys into the building.

The stairwell was dank and reeked of excrement. It was certainly not the luxury accommodation she had imagined Richard living in. *Perhaps that is why he chose the place as his hideout.*

As soon as they reached the second-floor landing, a rope snaked across the floor, entwining itself around Alannah's shins and pulling her down. She reacted with a sword strike across the tether.

Tyler's outstretched hand helped her to her feet, and the four of them charged into Richard's open apartment as one cohesive unit. Their backup soon followed, filing in behind them. Before long, they had Richard flanked with about twenty armed men.

Alannah glared at him. 'Any last words, Richard?'

'Do you honestly think you have enough force to take me down?'

Her lips curled into a vicious grin. 'Oh, I know we have enough.'

Richard's hand moved forward, directing a kinetic shockwave toward them, but Alannah brought up her Aether shield to block and rebound it. The blow sent him flying into the troops behind him. He struggled free of the man's hold, grabbing his sword and charging at Alannah.

She was ready for him, meeting his attack with a parry. It was satisfying to be able to fight him on equal footing at last.

They exchanged blows for what felt like an eternity, while one of the others would try to cut in every so often, but each time they did, Richard would send them flying. After about the tenth intervention attempt, Richard was sweating, and his footwork slackened. This was the opportunity Alannah needed. Having let him think her moves were predictable and her mind readable thus far, she used one of the mental bluff tactics Tara had recently taught her and went in for the kill. As Richard swung to his right, Alannah aimed for his left side.

A split second before she hit him, Richard dropped to his knees and released his own bubble, sending Alannah flying back into Tyler's arms. 'Are you okay, beautiful?'

She stood up straight. 'Yeah. I'm fine. But what is he doing?'

Richard hunched over on the floor, chanting to himself. Rather than a white radiance of Aether, his shield glowed red.

They heard screams from outside and Jaxon's radio sprang to life:

'Requesting back… *Ahh!*'

'*What the hell is that?*'

'*Oh God, somebody help us.*'

'*They're coming out of nowhere!*'

Alannah exchanged a frown with Jaxon. 'Damnit! He's summoning demons. Jaxon, we need to save those guys out there.'

He nodded his agreement. 'If I take a few of these guys, can you manage in here?'

'I hope so. Either way, we can't leave those men at the mercy of a demon incursion.'

As Jaxon ran from the room, Richard rose to his feet with fiery tendrils flicking out of his shield like a crimson corona.

Tyler's eyes bugged out. 'Gods! Is he summoning hellfire?'

'Afraid so.' Alannah closed her eyes and drew on the strength of her Aether connection and on the conviction of her faith. She did not know of any offensive spells that channelled the Celestial element, so she improvised, drawing on the power of the Gods to smite the fiend who defiled her own realm simply by living in it. If the stygian element could nullify earthly magic, she reasoned Aether could nullify nether.

'Um, Alannah? That's some impressive afterglow you got going there.' Tyler's mouth gaped open.

As Alannah's power intensified, she laughed. 'Just stand back, honey. I feel my climax coming on.' She winked and turned to face Richard.

'Hot damn,' Tyler muttered.

Advancing on Richard cautiously, Alannah maintained eye contact to the best of her ability. His eyes had turned mostly red by this point and looking into them felt like staring at the sun for too long. When one of the flares flicked out at her, it withered away the moment it touched her forcefield.

But another tendril lashed out to her right and she heard Tyler scream.

She spun around to see him bound by a burning tentacle squeezing his waist. He thrashed about, trying to cut it off with his sword to no avail.

'*Tyler!*' Alannah cried out as she ran to him. Extending her own sword within her Aether field, she released him, drawing him close, and wrapping her arms around his waist, she instinctively healed his burnt flesh.

Tyler remained gobsmacked and speechless as she pulled away and returned her attention to Richard.

More tentacles reached out to grab the unconscious guys who had fallen to his kinetic blasts.

'*Enough!*' Alannah bellowed across the room.

He turned and snarled at her with a noise sounding more monstrous than human.

She rushed at him, cutting through his barrier, and driving her holy blade straight into his heart.

Richard dropped to the floor and tried to speak but coughed instead.

Alannah stood over his limp body and watched as his eyes glazed over. 'Enjoy an eternity rotting in the Underworld, you piece of scum.'

A moment later, a black wisp emerged from his body and sank into the earth.

Relief washed over her like summer rain before she collapsed into a set of waiting arms.

Chapter Twenty-Four

aking up, Alannah found herself in what appeared to be a hotel room. When she glanced at the clock, she realised she must have slept most of the day because the sun would be setting soon. She got up and peeked through the bedroom door, finding the other guys chatting in a lounge area. After getting dressed, she slipped out of her room to join them.

Tyler grinned at her. 'Hey beautiful, how'd you sleep?'

'Great actually. Where are we?'

'Sydney still. When you collapsed after the fight, we decided it was best to check in to a nearby hotel to rest. Don't worry, the Council paid for it.'

'And Liam?'

Some of Tyler's smile faded. 'He's still recovering in Broken Hill. We can head back there as soon as you're ready.'

Alannah was in Australia's most lively city on a Saturday night and while it would be nice to return to Liam's arms, she knew he needed more recovery time. *Besides, he is in safe hands.* She directed her grin toward Tyler. 'How about we hit the town for a victory celebration before heading home?'

He jumped up from the couch. 'Heck yeah! I'm so down for it. What about you guys?'

Jaxon laughed. 'I think we deserve a drink or ten.'

'I'm in,' replied Shane.

Tyler's arm rested on her shoulders as he guided her back to her room. 'How's about you conjure up something sexy to wear, and I'll show you the best magic club in Sydney.'

'Sounds super.' Alannah broke free of his hold and retreated to the privacy of her room where she got ready. When she stepped back out in her black lace skater dress and fishnet stockings, all three jaws hit the floor.

'Gods, woman! Are you trying to get me killed? How am I supposed to keep my hands off you now?' Tyler rose and stalked across the room toward her.

'You said to wear something sexy. Now where's this club of yours?'

The night club hosted a mix of magical races mingling around the numerous bars and dancing intimately close on the dancefloor while a Satyr DJ pumped out Egyptian tribal beats.

Tyler found them a booth, pulling Alannah in close to him. No sooner had they sat down, than a half-elf waitress took their drink orders.

Alannah cast wide eyes over her surrounds. 'Wow. This place is incredible.'

'I'm glad you think so,' Tyler beamed.

As she took in the sights, a shiver gripped her spine and all the hairs on her body stood to attention. *Is someone watching me?* Scanning the room failed to reveal any such observer. When their drinks arrived, the group eased into some light-hearted discussion, but Alannah could not shake the prickly sensation from her skin.

Several drinks later, the awareness remained, although the buzz of the alcohol helped to dull her worries. Glancing at Tyler, he rewarded her with the warmest smile, so she grabbed his hand and dragged him out of the booth. 'Come on, let's dance.'

As soon as they reached the dancefloor, Tyler's hands beelined for her hips. Alannah encircled his neck with her arms and pressed her body close to his, letting him grind against her.

His lips pressed against her ear. 'Gods! This is like the sweetest form of torture.'

'Uh huh.'

'I've been hard for you ever since seeing the way you handled yourself in combat. Harder still when you plunged a blade deep into Richard's heart.'

Alannah sighed. 'Sounds like something he would have said.'

'So, this other guy I remind you of, is he like your ex or something?'

Inhaling deeply, she caught a whiff of Tyler's spicy cologne. Along with the spiky fringe and lack of piercings, it was one of the few differences to remind her he was not Brendan. 'Yeah. An ex who didn't just break my heart but shattered it into millions of tiny pieces.'

'I'm sorry to hear that. What about me reminds you of him?'

'You're overtly flirting even though my heart belongs to someone else. But also, you could easily pass as his twin.'

'Is he attractive?'

She rolled her eyes as she looked up into his gleaming gaze. 'Extremely.'

His hand moved to her arse. 'Then I'll take it as a compliment, Alannah.'

'Please, call me Lana.' She pressed her head into his solid, muscular chest.

'Did *he* call you Lana?'

'Yeah.'

He sucked in a sharp breath. 'I'm not him, Lana, but if you need to believe I am for one night, I'd be more than happy to oblige.'

Alannah peered up into green orbs peeking out from beneath long, thick lashes. Before she could let logic and decency get in the way, she crashed her lips into his. When she came up for air, the uncanny sensation she felt before had gone, replaced with a feverish rush of desire coursing through her blood. 'Let's get out of here.'

Tyler did not hesitate to escort her from the club and back to their hotel suite. They sank onto her bed in a series of fiery kisses, hastily removing each other's clothes in the process. When there were no more layers between them, he sat back and pulled on a condom. Leaning over her, he stroked her cheek. 'Who do you want me to be, Lana?'

She took a deep breath. 'Brendan.'

He climbed astride her. 'And what do you want me to do?'

'I want you to fuck me rough and hard.'

'Then I will.' He drove himself deep inside her and for a few glorious hours Alannah forgot all the heartache and focussed on the pleasure Brendan brought her.

Rested and healed, Liam stepped outside Tanya's house at first light and magiported his way to Sydney, following the instructions Jaxon had given him over the phone. His insides were buzzing from the news of Richard's defeat. He could not wait to scoop Alannah up into his arms and kiss his praise all over her soft body.

The directions were reliable, and he found the place without any hassles. Jaxon had advised him Alannah was still sleeping after a big night, so he tapped softly on the door.

'Hey man,' Jaxon whispered and shook his hand before letting him into the large four-bedroom suite. 'How was the trip?'

'Fine.' He cast an eye around the place and noticed the other guys were not up yet. 'Which room is Lana's?'

Biting his lip, Jaxon hesitated a moment. 'Uh, that one.' He pointed to the first door on the left.

'Thanks.' Liam headed for the door.

But Jaxon jumped in front of him and gripped his shoulder. 'You probably shouldn't go in there.'

'It's okay, Jaxon. Lana won't mind. We've been together for years.'

Jaxon cursed under his breath. 'You should still wait for her.'

What the hell is Jaxon's problem? Is he trying to protect me? Something heavy took root in the pit of his stomach. They had not told him what condition she would be in.

Barging past the warlock blockade, he burst into Alannah's room. Liam did not expect the sight that greeted him, but it still broke his heart. Her naked limbs entwined around the man who wore Brendan's face.

Liam's initial instinct was to kick the shit out of Tyler, with storming out of the room a close second. But glancing at Alannah's peaceful face, he remembered the promise he had made her and the hell Brendan had put her through. Fighting against all his violent and bitter urges, he slumped down next to her, kicked off his shoes, and climbed under the covers to hold her.

Alannah stirred from her sleep, moaning as her eyes fluttered open. When she registered Liam's presence, she sat bolt upright. '*Crap!*' Her forehead wrinkled as she studied him.

Her sudden movement woke Tyler who gasped at Liam, rolled out of the bed and ducked beside it.

'I… I'm sorry, Liam. I—' Alannah tried to explain.

But he cut her off by pulling her into his arms. 'It's okay, baby. I know you're still hurting, and I understand. Please rest assured I'm serious about my promise. As long as you still love me, I will never leave you again. Not unless you want me to.'

She gaped at him. 'But I cheated on you.'

'I'm not sure you did. I won't pretend I'm pleased with how things turned out, but it's not like we properly defined our new relationship. I'm willing to move past this if you are. Do you still love me, Lana?'

Tears welled in her eyes. 'Yes.'

'Do you still want to be with me?'

She nodded. 'Yes.'

'I love you too, princess.' He claimed her lips with his own, letting his forgiveness show in the fervour of their kiss. Liam was vaguely aware of Tyler sneaking out of the room and closing the door. They were alone in bed and Alannah was still naked. It was the perfect opportunity to show her how much he still loved her.

Waking up for the second time that day was surreal for Alannah. She could not believe how rational and understanding Liam had been.

He smiled at her when her gaze fell upon his. 'Morning, sunshine.'

'Hey. Is it still morning?'

'Barely. Have you rested enough?'

'Yeah. I guess we should get moving. I need a shower first, though.'

Liam rose and followed her to the ensuite bathroom. He did not even bother asking if he could join her. They had reached that level of comfort in their relationship years ago. *Why should we start over again with the formalities?*

When they both finished getting ready, they stepped out into the loungeroom to say goodbye.

'We should be getting home,' Alannah announced. 'I want to thank all of you for your help. I couldn't have defeated Richard without you.'

Jaxon smiled. 'You're most welcome, both of you. I mean in every way possible. Please don't hesitate to call on me in Broken Hill whenever you want or need.'

'Likewise, man.' Liam shook his hand.

Alannah pulled him into an embrace before giving Shane a farewell hug. Tyler hunched his shoulders, hiding his hands in his pockets and carefully avoiding eye contact with Liam. But as she pulled him into her arms, there was no air of discomfort between them. She whispered a soft 'thank you' to which he replied 'no, thank you, beautiful' before pulling back.

She returned to Liam, who grabbed her hand and led her out of the suite, out of the hotel, and out of Sydney.

Alannah's mouth watered at the Summer Solstice feast laid out before her. 'Wow, Aunt Nora, you've outdone yourself this time. But there's too much food for the four of us.'

Nora beamed. 'There won't only be four of us. We have several guests arriving shortly.'

When Alannah glanced at Liam, she noticed the mischievous glint in his eye. 'Wait! You know who's joining us, don't you?'

'Maybe.'

She narrowed her gaze on him. 'Who is it?'

'Telling you would ruin the surprise.' He grinned.

'Hmph. Keep your secrets.' As Alannah crossed her arms, the doorbell rang.

'Would you get that please, hun?' Nora directed her question to Alannah.

After casting a suspicious eye Liam's way, she rose to greet their guests. As soon as the door swung open, she squealed with delight at the five friendly faces. 'Oh my Gods, what are you guys doing here?'

Jaxon grinned. 'It was Liam's idea and apparently your aunt and uncle loved it.'

Liam drew close behind her. 'I figured it was the least we could do to repay our debt of gratitude.'

Jaxon, Shane, Tanya, Tyler, and his friend Samantha were all there. It had been almost three weeks since they had helped her defeat Richard and she had only seen them once since then, although she had also kept in contact via social media and text. The civility of Liam and Tyler's friendship amazed Alannah. Then again, Liam did not know about her more recent escapades with Brendan's doppelganger.

Once all the handshakes and hugs were out of the way, Alannah showed their guests into the dining room.

Alannah watched as everyone finished plating up their meals. 'So, what's the latest in Sydney?'

'Actually, I have an announcement to make,' Jaxon replied.

'Oh?' Alannah sat upright.

He grabbed Tanya's hand. 'This wonderful woman has agreed to marry me.'

Alannah cupped her hands to her mouth for a moment before jumping up to hug them both. 'That's tremendous news.'

A round of congratulations and cheers followed.

But as soon as Alannah took a sip of her champagne, the contents of her stomach decided to come back up, leaving her precious little time to rush to the toilet.

Liam dashed after her. 'Are you okay, babe?' Kneeling, he held her hair back.

When the worst of it was over, she collapsed against the wall. 'Actually no. I feel dreadful.'

He took her hand in his to offer a reassuring squeeze.

Nora appeared in the doorway. 'What's wrong, honey?'

Tyler's concerned face appeared behind her.

'I threw up. I must have some kind of stomach bug. Surely it wouldn't be your food, Nora.'

Nora shook her head. 'You're a pure mage. We don't get infections.' She smiled. 'Alannah, sweety, I think you might be pregnant.'

But when Alannah's forehead puckered, Nora's smile dropped.

'*Oh Gods!*' Tyler quaked.

'Chill, man. It's not likely to be yours.' Liam's grip on her hand tightened like a vice. 'Mum, get Dad in here, *now*.'

Nora nodded and disappeared.

'How do you know it's not mine?' Tyler's voice trembled.

Liam glared at him. 'You used protection, right?'

'Yeah, but—'

'Morning sickness usually takes at least four weeks to manifest,' Liam cut in.

'How do you know that?' Alannah was ignorant of such facts herself.

'I did some research after you told me about… you know.'

She realised why Liam was edgy. Tyler was not the only unlikely candidate. Alannah felt the walls closing in on her, more bile rose, and she leaned over the toilet a second later.

When she finished, Liam helped her up so Ross could examine her in the adjacent guestroom, where she laid down on the bed.

After touching her abdomen for a few minutes, Ross looked into Alannah's eyes with his best attempt at a neutral expression. 'You are definitely pregnant.'

Liam paced the room. 'Is it his? Did my arsehole brother do this to her?'

Tyler sat on the edge of her bed with wide eyes. 'Brendan's his brother?'

She gave him a nod as tears threatened to break free.

Ross sighed. 'If you give me some peace and quiet, I can determine the gestational age.'

'Come on Tyler, honey. Let's give them some privacy,' Nora suggested.

He nodded and followed her out.

Liam lowered himself into an armchair beside the bed.

Ross resumed pressing his hands to Alannah's abdomen and closed his eyes as he did so. She wondered what sort of spell enabled him to learn so much about the baby growing inside her. *Wow.* She had not fully grasped the fact yet. *There is actually another person growing within me.*

Several minutes later, Ross opened his eyes and smiled at her, a reassuring sign. 'Alannah, you have a special child on the way—a Beltane baby.'

Liam's eyes lit up and he pounced on the bed, pulling her into his arms. 'That is such a relief. Congratulations, my love.' Of course Liam would be delighted. He did not know whom she had spent Beltane with, nor would he ask.

But it felt like another piece of her soul crumbled away as Alannah hid her face in Liam's shoulder.

When he drew back to study her face, she forced a smile. He stood and helped her up. 'Come on. Let's go tell the others.'

No time like the present to put Grandma's training into practice. When they reached the dining room, Alannah looked at the faces staring back at her. 'So, um, I've kind of got some big news of my own. I'm pregnant with a Beltane baby.'

Worry lines softened and beaming smiles filled their faces.

Nora squealed and hugged her. 'I'm thrilled for you, honey.'

Tanya grabbed her next. 'Congrats, dude. That's awesome news.'

Tyler pushed his way through the crowd of well-wishers to squeeze her tight. 'That's a big relief, hey beautiful?' He chuckled. 'Seriously, though, congrats.'

Jaxon and Shane demanded their hugs before the party could return to some semblance of order; after which, Alannah relaxed thanks to the exquisite food and affable company. But as the evening wore on, she fell quiet.

Liam leaned in close, placing a hand on her arm. 'Hey, are you okay?'

'Yeah, just getting tired.'

'I guess I better get the two of you home.' He grinned.

'Are you honestly okay with me carrying another man's baby?'

'Lana, this isn't just some random guy's child. You have a blessed baby. I am more than okay with it. But even if you hadn't conceived him or her at Beltane, I would be happy to raise the kid as my own.'

This time her smile was genuine. 'Really?'

He nodded.

'Even if it was his?'

Liam frowned. 'Especially if it was his. Although, happy might not be the best word to describe my emotions in that case. I'm angry at him for what he did to you, but I wouldn't abandon you or the child.'

Alannah pursed her lips, fighting back more tears. 'Thanks.' *But there is still no way in hell I'm telling you or the child who the real daddy is.*

The small island housing the Gaeilge Shores Sailing Club was a feast for the senses on New Year's Eve. Twinkling lights adorned every single structure, including the gazebo hosting a live jazz band. Food carts scattered about the place, producing mouth-watering aromas making Alannah's stomach somersault. Most of the town's population showed up for the biggest party around for miles.

'Here you go. Curly fries and a dagwood dog as requested.' Liam smiled as he handed her the food.

'Thanks.' She pecked him on the lips, before gorging on her second dinner for the evening.

He watched her with amusement. 'I hope all this eating isn't an avoidance tactic.'

She pointed to her belly with a concertina of fried potato goodness. 'I'm feeding two people, remember.'

Liam arched his brows. 'You know that's not a real thing, right? You'll just end up getting fat.'

Alannah gasped. 'Take that back, Liam Winters, before I kick your arse.'

He laughed. 'I'd love to see you try, babe.'

After dropping her food on a nearby bench, she advanced on Liam with a ferocious glare. Laughing, he made a run for it, so naturally she gave chase, ending up in the one place she had been evading: the club rooms. Liam tackled Alannah, pulling her into his side in time to catch some unwanted attention.

Kieran approached them. 'Ah, there you are. I've been hoping to catch up with you, Alannah.'

The humour vanished from Alannah's features. 'Uh, hello, Your Honour.'

'I wanted to commend you on a job well done with Tara and my… uh, Richard. There is still a vacant seat on the Council if you would like to return to it.'

Alannah's mouth gaped open. 'Really?'

'Yes. I feel it is the least I can do after everything Richard put you through.'

Monique sidled up next to Kieran and smiled. 'The girls would love to have you back too.'

She frowned at Monique. 'What happened to making me pay for exposing your uncle?'

Casting her eyes to the floor, Monique shifted her weight awkwardly. 'I uh—I think I misdirected my anger. I'm sorry, Alannah. What he did to you was wrong.' Lifting her gaze, Monique's eyes pleaded with her. 'Please reconsider the lobby group. We could use your help.'

'I won't spare it a second thought.'

Monique pouted.

'What I mean to say is, I'm in. The women's group and the Council. I want my positions back. Although I will need to take maternity leave in about thirty-three weeks.'

Father and daughter Lane both stared with slack jaws.

Liam took his cue. 'Alannah and I are expecting a blessed baby.'

'Well, I believe congratulations are in order.' Kieran shook Liam's hand.

'Excuse me, but did I hear right?' Jessica interrupted. 'Did you say Alannah's pregnant?'

Alannah nodded. 'With a Beltane baby.'

Jessica squealed and hugged Alannah before dashing up to the stage to grab the microphone. 'Excuse me ladies and gentlemen. Alannah and Liam Winters have an important announcement to make. Get up here, you two.' Her arms summoned them with more enthusiasm than a cheerleader.

After rolling her eyes, Alannah let Liam drag her up there. Jessica handed her the microphone, so she took a deep breath and let the news spill out. 'This is awkward, but you will hear it on the rumour mill anyway. I am pregnant.' She caught a few wide-eyed glances amongst the assembly, namely those of her friends who did not yet know. Cara, the only other person she had told since the Solstice, gave her an encouraging thumbs up.

A dark figure up the back of the room stepped forward. 'So, which cousin is the baby daddy?' Caleb gibed.

Liam winced, grabbing the microphone from Alannah. 'Tradition forbids us from asking who the biological father is because Alannah is carrying a baby conceived at Beltane.' Ignoring the murmurs and hoots from their audience, he turned to face her and smiled. 'Lana, I promise to love and cherish both you and the child the Gods blessed you with. I will help you raise the kid as though he or she is my own. Not because of any sense of duty or honour, but because you are the light of my life, and I cannot imagine a world without you.' He dropped to one knee in front of her, pulling a ring from his pocket. Alannah's gasp echoed through the crowd. 'I adore you, Alannah Winters, and if you would do me the honour of becoming my wife, I promise to devote the rest of my life to keeping you safe and happy.'

Tears trickled down her face as she stared at Liam in stunned silence.

He gulped. 'Lana, baby, will you marry me?'

She nodded fervently until she found her voice. 'Yes. Very yes.'

Liam slid the white gold ring onto her left hand, and she noted the Celtic love knot surrounding a large garnet. He rose and pulled her in for a passionate kiss, earning them all manner of cheers and whistles. As soon as they came up for air, their friends accosted them.

When the onslaught of well-wishers eased, Alannah ducked outside for some fresh air.

Liam drew close behind her. 'Come on. I want to show you something.' He grabbed her hand and led her down to a private spot on the beach. 'I was actually planning to propose to you here, but it felt like the right moment back there. I'm sorry if I embarrassed you.'

'It's okay. You ought to know I'm not self-conscious. I just feel overwhelmed by everything. Can we sit down for a bit?'

'Of course. There's still something I want to share with you here.'

'Oh?'

Laying back on the sand, Liam pulled her atop him. 'I've always wanted to make love to you here.'

She squinted at him. 'This is a public place, Liam.'

He smirked. 'I thought you said you weren't self-conscious.'

'It's not that. I'm surprised *you* want sex on the beach.'

'Why not? The ocean is my home away from home. So, will you…'

Alannah decided they had wasted enough time talking about it and stifled his words with a kiss as her fingers pulled at his fly. A few minutes later she rode him hard and surfed the waves of her orgasms.

There must have been some magic in the air because as they both reached their climax, the sky lit up with the midnight fireworks.

To be continued…

What's Next?

Thank you for reading *Winter's Maiden 2*. Reviews are the lifeblood of authors, and they make a huge difference to the success of a book. Could you please post a review to one or more of the following sites?

Goodreads
BookBub
Amazon
Other Bookstores

Read all about Brendan's adventures during his time with Bridey in *Winter's Thrall*.

Alannah's story will continue in *Winter's Mother 1*, coming November 2022.

Bonus Content

I appreciate that not all my readers like much explicit content. For those of you who do want a little more, you can read the rest of the Beltane chapter in all its graphic glory…

Winter's Maiden 2: The Heat of the Beltane Fires

If you are keen to read this bonus content, you can access it on the 'Freebies' page of my website: www.starlaarts.com

Winter's Thrall

Winter's Magic Part 2.5

L. STARLA

Note from the Author

Trigger Warning *Winter's Thrall* is a dark paranormal romance with strong sexual content that blurs the lines of consent. It also includes graphic m/m, BDSM, and incest scenes. Feel free to skip ahead to *Winter's Mother 1*, the next main entry in the series if such matters are likely to offend or be a psychological trigger.

While this book contains scenes with dubious consent, I do not condone such behaviour.

Remember, Rape Fetish does not equal consent. BDSM scenes should *always* be sane, safe, and consensual. Establish rules, limits, and safewords before you play.

If you are a victim of sexual assault, please consider reporting the crime immediately by ringing emergency services.

For post assault support, I recommend reaching out to a professional, confidential counselling service such as:
    1800RESPECT in Australia (Ph 1800 737 732)
    RAINN in the United States (Ph 800 656 4673)
    SUPPORTLINE in the United Kingdom (Ph 01708 765 200)

Dedication

—This book is for fans of Brendan Winters. After falling in love with him myself, I knew he needed his own story. Happy reading!

Epigraph

"Go where the pain is, go where the pleasure is."
— Anne Rice

Book 2.5 Playlist

"The Mystic" by Adam Jensen
"Horns" by Bryce Fox
"Flesh" by Simon Curtis
"2 Wicky" by Hooverphonic
"Undisclosed Desires" by Muse
"I Come With Knives" by IAMX
"Saptak-Samaya Mix-Solace" by DJ Cary
"Give Up" by The Beautiful Monument
"I Don't Know Why" by Imagine Dragons
"Mantra" by Bring Me The Horizon
"Complications" by Interpol
"The Crawl" by Placebo
'Bloodline" by Northlane
"Novocaine" by The Unlikely Candidates
"Animal" by Badflower
"Underground" by MISSIO
"Stranger" by Johnny Hollow
"Endless Reverie" by Azam Ali
"The Allure" by Beats Antique
"My Empire" by Windwaker
'Bed of Thorns" by Gary Numan

Playlist available on Spotify.

The Cast of Characters

Pure Blood Mages

Brendan Winters AKA **Jet** (Pure-mage Enchanter, Slave)

Alannah Winters (Councillor, Conjurer, Dress Maker)

Liam Winters (Councillor, Warlock, Police Officer)

Jaxon Hayes (Warlock, Police Officer), from Broken Hill

Kevin Doyle (Broken Hill District Council Head, Mayor)

High Magus O'Grady (NSW High Magus, Mayor)

Acolyte Carran (Spiritual leader), from Sydney

Other Magicals

Caleb Hawthorn AKA **Stirling** (Fae- Endarkened, Gangster)

Bridey Hawthorn AKA **Lady Violet** (Fae- Endarkened, Crime boss), Caleb's older sister

Tyler Quirke (Half-mage Warlock, Police Officer), Brendan's doppelganger

Shane Walsh (Half-mage Warlock, Police Officer), from Broken Hill

Samantha Harrison (Dark mage Abjurer), from Sydney

Levi Delaney (Half-mage, Head Slave)

Damien (Dark mage, Cult member), from Sydney

Melanie (Dark mage, Cult member), Damien's partner from Sydney

Maurus Hawthorn (Dark mage, Slave trader & Cult member), Caleb & Bridey's father

Tara Winters AKA **Lady Scarlett** (Lich, Crime Boss), Brendan's Grandmother

Jacob Bennett (Boggart, Gangster), Brendan's best mate

Cara Hughes (Half-mage Shaman, Conservationist), Alannah's best friend

Nick Patterson (Orc, Orchardist)

Ben Sanders (Weredingo, Vet Assistant)

Connor Foley (Half-mage Abjurer, Marine Biologist)

Bailey Dougherty (Half-mage Warlock, Bartender)

Bianca Oakley (Fae- Wood Nymph, Cabaret Singer)

Amy Smith (Dwarf, Metallurgist & Council Blacksmith)

Prologue

September, during the early events of Winter's Maiden 2.

Sensing him close by, Bridey surveyed the dingy country pub. The news of Daddy's thugs tracking him down had thrilled her to bits. And there he was. Grinning, she gave his group a cursory glance confirming her prediction: Caleb had befriended an assortment of magical people.

It pleased her no end that her brother instantly recognised her, even after all their years of separation. She had missed him and hated her mother for tearing their family apart. When she reached his booth, she drank in the sight of him: from his high cheekbones and chiselled jaw to his long black locks and delicious piercings. 'Hello, Brother dearest.'

'Bridey? W-what are you doing here?' Caleb's shocked reaction was not what Bridey had hoped for.

The guy sitting beside Caleb gripped her brother's shoulder in a show of support. 'Well, well, well. The wayward sister returns.'

Holy shit! When she scrutinised him, he took her breath away. She'd never seen such a fine specimen of a man. Bright green eyes glared at her from beneath dark, choppy hair. A silver ring adorned his prominent brow and a five o'clock shadow accentuated his jaw, drawing attention to luscious lips. And that was merely his outward appearance. Even the man's aura was sexy. She had to know him in every way possible. 'And you are?' The way he studied the air surrounding her intrigued Bridey. *Is he an enchanter too?*

'Brendan Winters. Perhaps you've heard of me?'

Bingo! 'Oh, indeed. The infamous enchanter of Gaeilge Shores. I didn't realise my brother had such interesting friends. Mother did such a stellar job of hiding him from me.' She looked at Caleb and smiled. 'Relax, darling. I'm not going to hurt you. I'm here on business and I'd like your help connecting with the magic community in town.'

'Just business?' Caleb asked.

'Yes, sweetheart. *Just* business. Unless you want more.' When he visibly shivered, she could not hold back the laugh. 'Oh, Caleb... you are precious. And far too much like our sweet Mother. But your friends?' Her eyes travelled around the group, settling on Brendan. 'I think your friends will be a lot of fun. And I'm all for mixing business with pleasure.'

Intense lust flickered in Brendan's aura as his lips parted.

Bridey narrowed her gaze. 'May I sit?'

He shrugged. 'It's a free country.'

When her backside perched in his lap; Brendan rewarded Bridey with the sensation of his arousal. She could not help herself as she writhed against him, drawing an odd sound from his pursed lips.

Their dry humping did not amuse Caleb and she detected a hint of jealousy on top of his disgust.

The mage with spiky hair rose. 'I'm getting another round of drinks. Who's in?' The rest of the group pushed their glasses forward.

She smiled at Spiky. 'I'll have a Purple Haze, thank you darling.'

He frowned at her. 'A what?'

'*Pur-ple Haze*. It's a cocktail. Don't tell me this backwater doesn't know about cocktails!'

'Sure, we know about cocktails. We're just not pretentious enough to care.' Spiky was also sassy.

'Oh dear. I see I'm going to have my work cut out for me with you. What's your name, handsome?'

After a moment of hesitation, he replied, 'Bailey. Bailey Dougherty.'

Remembering the sign on the door, she gasped with delight. 'As in *the* Doughertys? Owners of this fine establishment?'

'Exactly. So, I suggest you show this *backwater* more respect if you don't want piss in your fancy-schmancy drink.' Bailey turned on his heels and strode off to the bar.

'Wow. What a gem.' Bridey turned back to her brother. 'So Caleb, who else do we have here?'

He introduced the rest of his friends.

Bridey noticed how most of the other guys at the table stared at her with hungry eyes, especially the orc and werepup. If she played her cards right, she could bank on a wild night without compulsion. Taking them willingly provided a more exciting challenge, although she'd settle for using her old tricks if necessary.

Chapter One

Eleven weeks later: the day after Brendan sees Liam kiss Alannah.
(This occurs prior to Alannah's showdown with Richard.)

Brendan's eyes fluttered open and landed on the dark fae enchantress in bed beside him. 'Oh Shit!' He had several regrets in life, most of which involved Tinder. But looking upon Bridey's sleeping form hit him with a compunction which trumped the lot. In a moment of weakness, he had divorced his soulmate and sold himself into the service of a woman he despised.

Feeling the call of nature, he rose from the bed and froze when he discovered metal cuffs around his ankles, tethered to long chains. He bent over to inspect his bonds. 'Cold iron. Damnit!' The material blocked magic and the locked restraints held tight. Even if he could channel a useful mana source or tune into any ley lines, there would be no escaping his shackles. At least the chains had enough length for him to reach the bathroom.

When he returned to the bedroom, Bridey—or Lady Violet in business circles—sat up and gawked at him hungrily. 'Morning, handsome. How do you feel? Has the pain gone away?'

He glared at her. 'The physical pain has.'

'Excellent. I have fulfilled my end of the bargain, now let's discuss yours.' She held out a contract. 'I honestly thought you would've learned your lesson last time you signed one of these without reading the fine print.'

Snatching the page, Brendan stared in horror at his signature, a bloody autograph beneath seven clauses:

1. *The subject, Brendan Winters, has agreed to enter a period of sexual servitude in service of Lady Violet.*
2. *The agreed period for this contract is one full calendar year from the date of signing.*
3. *Sexual servitude requires complete submission to Lady Violet, who invokes the right to insist upon any sexual act she desires.*
4. *Failure to submit may lead to the use of compulsion or result in punishment within Lady Violet's dungeon.*
5. *The subject will dress and act according to Lady Violet's every whim and show due respect to all other members of her household.*
6. *The subject may not leave Lady Violet's residence during the period of servitude except under her express orders.*
7. *Attempts to escape will result in punishment within Lady Violet's dungeon and may risk the wellbeing of other members of the Winters Clan.*

This is much worse than the Rhapsody production contract. The chains rattled as he slumped down beside her and tugged at them. 'Are these necessary?'

'I could hardly have my latest acquisition running off in the middle of the night, could I? When you earn my trust, I will permit you to move freely through my home. They are a precaution until such time.'

Brendan groaned. 'How am I supposed to earn your trust?'

'By doing everything I ask and not making any escape attempts when I loosen your tethers.'

'Can I at least go home first and put my affairs in order?'

Lady Violet laughed maniacally. 'Do you think I am stupid, Brendan? I will send Caleb to deal with your apartment when the time is right. For the next twelve months, this is your home, sweetcakes. And when you do step outside, you will remain by my side. Is that clear?'

His last sliver of hope disintegrated as he looked at her with frosty, dead eyes. 'Perfectly.'

'Good. Now get yourself cleaned up. I expect to see you at breakfast in twenty minutes. Levi will collect you at the appointed time.' She strode across the room and left, not bothering to dress before stepping out.

After letting out the mother of all sighs, he pulled himself up and dragged his feet along the floor. Showering challenged him, with his chains tangling several times. He usually preferred to take his time bathing, allowing himself to relax, but it was an impossible task in his current state. So, he sprayed himself with scalding water and wrapped a towel around his torso.

Stepping out of the steam cloud, he found a shirtless guy waiting for him. By all appearances, he was a half-mage; tall and slim, although well-toned, with tanned skin and a small goatee. Aside from the spiked leather collar around his neck, he wore only a pair of faded, ripped jeans.

Brendan jumped. 'The fuck, man? You startled me.'

'Sorry. Brendan, is it?'

He nodded.

'I'm Levi. Lady Violet told me you were expecting me. Here are some clothes.' He dropped the pile of clean laundry on the bed. 'I hope they're an adequate fit. I have filled your drawers with much of the same. There are also some suits and special outfits hanging in the wardrobe, but you can only wear those upon Lady Violet's request.'

Glancing over the options, Brendan observed an assortment of jeans and leather pants. 'There are no underpants or tops here.'

'She only grants such luxuries when we escort her outside.'

Brendan gaped at him. 'For real?'

'Yes. Lady Violet likes to see as much of our bodies on display as possible and she wants us ready to service her at a moment's notice. We only get pants because of her more… conservative clientele.'

He noticed the bruises on Levi's torso. 'So, you're one of her sex slaves too?'

Levi winced. 'I prefer the term *submissive*, but yes, I am essentially a slave.'

Brendan began rubbing himself dry. 'How many of us are there?'

'She likes to keep our number at seven.'

He snorted. 'What? One for each night of the week?'

Levi laughed. 'If only. No, Lady Violet has a thing about the number seven being auspicious or some shit. But I think she also likes to have a variety of men to cater to each of her different tastes. You should expect her to call upon you several times a week… possibly more, given you're her new favourite.'

Throwing the towel aside, Brendan picked up a pair of black leather pants.

As he stood upright, Levi cast an appreciative eye over Brendan's naked body, lingering a while at the sight of his Prince Albert piercing. 'I can see why Lady Violet likes you.'

Brendan was no slouch when it came to his physique, and he knew his other assets were desirable. 'No offence man, but I'm not into dudes.'

'None taken, but you should know your sexual preference means nothing to Lady Violet. If she wants you to sleep with a man, you will do it if you know what's good for you.'

His eyes bugged out. 'What happens if I refuse?'

'One of two things: either she will compel you to do it, or she will beat you to within an inch of your life.'

Brendan gulped. 'Is that what happened to you?'

Levi smiled. 'No. I actually enjoy the way she marks my flesh.'

With a cocked brow, he shot Levi a dubious look. 'Really?'

'It may come as a surprise to you at this stage, but most of us have grown quite fond of Lady Violet. So, don't get any funny ideas about running off.' With a wave of his hand, Levi released the cuffs from Brendan's ankles. 'You will only need to wear these in your room.'

Brendan slid into the tight pants that clung to every ridge and valley of his sculpted legs, emphasising the bulge between them. *May as well look the part.*

'Excellent choice,' Levi nodded his approval. 'Those pants are sure to please Lady Violet. She also insists you wear this.' He stepped forward and attached a collar resembling his own to Brendan's neck.

He brought a hand up to test the feel of the thing. The spikes were sharp, made of cold iron. Not enough to stop him channelling mana, but they would prevent him from magiporting.

'Come on, let's get some breakfast. We must not keep Lady Violet waiting.'

The moment Maurus Hawthorn walked into the dining room that morning, Caleb stiffened. He wasn't in the mood for one of his father's lectures. But when Dad planted his larger-than-life presence directly next to him, Caleb knew that's exactly what he was in for.

Maurus scowled at him. 'Put a shirt on, Son. You look like one of your sister's slaves.'

He snorted. 'I may as well be, with all the demands she makes of me.'

His dad's fist clenched on the table. 'You ought to show her more respect. Bridey adores you.'

'She has a sick and extremely twisted way of showing it.'

As if on cue, the devil herself walked into the room and smiled the moment she spotted Maurus. 'Hi Daddy!' She ran into his arms, falling into his lap as they kissed.

Ick! Caleb still couldn't deal with the level of intimacy they shared. His whole family was all sorts of messed up.

Dressed in one of her many purple corsets and black miniskirts, Bridey moved across to Caleb and straddled him. 'Morning, sweetheart.' As her skirt hitched up, his sister's slick arousal soaked into his jeans and her mouth claimed his with the hunger of a starved lioness.

Caleb detested how remarkable her lips felt pressed against his, how sweet she tasted, and most of all, how much his cock responded to her. 'I didn't realise I was on the breakfast menu.'

Bridey dabbed his nose with one of her manicured fingertips. 'Caleb, dear, you are always on my menu.' She moved to her own chair to his left and watched as servants spread the actual food on the table.

'Have you started training yet?' Dad's gruff voice pulled Caleb's attention away from Bridey's huge breasts.

'No.'

Maurus growled. 'I've been patient with you, Son, because of what your mother did, but I'm done waiting. You could be a great necromancer, Caleb. It's about time you lived up to your potential.'

'Not gonna happen. I don't wanna go dark.'

His dad chuckled. 'I've got news for you, my boy: your soul is already damned. You may as well embrace it.' Then all signs of humour fled. 'It's time to man up and start pulling your weight in this family. You have two options: either join my business or Bridey's.'

Caleb hated the idea of working for his father. From what he'd gathered, it was more of a cult than a company: one practising some of the darkest magic known to mage kind. It made Bridey's life of crime look like a teddy bear's picnic. 'Fine. I'll join the Dark Syndicate.'

Bridey gasped and clapped her hands together. 'Oh Caleb, do you honestly mean it?'

He looked at her and nodded.

She pulled him into a firm embrace. 'I love you so much! I can't wait to work together.'

A young woman in a skimpy French maid costume announced, 'Breakfast is ready.'

Bridey pulled out of Caleb's arms. 'Thank you, Isabelle. The seven may enter.'

The maid bowed, turned, and opened the door for Bridey's harem.

Caleb had been dreading this moment since the previous night.

As soon as Brendan entered—head lowered, as expected of a slave—Caleb observed how Bridey's eyes lit up. Her reaction didn't surprise him either. He had never seen a man pull off tight leather pants so well. The bastard even rocked the slave collar better than anyone else. Ironically, the whole outfit on Brendan's imposing frame made him look more Dominant than submissive.

Maurus erupted from his seat. 'Are you insane, Bridey?'

Having thought as much for ages, Caleb couldn't help the snigger.

Her jaw dropped open. 'What's wrong, Daddy?'

Dad thrust a hand toward Brendan. 'This. Him! Surely you realise your latest catch is a pure mage. Don't you think the Council will notice he's missing?'

Bridey moved across the room and encircled the shoulders of her latest prize with her arm. 'Don't be silly. Brendan here came to me willingly. Didn't you handsome?'

Brendan's gaze lifted and immediately fell upon Caleb. 'Yes, Madame.'

Pure delight registered in her expression.

Maurus shook his head. 'He must be a spy. You cannot trust him, sweetheart.'

'He is not just any pure mage. We have history. Brendan, honey, this is my dad, Maurus. Please explain the situation to him.'

Stepping forward, Brendan offered his hand to their unimpressed father, who shook it reluctantly. 'It's a pleasure to meet you, Sir. Your daughter refers to my involvement with the Dark Syndicate. I was the original source of Rhapsody.'

Caleb almost choked on his coffee. This was news to him. He hadn't realised all those previous visits had been business calls. After Bridey told him about the time she'd fucked Brendan,

Caleb had assumed a more sexual relationship existed between them.

Maurus narrowed his eyes on Brendan. 'Let me see your aura.' A moment later he grinned. 'Well, I'll be damned a second time. A bloodline mage with balls enough to dabble in the dark arts.' He glared at Caleb. 'Yet my own son, born with a tainted soul, won't even practise a modicum of necromancy.'

Christ! Even my old man prefers Brendo.

Dad turned his attention back to Brendan. 'What clan are you from, son?'

'The Winters clan, Sir.'

'No shit? You're *the* Brendan Winters?'

Caleb rolled his eyes. *Trust a fellow womaniser with a track record more infamous than Dad's own to impress him.*

Maurus clapped a firm hand on Brendan's back which didn't even make him flinch. 'So, it took a minx like my baby girl to reel you in, huh?'

'Ha! You are precious, Daddy. I wasn't the woman who stole his heart, but I do get the honours of mending it after the bitch went and broke it.' Bridey took Brendan's hand and kissed it.

'Is this true?' Maurus asked Brendan.

'Yes, Sir. Alannah, my soul mate, betrayed me. Lady Violet severed the link for me.'

Caleb had seen and heard as much when Brendan's miserable arse came crawling back to Bridey. He couldn't believe Alannah would do such a thing, but Brendan had seen it with his own eyes.

The old man offered him a nod. 'Women can be vicious creatures. I've had my fair share of heartache too, son. But stick with my girl here and she'll treat ya right.'

Bile rose in Caleb's throat because Dad knew shit about women. Mum leaving was his fault. Dad had corrupted Caleb's sweet sister and turned her into the monster who, in turn, took Caleb's innocence. Mum was only trying to protect him.

'Yes, Sir,' Brendan replied.

Caleb missed the flippant Brendan he once knew. *Is this all an act of compliance to protect himself from Bridey's wrath, or has Alannah majorly damaged him?*

Everything about Maurus Hawthorn sickened Brendan. Knowing this man's history did not help, but even if it had been a true first impression, there would be nothing to recommend Maurus. The long black hair—moustache and beard—along with the biker tattoo sleeves all added to the sicko sleaze vibe. But his aura spoke extensively for him: a pure black soul covered in a thick layer of lust pulsing brightly every time he looked at his daughter. It went some way in explaining Bridey turning out the way she had.

Brendan could clearly see Caleb's hatred for his father, but the jealousy oozing from him was a mystery. *Did Bridey stick her claws into Caleb that deep?*

'Come on, handsome, I'd like to sit with you for breakfast.' Bridey tugged on his hand, pulling him onto a chair. Of course, her idea of 'sit with' meant making a seat of Brendan's lap.

His famished stomach groaned at the sight of the feast laid out on the table. He wondered how he would actually eat with a fae enchantress perched atop him. Fear prickled across his skin as he glanced at the other slaves who took positions on the floor around her feet. They were all skinny men, with pale complexions and hair that varied in length from medium to long. Brendan could see how he fitted the aesthetic, although his muscular build stood out like a tall poppy. *Does she starve these guys? Will I wither away too?*

With a heeled boot pressed into Levi's back, Bridey leaned over the table and filled her plate with an assortment of fruits and pastries. Once she had served herself, Caleb and Maurus followed suit.

After throwing a few scraps to the floor for the other guys to fight over, Bridey turned to straddle Brendan. 'Don't worry, handsome. You will all get a chance to eat the leftovers once I have finished. She handed him her plate. 'Feed me.'

His eyes widened with shock, but he smacked the metaphorical mask back on his face, remembering what Levi had told him. 'Yes, Madame.' Brendan took the dish and broke the food into smaller chunks. He brought a piece of croissant to her lips.

She grazed his fingers with her teeth as she took the pastry into her mouth. The gesture was too damn hot, and he felt himself slipping. As soon as she had swallowed her mouthful, Bridey sucked on his fingers with a lascivious gaze piercing the last of his composure.

'Fuck!' He exhaled the muttered curse.

Bridey beamed as she ground against his hardening cock. 'Later, handsome.' She opened her mouth for another bite. Brendan continued to oblige, and as he lifted a grape, she flashed him a wicked grin. 'I want to take those from your teeth.'

Oh hell! It amazed him how this woman could turn something as simple as breakfast into an act of foreplay. Gripping the fruit between his teeth, he braced himself for the contact. But nothing could have prepared him for the heat of her lips as they pressed against his. Memories of their first night together flooded his mind. Her kisses were still among the most erotic he had ever experienced. Logically, he knew she achieved this through her magical attunement to his senses and emotions, pulling the same tricks he often used to enhance the experience; but his body still responded favourably to her touch.

'Mm, delicious.' She licked her lips and eyed the plate to indicate she wanted more.

This time, she bit into the grape with her lips pressed against his, letting the juices explode into his mouth. It was the sweetest torture to have his stomach grumble while the rest of his body cried out for more of what Bridey could offer. Yet his mind and soul wanted none of it. He could not have been more conflicted if he was Parliament.

A sudden commotion broke the spell between them, and the maid appeared at their side. 'Sorry to interrupt, Madame, but Lady Scarlett is here to see you.'

Bridey tensed and swivelled around to face the girl. 'Thank you, Isabelle. Let her in.'

'Yes, Madame.'

When Isabelle stepped aside, Tara burst into the room like a storm cloud. As soon as she spotted Brendan her eyes flashed with lightning, and she unleashed her fury on Bridey. '*You stupid girl!* I warned you to keep your hands off him. Do you have any idea what you have done?'

Bridey scoffed. 'I'm sorry, Madame, but I'm not the one who broke his heart. Your precious Alannah did that without my help. No offence, but I still don't get what you see in the girl.' She leaned into him and rubbed his bare chest. 'Brendan, on the other hand… I can definitely see his potential.'

Eyeing him, Tara spoke to Brendan telepathically, '*Does she speak the truth about Alannah?*'

He opened his mind to his grandmother, letting her see for herself as he replayed the memory of Alannah leaping into Liam's lap and kissing him. The recollection emotionally traumatised him, but at least the physical pain he had felt as their souls separated had dissipated. Bridey's ritual had successfully severed their link.

Tara's wide eyes betrayed her surprise. 'Is there some way you misread the situation?' she asked aloud. 'Alannah has the entire Council looking for you, Brendan. She is worried about you. When I sensed you here, I assumed my misguided *employee* was holding you against your will.'

More doubts plagued his mind. *Why does Alannah care about me? What am I missing?*

'Shit!' Maurus cut in. 'See, sweetheart, this is why I warned you to stay away from the bloodline mages.'

'Relax, Daddy. Brendan wants to remain hidden, don't you, my dear?' Bridey's nails dug into his thigh as she smiled at him sweetly.

Shielding his thoughts from Bridey's mind reading, he nodded. 'Yes, Madame.' Addressing Tara telepathically, he admitted to selling his freedom. *'I'm one of her slaves now, please get me the hell outta here.'*

Tara gave Bridey a sidelong glance. 'If Brendan is not your prisoner, why is he wearing a slave collar?' Her own thoughts entered Brendan's mind. *'You are not ready, darling prince.'*

'A mere formality,' Bridey continued. 'We have a mutually beneficial arrangement, which I assure you he enjoys as much as I do.' She squeezed his hard nipples to emphasise her point, drawing a pleasurable moan from his throat. 'See? What I'd like to know, Lady Scarlett, is how you were able to sense him here when I have wards up strong enough to conceal this place from the Council's detection magic.'

'Not ready for what?' Brendan demanded.

'Not ready to leave here, to return to Alannah.'

'*Please, Grandmother, I'm begging you. Don't leave me to rot in this place.*'

Tara's arctic eyes pierced him with shards of ice. '*Enough! My word is final. Accept your fate and wait for the right time.*' She returned her attention to Bridey. 'Some magic is more powerful than anything of Earthly origin.'

Bridey sighed. 'Always so cryptic. I may not channel Aether or nether, but I know they can't be used in scrying spells. You are not soulmates, so the only other possibility is blood magic, which would require….' Her voice trailed off as her eyes flicked back and forth from Brendan to Tara.

Tara laughed drily. 'Has it taken you this long to figure it out, Violet?'

Caleb furrowed his brow. 'Wait, what's going on?'

Brendan bit his tongue.

Bridey ignored him as her eyes narrowed on Tara. 'You died.'

'A minor inconvenience for a lich, I assure you.'

'The fuck?' Caleb glared at Brendan. 'Did you know?'

He nodded. 'Kinda hard to fail in recognising one's own grandmother.'

'Was this why the Council were cagey about letting us in to watch Alannah's trial? Because they discovered the truth and wanted to cover it up?' Caleb asked.

'Alannah's relationship with me was the premise of the trial.' Tara admitted. 'They charged her with treason and the practice of illegal magic… magic I taught her.'

With eyes bulging, Caleb whistled a single note. '*D-amn.* How'd she get outta that mess?'

Tara directed her gaze toward Brendan and smiled. 'She had an excellent lawyer.'

Caleb shot him a look. 'You represented Alannah?'

Brendan nodded.

'Gods, dude. Is there anything you don't excel at?' Although light-hearted, Caleb laced his words with envious undertones.

He could think of plenty of his own flaws and failures, but he did not want to go there. Especially not in present company.

'I still do not trust you, Violet,' insisted Tara. 'As a show of good faith, you will accept Brendan's help on your next job.'

'Wait, don't I get a say in this?' Brendan demanded.

Tara grinned at him. 'Trust me, darling prince, you *will* want in on this job.'

Chapter Two

'Fuck, I swiped right accidently.' Tyler Quirke threw his phone down on the station's break room table in disgust. Like most of the Council's warlocks, he had pursued a career in law enforcement.

Jaxon Hayes dived for the discarded device. 'You aren't still wasting your time with that app, are you, Quirky?' he teased Tyler affectionately. Jaxon may have been his superior in the Council and on the force, but they had always joked around and taunted each other like best mates.

Tyler groaned as he reached out a hand. 'Piss off, Hayes. And give it back.'

'That's Inspector Hayes to you, Sergeant.' Jaxon flashed his pearly whites before looking at the girl's profile.

'You know we can't all have your luck with women, *Inspector*,' Shane pointed out as he sat down with his coffee. In a country town like Broken Hill, warlocks often stuck together, and Shane Walsh had always been a great team player, even though his half-mage blood made him less powerful than the others.

Jaxon gazed off into the distance a moment. 'You're right. Tanya's pretty special.' He returned his attention to Tyler's phone. 'But what's wrong with Samantha? See, she's a hottie. Oh, and she likes cooking, camping, and hunting.'

Tyler snorted. 'Read on.'

'So, she has a thing for knives. What's the problem?'

'She sounds like a damn psycho, that's what.'

Jaxon slid the phone across the table and laughed. 'I dunno man, she could add some much-needed spice to your sex life.'

Tyler grabbed his phone back. 'Christ, bro! I may be into some kinky shit, but blood-play isn't my thing.'

'No? Then why did you date the v—'

Shane cleared his throat as one of the human officers entered the room.

'—ery hot chick with the teeth?' Jaxon asked.

'I told you, nothing weird happened with her.'

Jones, the human officer, approached Jaxon. 'Sorry to interrupt, Inspector, but the mayor is here to see you.'

'Thanks, Constable. Let him know I'll be there in a minute.' As soon as Jones left, Jaxon rose. 'Come on lads, this might be field work.' That was code for warlock duties, since the Mayor of Broken Hill also led the Mages Council for the Orana region.

When they reached Jaxon's office, Kevin Doyle sat in one of the visitor's chairs with a cup of tea. Jaxon settled into his own seat. 'Greetings, My Lord.'

'Councillor.' Doyle inclined his head a fraction of an inch toward Jaxon before glancing at Tyler and Shane. 'Ah good, I see you have come prepared. Hello Warlock Quirke and Warlock Walsh.'

Jaxon closed the door. 'Figured you'd have some Council business.'

'Well, you ain't wrong. The missus caught a whiff of something dodgy east of here, just out of town.' Councillor Doyle was married to Vivian, the Council member for Organic mana. If she sensed something, the chances of foul deeds were likely.

'Any particulars?' Jaxon sat in a chair, opposite Doyle.

'She said it was blood magic. Might be a vamp nest, but still worth checking out.'

Jaxon shot Tyler an impish grin. 'Might be Quirky's latest date.'

Tyler rolled his eyes.

'I don't think I want to know what you mean, Councillor. Anyway, I'd suggest getting out there while you still have plenty of sunlight, in case you are dealing with some rogue bloodsuckers.'

'Yes, of course, My Lord.' As soon as Doyle took his leave, Jaxon turned to them. 'Right, lads, gear up and meet me out the front of my house in twenty.'

The second Tyler got home, he switched out his standard issue police pistol for a blessed dagger, strapped a matching sabre to his belt, and cast a basic glamour spell to hide it from non-magical eyes. His blood was pumping with anticipation as he ran the few blocks between his and Jaxon's house. It had been a while since he had seen any decent action, both in and out of the bedroom. While combat was not his preferred rush, it still satisfied some of his darker urges.

Jaxon shook his head when Tyler arrived. 'You didn't waste any time! A tad too eager perhaps?'

'I've been chomping at the bit for a decent fight lately.'

'Easy tiger. We don't even know what we're dealing with yet.'

Tyler shrugged. 'I'm sure it will present some form of challenge.'

They jumped in Jaxon's patrol car as soon as Shane got there and headed east. Things were calm and quiet as they cruised along. Several townsfolk stopped to wave, either because they were polite law-abiders, or because they were chicks looking for another round with Tyler.

Tyler did not dislike the local girls, they simply bored him. He put it down to his restless nature and the desire to move on to a more exciting life.

Following the directions to their GPS coordinates took them along a dirt track for the second leg of the journey. Their destination was an old weatherboard shack with a rusted tin roof, which they could only see with the aid of glamour-piercing sunglasses.

Jaxon whistled as he exhaled. 'Someone didn't want the Council to see this place.'

Cocking his glasses, Tyler agreed. 'I'd love to meet the conjurer who imbued these. Damn nifty things.'

'I also hear she's a babe,' added Shane.

'And way out of both your leagues because she's a bloodline mage,' Jaxon explained.

'Typical,' Tyler huffed. He hated the stupid class system dictating who a mage could partner with. Besides, he was ninety percent: practically pure. One great-grandfather diddled the maid and fathered the bastard line of Quirkes. It was quite the scandal when Tyler's mum discovered Dad was not a pure blood. And Tyler figured himself as skilled as a bloodline warlock, so why couldn't he bone the same women?

'You boys ready?' Jaxon's voice brought Tyler back to the present situation.

'Yep,' Tyler replied.

'Yes, boss,' Shane called out from the back of the sedan.

'Walsh, you cover the rear flank, while Quirky and I suss things out,' Jaxon ordered.

'Got it.' Shane slipped away and snuck around the back.

Taking point as usual, Tyler tried the door and found it locked. Nothing his deft hands and a quality lockpick could not handle. A few minutes later they stepped into a slaughterhouse where the butcher was using a cursed blade and chanting in some cultish language as she slit open the sacrificial lamb.

The woman looked up and snarled at her intruders.

Jaxon chuckled. 'Well look at that. If it isn't Knife Girl!'

'What's the job?' Bridey's bare arse-cheeks remained firmly planted in Brendan's lap. He wondered why she even bothered with the sorry excuse for a skirt.

'Information gathering, with probable theft down the line. Oh, and it will mean relocating to Sydney,' Tara replied.

'Why would *I* want any part of this?' Brendan asked.

'Well for one thing,' Tara explained, 'if you do want to avoid Alannah, the move will put plenty of distance between you. But I also imagine the nature of the information itself will interest you.'

His eyes narrowed on her. 'Go on.'

'A tribe of Egyptian elves recently moved to New South Wales and set themselves up along the Hawkesbury River. They are a reclusive bunch, but from what my sources tell me, they have befriended a local dark cult. I want to know everything you can get on these elves; especially their secret magic.'

'When you say tribe,' inquired Brendan, 'Do you mean these elves still practise their traditional way of life?'

'To some extent, yes.'

'Shit! They could be the last living link to the Ancient Egyptians,'—whom Brendan understood to be the most powerful mages of all time.

'Now do you understand the significance of this job?'

'Hell yeah.'

Bridey leaned in, pressing her breasts against him. 'Will you work with me, handsome?'

Brendan considered his options carefully. If he refused the job, he would get more time apart from Bridey, but then he would likely die of boredom while stuck in her house. Dangerous though it might be, this work presented him with a chance to learn some fascinating magic lore, possibly new spells, and it might provide a golden opportunity for escape. He grinned at his captor. 'Yes, if it pleases you, Madame.'

After sucking in a sharp breath, Bridey kissed him fervently. When she pulled back, her heavy lids sat upon dark eyes burning with lust. 'It pleases me very much.'

'Ahem… here are the details.' Tara dropped a large envelope on the dining table.

Bridey reached her hand out and Isabelle, the maid, clambered to bring her the package.

With Bridey distracted as she flicked through the documents, Tara drew Brendan's attention as she spoke in his mind. *'Do not despair, darling prince. I have seen glimpses of your reunion in the future. There is still hope for the two of you.'*

Brendan knew exactly to whom she referred, and her words were like CPR to his soul. *'Thank you, Grandmother.'*

'Right. I will leave you to it.' Tara strode out the room.

Bridey leaped to her feet. 'This is exciting!' She turned to face Brendan. 'Come and see me as soon as you've eaten.' After pecking him on the lips, she skipped off like a schoolgirl: *a seriously hot schoolgirl.*

Blinking, Brendan dismissed the visions of Bridey in plaid skirts as he became aware of the death-stares from eight men. 'What?' He directed the question to Caleb.

'You've been her slave for a day, and you are already getting special treatment. They resent you for it and I can't say I blame them.' Caleb let his chair screech along the wood floor as he pushed it and stormed off.

'I will watch you closely, son.' Maurus's voice drew Brendan's attention. 'I hope you don't give me any reason to lose my newfound respect for you.'

'Of course not, Sir.'

The senior Hawthorn left Brendan alone with his fellow slaves, none of whom spared him a second glance as they dug into the food.

Caleb found Bridey in her suite, absorbed in work at her desk. The light rap of his knuckles against the open door got her attention, but he didn't wait for an invitation.

When he settled on the end of her bed, she spun around in her gas-lift chair and smiled. 'I love it when you come to my bed willingly.'

'Cut the crap, Bry. I want to know where I stand with this Sydney job.'

With two long strides, she crossed the room and straddled him, running a fingernail along his hairline. 'Do you still want to join the Syndicate?'

He took a deep breath before replying, 'Yes.'

'Then you have a choice. You can either stay here and hold down the fort for me, or you can join me in Sydney. Either way, I could use your help.'

Feeling rejected, he closed his eyes. 'So, you don't really want me to go with you?'

She pressed her forehead to his. 'Of course I do, sweetheart. Why would you think otherwise?'

'Because you're giving me the option to stay and… because you've got Brendan now.' He opened his eyes again.

'Oh, sweetie, I gave you the option because you deserve to make the choice. You have been good to me lately; I hoped you would want to come with me. As for Brendan….' She ran her hands along Caleb's bare chest. 'You need to understand he will never replace you. You are my first love and will always hold a special place in my heart.'

He huffed. 'I thought that was Dad's honour.'

Wide eyed, she shook her head. 'Not like that, honey. Dad touched me in a lot of ways, but he didn't fuck me before I turned eighteen. Nor did he ever steal my heart like you did.'

Caleb's breath stuck in his throat, and he whispered a curse. *Why couldn't she love me like a brother?* 'Why didn't you tell me I took your virginity?'

'I thought you'd realised. I mean there was blood on the sheets and everything.'

Thinking back to his first time, Caleb recalled how scared and clueless he'd been about the whole ordeal. It wasn't a happy memory. 'I guess I didn't think to look at the aftermath.'

'Well, now you know.'

'Why'd you do it? You could have had your pick of the boys you went to school with, so why'd ya pop your cherry by raping your twelve-year-old brother?'

Gasping, she jumped out of his lap. 'Is that all it was to you?'

He groaned. 'Come on Bry, don't sugar-coat it. You knew I was petrified, so you compelled me with magic.'

'Oh, you want to play it like that, hmm?' Narrowing her eyes, she shoved her hands against her hips, acting like the bossy brat she'd always been. 'What about those bedroom eyes you often gave me both before and after it happened? And don't think I hadn't noticed all the times you jerked off to fantasies of me. You can't tell me you didn't want me as bad as I wanted you.'

'I was a pubescent boy, Bry. I got hard for anyone with tits and arse. Didn't mean I was willing to go through with it, especially not with my sister.'

'I thought you loved me and wanted me… that's why I did it.' When her eyes watered, Caleb wished for an attunement to emotions because he would have given anything to know if she was manipulating him. 'You can be so dense, Caleb.' She spoke between sobs, slumping beside him. Grabbing his hand, she used it to wipe her tears. 'What could I possibly hope to get out of you by faking these?'

'Shit! I… I don't get it, Bry. Why me?'

'The better question is why not you?'

'I dunno, how about the fact I'm your br—'

'Shush.' She pressed a finger to his mouth. 'It was a rhetorical question, and I haven't finished. There is a lot to recommend you, Caleb. I know you don't tend to let others get close to you. You haven't had many people reinforce your worth. I count myself among one of the lucky few to know the real you and I love everything about you, sweetheart.'

Her words clawed at his heart like briars, entangling themselves in the mess of what he felt for her. He stretched out on the bed and dragged his hands down his face in frustration.

Bridey took the opportunity to mount him, pinning his arms to the bed. 'You're not a pubescent boy anymore, Caleb. And I'm not using my charms, so how do you explain this?' She thrust herself against his growing erection.

'It's exactly what you think it is. I won't deny how these days you turn me on like no other woman can, but that doesn't make it right—'

'Do I strike you as someone who cares what's right?' Her face hovered centimetres above his.

'Well, no, but—'

'Let it go, sweetheart.' She kissed him deeply, her writhing prompting him to moan into her mouth.

In that delicious moment he wanted nothing more than her.

But a knock at the door prompted her to sit up, killing the mood. 'Come in.'

'Sorry for interrupting, Madame, but you asked me to come and see you straight after breakfast.' Brendan's voice pounded the nails in that moment's coffin.

And Bridey's response buried it deep. 'Not a problem, handsome. Please take a seat.'

Flipping his head to the side, Caleb glared at Brendan, who hesitated once he'd read the situation.

'I can always come back later.'

'Don't be silly. Sit here.' She patted a patch of bed directly beside her and Caleb. 'As my two favourite men, you will see a lot more of each other anyway. In future, when one of you walks in on something involving either of you, I want the other one of you to join in. Do you understand?'

'Yes, Madame.' Brendan didn't bat an eye. Caleb knew he'd taken part in all sorts of gangbangs before—a threesome with a brother and sister probably didn't faze him.

Looking down at Caleb from the perch she made of his crotch, Bridey's eyes filled with expectation.

Caleb exhaled sharply. 'Fine. Whatever.'

She beamed. 'Splendid. Now, let's talk business.'

Brendan took his seat on Bridey's bed even though it was all kinds of awkward. She did not even move from her position atop Caleb, who at least wore his black jeans. Brendan knew it was only a matter of time until Bridey demanded the aforementioned threesome, but he still could not stomach the idea. Sharing a woman with friends was not the problem—he had done so plenty of times. But the thought of involving Caleb in the act was sickening, especially if Caleb was not consenting. Then again, glimpses of Caleb's aura and attitude recently made him wonder if the siblings' relationship dynamic had evolved.

Bridey looked at Brendan. 'Caleb has chosen to join the Syndicate, although I'm still waiting to hear if he plans to stay here or join us in Sydney.' She returned her attention to her brother.

That she gave Caleb a choice when she could have compelled him surprised Brendan.

Caleb stared at her. 'I go where you go.'

A gleeful squeal escaped her as she bent down to peck his lips. 'I'm thrilled to hear you say it. Oh, and Brendan dear, if you are going to be working with me, you will need to join the Syndicate in an official capacity too.'

Shit! I didn't think about that.

'Which brings me to my next point. You will both need codenames.'

Brendan's mouth gaped open. 'I didn't think your grunts got those.'

With a sudden click of her finger, a leash appeared in her hand. It connected to Brendan's collar, and she used it to reel him in. 'You are precious, handsome. You might be my slave on an intimate level, but when it comes to work, you will have a more elevated rank. You will both be my captains.'

Caleb stretched his arms, tucking his hands behind his neck. 'What's it mean to be a captain?'

'You must protect me, but you will also command your own teams of soldiers and associates.'

Caleb's face lit up. 'Sounds like a pretty sweet deal. So, what's my name, Bry?' He gave her a pelvic thrust, toppling her balance, and bringing her face-to-face with him.

Yup, definite change in that relationship.

She moaned. 'If you keep this up, sweetheart, I will have to take you right here and now.'

He replied with a smug grin.

'*Caleb,*' she warned.

'Hmm?'

Bridey sucked in an audible breath. With a flick of her wrist, the bedroom door slammed shut and the lock clicked into place. She tugged Brendan's tether before releasing it and letting it vanish. 'Remove your pants, slave.'

Gods no! 'Yes, Madame.' Brendan's hands trembled as he pulled at the waistband. He did not want this. *But what else can I do?* If he refused, she would either compel him or beat him. *And what's up with Caleb?*

Glancing at the bed answered his question in a literal sense when Bridey made quick work of removing her brother's jeans. 'Fetch two condoms from the nightstand, slave.' Her voice was low and breathy.

'Yes, Madame.' Once free of the tight leather garment, he reached across to the drawers and grabbed a couple of foil packets and tossed them on the bed.

Bridey opened one. 'Put the other on yourself.' With eyes fixed on Caleb, she failed to see Brendan's predicament.

For the first time in his life, Brendan was sporting a sponge dick.

Ascending upon Caleb, Bridey groaned. 'What are you waiting for, slave? Take me from behind.'

She was riding Caleb at a leisurely pace, drawing various guttural noises from him. Nothing about the scene suggested a lack of willingness.

A moment later, Bridey shot Brendan a look of displeasure. Her eyes lowered and she gasped. 'Oh dear.'

When she stopped moving, Caleb's head lolled to the side, and he sniggered. 'So, it *can* happen to the great Brendan Winters.'

Brendan's cheeks flushed from anger and humiliation. 'Shut up, bro. You're not helping.'

'Why would I want to help? Also, I'm not your damn bro.'

'*No, but you are hers!* You know… the woman you just shoved your cock inside?' he seethed, unable to contain his outrage anymore. *How do neither of them see the wrongness of the whole sordid affair?*

Caleb snorted. 'Oh, now you have a problem with fucking family members?'

Brendan saw red as he rushed at Caleb with a clenched fist.

But Bridey compelled him to halt. 'What the hell is going on with you two?'

'You're the enchantress, Bry. Why don't you tell us?' Caleb retorted.

Bridey withdrew from Caleb and stood up. 'Your jealousy is clear as day, sweetheart, but what I'd like to know is why. And what is *your* problem, Brendan? The two of you used to be friends.'

Throwing the useless condom aside, Caleb sat up and pulled a blanket across his lap. 'All the single girls in town couldn't satisfy you, could they Winters? You had to fuck with the ones who weren't yours. You're a bigger arsehole than your brother.'

Brendan's eyes narrowed on Caleb. 'You aren't just talking about Bridey, are you?'

Caleb gave him a slow clap. 'Somebody give this man a medal.'

He pulled up the desk chair and collapsed in it. 'I should have figured she got to you too.'

'That stupid *bitch*,' Bridey spat. She sat on the bed and grasped at Caleb's hands. 'What did she do to you, honey?'

'She didn't *do* anything. Not directly.'

Bridey shook her head. 'I don't understand how she could have such an effect on men without using magic.'

'It's called natural beauty, Bry. Look it up.'

Slap! Her hand struck Caleb's cheek, leaving a bright red impression.

'So now we're back to the foreplay, huh?' Caleb hissed. 'Although you might want to get some Viagra for Mr. Flaccid there.'

'Enough, Caleb! Stop acting like such a brat. Now, I suggest both of you quit pining after Alannah like she's a wonderwall and grow up.'

Ouch! Talk about a boot up the arse of reality. 'With all due respect, Madame, I am trying, but I can't easily erase her from my heart with the wave of a magic wand. What I felt for Lana was deep. I still love her as much as I hate her.' The truth of Brendan's own words came as another blow.

Bridey nodded her understanding. 'I'm sorry, handsome. I'm only trying to help. I get furious when I think of what she did to you, and to learn she sank her claws into my sweet Caleb's heart too? It's unforgivable.'

Caleb laughed derisively. 'Like you can talk, Bry.'

She shot him an angry look, but her face softened as Caleb's meaning registered. 'You really *do* love me?'

'How can you of all people not see?'

'It's a side effect of being an enchanter,' Brendan explained. 'We are blind when it comes to reading the love others feel for us.'

'Is that true?' Caleb asked.

'Yes,' Bridey replied.

Caleb exhaled through clenched teeth. 'You don't need to worry about what I felt for Alannah. You pushed those feelings aside when you came back into my life and bulldozed your way into my heart.'

She leaped into Caleb's arms, pushing him back on the bed and kissed him passionately. *Christ! Not again.* A few minutes later she came up for air. 'You are dismissed for now, slave.'

Thank the Gods!

Chapter Three

hit! No wonder Tyler recognised the redhead in black velvet robes kneeling before them. 'Told you she was trouble.' *What was her name again? I think it started with S. Sally maybe?*

'Stop right there, miss,' Jaxon ordered. 'With the authority vested in me by the Council of Mages, I order you to drop your weapon and raise your hands slowly above your head.'

The dagger slipped out of her grip as she obeyed Jaxon's orders. Tossing her head back, she gave them a better view of her perfect lips and nose, both accentuated by piercings. As soon as her wicked gaze—lined heavily with black makeup—landed on Tyler, she gave him a lascivious grin making his cock twitch. 'Are you going to arrest me, officer?' Even her deep, husky voice sounded sexy.

Fuck! Tyler glanced around to see if he could spot the film crew.

'Damn straight we are.' Jaxon stepped forward with a pair of cold iron cuffs. 'We are taking you in under suspicion of practising illegal magic. Will you come without a fight?'

'Only if *he* takes me.' She gave a slight nod toward Tyler.

Jaxon muttered a curse under his breath as he handed the manacles to Tyler and prepared a lightning bolt in his fingers.

Tyler approached her cautiously. Grabbing her arms, he restrained her. *Or was it Sandra?*

She reversed into him and tilted her head up to look into his eyes. 'Hey, hot stuff, do you enjoy tying up girls?'

Shoving her forward, Tyler tried to ignore how incredible she felt pressed against his body. 'You are not obliged to say anything, however anything you do say can be used as evidence against you.'

'Mm. I'd love to have *you* used against me.'

'I'm sure I can arrange it… just not in the way you're hoping.' *No, not Sandra.*

After licking her lips, she shrugged. 'Your loss.'

'I doubt it.'

'If that's so, why did your dick salute me?'

Samantha. That had to be her name. Thankfully, they reached the car before he needed to reply, and Tyler handed Knife Girl off to Shane, who sat with her in the back.

When they reached the station, Probably Samantha refused to budge.

'Step out of the vehicle miss.' Jaxon's tone was firm.

'I said I wanted Hot Stuff to take me.'

He sighed, stepping aside. 'Sorry, Quirky. She's all yours.'

Annoyed, Tyler pulled her out of the car without a word.

'Mm. I see you like to play rough too.'

Their first stop was the shielded evidence room, bringing them to the moment Tyler had both dreaded and anticipated. He frisked her robe to check for concealed weapons or magical tools.

'Are you going to strip search me now?' *Why does she have to sound excited about it?*

'Yes. We must follow standard protocol,' Jaxon replied for him.

Tyler removed her robe, freezing in awe of the art all over her body. A few occult symbols mixed with colourful, feminine imagery, and an Aquarius design took pride-of-place on her back.

Samantha glanced over her shoulder, smiling when she realised what had stolen Tyler's attention. 'Do you like my ink? I designed them all myself, although I couldn't draw the final pieces on my back for obvious reasons.'

'You're a tattoo artist?' He stepped closer and traced the design with his fingers, covering her soft skin in goose bumps.

'Uh huh.'

'*Quirky*,' Jaxon warned. 'Stop getting distracted by the pretty lady and do your job.'

Tyler placed the robe in the red evidence tub and removed her cuffs. 'Please take off your bra and underpants.

'Ooh. Are you sure you wouldn't prefer the honours?'

He smirked at her. 'Sorry, it's against the rules.'

She pouted, but complied, handing each undergarment to him in the process.

When she stood naked before him, Tyler's pulse quickened, sending blood to all the wrong parts of his body. *So very wrong.* 'Please squat and cough.' He tried to sound unaffected, but his shaky voice betrayed him.

'As you wish, officer.' Samantha crouched in front of him and coughed.

After inspecting her mouth, Tyler pulled on a pair of nitrile gloves to continue the cavity search. As his fingers brushed against her delicate folds, he wished the thin layer of rubber on his hands could do more to desensitise him, especially when her muscles clenched around him, and she moaned.

'Oh my. Straight to third base and we haven't even kissed yet.'

Hot damn! Once I'm done with work for the day, I am gonna bone the first available redhead I can find. 'All clear.' He rose, returning her underwear. 'Put these back on.'

She huffed. 'You haven't even brought me to climax yet.'

'And I never will. Now get dressed.' He handed her a set of teal prison clothes since they needed to confiscate her magic robe.

They escorted a dressed and restrained Samantha to the interrogation room.

Still standing, Jaxon set his phone to video. 'Please state your name for the record.'

'Samantha Harrison.' Her hazel eyes remained glued to Tyler as she spoke. 'What's *your* name, sexy?'

'I'm sorry, Samantha,' Jaxon explained. 'But you don't seem to understand how this works. My colleague and I ask the questions. Not you.'

Sitting back, she crossed her legs and arms and pressed her lips together.

Jaxon dropped into one of the chairs across from her. 'Now, what were you doing in the ritual circle?'

No answer.

'You were performing blood magic, weren't you?'

She remained tight-lipped and focused on Tyler who slouched against the wall.

He sighed. 'My name is Tyler.'

Samantha smiled. 'Thank you, Tyler. Are you going to ask me out on a date?'

'No.'

'That's okay. I'm cool with a casual hook up if it's all you want.'

Tyler leaned forward, pressing his palms into the Laminex between them. 'Let me get something through your thick head, sweetheart. This fantasy involving me you've got goin' on? It. Will. *Never*. Happen. I suggest you stop testing my patience, because my boss here is actually the good cop and you really don't want bad cop Tyler to come out and play.'

She gulped. Hard.

Like my cock. And unleashing his inner wolverine did not help contain his arousal. 'Now answer the boss' questions.' Sitting down to hide his evident lust, Tyler reclined into the back of the chair and crossed his arms.

'I was doing it to hide myself.'

'Hide yourself from what?' Jaxon asked.

'Don't you mean from whom? I won't answer the question unless you offer me full witness protection.'

Tyler laughed. 'You're a suspect, not a witness. We don't need to offer you shit.'

'Fine. I won't give you inside information on the biggest criminal organisation in the magic world.'

'And what organisation would that be?' he scoffed.

'I told you: protection first, then I talk.'

Jaxon sighed. 'Fine. If you tell us something useful, I promise the Council's protection.'

'You actually are the good cop, huh?'

'Yes.'

'I have one more condition.'

'For fuck's sake. What?' Tyler threw his arms up.

'When you verify my initial intel, I want a full pardon.'

He sucked in a deep breath.

But Jaxon beat him to the post. 'If your word is true, you have ours. Full protection and reprieve from anything linking you to their crimes. Now start talking.'

'Have you ever heard of the Obsidian Cult?'

Tyler's jaw hit the floor. 'Shit!'

Bridey's kiss was the ultimate contradiction: bittersweet, soft yet hard, taking Caleb to the Celestial and Stygian realms all at once. And it made him want her more, despite how much he despised the idea.

She yanked the blanket away, rendering him naked and vulnerable. 'I've got to have you now, Caleb. I need you inside me.' After rubbing against him for a moment, Bridey pushed herself onto his dick.

'Ah, fuck!' It felt even better than usual, especially when she moved against him. Until he realised why. 'Holdup, Bry! I'm bareback here.'

Grinning, she removed her corset and continued thrusting. 'I know. You feel so damn good.'

He grunted. 'So do you.' Sucking in a breath, he pressed his head firmly into the mattress.

'What's the problem, sweetheart?' Her muscles tightened around him.

'I'm not going to be able to hold back if you keep that up.'

Squashing her enormous breasts against his chest, she let her breath tickle his neck and ear as she spoke, 'I don't want you to hold back.'

His skin tingled all over. 'Are you crazy, Bry? I can't come inside you.'

'Why not?'

'You're my sister. What if—'

She cut him off with another Earth-shattering kiss. 'I told you to let it go.'

Caleb squeezed his eyes shut and tried to focus on the pleasure. But it was no use. It was like she had transported him back eight years: that first instance was the last time he had experienced unprotected sex. 'I'm trying, Bry, but I can't.' His arousal began to soften as he opened his eyes.

Anger flashed in her gaze. 'Don't you dare pull back from me.'

Like that's gonna help! 'I can't do this, Bry,' he rasped.

'You can and you will.' Her eyes flickered with violet flecks as a familiar floral fragrance invaded his senses.

Oh Gods, not again! He could feel her intruding in his mind, breaking apart his inhibitions with her intoxicating presence. His traitorous cock responded even before his willpower broke. And as soon as it did, she rode him hard like a savage beast, tearing the last of his resistance to shreds. Caleb lost himself in the ecstasy of the moment. There was nothing like sex with an enchantress employing all her magic tricks.

She wrenched a climax from Caleb, exploding a million stars in his mind.

But when he recovered his wits, the rapture turned to resentment. Silently fuming, he sat up and slipped into his jeans.

'Caleb, honey, what are you doing?'

Ignoring her, he strode out of the room and slammed the door.

Bridey raced into the hall a second later, still naked except for the ridiculous mini skirt.

'*What is your problem, Caleb?*' she screamed.

'You and your damn mind games, that's what!'

'*Excuse* me?'

He slammed her into the wall with a vice grip around her throat. 'One minute you're dangling free will in my face like a mouth-watering steak, the next you throw it to the dogs. You can't have it both ways, Sis. Either turn me into one of your mindless slaves or listen to me when I tell you to stop.'

When it appeared like she was struggling to breathe and trying to talk, he released his hold.

'Is everything okay here, Madame?' Levi's hot breath tickled the back of Caleb's neck.

Glancing over his shoulder, she nodded. 'Yes, thank you, slave. Please leave us.' She turned her attention to Caleb. 'Maybe you should stay in Adelaide.'

Her words stung like a bitch, but he figured she was manipulating him—again. 'Maybe I will.'

Tears pooled in her eyes.

'See? Two can play at that game, Bry.'

'I'm serious, Caleb. I think you should have some time alone to decide what you want because I'm not the only one playing mind games, little Brother.'

He snorted. 'Right. And in the meantime, you can get nice and cosy with Brendan.'

'This is exactly what I'm talking about, sweetheart. You harp on about how wrong it is to be fucking me—how much you hate what we have—yet you start spraying about the place like a tomcat as soon as I become genuinely interested in another guy. You don't own me, Caleb. No man ever will.'

'No. Only *you* get to own people.'

'I don't expect you to understand what I have with my slaves, but they do enjoy serving me.'

'Oh really? Is that why you compel them into preforming depraved acts no sane man would consent to?'

Bridey clenched her fists and her jaw. She never could stand it when Caleb proved her wrong. 'I only do it to free them of the shame they would feel by making the choice. They get as much pleasure out of doing that stuff as I do.'

He gaped at her in disbelief. 'Christ, Bry. Is this what you tell yourself to deal with your own guilt, or is remorse a foreign concept to you?'

She glared at him. 'You can stay in South Australia until you have cooled off. *When* you decide you can't live without me, we will discuss your move to Sydney. But don't expect me to change, Caleb. You will have to accept me for who I am and be prepared to utterly surrender yourself to me.'

'Don't you mean "*If*"?' He walked away from her, unable to bear the torture of gazing upon her glorious body while her wicked mind toyed with him. When Caleb reached the main parlour, he spotted Brendan lounging in front of the big screen television. When Brendan looked up, Caleb scowled. 'I hope you enjoy the Bridey rollercoaster.'

He stepped into the lift to the carpark, to his piece of crap Corolla, and all the way back to his nominal home. It was odd to think of it as home, given how he'd scarcely been there in the last two months.

The Obsidian Cult. Tyler had heard rumours, some of which made his skin crawl.

Jaxon shifted in his seat. 'The Cult is nothing more than folklore: urban legends to scare the kiddies.'

'That's where you're wrong, officer,' replied Samantha.

He huffed. 'And what makes you the expert?'

'I never said I was an expert, but I know they are real because they recruited me.'

Arms still crossed, Tyler stroked his chin with the thumb and forefinger of his right hand. 'How do you know they aren't some sect of dark mages with delusions of grandeur?'

She tensed, then took a few deep breaths. 'Why do you think I resorted to blood magic to try and hide from them? These guys don't want to be known for who they are. They assimilate with other gangs, hide behind corporate logos, and infiltrate governments. I had no idea who employed me at first. By the time I learned the truth, it was too late. I barely escaped with my life and now I have a great big target on my head.'

'Shit!' Tyler rose and paced the room. 'Is this why you didn't resist arrest?'

She nodded.

'What did they hire you for?'

'I'd rather not say.'

Jaxon sighed. 'You have my word that what you say will not incriminate you. We just need to understand what or whom we are dealing with.'

The look of trepidation she gave Tyler almost winded him.

'Please sit down, Quirky, you're making our witness too nervous.'

Sinking into his chair, Tyler attempted a reassuring smile. 'You have my word too, Samantha.'

After a minute of silence, she lowered her gaze, staring down at a dot on the table. 'My skill as a hunter got their attention. They sent me after wild animals and the odd rustling job at first. Then I was taking down big burly men. My employer assured me these thugs were the lowest forms of scum to walk the Earth and I was doin' society a favour. I didn't mind. I enjoyed the thrill of the chase and fed on the fear and disbelief in their eyes when they realised a chick had bested them. But when I was asked to capture innocent women and children and bring them in alive, I began to question things.'

Tyler tapped his finger on the table.

Jaxon was doing well to maintain his mask, although his left eye twitched. 'What happened to the innocents you kidnapped?'

'I don't know.' Samantha's voice trembled. 'They caught me snooping when I was looking into it. The rest is history.'

Being sexy as fuck was bad enough; why'd she have to go and strum my sympathy chords, damnit? 'So where can we get our hands on these arseholes?'

Samantha peeked up at Tyler from beneath her long lashes. 'My contact operated out of an abattoir in Mulgrave.' The look in her eyes was indecipherable, but it sure as hell turned him on.

For a moment, Tyler wished he could channel emotions. When the left side of Samantha's lip curled up in a knowing expression, he wondered if she was. *Shit! Now I'm in trouble.* 'What are your attunements, Samantha?'

'Senses and organic mana; classic abjurer. Why do you ask, Hot Stuff?'

'Because it's my job.'

This time the right side of her lip joined its friend. 'I am registered. You could've looked me up.'

'Really? I figured you for more of a rogue. Besides, abjurers heal people, not kill them.'

'I wasn't always a naughty girl. At least not in the legal sense.' She winked at him.

Captivated by her smile, Tyler propped his elbows on the table and steepled his fingers beneath his chin. 'Do you have any other attunements I should know about?'

Leaning forward, she brought her face as close to his as the table would allow. 'I don't need to channel emotions to know how hard you are for me right now, sweetheart. The lust in your eyes is plain to see.'

Tyler felt like a sailor stranded on the rocks by the siren filling his vision. And his quickened pulse thumped, mimicking the crashing winds drowning everything around him.

'Quit the flirting, Quirky.' Jaxon's distant warning cry drifted across the stormy seas.

Reclining in her chair, Samantha broke the spell and grinned smugly.

So much trouble.

Brendan dozed on the chaise longue as removalists bustled about, packing and moving Bridey's belongings. He'd given up on the mind-numbing tripe on TV hours ago. The viewing had become increasingly more difficult as the workmen continued to walk in front of the screen.

The one time he attempted a change of scenery, Levi dutifully informed Brendan of the requirement to stay indoors. Even his bathroom breaks were supervised. Sighing, Brendan sprawled out on the couch and took the opportunity to be lazy. It was still preferable to being chained to his bed.

'Why don't I get tied up in *this* room?' Brendan asked as Levi sat in the armchair next to him.

'I'm sure I could arrange it, handsome.' Bridey's voice startled him as she crept up behind the sofa. 'My purple bondage rope would look spectacular on your porcelain complexion.'

The thought of soft tethers stroking his skin while she had her way with him terrified him as much as it thrilled him. He shoved the image aside, hoping Bridey did not catch a glimpse. 'Not what I meant.'

She perched on the armrest and leaned into him. 'I know, but I think it's what you want.' Her fingers brushed his face.

Shit! He had to be more careful about letting his guard down around such a skilled mind reader.

'But to answer your question, this is my public parlour. I don't wish to alarm the clients of my more legitimate business operations with the sight of chained-up slaves. And I know you are well supervised here.' Bridey gestured toward Levi who continued to watch Brendan.

'In other words, you don't want them to know we are your hostages.'

Bridey grinned as her hand cupped his chin. 'You're not just a pretty face with a delicious body.' She repositioned directly above him, and Brendan instinctively brought his arms up to prevent her from falling. Her tongue caressed his lips before it plunged into his mouth.

He groaned as pleasure seized his body and held it for ransom. His grip around her sculpted hips tightened as she kissed him.

'Undress me,' she whispered the command in his ear, almost like a plea.

'Are you sure?' Brendan glanced around the room. 'There are still workmen here. Surely your room would be more suitable?'

'They won't mind. Some of them might even enjoy the spectacle. So, let's show them how well Brendan Winters performs.'

Oh hell. Exhibitionism with an audience was one of the few things left on his sexual bucket list and she was waving it before his raging hormones like a red flag. Brendan was beyond thinking or caring who ignited his desires.

He unzipped her corset at a leisurely pace, wanting to savour the experience, but also needing to get his breathing under control. As Bridey's chest sprang free of its fetters, Brendan thought of two young puppies let off their leashes, bounding and playful. Another jolt of lust surged through him, and he felt the sudden urge to taste them. *By the Gods!* He could have sworn he tasted the tart sweetness of stone fruit on his tongue and wouldn't have been surprised to see juice dripping from where his mouth had been.

Her head tilted back, and she let out a drawn-out moan. Looking back at him from beneath droopy lids, she brought her thumb and forefinger into her mouth and sucked on them a moment. Those moist digits clamped on to his left nipple as she prepared her other hand the same way.

Christ! He desperately needed to be free of his tight leather pants. Naturally, Bridey acted on his wishes, knowing exactly what he desired. After pulling them from his ankles, she rose and slid her skirt down in a slow, deliberate fashion. Brendan noticed the crowd of spectators who had stopped working. A few stood there aghast, but most of them were grinning either from amusement or arousal. Acknowledging their presence only enhanced the rush of excitement he experienced.

She sidled over to a locked cabinet from which she extracted some rope, making his breath hitch. As she returned, the sight of her curvaceous body moving in a gradual, provocative manner, while holding purple rope between long, slender fingers, was superheating his blood. Arriving at the edge of the lounge, she motioned for him to sit up. 'It's time we made some of your wildest fantasies come true. But first, I want to be sure this is what you truly want.'

Stunned, Brendan stared at her. *Why is she asking me for consent? Is it part of her pretence for the benefit of our audience?*

'Are you willing to surrender yourself to me here and now, Brendan?'

'Mm, yes.'

She pushed him back into the corner of the seat. 'Stretch your arms out across the backrest.'

As he followed her instructions, Brendan relished the sensation of his skin gliding over the velvet upholstery, all while keeping his gaze pinned on the woman's elven facial features: her high cheekbones and small nose with soft, silvery skin; almond eyes and high, rounded brow highlighted with dark, purple eye makeup; glossy, heart-shaped lips; and pointy ears accentuated with lines of dainty white gold studs; all framed with long, black, lustrous locks.

When she knelt to strap him down, he closed his eyes to focus on the silken texture of the braided cord and the delicate scent of violets washing over him.

'Look at me, handsome.'

The level of intoxication she had already inspired made it difficult for his eyes to open. But a look of fierce hunger rewarded Brendan for his efforts. Bridey impaled herself upon him. He inhaled sharply between clenched teeth. Everything felt extraordinary as her nails clawed his skin and she writhed against him.

'Mm. You have the most breathtaking cock, Brendan. I love the way it rips my cunt open.' Her rough voice sounded close.

'Fuck!' he rasped. He would have said more if he could, but she rendered Brendan Winters speechless.

Quickening the tempo; their bodies collided together in a symphony of panting, slapping, and squelching bringing his senses to new heights. Climbing that mountain eventually brought him to the peak of ecstasy from which he plummeted into the dark abyss of delirium.

Once partial lucidity returned, Brendan became aware of Bridey's warm body clinging to him and her relaxed breaths tickling his neck.

'Wow.' Fucking phenomenal.

Bridey looked into his eyes. 'See how perfect we are together? If you stick with me *and* behave, every time can be like this.'

Chapter Four

As soon as they got to Sydney, Bridey insisted on a housewarming. Of course, her idea of celebrating meant a weeklong orgy that kept Brendan run off his feet, which he actually spent little time on. In fact, they were the part of his body doing the least amount of work, with his brain a close second.

'Mm. You have incredible stamina, handsome.' Bridey collapsed beside him on the plum, silk sheets of her enormous canopy bed.

Leila, one of her endarkened guests, slept soundly on Brendan's other side despite the blaring tribal fusion beats coming through every speaker in the house. Glancing at Leila's partially uncovered breasts stirred his dick within minutes of use, making him extremely grateful Bridey had chosen to share him with all her new female acquaintances. *What had Bridey just said? Oh, right… stamina.* He rolled to face her. 'Might have something to do with how much I usually work out; not that I've had a chance to lift weights since moving in with you, Madame.'

'You raise a good point. I was going to get Caleb to pack your things and send them over, along with that sexy car of yours. But he can't do anything until you ring your family and let them know you are okay.' She stood up and walked over to her wall safe. When she returned, she was holding Brendan's phone.

'This should be entertaining.' Her eyes gleamed sadistically. 'Talk to Liam. Let him know you are fine.'

Damn it. He was hoping to call Alannah. *Of course, Bridey would never allow direct contact with her.* He would have to think of a way to send a coded rescue plea through his dense brother.

Bridey hit the call button and handed him the phone.

It took a while for Liam to answer. 'Where the hell have you been?'

'Chill, bro. What's got your knickers in a twist?' Brendan shouted, turning to Bridey and asking her to turn the music down with a hand gesture.

Liam growled. 'Are you serious right now? You disappeared for over a week without telling anyone. I half expected to find you dead in a ditch somewhere. Now I'm thinking I'll be the one to put your corpse in said ditch.'

Once the beats stopped, Brendan poured all the acrimony he could muster into his voice. 'Woah bro, that's pretty harsh, especially coming from you right now.'

'I warned you to keep your hands off her.'

Brendan laughed at the irony. 'Relax, man. It was just a fun tumble in the hay. I doubt it meant much to her, considering she has you again now.' He braced himself for the necessary lie forming part of his plan. 'And you can tell our princess it meant about as much to me too. Oh, and if she doesn't believe you, let her know I severed the link and I'm now whiling away the hours in the arms of a real woman—one who takes care of all my darkest desires.'

Bridey giggled with delight.

'If you're content in your newfound *happiness*, why call me? What the hell do you want?' Liam spat.

'I wanted to say goodbye now that I've settled into my new home beyond the state borders. Plus, I had those messages for you to deliver to Lana.' *Please deliver the damn message, bro.*

'I'm glad you left town, Brendan, because you've saved me a homicide charge.' Liam's deadly serious tone suggested he had missed the hidden meaning.

But Brendan figured only Alannah would get it.

Liam continued, 'And I mean it when I say, if I see you again, I will kill you for what you did to Lana. Good riddance, *Brother*!'

Brendan laughed nervously as Bridey took the phone and ended the call. 'You're right, that was amusing. Things will certainly get interesting the next time I see Liam.'

Bridey was rubbing his back. 'Don't worry, handsome. You don't have to see him ever again if you don't want to.'

Wouldn't that make a pleasant change? Pity it would also mean no more Lana.

'I love how you think of me as the real woman in your life. Shall we explore some more of those dark desires you mentioned?'

'What did you have in mind?'

'I was hoping you would tell me. They are your desires, after all. What's something you want to try, but never have?'

'Hmm. A toughie. I mean, what haven't I tried?'

'Has anyone ever explored this part of your body?' Reaching around, her finger pressed firmly against his back passage, causing his whole body to tense up.

'No.'

Bridey's eyes widened. 'Haven't you ever been curious?'

'Not really.'

'Come on, let's try it. It is only fair given how much you take *my* arse.'

Brendan snickered. 'Yeah, but you enjoy it. A lot.'

'And what's to say you won't enjoy it if you never try?'

He sighed. 'Fine.'

She clapped gleefully. Producing some lube and a set of anal beads from the side drawer, she pointed to the bed. 'On your hands and knees, slave.'

Surprisingly, the simple order turned Brendan on. He had always fancied himself more of a Dominant. *Am I a switch?* Once in position, he practised some deep breathing exercises to relax his body. Did not help much when the lube invaded his senses. 'Hmph, that tickles.'

'Does this tickle?' Her fingers were rubbing his entrance.

He sucked in a sharp breath. 'No, it feels spectacular.'

'And what about this?' The first of the beads penetrated him.

'Fuck, it hurts! But in a good way.' He screamed out in pain as she rammed the rest of the toy into him.

She eased them out, then thrust into him again. Bearing down into it, he found after a few repeats he felt more pleasure than pain. 'I think you're enjoying this,' she whispered.

'Uh huh.'

'That's great because I have plans for this gorgeous arse of yours.'

Oh hell.

Looking up from his *Candy Crush* game, Tyler watched as Jaxon entered the break room in a huff.

He pushed Tyler's feet off the table and nodded a silent greeting toward Shane. 'Still no progress from the Sydney warlocks.'

After regaining his balance, Tyler frowned at Jaxon. 'That was our damn lead! *We* should be investigating the cult. I don't give a shit about jurisdictions.'

'No, but the Council does. Unless they find evidence of a global, or at least national threat, we can't do anything.'

Violently pushing his chair back, Tyler leaped to his feet and paced the room. 'The longer they take to verify Sam's statement, the longer she is cooped up in a holding cell. It's not fair on her.'

Shane snorted. 'You only want her out so you can nail her to your bed.'

'Shut up man.' Tyler glared at him.

'Am I wrong?'

The sound of Jaxon's pager saved him from the need to confess. 'A mage magiported into town. I'm gonna check it out.'

'You need our help, boss?' asked Shane.

'No. The Council didn't detect a threat. Probably a tourist. They only need me to greet our visitor.'

Tyler sighed as Jaxon left.

'So, am I wrong?' Shane wore a smug grin Tyler wished he could wipe away with a fist.

He slumped back in his chair. 'Wouldn't *you* enjoy a bit of her southern comfort, given the chance?'

Shane chuckled. 'She might be hot as hell, but that's exactly where she'll take you.'

'Fuck! I'm halfway there already. I can't get her out of my head, Walshy. She's haunted my dreams for the last week, driving me to daily sheet changes.'

'Damn! You've got it bad. Have you tried a substitute? There are plenty of chicks on the Quirky waiting list.'

'Yeah. Once. Didn't help much.'

'Hmph.'

A moment later, Shane's phone rang. 'Hey boss … yeah of course.' He hung up and turned to Tyler. 'Gear up and meet at Jaxon's in ten.'

'On it.'

When Tyler entered Jaxon's lounge room, he blinked twice and pinched himself to be sure he was not dreaming. Sure enough, the stunning woman standing before him was real. As were her hourglass curves, showcased by a snug fitting black singlet top and short skirt. '*Hot damn!*' he muttered under his breath. *What I wouldn't give to bend her over the couch right now.*

Jaxon rolled his eyes. 'This is Alannah, and she needs our help.'

Tyler's eyes trailed upwards from her boots, taking in every glorious inch of her shapely figure, pausing a moment at her perky tits. But gazing upon her face stole the breath from his lungs. Luminous, black hair crowned her proportioned oval face. And her wide eyes fixed on him. Grinning, he rose along with his arousal, extending a hand to greet her.

'This obnoxious flirt is Tyler Quirke,' explained Jaxon.

As she went for the shake, he turned her hand over and brought her knuckles to his lips. 'It's my pleasure, Alannah.'

She laughed. 'I'm sure it is, but don't go hogging all the enjoyment.' Her deep, sensual voice could have been talking about the rain in Spain and he would have heard 'Please take me now.'

'Trust me, beautiful, I'm extremely generous in that department.'

Alannah released his hand and snorted. 'That's what they all say.'

Shane whistled through his teeth and stepped in front of her. 'Hi, Alannah. I'm Shane Walsh.'

'Hi, Shane,' she replied as she shook his hand.

'You'll have to excuse Tyler, here. He's starstruck. I mean, just the other week he was going on about how much he'd love to meet the conjurer who made those glamour-piercing glasses and here you are, in the flesh.'

Tyler gaped at her. 'You made those? Holy shit!'

Shane slapped him on the back. 'You have no effing idea, do you Quirky? Try following some relevant news for a change.'

'There's plenty of significant stuff reported on social media,' Tyler retorted.

'Oh really? When was the last time you saw the Council of Mages post on Instagram?'

Jaxon cleared his throat. 'Guys, please. As riveting a debate as this is, Alannah has an urgent matter requiring our attention.'

Tyler directed his focus on their gorgeous guest. 'Sorry, beautiful. I'm all yours.' He offered her a wink.

Returning his smile, she kept her gaze on him. 'I need help taking down Richard Lane. Do you know him?'

Terror replaced Tyler's mirth. 'Now that's a name I know all too well. Are you telling me he is in my backyard?' From what Tyler had heard, Australia's previous inquisitor was a nasty piece of work who the Council exiled for his archaic methods of interrogation.

She nodded. 'He took me and Liam hostage as part of his revenge plot. I barely got out, but Liam is still there.'

'Liam?'

'Liam Winters. My um, boyfriend.'

Everything clicked. *That's where I know her from!* Tyler felt enraged on Alannah's behalf for all she must have endured at Richard's vile hands. 'Tell me where he's at and I'll pulverise the arsehole for you.'

'Your enthusiasm is admirable, Quirky,' said Jaxon. 'But this is not the time for one-man heroics or half-cocked plans. We need to sit down and talk strategy.'

'Right, of course.' Tyler sat on the sofa. 'What do we need to know, Alannah?'

He did not expect her to sit next to him, let alone close enough for their thighs to touch. But Tyler sensed Alannah would be full of surprises.

After commandeering the jukebox to play all the tolerable metal and rock available, Caleb sank back onto his usual stool at the bar of Doyle Dougherty's, the only pub in Gaeilge Shores. 'You've gotta talk your dad into updating that piece of shit.'

Bailey glanced up from polishing glasses. 'Even if he did, it's not likely to have much to our taste on it. Another pale ale?'

'Better make it something stronger.' Caleb pulled out his e-cigarette.

'Seriously, man? You're gonna get me in trouble again if you smoke in here.'

He took one drag and put it away. 'Sorry, Bay. I needed a smidgen to take the edge off.'

Bailey pushed a bottle of Jameson's along with a chilled whiskey tumbler across the bar. 'Do you realise you've been in here every afternoon for the last week? And your mood has been spiralling each time?'

'What's your point?' He poured a measured shot over the ice and watched in fascination as it swirled around the frozen chunks of water.

'You gonna tell me what's clearly eating at you?'

'Nope.' A large swig of liquor warmed his insides.

Bailey sighed. 'Maybe you should get a job. As much as I love your constant cheerful company, the day drinking habit isn't helping.'

'I have a job. I just tend to work nights.'

His spiky-haired warlock friend stared at him. 'Really? What is it?'

'Nothing I should be telling one of the Council's pets about.'

'Oh hell. Don't tell me you've gotten mixed up in the family business.'

'Fine. I won't.' Caleb skulled the rest of his drink and poured another.

'You're lucky I don't also work for the cops.'

Caleb sniggered. 'No way in hell I'd be mates with you if you did. I can't stand the smell of bacon.'

'See, this is what I don't get about you, man. Your vegetarianism clearly isn't for your health because of how much you drink and smoke. It can't be because of ethics if you're working the unseelie circuit. Why bother?'

He glared at Bailey. 'Do I question your lifestyle choices?'

'No. But mine aren't all shit.'

Caleb groaned. 'Look, bro, I don't do anything to violate animal rights. It's the true-blue[4] reason for my diet. Besides, I never said I was happy about my job. I was given two options, so I went with the lesser evil.'

'Is this what's eating at you?'

'Partly.'

Bailey leaned toward him. 'When was the last time you got laid?'

---

[4] Genuine

He snorted. 'Why do you assume this has anything to do with sex?'

'I didn't before, but with that reaction I'm almost positive it does. I only meant to imply sex can be an effective stress reliever.'

'Unless it's the cause.'

Whistling as he exhaled, Bailey poured himself a shot from Caleb's bottle and threw it back. 'So, Bridey's up to her old tricks again?'

'You sure you're not a mind reader, Bay?'

'I wish I was sometimes. It'd make understanding you a helluva lot easier. You know you can press charges, right? The Council frown upon magic compulsion, especially when used in sex crimes.'

He slumped forward with his elbows on the bar. 'It's not that simple, Bay.'

'Why not? Way I see it, if she did you wrong, you have every right to seek justice.'

'Because I don't *want* to. I love her, man. As fucked up as it sounds.'

'It's not wrong to love your sister, even if she *is* a manipulative whore.'

Caleb scowled at Bailey. Even though he agreed, he hated hearing other guys talk derogatory shit about her. 'It *is* wrong the way I love her.'

Bailey's eyes widened. 'Christ! You don't actually enjoy what she does to you?'

'It's not always non-consensual and even when she enthrals me, she does it in a pleasurable way. I don't feel all the shame and mortification until after the fact.' Caleb downed another shot, and another. Sorrow was not the only emotion he was hoping to drown.

'Shit! You've gotta get away from her, Thornsy. She's poisoning you.'

'You think I don't know? Besides, she moved interstate last week, so there's plenty of distance between us. Problem is I fucking miss her.'

Bailey shook his head. 'You should date other people. Experience some healthy relationships, or even some meaningless hook ups if that's your thing. Anything to get your mind off her.'

'Right, 'cause it's easy to pick up in a town where everyone knows who I am.'

'You'd be surprised. Try casting your eye around the pub tonight. If you see anyone you're attracted to, make a move. If they turn you down, shrug it off and move onto your next prospect.'

'Fine. Whatever. Can we drop the subject now?' A commotion at the door did exactly that. When he turned, Caleb glimpsed his two favourite redheads entering. 'Holy shit! Jacob's back!' He hadn't been alone in Sombre Town lately: the whole friendship group felt the loss of Jacob when he'd disappeared ten days ago.

A bunch of their other friends filed in after Jacob and Cara, taking up residence in their usual booth.

Caleb joined them, directing his initial fist bump and greeting with the impish boggart. 'Hey man, it's great to see you home safe.' He noticed the bruises and gashes on Jacob's face. 'Although you don't look too sound.'

'Richard Lane kidnapped and tortured me, so I've seen better days.' Jacob pulled Cara onto his lap, freeing space for Caleb to sit next to him. 'At least I'm free, which is more than I can say for Alannah right now.'

'What?' Nick roared across the table. Along with every other guy in their group, the orc was a member of the Alannah

Winters fan club and could probably become the new president with Brendan out of the picture. 'Why didn't you say something earlier? And why are we sitting here rather than getting her back?'

Jacob frowned. 'The Council have it covered. They don't want us non-mage folk interfering.'

A loud growl slipped from Ben. 'What about Bailey, Connor, and Cara?'

'If things escalate, the Council might summon them, but Richard is in New South Wales right now. They are only mobilising units over there.'

'By the Gods! Way to make us feel helpless,' replied Connor. 'Is Brendo with her? Did Richard capture him shortly after you?'

'No, he's been… wait! Did you think Brendan was missing all this time?'

Most of the group nodded.

Oh hell!

Jacob shot Caleb a look. 'Why don't you guys ask Thornsy? He knows what Brendan's been up to.'

All eyes turned on him.

Cara's dagger stare stung the most. 'What the hell? How could you?'

Chapter Five

'Because he's hurting.' Bianca offered Caleb a sympathetic smile across the table. 'He hates Brendan for what he did.' It was easy to forget how insightful the nymph could be. She didn't make a habit of flaunting her magical gifts in public.

Caleb began comparing her to Bridey. What the nymph lacked by not being attuned to senses mana, she made up for with empathy and a virtuous soul. 'It's true,' Caleb explained. 'Brendan left Alannah and ran off with my sister.'

'What?' Cara gaped. 'Don't tell me the bitch enthralled him?'

Caleb winced. 'No. I know what her magical compulsion looks like better than anyone. Brendan went with her willingly.'

'But why? Alannah was his soulmate.' Tears welled in Cara's eyes.

'Fucked if I know why Brendan does what he does. Apparently, his soul is tainted now, which could have something to do with it.' He stole another peek at Bianca.

'No! I don't believe you!' exclaimed Cara.

'It's true,' Bianca explained. 'I saw his darkened aura myself almost two months ago.'

'But why?' Cara repeated.

Jacob visibly squirmed beneath her.

Caleb didn't miss a beat. 'Damn it, Jacob! Don't tell me you were in on that racket too?'

The boggart hung his head as Cara slid off his lap, pushing Caleb down the booth, and stared at Jacob.

Bailey approached the table. 'What's this about a racket?'

'I can't say,' Jacob replied sheepishly. It was no secret to their friends Jacob worked the unseelie crime scene, but as far as they knew, he only committed petty theft, so Bailey generally turned a blind eye.

Caleb leaned forward on the table to look past Cara, directing his glare at Jacob. 'Was it your idea, or his?'

Jacob gulped and hesitated. 'Mine.'

Bailey tapped the end of the table. 'Is someone gonna fill me in here?'

Jumping up, Nick pulled Bailey aside to explain the situation while Caleb scowled at Jacob. 'So I guess I have you to thank for Brendan stealing her from me.'

'Those two nymphomaniacs didn't need any help to find each other,' Jacob replied. 'You saw the chemistry between them when she first arrived in town. I had nothing to do with that. Maybe Brendo prefers sluts who can pull the same magic tricks he does. Could explain why he kept going back to Bianca's bed.'

Cara gasped. 'Jacob! Take that back!'

Connor cleared his throat. 'If you weren't still recovering from Richard, I'd drag you outside and beat the shit out of you right now, Jacob.'

'Naw, has the little subbie finally found a pair?' Jacob scoffed.

Amy, Connor's dwarven Dom, shot Jacob a death glare.

Even as his eyes wandered in Bianca's direction again, Caleb couldn't hold back the snigger.

When Bailey and Nick returned, the tension around the table was thicker than Daddy Hawthorn's criminal record.

'Let me get this right,' Bailey interceded. 'Brendo got into something highly illegal that brought him closer to Bridey and set him on the path to dark mage wonderland. Oh, and Jacob hatched this scheme?'

Jacob's Adam's apple bobbed as he nodded.

'It doesn't take a degree in rocket science to know what you bastards have been up to.'

Most of the group looked at Bailey with inquiring eyes as Jacob paled.

'Come on guys. What was the biggest criminal news of the magic community all year?'

'The Inquisitor getting shafted?' Connor suggested.

'Rhapsody.' Everyone shot Ben a surprised look. Their weredingo friend had remained relatively quiet up to this point. 'I figured it was the drug Brendan gave me at The Vault. Trial batch?'

The wide-eyed boggart gradually bobbed his head.

'What the hell, Jacob?' The tears were trickling down Cara's face by this stage.

Someone drew up alongside Caleb. When he turned, Bianca extended a hand and smiled down at him. 'Come on, sweetheart, let's leave them to sort out their shitstorm.'

Curious to know what Bianca was proposing, he took her hand and slid away from the booth. Once outside, they walked alongside each other in silence for a few minutes. There was a gentle sea breeze in the air, and Caleb almost forgot it was the start of summer.

'Do you want to talk about it?' she eventually asked.

'About what?'

'Your feelings for Bridey. What happened with Brendan. Any of it.'

Caleb sighed. 'Not really. I need to forget her.'

'I understand.' She stopped walking and pressed herself close to him. 'I can help with that.'

His breath stuttered. If she had made the offer two or more years ago, he would have her pinned up against the nearest wall within seconds. Bianca had been one of his two biggest crushes ever since he moved to Gaeilge Shores. But they'd become good friends of late. 'I don't know, Bee. What if this messes with our friendship?'

'You know I'm capable of doing friends with bennies.' She was right. Brendan wasn't the only guy in their group she'd slept with. Nick and Ben had fucked her on several occasions. There was even a threesome with Jacob and Cara.

But Caleb's brain was wired differently. 'I don't know if I am.'

She ran her long, slender fingers through his hair. 'If you decide you want more after spending one night with me, we can cross that bridge then. But right now, I can feel how much you want me. Are you going to deny what you need?'

Looking over her shoulder, Caleb noticed they'd reached his cottage. When his attention returned to her face, he backed her into his front door, caging her in his arms. 'I prefer things rough, Bee. Sure you still wanna give me what I need?'

Bianca grinned. 'Do I look afraid to you?'

His mouth clamped down on hers as his right hand fished for keys in his pocket. Once inside the house, they undressed frantically between bursts of kissing on the way to Caleb's bedroom.

Caleb woke from his lustful haze hours later. Bianca had drifted off beside him, but his own frayed mind didn't release him from its clutches. Not as a train of thought barrelled into the station: *sex with Bianca was great and all, but it doesn't compare to what Bridey can offer. I really can't live without her.*

Peering out of the limousine window, Brendan watched as their demon driver merged with traffic on the M7. 'Explain to me: why are we traipsing across the city to meet these people in a Gods forsaken nightclub when we moved to Windsor to get close to them?'

'Two reasons, handsome. Their need for anonymity and our desire to impress. This isn't any club. It is the premier nightlife spot for the magical community, not only for the state, but the whole nation. You'll see.'

He sighed, wondering what sort of impression his black mesh top and tight leather pants would have on these dark mages. *At least I get to wear shoes.* But as they pulled up outside the Darlinghurst club forty minutes later, Brendan understood why Bridey had chosen the outfit. All manner of magical races were filing into the place, but their dress code was the one thing they all had in common: sexually provocative.

Bypassing the queue thanks to Bridey's VIP status, they stepped inside. Deafening tribal fusion beats assaulted Brendan's ears. The genre had become flavour of the month because of Sydney's latest elvish immigrants. He did not mind the music, but it could have lost some decibels.

Bridey encircled him in her arms and pressed her lips against his ear. 'I can see a few Council mages around. I'm going to cast selective glamour to conceal us from them.'

'Good thinking,' Brendan agreed.

As the shimmering spell enveloped their bodies, she pulled him up some stairs and stopped at a VIP booth. 'Get me a

Purple Haze, will you handsome?' Bridey slipped a wad of cash into his hand and sat down.

'Yes, Madame.' As he made his way across the mezzanine, Brendan caught sight of someone who made his heart stop for a split second.

She sat alone in a booth directly below, watching the dancefloor until three guys joined her. They were all mages, although Brendan did not know any of them. More importantly, there was no sign of Liam anywhere.

His heart was pounding. *Shit! Did Alannah understand my message? Is she here to find me? To free me?* He was pushing through the crowds towards her when a hand grabbed his arm.

'Where are you going, handsome? I hope you're not trying to escape?' Bridey gestured toward his collar, reminding him of the invisible tether binding Brendan to his master.

Panic seized him for a moment. 'Uh, no. I'm heading for the bar.'

Bridey eyed him suspiciously. 'There's one up here, over there.' She pointed to their nearest drinks counter.

'Right, of course.' He smiled and ordered their drinks.

When he returned to their table, the dark mages had joined her. Bridey presented him using his Syndicate codename: 'This is my partner, Jet. Jet, this is Damien, and Melanie.'

He shook each of their hands as Bridey introduced them. When they sat down, Brendan tried his best to engage in the small talk, but he was restless, with eyes constantly shifting to Alannah. When he saw her move onto the floor, he decided to try his luck and offered Bridey his award-winning smile. 'Shall we dance?'

'A wonderful idea, hon. What do you guys say?' She directed her question to their guests.

'I'd love to,' the blonde bimbo known as Melanie beamed.

'Well, I'd hate to disappoint such a beautiful lady,' replied Damien, nodding with his head full of hair gel while taking Melanie's hand.

Brendan led them to a prime position where he could observe Alannah without alerting Bridey to her presence. Their proximity allowed him to see how close she was dancing to her male companion. *Too damn close.* Brendan pressed up against his own partner and let her grind against him while he tuned into Alannah's conversation with heightened hearing.

The guy's lips pressed against her ear. 'Fuck! This is like the sweetest form of torture.'

'Uh huh.' Alannah's voice slurred a fraction. *She must've drunk a bit.*

'I've been hard for you ever since seeing the way you handled yourself in combat. Harder still when you plunged a blade deep into Richard's heart.'

What the hell? Did that sleaze infer she'd killed Richard?

Alannah sighed. 'Sounds like something he would have said.'

'So, this other guy I remind you of, is he like your ex or something?'

Shit! Were they talking about me? Upon closer inspection, Brendan noticed the guy's uncanny resemblance to himself.

Alannah took a deep breath. 'Yeah. An ex who didn't just break my heart but shattered it into millions of tiny pieces.'

Her words pierced his soul with regret. *Gods, Lana! What have I done?*

'I'm sorry to hear that. What about me reminds you of him?'

She's clearly not over me if she's slow dancing with my stunt double. He was on the verge of cutting in and showing Alannah how sorry he was.

But her response stopped him. 'You're overtly flirting even though my heart belongs to someone else. But also, you could easily pass as his twin.'

Her heart belongs to someone else. Is she talking about Liam? A fresh jolt of pain seized his chest. But he questioned the logic. *Why is Lana out with this guy rather than Arse Face?*

His clone's hand moved to Alannah's backside. 'Is he attractive?'

'Extremely.'

'Then I'll take it as a compliment, Alannah.'

'Please, call me Lana.' She pressed her head against his chest.

No way! There were only two people in the world she liked using that name. Brendan was not about to let some impersonator take his place. He broke free of Bridey's grip and moved towards Alannah.

'Where do you think you're going?' Bridey had crept up behind him. She tugged on his collar with a short leash that would have been invisible to onlookers. Spying the source of Brendan's interest, she laughed. 'Do you honestly think she is going to take you back? She's clearly enjoying another man's company.'

Brendan scowled at his captor and turned back to Alannah. Dread filled his gut as he watched her kiss his double. The savage, ferocious kiss reminded him of the passion they had shared.

'Although,' Bridey continued, 'that guy does look a lot like you. Maybe she never stopped loving you after all.' She paused as if to let it sink in as her arms slithered their way around his waist.

And boy, did it sink in!

'Not that it matters now. You broke her heart and all faith she ever had in you by severing your soul link. Not to mention your debt to me. I still own you, Brendan, so don't even think about running off with another woman.'

Bugger what they say about fate. Bridey Hawthorn is the cruellest mistress.

She dragged him back to their booth, releasing the tether a moment before Damien and Melanie came into view. 'It's time for business. So, get your head out of the clouds and focus.'

Brendan huffed as she slammed him down in his seat and straddled him.

He could hear Damien titter. 'I hope we aren't interrupting.'

'Not at all,' Bridey drawled in her deepest, most seductive voice. 'Why don't you join us?'

Melanie giggled. 'Sounds delightfully naughty.'

Fighting the urge to roll his eyes, Brendan shut them instead. A moment later, their booth became a heated make-out session. But he tuned it all out, unaware who was touching or kissing him most of the time. All he thought about was his desire to be free so he could return to Alannah.

'Would you like to come back to our place?' Bridey's voice drifted through the fog.

'Mm, yes please.' Melanie, groggy with lust, sounded close.

When awareness returned to Brendan, the dark mage chick was in his lap. Realising his fingers probed her insides did not even shock him, but his instinctive channelling of emotions and senses concurrently did. *When did I start doing that? Was it because I was thinking of Lana?*

'Nothing would please me more,' replied Damien.

As they made their way to the exit, Brendan pulled Bridey back out of Damien's earshot to query her, 'I thought we were supposed to be working, not fucking around?'

'Oh, you are precious. We *are* working.'

A sickening understanding struck him. 'Is this what you've been doing for the last week? Working the scene by fucking all our contacts?'

'It's what *we've* been doing, handsome. Don't tell me you haven't been taking the opportunity to gain intel from their vulnerable minds? I certainly have.'

'Uh, no. I thought we were just having fun. You didn't tell me they were leads. In fact, you've told me shit. This is not how a business relationship works, *Violet*,' he spat.

She growled. 'That's *Lady* Violet to you, *Jet*. And don't forget I am still your boss when I'm not your Mistress. I'm the one giving the orders.'

Bitch! 'What will Lady Scarlett say when she hears you've been keeping me in the dark?'

Bridey laughed. 'She won't be hearing much of anything anymore.'

He halted and someone ploughed into his back.

'Watch it, mate!'

Brendan spun and glared at the goblin who gulped and backed away. Turning back to look at Bridey, he ignored her scowl. 'What do you mean Lady Scarlett won't hear much anymore?'

'Exactly what it sounds like. She's dead.'

Shaking his head in disbelief, he pulled Bridey in close. 'Are you sure she's gone this time?'

'Yes. They destroyed her soul crystal first.'

'But how?'

Bridey grinned malevolently. 'This is the best bit, actually. It was none other than your beloved Alannah who killed her.'

He was utterly gobsmacked. 'That can't be right.'

'Well, I can't imagine the official Council reports getting it wrong. Now, hurry along. We can't keep our guests waiting.'

Brendan resumed walking, masking the grief threatening to burst through its dam. He swallowed against the lump pinching his vocal cords. 'So… who's running the Syndicate now?'

'We are yet to decide. It's customary to allow a week of mourning before the upper echelons gather at a summit to vote in the next Boss.'

Interesting. 'I presume that includes captains.'

Bridey sighed. 'Usually.'

'I want to go.' *This could be a convenient opportunity to undermine her.*

'I suppose I can arrange it. They will expect to see you and I could use your vote anyway.'

'Good.' With newfound enthusiasm for his work, Brendan pushed forward and caught up with Damien and Melanie, slipping an arm over each of their shoulders. 'Sorry to keep you waiting. The missus and I bumped into an old friend.'

'Not a problem,' Damien smiled.

Grinning, Brendan opened the limo door for them.

Bridey cocked a brow at him on her approach. 'What's your angle, Jet?'

He narrowed his eyes. 'Just doing my job, Madame.' The brutal kiss he savaged her with left her moaning for more. *Yup, I still got it.*

<h1 align="center">Chapter Six</h1>

As soon as Alannah and Liam left, Tyler collapsed onto the couch of the Darlinghurst hotel with a big dumb grin painted across his face. 'Mm. Best night of my life.' He replayed the highlights in his mind. Like the way Alannah clawed at his back when he nailed her in missionary, or the sight of her chest bouncing as she rode him. *Fuck!* The memories alone aroused him.

Shane pushed Tyler's legs aside and joined him. 'Pity she has a boyfriend.'

'Don't be such a buzz kill, man.'

Jaxon took one of the armchairs. 'You're damn lucky Liam didn't kick your arse.'

He shrugged. 'At least I would have died happy.'

Sipping on his coffee, Shane studied Tyler across the steam wafting from his cup. 'Does this mean you're finally over Samantha?'

'Ha!' He had not thought about the firecracker dark mage with red hair since meeting Alannah. 'I guess Lana did *me* a service too.'

Jaxon picked up the room service menu from the coffee table. 'I'm almost afraid to ask, but what are you talking about?'

Alannah had opened her heart to Tyler and told her whole tragic love story over the course of the night. Sex was not the only therapy he had provided her, and he explained it all to the guys.

Shane shook his head. 'Wow. Brendan sounds like a real jerk. To think I used to idolise the guy for all the no-strings pussy he could reel in without repercussions.'

Jaxon sighed.

'What?' Shane jerked his head toward Jaxon.

'Could you be any cruder, Walshy?'

Shane smirked. 'Probably, but that's more Quirky's department.'

Jaxon's phone filled the hotel suite with the sound of Ed Sheeran singing 'Shape of You', so he took the call to his room.

'Hmm.' Shane looked at Tyler thoughtfully.

He lolled his head to the side dreamily. 'What?'

'It looks like you've gone from a ridiculous obsession to an impossible one.'

'She'd consume your thoughts too if she'd rocked your world half as well as she did mine. Lana reminds me of wild strawberries. You wanna know why?'

'Go on.' Shane loved hearing about other people having sex almost as much as he loved watching it.

'She smells and even tastes like strawberries. And she becomes a ferocious animal in bed.'

Shane shifted to accommodate his own obvious arousal. 'Yeah, I heard her through the walls.'

Tyler closed his eyes, allowing flashbacks to occupy his mind. 'I haven't even told you the best part.'

'Oh hell. I'm gonna need a cold shower in a minute.'

'You're not alone. I'll never forget the red marks I left on her soft, milky skin. Lana is a serious masochist.'

'Shit, man. She sounds like the perfect yin to your yang. It's unfortunate she's a bloodline mage, not to mention taken.'

He could not hide the wicked grin creeping across his face. 'I reckon she'll be back for more.'

'Why?'

'She told me a secret about her relationship with Liam. Suffice to say, they are not the most compatible pair. I'll happily sit on the sidelines if it means I'm the one who gets to bring her immense pleasure.'

Shane punched him in the arm. 'You dirty little homewrecker.'

Tugging his arm back, Tyler feigned injury. He leaped at Shane and tackled him to the ground.

They were still grappling when Jaxon returned. 'I don't know if I've walked onto the set of a gay porno or the WWE.'

Pinning Shane's chest to the floor in a Half Nelson, Tyler looked up and grinned. 'You're in time to see my boom boom boom.'

'Please spare me. Besides, we have Council work to discuss.'

Clambering off his opponent, Tyler returned to the couch. 'I'm all ears.'

After stretching out a crick in his neck, Shane joined them. 'After that beat-down I'd say you're all muscle,' he whinged.

'I don't usually hear any complaints about this bod from the ladies.' Tyler returned his attention to Jaxon. 'What's the job, boss?'

'The Council confirmed Samantha's intel. They have approved her release and protective custody on the condition I organise it.'

'That's great news,' Tyler replied.

Jaxon sat in quiet contemplation for a moment. 'After last night, I guess Quirky won't be interested in working with Samantha anymore.'

His ears pricked up. 'Ah, what?'

'High Magus O'Grady suggested we provide the protective detail and use our position to continue gathering information.'

'How so?'

'Moving to the City for one thing. But we would also have to live with Samantha.'

Tyler thought back to his brief encounters with the fiery redhead. Residing in such proximity to her would be dangerous yet exhilarating. He prayed for the fortitude to withstand the inevitable heat. 'Count me in.'

Having seen her guests out, Bridey returned to her bedroom. She was glad to be rid of the dark mage couple and the stench of their cigarette smoke, not to mention the girl's irritating giggle. A change of clothes would be essential. She went straight to the large mahogany wardrobe to select her outfit. *Which shade of purple today?* Turning, she threw the thistle-coloured corset on the bedroom bench and jumped. 'Shit! You startled me, handsome. I didn't realise you were still in here.'

Brendan's naked body was sitting on her bed and his muscular arms bulged as they rested upon bent knees. *He truly is picture-perfect sex appeal.* The left side of his lip curled in unison with his pierced brow. 'You never gave me the order to leave.'

The expedience of his obedience is impressive. As she knelt against the edge of the mattress, her silk robe gaped open, and he devoured the view she offered with hungry eyes. *How does he reduce me to a quivering teenage girl just with a look?* Feeling the need to recover her sanity, Bridey glanced at the door and waved dismissively. 'You may leave, slave.'

But he did not move. 'I thought you might like to hear what I learned from reading Melanie's mind.'

Adolescent brain instantly transformed to criminal mastermind as Bridey's attention jerked back. 'And what, pray tell, did you garner from that minute head of hers?'

'I'll tell you on one condition.'

After sliding across the soft sheets, she pushed Brendan's knees down and straddled him. She combed her fingernails through his thick, black hair. 'Are you trying to negotiate with me, slave? I could compel the information from you.'

'Or you could tell me what you got from Damien. I want to help with this mission, but to be effective, I need to know everything you've learned about these people.'

Moving her hand to his chest, she forced him back against the bed. 'I'm the only one who gets to do the pushing.' Lust-filled intent replaced his smirk, and she felt his arousal growing. 'Mm, I love how easy it is to turn you on.'

He thrust against her. 'I could say the same about you, Madame. You're dripping all over me.'

Parting her lips, Bridey tried to catch her breath and reel in her pulse, but both had long since bolted. Control was slipping from her grasp, and she hated it. She brought her palm firmly across Brendan's cheek, leaving a bright red handprint.

Brendan did not flinch. In fact, he replied with a shit-eating grin as he prodded at her opening again.

She slapped his other cheek with greater force before lunging on his cock and taking him with all the frenzy of a possessed woman.

Five glorious orgasms later, she pulled back, depriving him of his own climax.

He glared at her. 'Why doth you leave me so unsatisfied?'

'Because I'm the boss and you will tell me what you know if you want more.'

The insolent bastard shrugged and wrapped a large hand around his erection. Maintaining eye contact, he stroked his shaft, and swirled his thumb through the glistening drop that had formed on the tip.

Bridey's eyes kept flicking between his gaze and the sight of his desire. *And damn—but it looks incredibly hot. He must know he's playing with fire. For every inch of power he attempts to wrest from me, I'll yank back more.* Wrenching his hand away, she restrained his wrist along with its partner, using the manacles fixed to her bed. 'Try coming without me *now*.'

A low growl sounded from deep in his diaphragm.

'Tell me.'

'Melanie observed my tainted soul and thought about the reward she'd get for recruiting me, a bloodline mage, into the Cult.'

She rose and stamped her foot. 'Damn it! How did she know who you were?' Her eyes narrowed on him. 'You didn't tell them, did you?'

Brendan's expression was incredulous. 'No. But if she could read my aura, she would have seen how strong my magic is. It's not hard to pick the partials from the pures when you know what to look for. We could work this in our favour. I could be your inside man.'

Her eyes travelled over his arousal as she licked her lips. Bridey had to admit his idea was brilliant. 'Would you like to be inside?' She offered him a suggestive look.

'I'll penetrate anything if it pleases you, Madame.'

Oh hell. There I go, turning to mush again. With one swift movement, she mounted him. This time Bridey did not stop until she milked him for every last drop, tearing a guttural cry from him.

With her face pressed against his chest, she listened to the sound of his beating heart: erratic at first, but it gradually settled.

'What did you learn from Damien?'

Tilting her head up, she peered into his big green eyes. 'You mean other than how useless he is at pleasuring a woman? Not much. I bet you ruined Melanie for him.'

A satisfied smile appeared on his face. 'Good.'

'Don't tell me you actually enjoyed fucking that bimbo?'

'Gods no! But *she* had a wonderful time which makes my job easier.' His eyes gleamed wickedly.

Sitting up and still astride him, Bridey brushed her fingers over his skin, starting from his shackled wrists, down his arms and across his torso. Goosebumps prickled his flesh and he bucked against the restraints. 'I think I'm really going to enjoy plotting and scheming with you, Brendan Winters.'

Something about Samantha's wide-eyed awe stirred more than Tyler's hormones. He studied her as she took in the luxury of her new Darlinghurst house. *Our new home.* The hallway opened into a dining room furnished with a solid ebony table and six high-backed, black leather chairs.

Walking through the dining room brought them to the living room and back to the front of the house. Suede couches, a Persian rug, and a large, wall-mounted television were the main features of this space. 'This place is astounding,' she rasped.

'You've only seen two rooms so far.'

She nodded. 'And their combined floorspace already is bigger than my poky flat in The Rocks.' When they moved into the galley kitchen, her jaw dropped.

The modern interior of white granite and black timber contrasted starkly with the terrace's Federation façade. *The Council must have renovated the place recently.* 'Come on, I'll show you to your room.'

After climbing the first flight of stairs, Samantha paused at the landing, glanced down the hall, and back at Tyler as he ascended to the top floor. 'What are all those rooms?'

'This is Jaxon, Tanya, and Shane's floor. We are up here.'

'Oh?' She dragged her tongue across her bottom lip as desire filled her eyes.

Tyler had hoped his time with Alannah would have helped him build some resistance to Samantha's charms. *Alas no.* Gulping, he spun around and jogged up the stairs.

'Who's Tanya?'

'Jaxon's woman. She's an abjurer like you, but bloodline.' Walking along the upper corridor, he tapped against a closed door. 'This is my room.' He continued to the end. 'And here is yours.'

Brushing past him with deliberate contact, Samantha beelined for the bed and sat on the crisp white linens. She leaned back on her elbows and smiled at him. 'Are the separate rooms necessary, Hot Stuff? This big ol' bed is too much for just me.'

He cursed under his breath as his dick twitched. 'They are… essential.'

'I give it a week, tops.'

'What do you give a week?'

'You. Before you stop resisting the urge to keep me warm at night.' She winked at him.

Tyler strode across the room. Raising his right leg, his foot rested on the end of her bed. 'Only a week, huh? I'm offended you have so little faith in my willpower.'

'On the contrary—a week is much more than I'd give most men.'

'You're rather sure of yourself.'

'You don't believe me?' She crawled across the bed toward him with a cocky grin.

'No.' He should have pulled back, but his more stubborn, defiant side won out and he stood his ground. Instant regret surged through him as her hand ran along his leg and up his thigh.

'Tell me, hottie, why did you take the room next to mine?'

'It's where Jaxon put me.'

'Did you disagree with him over it?'

His jaw clenched as he fought the temptation to lie for the sake of argument. 'No.'

'Curious.' Her hand moved to his waistband and tugged at the zip of his blue uniform pants. The proximity of her face and his crotch had not escaped his attention either.

A throat cleared from the doorway, and he cussed below his breath while jumping back. Jaxon glared with stern disapproval. 'I hope I don't have to pull you off this case, Quirky. Miss Harrison is an official informant now. All intimate contact with her is strictly out of the question.'

'Won't be a problem boss, but how can Samantha be an informant when she is in protective custody?'

'To begin with, she will talk us through the details of every hunt she went on. If we need more, we can disguise her.'

She went pale with fear. 'I… I can't go back to them.'

Jaxon stepped inside the room and crossed his arms in a stoic pose. 'Don't worry, Miss Harrison, we do not intend to put you in dangerous situations. If we take you out in the field, we'll surround you with warlocks.'

Tyler shook his head. 'I can't believe you would consider any form of fieldwork for Sam. It's too risky.'

'We will assess the risks when the time comes. For now, I suggest you both freshen up, then join me in the living room so we can get to work.' Jaxon left them alone again.

Samantha smiled warmly as she rose. 'I think I'm growing on you, Tyler.'

'What gives you that impression?'

She drew close and placed her hands on his chest. 'Well for one, you're worried about me.'

'Concern for your safety is in my job description.'

Her lips curled into a smirk. 'What about giving informants nicknames? You called me Sam before. Only my friends use that name.'

He feigned a gasp. 'My Gods! You have friends?'

'Deflection and denial won't hide the truth from me, sweetheart. I look forward to breaking down all your defences and inhibitions.' She sauntered past him and into the bathroom.

Desperate for release from the tension mounting in his balls, Tyler headed straight for his room. After stripping out of his uniform, he collapsed on the bed and closed his eyes. Calling upon memories of Alannah, he bolted toward the climax.

'Mm, quite a show.'

Tyler jack-knifed and grabbed a pillow to cover his lap. 'How long have you been standing there?'

The sight of Samantha in the doorway in a towel was wreaking havoc with his determination. 'About a minute. I came to let you know the shower is free.' She gave him a wicked grin. 'Were you thinking about me?'

'No.'

She shrugged. 'Perhaps you need more inspiration.' Letting her towel drop, she strolled forward. Her brightly inked, curved body was magnificent. Her tits were not exactly large, but they were firm and perky. A tattoo adorned her left side: a heart within a circle of flames with fiery tendrils sprawling across her skin and setting the rest of her chest ablaze.

The enchanting fragrance of coconut wafted across the room and surrounded him. He could feel a lump forming in his throat, making swallowing difficult. 'I think we need to establish some share-housing rules and boundaries.'

'What's the point? I don't follow rules anyway,' Samantha grinned.

'Figures. Even so, I want you to know my bedroom is off limits.'

Samantha reached the end of his bed, standing before him in all her naked glory. 'Then put a lock on the door.'

'Fine, if that's what it takes. Now please excuse me.' He bolted from her intoxicating presence and sealed himself in the bathroom. But his new surrounds did little to break her spell. The odour of a tropical paradise filled his senses. When he stepped into the shower, he found her coconut body wash and banana haircare products. *No wonder she smells edible. Oh Gods! I am in serious trouble.*

Except for the floorplan, Bridey's new house was essentially the same as her previous den. Caleb took in the sights as he entered. All the same purple velvet and black leather furnishings; the same old-style décor and lighting making the place look like a brothel. He knew this was intentional because business for his sister generally involved the art of seduction. And she'd made it perfectly clear she wouldn't be changing for him, putting the onus on him. *That's fine, sweetheart. You want a new me, you'll get a new me.*

A wolf-whistle greeted him the moment he stepped into the parlour. Levi followed up the praise by blatantly checking him out. 'Looking sexy, My Lord.'

I guess I can pull off leather too. He'd worried about overdoing it with the leather trench coat, leather pants, and tight, black mesh top. But Bridey did love the material. *Speaking of Bridey….* 'Tell me, slave, where is my sister?'

'Lady Violet is in her chambers. Third on your left down there.'

Descending the stairs, he followed Levi's directions and found a closed door. Banging, screaming, and moaning permeated through the walls. He considered finding his own room and sneaking in a nap before dinner.

Then Bridey's cries stopped him in his tracks. *'Fuck me harder, Brendan! Tear me open with your massive cock!'*

Jealousy reared its ugly head and all sense of propriety fled as Caleb barged into the room. But he didn't achieve the grand entrance he'd hoped for. They were both facing away from him and the noise they made drowned his booted footfalls. Feeling awkward, he wondered how he should announce himself. In the end, Caleb slammed the door shut and leaned against it with arms crossed.

'The fuck?' Brendan glanced over his shoulder. His jaw dropped at the sight of Caleb.

'What now?' Bridey grumbled as she pulled away from Brendan and turned to face the door. Kneeling naked on the bed, she gasped. 'Caleb?'

He took a moment to appreciate the view and gave her a sly grin. 'Surprise, Sister dearest.' Warm tingles spread across his body as she scanned him with hungry eyes.

'To what do I owe this honour?' Bridey employed her deepest, most seductive voice.

Pushing off against the door, he crossed the room and stood before her, paying no heed to Brendan. 'I decided I couldn't live without you, Bry.'

Her eyes lit up as she ran her hands along his jacket seams. Tugging it off, she let the heavy garment drop with a thud on the wooden floor.

Manicured nails touched his nipple rings a second later, teasing them through the thin veil of mesh fabric. The result was immediate, and Caleb's knees sank to the mattress as pleasure shot through him. He pulled her into his arms and kissed her savagely.

Pivoting, Bridey pushed him onto his back. 'Remove Caleb's boots, slave.'

At first, he thought it weird to have a slave remove his shoes, but this was Brendan. Caleb also felt some perverse pleasure in the way Bridey ordered Brendan to degrade himself on Caleb's behalf.

'Yes, Madame.' Brendan's voice betrayed a hint of reluctance.

If Bridey noticed, she ignored it as she continued kissing Caleb. Her tongue toyed with each of his three lip piercings with renewed interest. It plunged into his mouth and circled around his tongue ring. 'Mm, have I told you how much I love all these?'

Caleb met her gaze and smiled with smug satisfaction. 'Once or twice.'

At the sound of his second boot hitting the floor, Bridey commenced removing Caleb's pants, freeing him from their restrictive hold. As she lowered herself onto him, she eyed him intently.

He knew she was testing him because she hadn't bothered with protection. Caleb maintained the eye contact, refusing to flinch or succumb to any of his misgivings.

She moved gently at first, her breasts quivering in the undulating motion. Moans slipped out each time he entered her.

The doubts still crept in. *This is your sister, you sick bastard!* But he focussed on the blissful expression on her beautiful face. *Let it go, Caleb.*

'Join us, slave,' she rasped, still with her attention on Caleb.

'I'm sorry, Madame, but I can't,' Brendan replied.

With a sigh, she turned to face Brendan. 'That was an order, slave. Do I need to compel you?'

'Probably. I'm not gonna be able to perform without some magical assistance.'

Caleb rolled his eyes. *Here we go again.*

'Why?' Bridey asked. 'You are normally insatiable.'

'It's the whole incest thing. Big turn off, I'm afraid.'

The distraction brought Bridey's movements to a stop, impacting on Caleb's desire. But he was determined to stick with it this time, so he thrust into her.

A loud groan escaped her. 'If Caleb can get over it, why can't you?'

His next thrust made her collapse against his chest. 'Forget Brendan. Let me ravish you.'

'But I want you both at the same time.' She sounded like a whiney brat rather than a grown arse woman. 'I have an idea. Brendan, lie down next to Caleb.'

Brendan hesitated but eventually obeyed her.

Bridey climbed off Caleb and retrieved a blindfold from her bedside drawers which she placed over Brendan's eyes. Next came the leather cuffs around his wrists. 'I want you to forget Caleb's presence. Focus on me.' She spoke into Caleb's mind. *'Once you can see him getting into it, take me from behind.'*

Why doesn't she compel him like with all the other slaves? The thought brought a few insecurities to the surface of his mind as he watched Bridey pleasure Brendan back to a heightened state.

By the time the two of them were going at it, Caleb lost all desire to join in; he was too green with envy. Rolling out of bed, he grabbed his pants, and snuck out of the room. He leaned against the wall to dress. Reclining his head, he winced and shut his eyes as the sounds of Bridey's orgasms washed over him.

'Wow. Things must be getting serious between them if she's even shutting you out.' Levi's voice prompted his eyes to flick open.

'What do you mean?'

'The rest of us slaves have had bugger all time with Lady Violet since moving here. She doesn't just favour Brendan, she has him in her bed all night, every night and then some.'

'Shit! Really?'

Levi nodded.

Things were worse than Caleb thought. *Brendan is going to be a problem if I don't do something about him.*

Chapter Seven

When Tyler had cooled off, he made his way to the living room. But the efforts he had gone to with the cold shower were all in vain when he beheld the scene before him. Again, he found himself checking for cameras before returning his gaze to the fox lying on the floor. Denim short shorts barely covered her arse cheeks and her legs swung like scissors as she read her magazine. 'Is there something wrong with the couch?' Tyler asked.

Rolling onto her back, she faced him with impish eyes. 'I'm sure it's fine, but I feel more at home on hard surfaces.'

He tried to control his breathing, but her transparent white singlet top did not help, especially since it revealed her obvious lack of bra. Thoughts of ruining the rug along with his sanity and career filled his mind. For once, he was thankful for the cockblocker in the room.

Jaxon shook his head in disapproval of Tyler's obvious affliction. 'Sit down, Quirky. We have work to get on with.'

Tyler took the sofa, at which point Samantha decided the plush seat next to him was suitable after all.

'Let's start with the details of the first time you killed a person,' Jaxon suggested.

'What do you want to know?'

'Everything.'

Samantha gulped and looked at Tyler with wide eyes.

He attempted a reassuring smile as he nodded for her to spit it out.

'It started about two years ago now. I was almost seventeen at the time.' Clutching Tyler's hand, she curled up against him.

Tyler's heart ached for her. To be a hardened criminal by seventeen suggested the girl had lost her innocence at a young age. He wondered what her youth had been like.

'I was delivering my latest game to Mr. Black at the abattoir:

After paying me in cash, he handed me a manilla folder. 'This is your next assignment.'

I gasped at the file. 'What you are suggesting is murder.'

'Read the man's bio and you'll see how you're doing the world a favour.'

A second glance showed my target was a felon with several charges of assault, drug trafficking, and even rape. His real name was Andrew Short, but he was a notorious gang leader better known by the alias Sharp Knuckles.

Tyler exchanged a glance with Jaxon. They both remembered the name, but the media reports claimed he had died of a drug overdose.

'What does this man have to do with you?' I asked.

'Let's just say he is a spanner in the cogs of business.'

If Mr. Black had dealings with Mr. Short, I didn't want to know the specifics, so I took the job description and left.

According to my briefing, I was required to make his death look like an overdose, which meant getting close and personal. I shuddered at the thought. But I was uniquely adept at illusionary magic for an abjurer and as far as I knew, Mr. Sharp was only human. So, I organised a meeting through my old gang contacts.

Jaxon was engrossed in her tale, leaning forward like an attentive child listening to his favourite story. 'Old gang?'

'Nothing as organised as the Knuckle Heads. We were a bunch of magical street kids who stuck together. Most were unseelie, but a few of us were otherwise.' Samantha continued her story:

When I met Sharp Knuckles, he warmed to me straight away. Too warm if you ask me. The guy was an absolute sleaze who couldn't keep his hands to himself. But I didn't let it deter me, instead using it to my advantage. I played the drug-running angle, starting small to build trust. Eventually, I got my hands on a shitload of methamphetamine.

The night before I was scheduled to make my first meth run, Knuckles invited me to party with him in his room. Seizing the opportunity, I went prepared with two preloaded syringes. One a placebo, the other a lethal dose of ice.

Things started out much as I had envisioned. We shared a couple of whiskeys while listening to shitty RnB, all with his arm draped over my shoulders. When he begged me for a striptease, I figured there was no harm in it if he kept his own clothes on, so I complied. It took a lot of restraint on my part to hold back the bile when he began jerking off to my performance.

Then came the moment of truth. He approached me with hungry eyes and grabby hands. 'I gotta fuck you, baby.'

I smiled sweetly. 'Yeah, okay, but why don't we make it feel fantastic?' Pulling out the needles, I held them up. "You can deduct these from my cut."

Knuckles laughed heartily for a full minute. 'Come on, sweetheart. You and I both know you don't need to use drugs to enhance the experience. Let's cut the crap and both agree to use our attunements to heighten each other's sense of touch.'

I gaped at him in wide-eyed wonder.

He feigned shock. 'Wait? Didn't you know I'm magical too?' Dropping his extremely powerful glamour, he revealed himself as a dark elf. He sauntered forward.

'Um, I think I should go.' I tried backing away, but my legs hit the bed.

'There's no way you're gonna leave this room tonight, baby. Not after getting me all hot and hard.' He pounced on me, pinning me to the bed with his muscular frame.

When I screamed, he muffled my cries with his vile mouth. But common sense, or perhaps it was my survival instinct, kicked in and I realised it was in my best interest to play along. Letting him think I was enjoying the way he defiled my body would ensure my freedom afterwards.

That was exactly how it played out, and as he dozed beside me in bed, I stuck him with the needle. I used my

organic attunements to increase the rate of uptake. As soon
as I was sure of his demise, I dressed and slipped away.

The story horrified Tyler. Knowing the lengths she had gone to churned his nauseous gut. 'Did you end up using sex to get to the other guys you assassinated?'

'A few, but not the majority.'

Jaxon's furrowed brow suggested equal displeasure. 'Did your employer know Mr. Short was a dark elf?'

'He denied all knowledge, but I suspect he, or at least someone in the Cult knew.'

'What makes you think that?'

A smug grin took over Samantha's visage. 'Because every other man I killed was a magical disguising themselves as human.'

Feeling parched and famished from hours of sex, Brendan made his way to the kitchen. After turning on the light, he dashed for the fridge and grabbed the orange juice. When he spun toward the breakfast bar, he didn't expect to see anyone sitting at it. 'Christ! What the hell man?'

Caleb sat alone, sipping from a whiskey glass, and glaring at Brendan.

'Why are you drinking alone in the dark?'

'Why are you always banging my sister?'

He chugged a mouthful of juice from the carton and slammed it on the bench. 'Is that what this is all about? A pity party because you can no longer have your own sick way with her whenever you want? I don't get you, man. Since when did you go from being Bridey's biggest hater to the president of her goddamn fan club?'

Caleb rose and faced off against him. 'Shut your mouth, Winters. You have no idea what you're talking about.'

'No? So, you're not jealous because I get to fuck Bridey more than you?'

Seething rage boiled in Caleb's features. *'I. Said. Shut. Up!'* He attempted to shove Brendan back. But the effect was almost comical given their size difference. The scrawny goth had nothing on Brendan's build of pure muscle. Caleb did not appear to care.

Brendan was getting sick of Caleb's attitude, especially since it wasn't like Brendan had a lot of choice when it came to Bridey. 'Or what? You'll hit me? Go for it, Thornsy. Take your best shot, you filthy sister-fucker.'

Caleb's right fist collided with Brendan's left cheek, immediately followed by a left hook to the jaw.

Brendan staggered, shocked at the force behind Caleb's punch. Slamming into his opponent, he decked Caleb and followed up by pinning him to the floor. 'Why did you follow her, Thornsy? You had your chance at freedom and squandered it.' He became vaguely aware of footsteps running throughout the house.

'You don't get it, do you?' Caleb spat. 'I was never her slave. I sought Bridey out willingly. I don't just love my sister. I'm in love with her.'

A gasp drew Brendan's attention to the doorway and a shocked Bridey. 'Step back, slave.' As soon as he rose, she ran to Caleb and pulled him up and into her arms. 'Oh Gods, are you okay, sweetie?' She studied Caleb's black eye. 'Levi, get Marcus.'

Levi's gentle reply of 'Yes, Madame,' came from the hall as he retreated.

Bridey turned a lethal gaze on Brendan. 'What the hell is wrong with you?'

'Your brother's attitude problem, that's what.'

'Have you forgotten your place, slave? You must never raise a hand against me or mine.'

Caleb wore a satisfied smirk for all of one second before Bridey turned back to him — then he gave her an apologetic expression. 'I'm sorry, Bry. I lost my shit when he called me a *filthy sister-fucker*.'

Again, she turned the stink eye on Brendan. 'Did you really insult my dear boy with such putrid language?'

This was ridiculous. He felt like he was back in primary school. 'Yes.'

'Yes what?'

'Yes, Madame.'

Marcus rushed into the room a moment later and got to work on healing Caleb's injuries.

'So, you provoked him?'

Brendan threw up his hands in a defensive stance. 'Oh, you want to play the blame game? Caleb's unhinged because of you and I'm at the end of my own damn tether because of Alannah. It all comes back to you bitches.'

She stormed across the room and slapped him hard across the bruised cheek.

It hurt like hell, but Brendan was beyond caring.

'Levi, lock Brendan in the dungeon for the rest of the night.' Her eyes narrowed on Brendan. 'Perhaps some solitary confinement will help you cool off.'

A set of large hands grabbed Brendan and led him away. He did not worry at first because he expected to see more of a BDSM playroom. While he was not wrong about the room's intended purpose, there was more of a medieval torture chamber aesthetic to the place. Numerous sets of cold iron chains dangled from the stone walls, a steel spanking bench sat to the right, and a wooden cross to the left. There were no soft furnishings or silken ropes in sight. *Bridey likes to play extremely rough. No surprises there.* He turned to face Levi, who was tying him to the St. Andrew's Cross. 'Is this where she flogs you?'

'In theory. She hasn't touched me since we moved here.'

'Don't tell me you're envious too?'

Levi scowled at him. 'Do you realise she hasn't spent time with any of us lately? Lady Violet has focussed one-hundred percent of her attention on you.'

'That's not true. She's been working.'

'With *you*.'

Brendan bit his lip. There was no point arguing.

'At first I thought I'd outgrown my use because her sadistic streak had gone. But now it seems you'll replace me there too.'

His pulse was racing, and a cold sweat dripped from his brow. 'What do you mean?'

Levi ignored him as he continued securing the bonds. He walked to the exit, pausing to look over his shoulder. 'Enjoy your flogging, Brendan.' He flipped the light switch and closed the door.

The room plunged into complete darkness. Brendan had never experienced pure pitch black before. Not even living in the country, away from the light pollution of the city, had prepared him for this. At least there had been the moon and stars back then. This sealed underground chamber did not allow a crack of light to enter from the rest of the house, too dim even for a single shadow. Every creak and groan in the building's foundations stole his breath. Each sound toyed with his wild imagination. Living in a world of magic—knowing ghosts, ghouls, and demons were real—only enhanced his fear during the bleak solitude. Pushing anxiety aside, he calmed his breathing and attempted sleep.

As with any night when he closed his eyes, his thoughts returned to Alannah. He missed her more than ever, craving the feel of her soft skin, her strawberry-scented hair, the sound of her laugh, and the look of desire in her eyes. Not to mention her sweet, musky taste. He loved the way she tingled on his tongue. *If I ever get the chance again, I swear to the Gods I will feast upon you, Lana.*

Memories of all the intimate times they had shared came flooding back, making him stiff as a board with no means of relief. Ironic how Bridey was not the instigator of his true torture.

With a grunt, Tyler startled himself awake. 'Shit! I must have dozed off. Sorry guys.'

'Sleep well?' Samantha's voice sounded close. Too close.

As awareness of his position set in, he realised where his subconscious had decided to rest his head. *Those soft things aren't cushions, are they?* Jolting upright on the couch, he blinked and gave her a sheepish smile. 'Sorry.'

'Trust me, sweetness, if it bothered me, I would have moved.' She brought her thumb up to his chin and wiped at something. 'You were drooling.'

A brief inspection revealed a wet patch on her top turning the white fabric even more transparent. Mesmerised, the crick in Tyler's neck ceased to worry him, no longer the stiffest part of his body.

'Oh good, Quirky's awake.' Jaxon entered the room with a coffee in hand.

'I'm gonna grab myself one of those.' He dashed into the kitchen and took his time fixing a drink. Glancing at his watch, he noticed it was 3AM. *Have they been up working all this time?*

After a few deep breaths, Tyler returned to the living room. 'Woah!' The number of police files littering the floor had more than doubled since he nodded off.

'Walshy printed out the last one.' Jaxon placed the profile at the end of the bottom row.

'Where is he now?'

'Turned in for the night. Unlike some members of the team, he's been awake this whole time.'

Tyler gave Jaxon a guilty grin. 'Did he do a stat analysis for us first?'

'Here.' Jaxon shoved the report in his face.

He took it and sat on an armchair to maintain necessary distance from Samantha. Sipping on his coffee, Tyler flicked through the summary. *Christ!* She had killed fifteen men in two years: two dark elves, seven endarkened, two goblins, two ogres, one dark mage, and a gorgon. But no obvious patterns. 'A gorgon? Wow, I didn't think we had many of those in Sydney.'

'You'd be surprised,' replied Samantha.

'Please tell me you didn't sleep with'—he checked the gorgon's name—'Mr. Ambrose.'

She bit her lip, telling him all he needed to know.

Images of her blindfolded and tied up in a dark dungeon filled his mind. 'Fuck!'

Samantha laughed. 'Don't worry. It was actually a pretty wild night.' When her gaze met his, her eyes widened and her mouth formed an 'O.' 'You weren't worried, were you?'

Holding his breath, he shook his head.

'Oh my. I knew there was a reason I felt drawn to you.'

'Quirky!' Jaxon broke their heated stare. 'Get over here.' He handed Tyler a marker. 'Make yourself useful.'

'Ouch, boss.'

Jaxon ignored his comment as he moved between the files. 'What do all these guys have in common? Why did the cult target them?'

'You mean aside from them all being magical?'

'There has to be more to it, but you may as well list it.'

Tyler stepped up to the large whiteboard mounted on the wall and wrote MAGICAL in big bold letters, along with the other obvious factor: MALES. 'Well, they're all criminals.'

'Uh huh.' Jaxon's gaze drifted far away.

'I guess by extension they would all be dark. The two goblins are the only possible anomaly there, but if they were crooks—'

'Samantha, do you know if those goblins had black souls?' Jaxon cut Tyler off.

She shrugged. 'I don't know for sure, but they were scumbags, so I wouldn't put it past them.'

Tyler added MALEVOLENT and MURKY SOULS to the list. 'Sam, you mentioned these guys were all disguised as humans. What exactly did you mean?'

'Well, they used strong glamour, making it hard for other magicals to detect their true nature. They weren't registered with the Council either.'

MASKED and MISCREANTS.

'Ho-ly shit!' Jaxon exclaimed as he rushed from one file to the next.

'What is it, boss?'

Jaxon fell silent while he continued checking the facts. When the Inspector looked up, his expression cried Eureka! 'They were all suspects for murders committed shortly before Samantha killed them.' His focus shifted to Samantha. 'You might have been the clean-up crew.'

Tyler wrote MURDER SUSPECTS, pleased he was able to use another M word.

When Jaxon looked at the board, he rolled his eyes. 'On that note, I'm gonna call it a night. Quirky, I want you to pull up everything in the system on the murder cases these guys were linked to. Tomorrow we will compile and compare the data.'

'Sure thing.' Tyler followed Jaxon upstairs, veering right to enter the office.

As he sat down at the computer desk, Samantha drew close, placing her hands on his shoulders. 'What can I do to help?' She began to massage him.

Tyler sucked in a deep breath. 'As enjoyable as that feels, Sam, it's a serious distraction.'

'Um… sorry.' She sat on the chair next to him with an expectant look.

'Maybe you should get some sleep. You must be exhausted.'

'Nah, I'm good.'

'Okay, fine. You can take notes for me. Fire up that laptop and open a new spreadsheet. Title the columns: name, age, race, gender, home, and cause of death.'

Samantha gave him a blank look.

'What?'

'I uh, don't know how to do any of that.'

'Seriously?' He felt his mouth gaping open.

'I dropped out of school at the age of thirteen. I haven't used a computer since year seven, and even then, I sucked at it.'

'Oh. Can you write with a pen?'

'Yeah.'

He grabbed a notebook and drew the table up for her. 'Here, jot the notes on this.'

'Thanks.'

He grabbed the summary file and entered the first name into the police database, which linked directly to a murder case. 'Jannette Dawson, sixteen-year-old human girl from Surry Hills. Cause of death was exsanguination resulting from sharp force trauma to the carotid artery.'

'Ah, what does that mean?'

Tyler sighed, gaining a new appreciation for his competent colleagues. 'Blood loss, neck wound.'

'Okay, got it.'

He eyed her sceptically before glancing at the page. Surprisingly, her writing was neat, and all the information was there, although she had used the astrological gender symbol, and the cause of death was a drawing of a neck with blood dripping from it.

'Artist, remember?'

His gaze shifted to the ink on her chest before meeting her eyes. 'How could I forget?'

She grinned knowingly.

Tearing his eyes away from her, Tyler returned his attention to the screen. After hitting PRINT on the case file, he punched in the name of the next suspect. 'This time we have Sarah Woods, another human girl, aged fourteen, from Parramatta. Same cause of death.'

As they continued compiling the details, the link became obvious. 'They're all teenage girls who died in the same way. Tying them all to different suspects is what kept the human police from calling it a serial killing. I wonder why the Cult picked these girls.'

'Seems obvious to me.' Samantha was leaning back with her bare feet propped up on the desk. 'They were used for blood magic and if I were to hazard a guess, I'd put money on their virgin status. Human virgin blood is a lot more potent than lamb's blood.'

Hot damn! Her smarts made him ache for her even more. 'Question is, were those men trying to hide like you, or were they performing a ritual for the Cult?'

Bright light washed over Brendan, forcing him to squint. After blinking a few times, his eyes adjusted to the new luminescence.

'Tsk, tsk. You've been fantasising about her again. You ought to stop tormenting yourself.' Bridey stood before him holding a cat o' nine tails.

Shit! Levi had been right. 'Are you going to beat me now, Madame?'

Stepping close, she stripped him, freeing the erection from the confines of his pants and gripping it firmly. 'Would you like a flogging, slave?'

He sucked in a sharp breath, savouring the way she enveloped his dick in her warmth. 'W… what kind of a question is that?'

'A simple one. Would you like to meet the cat?' She moved back, releasing her hold of him.

Brendan's eyes widened as he shook his head adamantly. 'No, Madame.'

'No? What a shame.' With a sudden flick of her wrist, she struck him across the chest.

'*Ah, fuck!*' His skin burned from the whip's sting.

Bridey's grin turned malicious, reminding him of all the reasons he despised her. 'I thought you enjoyed receiving pain as much as you loved giving it.'

'Not *that* much pain,' he rasped.

'You know the deal, handsome.' Her hand returned to squeezing him. 'Sink into it.'

Her behaviour would disgust Brendan's kinkster friends. There was nothing sane, safe, or consensual about Bridey. The woman was a deviant who subscribed to the old libertine way of life, and she gave the Marquis de Sade a run for his money. *Was it any wonder the original sadist was also endarkened?*

Crack! Another blow, this time to his stomach.

A guttural cry escaped him. This time Brendan closed his eyes to regulate his breathing. His arousal was waning, but Bridey's hand brought it back with a vengeance mere seconds before punishing his left thigh. *At least the pain is more tolerable this time.* As Bridey oscillated between hurting and pleasuring him, the sensations merged, and he felt himself slipping into a euphoric trance.

When lucidity returned, Marcus was dressing the wounds left by the lashings. A quick glimpse of his surroundings told him they were on his own bed. Bridey sat on the edge of the mattress, half a metre from him, looking pleased with herself. The rest of the slaves stood around the room like silent sentinels mocking his stupidity.

Caleb was there too, front and centre with a smirk showing how much he was revelling in Brendan's humiliation. 'It doesn't pay to anger my sister.'

The left side of his lip curled up. 'Depends who you ask. I think I understand what Levi sees in her now. And it looks like I found another way to please my mistress.'

'Fuck you, Winters!' Caleb charged at him, pinning his throat in a choke hold.

'*Caleb!*' Bridey screamed. 'Stop it.'

He pulled his hand back, but Caleb still towered over Brendan with a menacing glare.

Once Marcus finished, Bridey drew closer. 'This feud needs to end. Right. Now.'

'Like it's that easy, Bry.' Caleb gave her an incredulous look.

'Sure it is. The two of you used to be friends. You need to kiss and make up.'

Oh hell.

'What are you suggesting?' Caleb asked.

Bridey sat back and crossed her arms with wicked intent in her eyes.

Caleb paled. 'You didn't mean literally, did you?'

She nodded. 'You are both harbouring a lot of aggression and animosity for one another. I want to see the pair of you fuck the hostility out of each other.'

'No way.' Caleb began backing away from the bed.

'Don't make me compel you sweetie.'

'Are you going to compel him too?' His arm flung toward Brendan. 'Because I doubt he wants this either.'

Bridey stood in front of Caleb. 'I don't need to because, unlike you, Brendan submits to *all* my requests.'

Caleb hissed but stood his ground.

Mounting Brendan, Bridey kissed him, flooding his senses with her strong, feminine power. She paused. 'Slaves, don't let Caleb leave.'

Brendan peeked over Bridey's shoulder and saw Caleb attempting an escape. But Bridey claimed his mouth again, stealing all his attention. The way she devoured him while her fingers toyed with all the sensitive parts of his body drove him to distraction.

A moment later he was inside her and she employed the reverse cowgirl position. 'Come to me, Caleb.'

When Caleb wavered, Levi pushed him forward. He reluctantly crossed the remaining distance.

'Strip for me please, sweetheart.' Bridey spoke with a soft, pleading tone as she continued to grind against Brendan.

Much to Brendan's surprise, Caleb complied, removing his black mesh top, and inching off the leather pants.

'Now kiss me.'

This time there was no hesitation when Caleb straddled Brendan's thighs to reach Bridey.

Brendan closed his eyes to avoid watching the siblings sucking face. Instead, he focused on probing Bridey's welcoming depths. He felt disappointed when she retreated. But the weight of a warm body filled the void and soft lips crashed against his. They could have belonged to a woman's mouth except the piercings gave their owner's identity away. His eyes shot open in shock and met with Caleb's.

Pure desire sizzled in Caleb's aura. 'Can we please get this over with? And don't get any funny ideas, 'cause I'm only doing this for Bridey.'

'Fine.' He closed his eyes and let Caleb kiss him again. Without thinking, Brendan channelled his attunements, heightening what they felt.

Before long they were both moaning as they writhed together. The noise was like an alarm sounding in Brendan's brain as realisation hit him. The experience was a huge turn on, and upon inspection, it fuelled Caleb's lust too.

'Turn over so I can fuck you.' Caleb issued the order in a breathy voice.

Why did that have to sound so damn hot? Brendan obeyed without a second thought. The next surprise came when he discovered surrendering to Caleb's sodomy felt better than sex with Bridey.

Chapter Eight

The room was peaceful, dimly lit by the afternoon sun peeking around the velvet curtains. The only movements were the rise and fall of two breathing chests; the only sounds were the breaths escaping their mouths. Brendan felt grateful Bridey had chosen to give the guys some privacy in the end. Shifting onto his side, he took a moment to gaze upon Caleb, who had closed his eyes. 'Hey, are you sleeping?' He kept his voice to a low whisper.

'No,' Caleb replied without opening his eyes.

'Do you still hate me?'

Caleb sighed, pausing before he answered, 'No. Do you? Hate me, I mean?'

Well, I'll be damned. Bridey's insane plan worked. 'No.'

His eyes fluttered open, and his head turned to face Brendan. 'So what… does this mean we're friends again?'

'If you want. I never had a problem with *you*. It was your attitude getting on my nerves.'

'Fair point.' Caleb snorted. 'I dunno about being friends after that, though. Every time you talk, I'm gonna remember your girly pleas for me to go harder.'

Brendan punched him playfully in the arm. 'Come on, man. You loved it as much as I did.'

'Shut up, Winters.'

He could not hold back the chuckle. 'Not until you admit how much you love my arse.'

'Not gonna happen.' Caleb wore a smirk big enough to cover his naked body.

A body Brendan felt strangely attracted to. *Men didn't turn me on before. Why now? What's changed?* He leaped at Caleb and tackled him.

They both laughed as they grappled each other. Inevitably, Brendan won their wrestling match, pinning Caleb to the mattress. As he looked down upon his goth friend, the humour between them escalated to heated desire. The bright red lust flickering in Caleb's aura was beckoning him. *Is this really what I want?* Typically, he let his hard dick answer as his lips pressed against Caleb's.

When his arousal turned into a savage need, Brendan growled into Caleb's ear before asserting himself in a gruff voice. 'Now it's my turn on top.'

Caleb's eyes shot wide open, but he nodded. 'Please go easy on me. I've never… you know?'

Gods! Caleb is an anal virgin, yet he is offering himself to me! The thought alone drove Brendan wild. 'I understand. Let me know if you need me to stop at any stage.'

'Will do.'

Brendan sat back, allowing Caleb to move into position as he grabbed the lube. When his attention returned to the naked man before him, the resemblance between Caleb and Bridey's bodies astounded Brendan. *Especially from this vantage point.* With long black hair cascading down the silvery skin of his narrow shoulders and back, even his arse was small like hers; although it had a firmer, more masculine shape to it. 'Gosh, you look pretty, Thornsy.'

'Shut up and fuck me already.' His body trembled.

Floored by Caleb's nerves combined with willing desire, Brendan pressed his chest against Caleb's back, embracing him from behind. He trailed kisses up Caleb's right shoulder blade before sinking his teeth into the shoulder itself.

Caleb groaned as his body bucked against Brendan.

Fire ignited between Brendan's legs, prompting him to pop the cap on the tube he was holding. He lathered the stuff liberally along his shaft and over Caleb's tight little hole, before testing the waters with a single finger.

Caleb moaned.

'How does this feel?'

'Awesome. Truly fucking awesome.'

He continued working Caleb up to the moment of truth. Reaching around, he gripped Caleb's cock before plunging his own deep inside him. 'Does it still feel good?'

'Gods yes!'

Confident Caleb was not about to cry out in pain, Brendan let himself get lost in the pleasure until their bodies collapsed together.

Once he had caught his breath, Caleb cracked up laughing.

Brendan smiled, trying to stifle his own laugh. 'What?'

'I doubt Bridey banked on this.'

'This?'

'Us. Enjoying the sex. I wonder if it screws with her plans.'

'You know, I suspect we are right where she wants us. Think about the times she pushed for a threesome with us. Plus, there's the way she's been grooming me for anal.'

Caleb snuggled up against Brendan's side and eyed him warily. 'Are you telling me you'll only want more sex with me if it's on *her* terms?'

'No, but….' His arm instinctively came up to encircle Caleb's back and his fingers entwined with his long locks. 'You know I don't have a lot of say with your sister. I'm still her slave.'

'See, I think you're wrong. Officially, you might be her slave, but you are the only member of The Seven who chose servitude. And you're one of few men she has seduced without using magic. In fact, she hasn't *ever* compelled you.'

Pressing his hand against Caleb's back, Brendan froze. 'Shit! It can't be true, surely? What about….'

'Ben and Nick? She admitted to using magic to charm them before telling me you were… special.'

The jealousy Caleb had exuded began making more sense to Brendan. 'Special?'

'Yeah. I think she has genuine feelings for you. Given that, I bet you have more power in your relationship with her than you realise.'

'I never thought of it like that.' Grinning, Brendan contemplated the ways he could use those feelings to his advantage.

Samantha had gone back to haunting Tyler's dreams again. Vivid images of the fiery redhead submitting to him filled his mind even as he woke in a searing, sticky haze. He failed at all attempts to throw back the bedding until he was cognizant enough to realise his legs had tangled in the sheets.

The Sydney sun blazed through the sheer white curtains, but it did not bother him half as much as the humidity. The stifling atmosphere already made him miss Broken Hill's hot, dry summers. After flicking on the air conditioner, he slipped on his thinnest robe and headed to the bathroom.

Still in a bit of daze, he locked the door behind him and let the robe fall to the floor before pulling back the shower curtain. *Christ! Am I still dreaming?*

Her naked body stood before him with droplets of water trickling down her chest and beading on her strawberry buds. 'If I knew you were planning to join me, I would have waited. Although, I don't mind showering again if it means getting wet with you.' Samantha's deep, husky voice broke his trance.

'Shit! Sorry. I didn't know you were in here.' Tyler stepped back, reaching for a towel.

But she charged into him, wrapping her arms around him, and bringing her bare skin flush against his. 'Honestly, Tyler? When are you going to stop denying the chemistry between us?'

Storm clouds gathered in and around his head as he glared at her. 'I'm not denying anything, Samantha. I'm just not acting on my desires.'

'Why not? Can't you see how much I want you?' One of her hands travelled down his back and cupped his left arse cheek.

The breath he released through his clenched teeth sounded like a snake hissing. 'You know why. Or have you forgotten the boss' rules? If anything happens between us, they'll take me off this case. My job is also at risk.'

A finger on her other hand skimmed along his waist, covering his flesh in goosebumps. 'Only if we get caught. I'm an expert at evading the authorities when I want to.' Stepping back, she tugged at his hand before retreating into the tiled alcove. 'Come on, Tyler. Stop agonising over the rules and take what you want for a change.' She turned the water back on, all while keeping her eyes locked on him.

He should have seized the opportunity to get the hell out of there. But there was something mesmerising about the sight of the water gushing down over her. *You need to leave, you idiot. Like. Right. Now.*

'What are you waiting for, sweetness?'

He went to turn away.

…

But he did not.

…

Because his feet, along with the rest of his body, betrayed him. He crashed into her, pinning her to the wall with his bodyweight as his mouth devoured her. The kiss was brutal, as were the rough hands gripping her tightly. Even more savage was the way he thrust his cock into her.

She yielded to his touch, gripping him with her tight walls and moaning.

As he came, Tyler unleashed all his pent-up frustration and rage into her. It was the first time he'd experienced angry sex. And as he came down from the high, he felt dirty and ashamed. After a quick rinse under the water, he scowled at Samantha, who was still revelling in her afterglow. 'Happy now?' Grabbing a towel, he made his escape, slamming the door behind him.

Samantha barged into his room. 'What the hell is wrong with you, Tyler?'

I must remember to put a lock on that thing. Tyler huffed. 'What's wrong with *me*? You're the one who seduced me, despite my warnings.'

'Don't project your bullshit on me, sweetheart. You wanted it as much as I did. I'm not an enchantress, Tyler. You exercised free will. Along with some extremely hot muscles, I might add.' She smirked at him.

'You don't even care what this could do to me, to us?'

'I care. I'm just not worried.'

He collapsed on the bed, combing his fingers through his hair. 'I lost control back there, Sam. Didn't I scare you?'

She sat beside him, her hair dripping all over them and the quilt. 'Not at all. I loved it. I'm not a fragile cupcake. I can take everything you dish out and then some. More importantly, I want to.'

'Fuck! Do you understand what you're suggesting?'

'Of course. I can sense darkness deep inside you, Tyler. You don't need to hide your true self from me. Give me all your violence, let me be an outlet for your aggression.' She climbed into his lap.

He stared at her in wide-eyed amazement. 'What if I really hurt you?'

Samantha smiled. 'Kinda the point, hun.'

'No. I mean like serious bodily harm.'

She shrugged. 'I can heal myself with magic. You don't need to worry about boundaries with me. Imagine how liberating it will be.'

He closed his eyes to think carefully about her proposal. It posed a higher risk than the possibility of getting caught with his dick inside her. Yet he could not suppress the urges clawing at his insides, fighting for their chance at freedom. Tyler looked into her eyes. 'Do you honestly want to submit to me with no limits?'

'Yes.' There was no hesitation or doubt in her reply.

Instantly hard, Tyler's eyes narrowed on her. 'I want you to drop to your knees before me.'

And she did.

The way Brendan held him—playing with his hair and caressing his skin—made Caleb feel vulnerable. He didn't like being defenceless, especially with someone who changed partners more often than underwear. But that's how Brendan was with women. *Perhaps he'll treat a man differently, treat* me *differently. Gods! Why am I thinking like this? It was just sex. So what if it was mind-altering and out of this world? It was still just sex.*

Was it though? Caleb couldn't help but wonder why Brendan continued to hug him well after the fact. He tried reminding himself they'd both done this for Bridey: she was the priority here. But it was useless to continue denying the feelings he'd harboured for Brendan all this time.

'Oh hell, Thornsy! Have you honestly been crushing on me for years?'

His breathing quickened as he tried to pull away, but Brendan's strong arms stopped him from moving. Unable to escape, Caleb conceded, wrapping his arms around Brendan. 'Have you been reading my mind this whole time?'

'Hard not to when you're thinking so damn loud. And for the record, I didn't drop every woman I slept with.'

'No? Name one.'

'Alannah.'

'Really? 'Cause from where I was sitting, it looked like you ghosted her big time.'

Brendan's grip on his hair tightened and he tugged at Caleb's scalp producing a delicious sting. 'That's not fair, and you know it. I left because she couldn't keep her hands off Liam. I thought she was the one, Thornsy. Hence the soul link; not that I knew we were making the ultimate commitment at the time, but when I did know, I was all in. I even made attempts to start a family with her during *and* after Beltane.'

'Shit, man! I'm sorry. I had no idea you'd fallen so hard and deep with her.' Caleb relaxed back into Brendan's embrace.

'It doesn't matter now, does it?' The sorrow in Brendan's voice came across loud and clear.

'What if you tried talking to her?'

'I can't. Bridey won't let me contact her. Besides, I made my Gods forsaken bed. Now I gotta lie in it.'

Resenting the implied rejection, Caleb shifted and looked down into Brendan's bright green eyes. 'Are you saying you don't want to be here?'

'Honestly? I didn't at first. But things are more complicated now.'

'Complicated how?'

'Well, there's the job I took on, for one thing. I've become invested in pursuing the secret knowledge Tara was referring to. And now there's you.'

Caleb's heart skipped a beat. 'Don't toy with me, Winters.'

'I'm not. You weren't the only one blown away by the experience we shared, Thornsy. It's been a real eye-opener for me. I've never fancied a dude before. Yet here we are, and I don't feel the least bit uncomfortable. I don't know if it means I've been so deep in the damn closet I got lost in Narnia, or if it's something I only feel with you. Like maybe you're a refuge in the sea of Bridey's madness. Whatever the case may be, I'm thankful for your company.'

He nodded and resumed resting his head on Brendan's chest. A snigger escaped him a second later. 'You think Bridey's crazy?'

'Come on, man, you know her better than anyone. Don't tell me you disagree.'

'I don't. I've always kinda thought it. You don't like her much, do you?'

Brendan took a deep breath and held it in his lungs.

'Don't worry. The truth won't offend me and I sure as hell won't tell her.'

He exhaled audibly. 'Sorry, bro, but I despise the bitch.'

'If that's the case, why do you do everything she asks without her compelling you?'

'I'm terrified of what she'll do to me and those I care about.'

Caleb sighed. 'I'm sorry.'

'What for? It's not like you have any control over her behaviour.'

'I know. But she's still family and I can't help but feel partially responsible. I'm also sorry for my irrational jealousy.'

Brendan's hand went back to playing with his hair and stroking his back. 'Don't sweat it, Thornsy. It wasn't irrational when you thought things were serious between me and her, or when you thought I was acting with complete free will. What is illogical is what you feel for her. Are you seriously in love with the whack job?'

'I know it's absurd, but yeah. She got under my skin when I was young. I never told you the full story of my childhood, or the relationship I shared with Bridey. The two of us were extremely tight before Mum took me away. Things weren't always sexual, either. But when my wet dreams and fantasies started, she was the object of every one of them.'

He froze. 'Christ! Are you saying you wanted her to rape you?'

'Yes and no. When she tried to seduce me, I was petrified; not of her, but of what I felt for her and the wrongness of it all. That's why she compelled me. I still hadn't come to terms with my feelings at the time and resented her for forcing herself on me.'

'Understandable.' His petting continued.

'I didn't get over the incest factor until the recent period of separation from her, when I had time to think. Honestly, I'm now more bothered by the fact she keeps sex slaves.'

'Well, the slavery thing *is* pretty disturbing. Is there anything you can do to set them free?'

'Believe me, I've tried talking her into letting them go. But she wouldn't budge on the issue. I even threatened to aid in their escape, but she only laughed at me, claiming she'd find a new Seven after Dad's thugs hunted down and killed the others.'

'Oh hell!'

'My thoughts exactly. So, in the interest of their safety and my own sanity, I leave well enough alone on the topic.'

'I'm almost afraid to ask, but what fate befell my predecessor?'

'Oh, she's still around, she just doesn't get counted among The Seven anymore.'

Brendan surged upright, resting against the headboard. 'She? Do you mean the maid?'

'Yeah. Isabelle was her first slave. She was a gift from Dad whose company deals in people trafficking, among other horrors.' Feeling the urge to kiss Brendan's gaping jaw, Caleb straddled him and claimed his mouth.

A familiar laugh sounded from the doorway. 'Are the two of you still going at it? I guess it's fair to assume you have resolved your issues with each other, yes?' Bridey stepped up beside the bed and placed a hand on Caleb's shoulder. 'I hate to interrupt such fun. In fact, I wish I could join in, but we have an important dinner meeting. I need both of you to shower and suit up.'

Caleb groaned. 'Suits? Seriously? What sort of meeting is it?'

'Syndicate business. And I need both of my captains looking sharp.' She left the room.

Reluctantly, he tore himself away from Brendan and rose to his feet.

Brendan followed, making his way to the ensuite bathroom. Pausing at the door, he turned and grinned lasciviously. 'Wanna join me in the shower?'

Joy mixed with desire rushed through every one of Caleb's blood vessels. 'Hell yes.'

Dressed in black Armani, walking alongside Caleb who wore the same, Brendan felt like he had stepped off the set of a *Men in Black* film.

Caleb's mind wandered elsewhere though, as he kept stealing glances. *'Why does he have to look so fucking sexy in that suit?'*

Brendan grinned at his new lover and spoke telepathically. *'Would you rather I wear nothing?'*

'I'm trying to focus on business, Winters!'

'Hey, I can't help it if I'm too sexy for my clothes.' Brendan smiled to himself. *Damn, it feels good to joke around and flirt again.*

Caleb groaned. *'If I soil this suit, I'll make you clean it by hand.'*

Brendan laughed as they entered the dining room, but his humour faded as soon as he spotted their guests.

Bridey remained seated at the table. 'Ah, Jet, I assume you remember Damien and Melanie?'

Rising from her chair, Melanie beamed at the sight of him. 'Hi, handsome.'

After closing the distance, Brendan took her hand and kissed her knuckles. 'It is a pleasure to see you again, My Lady.'

And… cue the giggles. 'Oh, please Jet, you don't need to act formal when I know what an animal you are in bed.'

Caleb choked on his snigger.

All eyes cut to him.

'Oh dear, sweetheart. Are you okay?' Bridey approached her brother.

'Yes, sorry Madame. Something got stuck in my throat.'

With her arm around Caleb, Bridey glanced back to the pair of dark mages. 'I'd like to introduce Stirling, another of my captains.'

Damien stood to shake Caleb's hand. 'Any relation to Lady Violet here? You look alike.'

'Yes we're—'

'Cousins.' Bridey broke in. 'First cousins on my mother's side.'

Interesting. Why is she concealing their true relationship?

Brendan exchanged a look with Caleb who answered with his thoughts: '*She probably intends to jump my bones in front of them.*'

Something did not add up though. '*I can't imagine incest turning these guys off. They're as deviant as Bridey, possibly more,*' Brendan replied telepathically.

Melanie took Caleb's hand and batted her eyelashes at him. 'It is a pleasure to meet you, Lord Stirling.'

'*Ick, Winters, I can't believe you fucked this chick.*'

'*You make it sound like I had a choice.*'

They all settled in for drinks and appetisers, with Brendan and Caleb flanking Bridey.

Damien watched Isabelle with a lecherous eye as she delivered dishes to the table. 'Your hospitality is exceptional,

Lady Violet. I do hope you have another wild night of debauchery planned for us this evening.'

'It's certainly on the cards, but I thought we should discuss business first.'

Licking his lips, Damien reluctantly returned his attention to Bridey. 'Oh? What did you have in mind?'

'I represent an organisation that wants to connect with yours.'

Damien's brows bounced off his hairline. 'You work in the meat industry?'

Bridey laughed. 'Don't play coy with me, sweetheart. I'm not talking about your corporate front. I refer to your dark mage cult.'

A stern frown crept across Damien's features. 'I don't know what you're talking about.'

'Plausible deniability—I get it. But you forget we run in the same circles, Damien. Plus, my father is also a Cult member.' The sound of her biting into a carrot stick filled the ensuing silence.

'What's your father's name?' Damien eventually asked.

'Maurus Hawthorn.'

Damien's eyes bugged out. 'You're Lord Hawthorn's daughter?'

Bridey's eyes gleamed wickedly. 'That's what I said, yes.'

'I thought his kids were dark mages too. I didn't realise the old cad bedded an elf.'

'Daddy prefers to keep his family life private, so it's no wonder you didn't have your facts straight.'

Caleb coughed again.

She shot him a warning look. 'Isabelle, darling. Would you get Sterling some water?'

'Certainly, Madame.' The maid poured Caleb a drink from a crystal decanter.

'Do you understand I'll need a show of good faith before we forge any sort of allegiance?' Damien continued.

'Of course. I will also require something of you.'

'Such as?'

'Jet here wants someone to school him in the dark arts. It would give me immense pleasure if you would take my beloved under your wing.'

'The fuck?' Caleb's thought screamed at Brendan.

Damien looked extremely pleased by the prospect. 'Is that so, Jet?'

'Yes, sir. I've only had a chance to dabble thus far and now I have a thirst for more.'

'He speaks the truth, honey,' explained Melanie. 'I have glimpsed his tainted soul.'

'Very well. I am willing to bring Jet into the fold. But I also have a job for you, Lady Violet.'

'Go on.' Bridey gestured with her delicate fingers before daintily bringing an hors d'oeuvre to her lips.

Unless they knew her like I did, most people would have a hard time imagining the brutal force those hands were capable of.

'A client of mine requires an artifact that is currently locked up tight in the Ancient Egyptian collection of The Australian Museum. I want you to retrieve this item for me.'

'And what is this treasure you seek?'

'A lazurite scarab. You are welcome to anything else you find in the collection.'

Bridey leaned over the table, letting her breasts fall free from their cage of corsetry. 'A generous offer. Consider the job done.'

Damien's eyes glued themselves to her chest as he sipped his sherry. The way he fell for her feminine charms was almost laughable, but Brendan remembered being in the same boat when he had first met the enchantress. Damien tipped his glass to her. 'I am pleased to hear it, My Lady. When can I expect my delivery?'

'I will require some time to plan a job this big. And my organisation is having a leadership conference in a few days. I'll need at least two weeks to pull it off, possibly three.'

The letch licked his lips. 'Marvellous. I look forward to working more *closely* with you.' He turned to face Brendan. 'As I'm sure my wife looks forward to working with you, Jet.'

Brendan employed his most charming smile. 'Indeed, sir. When can I start my training?'

'Tomorrow night if Lady Violet can spare you for a few hours.'

Bridey leaned into her brother and ran her hand along his arm. 'It's true I'll miss him, but I'm sure Sterling will happily keep me company in Jet's absence.'

'I'm sure he will.' Damien winked at Caleb.

After several courses and a lot of dull small talk, the meal was wrapping up. Isabelle was collecting the empty plates. As she reached for Damien's, he groped her arse. Shock registered in her expression, but she hid her surprise well and kept a firm grip of the crockery.

'Isabelle, darling, why don't you leave those for now and show our guests to their room?' Bridey grinned knowingly at Damien. 'Please make yourselves quite at home and my captains and I will join you shortly.'

'Thank you, Madame.' Damien rose, along with Melanie, and eagerly followed the maid.

As soon as the dark mages were out of earshot, Caleb turned to Brendan and chided him in a hushed voice, 'Are you insane, Winters? Do you have any idea what you're signing up for with those guys?'

'Relax, Thornsy. This is our best way to get someone on the inside. I know what I'm doing,' replied Brendan in a whisper.

Bridey placed a reassuring hand on Caleb's shoulder. 'He's right, sweetheart. Brendan is smart. You don't need to worry about him.'

Caleb looked sternly at Brendan. *'I hope you don't do irreparable damage to your soul.'*

Chapter Nine

Awareness of someone beside him woke Brendan from his slumber. The silk sheets caressed his bare skin as he stirred, and he savoured the comfort of his soft bed. *I could get used to such luxuries.* He opened his eyes, hoping for the brother, but the sister greeted him.

'So? How'd last night go?' Bridey asked in a shrill voice he might have expected from a cheerleader but not from his criminal mistress.

He groaned. 'What time is it?'

'Nine.'

'Christ! I haven't even had six hours of sleep yet and you're already hounding me about work?'

Her hand slid down his bare torso. 'Would you rather play first?'

'As a general rule, I always prefer playtime.'

With a delighted laugh, Bridey pulled back the covers and grabbed his morning wood. 'Give me the cliff notes and I'll make it worth your while.'

With a sigh, Brendan cast his mind back to his training session with Melanie and Damien. 'Not much to report. It was mostly an initiation ceremony where I got to meet a few other cultists. They were all pleasantly surprised to see me there.'

'Initiation? Already?'

'Of course. They needed to open me up to the Stygian element before I could start my practical training.'

'I figured they'd start with theory.'

He shook his head. 'They use a congruent approach.'

'Curious.' Bridey lurched forward and sat astride him. 'That's enough business for now, don't you think?'

It often amazed Brendan how a woman he detested could bring him such incredible pleasure. *I must be even better at compartmentalising my emotions these days, and there's no denying her beauty.* Especially not as she rocked back and forth in a slow, gentle rhythm, her chest bouncing. Or with the look of pure joy painted on her face as she took him deep inside, surrounding him with her soft, silky warmth.

As their mutual desire mounted, the most erotic moaning noises escaped her throat. 'Enchant me, handsome. I want to feel your magic.'

Brendan froze. He did not use his magic on Bridey because he did not want her to channel him at the same time. The last time he did so with a woman had ended in disaster.

'Relax, sweetheart. I promise I won't go linking our souls. I want to know what it feels like to be on the receiving end for a change.'

'Okay, fine.' Flipping Bridey onto her back, he took charge. He needed full sensory awareness, which he could only achieve when he was in control. Brendan commenced with touch, tuning into the feel of her soft skin beneath his fingertips. As he tapped into the power, he amplified the sensation.

'Oh my.' Her breathing became heavier, her moans raspier.

'I've only just started, Madame.' Sound and sight came next. He focussed on the orgasmic grunts and whimpers escaping her throat and the way her gorgeous body jolted as he thrust his fingers inside her, letting the magic flow through him and into her.

Welcoming her natural, floral aroma in his nostrils, he dove between her legs and tasted her tangy juices. *Gods! I could get addicted to this flavour.* Brendan feasted on her, bringing forth countless waves of her ecstasy and lapping them up like a thirsty dog.

Finally, he channelled her emotions: lust and… *Oh shit! No way! Surely she's projecting what she feels for Thornsy.* Pushing the bombshell aside, he concentrated on her carnal hunger, letting it fuel his own arousal as he drove himself into her.

A bright flash behind his eyes blinded him as they exploded together, then darkness took him into a semi-conscious state of euphoria.

Bridey wrapped herself around Brendan when he stirred. 'You were spectacular, handsome.' She looked down into his eyes with a peculiar expression.

'What? Why are you looking at me like that?'

She bit her lip and smiled. 'You came back.'

Confused, he looked at her blankly.

'You left the confines of my house without supervision, and you came back to me. You didn't even try to escape.'

Fuck! It did not even occur to Brendan she was not keeping tabs on him when he was out.

'I've become extremely fond of you, Brendan, and I suspect I'm growing on you too.'

No! Please, Gods, no! When Caleb spoke of genuine feelings, Brendan did not think he had meant serious sentiments. He shrugged. 'Perhaps. The sex *is* out of this world.'

'Mm. You're not wrong.' She claimed his lips in a passionate kiss. 'If you keep up this good behaviour, I might end your contract of servitude early.'

Hope surged through him. 'Really?' She nodded. But then suspicion took root. 'Why?'

'Because I think you and I would be great together… as equal partners.'

Brendan's heart sank. She was not talking about true freedom. Not from her.

'I'd even go so far as to put money on the fact that by the time I remove this,' Bridey carefully touched the spikes of his collar, 'you will choose to stay with me.'

Oh hell! You may as well add delusional *to her list of crazy, right alongside* psychopathic. 'You seem sure of yourself, Madame.'

'You doubt my ability to show true affection, don't you?'

'Not as much as my own heart's ability to feel much of anything anymore.' The truth of his own words slapped him hard across the face.

Bridey smiled sympathetically. 'If that's the case, handsome, I'm already halfway there.'

Samantha smiled as she gazed at Tyler dozing beside her. One of his strong, masculine arms draped across her chest, almost pinning her down. In a few hours he would make his exit, usually leaving once she'd drifted off. She understood why he couldn't spend the whole night in her bed—the risk was too high—but waking up alone still sucked.

I'll just make the most of this moment. He was easily the best-looking man she'd ever seduced. *And the sex is unreal!* The last four nights had been the wildest ride of her life, which was saying something for a kinky submissive with her wealth of experience. Their chemistry was off the charts and their relationship had genuine potential, which saddened Samantha because she should *not* fall for this guy.

As her eyelids drooped, Samantha sighed. Staying awake to watch her lover sleep wasn't the only reason she held the Sandman at bay for as long as possible. Her dreams had always disturbed her and ever since she started working for *him*, she dreaded her nightly visions.

But the riptide of fatigue pulled her under, and Samantha soon found herself washed up among some reeds on the banks of the Nile. Kek's intimidating form appeared, greeting her with a rictus grin showing his sharpened teeth. *'Good evening, Samantha. How are things progressing?'*

'I have the warlocks busy following your false leads.'

'Excellent. And the doppelganger? Is he ready?'

'I have unleashed his dark side, as requested.'

The dark elf brought his hand up to her cheek and devoured her with his hungry eyes. *'I have felt much of what he has done to your body, and it has given me great pleasure. You've done exceptionally well, my dear. But do you think he is ready for the next step?'*

The worst thing about dreamscape telepathy? Not being able to lie or suppress one's thoughts from the oneiromancer. She desperately wanted to tell him 'no,' to buy more time. *'Yes. They are already talking about sending someone in undercover.'*

'Good, because we have already recruited the Original. Make sure they send the doppelganger.'

'Yes, sir.'

His arm snaked along Samantha's waist, spinning her around and pressing his body against her back. *'Now get on your hands and knees for me.'* He whispered the order harshly in her ear.

'I don't want to, sir.'

'Oh? So, you want to play that old favourite, hmm?'

Damn it! Why did I ever tell him about those fantasies? 'No. I'm not in the mood.'

'*Well too bad, Samantha.*' He pushed her to the ground.

Her once-clothed body was instantly naked and clambering in the mud of the riverbank.

Kek grabbed a handful of reeds and bundled them into a makeshift whip to flog her.

The blood-curdling cry spewing from her mouth only encouraged him further.

'Sam? Please wake up!'

Samantha crashed back to reality; heart racing and sweat pouring off her as she sat up in bed.

Tyler pulled her into his arms. 'Christ! You worried me with all the screaming and thrashing about. Are you okay, baby?'

'Yeah. It was just a nightmare.'

'Your subconscious sure did a number on you. Fuck! You're still shaking.'

She was. But as he held her close and comforted her, the gravity of her situation sunk in. For the first time since childhood, Samantha cried. Big, hideous sobs broke free from her as the tears streamed down her face.

Lifting her chin, he peered deep into her eyes. 'Hey, sweetheart, what's wrong?'

'I think I'm in love with you, Tyler.'

Stepping from the boat, Brendan gaped in awe of his weekend lodgings: a private island resort. White, luxury apartments lined the curved beach, with a large conference centre to the north and an entertainment complex to the south. The Syndicate spared no expense when it came to their comfort. When he glanced back at his companions, the setting sun captivated him as it painted the crystal-clear ocean with vibrant shades of red, pink, and orange.

Laughing, Bridey linked her arm with his. 'These summits are as much an excuse to party as they are business. Naturally, we have exclusive use of the place. There won't be any humans to worry about.'

'What about the staff?' asked Caleb.

'All unseelie. The Syndicate owns the entire island.'

''Course they do.'

She took Caleb's arm. 'Don't you mean *we* do? You are a part of this too now, sweetness.'

'I know, but it hasn't sunk in for me yet. Maybe if you gave me more responsibilities and more actual work.'

Bridey motioned for them to continue walking. 'Well, I could use more help with this museum job. Why don't the pair of you look over my plans and give me some advice? When we get home, that is.'

'Yeah, fine.' Caleb sounded unenthusiastic. So yeah, he sounded like Caleb.

The seed of a plan planted itself in Brendan's brain. 'What if you let us oversee the whole operation? We are captains, after all. Let us command our teams.'

Wide-eyed-panic struck Caleb's visage. '*What the hell, Winters?*'

'*Roll with it, Thornsy.*'

Bridey stopped to consider his suggestion. 'Okay.'

Adrenaline surged through him. 'So, you'll let us run this job?'

'Yes, but I want you to give me a full run-down of your plan before you put anything into action. I need to feel confident you won't botch things.'

Brendan smiled. 'Of course.'

'Now let's go have some fun.' Bridey urged them towards the southern end of the island. She led them through crowds of fae and dark mages who mingled in the casino, introducing them to all the important folk as they went.

'I didn't realise Australia had so many Syndicate leaders,' Brendan commented as they moved across to the restaurant. He noticed the complex also housed a nightclub, movie theatre, and games arcade.

'They aren't only Australian, handsome. This is the entire Oceania branch of the Syndicate.'

Their evening meal dragged. Sure, the gourmet food was exquisite, but Brendan had seen kiddie pools deeper than the boot lickers and toffee-nosed arseholes hovering around Bridey. Syndicate politics put him in mind of high school cliques, and he'd never had the patience for such bullshit.

Glancing around the table, his eyes fell on Caleb, who concentrated on the plate in front of him. Caleb had barely spoken to him since their intimate encounter three days ago and Brendan suspected it was an avoidance tactic. When he probed Caleb's mind, he found it locked up tight. *Yup, definitely evading me! But why? Was it something I said? I know I rocked his world, so….* He tried to humour Caleb telepathically. *'Thrilling dinner conversation, hey Thornsy?'*

That got him a look, or more of glare. *'I'm sure it is, if you find supply and demand curves sexy.'*

Brendan laughed silently. *'Come on, man, the only curves I found sexy in Year Twelve economics were Miss Harper's.'*

'You're such a pig, Winters.' The bitter tone of Caleb's thought fell short of the intended insult thanks to the grin tugging at his delicate lips.

'Yeah, you remember that hottie, too.' Ice-breaking mission success.

Moving into the cocktail lounge, Bridey encircled her two captains in her arms. 'Why don't you boys go have some drinks and unwind while I mingle for a bit?' She left them both with a peck on the cheek before disappearing in the crowd.

Brendan followed Caleb, who beelined for the bar where they both ordered straight whiskey. Spotting a quiet table in the corner with a couple of free seats, he gestured for Caleb to follow. When Caleb refused to budge, Brendan grabbed his arm and dragged him across the room.

'What the hell, man?'

Plucking the drink from Caleb's hand, Brendan put both their glasses on the table. He pushed Caleb up against the wall, caging the man between his arms. 'I wanna know what's going on inside that pretty head of yours, Thornsy. Why have you been avoiding me?'

Quick, shallow breaths slipped through Caleb's soft, kissable lips.

Brendan narrowed his eyes. 'You know, I thought you would have snuck into my room at least once in the last few nights.'

'I figured you were busy.'

'Bullshit.' He pressed his body hard up against Caleb's and fixed his gaze on the silver-lined mouth a moment before meeting the dark-brown eyes staring coolly back at him.

'Back off, Winters.'

'Oh, we're back to your antagonistic tripe, now are we? I honestly thought we'd moved past that after fucking each other stupid.'

Caleb sighed. 'It's not that.'

Unable to control the urge to touch, Brendan brought his fingers up to Caleb's face, caressing the soft, glimmering skin covering his well-defined cheekbone. 'What is it?'

His sinfully gorgeous eyes closed. 'I can't do this with you.'

Brendan's messed-up heart slammed against the walls of his chest. *I've only just discovered these feelings for Caleb and he's already slipping through my fingers.* 'Why? Did Bridey tell you to stay away from me? Because she didn't say anything about this,' he waved at the small amount of air between them, 'to me.'

'No.'

'Then what?'

Caleb filled his lungs with a deep breath and opened his eyes. 'I don't think we should be intimate again.' A hint of salty sadness brimmed his eyes.

Brendan's pulse was hammering by this point. 'I hear your words, Thornsy, but they don't make any sense. I thought you wanted me?'

'I did.' The past tense punched Brendan in the gut.

'But you don't want me anymore, huh?' Brendan pulled away to grab his drink and knock it back in one mouthful. His attention returned to Caleb, but this time he kept his distance. 'Nah, I get it. You were bicurious right? One day of mind-blowing sex with me was enough to satisfy your little crush. Now you can go back to your incestuous obsession with a psychotic bitch.' He slammed his glass down hard enough for a shard of ice to leap out and plummet to its death. Storming across the room, he returned to the bar for another shot of Ireland's best medicine.

'Trouble in paradise?' A rich, feminine voice startled him.

Turning around with a fresh refill in hand, Brendan beheld the most buxom blonde he had ever seen. Golden hair fell in loose curls around the plunging neckline of a light-orange cocktail dress. Looking her up and down, he tried to keep his tone polite despite the surge of desire he felt. 'Excuse me, Madame?'

'I could not help but notice the spat you had with your lover over there.' She gestured toward Caleb, who sat alone at the corner table, looking at his phone.

'Oh. He's not my lover.' *But hot damn, you could be.* 'Can I get you a drink, Lady….'

'Amber. They call me Lady Amber.' She reached her hand out, not to shake, but as though she expected him to kiss it.

Brendan accepted her invitation willingly, even though she gave off haughty snob vibes. If Bridey had taught him anything, it was how he did not need to like a woman to appreciate her beauty. And Amber projected beauty in spades. 'And they call me Lord Jet.'

'I would love a martini, thank you, Jet.'

After getting her drink, they moved to a nearby couch where Brendan sat as close to Amber as respectfully possible.

'Tell me, Jet, are you vying for the top spot?'

He snorted. 'Ah, no.'

'Why not?'

'Well, I'm pretty new to the Syndicate for one. And I'm only a Captain.'

When she smiled, her brilliant green eyes lit up the room. 'Your current rank shouldn't matter. Bloodline ties to the previous Boss, however, would count in your favour.'

Surprised, Brendan felt his eyes widen. 'You know who I am?'

'Yes, I do. I make it my job to know all the big names in the magic world, but I also have a particular interest in your clan.'

Okay, that's a tad creepy, but I'm not gonna complain about having such a sexy stalker.

'I think you have a valid claim.'

He shrugged. 'Politics isn't my thing. I detest the idea of brown-nosing and selling myself.'

'Is it just the campaigning, or do you dislike having authority?'

Brendan scanned the room for Bridey and spotted her hanging all over some endarkened man in a flashy pinstripe suit. She remained oblivious to his conversation. When his focus returned to Amber, her ample cleavage caught his eye. *Oh, the things I could do to that rack!* Licking his lips, he threw his right arm across her backrest and leaned in closer. 'Don't get me wrong, My Lady. I love power and control as much as the next dark mage, but I'm more of a doer.'

'Curious.' She appeared lost in thought for a moment before turning to face him. 'If you are not planning to make a bid for the position, would you consider voting for me?'

Hell yes! She's gotta be a better option than Bridey. He placed his left hand on her knee and gave her his best bedroom eyes. 'I might be persuaded.'

'I think I am too old for you, sweetheart.'

'What's a few years? I'm honestly not bothered.'

'Trust me, Jet, the age gap is much bigger than you realise.'

He studied her carefully. 'You must be using some serious mojo to glamour yourself, because you don't look a day over twenty-five.'

Amber laughed. 'More than you know. Your offer is both gratifying and tempting, but I must decline your advances.'

Brendan did not bother to hide his disappointment or remove his hand from her. 'Is there any way I can change your mind?'

'Trust me when I say you will thank me later for resisting your charms. Besides, I think your friend is getting jealous.'

Following her line of sight, Brendan's eyes locked with Caleb's. While schooling his poker face, he failed to conceal the murky-green aura from Brendan's prying gaze.

'I tell you what. If you vote for me and I win the election, I will make it worth your while.' She was grinning when he turned back to face her.

He could not say no to such a gorgeous smile. 'We have a deal, My Lady.'

Amber rose to her feet. 'I am glad we have reached an understanding. Please excuse me, My Lord, but I have some *brown-nosing* to do.' With a wink, she walked into the crowd.

He sighed as she disappeared. Closing his eyes, Brendan reclined his head. *Two rejections in one night? I must be losing my touch.*

A shadow moved in front of him, blocking some of the light filtering through his eyelids. 'Was she like the first woman ever you couldn't seduce the panties off?'

Brendan growled as his eyes flicked open to glower at Caleb. 'Either fuck me, or fuck off, Thornsy.'

'Wow! You sure know how to flatter a guy. Don't tell me you—'

'Hmm,' he cut Caleb off before the damn fairy could spew forth anymore attitude. 'You're still here, which means you're either deaf or begging to be my bitch tonight. I'll give you five seconds to start walking away.'

That shut Caleb's trap, but he did not move.

'Five.'

Intense dark eyes stared back at him.

'Four.'

A wisp of hair fell across his brow as his head inclined.

'Three.'

Caleb's lips parted. *Those damned lips.*

'Two.'

Brendan jumped to his feet, ready to take what he wanted. But Caleb remained still.

'One.'

Seizing Caleb's ponytail with one hand as he slid the other around his waist, Brendan pulled Caleb's body flush against his. 'Time's up, Thornsy. Now you're mine.'

Chapter Ten

Dumbstruck, Tyler stared at Samantha in shock. Her confession of love was the last thing he expected from her. Like, ever. Her emotional state compounded the strangeness of her words. 'Ah….' *Nope. Still no words.*

She blinked her big, brown eyes, red and puffy with tears that continued to flow.

'But how? I mean, we've only known each other a couple of weeks.' *Not even enough time to make sense of my own feelings.*

Pulling out of his grip, she turned away. 'I… I'm sorry. It slipped out. Forget I said anything.' Her tone did not carry resentment; nothing but remorse and anguish.

'Hey.' He closed the gap between their bare bodies, enfolding her with his arms. 'It's okay. I'm surprised and confused. I….'

'It's not okay, Tyler. I'm the last person on Earth you should be with. We shouldn't be doing this.'

The cause for her concern started to make sense. His lack of reciprocation was not what upset her. Tyler placed a comforting hand on her arm. 'I know I worried about delving into the forbidden before, but I've moved past those fears. I honestly don't care if I lose my job over this, if it means I can be with you.' He did not know if it was love yet, but those were some strong feelings. 'You've grown on me, Sam. What I feel for you is deeper than—'

'Stop it!' she cried. 'You don't understand. I'm toxic, Tyler. This has nothing to do with *your* boss.'

Alarm bells rang out and dread festered in his gut. 'What do you mean?'

'I… I can't tell you.'

'Sam, please,' he pleaded with everything he had.

'I mean I… lit… rally can't… ss-say. Just… please don't… under the covers.'

Holy. Shit. 'Non-disclosure spell?'

She blinked at him. Twice. It was all he needed to confirm his suspicions.

'Fuck!' Tyler leaped out of the bed and paced the room. Millions of questions formed in his mind, but there was no point asking her any of them. 'I gotta find a way to break the spell.' He paused mid-stride and spun to face her. 'Would you stop me from lifting it?'

Her head hesitantly shook as if testing her limits. 'No,' she whispered.

Complete ignorance with dispelling such magic became the main problem. 'I need some time alone to think.'

Samantha nodded her understanding with eyes full of sorrow.

After slipping into his jeans, not bothering with the rest of his clothes, Tyler shut himself away in his own room and collapsed on his bed. *I ought to tell Jaxon about this, but that will mean admitting to my relationship with Sam. Not to mention the shit it would land her in.* Being honest with himself, he realised that despite her betrayal, he still cared for Samantha. *Gods, I am messed up!*

But if I can't turn to the Council for advice, then who? After racking his brains for several hours, the sun began to rise, and the answer came as his phone sprang to life with a text from Alannah: HEY, ARE YOU AWAKE YET?

Not bothering with a written reply, he hit the call button. 'Hi, beautiful. What's up?'

'Me. I couldn't sleep last night.'

'Thinking about him?' Tyler was not sure if she wanted to hear the jerk's name, so he played it safe.

'Yeah. It feels wrong to burden Liam with this. I hope you don't mind?'

'I don't mind, Lana. Not at all. What were you thinking about?'

'How much I miss everything about him. I don't understand why he left me.' Her voice cracked.

'Neither do I, gorgeous. There's no way I would have.'

'I was sort of wondering if…,' her voice trailed off.

Tyler's heart skipped a beat. 'Did you want to see me again?'

'Uh huh.'

His blood surged with the unspoken meaning. Tyler figured he must be an emotional masochist because what he wanted from Alannah was more than she could offer, but he would take what he could get. 'Tell me a time and place and I'll be there.'

'Really? I mean, are you honestly okay with this?'

Tyler sighed, smiling to himself. 'Yes, Lana. You're a phenomenal woman and I'd have to be crazy to say no to any intimate contact with you. But more than that, I know you need a good friend right now. And frankly, so do I.'

'Shit! I'm such a selfish bitch. I didn't even ask how you were. I'm sorry, Ty.' The way she shortened his name did not escape his attention. And Gods help him, but he loved it.

'It's okay, beautiful. I know you're going through a rough patch, and I want to be here for you.'

'Thank you. What's been bothering you?'

'Christ! I don't even know where to start.'

'Are your troubles work related, or something more personal?'

Closing his eyes, he thought about how to broach the topic before giving up on the idea of sugar-coating things. 'Both. I've managed to mess everything up big time. All because I couldn't keep my pants on.'

Alannah made that adorable snort of hers. 'Tell me about it.'

Tyler loved how well she understood him. So, he told her all about Samantha, from the way he had met her in Broken Hill right up to the two big bombshells she had dropped. And his new best friend listened attentively, giving him endearing noises of acknowledgement and words of encouragement as he went.

'Wow. That's huge, Ty. How do you feel about her?'

'I like her a lot. I was on the verge of entertaining the idea of a serious relationship, but when she admitted to her deception, I instantly forced my heart to apply the brakes. Now I'm confused. I thought we were having a bit of fun, then she tells me all that. Before I can do much else, I need to break the non-disclosure spell. You don't happen to know much about dispelling mind control magic, do you?'

'I imagine it's like nullifying any other spells. I don't have a lot of experience with this stuff, but I'm guessing one could use nether, like how Richard negated your attacks.'

Tyler sat up surprised. 'That was nether?' He paused for thought. 'Wait, how did you know?'

'Promise not to freak out?'

'Might be too late.' *Is Alannah dabbling in dark magic?*

'I'm attuned to nether, but it's not as sinister as you might think. I don't use it for nefarious purposes, and I have a safe way to channel it.'

'What if it taints your soul, Lana?'

'I guarantee it doesn't. If you like, I could have a go at dispelling whatever magic is holding Sam's tongue.'

'Are you sure it's safe?'

'Yes, Ty. It's perfectly safe.'

'Then, yes please and thank you.'

Half a laugh slipped from her. 'Hey, it's the least I can do, considering what I'm asking of you.'

'Believe me, gorgeous, that has its own rewards. Speaking of which, you haven't named a time and place yet.'

'I was thinking of meeting you at the hotel in Sydney. I'm sure you know the one I mean.'

Memories of his wild night with Alannah flooded his mind. 'Mhmm. When?'

'In two hours? Text me with the room number once you've checked in. You can introduce me to Samantha tomorrow.'

'Will do. I'll see you soon, okay Lana?'

'Okay. And thank you, Ty.'

Tyler was like a tornado, rushing to shower and get ready. On his way out of the house, he knocked on Shane's door.

Shane took one look at him and grinned. 'Hot date?'

'Damn straight. Would you mind keeping an extra eye on our charge today?'

'No probs, man.' Shane bumped fists with him. As Tyler turned to leave, he called after him, 'Oh, and Quirky?'

'Yeah?'

'If you're meeting who I think you are, please be careful.'

'Of course.'

Walking the few blocks needed to reach their hotel room gave Tyler time to think about the two chicks at the centre of his life. *Of all the women I take to bed, why do I have to fall for the ones I can't or shouldn't have?* There was no way he was going to admit it to Alannah, but he was already drowning in the depths of what he felt for her. Problem was, she only wanted him as a best friend with totally messed up benefits.

As for Samantha? Knowing there was a chance Alannah could help break the non-disclosure spell gave him hope. Pending what his Firecracker had to say, he was prepared to forgive her. Not only were the last few nights with Samantha the best in his life, but Tyler felt a genuine connection with her. Smiling, he thought about Samantha the rest of the way to the hotel.

Now you're mine. Brendan's words resonated in Caleb's damned, filthy soul, pushing aside all his fears, and arousing him more than he thought possible. The way Brendan's lips savagely crashed into his own burned hotter than hellfire.

Wasting no time, Brendan dragged him out of the cocktail lounge and straight for their suite, kicking open his bedroom door with a terrifying force that excited Caleb. He threw Caleb down on the bed and literally ripped the clothes from his body.

Whether Caleb was born with his submissive nature, or if his sister had cultivated the tendency, he would never know. But he was certain Bridey had shown him how much he needed the pain, the humiliation, and most importantly, the loss of control. These were all things he knew Brendan could've given him once, but in the last two weeks he had seen circumstances—along with two certain women—crush Brendan's soul, leaving Caleb to wonder if those fires of passion had fizzled. That night, he saw the spark of dominance rekindle Brendan's flame.

The heat blazed. The physicality felt brutal. Unlike the first time, Brendan didn't go easy on him, which made the night perfect. *His* Brendan—the man whom Caleb had fallen for before any women had ruined him—was back. Not only that, but this time he was making Caleb's wildest fantasies come true.

With their carnal needs satisfied, Brendan's nurturing side returned as he held Caleb in his arms and toyed with the tangled tendrils of hair falling around his shoulders. 'Don't ever pull away from me again, Thornsy.'

'I'm sorry. I kinda freaked out.'

'Why?'

'Several reasons, but if I had to narrow it down, I'd say your inevitable rejection scared me.'

Pursing his lips, Brendan exhaled sharply, whistling as he did. 'You're already writing me off? How about giving me a chance to show you I can be serious?'

'I said I'm sorry, okay. I honestly didn't think you wanted more than sex. Not that I'm complaining about that. *Especially* this time. But—'

'Wait up. What do you mean *especially* this time?'

Sprawling his arm across Brendan's chest and entwining their legs, Caleb yielded further to the embrace. 'It was exactly what I needed, what I desired. The violence, the complete surrender.'

'Oh? You prefer it rough, huh?'

'Gods yes!'

'Good to know. Extremely good to know. Now, go on.'

'Given I'm the first and only man you've fucked, I figured *you* were the bicurious one. I thought I was some passing phase and as soon as you were free of Bridey, you'd dump me and go back to being straight.'

Brendan sighed. 'Does it matter if you're the only guy I'm attracted to? The point is I *am* into you.' His face transformed with a wicked grin as he leaned closer to Caleb's ear. '*Really* deep into you.' The gruffness of his voice sent Caleb's mind reeling as goosebumps covered his body.

'Brendan,' he warned.

A hand clamped down on his mouth as Brendan straddled him. 'Shoosh, Thornsy. Neither of us know what the future holds. Let's make the most of our time together now. I want you, okay? And not just for that pretty little arse of yours.'

His eyes widened in surprise for the briefest of moments.

Claiming every inch of his body, Brendan ravished him again. And again.

Winters sure does have some stamina. 'What else do you want me for, if not just my arse?' Caleb asked as they collapsed hours later.

'You, Thornsy. I want all of you. I get enough meaningless sex from your sister. The woman's a relentless nymphomaniac.'

Caleb laughed. 'I couldn't agree more. What was the deal with the blonde broad in the orange dress? Were you trying to make me jealous?'

'So, you *were* envious of her, huh?' Mischief glimmered in his eyes. The same look had attracted Caleb the first time they'd met:

Caleb followed Locky to the courtyard where they claimed one of the lunch tables. They had clicked the moment they sat beside each other in homeroom and stuck together for the rest of the morning, helping each other survive their first day of high school. Where the goblin had grown up in the town, Caleb had recently moved there with his mum, so he didn't know any of the kids in the area.

The moment he planted his arse on a bench, a foul stench emerged from behind, followed by a deep, taunting voice, 'Hey freaks, you're in our spot!'

Turning to face the troll, Caleb gulped at the sight of the guy's enormous tusks. Still he wasn't about to let a bunch of bullies push him around. He made a show of sniffing the table. 'Funny. I can't smell your scent here. I guess it's been a while since you last marked your territory and since there aren't any reserved signs, I'm thinking it's fair game.'

The troll lifted Caleb up by his collar, exhaling putrid fumes that made him feel dizzy. 'Listen up faggot! I know ya new in town, so I'll give you one last warning. Take your green boyfriend and fuck off outta my spot!'

'Yo, Chad! It's time you and your buddies took a hike back to Hicksville.'

Looking over his shoulder, Caleb spotted two guys. Judging by their auras they were both magical, although the shorter one oozed so much power that he could only be a pure mage.

'What the fuck do you want Winters?' Chad dropped Caleb and he scrambled to regain his footing.

Winters… where have I heard that name before?

'You hard of hearing old man?' asked Winters. 'I told you to get lost, scram, beat it, piss off. This spot now belongs to me and my friends. Oh, and next time I hear you spouting homophobic nonsense, I'll make you and your

mates all fall in love with each other so hard you won't be able to resist fucking each other to death.'

The troll gaped at him. 'You wouldn't dare? The Council frowns on that shit.'

Winters grinned slyly, and something twinkled in his emerald eyes, stealing Caleb's breath in the process. 'Screw the Council. Besides, who would they believe? One of their own, or a bunch of low life trolls?'

Chad huffed and marched away with his friends in tow.

Sitting at the table, Winters stretched out across the bench, looking like a fucking sex god with his long limbs sprawled out and his beaming smile. 'Ignore those wankers. They think anyone who doesn't conform to their drab sense of fashion is gay. I swear to the gods they are more conservative than the Council. Just don't let 'em get you alone off campus, yeah?'

'Cheers man.' Caleb sat opposite Winters. 'I wasn't too worried about Chad. I can hold my own in a fight, but you probably saved me from getting detention on my first day.'

Winters snorted and glanced at Locky over Caleb's shoulder. 'Hey Munroe, you gonna take a seat, or do you plan to hover about behind the new kid like his shadow?'

'You do realise Caleb and I are unseelie, right?' Locky asked timidly.

'Dude, my best mate here is cursed.' Winters gestured to the guy with long black hair who was now sitting beside him. 'Does it look like I give a fuck what race you are?'

Upon closer inspection, Caleb realised that the guy with long hair also had luminescent eyes. Like a vampire.

Hot damn. If those guys are lovers, I really hope they let me in on some of that action. Locky slumped into the chair next to him and Caleb sensed him fidgeting. Is he just as turned on by them as me?

'So, Caleb, right?' Winters' silken voice brought him back to the moment and he nodded. 'I'm Brendan Winters, and this surly fucker is Austin Pearce.'

Caleb's thoughts returned to the present and he considered Brendan's question of jealousy. 'Maybe a tad. Although, I'd be a hypocrite to expect exclusivity.'

'Right! It'd be impossible with Bridey around.'

'Exactly. But you're evading my question, Winters. Come on man, she was hot *as*. Were you genuinely flirting with her?'

'Of course I was. Although I think she only wanted me for my vote rather than my mad skills in the bedroom.'

Caleb sat up. 'Wait, what? She's running for the boss' job?'

'Yup.'

'So, how are you intending to vote?'

'I....' Brendan bit his lip to hold his tongue, worry evident on his face.

He caressed Brendan's designer stubble, loving the masculine feel of it against his skin. 'It's okay. I won't tell her. But you'd better prepare for the fallout when Bridey doesn't find your name among the list of people voting for her.'

'Shit! It's not a blind ballot?'

'Not exactly. The votes are cast with magic. The candidates will only know if you selected them.'

Brendan closed his eyes as he considered Caleb's words. When they opened again, something devious flickered in his dark, sinister expression. 'Voting isn't compulsory, right? I can tell her I refused to vote.'

'It's an option, but she'll still crack a fit. Personally, I'd rather not risk her wrath, so I'll be voting for her.'

'Yeah, but you're in love with Bridey. It makes sense you'd want to back her.'

If only things were so simple. 'Honestly, I'd rather she didn't take on the Boss' job. It'd mean less time to spend with her and more pressure on all of us.'

'I didn't consider that. I've got enough on my plate with the Cult. Yet another reason to vote against her.'

Caleb shook his head. 'You're a braver man than me, Brendo.'

Brendan huffed. 'Hardly.' The room fell silent as they both lost themselves in thought. After what might have been half an hour, possibly more, Brendan propped himself up and looked down into Caleb's eyes. 'Humour me, here, Thornsy. And please don't freak out or take this question the wrong way. But hypothetically speaking, if you had to choose between me or Bridey, who would you stay with? Like if I were to leave your sister's service next week, or even next month, for example, and you were forced to make the decision.'

Oh hell. How could I not take it the wrong way? 'Brendan,' he whispered, 'I don't think I can make a choice.'

A smile tugged at Brendan's lips. 'Does that mean you love *me* as much as you do Bridey?'

The sly bastard! I gotta hand it to him though. 'Yeah, it does.'

Tyler felt like he was living in a fantasy role-playing game when he awoke well-rested. He rarely slept soundly; less so when worries plagued his mind, and he had plenty of those. But holding Alannah Winters and talking to her between bouts of passion compounded with sex-induced fatigue produced a full-night's sleep.

The dark-haired angel stirred in his arms, opened her eyes, and smiled at him. 'Morning.'

'Afternoon, gorgeous.'

Alannah groaned. 'Already? Damnit. I'm not ready for reality yet.'

Tyler sat astride her, hovering close to her face. 'I'm happy to keep pretending. What if we run away to some remote island paradise together?'

Her arms encircled his waist. 'Sounds tremendously tempting, but I have a boyfriend back home who would miss me.' She sighed. 'And I'd feel guilty pulling a *Brendan* on him. Not to mention all my other responsibilities. Besides, you have Samantha to worry about. I want to help the pair of you.'

Leaning in closer, he kissed the soft patch of skin beneath her ear. 'You're an extraordinary woman, Lana.'

She quivered in response to his light touch. 'Okay, maybe once more.' Her voice became breathy as her fingernails dug into the firm muscles of his backside.

Pulling back a hair's breadth, Tyler gave her a serious look. Things felt more real in that moment, as though she was seeing *him* rather than her ex. 'Are you sure?'

'Yes, Tyler. I'm sure.'

Tyler's heart soared at the sound of his name on her lips. He wasted no time tearing open the foil packet and preparing himself to sink into her.

Once Alannah caught her breath, she laughed. 'Gods, I think I'm addicted to sex with you, Ty.'

His wide grin failed to hide the thrill her words gave him. 'Well I'm not gonna complain, although your boyfriend might.'

When she rolled on to her side to look at him, there was an impish gleam in her eyes. 'What he doesn't know won't hurt him.'

Tyler's eyes shot open wide with shock. 'Liam doesn't know you're with me?'

'Hell no! He'd lose his shit. The first time was okay because things were still in a state of flux. But I doubt he would be so cool about it now.'

'Fuck! So, where does he think you are?' This was indisputable cheating and Tyler was complicit. Yet the fear of Liam's wrath was much stronger than any hint of guilt.

'He thinks I'm visiting my old Melbourne friends.'

'If Liam catches us….'

'He won't. It's why I came to Sydney. Please don't worry about him, or me.' She left the bed and walked toward the bathroom. 'Let's shower and go deal with your girlfriend.'

'She's not my girlfriend, Lana.'

When she reached the door, Alannah paused as she gripped the handle. Glancing over her shoulder, she offered a spectacular view of her perfect porcelain skin and the womanly curves of her hips and backside. 'Not yet, she's not.'

After checking out of the hotel, Tyler took Alannah to the safehouse in Darlinghurst. He was relieved to learn Jaxon was out with Tanya.

Shane's eyes remained glued to his game of *Overwatch* when they entered the living room.

Tyler laced his fingers with Alannah's and squeezed her hand as he approached Shane. 'Where's Samantha?'

'Moping in her room.' The brief distraction proved lethal to his game's avatar. He flung his controller onto the coffee table in a huff and looked up at them. 'Holy. Shit! Alannah?' He leaped to his feet and pulled her into a bear hug. 'It's great to see you again.'

She laughed. 'You too, Walshy.'

'What are you doing here?'

'I'm about to make Tyler's threesome fantasies come true.' She winked.

Tyler spluttered. 'Shit! How'd you know about those?'

Alannah linked her arm with his and grinned. 'Oh, come on, you're nothing if not predictable, Ty.'

Shane's jaw hit the floor. 'Can I watch?'

This could make for a convenient cover story. Tyler turned and called over his shoulder as he guided Alannah towards the stairs, 'Maybe next time, Walshy.'

Canned laughter permeated Samantha's closed door, so he pounded his fist against the timber.

'Come in.'

Tyler felt his cheeks flush at the sight of Samantha sprawled out on her bed in a pair of blue satin boxershorts and matching camisole.

Her focus shifted from the television to the woman standing beside Tyler, and she visibly tensed.

Closing the door behind him, Tyler approached her cautiously, unsure if she was about to strike out like a cornered animal. 'Sam, this is Alannah. She's here to lift the spell.'

Samantha's eyes darted between Tyler and Alannah several times before settling on him. 'A bloodline mage? Are you for real?'

'It's okay, Sam, you can trust Lana. She's not exactly on speaking terms with most of the Council right now.'

Alannah smiled. 'Hi Samantha. Tyler's right. I don't play by the rules. I can see you're a dark mage and it doesn't bother me. I want to help you.'

Samantha eyed her sceptically. 'Why?'

'Because I care about Tyler, and he cares about you.'

Her eyes drifted back to Tyler. 'Really?'

'Yes.' He closed the rest of the distance between them and sat on the bed. Up close, he saw evidence of prolonged crying in her bloodshot eyes. His heart melted for Samantha, prompting him to bring a hand up and tuck several strands of vibrant red hair behind her ear. 'I'm not going anywhere, Sam, but I need to hear what they've roped you into.'

'Okay. What should I do?'

Tyler directed a questioning gaze toward Alannah.

'Sit cross-legged on the bed for me.' Alannah retrieved a large white crystal from her handbag. She sat in front of Samantha, mirroring her stance with their knees touching, and placed the crystal in her lap. 'Lean forward and close your eyes.'

Samantha obeyed without question. Tyler was not prepared for what came next and almost embarrassed himself when Alannah grabbed Samantha's neck, pulling her face in close to her own. At first, he thought they were about to kiss, but Alannah simply pressed her forehead to Samantha's. *Wishful thinking, I guess.* They still looked incredibly hot together and Tyler's imagination was running wild.

Several minutes later, Alannah leaned back and looked at Tyler. 'I think it worked. Ask her a couple of test questions.'

'Sam, have you been working with the Cult even after coming into our protective custody?'

Remorse showed in her eyes as they met his. 'Yes.'

'But we blocked all of your telecommunication channels and heavily warded the house. How are you in contact with them?'

'Through dream telepathy.'

'I....' Tyler stammered. 'I didn't know that was even a thing.'

'It's definitely a thing. The nightmare you woke me from was one such dream.'

He glanced at Alannah. 'Have you ever heard of dream telepathy?'

'No.'

'It's dark elf magic,' Samantha explained. 'And something unique to those of the Cult. They like to guard their secrets well.'

'Are they actually the Obsidian Cult?' Tyler noticed Alannah jerk back in surprise. *I guess I left that detail out of the briefing.*

'Yes, although it's a name they created to inspire fear in the wider magic community while hiding their true identity.'

'Who are they?'

Samantha shrugged. 'I don't know. Only first tier members are privileged to that information. My master is one such elf, but I am only second tier, which is as far as mages can advance. The inner circle restricts access to pure blood dark elves who are born into the ranks.' Her eyes moved to Alannah. 'Like with Council mages.'

'Are they also misogynistic arseholes, like the Council?' Alannah's question made both Tyler and Sam chuckle, easing the tension in the air.

'No. The Cult has as many women as men.'

Tyler took a deep breath before asking the big one: 'What do the Cult want with me?'

Samantha's hand slipped into his and squeezed it hard. 'They want to recruit you and corrupt your soul.'

A single laugh burst forth from Tyler. 'Right, how do they expect to achieve that?'

'By using me to get to you; to make you think you are going undercover to expose them. Once they have you, they can use mind control to trick you into performing dark magic.'

'Christ!' Tyler stared at her in shock. 'Why me?'

'Because you're a doppelganger.'

The Dark Syndicate sure knew how to party, and they did it hard. Lots of sex, substance abuse, and loud music. All day and all night. By the time Sunday afternoon rolled around, Brendan felt wrecked. He had done well to avoid the politics and make the most of the fun times. Problem was, the situation at hand called for intellect and strategy.

It was time to vote. They all assembled in the conference centre where the three candidates sat on the stage awaiting the results. Lady Violet, Lady Amber, and Lord Slate were their options. The administrators mandated complete silence. A large wall clock marked the seconds, filling the auditorium with a merciless ticking, reverberating with an eerie echo.

As soon as Bridey shifted her gaze from Brendan's general direction, he withdrew the enchanted parchment and quill pen given to him upon entry. After sharing a look with Caleb, who sat beside him, he pierced his thumb with the nib. An unfortunate aspect of being a Syndicate member was the need to participate in blood magic, but it was the only way to cast his vote. He wrote LADY AMBER on the paper, watching as the writing disappeared from the page. He popped them in his pocket and turned an anxious eye to the timepiece counting down the last few minutes until the deadline.

A bell chimed at 6PM and the returning officer, a short, grey-haired dark mage, rose from his seat on the stage. 'All votes have been cast. You have chosen our new leader.' He produced three old-fashioned scrolls and eased each one apart, keeping the room in suspense longer than necessary. After comparing the results, he looked up at the crowd. 'Your new elected official is Lady Amber.'

As Brendan breathed a sigh of relief, Bridey gasped, grabbing for the scrolls. 'Give me those.'

Frowning, the old man pulled back. 'Lady Violet, please. Show the respect and decorum expected of someone with your title.' He handed her the one scroll she could see and gave the others to their respective owners.

'The stage is yours, Lady Amber.'

'Thank you, my Lord.' The knockout blonde rose and took the microphone. 'I am honoured most of you continue to put your trust in my family. My sister was an excellent leader before me, and with the help of my great nephew, I promise we will do our best to fill the shoes of a powerful woman.' She gestured toward Brendan.

What. The. Actual. Fuck?

'So, without further ado, I would like to introduce my Second in Command, Lord Jet.'

All eyes turned on him, but none of them worried him more than Bridey's lethal glare.

Chapter Eleven

'A what now?' Tyler knew the term, but not the significance.

'A doppelganger,' Samantha repeated without explanation.

'Okay, babe, pretend for a moment I have no idea what you're talking about.'

'You are the non-related, identical twin of another. Humans use the term frivolously, but in our world, there is magical significance to such phenomena.'

'Shit! I never even stopped to think about the reason you look like him.' Alannah jumped up from the bed and grabbed her bag.

Samantha gasped. 'Alannah knows the Original?'

'Now I'm insulted. What makes you think I'm not the Original and that jerk's the copy?'

Alannah returned to them a moment later with her phone in hand.

'Trust me, Hot Stuff,' Samantha explained as she grasped his hand, 'this is not something to take offence over. The Original is usually the first of the doppelganger twins to fall into darkness. In your case, the other guy's soul was tainted first. But if he is a pure mage, it's unlikely he carries the doppelganger gene.'

'I don't know why I never thought to show you this before.' Alannah thrust her phone under Tyler's nose.

When he looked at the image on the screen, he needed to blink several times to be sure his eyes were not playing tricks on him. He wondered if Alannah had taken a candid photo of him. But that could not be it. This had to be a picture of Brendan because the hairstyle differed to his own and the man sported an eyebrow piercing. 'Damn, this is creepy. I can see why you found comfort in my arms, Lana.'

Samantha squeezed his shoulder. 'Wait, what am I missing here?'

He handed her the phone. 'He is Alannah's ex-boyfriend, Brendan Winters.'

'Ex-soulmate,' Alannah corrected. 'We made the ultimate commitment, then he up and left me without saying a word. I thought he had been the victim of a violent crime at first, but he rang his brother to gloat about running off with another woman. I was still grieving my loss when I met Tyler.' She bit her lip.

'And slept with him because he looked like the man you love?' Samantha finished for her.

'Yeah.' Alannah avoided eye contact with Samantha.
Talk about awkward!

Thankfully, Samantha acted cool, despite knowing he had also been intimate with the other woman in the room. 'Winters, huh? It makes sense Tyler's double would belong to such an infamous clan. I mean, look at who his grandmother was. From what I've heard, there is usually at least one who turns dark in every generation.'

'Gee, thanks,' Alannah huffed.

When Samantha looked perplexed, Tyler jumped in, 'Alannah is also a Winters. She's Brendan's cousin.'

Samantha mouthed a silent 'Oh', and her expression softened. 'I wasn't trying to offend, Alannah. I know you view dark mages in a negative light, but don't forget what I am.'

'I uh….' Alannah clamped her mouth shut.

'It's okay. I'm used to it. I was born and raised a dark mage, and like my parents, I've been able to keep my sense of humanity by moderating my behaviour. But I've seen how far down the rabbit hole some go. The darkness consumes them in their quest for power and they lose their sense of morality and empathy, if they even had any to begin with. My master, however, is pure evil, like most of his dark elf kindred.' She turned to look deeply into Tyler's eyes. 'I'm afraid of what will happen if they give you a taste of power. Your innate goodness is one of the things I love most about you.'

There she goes strumming at my heartstrings! Without any thought to his surrounds, Tyler pulled Samantha in for a deep kiss. Before long he was pinning her to the bed as their passion intensified.

After clearing her throat, Alannah spoke: 'I'll take that as my cue to leave you to it.'

Samantha broke away from Tyler's lips and grinned at Alannah. 'You could always join us.'

Hot damn! His fiery redhead was pushing all the right buttons.

The sound of Alannah's footsteps approached the bed. 'Is it what the two of you really want?'

Sitting back on Samantha, he turned a lascivious gaze toward Alannah. 'That didn't sound like a refusal. I think it goes without saying how keen I am to have you both at once. But what do *you* want here, Lana?'

Alannah kneeled behind him, straddling Samantha's legs as she slid her hands down his back. She yanked his t-shirt over his head. 'I want to bring you immense pleasure, Ty. It's the least I can do considering….'

'Fuck!' He leaned back into her and groaned as Samantha's hand trailed down his front. 'I thought you were joking before, Lana. To cover up what we had planned.' A second later, Tyler's arousal sprang free of his jeans, finding a new home in Samantha's tight grip. He sucked in a deep breath.

'With Shane you mean?' Alannah's husky voice asked in his ear. 'Yeah, I was joking then. But does *this*,' reaching around, her fingers found his nipples, 'feel like a joke now, babe?'

Tyler melted. At the mercy of the two sexiest women he had ever known, he lost himself in the intense sensuality of the moment. Somewhere deep in his mind he knew there were more important things to worry about, but there was no way in hell he was letting reality spoil his fun.

His fellow Syndicate members applauded as Lady Amber beckoned Brendan to the stage. But he remained frozen by the bitter rage pouring from Bridey.

Caleb leaned his head on Brendan's shoulder. 'Oh hell, Jet, you are in serious shit with our mistress.'

'Yeah, no kidding. I swear I had no idea who Lady Amber was, or what she had planned for me.'

'Hardly matters now. You may as well embrace your moment of glory. We'll deal with my sister later.'

He shot Caleb a look. 'We?'

'Of course, man. I'm hardly gonna leave you to fend for yourself. Now go, show these people how badass you are.'

Hesitantly, Brendan rose and walked up to the stage. His legs faltered as he ascended the three steps to the raised platform.

But he kept all his nerves bundled deep inside, mastering his passive mask.

Thankfully, he did not need to address the crowd. Lady Amber took care of that as he stood beside her. 'Consider me the Syndicate's public face. I grant Lord Jet the same decision-making powers I hold in this position. When dealing directly with him, I expect all of you to treat him as my equal.'

By the Gods! How did my life change so drastically? I'm a big deal crime boss! If only Jacob could see me now.

Once the formalities finished and most people had dispersed, Brendan remained standing with two scary-as-fuck women flanking him. He could also see Caleb hovering in the wings.

Bridey strode up to Lady Amber, pulled Brendan into her arms, and stared up at the tall blonde with a ferocious snarl. 'I don't know who you think you are, or what you're playing at, but Jet here is mine, not just in Syndicate business either. You see, he is under contractual obligation to remain in my service for an agreed time, making it next to impossible for him to be at your beck and call.'

Amber let out a haughty laugh. 'You are under the mistaken impression you have any say in this matter. I am your Boss, Violet. And now, so is Jet. He will no longer be taking orders from you. I could not care less about your contract. It is now,' she paused to close her eyes and click her fingers, 'officially null and void.' The abhorrent agreement appeared before their eyes, hovering in the air as it disintegrated into speckles of white dust. 'You should have known better than to mess with the Winters clan. My sister expected you to work with him as an equal partner, but she did not trust you to comply with her request. Do not think, for one second, I am unaware of everything going on behind your closed doors.' She glanced at Brendan.

'Meet me in my rooms once you have resolved anything you need to with this woman.'

Stunned and wide-eyed, Brendan simply nodded.

Satisfied by his response, Amber turned and marched away with a graceful yet determined manner.

As soon as they were alone, Bridey grabbed Caleb in a chokehold and glared at Brendan. While it did not look like she was restricting his airways, Caleb yelped hoarsely in a show of distress. 'You may have won your freedom, Jet, but don't forget I still have the one person you care about. If you wish to continue seeing my brother, you will reside under my roof and follow my rules.'

'What? So, now he's your slave because I'm not?'

Her visage took on a malicious grin. 'No, Jet, I don't need to make him my slave.' The hand gripping Caleb's throat gradually slid down his front and into the waistband of his pants. 'This man loves me unconditionally. He always was and always will be *mine*. I am willing to share him with you, but only if you continue with our former living arrangements.'

Caleb's neck arched against her shoulder, and he groaned as Bridey's hand wrapped around his growing arousal.

Brendan shook his head in disbelief. 'I can't believe how fucked up the pair of you are.'

Two pairs of dark eyes scowled back at him, and Caleb's adopted a wicked gleam. 'And you're as sordid as we are, so don't pretend like this doesn't turn you on.'

Damn him for having a wise mouth Brendan desperately wanted to kiss the shit out of. Damn him for looking hot as hell with Bridey's hand down his tailored suit pants. And damn him for being right. He felt his jaw clenching as he considered their words. 'I need time to think about it.'

Bridey inched forward with Caleb still between them.

While tempted to act upon the tension both in the air and in his trousers, Brendan had too many questions that needed answering, so he stepped back. 'If you'll excuse me, I have an important business meeting.' He turned to leave the stage.

'Oh, one last thing, handsome.'

He peered back over his shoulder. 'What?'

'To sweeten the deal, I will provide you with full protection from the authorities when you are working. But if you contact Alannah, our arrangement is off.'

He could not understand her Alannah-induced paranoia, but since Brendan had no intention to open old wounds, Bridey's deal suited him for the time being. 'Fine. But I only wear the collar in the bedroom, and you will grant me the freedom to come and go as I please. Outside of your home, *I am your* boss.'

She smiled victoriously. 'Of course, My Lord.'

Waking up between two gorgeous naked women, Tyler pinched himself multiple times, but reality did not sink in until he looked at the clock. *Shit! It's Sunday morning already.* He feared Jaxon had looked in on Samantha and found their limbs entwined. Although, he had bigger problems to worry about.

Samantha stirred and smiled at him. 'Hey, Hot Stuff.'

'Morning, Firecracker.'

She giggled. 'Nice nickname.'

'That's what I thought. I'm gonna grab us some coffees. Be right back.' He leaped out of bed and slipped into his jeans. Ducking out of the room, he took the stairs two at a time.

When he reached the kitchen, Jaxon was sitting at the breakfast bar. He looked up from his newspaper and glared at Tyler. 'Are you out of your mind, Quirky? I told you no fucking the informant.'

Well, that answers my previous concerns. 'Too bad I don't give a damn about those stupid rules.' He turned on the coffee machine, effectively ending the conversation with its spluttering.

Jumping in as soon as Tyler finished making the espressos, Jaxon persisted, 'Well I hope it was worth it and you made the most of your night with Miss Harrison, because it will be your last time with her.'

Tyler put the drinks down and stood directly in front of Jaxon. 'Yeah, I don't think so, boss. You see, because of my intimate involvement with Samantha, I've been able to crack this case wide open in ways you can't even begin to imagine. If you promise to keep your mouth shut, I will fill you in this afternoon; otherwise, I'll be taking Samantha with me when I leave.'

'You're playing with fire—you know that, right?'

'Yeah, well maybe I like getting burnt.' He grabbed the three beverages and carefully took them into Samantha's bedroom.

Both girls were sitting up, giving him the best sight to behold: their bare chests on display. Alannah's eyes lit up when she spotted the steaming coffee mugs. 'You are a legend, Ty.'

'Speak for yourself, beautiful.' With the drinks distributed, Tyler sat between them in the same spot he had woken up in. After imbibing several mouthfuls of caffeinated delight, he focussed his attention on Samantha. 'Tell me everything you know about doppelgangers.'

'The Egyptians call you *altaw'am alsihriu*, which means magic twin. The term doppelganger is of German origin. From what I understand, *you* are the descendent of an Egyptian god or goddess. I'm not sure which one—the Cult guards that secret. But thanks to your magical ancestry, certain traits, like your physical appearance, mystically replicated those of another magic user upon the moment of your conception.'

'Hmm. I guess I have my great-grandfather to thank. He had an affair with his half-mage maid and diluted the Quirke bloodline. I'm guessing my great-grandmother was a doppelganger and I wonder if old gramps knew anything about it.'

Samantha shook her head. 'Unlikely. I doubt *she* even knew. The Cult like to keep this knowledge under wraps and it is rare for doppelgangers to live in the same country as their Original, let alone meet them. But when the opportunity arises for the Cult to bring you together with your Original, they jump on it. You are the reason a number of inner circle members recently moved to Sydney.'

Alannah leaned forward to peer at Samantha across Tyler. 'What do you mean, "bring them together"?'

She sighed. 'I'm sorry, Alannah, but the Cult already have Brendan. If they recruit Tyler and tempt him, it will set him on the dark path. Once they taint his soul, they will be able to bring the pair together to practise dark rituals of immense power… the sort with catastrophic results.'

When he looked at Alannah, Tyler saw several tears trickling down her pale cheeks. He wiped a few of them away with his thumb. 'I'm sorry, beautiful. I know this must be hard news to swallow. But I promise I won't go anywhere near this cult. I won't let them use me and Brendan against you or anyone you love.'

All she could manage was a slight nod.

He brought his arm around Alannah's shoulders to comfort her, then turned back to Samantha. 'How did you get mixed up in all this?'

'My parents groomed me for the Cult, but until the inner circle moved to Sydney, I only worked on the outskirts. But Kek, my new master, took an interest in me and brought me into the

second tier through mind control and… other manipulations.'
She did not need to say more for Tyler to understand the
implications. Samantha trembled.

With his free arm, Tyler pulled her close to his chest. 'Hey.
It'll be okay.'

'I'm legitimately in danger now, Tyler. The next time Kek
contacts me, he will detect my betrayal.'

'Lana?'

'Hmm?' Her head was also resting against him as she
snuggled into his side.

'Are you able to block the Cult's access to Samantha's
mind?'

'I don't know. Possibly. It would be easier to keep such
shields in place if Samantha was able to channel the Stygian
element too.'

Samantha huffed. 'Fortunately, my dark mage initiation
opened me to nether.'

Sitting up, Alannah dried her eyes and forced a smile. 'I
guess I'd better shower and dress now 'cause it looks like we're
in for a long day.'

Tyler's eyes remained fixed on the sight of Alannah's arse
until she disappeared into the hallway.

Once the door closed, Samantha whispered to him, 'You're
in love with her, aren't you?'

He gazed into her hazel eyes. 'She's not the only woman
I'm in love with.'

A boggart with copper-coloured hair guarded the room Brendan
needed to visit. 'Greetings, Lord Jet. I am Lady Amber's captain.
You can call me Rusty.'

'Thank you, Rusty.' He wondered if Rusty was any relation to Jacob, although most boggarts looked the same to him. It was unusual to see one in the upper ranks of the Syndicate, but not unheard of. Unlike the seelie fae who rank their folk according to race, the unseelie earned their positions through merit. Given how boggarts were one of the least magical fae, they needed to prove themselves through their wit and cunning in the criminal world.

'My Lady is expecting you, please head straight in.'

Brendan nodded and entered through the door Rusty opened for him, finding Amber sitting on an elegant chaise longue.

'Please make yourself at home,' she insisted with a nod toward one of the matching armchairs.

Sitting on the antique, he realised her deliberate choice of words had not included 'comfortable' with good reason. This furniture was the next best thing to medieval torture devices.

'I imagine you have a few questions?'

He snorted. 'To put it mildly.'

'Give me a moment.' Closing her eyes, she cast a series of spells, the last of which popped Brendan's ears. 'I have warded the room so we can speak freely. Ask away.'

'Are you really my great aunt?'

Amber dropped her glamour, revealing herself for the lich she was: hair and eyes both faded to white, and ribs showing through the semi-transparent skin of her chest. Yet her face remained vibrant and firm. 'Yes, Brendan. I am Dana, Tara's sister.'

Feeling nauseated by the memory of his own seduction attempts, he shifted his focus to a spot on the wall to ground himself. 'Why didn't you tell me before the vote?'

'Because it was not safe. The enemy has spies everywhere, even among the most irreputable organisations.'

'I don't understand.'

'It is too soon to explain the nature of our enemy, but I want you to understand the Syndicate is your grandmother's legacy, an asset for you to use in your quest for knowledge and power. But also, a means of protection and disguise. She intended for you and Alannah to take the reins together, but I heard the two of you had a falling out.'

Gobsmacked, he did not even register Dana's last comment about his relationship with Alannah. 'Wait, are you saying Tara built this organisation for me and Lana?'

'More like rebuilt it, but yes. When she could not use her previous role as Queen of the Cursed to control Alannah, she realised there was more to gain by elevating the girl to her full potential. She also discovered… things. *Your* role in this is critical, but perhaps you can both conduct your own research separately until the pair of you reunite.'

Brendan scoffed. 'Any form of amicable reunion is unlikely at this stage. Her actions destroyed me, and I reacted drastically, hurting her just as much.'

'Oh, the young and foolish heart. Do you still love her, though?'

He closed his eyes to search his soul. 'Yeah, I do. But I hate her too.'

'Do you care about her enough to want what is best for her?'

'Yes.' He did not even need to think about it. Despite how much she had broken his heart, he would always care about Alannah.

'Then running the Syndicate and using it the way Tara intended will provide an opportunity for you to help Alannah, even if only at a distance for now.'

He nodded his agreement, mulling over Dana's words. 'What do you mean run the Syndicate? I thought that was your job and I am your 2IC?'

'I have my hands full as leader of the cursed and this is your Syndicate, not mine. I only intend to be the face because you dislike politics. You are the true leader, at least until you are ready to bring Alannah on board.'

Brendan combed both hands through his hair. 'I have no idea how to lead these people.'

She offered him a sympathetic smile. 'I am here to help with your transition. But, before we get to the ins and outs of upper-level management, I would like to hear about your progress with the Egyptian elves.'

He cocked a brow in surprise. 'You knew about that job?'

Dana laughed. 'Of course. I was Tara's wing-woman. She kept me abreast of all her work and vice versa. Until I took over as the Queen, I was the one working from the shadows, gathering intel, and making secret deals on her behalf. She used her defeat at Alannah's hands as an opportunity to trade places and keep her identity hidden.'

'I assume you refer to her first defeat. From what I hear, Tara's true death was also Lana's doing. But I honestly don't understand why. I thought Alannah was on Tara's side?'

A conspiratorial grin crossed his great aunt's face. 'That is what Alannah wanted the world to think. Richard was the one who murdered my sister and Alannah avenged Tara's death.'

Brendan wished he had been there to see Alannah finish the arsehole.

'So, about these elves?'

'Oh right.' He forced his mind away from the woman who had turned his world upside down. 'Violet used her contacts to become acquainted with some Egyptian elves and their local dark mage associates. The closest we got is my joining a cult.'

Dana's eyes widened with surprise. 'Did the cult initiate you?'

'Yup. But it's all I've done so far.'

She leaped up from her chair and grabbed a book from her suitcase. After handing it to him, she returned to the couch. 'Have a look through this book and tell me if any of those sigilla match the one used by the cult who recruited you.'

Flicking through the book, Brendan noticed it was a handwritten research log of dark mage practitioners. 'Did you compile this?'

'Yes.'

Returning his gaze to the journal, he paid closer attention to the magic symbols until he was certain he had found the applicable motif. After reading the name of the associated cult, his eyes bugged out. 'Holy. Shit.'

'You found it? Let me see.'

He handed her the book with the page open to a hieroglyphic sigil.

Dana's brows rose as she glanced back at him. 'Are you sure this is the one?'

'Yup.'

'In that case, your job got a whole lot more interesting and significantly more dangerous.'

Chapter Twelve

When Brendan found Caleb alone in his room, anxiety radiated from Caleb's aura in plumes of burgundy smoke as he sat cross-legged on his bed, vaping his lungs out. One of these days he was going to have to teach Caleb how to conceal his aura. But it could wait until things were less strained between them. He approached from behind and placed a comforting hand on Caleb's shoulder. 'You're not the only one feeling nervous.'

Leaning back against Brendan, Caleb's free hand found his. 'I still can't believe you volunteered to organise this shit-show. You weren't even the boss man at the time.'

In the week since the vote, Brendan had dedicated most of his time to planning the crime they were about to commit. A grunt slipped from his lips as the weight of Caleb's head pressing against his crotch stirred his arousal. But it was not the time to give in to his carnal desires, so he dropped to the bed beside Caleb. 'I'm gonna be honest with you, 'cause I think you deserve to know. When I first suggested taking on this job, I had an ulterior motive, though it's no longer relevant.'

Caleb's jaw dropped. 'Shit! You were gonna try to escape, weren't you?'

He nodded.

'So that's it: you were gonna leave me, like you left Alannah?'

Feeling ashamed, he lowered his gaze to his hands. 'If you weren't in love with your sister, I would have taken you with me. But I know you can't live without her. Doesn't matter now that I'm free.'

'It *does* matter to me, 'cause of how much I love *you*, Brendan.' Tears trickled down Caleb's silver cheeks. 'You didn't care enough to stay.'

'Hey,' Brendan wiped away the droplets of anguish, 'don't forget, even as a free man, I chose to stay here.'

Bitterness filled Caleb's eyes as he glared at Brendan. 'Only because Bridey offered you protection.'

'Icing on the cake, Thornsy. *You* are the real reason I'm still in this house.' Brendan claimed his mouth in a fervent kiss, then jerked back, before things escalated to the sort of all-consuming passion that can last the whole night. 'Come on, we'd better get to work.'

Caleb's voice turned breathy. 'Yeah.'

Dressed all in black, Brendan drove Caleb and Levi to their rendezvous point in Kings Cross. It was gratifying to get behind the wheel of his Jag again after what seemed like months. In reality, a trifling shy of four weeks had transpired since he walked out of Alannah's life.

They pulled into the unmarked warehouse and let the roller-door close before getting out of the car. Climbing the steep ladder in gloomy darkness brought them to a cramped office in the loft space. Three other guys and two girls sat around the table, talking in hushed voices while they waited.

Brendan retrieved the tablet from his pocket and pulled up his notes. 'Hey everyone. Have you all reviewed the schematics and schedule?'

The chorus of 'Yes, sir' felt oddly formal, but Brendan knew he would need to get used to it.

He turned to the newly recruited endarkened guy. 'Kyle, did you manage to get a police radio scanner and Council comms interceptor for the getaway car?'

'Yes, sir.'

'Excellent. Any questions before we start?' His eyes scanned the group.

'Yes, actually,' replied Kyle. 'I was wondering how we are all gonna fit in my car?'

'Well, Zach will be staying here, and Mason is taking his motorbike.'

'Still makes six of us.'

Sierra, the four-foot-tall pixie stood and approached Caleb. 'Do you think I could ride in your lap, sugar?'

When Caleb cautiously glanced at him, Brendan was grinning. Caleb was gorgeous, but he was not accustomed to being hit on. Caleb smiled at Sierra. 'Um, yeah, sure.'

'Right,' continued Brendan, 'with Erin up front, the rest of us should fit easily in the back. Come on, time's a-wasting.' He led them all downstairs to the black Subaru WRX Kyle had recently modified with bulletproof, tinted windows.

They all stopped beside the vehicle, allowing Zach, their illusionist, to cast strong glamour spells on each of them. The idea was for them to be invisible to the untrained eye. It would take an extremely powerful mage to pierce through such a strong veil and there were not many of those around. But they all knew the spell would only last an hour, which made Caleb's role as timekeeper critical.

As the initial team member to gain concealment, Brendan would lose his cover first. But he was their enchanter, so he ought to be able to get himself out of trouble if it came to it. Caleb set the master timer going, while each person set their own watches as soon as Zach cloaked them.

Things were cosy in the back seat, but Brendan did not mind pressing himself up against Caleb and the sexy pixie who snuggled into them. Levi did not even blink an eye at the apparent intimacy the guys shared. After all, the other members of Bridey's household knew all about their sexual relationship.

The Australian Museum came into view within record time thanks to Kyle's driving skills and his souped-up Subie[5]. They parked at the bus stop outside, waiting for Sierra to perform her magic. With her attunement to nether, it was her job to bypass any wards protecting the building.

During this time, Erin got to work on the human security systems using her hacking skills. Being half elf, her magic abilities were limited, but she made up for it with her smarts. 'I'm in,' she announced, even before Sierra had finished.

'And?' Brendan asked.

'The alarms are disabled, and I looped the camera feed.'

'Good.'

A steel gate opened, granting them access to the business entry and Kyle moved the car behind the large stone wall. Mason arrived on his bike a minute later. The orc was their hired muscle and with any luck, they would not need him. But it always paid to prepare.

With a sigh, Sierra leaned back into Caleb's arms. 'Those were some strong wards, but I got 'em all.'

Brendan gave her a seductive smile. 'Great work, sweetie. Let's go, guys.' Except for Kyle, they all piled out of the car, meeting Mason at the door.

---

[5] Subaru

Brendan planted a quick kiss on Caleb's cheek before sending him to his lookout post by the gate. While Levi made use of his magic lockpicking skills, Brendan tested his telepathic comms. '*Can everyone hear me, over?*'

The replies came in their designated order starting with Caleb, '*Stirling reading you, over.*'

'*Erin reading you, over.*'

Kyle, Levi, Mason, and Sierra checked in. The door opened for them as soon as Brendan had finished confirming a connection with all his present team members.

Being the spell breaker, Sierra took point, followed by Levi, Erin, Brendan, and Mason. She followed the map on her iPad, leading them past a series of locked offices, up the stairs, and directly to the Ancient Egyptian collection. A few pieces of art on plinths surrounded the central exhibit—a large black sarcophagus containing 'The Black Mummy.' Glass cases lined the walls, displaying an assortment of artifacts from earthenware pots to gold statues of the gods. The shiny blue beetle was easy enough to find alongside some other magic jewellery. '*This display case is warded.*' Closing her eyes, Sierra channelled the stygian element to dispel the protections.

After a quick scan using one of her electronic gadgets, Erin smiled as her thoughts filled Brendan's mind. '*No further electronic systems.*'

As soon as Sierra gave him the all-clear, Brendan nodded toward Levi, who made quick work of the lock. Brendan grabbed the scarab and two other items catching his eye: a shimmering gold ankh pendant on a chain, and a lazurite cartouche. He let the others each select their own treasure as part of their cut. They knew the extra item he took was for Caleb and Levi claimed the loot for Kyle and Zach.

Kyle's voice boomed in Brendan's head. *'Council en route, over.'*

Shit! 'We've gotta go, now!'

Mason was still choosing his prize and Sierra pouted at Brendan. *'I haven't got mine yet!'*

Brendan wanted to groan, but he held back, not willing to risk making a sound and alerting the guards. *'Fucking hurry! We've got unwanted company coming.'*

With everything out in the open, it was a relief for Tyler to be able to hold Samantha in his arms whilst watching television in the living room. Jaxon did not exactly like it, but he was not going to stop them. Aside from playful hints of jealousy, Shane did not care.

Samantha had redeemed herself by giving them all the real intel she could. Of course, striking the Cult at their core was going to be a big undertaking, one that would take time to plan. In the meantime, Tyler was going to enjoy every moment he got with his Firecracker.

As she laughed at the sitcom, Tyler's gaze focussed on Samantha. With a glance, she caught him looking at her. 'What?'

Tucking a strand of hair behind her ear, Tyler smiled. 'Just admiring the woman I love.'

Her eyes bugged out. 'I didn't know Tyler Quirke could be so cheesy.'

He laughed. 'I was going for sweet and romantic. But hey, if you're not into hearts and flowers, I could stick to wildly inappropriate.'

After biting her lip for a second, she grinned. 'I love your wild side, but I can handle romance so long as you don't lock your beast away when in the bedroom.'

'Ah hell, I don't think that's even possible with you.'

'Glad to hear it.' She leaned in to claim his lips in a fierce kiss.

But Jaxon's voice killed their moment. 'Gear up Quirky, we've got an urgent job to attend.'

Tyler whipped his head around to face Jaxon. 'What?'

'Probable Cult-related robbery going on in the city. We have to move *now*.'

He rose to his feet. 'But what about Sam?'

'Shane and Tanya will stay here to watch her.'

'Why can't Shane go with you instead?'

'Because I need *you*.' Jaxon swapped over his guns for a bunch of imbued blades.

Samantha jumped up from the couch. 'But what if this is a trap to capture Tyler?'

Jaxon scowled at her. 'Your concern is endearing, really. But Quirky is more than capable of holding his own in a fight.'

Pulling her into his arms, Tyler kissed Samantha on the forehead. 'He's right, babe: I'll be fine. Stay close to Shane and don't let anyone in while I'm gone, okay?'

She nodded and pressed her lips to his fleetingly.

Having armed himself, Tyler followed Jaxon outside. 'So, what's going on here?'

'I got a call from the High Magus. The wards at the Australian Museum went down, which can only mean one thing.'

Puzzled, Tyler looked at him blankly.

'Someone is going after the artifacts the Council stored there for safekeeping.'

'How do we know this is Cult business? Surely the City's regular warlocks can handle this?'

'Well for one thing, most dark mages wouldn't have the means to break into this place. Plus, those artifacts they are after are Egyptian—Ancient to be precise.'

'Shit! Sam said her master was Egyptian.'

Jaxon glanced at him with an arched brow. 'Exactly.'

They magiported to the station and Jaxon jumped behind the wheel of his patrol car. It did not take them long to negotiate traffic with the sirens blaring. When they arrived, Tyler could not see anyone.

Jaxon grabbed his glamour-piercing glasses from the console and put them on. 'Christ! Put yours on too, Quirky.'

As the lenses slipped in front of his eyes, the scene came into focus. A group of people wearing balaclavas were running from the opposite side of the building toward a black Subaru, while two more guys approached their patrol unit. Tyler jumped out of the car, along with Jaxon who sent a kinetic shockwave designed to knock their opponents to the ground.

But the guy in front put up an Aether shield in time to deflect the blow, causing it to rebound.

Despite bracing himself for the impact, the spell pushed Tyler back a couple of feet. 'These two guys are the distraction, boss. We gotta get the rest of 'em.'

'On it. Keep these folks busy.'

Retrieving a sword from its hilt, Tyler advanced on the front man. It was curious how they had put the skinny guy up front when the man behind him was clearly stronger and the only one drawing a weapon. Skinny Guy appeared frozen in place with his gaze locked on Tyler. *What the hell? Why isn't he preparing to fight?*

'*Fuck!*' Jaxon cried as his second attack rebounded off the shield and he fell on his arse.

The transitory distraction allowed Muscle Man to run at Tyler, almost catching him off guard. But Tyler parried at the last second. *Damn it! These guys know exactly what they're doing. I need to take out the man attuned to Aether if we are gonna have any hope of getting attacks through.* With that in mind, Tyler shifted the sword fight toward his target.

As the sound of swords clashing filled the night air, Tyler ducked and wove until he was in arm's reach of the other man. Lunging, Tyler pulled Skinny Guy up to his chest and pressed the sharp edge of his blade against the silvery skin of his throat. 'Drop your weapon,' he demanded of Muscle Man, 'or your friend will lose his head.'

'Stirling! No!' The pained cry pierced the night, and it came from one of the men who had reached the getaway car. It sounded like the distressed call of someone who deeply cared.

A brother? Or maybe a lover? Tyler was not about to shift his attention from the man wielding a sword to see who it was, though. He applied a touch more pressure, letting blood trickle down his captive's throat. 'I said drop. Your. Weapon.'

His opponent obeyed this time, letting the sword fall noisily to the concrete.

'Hands in the air where I can see them.'

The guy's sleeves slipped back over his wrists, and his biceps bulged as he extended his arms upward. The olive-coloured skin showing through and the horns protruding through the ski mask suggested the man was an orc.

Odd to see them siding with the bad guys. He must be a mercenary. 'Surrender now and I will put in a good word for you.'

He nodded his thanks and let Tyler handcuff him to Skinny Guy. Without the threat of immediate danger, Tyler looked at the other group and noticed them trying to pull one of the guys into the car. The one who hesitated exchanged a look with Tyler's prisoners as Jaxon approached the car with a fireball forming in his hand. Seconds later, the other man let his associate drag him away and the car sped off into the distance.

Jaxon lobbed his fireball, but it did not reach them in time. *'Damn it!* Come on Quirky, we may as well see what we can get out of these arseholes.' He stormed off toward the car and opened the back door.

Tyler clamped separate pairs of cold iron cuffs on each of the robbers and removed their masks, confirming that Skinny Guy was endarkened. *Sam didn't mention the Cult was recruiting them too.* Not that it mattered. He had always considered them to be the scum of the Earth. With no care for the unseelie man's comfort, he pushed him into the back of the car, along with the Orc, and climbed in next to Jaxon.

The warlock manhandling Caleb could've been his lover's twin. Combining the disconcerting resemblance with the rough treatment evoked a similar response in Caleb's body to when Brendan touched him. It almost didn't matter that this guy's intentions were anything but sexual.

When they reached the evidence room, the Brendan lookalike released the cuffs on his hands. 'Lose the clothes.'

This must be the infamous warlock strip-search I've heard so much about. It was embarrassing how much his dick twitched at the thought. Remembering the reality of his predicament helped to subdue his arousal as he slipped out of the plain black clothes, leaving his jeans and underpants until last.

While the sexy warlock explored Caleb's depths, the other one snickered.

'What the hell are you laughing at, Hayes?'
'I think he likes that a bit too much, Quirky.'

When Quirky—or whatever the hell his name was—looked between Caleb's legs, he swore. Jerking his hand back, he shoved Caleb, knocking him to his hands and knees. 'Get dressed.'

It was a relief to reclaim his clothes and sit with a table between him and Quirky. But when Caleb realised he was in an interrogation room, panic seized his heart in a vice.

The blond warlock set his phone to film their conversation, sat back and stared at Caleb a moment. 'I am Warlock Jaxon Hayes, and this is Tyler Quirke. Please state your name for the records.'

Caleb remained silent.

Jaxon sighed and retrieved the evidence bag containing Caleb's wallet. After snapping on a pair of blue nitrile gloves, he retrieved several cards from it. 'Are you Caleb Hawthorn?'

He nodded.

Tyler sniggered. 'What's wrong, faggot? Cat got your tongue? Oh wait, you probably don't put that thing near pussies.'

With a sneer, Caleb replied, 'Listen, you homophobic arsehole: just 'cause I like fucking men, doesn't mean I don't love women too.'

'Hey, I don't have a problem with gays, or bi people. It's criminal trash like you I detest.'

'Quirky, please,' Jaxon reprimanded his partner before turning his attention back to Caleb. 'What were you doing at the museum?'

'I was on a school excursion. What the fuck do you think I was doing there?'

'Do you admit to being party to the theft of several magic artifacts?'

Caleb shrugged. 'Maybe we were borrowing them.'

'Right, because unseelie scum like you are known for returning the shit you take.' Vitriol oozed from Tyler's tone.

'Oh, on top of being sexist, you're a racist bigot too?' Caleb challenged him.

'Don't make me shut that smart mouth of yours.'

A grin crossed Caleb's lips as he pressed them tightly together.

'Shit! We want him to talk, Quirky.' Jaxon raked his hands through his hair with a frustrated huff. 'Who were you working for tonight, Caleb?'

'A friend.' As much as he tried to avoid it, Caleb couldn't help casting lustful eyes at Tyler. *He looks so much like Brendan. Those deep-set emerald eyes, the perfect fucking jawline with enough stubble to graze my skin….*

'Can you be more specific?' Jaxon continued the questioning while Tyler glared at Caleb.

'No.'

'Why not?'

'I don't wanna.'

Tyler squirmed. 'Why the hell do you keep looking at me with bedroom eyes?'

Caleb couldn't keep the wicked grin from his face. 'You look like someone I know.'

With wide eyes, Tyler snatched the evidence bag with the loose contents of Caleb's wallet. 'South Australian licence,' he mumbled. 'Do you know Brendan Winters?'

His lips continued curling upwards. 'You might say I know him *very well*.'

Tyler paled, and his mouth fell agape when the implication hit home. 'Do you have a sister named Bridey?'

Taken aback by the leftfield question, Caleb's expression turned serious. 'Why do you ask?'

'Answer the damn question.'

'Yeah, I do.'

Rising from his seat, Tyler tossed Caleb's stuff on the table. 'These guys are Dark Syndicate.'

'Yeah but remember what your friend said about Brendan?' replied Jaxon. He turned back to Caleb. 'Have you or your sister joined any cults recently?'

'Hell no. We don't touch that shit.'

Tyler scowled maliciously. 'And what about your beloved Brendan?'

He tensed. 'What about him?'

'Has *he* joined any cults?'

Hiding his trembling hands under the table, Caleb steadied his breathing. 'I don't know, you'll have to ask him.'

'I guess I will. You gonna tell me where I can find him?'

'Is the Arch Mage a woman?' Caleb scoffed.

'You know, we could call Brendan or Bridey from your phone and trace the call,' Tyler explained.

Caleb laughed, knowing they wouldn't be able to find those numbers in his contacts. 'Yeah, good luck.'

Tyler dropped Caleb's phone on the table. 'I guess you'll have to take us home to meet the family.'

'Not gonna happen.'

'Oh, you don't want to go home? Let's see if you still feel that way after a few days in the lockup.' Tyler pulled him out of the chair and dragged him down to the basement of the cop shop. After shoving him into a cell, he removed the cuffs and locked the cage-like door with a big-arse smirk. 'Be sure to let the guards know when you are ready to post bail.'

Flying through the front door, Brendan did not even stop to don his collar as he sought out Bridey. He flung the bedroom door open and found her riding Damien like a rodeo bull.

'Jet, sweetheart, what's going on?' Bridey's voice betrayed her apprehension.

He tossed the scarab on the bed. 'There's your damn beetle, now please leave us, Damien.'

Bridey sat back on the bed to let Damien gather his things and get dressed.

Damien inspected the artifact and smiled. 'Thank you, Lord Jet. I'll be in touch,' stopping once more to shake Brendan's hand on the way out.

He watched to be sure Damien was out of earshot before turning back to Bridey. This time, he did not hold back the emotion in his voice. 'They got him, Bry. The Council got Caleb!'

'Oh Gods. What happened?' The fear in her eyes was plain to see.

'A couple of warlocks rocked up as we were leaving.' Brendan gulped back the lump forming in his throat. 'One of them grabbed him and held him at sword point and forced Mason to disarm. I wanted to go after him, but Levi and the others held me back.'

'He was doing his job protecting us,' Levi explained from the doorway. 'You knew there was a risk of this happening.'

'Doesn't make it any easier to deal with. I'm so fucking sorry, Bry.' The tears sprang free.

Leaping from the bed, Bridey embraced him. 'Please give us some privacy, slave.'

'Yes, Madame.' Levi closed the door, leaving Brendan alone in Bridey's arms.

'It's not your fault, handsome.'

'Yes, it is. You heard Levi. Caleb got caught trying to protect me. And it was my goddamn plan. I screwed up and—'

'Shh.' Bridey pressed a finger to his lips. 'I reviewed the plan with you, and it was flawless. Obviously, the Council has magic technology beyond our understanding.'

'Shit!' Brendan lifted his head to look into her eyes. 'They were wearing glasses. Must have been how they saw through our glamour.'

'Interesting. Sounds like the work of a powerful conjurer.'

'How can you be calm about this? Aren't you worried about Caleb?'

'Of course I am,' Bridey sighed. 'I'm trying to be strong for you, handsome.'

The raw truth in her eyes floored him. This woman was hurting as much, if not more than Brendan, but she was putting his needs first. It threw all his previous opinions of her out the window. He pulled her against him, holding her tight.

'I have a few contacts I can call tomorrow. With any luck I should be able to get him out of there.'

'Fuck, I hope so.' He dug his fingers into her shoulder blades.

She ran soothing strokes along his back. 'Trust me, sweetie, Caleb's gonna be okay.' With a tug of her arms on his, Bridey drew Brendan down into her bed where she wrapped herself around him. She continued to comfort him with her gentle touch, helping him drift off to sleep. It was the first time he had shared Bridey's bed without her demanding sexual gratification. And for once, he got a proper feel for the real Bridey Hawthorn.

Chapter Thirteen

It came as a surprise to Brendan when his waking thoughts were of the beautiful woman in his arms. And they were not unpleasant like the usual kneejerk reaction he got to finding himself in bed with her after the sexual frenzy wore off. He had come to understand why her inner aura was not pitch-black. The sensitive violet patches of her soul had made themselves known. *Is that why she's obsessed with the colour purple?* These thoughts filled his mind as he admired her sleeping form.

She must have sensed him looking at her, or perhaps he moved too much, and before long she stirred and opened her eyes. Speaking with a gruff voice, she slid a hand down his bare back. 'Morning, handsome.'

At some point during the night, Brendan had stripped away the clothes obstructing his comfort, always preferring to sleep naked. He glanced at the clock before smiling at her. 'Afternoon, beautiful.'

She sucked in a breath as a grin curled her lips. Seconds later, she jack-knifed. 'Shit! I need to make those calls for Caleb.'

When she began to rise from the bed, Brendan pulled her back. 'Wait a sec.' Gathering her into his lap, he kissed her lips; not with the usual ferocity they shared, but a slow, sensual kiss. He heard a soft moan escape from her as he drew back. 'Thank you for last night, Bry.'

Pressing her forehead to his, she whistled through pursed lips. 'No one has ever kissed me like that,' she whispered. The confession painted her in a vulnerable light and broke through a crack in the shield he had erected around his heart; one of many hairline fractures her brother had made when chipping away.

'Not even Caleb?'

'No. My relationship with him is beyond complicated.'

'I can see that. How many times have you been in love before, Bry? I get the impression you've had your heart broken as severely as I have.'

She closed her eyes a moment, as though she was holding back the threat of tears. When they fluttered open again, she took a deep breath. 'Before you, Brendan, there was only ever Caleb. He's the one who broke my heart.'

'How so?' He kept his voice soft and encouraging.

'When we were younger and our relationship turned sexual, he kept pushing me away even though I could read his mind and his emotions enough to see how much he wanted me. Eventually he told our mother I had raped him, prompting Mum to run away and hide him from me.'

'I guess it would be devastating. You know he loves you now, right?'

'I know he loved me even then. But sometimes love isn't enough to overcome our fears.'

It was the crux of Caleb's problem. He had been afraid of what it would mean to allow himself the pleasure of his sister's affections. 'I'm guessing your mum is where he got his strong moral compass from?'

She adopted a lop-sided grin. 'We both did, but Dad skewed mine a lot over the years.'

'How did such a pure-hearted elf end up with your old man?'

'It wasn't her choice. My dad works in the slave trade, and she was one such victim. He took a liking to her and kept her for himself.'

'Fuck! That's heavy.' Brendan paused to let it sink in. 'Are all of your other slaves from him?'

'Yeah, they are,' she admitted. This was the side of Bridey he did not get.

'You've gotta set them free, Bry.'

Tension started to lock her up and she pulled away.

But Brendan was not about to let her true self escape. He grabbed her shoulders and looked deep into her eyes. 'Listen to me, beautiful. I know you still have some good left in your soul. You proved it to me last night. This woman, the real Bridey Hawthorn, she is the one I can feel myself falling for and she is probably the one Caleb loves. I want to see more of her and less of the persona you created for your father.'

Bridey's eyes widened as droplets trickled from them.

'Do you really love me?' he asked.

'Yes, but Dad—'

'Your old man isn't here. You can be your own woman now. Please, will you free those slaves? For me?' He pleaded with everything he had; magic tricks included.

'Okay.'

Smiling, Brendan kissed her deeply again before letting her go. 'Thank you. Now, let's get Caleb out of prison.'

As Samantha's fork slipped out from between her lips and she bit into her piece of ravioli, Tyler realised he was a captive audience. No one made eating look as sexy as she did. But the sound of Jaxon's phone ringing broke his trance.

Jaxon glanced at the caller's name. 'It's High Magus O'Grady.' He picked up the device and answered the call. 'Hello, Your Honour … *What?* … Did you try to stop them? … I see … Were you able to get his current address? … Understood. Thanks for letting me know. Bye.'

Tyler looked at him expectantly as he hung up.

'The Council dropped the charges on Caleb Hawthorn and let him go.'

'*The fuck?* Why would they do that?'

'The call came from above O'Grady. He couldn't stop them. As for why, he couldn't say.'

'Are you telling me we lost our best lead on tracking down Brendan Winters?'

'Afraid so.'

'*Damn it!*' Having lost his appetite, Tyler pushed his dinner plate into the middle of the table, standing to pace the room. 'So, we're back to square one?'

'Not exactly. We still have Samantha's intel,' Shane suggested.

'Right, because poking the wasps' nest is such a smart plan.'

'What if you follow the wasps from the nest?'

'What the hell are you talking about, Walshy?'

'He means a stakeout, Quirky,' Jaxon explained. 'If we watch their HQ, we can track the people coming and going, learn who lives where. We could pick them off one by one. Who knows, we might even spot Brendan in the process.'

Tyler flopped back onto his chair, letting Samantha soothe his nerves with a gentle caress of his thigh. 'Sounds like a slow process, but I guess it's our best shot now. It's frustrating when we almost had the guy in our grasp.'

After scraping up the last of his pasta and swallowing his hefty mouthful, Shane let his cutlery clatter onto his plate. 'What's important about catching this Brendan guy anyway?'

'You're kidding right?' Tyler asked. 'Did you not hear what Sam said about me being his doppelganger and what the Cult plan to do with us?'

'Sure I did. But how does catching Brendan, as opposed to any of the other cult members, help us?'

'Because if they don't have Brendan, they can't use *me*. Without him, it's a lot safer for *me* to enter their premises and help take them down.'

Returning from a short trip to the kitchen, Shane popped the top off his second beer. 'So what? You kill him to eliminate the threat?'

Tyler huffed. 'I wouldn't mind after what he did to Lana.'

'Quirky, you know we can't. We have to operate within the law,' Jaxon reminded him.

He put his hands up in a surrendering gesture. 'I know, boss. I was kidding. We only need to keep Brendan locked away and out of their reach when we attack. After the museum job, he's up for some hefty criminal charges anyway. Should be enough to put him away for several years.'

Shane laughed. 'Those larceny charges won't worry him as much as the whole drug operation he started back in SA. He's looking at life for that alone.'

'Excellent point.'

Jaxon gave up on his own dinner and sighed. 'If the powers that be don't let him off like they did his boyfriend.'

Shane shot Jaxon a surprised look. 'His *boyfriend*?'

Samantha and Tanya also looked on with intrigued expressions.

'I guess we forgot to mention those juicy details. Apparently, Brendan bats for the other team now, or possibly both. Oh, and that Caleb guy we arrested was his lover. We worked it out when he kept giving Tyler bedroom eyes while confessing to knowing Brendan,' Jaxon paused to add air quotes, '"very well."'

Tyler shivered. 'It was totally disturbing. Not to mention his reaction to the strip search.'

Samantha cracked up laughing. Once she calmed down, she bit her lip for a few seconds. 'I'm sorry, babe, but that was too funny.'

He groaned. 'I'm glad you find it amusing.'

She grinned. 'First Alannah, then Caleb. I wonder who your doppelganger charms will work on next?'

Shane prodded Tyler's arm. 'Ah hell Quirky, you better be careful if you visit Brendan's hometown. I heard he was a bigger slut than you.'

'Speaking of which, Liam invited us to their family's Solstice dinner on Friday night,' Jaxon informed them.

'Really?' Tyler paused for thought before continuing, 'What about Sam?'

'I asked him if you could take a plus one and he said it's fine. Honestly I think he's relieved your attention diverted from his woman.'

Swallowing a lump of guilt, Tyler chose not to remind them of his recent liaison with Alannah. 'Fair enough, but is it safe to take her?'

'Safer than leaving her. Besides, the dinner is at his parents' house and the place has even more protection than this apartment. Apparently, those wards kept Tara out when she threatened Alannah.'

Tyler breathed a sigh of relief. 'Good to know.'

Grabbing Tyler's arm, Samantha squeezed it and smiled up at him. 'It'll be nice to get out of this place for a change of scenery.'

'Are you sure?'

'Yeah, it's safe if we magiport straight there. Plus, I'd like to see Alannah again too.' A sly grin formed on her face, hinting at their shared memories.

'I guess it's a date.'

'Don't mention anything to Alannah about the dinner if you chat with her on social media before Friday night. Liam wants it to be a surprise.'

'Noted.' Having curbed his initial irritation, Tyler sat down at the table and resumed his meal.

When Bridey's demon driver dropped Caleb home, his first thoughts turned to ensuring Brendan's safety. Not having a friendly face to meet him at the police station sucked, but he understood the risks such an appearance presented to both Bridey and Brendan.

Neither Levi nor Isabelle greeted Caleb when he walked through the hall, much to his surprise. Voices drew him to the parlour, where Brendan sat extremely close to Bridey as they studied some paperwork together. Lifting their eyes to spot him, both of his lovers leaped to their feet, letting papers fall to the floor as they rushed to embrace him.

'Are you okay, sweetheart?' Bridey scanned his body. 'Do you need a healer?'

'I'm fine, Bry. They healed my battle injuries in prison.'

Brendan's fingers gingerly touched Caleb's neck as he inspected his throat. Seemingly satisfied the gash from Tyler's sword had vanished, Brendan pulled him closer and kissed him deeply. The greeting made his heart flutter and his toes curl.

'I take it you're okay?' Caleb asked him with a breathless voice.

'A hell of a lot better now you're home,' Brendan admitted.

Knowing Brendan cherished him brought a smile to Caleb's lips. The men hugged again, and Caleb doubted he'd ever get enough of feeling Brendan's body against his own.

Bridey pressed herself into Caleb's back, placing her hands on his shoulders as she peppered kisses along his neck and whispered, 'Welcome back my love.'

Pivoting to face Bridey, Caleb devoured her lips. Coming up for air, he glanced over Bridey's shoulder, and the pages on the floor caught his attention. 'What were the pair of you working on?'

'Looking at some resumés of potential household staff,' she replied.

He gave her a puzzled look. 'Why?'

Her beautiful, dark eyes lit up. 'I freed the slaves, so now I need some legit servants.'

Caleb's mouth gaped open. He threw his arms around Bridey and squeezed her tight. 'I'm damn proud of you, Bry. What brought you to that decision?'

'Brendan helped me come to my senses,' she explained.

Leaning back into Brendan, Caleb peered up at him. 'You never cease to amaze me, Winters.'

Brendan's eyes gleamed with wicked intent. 'Mm, you can thank me later, Thornsy.'

Bridey and Brendan flanking him spiked Caleb's arousal. He loved the contrast between her soft curves and his hard muscles. 'Why wait?' He felt thankful for the opportunity he'd had to shower at the decoy house on the way home because he could not wait to rip his clothes off.

Bridey stepped back. 'Mind if I watch?'

Having something else in mind, Caleb grabbed her arm and reeled her back in. 'I'd rather you join us.'

'Brendan?' Bridey asked, likely seeking reassurance because the three of them had not attempted another threesome since their earlier disasters.

'Don't worry, Bry, I have zero inhibitions left,' rasped Brendan as he pressed his arousal against Caleb's backside.

What happened in my absence? The way they squashed Caleb between them, kissing passionately over his shoulder, suggested something significant. Four weeks ago, the sight of them sucking face had stirred some different emotions, but there was no longer room for jealousy or trepidation between any of them.

As Brendan withdrew from the kiss, his hands found the hem of Caleb's t-shirt and he removed the garment. His fingers trailed down Caleb's back while feathering kisses along his neck. A frenzy of undressing followed amidst moments of passion as they stumbled into the guestroom.

When Caleb's gaze fell upon the bed, he found Bridey adopting a submissive position for the first time in the history of their relationship. *Things are definitely about to get interesting.*

The afternoon sun was peeking through the blinds of the guestroom when Brendan awoke. The previous night had been incredible, and he found himself cursing the former hang-ups that had prevented him from enjoying both Hawthorn siblings together in the past. Hours of pure erotic delight with the three of them taking turns in the middle had made for one of the most sexually satisfying nights of his life.

Rolling on to his side, he found Caleb sleeping soundly, but no sign of Bridey. *She must be working*. Brendan figured he should be doing likewise, but he could not draw himself away from the breathtaking sight before him. Caleb looked like a dark angel, or what Brendan imagined such beings would look like if they existed.

'Are you being a creeper, Winters?' Caleb's lips curled as he spoke with a gravelly morning voice.

Brendan laughed. 'Depends on whether you were actually sleeping.'

His eyes shot open, and the grin widened. 'I'm sure I was at some point, but that's beside the point if you thought I slept while you were watching me.'

'What can I say? I've grown fond of your pretty face, Thornsy.' Leaning in, he crashed his lips into Caleb's. Brendan broke away from the kiss before he lost his last sliver of willpower. There would be plenty of time to give in to such desires in the near future, but he needed to say something while he had Caleb alone.

Cupping Caleb's silvery cheek in his hand, Brendan looked deeply into his lover's eyes. 'You freaked me out, Thornsy. Getting yourself captured… I feared the worst. The thought of them taking you from me before… before I could tell you.'

Caleb's expression turned serious with concern. 'Tell me what?'

He hated how hard it had become to talk about his true feelings. *Damn you, Lana!* Brendan gulped. 'You've worked your way into my heart in a way I thought would be impossible with how broken it was.'

Caleb's eyes widened.

Moving directly on top of him, Brendan pinned Caleb down as a way of bracing himself for the words that followed. 'I'm… in love… with you, Caleb.'

A sharp breath slipped through Caleb's lips a moment before he pulled Brendan down for another sensual kiss. As their passion intensified, the feel of Caleb's tongue ring brought back memories of other ways he had stimulated Brendan with the tiny barbell. And it was not long before they made new memories.

Brendan caught his breath. 'I fucking love your tongue, Thornsy. I'm thinking of getting my own venom piercing so you know how superb it feels.'

'Christ! I already fall apart when you go down on me. You don't need to improve on anything there.'

'Really?'

'Absolutely. How the hell did you get them expert skills without any experience before me?'

Brendan shrugged as he smirked. 'Natural talent, I suppose.'

Caleb's fist bumped Brendan's arm. 'Smug bastard.'

His smile grew. 'Oh, but you love me all the same, right?'

This time Caleb mounted him. 'Yeah, I do, Brendan. I love you.'

They spent the rest of the afternoon expressing their love for each other in every possible way.

There was a time when Brendan looked forward to the Summer Solstice. As he walked the empty halls of the inner-city office block, he imagined the smell of his mum's cooking wafting through the building. Spending the holiday alone made him realise how much he missed his mother. *Next chance I get, I'm gonna give Mum a call.*

He could have joined the Hawthorn family, but it would have meant returning to Adelaide and he was not ready. Nor did he fancy seeing their scumbag father again. Besides, with most of the magic community busy celebrating, it was the perfect time for Brendan to catch up on some Cult reading.

Turning one last corner brought him to the library. He swiped his key card against the security panel and sent a silent thank you to Erin when the door unlocked. *Hacker girl is a damn genius.*

By the Gods! The place was huge. Thankfully, the Cult organised books logically, so it did not take him long to find what he was looking for. Most of the books were in Arabic, but he had come prepared with a translation app on his phone.

He pulled out one volume entitled *Magical Artifacts of Ancient Egypt* and continued scanning the shelves until he found several leatherbound works with unlabelled spines. He grabbed the first of them and discovered he was holding an Egyptian book of Shadows belonging to the Arafa clan. Grabbing more of them revealed a whole collection of spell tomes from all the major mage clans of Egypt. *Talk about the fucking jackpot!*

Brendan took them all to the photocopier near the reading desks and got to work on his reproductions. He would have taken them, but he knew the wards would alert the inner circle if any of their precious books left the room.

Unfortunately, the mindless task gave him time to reminisce on better times and to imagine what would be happening at Cailleach Estate in his absence. He knew his parents would decorate the house in bright, warm colours symbolic of the sun and Mum would be baking her traditional pumpernickel bread while Dad roasted meats on the Weber. *Who would be there this year?* They usually invited a couple of friends, but never the same people.

A noise from down the hall broke his reverie and prompted him to take cover. He smacked the off switch on the photocopier and ducked behind one of the solid oak desks along the wall. Turning off his torch plunged the room into darkness. Minutes later, a security guard walked into the room and casually strolled through the bookshelves, checking each row with his own torch.

Brendan's heart was pounding fast, and he could feel his grip on the pile of books slipping.

Having inspected the shelves, the man moved to the reading area.

Shit! I forgot my copies. Please don't look at the photocopier.

As the half-mage guard approached the machine, the top book on Brendan's stack toppled onto the floor, diverting the man's attention in his direction.

Fuck! Thinking quickly, Brendan intruded on the guard's mind, pushing past the mind shield, and convincing him the sound came from another room down the hall. He breathed a sigh of relief as soon as the guard left. *That got too damn close.*

After waiting for the guard to move on to a different floor, Brendan hurried the last of his copying and shoved the books back in their place. He put his duplicates in a large box and hauled them out to his car.

In the comfort of his own office, he flicked through the book on artifacts, finding the two treasures he had taken from the museum and worked on translating the Arabic text.

The ancients imbued the agate ankh with the power of healing. Anyone with magical blood can use the charm to heal their wounds without needing to channel mana or cast any spells.

Glad he had chosen the shiny piece of bling, he moved on to the next entry.

Scholars believe the Cartouche of Set was used to summon the God as part of a dark mating ritual. But along with the artifact itself, the magic world lost this knowledge centuries ago.

Brendan furrowed his brow. *How did the Cult not realise it was right under their nose? Surely they scoped out the contents of the case before arranging the job?* He turned several more pages, looking for the final item of interest. When he found it, he got his answer:

The Lazurite Scarab provides a direct connection to all Celestial beings and the Egyptians may have used it in the original immortality rituals.

His mouth dropped open. *With the beetle, they don't need the cartouche.* The significance of the second part of the entry also struck him. *Are they planning to become liches?*

Brendan's mind was spinning when he left his office the next day and drove home. When he checked Caleb's room, he found it empty. Looking in Bridey's quarters, he saw them both wrapped in each other's arms, sleeping soundly. He smiled at the sight. *They make such a cute couple.*

Not wanting to disturb them, he eased the door shut and headed to his bathroom. What he needed more than anything was a scalding shower to soothe his aching muscles. Scorching water poured down around him when Brendan sensed someone. Opening his eyes, he turned toward the intruder.

'Hey, handsome. Mind if I join you?' Bridey stood naked at the entrance to the shower cubicle.

'Mm, not at all.' He reached out to grasp one of her hands, pulling her in close and kissing her. Closing his eyes, Brendan pushed aside all the dark secrets he had learned to focus on Bridey. *She feels incredible in my arms and against my lips.* He slipped his fingers inside her, bringing forth a deep groan vibrating against his mouth as he continued to kiss her.

She whipped her head back. 'Oh Gods! Fuck me, Brendan. Fuck me *now*.'

Backing her up against the tiled wall, he leaned in close to her ear. 'No.' Stepping back an inch, he observed her reaction.

Gobsmacked, she stared at him in disbelief.

With a wicked grin, he pumped his fingers twice more before removing them. He pressed his arousal against the entrance to her quivering core. 'I'm not gonna fuck you this time Bry. Do you wanna know why?'

'Yes,' she rasped.

'Because I want to make love to you. Do you know why?'

With wide eyes, she replied by shaking her head.

'Because I love you.' He eased himself into her and let his instincts take over.

As they came together, Bridey collapsed against him. Brendan rinsed them both before turning off the taps. He wrapped her in a towel and carried her into his bedroom. Snuggling with him on the bed, Bridey smiled sweetly. 'Another astonishing first, thanks to you.'

'Christ! You've never made love or had gentle sex before?'

'No.'

He was beginning to understand Bridey. She was a broken woman, the product of a horrid upbringing where she never learned how to love. *Question is, am I too late to fix her?*

'What about you, Brendan? With your love of kink, I can't imagine you doing that much.'

'My tastes have nothing to do with it. I believe a loving relationship requires a balance of tender and kinky moments. I reserve sex like that for people I love, Bry, and there have only been two such other people.'

She sat up surprised. 'Two? I assume *she* was one of them, but the other?'

'Is Caleb.'

Bridey grinned widely. 'I am thrilled to hear it, handsome. You've been good for him, for both of us.'

He laughed. 'And you've been strangely good for me. In a dark and twisted kinda way.'

'Hmm. Speaking of dark and twisted, how did your work go last night?'

'Brilliant actually.' He told her about the scarab but kept the rest to himself. 'I think I have all I need from the Cult. Now I need to work on my exit strategy.'

'Exit strategy?'

'A way out of the Cult. I don't want to get messed up with anymore of their shit.'

'Why can't you tell them you're leaving?'

Brendan sighed heavily. 'Because they made me sign a blood oath, swearing lifetime service.'

Chapter Fourteen

'This is one hell of a way to spend Christmas Eve,' Tyler complained as he settled in alongside Jaxon in the front of their stakeout vehicle—a black SUV with tinted windows. *Totally not suss at all.*

'Why do you care about Christmas? You're not even human, let alone Christian.'

'I know, but I love capitalism.' He paused to sip his steaming coffee. 'And those cheesy movies. I was hoping to watch *Home Alone* with Sam tonight.'

Jaxon sighed, reaching into the backseat to produce a large cardboard box. 'Here, Merry Christmas. I hope this makes up for it.'

Tyler looked at the Krispy Kreme logo and smiled. 'You bloody legend!' He grabbed one of the cream-filled delights and handed the box back to Jaxon. 'Mm, yum,' he spoke with his mouth still half full of caramel.

After rolling his eyes, Jaxon returned his attention to the office building Samantha had told them was the Obsidian Cult's Australian headquarters. 'So, I've been meaning to ask. Will you be my best man?'

Licking the cream from his fingers, Tyler stared at him stunned for a moment. 'Ah, hell yeah.'

Jaxon announced his engagement to Tanya two nights ago at the Solstice dinner Alannah's family had hosted. 'Don't look surprised, Quirky. You're easily my best mate, so it stands to reason I'd ask you.'

'What about Walshy?'

'Why do you think I always take you on missions and leave him to watch Samantha?'

'I dunno. I figured you wanted to keep me away from Sam as much as possible.'

Jaxon laughed. 'No, you idiot. It's because I trust *you* with my life, more than I can Walshy. You're a skilled warlock and a loyal friend.'

'Hmph.' Tyler gave Jaxon's words some thought. 'That's cool. Speaking of weddings, do you think Liam will propose to Lana?'

'Given she's pregnant, you mean? Seems likely to me. Liam's nothing if not traditional when it comes to family values. Do you think she'll accept?'

A dejected sigh slipped from Tyler's mouth. 'Most likely. I know she loves him, and he provides her with much needed stability. Especially now she has a baby on the way.'

'You sound disappointed. I thought you were over her. And what about Samantha?'

'I love them both, Jax. I kinda hoped I could've had two women. Like a ménage à trois, you know? But at the same time, I need to stop kidding myself because I know what she does with me relates to her unresolved feelings for Brendan.'

'Yeah, it's pretty messed up.'

'That jerk *did* mess with Lana something awful.'

'Shit!' Jaxon's attention shifted back to the task at hand. 'Pass me those binoculars, Quirky.' He took them from Tyler's hand and looked at a shadowy figure in the distance. 'He's the same dark mage we saw the other night. I think we should follow him.'

Tyler grabbed the spying aid and confirmed what Jaxon had seen. The man with dark slicked-back hair was getting into a black convertible. 'Yeah, it's him alright. Let's go.'

Jaxon trailed the dark mage carefully, keeping a few cars behind to avoid detection. Their drive came to a stop outside an old house in Windsor. 'Call Walshy and get the lowdown on this place.'

Bringing up his contacts, he rang Shane.

The sound of gunfire blasted across the phoneline until Shane muted the television. 'Hey man, what's up?'

'I need you to run a property search.'

'No probs. Text me the address and I'll send you the deets.'

Shane's reply came within ten minutes, and Tyler read it out to Jaxon, 'The title and deed belong to a Finn Ryan, who obtained ownership in 1954. Walshy is looking up this man now.'

'That would mean the owner is approaching ninety at least. I doubt this dark mage is Finn, but I suppose they could be relatives.'

'Maybe.' Tyler chowed down on another doughnut while they waited.

Tyler's message tone sounded an hour later. 'Holy. Shit. Check this out. It can't be a coincidence.' He handed his phone to Jaxon.

'Indeed. Looks like we have our new lead.'

Brendan's idea of festive tradition involved Christmas themed horror movies. While some things would never change, everything was different this year. Rather than holding Alannah in his arms, he was embracing Caleb whilst watching *Eyes Wide Shut*. Even their entertainment was more thriller than horror. At least he could send his hands exploring during the more titillating scenes.

'Things are getting a bit hot, Winters.'

'Mm, is that so, Thornsy?' He breathed heavily into the crook of Caleb's neck. 'Are you talking about the flick or what I'm doing?' To emphasise his question, Brendan plunged his hand inside Caleb's pants.

Caleb sucked in a sharp breath. 'The combination. *Ah Gods*!'

Pleasuring his lover without *needing* magic gave Brendan immense satisfaction. The thought alone drove him to maximise Caleb's gratification.

As the film ended, Caleb tilted his head, diverting his attention. 'Listen. It sounds like Bridey has company.'

Grabbing the remote, Brendan muted the volume, revealing the tell-tale sounds of sex emanating up from Bridey's room. 'Curious how she didn't invite either of us to join the fun.'

'Maybe she thought we could use the alone time.'

'Since when has *our* privacy been a concern of hers? No, I'm guessing it's one of her *business meetings*. And if this is Syndicate business, I'd like to know who she is entertaining.' Brendan dropped the controller on the coffee table and made his way downstairs to Bridey's bedroom door. Pushing it open a crack, he peered inside and groaned at the scene.

Bridey was making a show of riding Damien, clearly faking her pleasure; it would take either an enchanter, or someone with intimate knowledge of her, to read the signs, however. Luckily Brendan was both and he knew the dark mage would not be a significant threat to his own relationship with Bridey.

He was about to turn and leave when Damien caught his eye. 'Hello Lord Jet, why don't you join us?'

Bridey's head turned in surprise, her eyes wide with panic.

'It's okay, I didn't mean to intrude. I'll just—'

'No, please, I *insist*.' Damien's voice carried a commanding tone Brendan felt would be foolish to ignore.

He stepped into the room, closing the door behind him, but he did not move any closer.

Keeping his eyes fixed on Brendan, Damien reached up to stroke the side of Bridey's face. 'Your woman is exquisite. It's kind of you to lend her to me.

Brendan snorted. 'Violet is her own woman, and she does as she pleases.'

'Are you not her boss now?'

'Only in matters of business. In the bedroom she is free to fuck whoever she wants.'

Damien looked up at Bridey. 'Is that so?'

She put on one of her seductive smiles. 'Yes, Damien.' Thrusting her hips against him, she reminded him what they were in the middle of.

Ignoring her, Damien returned his gaze to Brendan. 'I want you to watch Lady Violet fuck me. I want you to stand there, knowing I am the one making her come and you may *not* touch her while she is with me.'

Is this guy for real? Brendan leaned against the closed door and crossed his arms. 'Go on. Make her come.'

They resumed their ridiculous charade, and each time Bridey faked an orgasm, Damien turned to smile smugly at Brendan. *What a wanker.* All were relieved, for their own reasons, when Damien climaxed.

After cleaning himself, Damien sat on the edge of the bed and glowered at Brendan. 'Lady Violet tells me you plan to leave the Cult.'

Feeling hurt and betrayed, Brendan shot Bridey a death glare. 'Did she now?'

'Have you forgotten your initiation oath, Lord Jet? The only way a member leaves the Cult is on their deathbed. For your sake, I hope you are not considering deserting us.'

'Of course not, Damien. I don't know where my *subordinate* got such a ridiculous idea.' He infused as much bitterness as he could into both the words and the scowl he directed her way.

'I'm glad. We will expect to see you at the next new moon ritual.'

'Don't worry. I'll be there.' With a few long strides, Brendan was out the door, slamming it behind him. He hurried up the stairs, craving the fresh night air to cool off.

Tyler took his phone back and read through the genealogy stuff Shane had dug up.

'That means Finn Ryan is Brendan's great-grandfather, right?' Jaxon asked.

'Correct. Apparently, Finn arranged the marriage of Brady Ryan and Tara Winters without the pair ever knowing each other. He shipped Brady off to Adelaide in 1979 to marry Tara a week after her eighteenth birthday. Brady brought his wife back here for family holidays every year until his mysterious death at age thirty-four in 1989.'

Jaxon huffed. 'Mysterious indeed. I bet the crazy bitch killed him. Is old man Finn still alive?'

'There are no death records, but he disappeared. It looks like Tara took over managing the property on his behalf, renting it out for years.'

'Until her grandson shows up in town,' Jaxon concluded.

'I wonder how many other skeletons there are in the Winters family closet,' Tyler mused. 'They make my own family's secrets look as innocent as an episode of *My Little Pony*.'

'I dunno, man… some of those got pretty wild. Besides, learning the maid your great-grandfather had an affair with was of Ancient Egyptian descent, and that she carried this doppelganger gene is a pretty big deal.'

'True. I'd love to dedicate some time to researching my own family history. See if I can learn more about this gene and doppelgangers in general.'

'Which God do you suppose that line descends from?'

Tyler pulled up some recent searches on his phone. 'Well, Geb and Nut were the father and mother of Egyptian mages, so it's unlikely to be them. Bes and Ptah were the fathers of dwarves, Osiris was the father of orcs, Babi among a few others fathered the giants, and Kek was the father of gorgons. If you exclude the various nature gods responsible for creating elves, fae, and other beasts, that leaves Isis, Horus, and possibly Set because I don't know where he fits in. I'm sure there's a bunch of minor deities I'm missing, but that narrows it down a bit.'

'Isis being the Goddess of magic makes sense if the link you share with your Original, or whatever Samantha called Brendan, is magic. Also consider the fact you enhance the potency of each other's magic.'

'Interesting theory. Could it mean our own Dagda[6] has fathered a race of Celtic doppelgangers?'

Jaxon shrugged. 'Maybe, but we don't know if he has ever fathered any demigods and it's not like we can ask him.' Movement ahead got his attention, and he lifted the binoculars to his eyes. 'Shit! Does that look like Brendan to you?'

Grabbing the binoculars from him, Tyler watched as his mirror image walked along the front path leading from the house, stepped out onto the street, and headed in the opposite direction. 'Hell yes! I'm gonna grab him.' Without awaiting further instruction, he jumped out of the car and ran after Brendan.

As Tyler approached, Brendan glanced behind, but Tyler was not about to give him a chance to fight back. The instant their eyes locked; he sent a kinetic blast pushing Brendan to the ground. He immediately followed up with a lightning bolt strong enough to knock Brendan unconscious. Whipping out a set of cold iron cuffs, he secured Brendan's wrists and dragged him back to the car.

'Christ, Quirky!' exclaimed Jaxon. 'I hope you haven't fried all his braincells. Could make it hard to question him.'

He threw Brendan in the backseat and slammed the door. 'This is me giving zero fucks. The arsehole deserves a world of pain.'

As soon as Damien left, Bridey ran into the living room where she found Caleb dozing on the couch. No sign of Brendan. She darted through the house, searching every other room to no avail.

---

[6] The Dagda is the Celtic Father God of fertility, agriculture, strength, as well as magic, druidry and wisdom.

Shit! An inspection of the garage showed his car was still there. *He must be going for a walk.* She sighed and tried calling him.

'Hi, this is the voicemail of Darth Jet. I'm currently plotting to take over the galaxy, so you'll need to leave a message after the tone….'

After trying a few more times for good measure, she gave up. *Brendan must be royally pissed with me.*

Returning to the living room, she sat beside her brother and nudged him. 'Caleb, sweetie?'

He groaned as he stirred. As his eyes opened, he sat upright. 'What's wrong, Bry?'

'I messed up.' Her voice trembled and her hands shook like a tuning fork resonating with the song of trepidation in her heart.

Caleb surveyed the room. 'Where's Brendan?'

'He, uh, left.' She tried to inhale deeply, sputtering in the process.

Every muscle in Caleb's body appeared to tense. 'What do you mean, he left?'

'I don't know exactly. He might have gone for a walk. But he is upset with me and won't answer my calls.'

'What did you do?'

She could not hold back the tears any longer. 'I had no choice. Damien forced the truth out of me and confronted Brendan with it.'

Caleb pulled her into his arms and softened his voice. 'What truth, Bry? What's going on?'

He can be such a sweet boy. 'Brendan broke into the Cult's library on the night of the Solstice. I don't know everything he learned from his knowledge quest, but he did discover the significance of the scarab you guys stole for Damien. He also told me he wanted to find a way to sever ties with the Cult.' She choked back a sob.

With one hand caressing her back, Caleb pressed a soft kiss on her forehead. 'Hey, it's okay. Take your time.'

After a few deep breaths, she continued, 'Damien must have heard about the break-in because he came here tonight to question me, and he was able to use magic to force the truth out. Oddly, Brendan leaving the Cult concerned Damien more than the stolen secrets. Apparently, Brendan signed a blood oath tying him to the Cult for life.'

'Oh Gods, Bry! This is bad, real bad. If they force Brendan down the dark mage path, there is a high chance he could spiral out of control. He wasn't born into a life of dark magic like us. One taste of the power they can offer, and he could get hooked, like a drug addict. From what I've heard, bloodline mages are the most susceptible to corruption.'

Terror gripped her heart, sending it into a rhythmic fit to rival hardcore drumming. 'Crap! I didn't even think of the possibility.' She squeezed Caleb tight as she let the tears flow. 'What if it's already too late? What if we've lost him and it's all my fault?'

'Hey, look at me.' Caleb pulled back and peered deep into her eyes. 'This is *not* your fault, Bry. And Brendan's not about to turn dark overnight. It is not too late. We just need to find him. If he felt betrayed by you, doubtless he is screening his calls. Let me try.'

She nodded and sat back, watching as Caleb dialled Brendan with his own phone.

But Caleb frowned almost as soon as he tried. 'Straight to voicemail. I'll send him a text.' After typing out a message, he put his phone down and pulled Bridey back into his arms.

'I really do love him, Caleb.'

'I know, Bry. So do I.'

Chapter Fifteen

verything was dark, a chill seeped into his bones, and for one dreadful moment Brendan thought he was dead. But a splash of icy water over his head restored the final sliver of consciousness eluding him. Startled by the bright fluorescent light, it took him a few minutes to register his surroundings. Then he wished he were dead.

Cold iron bars lined the walls of the interrogation room. The only other person present was a blond warlock who towered over him with a scowl. 'About time you woke up.' He moved across the room and pressed a button on the intercom. 'Hey Quirky, our suspect has come to.'

The muffled sounds of the police station filtered in through the speaker box. 'I'll be right there.'

'What the hell's going on?' Brendan demanded. 'Am I under arrest?'

'Not yet. I brought you in for questioning. But given the shit on your criminal record, I don't hold out much hope for your freedom.'

Talk about the proverbial fucking frying pan fire.

A dark-haired man who looked strangely familiar walked through the door. 'Sorry if I missed anything, boss.' Distracted by his phone, he did not even look at Brendan.

'I haven't really started yet. I was explaining how we haven't yet arrested him.'

The new guy sat in a chair across the table, still looking at his phone. 'Right, let's begin.'

'Wait a minute,' Brendan interrupted, 'if I'm not in custody, I'm free to walk out of here and refuse to answer your questions, right?'

The man affectionately known as Quirky glanced up and snorted. 'Right, that'll sure help your cause. We'll subpoena your arse faster than your first fuck.' But as soon as his eyes fell on Brendan, his indifference turned into a bitter scowl.

'What my friend here is trying to say,' explained the other guy, 'is you can either cooperate now, or face the full force of the Council later.'

Brendan glared at Blondie. 'I know what a fucking subpoena is.'

'Good, I'm glad we have an understanding. So, what's your choice?'

Heaving out a sigh, Brendan reclined in his seat. 'What do you want to know?'

Blondie set his phone on the table and opened a voice recording app. 'I am Warlock Jaxon Hayes, and this is Tyler Quirke. Let's start with your name.'

'Brendan Winters.'

'Oh hell,' Hayes muttered as Tyler flew across the room and slammed a fist into Brendan's left eye.

'*That's from Lana, you piece of shit!*' Tyler screamed. 'And these are from me.' He pushed Brendan to the floor and continued to pummel him.

Tyler stunned Brendan, not only with the near-concussive blows to his head.

'*Quirky, stop it!*' Hayes cried out as he attempted to pull ninety kilos of solid warlock from Brendan. '*Get a hold of yourself before I take you off this case.*' With Tyler restrained, Hayes glared at Brendan. 'Get. Up.'

Brendan clambered to his feet.

'Sit. Down.'

Sensing Hayes was nearing the threshold where he flipped from good cop to bad cop, Brendan complied.

Hayes turned to Tyler. 'Are we going to have a problem here, Quirky? I can't have anything compromising the integrity of this case.'

'No, Sir. Let me have a few words, then we can move on.'

'Fine. Make it quick.' Hayes stopped the recording.

Tyler braced his palms on the table. 'Do you realise how much you broke Lana? Or was it your intention, you piece of dark mage scum?'

Who was this guy and why was he using the diminutive of her name? 'You don't know shit about my relationship with Lana, so shut the fuck up.'

'Oh? So, you didn't steal her away from your brother, and talk her into making the ultimate commitment right before running off into the sunset with some endarkened whore and severing the soul link?'

He gaped at Tyler, the brutal truth rendering him speechless.

'That's right. She confided everything to me. I knew her for less than twenty-four hours before she told me. Why do you think she would have poured her heart out to me when I was practically a stranger?'

Bewildered, Brendan shook his head.

Tyler leaned forward. 'Have you looked in a mirror lately? If not, I'm sure my face will do.'

Brendan's eyes widened with realisation. Tyler was the guy from the nightclub.

'I dunno if I should thank you or hate you for what followed because it was the best damn sex of my life. Problem was, she wasn't really fucking *me*.'

Shit!

'She'll never forgive you. I hope you realise that.'

Every muscle in Brendan's body tensed. 'Lana made her choice. She has Liam now.'

Tyler laughed drily. 'Right. And I'm sure she'll forget all about you when she marries him.'

Brendan shot him a look of surprise mingled with fear. *Did he seriously drop the M word?*

'It's inevitable. So, I hope you're happy with your whore and her brother, 'cause they're your lot now. That's if we don't throw your arse in gaol.'

The last of Brendan's hope pulled a vanishing act more impressive than David Copperfield.

Hayes sighed. 'Wrap this up please, Quirky. As much as I hate Brendan for what he did to Alannah, we have a job to get on with.'

'Yes, Sir,' Tyler replied with hesitation.

Brendan shifted his gaze to Hayes. 'Can I ask one thing?'

'What?' he clipped.

'How do you guys know Lana?'

'We helped her put Richard Lane and Tara Winters in the ground.'

Gods, I wish I'd been there to see her put a blade through the sadistic bastard's heart. 'Did she really kill Tara? I mean it wouldn't be the first time she tried.'

'Yep. I saw it with my own eyes.' Hayes smiled as he remembered. 'Blessed dagger in the heart, shattered soul crystal against the wall. It was glorious.'

Hmm, sounds like Lana pulled off a convincing act.

'Not as hot as when she took down Richard though,' Tyler added.

They both looked like a pair of lovesick puppies. *Yup, sounds like the Lana I remember. Breaking hearts wherever she goes.*

Hayes cleared his throat as he resumed the recording. 'Anyway, getting back to the issue at hand. Are you a member of the Obsidian Cult, or one of their contractors?'

'Shit! You know who those guys are?'

Tyler rose and leaned across the table, invading Brendan's personal space. 'Need I remind you; *we* ask the questions here?' He grabbed Brendan's throat in a choke hold. 'What's the extent of your association with the Cult?'

'Sit down, Quirky.' The other warlock spoke calmly.

When Tyler returned to his chair, he resumed glaring at Brendan.

'I'm a recent initiate.'

'Christ!' Tyler gritted his teeth. 'Do you know who those bastards are?'

He grinned. 'Yup. More than you do, I'd warrant.'

'What are you talking about?' asked Hayes.

'If you want to know more, you'll have to turn off your recording devices.'

His interrogators exchanged a look. Hayes nodded and turned off his phone.

Brendan looked at Tyler. 'And yours.'

Tyler's eyes widened. 'How?'

Brendan tapped the side of his head. 'Mind reader.'

'But this room is magic proof,' Tyler protested.

'Spooky.' Brendan leaned back and crossed his ankles. If these idiots did not know how enchanters worked, he was not about to enlighten them.

'We are his mana source,' explained Hayes, spoiling Brendan's fun.

He watched carefully as Tyler removed the digital recording device from his pocket and turned it off. When both sets of eyes returned to him, he cast the soundproofing ward he had recently learned from Dana. 'Between us, I may be a member for the Cult, but I don't work for them. I only joined them to gain access to their secrets.'

'Right. I almost forgot. You work for that Dark Syndicate slut,' Tyler scoffed.

A snigger slipped out. 'Puh-lease. I *own* the Dark Syndicate, in Australia anyway. But I don't represent their interests either.' Brendan hoped he could trust these guys since they were friends with Alannah.

Hayes narrowed his eyes, one of them twitching in the process. 'Whose interests do you serve?'

'The Winters clan.'

Pure hate poured from Tyler's aura like murky swamp mud. 'Like hell you do. How is abandoning your family in their best interest?'

'I don't expect you to understand the intricacies of my family's dynamics. One night of intimacy with Lana doesn't give you the right to judge us, and I sure as hell doubt it was enough to get the full story.'

This time Tyler leaned back and smirked. 'What makes you think it was only one night?'

'Well good for you, Tyler.' Brendan returned the smug expression. 'I'm glad Lana isn't restricting herself to my impotent brother. If you were hoping to get a rise out of me with that news, you clearly don't understand the Winters clan at all. There is only one man who could achieve such a result.'

Confusion spread across Tyler's visage in a series of fine wrinkles.

'He's talking about Liam,' explained Hayes.

'I wonder, Tyler,' Brendan went on, 'did Lana tell you how close she grew to Tara this year? Did you know Grandma was training the two of us in the art of deception as well as other… magics?'

Tyler shook his head in stunned silence.

'I didn't think so. There are few people she would trust with the knowledge. Certainly not the Council's pets.'

'So why are *you* telling us?' Tyler spat with bitter vitriol.

'Because I believe you both care about her. Am I wrong?'

'Yes, I care,' replied Hayes.

'I care about her a lot more than you do.' Tyler barely contained his rage at this point.

'Fuck off, Tyler. You've known her for what? A few months? I've been in love with the woman all my life. Don't mistake my emotional response to heartbreak as a lack of concern for her. I would still lay down my life to protect hers. Would you?'

Tyler's jaw hit the floor.

'I would,' confirmed Hayes.

'Of course I would.' Tyler's honesty was plain to see within the bright swirling sunset of his aura.

Brendan narrowed his eyes on Tyler. 'Even if it meant going against the Council?'

'Yes.'

He glanced at Hayes, who was carefully thinking about his reply.

'I would protect her from the authorities to the best of my abilities, but I would not taint my soul, nor risk my own woman's life.'

'I can respect that.' Brendan sat forward and leaned on the table. 'Lana needs allies on the inside.'

Tyler mirrored Brendan's stance. 'Why, what is she planning?'

'At this stage she is watching and learning. But according to Tara, knowledge is a dangerous asset in our world. There will come a time when Alannah knows too much for her own good.'

Tyler shook his head with a puzzled expression. 'So why seek such knowledge?'

'Because someone needs to uncover the truth. Speaking of which, did you know the inner circle of the Obsidian Cult refer to themselves as the Sons of Set?'

The warlocks exchanged a look and Jaxon leaned forward. 'Does that mean they are—'

'Direct descendants of the God? Yup. They are a different race of elves. You can call them dark elves since their souls are completely black.'

'I don't suppose you came across anything about doppelgangers in your Cult research?' Tyler queried.

'No, but I haven't finished translating everything. Why do you ask?'

'Why do you think we look like twins?'

'I can't say I've given much thought to your appearance, Tyler. You're not my type. Fucking you would be too much like masturbation.'

'Well maybe you should think about it, because you and I are the reason the Sons of Set are in town.'

Curiosity was getting the better of Brendan as he sat up. 'What do you mean?'

'I'm your doppelganger, or magic twin as they call us. I don't know the full story, but apparently, I descend from an Egyptian God, one who is not a progenitor of mages or any other common magic race, and I carry a gene that created a magic link between us. Aside from looking alike, we are amplifiers for each other's magic.'

'Colour me intrigued. What's your date of birth, Tyler?'

'Fourteenth of August 2002. Why?'

Brendan remained silent for a moment. 'I was wondering if we shared a birthday.'

'And do we?' Tyler sat on the edge of his seat.

'No, I'm a week older. Same star sign, though. I don't know if that bears significance on this doppelganger stuff. What I do find intriguing is the fact you share a birthday with someone else we know.'

Tyler's eyes bugged out. 'Do you mean Lana?'

'Yup.'

After an hour of waiting, Caleb felt restless. 'I'm going for a walk to see if I can find him.'

'On your own? Are you sure it's a smart idea?' Bridey sprang to her feet and grabbed his hand.

'Yes, on my own. What's wrong with that?'

'It's the middle of the night in a rough neighbourhood, sweetie.'

Caleb smiled as he pulled her in for a hug. 'I may not have Brendan's bulk, but I do know how to fight and look after myself. Worst case, I can run or magiport. I'll be careful, Bry. Call me if you hear anything, okay?'

'Okay.' She squeezed him tight.

Stepping outside, the first thing Caleb noticed was the warmth of the night air. With the way Bridey kept the house chilled, it was easy to forget the heat of the Australian summer, especially when he rarely did go outside. There were few people around, likely due to the Christian holiday. When he reached the local park, there was a gang of human kids all dressed in black hoodies who were vandalising some play equipment.

'Hey guys, check out the goth freak!'

They all laughed as they turned to stare at him.

Morons have no idea who they're messing with. He simply flashed the unloaded Glock on his belt as he grabbed his knife and twirled it in his fingers. The pistol was only ever a prop. Couldn't be too careful around magic users, after all: anyone attuned to the elements or matter could ignite the gunpowder of an opponent's firearm.

He continued walking and the thugs backed off when they saw he had no intention to fight. *Almost a pity. I could have used an excuse to blow off steam.* Despite what he'd said to reassure Bridey, the possibility of losing Brendan was getting to him. *Ironic how the woman who brought us together was the one to drive us apart.*

Spotting a payphone, he decided to try his luck as an unknown caller. *Not likely to work, but worth a shot.* It went straight to voicemail, again. Caleb slammed the phone down, an idea forming as he returned home.

Bridey ran to the door, looking crestfallen when she saw he was alone.

'I could try scrying?' he suggested.

'You can do that?' Bridey gawked at him in amazement.

With a shrug, he strode toward the ritual room. 'I'm attuned to cosmic and organic mana. How hard can it be?'

'So, you've never tried it before?'

'Not exactly. But I have been reading up on it, so I know what's needed.' When they reached the cellar, Caleb unlocked a chest of magic supplies and withdrew a set of maps and a bright green moldavite crystal on a silver chain. 'I need some of Brendan's hair. Would you mind retrieving a few strands from his brush?'

Nodding, she ran upstairs, giving him some much-needed peace and quiet to prepare. By the time she returned, Caleb had memorised the ritual steps and had everything else set up. He called the elements, cast the circle, and kneeled at the altar.

Not being a regular practitioner, it took several excruciating minutes to focus his mind. Eventually the mana flowed through him, and the crystal moved. The first map confirmed Brendan was still in New South Wales. Next, he narrowed it down to the metropolitan area. Finally, the crystal stabbed the page, pinpointing an exact location: The Darlinghurst Police Station. 'Fuck!' That was a place Caleb hoped he'd never have to return to.

Peeking over his shoulder, Bridey noticed where the moldavite had landed. 'Oh dear. Well at least he isn't with the Cult.'

Slicing his athame over the circle, Caleb jumped to his feet. 'How can you say that, Bry? You know how much shit Brendan is in with the Council? Those drug charges alone could be enough to get him a life sentence.'

Bridey reached out and drew him into her arms. 'I'll make some phone calls. I meant it when I promised him protection from the authorities. The Council can't touch us, sweetie, and I'm gonna make sure that applies to Brendan too.'

He gazed down upon her with narrowed eyes. 'How exactly?'

'Best if you don't know.'

'Quite the coincidence.' Tyler could not wait to share this detail with Alannah. He even smiled at the possibility of partying with her.

Brendan cleared his throat. 'What exactly do the Cult want with us?'

'They want to use us together in their dark magic rituals.'

An obnoxiously loud laugh burst from Brendan. 'I'm sorry, but the thought of a goodie-two-shoes like you getting mixed up with those arseholes is one of the funniest things I've heard in ages. I don't think you need to worry, Tyler.'

He groaned with irritation. Brendan's arrogance was getting on his nerves. 'I guess it might surprise you to know they came dangerously close to succeeding. According to my source, they have some cunning ways of tricking mages into joining them.'

The humour faded from Brendan's expression. 'How close? You didn't sign anything did you?'

'No. They haven't been able to recruit me yet, but I almost went undercover to investigate them which would have meant joining.'

Brendan sat back and sighed. For several long seconds he stared at the table, apparently lost in thought. 'If you want to take these guys out, I'm willing to help, but only on two conditions.'

'We don't make deals with scumbags like you,' Tyler scoffed.

'Quirky, please,' Jaxon warned. 'What are your conditions, Mr. Winters?'

'First of all, I want the Council to wipe my criminal record clean.'

'You have got to be kidding me!' Tyler was keen to lock the bastard away for life—an easy enough feat if they pegged him for the Rhapsody drug charges.

'I guess you guys are on your own with the Cult.' Brendan sat back and crossed his arms again.

'And what is your second condition?' Jaxon asked without blinking an eye.

A wide grin formed on Brendan's face as he turned his attention from Tyler to the real negotiator in the room. 'You can't arrest the inner circle. You need to kill them. All of them. This is critical because I guarantee no bars will hold them.'

'I can't make any promises, but I'll see what I can do.'

Tyler slammed a fist on the table. 'Seriously, Jax. What—'

'Shut it, Quirky!' Jaxon moved to the door. 'See this? It's a door you can walk through if you don't start towing the line.'

With a huff he sat back in his chair. 'Fine!'

Jaxon leaned against the door, crossing his arms. 'You need to put your personal qualms aside and focus on the bigger picture, Warlock Quirke.'

Shit! Official titles mean Jaxon is serious. Or pissed. Maybe both?

After an excruciating silence, Jaxon approached the table again. 'What exactly can you do to help us, Mr. Winters?'

'I can provide intel and access.'

'Keep talking.'

'I'll need a show of good faith first.'

Jaxon sighed. 'Give me a few minutes.' He grabbed his phone and headed for the door where he paused and pinned Tyler with a severe look. 'Behave yourself, Quirky.'

'Yes, Sir.'

Jaxon left the room, shutting Tyler in with the man he despised most in the world.

He turned an evil eye on Brendan. 'Why did you do it?'

'Do what?'

'Leave Lana without a word.'

An animalistic growl slipped from Brendan's throat. 'Have you ever been in love before, Tyler? I'm not talking about some crush or the butterflies you get at the start of a new fling. I mean real, all-consuming love where that person becomes your world.'

'I am now.'

'Christ! For your sake, I hope you're not talking about Lana.'

'No, not exactly. I have strong feels for her, don't get me wrong. But I was talking about my girlfriend.'

'Right. Now imagine you are essentially married to the woman, newlyweds at that, and she hooks up with her ex, someone you happen to despise. You don't simply hear about it but see it with your own eyes. Can you imagine how painful it would feel?'

'Yes but—'

'No buts, Tyler. Take a moment to think about how you would *feel*.'

Deciding to humour Brendan, Tyler closed his eyes and gave it some thought. Samantha's Cult master sounded like a nasty piece of work and seeing her choose to return to him would be pretty devastating.

'If someone gave you the option to instantly erase the pain, but you needed to take immediate action, would you?'

'I suppose I would,' Tyler agreed.

'Ah, but it turns out there's a catch you didn't think about because you weren't in your right mind. You've essentially sold both your soul and your freedom. So, you can't even talk through whatever issue there was between you and your woman. She is lost to you forever.'

Understanding was beginning to sink in for Tyler. He hated to admit it, but he almost felt sorry for Brendan. 'What did you see?'

'Lana was making out with Liam in the back of my parents' garden mere minutes after we had announced our soul link to the family.'

Tyler scratched his head. 'But she was in love with you. Why would she do that?'

Brendan let out a brief sardonic laugh. 'You know, I keep asking myself the same question.'

'Surely there was some misunderstanding?'

'Possibly, but it's too late now. The damage is done, and I can't contact her anyway.'

'Why?'

'That's classified.'

It was such a frustrating situation and he wished he had a magic band-aid to fix their relationship.

'So, what's the deal with you and the Hawthorns? Lana told me you ran off with Bridey, but I got the impression from Caleb you and he have a thing.'

Brendan's pierced brow arched. '*You're* the warlock who arrested him?'

'Yeah, along with Jaxon.'

'Curious how he didn't mention meeting my double.' He chuckled a moment. 'I bet he gave you hell. The man's got a major attitude.'

'One to rival yours, even.'

He nodded with a wistful smile. 'To answer your question, my relationship with Bridey is more complicated than astrophysics. But Caleb and I are very much in love—something that took me by surprise, considering I've never had any gay or bi tendencies before. We had been mates since starting high school together and I recently found out he'd had a crush on me all this time. Just when you think you know someone.' Brendan shook his head. 'I didn't even realise he was bi.'

Jaxon returned the next second holding a laptop. 'It took some serious string-pulling, but here.' He directed the screen towards Brendan. 'No record, no pending charges, and no open cases linked to your name.'

'Sweet. Thank you.'

'Now tell us everything you know about the Obsidian Cult.'

Slumping into the leather office chair, Brendan put his feet up on the solid oak desk and sipped on the expensive whiskey Tara had left behind. Dana had explained how his grandmother had owned this office building and she had left it to her two favourite grandchildren. While most of the spaces had tenancies, the tenth floor had been her headquarters and it was where he conducted his business as the new Boss of the Dark Syndicate.

He was thankful for the inner-city retreat and for Tara's exceptional taste in liquor, especially since he did not feel like going home yet. *What is it with the women I love betraying me? Am I wearing a sign inviting them to crush my heart into lifeless pulp?*

With a sigh, he picked up his phone, being careful not to disconnect it from the charger, and powered it on. A bunch of missed calls registered, mostly from Bridey, but there were a few from Caleb, along with a message: DON'T YOU DARE SKIP TOWN BEFORE GIVING HER A CHANCE TO EXPLAIN HERSELF. WE BOTH LOVE YOU.

Fuck! Even if Bridey is a deceitful whore, I still have Thornsy and I can't leave him. While he did not have any plans to leave before fulfilling his end of the bargain with Tyler and Jaxon, the thought of moving to another city had crossed his mind. *I guess I may as well confront the bitch.*

After knocking back the last of his drink, Brendan strode out of the office and hailed a taxi. The middle-aged driver attempted some small talk at first, but soon learned Brendan was not in the mood for chatting. As soon as they pulled into the Windsor driveway, he threw a bunch of hundred-dollar notes at the driver and didn't bother waiting for change.

The front door slammed into the wall from the force of Brendan's entrance, alerting the Hawthorns to his arrival. They raced into the parlour from the rear living area. Bridey's face lit up at seeing him. 'Oh Gods, Brendan, I'm—'

'Shut. Up.' Brendan was fuming as he approached her.

She must have sensed his foul mood because she began to retreat.

He rushed at her, pinning her against the wall and caging her with his arms.

'Brendan, please—' Caleb pleaded.

'Stay out of it, Thornsy. This is between me and your sister.' He glared at her a moment. 'Does love and loyalty mean nothing to you?'

'I'm sorry. I didn't want to tell him, but he pulled the truth from me with magic.'

'You expect me to believe a half-wit like Damien could break through your mind shields when I can't?'

Bridey's eyes widened with a mixture of fear and surprise. 'I… He must've had help from the inner circle.'

'Stop lying to me.' Brendan was seething.

'I'm not, I swear.'

'How did they break through your defences?'

She gazed at her feet with a shameful expression and tears trickled from her eyes. 'Damien threatened Caleb's life if I didn't let him in my head.'

'What the hell, Bry.' Caleb drew closer.

But Brendan turned and raised a hand to stop Caleb before resuming his position with Bridey. He could not blame her for protecting her brother, the man they both loved. 'Look at me, Bry,' he demanded with a softer tone. As soon as her eyes met his, Brendan's mouth crashed with hers and he kissed her violently. Clutching her arms with a vice grip, he pulled back. 'Thank you for looking after our Caleb.'

He spun away from her and grabbed Caleb, pulling him into a loving embrace and a deep kiss that made Caleb moan into Brendan's mouth. Those sexy little noises were driving him to distraction and before long, he dragged Caleb to the couch. He stripped him bare, taking a moment to appreciate his lover's slim build, soft, silvery skin, and dark eyes full of emotion. 'I'm so damn in love with you, Thornsy.' Brendan bent Caleb over the sofa and let his own body emphasise his point.

Chapter Sixteen

rendan's eyes were starting to glaze over as he read the latest management reports. This was the sort of dull shit he despised most about his new job. It was Friday and he was almost counting down the hours to the weekend. *Why can't the Syndicate take the week between Christmas and New Year's off, like most legit businesses?*

He welcomed the buzzing sound of his intercom, followed by his secretary's soft, feminine voice as it came through the speaker. 'Lord Stirling is here to see you, sir.'

A smile took over his face. *My final meeting for the week and the perfect distraction.* 'Let him in.' Reclining in his chair as the door opened, Brendan drank in the sight of Caleb dressed in a business suit tailored to perfection. As soon as the door closed, a whistle escaped his pursed lips.

Caleb offered him a lopsided grin. 'You wanted to see me, sir?'

'I always want to see you, and right now I'm dying to bend you naked over my desk.'

Ambling forward, Caleb unclasped the buttons of his jacket. 'Not that I'm complaining, but did you really call me into your office for sex?'

A short laugh slipped from Brendan's mouth. 'Well no. I have a sensitive matter to discuss, but now you're here and dressed like that, I find myself extremely tempted.'

He dropped the jacket over the back of a visitor's chair and moved around to Brendan, perching on the edge of the desk directly in front of him.

Springing from his seat, Brendan kissed Caleb passionately. But he pulled back before letting himself get carried away. With a sigh he sat down. 'As much as I'd love to see my fantasy become a reality, I still have a mountain of paperwork to get through before heading home tonight. I never realised running a criminal organisation would be like managing a legit company. Being a captain was a lot more exciting.'

'Indeed,' Caleb smirked. 'What can I *do you* for, Boss?'

Damn, it sounds and feels satisfying to hear him address me like that. All sorts of roleplay ideas filled his mind, but he gave himself a mental slap across the back of his head. 'I have an assignment for you. I know it's not exactly kosher for me to be calling on someone else's captain for a job like this, but I am banging your boss and I doubt she'll mind me borrowing you.' His lips curled up as the unspoken understanding passed between them. 'Besides, you're the only person I can entrust with the task and I'm hoping you won't mind the trip.'

'You need me to travel? Where to?'

'Gaeilge Shores.'

Caleb's eyes bugged out. 'Why?'

'I want to promote Jacob to be my captain and spymaster there. While I'm communicating most of the promotions in other towns via demon couriers, I feel this one deserves a more personal approach. I'm sure you can appreciate why.'

'Yes, of course.'

'I don't know if Jacob knows I'm Lord Jet. If he doesn't, please don't fill in the blanks for him. Let my identity remain a mystery for the time being.'

'And if he asks how he got promoted?'

'Tell him I went with your recommendation. Jacob is smart and skilled at what he does. I'm pretty sure the Syndicate only overlooked him before because he lacked connections. You can pretend your move to Sydney and position as Violet's captain brought you into my inner circle or some shit.'

'Yeah, I can work with that.'

Brendan grabbed the brown paper parcel he had warded with a tamper alert spell and placed it on the desk next to Caleb. 'This is his induction pack. Please see he gets it and no one else but Jacob opens it.'

'Will do. When do you want me to go?'

'Sunday.'

'But that's New Year's Eve,' Caleb pleaded.

'I know. Promoting Jacob isn't the only task I have for you. I would like you to attend the Council's party at the Sailing Club. The folks in those circles know you well enough, so visiting your mother and spending the night with your old friends won't arouse suspicions.'

Caleb took a deep breath. 'What do you want me to do?'

'Keep your ear to the ground and tell me all the gossip and rumours circulating around town. I'll get Jacob to do this in future, but I need you to bring me the latest news.'

'Sure this isn't a ploy to keep me from my sister's New Year's Party?' Caleb gave him a devious smile.

'Maybe.' Brendan gazed upon him. He was not ready for Bridey to introduce Caleb to her party scene, and he had made his sentiments on the matter known to both of the Hawthorn siblings. As much as he could, Brendan wanted to shield his precious Caleb from the worst of the Syndicate lifestyle. It was probably a fruitless endeavour with Bridey pulling most of Caleb's strings, but Brendan would still do what he could.

Caleb sighed. 'Fine. I'll go on Sunday and have a boring New Year's Eve. But you'll owe me big time for this.'

Sliding his hands up along Caleb's thighs, Brendan rose and pressed his mouth to Caleb's ear. 'Between Bridey and myself, I'm sure we have all your kinks covered. Perhaps we could spend tonight exploring them all with you.'

A shiver ran through Caleb's body and goosebumps rose on his neck. 'Mm, yes please.'

Brendan drew back and grinned at his lover. 'Great. I'm glad we could come to an understanding. I will, of course, compensate you for your work in the usual business manner as well. Just don't forget to keep your receipts.'

Wanting to catch Jacob before the party, Caleb arrived in town late Sunday afternoon and headed straight for the boggart's cottage house. He knocked on the decorative glass panel beside the door. Apparently, the house had been in the Federation style, but someone lacking in taste renovated the interior during the fifties and as a rental tenant, Jacob could not do much about the hideous 'retro' design.

Jacob's jaw dropped when he opened the door. 'Thornsy?'

'In the flesh,' he deadpanned.

'What brings you to your old neck of the woods?'

'Business, mostly. Can I come in?'

'Yeah, sure.' He stepped aside to let Caleb in. Jacob closed the door and lead him along the hallway and into the loungeroom. 'Have a seat. Can I get you a drink?'

'Got any cold beers?'

Half a grin touched Jacob's lips. 'Always.' He dashed out of the room and returned momentarily with a couple of pale ales. After handing one to Caleb, he sat across the small room. 'So, what can I do you for?'

'I assume you are aware of the recent Syndicate leadership elections?'

He nodded his head. 'Some guy known as Lord Jet now runs the show.'

Well, that answers my first question. 'He sure does. Lady Violet, my sister, is a part of his inner circle, which means I am too. She made me her captain by the way, so you should call me Stirling when other Syndicate members are around.'

'Christ, Thornsy! I never thought I'd see the day you followed in your father's footsteps.'

A growl escaped before Caleb could repress it. 'Trust me when I say the Syndicate is like charity work compared to what my father does. He gave me a choice: join his business or my sister's. The choice was easy.'

Jacob nodded his understanding.

'Anyway, Lord Jet asked me to deliver the news in person.'

'What news?'

'Well with the changing of the guard, he is hiring new spymaster captains and he wants you to be his man in this town.'

The redhead stared at him in amazement. 'Why me?'

'He wanted my recommendation, so naturally I suggested you. We may have had our differences recently, but you are still one of the best Syndicate members around these parts and I have to respect you for that.'

'Um… I don't know what to say.'

'Thanks will do,' Caleb replied drily.

'Yeah, ah thank you. So, what's my codename?'

'Red. He also asked me to give you this induction pack.' He withdrew the parcel from his satchel and gave it to Jacob.

'Cheers, man. Are you in town for long?'

'A couple of days. Figured I'd catch up with Mum while I'm here.'

'Most of the magical community are going to the Sailing Club tonight. You in the mood for a party?'

'Sounds good. I'd love to catch up with the rest of the gang.'

'Yeah, about that. I'm kinda on the outs with most of them now. They didn't take kindly to my corrupting influence on Brendo. Alannah is still friendly, and Ben tolerates me, but I tend to hang out with other unseelie these days.'

'Ah shit, man. I'm sorry.'

'Hey, it's not your fault. The truth was bound to come out eventually, since Richard told Liam and Alannah when he took them hostage.'

'Cara?'

'Left me.'

'Well damn. She was a decent woman. You seeing anyone else?'

'Nope. I'm flying solo for a bit. We could check out an unseelie club in the city tomorrow night if you're interested. Party together like old times?'

Caleb's instinct was to decline because he was already in two relationships, but it wasn't like either of his lovers expected him to remain exclusive when they weren't. He gave Jacob a mischievous grin. 'Yeah, okay. Dull party tonight, real one tomorrow.'

'That's the spirit.'

'Did you get in trouble with the Council?'

'The High Magus wanted to charge me, but Liam convinced Kieran to pardon me on the grounds I helped save him and Alannah.'

'Wow. The Council absolved you and proclaimed you a hero, yet Cara couldn't forgive you? What a bitch.'

Jacob shrugged. 'The betrayal was more personal for her and the other guys. Funny thing is Alannah doesn't blame me at all, and my fuck up affected her the most. Then again, she knew all about the drug trade back when she was in trouble with the Council and even helped Brendan get out of the business when they hooked up.'

This time Caleb was gobsmacked. 'Alannah knew? Brendan never mentioned.'

'Do you see Brendo often?'

Caleb tried to hide the warm smile threatening to show. 'You could say that. I do live with him.'

'Oh right, of course. He lives with your sister, and you moved there to work for her. Makes sense you would live with them too. How is he and how are things between the two of you? Last time we spoke, he wasn't exactly your favourite person.'

Caleb took a moment to approach his reply carefully. 'I smoothed things over with Brendan. And he is doing okay, all things considered.'

'Hmm, well at least he is okay. Come on, let's get ready for tonight.'

Caleb hadn't been wrong in his assumption regarding the Council's festivities. A bunch of food trucks, carnival rides, and sideshow games might have appealed to him when he was a kid, but it was entirely too wholesome for his matured tastes. The jazz band playing in the gazebo didn't do much for him either—not without Bridey present. She loved the chaotic excuse for music and would've pulled him onto the dancefloor. While he would have outwardly cringed and complained, secretly he would have loved dancing with her.

But Caleb wasn't there to have fun, so he did his best to catch up with all his old school friends and even mingled with his mother and some of her acquaintances to learn as much as possible.

Cara caught his attention as he wandered through the crowd inside the clubrooms. 'Hey, Caleb. How've you been?'

'Great, thanks. You?'

'I've been better. I suppose you heard about my breakup with Jacob?'

Unsure what to say, he simply nodded.

'You're living in Sydney with your sister now, right?'

'Yeah.'

'And Brendan?'

He could see where she was going with this, so he sighed. 'What do you want to know, Cara?'

'Why did he leave Alannah?'

A commotion on the stage saved him from an awkward conversation. Jessica Ó Máille was holding a microphone. 'Excuse me ladies and gentlemen. Alannah and Liam Winters have an important announcement to make. Get up here, you two.' She beckoned them with excited hand gestures.

Alannah took the microphone from her. 'This is awkward, but you would probably hear it on the rumour mill anyway. I am pregnant.'

Caleb's first thoughts went to Brendan. He stepped forward in the crowd to call out, 'So, which cousin is the baby daddy?'

After a visible shiver, Liam grabbed the microphone. 'Tradition forbids us from asking who the biological father is because Alannah is carrying a baby conceived at Beltane.'

Turning to face her, he spurted forth a bunch of mushy words that sickened Caleb. Dropping to one knee in front of Alannah, Liam pulled a ring from his pocket. 'I adore you, Alannah Winters, and if you would do me the honour of becoming my wife, I promise to devote the rest of my life to keeping you safe and happy.' There was a moment of silence between them. 'Lana, baby, will you marry me?'

Tears streaked Alannah's cheeks as she replied, 'Yes. Very yes.'

Bugger me! Brendan will lose his shit when he hears about this. As Liam slipped the ring on her finger, Caleb disappeared into the night. He needed to call Bridey about the situation.

She picked up after a couple of attempts. 'Hey sweetie, what's up?'

'Alannah Winters is pregnant.'

'Shit! Is the child Brendan's?'

'Yeah. Beltane baby.' He knew Brendan had been her only partner that night because he confided as much to Caleb.

'Damn it. If he finds out, there won't be any stopping his return to her. You can't tell him Alannah's pregnant. And you should advise Jacob to keep the news under wraps too.'

Caleb squeezed his eyes shut. He hated the idea of keeping such tremendous news from Brendan, but he understood it was for the best. 'I'll have a word with Jacob.'

'Thanks, hun.'

With a warm afterglow on his face, Jacob woke late on the second day of January, and made his way into the kitchen as recollections of the previous night played through his mind. When he reached the table, he found a note with Caleb's messy scrawl:

Thanks for a great night and for letting me crash in your bed ;-)

Sorry to love and leave you, but I had to get going and didn't want to wake you. You look too cute when you sleep. Until next time, try not to do anything I wouldn't do, LOL.

Regards,
Caleb.

Jacob smiled as he read it. *After last night, I'm not sure there is much Thornsy wouldn't do.* The unseelie club had been entertaining, but the afterparty they brought home with them was when the real fun began. Letting out a satisfied sigh, he went about brewing some coffee. He sat down in the loungeroom, letting the steam dissipate from his drink as he picked up the parcel Caleb had given him.

Ripping aside the brown paper, he found a small envelope affixed to a manilla folder which sat atop another wrapped package. A quick flick through the contents of the folder showed a bunch of induction papers and forms, all standard Syndicate stuff. But when he opened the envelope, he found a handwritten letter:

Hey man, sorry it took ages to get back in touch. Things have been crazy for me of late.

Jacob paused as the familiar tone of the writing struck him. *Is this Brendo?*

I bet you've already figured out who I am, yeah? See, this is one of the reasons I asked Stirling to promote you.

You are hell smart, and the Syndicate should've made you captain long ago. Ah well, their loss is my gain. I also need an ally on my side. It is hard to know who I can trust these days. And as much as I'd like to think Stirling is among the select few, our relationship has grown rather intimate of late, and love complicates things. Especially when it comes to the matter I am entrusting you with.

Jacob laughed. *Well shit! Brendo and Thornsy? I didn't see that one coming.*

I have made a deal with my other lover preventing me from contacting Alannah, so I need you to deliver the contents of the inner package to her. Do not, under any circumstances, let her know they came from me. She needs to believe this stuff came from her great aunt. It will give her enough context to understand their significance. The same will go for all future parcels I send you, most of which will arrive by demon post.

It pains me more than you'd know to keep this distance from her. I still love her, and I will forever regret the impulsive reaction that broke us apart and landed me in this mess. But for her safety, as well as my own, it is best we both move on with our lives. I hope you understand this and forgive me for what you must have perceived to be a real dick move on my part.

Are things okay for you and your woman? I'd ask you to send her my regards, but she probably hates me for what I did. And for what ought to be obvious reasons, you can't tell her I have contacted you to explain the situation. So just know my well wishes extend to you both.

Until next time, take care.
PS. Please burn this letter.

A pang of grief struck at Jacob's heart when he thought about Cara. *I guess Caleb will fill Brendo in.* A moment later, the implications of the letter struck him. *Brendan is Lord Jet, which means he has become the leader of the Oceania branch of the Syndicate.* Jacob did not know whether to cheer or cry for Brendan. *But Christ, Brendo! Being a Dark Syndicate Boss puts you directly at odds with the Council and the rest of your family.*

Jacob wondered if there would ever be any redemption for Brendan. *Will he remain estranged forever?*

Chapter Seventeen

ager for the news, Brendan gave Caleb a quick welcome home kiss before pulling him into their room and shutting the door.

Caleb laughed as Brendan shoved him onto the bed. 'Can't wait to have your way with me, huh?'

There was no way of hiding the tent situation in his pants from Caleb. 'True, but I will wait long enough to hear your rundown.' He sat beside Caleb and looked at him expectantly.

'Well Jacob didn't know you and Lord Jet are one and the same. The promotion surprised him, but I stuck to the plan, and he didn't get suspicious. He and Cara split, by the way.'

'What? Why?'

'She was upset to learn about his involvement in the Rhapsody business and she blamed him for corrupting you. So, she left him.'

'Christ! Did he look broken up about it?'

'Hard to say. I think he is avoiding grief by hitting the party scene hard. Speaking of which….'

Brendan's pulse picked up when Caleb's words trailed off. 'What?'

'Jacob and I took a couple of chicks back to his place last night and had our own orgy. Nothing like what you and Bry would've got up to on Sunday night, but it was still pretty hot.'

Thinking back to the number of chicks and dudes he had fucked on New Year's Eve; Brendan could hardly blame Caleb for getting some on the side. An impish grin formed on his face. 'I want the graphic details later.'

'Mm, thought you might.'

'What other news of home?'

Caleb told him all the small-town gossip—some of which was amusing, most made him yawn—and none of it related to Alannah.

'Anything else to report?'

'Nothing good.'

He took a deep breath, attempting but failing to calm his racing heart. 'Go on.'

'I'm sorry, Brendan, but they're getting married. Liam proposed to her on New Year's Eve.'

'Shit! He didn't waste much time, did he? I guess he realised his mistake.'

Caleb's hand squeezed his thigh. 'You aren't only talking about Liam's mistake, are you?'

'No. But she made her choice and now I have even less reason to go back.' Brendan pushed Caleb back on the bed, pinned him down, and grinned wickedly. 'And you keep giving me more reasons to stay here.' He ravished every part of Caleb's sweet body.

As the postcoital haze wore off, Caleb snuggled into Brendan's arms. 'Mm, I love this.'

'Me too, Thornsy.'

With a contented sigh, Caleb stared at the ceiling. 'When I was crushing on you hard back in our school years, I never once imagined I would end up in your bed, let alone getting to share you with Bridey.'

His fingers caressed Caleb's arm as thoughts raced through his mind. 'Curiosity is getting the better of me, Thornsy.'

Caleb stared into Brendan's eyes. 'How so?'

'Have you fancied any guys other than me?'

'Of course I have,' he snorted. 'I'm not as sexually repressed as you.'

'Piss off.' Brendan's fist playfully punched Caleb's arm. 'Any of the guys we went to school with?'

'Yeah, there were a few who got me hot under the collar, although never as much as you did. I even fooled around with one of them.'

Intrigued, Brendan propped himself up with one arm. 'Now you've piqued my interest. Care to share?'

'Well, it's not like he's gonna mind me telling you now. I had a casual thing going with Locky.'

'Ah hell. No wonder you took his passing so hard. I'm sorry, man.' As Brendan cast his mind back to their goofy goblin friend who had lost his life in the showdown with Tara, he tried to recall if there were any signs he might have missed but came up blank.

Caleb waved his hand in a dismissive gesture. 'It's okay. It was years ago and it's not like I was in love with Locky. Sure, I miss him, but no more than you or any of the other guys do. He was a decent bloke and a great friend.'

'Yup, he sure was. Did the two of you have anal sex?'

'Yeah, but I always topped.' That explained his initial instinct to top Brendan, despite his obvious preference for the reverse.

'So why didn't you ever give him a taste of your sweet arse?'

He shrugged. 'I dunno. We found a dynamic that worked for us and never thought to switch things up. We were still extremely new to the whole experience.'

'Fair enough. So, who else did you have the hots for?'

Caleb laughed. 'Are we still talking about guys here, or do you want the full list, including girls?'

'Let's start with the guys.'

'Okay, well from our old group there was Ben and Austin.'

Brendan nodded. 'Yeah, I can see it. They were both attractive men with luscious long hair.' Leaning in closer, Brendan tucked some of Caleb's own lustrous locks behind his ear.

Caleb listed a few non-magical guys before pausing to bite his lip.

'Oh Gods, who?' Brendan prompted, fearing the worst.

'Your cousin, Steve Maher.'

A half-laugh, half-sigh of relief burst from him. 'Seriously? That tosser?'

'Hey, I never said I liked the man, but he was sexy. Plus, he also had the hair thing going for him.'

'Okay, what about the chicks?'

'Oh hell, Winters. I was hard for half the girls in our year level.'

'Come on, Thornsy, I want specifics.'

'Fine. All the ones you fucked.'

Brendan twirled a strand of Caleb's hair around his fingers as his gaze heated. 'Were you keeping track of my sex life?'

'You might say I was living vicariously through it.'

'Well damn. So, which of my many conquests were you most attracted to?'

Tension visibly formed in Caleb's jaw. 'Do you have to ask?'

With a sigh, Brendan pressed a brief kiss to his lips. 'I mean aside from Lana.'

'In that case, I would have to say Bianca.'

Fond memories of simpler times flooded Brendan's mind when he thought of the cute little nymph he used to hook up with in high school. It had always been no-strings fun with her. 'Mm, would have been an incredible threesome.'

'You know I used to think the exact same thing.'

'Damn. There's a missed opportunity. Did you ever sleep with her?' Brendan asked. 'I heard she hooked up with some of the guys in our group, but I never pried.'

'I did actually. Only once though and it was immediately before I followed you and Bridey here. I wanted to forget the pair of you, but she made me realise what I was missing.'

'Christ! I didn't think she was that bad in bed.'

Caleb sniggered. 'I never said she was. It was just the sex felt so… shallow and empty. The experience didn't compare to what I'd recently shared with Bridey.'

'I know what you mean. Meaningless sex can be fun, but it is nothing compared to being intimate with someone you love.' Brendan ran his fingers along Caleb's smooth skin, evoking a rapid recovery for them both. When their eyes locked together, there was no denying the raw emotions flowing between them.

A knock sounded at the door and Bridey approached the bed. 'Room for one more?'

Caleb smiled at her lovingly. 'For you, there is.'

After throwing her clothes aside, Bridey climbed in to face Caleb, flanking him with Brendan pressing against Caleb's back. Three bodies entwined as they spent the rest of the night losing themselves in each other.

The musty old bookstore was a curious place to meet. A small bell jingled above the door as Brendan entered, alerting the old man who stood behind the counter. The geezer's inner aura was silver, and his Celtic knot pendant bore the symbol of Lugh, father of mages: signs suggesting a spiritual leader.

He eyed Brendan in amazement. 'Fascinating. You actually do look like his twin.'

'Don't you mean he looks like me? I'm the eldest.' Brendan smirked, offering his hand. 'Brendan Winters. You are an acolyte, yes?'

With a firm handshake, the mage nodded. 'Acolyte Carran. The others are waiting for you out the back.'

'Thank you, Your Holiness.' Without further ado, Brendan strode behind the counter and through a door labelled STAFF ONLY.

The warlocks did not look pleased. 'You're late,' Hayes commented, while Tyler glared at him.

'Apologies. I'm still not used to how ghastly Sydney traffic can be.' Brendan was not sorry, not when magnificent morning sex had been the real reason for his tardiness; but they did not need to know, nor did he care what they thought. He took a seat at the cheap Laminex table in the poky kitchenette. 'So, what's the plan?'

'Simple, really,' Tyler explained, 'I walk into HQ pretending to be you on a day when they are meeting in the boardroom and take them all out.'

Brendan burst out laughing. After catching his breath, a full minute later, he slapped his hand on the table. 'I'm sorry, but there is no way that will work.'

'Do you doubt my ability to impersonate you?' Tyler asked.

'Maybe, but it's beside the point. If it was easy to walk in on them, don't you think someone would have tried by now? They keep the place locked up tight.'

'Which is why we intend to hack their security system and forge ourselves an all-access pass with your name on it,' replied Hayes. 'Did you bring your key?'

'Here.' He gave them the plastic ID card on the black lanyard. 'But they have other security measures.'

Hayes snapped a few photos of the card, along with one of Brendan, and handed back the key card. 'Figured they would, which is why we need to take impressions of fingerprints and scan your retinas.' Pulling out a high-tech device, he connected it to a laptop and waved it in front of Brendan's eyes.

'The Council are more tech-savvy in these parts. I wonder, is it to compensate for anything?'

'Hardly,' Tyler scoffed, 'I haven't received any complaints yet and I don't even need to resort to magic to please the ladies.'

Hayes rolled his eyes. 'I don't think Brendan was referring to dick sizes, Quirky. And no, we are not lacking in power here, we reserve our energy for what technology can't do.' Next, he produced two slabs of putty. 'Press your thumbs and fingers into these.' After taking Brendan's print impressions, he placed the fresh moulds in the freezer.

An uneasy feeling came over Brendan as he gave up pieces of his identity. 'Promise me you'll destroy my fake biometrics once you've dealt with these arseholes?'

'Of course,' Hayes assured him. 'We are not crooks, and we have no interest in misappropriating these items.'

He turned his attention to Tyler in an attempt to shake off his apprehension. 'Say you get all the way to the boardroom; how do you intend to take them all out before they strike back with magic more powerful than that of any warlock?'

'The element of surprise should give me enough time to hit them all with a single chain-lightning attack.'

'Are you for real? That's like twenty guys. Do you know how much mana you would burn to hit that many targets at once? How much power you would need to channel? You could kill yourself.'

Tyler gave him a smug grin. 'I've been training for something like this all my life. I can easily manage twenty people.'

Not even Liam could pull it off. Brendan felt a newfound respect for Tyler. 'Well, fuck! I'd love to see you put my brother to shame in a duel one day.'

Pride beamed from Tyler. 'You think I'm more powerful than Liam Winters?'

'If you can pull off a chain attack of twenty or more, then yeah, easily. The most targets I ever saw him hit was like five.'

'It's true, most warlocks can't pull off a stunt like this,' Hayes explained, 'but Tyler has specialised where the rest of us tend to diversify our skill sets. Plus, I think the fact he is not a bloodline mage has driven him to prove he can fight like the best of us.'

Brendan stared at Tyler in wide-eyed astonishment. 'You're not a pure blood? Your aura is as strong as Jaxon's.'

'No, I'm only ninety percent. My great-grandfather had a bastard child with his maid who was not pure. She would be where the doppelganger gene came from.'

'Interesting.' Brendan gave it some thought for a moment. 'You said doppelganger genes came from one of the other Gods, right? Possibly a God of magic?'

'Yeah, why?'

'What if descending from these two different Gods makes you more powerful despite the slight dilution of your blood? Like with the enlightened and endarkened fae.'

'You know, I never thought of it that way,' Tyler admitted.

'Right, well we've got all we need from you for now.' Hayes rose to his feet. 'I'll call you on the burner phone when we are ready for stage two.'

'Okay. See you then.' Brendan took his leave, walking back through the bookstore and waving to the acolyte on his way out. Rounding the corner to the carpark, something moved in his peripheral vision, and he spotted a dark figure bolting down the street. *What the hell?* It was hard to make out any details, but Brendan did not need to see the man's face—he could recognise that arse anywhere. *Why the fuck is Thornsy spying on me?*

Drawing the curtain aside to look through her window, Samantha sighed as she watched Tyler leave. She hated spending time without him. Not only did she love and miss Tyler, but he was the most powerful warlock of the three, and thus more adept at protecting her.

Movement on the balcony beneath drew her eye and she noticed Tanya step out and sit on one of the deckchairs. The two of them had not had much chance to connect in the time they'd lived together, and it was not like Samantha had any issues with her. Seizing the opportunity, she joined Tanya. The gentle breeze tickled her skin when she stepped outside with a coffee in her hand. 'Mind if I join you?'

Tanya looked up and smiled. 'Please do.'

Glancing at the laptop on the small round table, Samantha saw the open Pinterest results for pagan weddings. Sitting beside

Tanya, she gestured toward the computer. 'How goes the planning?'

'Good. I've been compiling an inspiration board to collect ideas.'

'Neat. I've never been to a wedding before and now it looks like I'll be attending two this year.'

'Yeah, it's pretty exciting. I'm thrilled to hear about Alannah and Liam.'

Samantha could not share her enthusiasm, not when she knew the truth about Alannah's broken heart; all she could do was nod and shrug a silent reply.

'You're not pleased about the news,' Tanya observed.

'Hmph. I never was great at faking emotions. Honestly, I don't think Liam's a suitable match for Alannah.'

Tanya furrowed her brow. 'Would you rather see her raise the kid alone?'

'No. It's just….' She bit her lip to prevent the truth spilling out.

Tanya eyed Samantha suspiciously a moment, then her eyes widened as realisation dawned. 'You've got the hots for her too, don't you?'

A nervous laugh slipped out. 'Maybe.'

Tanya shook her head with amazement. 'That woman's ability to charm the pants off men,'—she cast her eyes over Samantha—'and some women, apparently… is uncanny. Especially when you consider she's not even an enchantress. Look, Sam, you know she's a pureblood, right? Even if she wanted to live with you and Tyler, her uncle would never stand for it.'

'I know.' Feeling dejected, Samantha stared into the distance. Alannah's situation contained bucketloads of unfair.

Distracted by her inner musings, she did not notice the black clad figure dropping onto the balcony from above until it was too late. He pressed a knife to Tanya's throat and clamped a hand over the woman's mouth.

'Not a sound,' the familiar voice spoke behind her, and Samantha's skin crawled off her bones and nose-dived from the balcony.

She spun around to face Kek, cursing herself for forgetting the wards did not extend beyond the walls of the house.

'Or your friend's blood will decorate this lovely balcony,' Kek continued. 'You've been a naughty girl, *Samantha,*' pronouncing her name with a thick Arabic accent, 'and you know what I do to disobedient girls, don't you?'

Is it a rhetorical question? She never could tell with him, so she gave him a curt nod.

'Your current assignment ends now. You will come home with me this instant. And if you cooperate, we will let the healer live.'

She looked over her shoulder at Tanya whose eyes pleaded with her, but Samantha could not tell if Tanya wanted her to stay or go. Not that it mattered—there was no way she would risk the woman's life. Samantha may have been a hunter and a killer, but there were already too many innocent lives weighing on her conscience. She mouthed her final words, *'Tell Tyler I love him.'* Slipping her hand in Kek's, she let him magiport her back to hell on Earth.

When Bridey asked Caleb to spy on Brendan, she assured him it was for Brendan's protection. But as he followed Brendan to the old bookshop in Darlinghurst, he wondered if she had been upfront with him. *What are you doing here, Winters?*

As he peered through the window using binoculars, he noticed the shopkeeper was an old mage of some sort. *Is he a dark mage?* For the bazillionth time in his life, Caleb found himself wishing he could read auras like an enchanter.

After a short greeting, Brendan disappeared into the back of the shop. There was no way to get a visual from this side of the building, so he moved around the back. *Damn it!* The only window was small and frosted, suggesting the room beyond housed a toilet. Settling on making do with audio alone, he snuck into some bushes alongside the carpark. At least the minute microphone he had planted in Brendan's wallet worked well enough.

The voices of the men he spoke to sounded familiar, but he could not place them. *And who are they plotting against?* At the first mention of the Council, Caleb's blood chilled, despite the warm summer sun. *That's where I know these guys from! What the actual fuck, Winters?*

As the man he loved continued to scheme with the Council's warlocks, Caleb felt his trust in Brendan dwindling. Mention of doppelgangers pricked his ears up, literally in his case. He had heard the term doppelganger used loosely before and it was fitting when applied to Brendan and Warlock Quirke, but knowing there was some magical significance tied to the Gods? *I'll have to investigate that.*

Thanks to his wandering mind, Caleb almost missed Brendan's exit. He made a mad dash for the street, racing toward his silver Corolla. It was imperative he got out of there before Brendan recognised his car. Taking the next left turn, he wove through some side streets and sped off along a highway.

After travelling a safe distance, he told his phone to call Bridey.

'Hey sweetie.'

'Hey Bry, I have some disturbing news. I caught Brendan collaborating with a couple of Council warlocks. They are planning something big. I don't know what, but it involves using Brendan's identification.'

'Hmm.' Bridey did not sound happy. 'Did you record their conversation?'

'Of course. I'll upload it to your secure drive on the cloud.'

'Thanks, hun. Which warlocks did he meet?'

'Hayes and Quirke. The same two who arrested me. Something else came up. Do you know anything about the magical significance of doppelgangers?'

'No. Why?'

'I think it's what Brendan and Quirke are, what with them looking like twins. Quirke mentioned something about having the doppelganger gene. I don't know what it means, but I'd like to.'

'I can look into it. Given your discovery, I think it would be prudent to keep an eye on Brendan at his office. Can you do that for me?'

'Sure.' Changing into the left lane, Caleb took the next exit and turned toward the city centre.

'Oh, and Caleb?'

'Yeah?'

'Please watch your back. I'm worried Damien has his eye on you.'

'Will do. Love you, Bry.'

'Love you too, Caleb.' She ended the call.

When he got to Brendan's office, he parked a safe distance down the street and watched as Brendan's Jag pulled into the parking lot beneath the building. Tuning in to the device he had planted, Caleb heard Brendan cursing under his breath as he rode the lift. As soon as he was in his office, the speaker crackled an awful lot. 'Fuck's sake. He's even bugged the office.'

Caleb's heart stuttered. *Shit! Winters is on to me! Did he see me at the bookshop?* A loud pop sounded through the speaker, startling him.

Brendan's voice spoke sternly, 'If you ever want to see me again, you will get your arse up here right now, Thornsy.'

Chapter Eighteen

Brendan waited impatiently for Caleb to appear, tapping his fingers manically against the oak desk he had perched himself on. As soon as the door opened, Brendan flew at Caleb, grabbing him and thrusting the door closed by slamming Caleb into it. 'Why the hell are you spying on me like this?' He produced one of the listening devices, shoving it in Caleb's face.

Caleb replied with a defiant glare.

'Do you want me to hurt you?'

The left side of Caleb's lips began to curl upward, but he kept his mouth shut.

Damn masochist! Brendan released Caleb and stepped back.

'I'm serious, Caleb. I want answers. *Now.*'

They became locked in a silent stare down and Brendan erected fresh walls around his heart. Stone cold granite walls. 'If this is how you want to play it, you can get the hell out of my face. I'm done with you and Bridey.'

The smirk vanished immediately from Caleb's expression. 'I was doing Bridey's bidding. I don't know what her reasons are, but she's had me keeping tabs on you since she first appeared in Gaeilge Shores. Could be for business, or… a more personal matter. How about you tell me why you are having secret meetings with a Council warlock? If you're planning to betray us—'

'*Hell no!* There's no way I'd betray you. Do you seriously doubt my love for you? After everything I've done to prove myself?' The tension building in Brendan's skull was giving him a headache. He rubbed his palm against the side of his face, trying to relieve the pain. 'I mostly kept you and Bridey out of the loop with this to protect you, but also to maintain the integrity of the mission. The less Damien can pull from your minds the better.' After striding across the room, he slumped into his chair. The stress ball on his desk called to him, so he grabbed it and imagined he was squeezing the life out of Damien.

Lowering his gaze, Caleb fell silent.

Brendan dropped the ball on his desk and rose. *Screw this, I need a drink.* He grabbed the whiskey decanter, poured them both a shot, and threw his back in one go before refilling his glass.

Caleb ignored his drink as he mumbled, 'I'm sorry for doubting you. I guess Bridey got in my head. The prospect of your betrayal hurt, and I didn't think. I'm really fucking sorry.'

'Ah hell, Thornsy. I'm sorry for snapping at you. Come 'ere.'

Caleb obeyed the request, taking up residence in Brendan's lap. As Brendan's arms encircled his waist, Caleb pressed his forehead to Brendan's. 'I can't think straight when it comes to you, Winters. You make me crazy.'

Brendan snorted, knowing exactly what that felt like. 'Love makes us all crazy. It's the one emotion that can turn even the most sensible and logical of men into babbling fools.' He pulled Caleb's lips down to his, kissing him gently.

Hesitantly, Caleb pulled back and looked reverently into Brendan's eyes. 'What's a doppelganger?'

Panic surged through Brendan. 'Shit! You heard my conversation?'

With a sheepish look, Caleb nodded.

'You need to get the hell out of dodge. I can get you a mind shield to keep Damien out of your head, but that won't stop him torturing you, or worse….'

Caleb shook his head. 'I can't leave you to fight those arseholes. And I'm not some feeble thing you need to protect. I can hold my own.'

'I'm not saying you're weak, but these guys are more powerful than any of us. What worries me most is the possibility of them using you to manipulate me. If they get me and Tyler in a room together and they have enough leverage, there is no stopping the unspeakable evils they could unleash on the world.'

'Is this to do with the doppelganger thing?'

'Yup. Tyler is like my magic twin, born with a mystic connection to me that enhances the magic we perform together. We don't know how much, but the Cult are hellbent on finding out. It's why the inner circle came to town.'

'Then we both leave,' said Caleb. 'Let's get out of Sydney. Go someplace they can't find us.'

'Not an option. They'll find us with scrying magic.'

'But if we use wards—'

'They are attuned to nether, Thornsy. They'll break the wards.'

'Not if we get a powerful abjurer to put them up.'

'And where are we supposed to find one of those? In case you've forgotten, I'm not exactly in favour with the Council at large, even if I'm secretly working with a couple of their warlocks.'

'What about your dad?'

'*No!*' Brendan shocked himself with the force behind his response.

Even Caleb visibly cringed.

After a gentle caress of Caleb's cheek, Brendan adopted a softer tone. 'Look, I'm not gonna spend my life running. We need to put a stop to these bastards once and for all.'

'If they are as formidable as you suggest, why not send the full force of the Council against them? Why is this task falling on the shoulders of two warlocks and an outcast enchanter?'

'Bah! The Council are too busy tripping over their own red tape these days. Without hard evidence, they won't initialise outright war. Tyler and Jaxon were their best chance of finding proof, but the whole doppelganger thing has complicated matters.'

Caleb sighed. 'Bunch of wankers, the lot of 'em. Surely you've got something to take to the Council after breaking into the Cult's library.'

'So far, I've got jack. I'm still working on translating most of it.'

'What about the stuff you stole from the museum?'

'There's nothing tying them to the robbery, Thornsy. That's why they got us to do their dirty work.'

'Yeah, but aren't you technically a Cult member now?'

Brendan's eyes widened with a lightbulb moment. Sliding Caleb off his lap as he rose, Brendan planted a big kiss on Caleb's lips. 'You are brilliant, my love.'

After deleting the audio file on her laptop, Bridey sat back and closed her eyes. *Why does Caleb have to be such an effective spy? Nothing good can come of this revelation.* She never wanted to know the truth, but it was too late.

As if on cue, her phone rang with Damien's name popping up on the screen. 'Hello, Lady Violet. Do you have anything to report?'

She desperately wanted to lie. 'Yes.'

'That's excellent news. I will get there soon.'

As the line went dead, Bridey considered her options for leaving the state, or possibly even the country. She would have to get her men first, which meant a trip to Brendan's office. Pressing her hand against the back panel of her wardrobe, she opened the secret compartment where she had stashed her emergency bag. With critical supplies in hand, she ran out to her brand-new purple Ferrari and threw the duffel in the boot.

'You aren't thinking of escaping, are you?'

Bridey's heart skipped a beat and chills crawled up her back, leaving a trail of goosebumps in their wake. She turned gradually, adopting a sweet smile before coming face to face with Damien. 'Of course not. I was preparing for a leisurely cruise, which I plan to take after we finish our meeting.'

Suspicion filled Damien's eyes. 'Is that so?'

'Indeed. I'm excited to take my new wheels for a spin. Do you like her?'

Damien cast a bored glance at the Ferrari. 'It's adequate, I suppose.' He grabbed her arm and dragged her across to his limo.

She tried to pull her arm free, but he gripped her tighter. 'Where are you taking me?'

'To the office, for the meeting you were about to skip out on.'

'Ow, you're hurting me.'

'I promise a lot more pain if you don't cooperate.' Damien opened a car door and shoved her into the back seat, climbing in to join her soon after.

'Why can't we stay here?'

'Because the Boss wants to meet you.'

A new wave of icy terror gripped Bridey's spine. 'You mean….'

'The inner circle, yes.'

'But why?'

Damien turned a severe gaze on her. 'No one questions their motives, and you would do well to remember that.' His expression softened, if only slightly. 'You know, we have a bit of a drive. Why don't we make the most of our time together?' He unzipped his fly. 'Come and ride me like the expert whore you are.'

Bile filled her throat. 'My services don't come free, Damien.'

'Always such a mercantile woman. How about you rock my world, and I won't tell the Boss about your escape plan.'

'No deal. He will get inside my head and uncover all my secrets anyway.'

'I suppose he will. Fine, name your price. And before you get any ideas, cancelling this meeting is not on the table.'

'I want to know all about doppelgangers.'

His lips curled up as he leaned in closer. 'Well, well. You have been a busy little spy. What have you learned thus far?'

'I know Warlock Quirke carries the doppelganger gene, which is why he looks like Brendan. And I'm guessing the pair of them are the reason your Boss is in town. But that's about all.'

'Well, your intel is spot on. I don't know everything about doppelgangers. The inner circle like to keep their secrets. But I do know Brendan and Quirke are like mystical twins who enhance each other's magic. That's why the Cult want them.'

The implications horrified Bridey. 'What makes a doppelganger?'

'Their bloodline. Quirke has different magical ancestry to most mages. In addition to descending from a creator God, he also comes from a God of magic.'

Fascinated, Bridey stared at Damien with wide eyes. 'So, Quirke is like an uber mage?'

'Pretty much. And the havoc he could wreak with Brendan at his side would be phenomenal.'

'What is the Cult planning to do with them if they succeed in getting their hands on Quirke?'

'That's inner circle business. I've told you all I know, now get over here.'

Resisting the urge to sigh, or throw up, Bridey slid across the seat and straddled Damien's lap. 'What do you want?'

Two large hands lifted her skirt and gripped the bare cheeks of her backside. 'I want to fill all of your holes with my seed. And I want you to enhance the experience with magic.'

'I'm not sure we'll have time to bring you to orgasm three times.'

He wore a disgusting smirk. 'Fair point. I have too much sexual stamina. Fine. I'll take your arse. It's not like you ever get off with me anyway.'

Shit! I guess my acting skills need some work.

'But I want you to start working me up with your mouth.'

As she dropped to her knees in the foot well of the limo's backseat, Bridey felt tempted to bite Damien's dick. The thought alone was far from professional, and it was the first time she had felt such ill will toward a client, but she couldn't help it. Everything about Damien repulsed her, the least of which being his filthy-tasting cock. When she shifted to give him access to her arse, she did not bother prepping herself. She wanted to feel something, and since pleasure was unlikely with Damien, she resorted to pain.

The sting of his entrance was intense, and Bridey screamed out.

Damien laughed. 'That didn't sound fake. Will I finally succeed in making you come?'

'Don't mistake my pain for anything more,' Bridey retorted.

His arms held her tight as he moved a hand between her legs. 'I made a mistake assuming you were a Dominant when, in reality, you are much more of a submissive.' Damien's fingers pressed against her sensitive core as he continued to rip her open with his thrusting. With lips brushing her ear, he whispered, 'Don't forget, I've been inside your head. I know all your dirty secrets. Your pussy salivates when Caleb challenges your authority. You love how Brendan flipped the balance of power in your relationship. You want those men to control you, to make you feel the way your father did. But the thought alone scares you, doesn't it Violet? You don't want others to see your weaknesses. Fear not, your secret's safe with me. But you're not.'

The moment he dug the nails of his other hand into her throat, Bridey unravelled in Damien's arms. He had found and pushed every one of her buttons. Only one other man had done that for her, and he was an enchanter.

When they reached the corporate headquarters in the wealthy part of Sydney's city centre, Damien led Bridey into a large office on the top floor.

The elf stepping out from behind the large mahogany desk grinned, showing off brilliant white teeth as sharp as a tiger's. His skin was as dark as night and a bald head emphasised his pointy ears.

She gulped as he stood before her. Bridey was tall, especially for a woman, but this man towered over her.

'Good day, Lady Violet. I am Grand Master Kek.'

With the board meeting taking place that afternoon, the warlocks had no time to waste. Tyler grabbed his comb and styling gel and moved into the bathroom where he had access to a mirror. He styled his fringe to resemble Brendan's and changed into the suit Jaxon had given him. Apparently, it was the same label Brendan wore when conducting business.

When he returned to the bookshop's kitchen, Jaxon was making the fingerprint overlays by pouring gelatine into the chilled mould. The fake ID sat waiting for Tyler on the table, already clipped to a black lanyard.

'Do I want to know where you learned to become a master in the art of forgery?' Tyler put the black strap around his neck.

'I assure you; my training was all above-board.'

'Oh, I'm sure,' Tyler winked for effect.

Jaxon rolled his eyes and returned the putty to the freezer. No longer distracted by high-tech espionage tasks, he took a moment to look at Tyler. 'Christ! Dressed like that and with the hair, you are the spitting image of Brendan.'

'Good. Should make this job easier.'

'Aside from the fingerprints, which need a couple more minutes, are you ready?'

'Yes, I think so. I have my real mana rings in my pockets. These are fakes but should do the trick.' Tyler held out his hands to show Jaxon the rings on his index fingers mimicking Botswana agate and blue lace agate, the two crystals used by enchanters.

'They look real enough to me. And your phones?'

'Both off. I'll leave my main mobile here to prevent the risk of tracking.'

'Great thinking. I'll do the same. Now *please* don't hesitate to call me if you need help. I hate sending you in alone to do this.'

'I know the drill. Don't worry.'

'Sit down and place your hands face up on the table,' Jaxon instructed as he retrieved Brendan's fake fingerprints.

Tyler watched in awe as Jaxon adhered the thin, rubbery coatings to his fingertips. Once they were all in place, he gave the glue a few minutes to dry before heading out to the car. They reached Australia's Obsidian Cult HQ, better known as Mara Holdings Pty Ltd. After learning the name's meaning in Arabic[7], he had snickered at the irony.

Jaxon pulled into the public parking garage across the street. 'Good luck.'

'Cheers, boss.' Tyler hated to think of this as a final farewell, despite the risks. Drawing things out would only further the impression, so he left the car without looking back.

The first security checkpoint was a breeze: all he needed was the swipe card and his award-winning smile.

The human guard gave him a polite nod. 'Greetings, Lord Jet.' The formality of the man's tone made Tyler feel like royalty.

Is this what it feels like to live in Brendan's world? He beelined for the elevator where he hit the button for the 40th floor. Studies of the building's schematics, combined with Brendan's intel, told him that while the Cult had multiple meeting rooms, the inner circle only ever held their board meetings on the top floor. Access to this level required fingerprint ID. Tyler took a deep breath and pressed his thumb to the touchscreen. When the red light turned green, he exhaled his relief.

The final checkpoint before the boardroom was a pretty, blonde receptionist. 'I'm sorry, sir, but you can't go in there. The board are having a meeting.'

---

[7] Mara means joy in Arabic.

Tyler turned on his charms. 'It's okay, they are expecting me. Perhaps Grand Master Kek forgot to tell you he summoned me?'

The blonde blushed. 'Certainly. Please go right ahead.'

Pausing at the door, Tyler was thankful for the wards surrounding the room. *The measures you use to prevent people eavesdropping on your thoughts and conversations go both ways and they are about to be your downfall.*

He drew on all his strength, all his power, as sparks tingled through his fingers. Stepping into the room, he let the chain lighting jump from his hands and strike everyone sitting at the table.

It all happened too fast. Tyler barely had time to catch Samantha's eyes at the head of the table before she fell to the floor with nineteen other bodies. 'Oh Gods!' He ran to her in a panic.

When he knelt beside Samantha to check her pulse, the door opened, and Tyler looked up to see a tall dark elf clapping his hands in deliberate mockery.

'Such a wonderful display of power Mr. Quirke. I can't wait to start working with you.'

Brendan's burner phone lit up. He put aside the book he was studying to read Tyler's message: STAGE 1 SUCCESSFUL, PROCEED TO STAGE 2. He rose and moved around to Caleb's side of the desk. 'I gotta go.'

'Why? What's going on?' Caleb stood upright, gravitating toward Brendan.

'The warlocks need me to carry out my part of the plan.'

'Which is?'

'To grab all the important books from the library.'

Caleb shook his head. 'You can't go into the place while Tyler's there.'

'It's okay. Tyler has taken down the inner circle. Only the plebs remain, and they don't know about all the doppelganger stuff.'

Relief washed over Caleb's face. 'Can I help? I imagine there are a lot of books to carry.'

'Sure. I could certainly use an extra set of hands and a pleasant view while I work.' The smirk on Caleb's face was as sexy as hell and it took all of Brendan's willpower to focus on the task at hand. 'Let's go now, before I forget what I need to do.'

It was a short walk to the Mara building from his own office block, which was just as well considering the summer sun's bite. They both carried large briefcases with them and for all intents and purposes, they looked like a pair of typical businessmen. No one would suspect them of carrying books full of ancient mystical secrets in those cases.

Brendan knew something was wrong the moment he stepped into the lobby and spied Damien sitting on one of the couches. The arsehole looked at him with a smug grin, raising the hairs on the back of Brendan's neck. 'Fuck! *Run Caleb!*' Brendan cried out as he turned to flee the building, but one of the security guards grabbed him before he got far.

Caleb froze.

Dread filled Brendan's gut like lead weights. '*I said, Go! Run!*'

Snapping out of his panicked daze, Caleb nodded and dashed outside before the other guard could catch him.

Damien sauntered over to Brendan. 'You didn't honestly think it would be that easy to take down the world's oldest and largest syndicate now, did you? I thought you were smarter than this. I'm disappointed in you, Jet—or should I call you Brendan?'

'Well at least I never disappoint a woman in bed. Did you know Violet faked every orgasm with you, or are *you* really that dumb?'

The biggest shit-eating grin filled Damien's face. 'Oh, I knew. I also know the orgasm I gave her in the back of my limo today was real *and* intense. You see, I discovered a secret about your woman, Brendan. I unlocked her hidden desires and now I have her tied up in the basement, begging for more. Would you like to see her?'

Brendan stood paralysed by fear. *If Damien has Bridey, he clearly intends to use her as leverage.*

'What's the matter, Jet? Cat got your tongue?' Damien turned and strode toward the lift. 'Come along, Harvey.'

The guard pushed Brendan forward and they followed Damien into the elevator. It was a brief descent to the basement. Brendan's eyes took a moment to adjust to the dim lighting of the underground space and when they did, he wished he could have stayed ignorant of his surroundings.

The room reminded him of the ritual cellar in his parent's house, only much grimier. There were also a lot more blood stains on the floor. But the semi-circle of St. Andrew's crosses sent his heart into frenzied palpitations. The wooden crosses bore naked women, all of whom were unconscious. His eyes scanned across the group, bulging from their sockets when they landed on Bridey's limp form. A red mist filled his vision. 'If you've hurt her!' He tried to rush toward Bridey, but Harvey held him back.

'Relax,' replied Damien. 'I gave her a mild sedative. She should wake in time to enjoy her front row seat to the dark magic show you will put on.' His hand gestured across the room to where two other men stood.

Brendan recognised Tyler, and the tall dark man fitted Melanie's description of Grand Master Kek. *The fuck? Was Tyler playing me all this time?*

'I can't say the same for Warlock Quirke's girl though,' Damien continued as he moved up to a woman with red hair and traced a finger along her face. 'I hear that lightning bolt packed quite a punch. Luckily, he didn't use lethal force, else we might have had less sway with him.'

Well, that explains it. Brendan cast his eyes over Tyler's girlfriend, surprised to see one of the Council's pets had been dating a dark mage. Another glance at Tyler showed the cold iron cuffs binding his wrists.

'Do you want to know the best part of our plan?' Damien crossed his arms and stood upright in a cloud of his own stinking arrogance.

'What?' Brendan asked impatiently.

'The best part is our backup plan: you see, in the off chance you let us kill Violet and Samantha, we have one of our men in Gaeilge Shores ready to assassinate the woman you *both* love. Pure genius. I love the synergy you doppelgangers bring to this circle.'

Brendan's whole body tensed. *How the hell did they know about Lana?*

'We make it our business to learn secrets,' Damien explained as though he had read Brendan's mind. 'Oh, and in case you think I'm bluffing….' He turned on a security monitor mounted to the far wall. It showed a live camera feed of someone watching Alannah.

'Shit!' It was the first thing Tyler had said since Brendan entered the room.

So, Tyler is in love with Lana too. The thought made Brendan feel sympathy for the guy.

'Here's how this is going to work,' Damien explained. 'The pair of you will participate in this ritual and we'll spare the lives of all four women.'

'Four?' Brendan glanced across the group of women, but no other faces were familiar. Sure it would be tragic if their innocent lives were sacrificed, but it was hardly leverage.

Tyler jerked his head toward the brunette between Samantha and Bridey. 'He's talking about Tanya, Jaxon's fiancé.'

'Indeed.' Damien stepped over to Bridey and stroked the side of her breast. 'Perform the ritual, the women live, and we will set them free. After they perform their part, of course.'

A sick feeling stirred in Brendan's stomach. 'What is the ritual?'

'A summoning.'

Brendan huffed. 'Neither Tyler nor I have the attunements for such magic.'

'Oh, but you do, Brendan. I made sure of it as part of your initiation. You see, our Dark Lord was banished to the Underworld. You will be channelling the stygian element to bring him forth, and Tyler here will enhance your magic to ensure you are capable of such a feat.'

Recalling what he had read about Set's dark mating rituals, the nausea intensified as Brendan realised what the Cult intended to do with the naked women in the room. 'Tyler won't be much use in those mana blocking shackles.'

Damien turned his attention to Brendan. 'We will release him once you invite him into the circle. If he tries anything, Harvey and I won't hesitate to hit the numbers we have on speed dial.' He nodded toward the security monitor for effect. 'Now, let's get this party started!'

Chapter Nineteen

He was running faster than ever before; running like his life depended upon it—because it did. If Caleb didn't escape the Cult's clutches, he was as good as dead because there was no way he would let them use him as leverage. *The Cult won't force Brendan to perform unspeakable evils on my account.*

Brendan's office was his first stop. He needed to pick the lock, since Brendan had secured everything before heading over to Cult central. Caleb grabbed the books they'd been reading, along with the translation notes and the blue cartouche. Too impatient to wait for the lift, he descended the stairs two at a time.

A quick peek out into the street assured him the coast was clear, so he made a dash for his car. *Now what?* Caleb glanced at the books on the seat beside him and sighed. Taking the only option remaining, he drove through the city and across the Harbour Bridge into North Sydney. After giving up on a legitimate spot, he parked in a loading zone and stormed into the Council Chambers.

The petite half-mage receptionist jumped at the sound of Caleb's brief case hitting the counter.

'I need to see High Magus O'Grady, *immediately.*'

'I'm sorry, but the High Magus is busy at the moment. You will need to make an appointment.'

'I don't give a rat's arse what his Lordship is doing. If he values his life and that of everyone else in this damn state, he will make time to see me *now*.'

'Are you threating us, sir? Because the High Magus does not take kindly to threats, nor do we appreciate interruptions by unseelie riff raff.'

Caleb laughed drily. 'Trust me, woman, I am the least of your worries right now. If you don't get the High Magus for me pronto, a cult of dark mages over in the CBD will bring hell to Earth and you can die knowing you had a chance to stop it, but let your prejudice get in the way.'

Gaping at him, she picked up her phone. 'Sorry to interrupt Your Honour, but there is a man out the front with an urgent matter. Something about a dark mage cult … Yes, Your Honour.' Dropping the handset in its cradle, she looked up at Caleb. 'He will see you now.'

Picking up his suitcase, Caleb marched on through the security gate, up the stairs, and onto the second floor of the Council's ivory tower.

High Magus O'Grady waited for Caleb at the door to his office. As soon as he glimpsed his visitor, he frowned. 'I did not expect to see one of the endarkened coming to me about this. What is your involvement with dark mage cults?'

He pushed past the High Magus into the office. 'My boyfriend went undercover to investigate one of them and now they have him in captivity.'

'And you expect me to drop everything to go rescue some unseelie?' O'Grady closed the door.

Caleb scowled at the High Magus. 'Firstly, my boyfriend is not unseelie. He is a pure mage. Secondly, the cult in question is one your own pets have been investigating and I believe they also captured Warlock Quirke.' He threw his briefcase on O'Grady's desk and flipped open the latches. 'Here is the evidence you need to mount an outright attack on the Cult's headquarters. I suggest doing so pretty soon because they have what they were looking for and are probably casting the ritual circle about now.'

O'Grady looked through the books and papers. 'How is this evidence? I can't even read most of it.'

'Those books are copies taken directly from the Cult's secret library.' He drew closer to the desk, handed O'Grady the cartouche, and flicked through the pages to where Brendan had made notes on the relic. 'This ancient artifact belonged to the Cult. But they don't need it anymore because now they have this.' Caleb skipped to the page about the lazurite scarab. 'This is what the Cult stole from the museum.'

Minutes passed in painful silence as O'Grady read Brendan's notes. He looked up with a furrowed brow. 'I still don't understand the significance of all this.'

Caleb rolled his eyes. *How could such a dumb fuck have become High Magus?* 'Did you miss the page explaining how the Obsidian Cult also call themselves the Sons of Set? They are dark elves born of an evil Egyptian God. Who do you think they want to summon with the Lazurite Scarab? I seriously doubt they are looking to invite Lugh around for tea and scones.'

With wide eyes O'Grady's attention returned to reading the page about the cartouche and the Sons of Set. 'Apparently they used to use this trinket in a dark mating ritual. Does that mean—'

'They want more dark elf babies? Yep. I can't imagine the women they are using in the ritual are willing volunteers either. I bet Set would be keen to stay a while once he comes to town since I doubt it's much fun for him in the Underworld.' Caleb had no idea if the Cult were intending to summon Set, but it made as much sense as any of the theories he'd toyed with, and it was the most ominous story to tell the High Magus.

'You can't be serious. It would take immense power to break Set's shackles and pull him from the Underworld.'

'With Brendan and Tyler as his doppelganger, they have all the power they need. Sorry, did I forget to mention that part?'

Brendan cast the circle much like he had done for years as a regular mage, only the Cult had inverted the pentagram he stepped around. Instead of calling upon the element of Aether at the apex, he lit a purple candle at the base to call upon nether, the stygian element. With Damien and Harvey watching from the sidelines, both with phones in hand, Brendan gulped before continuing. He invited Kek, along with two other dark elves, plus Tyler, into the ritual space, asking them, 'How do you enter the circle?'

They each responded, 'With a hunger for power.'

Once the others were kneeling, Brendan took his place at the altar where he touched the Lazurite Scarab as he read the prescribed invocation:

'Set, God of Chaos, we praise you in all of your forms. You are the dark that balances the light, the violence in our hearts, and the Divine Outcast. We present you with offerings and you are free to take those of your choosing. We ask only that you honour us and bless us with power.' He felt queasy as he spoke the words of offering.

Lifting his arms, he began chanting. 'We invoke thee Set: accept our offerings and live among us.' As the words left his lips, Brendan visualised Set in the fiery pits of the Underworld and imagined the God breaking free of his prison.

The rest of the group repeated the mantra with him and after a few minutes, Brendan felt energy surging through him, giving him an incredible rush. But the air changed in the room and his heart thumped wildly as a dark form materialised in the middle of the circle.

Breath rushed out of Brendan's lungs at the sight of the red ochre-skinned man with the head and tail of a beast. Set was easily seven foot tall. *Holy. Shit. An actual God stands before me.* He experienced true awe in the face of such terrifying beauty and unbridled power.

Set leered at the women strung up around the room, all of whom had awoken and were attempting to scream, but their gags muffled their cries. He said something in Arabic before approaching Brendan.

Unsure if he wanted Set's blessing—*or is it a damning?*—but too afraid to move, Brendan remained frozen in place, allowing Set's hand to rest upon his head.

A commanding voice filled his mind. *'You have done well, my servant. As a reward, I shall strengthen your conduits.'* Power flowed into Brendan, and it felt as though he was growing. But after Set's words, he understood his capacity to channel mana was expanding. Set moved around the circle, empowering the other participants.

As Set approached the women, Brendan's stomach lurched. The first victim was a buxom blonde dark mage. No one Brendan knew, but that did not diminish the horror he felt at the sight of her thrashing about when the seven-foot-tall beast of a man forced himself upon her.

Unable to watch the whole scene unfold, Brendan turned his gaze toward Bridey, who was the eighth and last in line, assuming Set planned to follow a linear path. Her expression betrayed anguish and dread as she watched the mating ritual unfold, knowing the same fate awaited her. When her eyes met Brendan's, they pleaded with him for clemency, for release from her bindings.

Tears slipped from Brendan's eyes as he projected his thoughts into Bridey's mind. *'Would that I could, but my own hands are metaphorically tied. I'm sorry, Bry.'*

She nodded her understanding and drooped her head in resignation. It was enough to shatter Brendan's heart and he hung his head in shame.

While Set took his time with each of the women, he did not need a recovery period. *He truly is a God*, Brendan thought bitterly.

As Set drew close to Samantha, Tyler jumped up and shouted, 'No! Not her!'

Set paused and turned to face Tyler with a look of disdain.

Kek snarled at him. 'How dare you disrespect our Dark Lord! Would you prefer to see her throat slit?'

'It would be more merciful than subjecting her to *him*!' He pointed angrily at Set.

Samantha nodded her agreement.

'Shall I contact our assassin, Master?' Damien pointed to the screen on the wall behind the women.

Brendan's heart skipped a beat.

Tyler paled and dropped to his knees. 'I'm sorry, Sam.' He tried to lower his head, but Damien, who knelt beside him, leaned over and yanked Tyler's head up, forcing him to watch as Set defiled one of the women he loved in exchange for saving the life of another.

Talk about a seriously fucked up trolley problem.

As Set finished with Samantha, the basement door burst open.

Brendan had never been so happy to see such a large bunch of Council warlocks. As they filed in, he spotted Hayes and pointed toward Damien and Harvey.

Hayes did not hesitate to lob two fireballs, dropping both douchebags to the floor in a pile of ash and bone.

Although surprised at first by the extreme force used, Brendan felt a perverse sense of satisfaction at seeing Damien toasted.

With the threat of Alannah's death out of the way, Tyler rose and sent a chain lightning attack at the three dark elves and their God. 'That's for Samantha, you arseholes!' The shock threw the elves back, either dead or unconscious.

But the bolt of electricity merely annoyed Set, who sauntered toward Tyler with a menacing scowl. A few warlocks tried to stop him, but he grabbed and flung them across the room, smashing their heads against the wall.

The remaining warlocks backed down like a bunch of cowards; all except Jaxon, who silently assessed the situation.

How does one stop an angry, rampaging God of chaos? That chapter was missing from all the mage textbooks.

With nowhere to run, Tyler visibly trembled as Set moved in for the kill.

Not willing to let the God of jerkdom crush Tyler, Brendan drew on his powers of persuasion as he leaped in front of Set. 'Hey Set, buddy, old pal. Why waste your time with these idiots, when there is a whole world out there waiting for you? Think of all the lovely ladies who are ripe for the taking.' He moved up and placed a friendly arm around Set's back, since he could not reach the giant's shoulders comfortably. 'I'm what they call an expert in the art of seduction. Why don't I take you out prowling for women?'

Set looked at him doubtfully. 'You are a powerful enchanter. Why do you bother with seduction when you can take them?'

Brendan grinned. 'Because there is more excitement in the chase when they are willing. But that's my preference and quite beside the point. I know a great place to find some magic babes far more worthy than these offerings. Would you like me to show you?'

Caleb chose that moment to appear, distracting Set, and blocking the door as he stood frozen in abject horror.

'Oh look, it's my friend Caleb. He knows how to party too,' Brendan added. 'The two of us could take you out on the town and show you a good time.'

'Mm, I am hungry for more women. Although I have not finished tasting the last of my offerings.'

Brendan waved a hand through the air. 'Bah. You don't want 'em. That one,' he pointed to Tanya, 'is as bland and boring as they come. She's only ever been with one man in her life. I mean come on; she has vanilla written all over her. And her,' he pointed to Bridey, 'trust me when I say you ain't missing much. I've been there, done that, along with most of the men in this city.'

Bridey's eyes bugged out at Brendan's blatant insult. *That's gonna take some apologising when I get home.* 'Surely you want excitement from the women you take. I know I do.'

'You make a fair point.' Set let out a hearty laugh, eroding the mountain of tension in the room. 'Very well. I trust you know this world better than I do now. Show me where to find the beautiful women.'

'Okay, but first, you'll need some glamour, so the humans don't run screaming.'

'But I like the sound of humans screaming,' Set insisted.

With a chuckle, Brendan slapped Set on the arm. 'A man after my own heart. Seriously though, you don't want the humans to see you in this form or they will send their soldiers to attack you. Trust me when I say human warfare has advanced a lot since you left. Some of the weapons they use are more powerful than anything magical.'

A wide grin formed on Set's face. 'I like the sound of these modern humans and their weapons. Will you show me some?'

'Of course. But glamour first.'

'Okay,' Set agreed.

Brendan cast a basic glamour spell making Set's head appear human, hiding the tail, changing his skin to more of a chocolate colour instead of dark red, and applying a black suit in place of the skimpy loin cloth. 'Okay, all set. Ah hell, I did not intend that pun, I swear.'

'It is okay. I liked your pun,' replied Set.

'Christ! Remind me never to introduce you to my brother.' Brendan seized Set's arm and led him out of the basement, grabbing Caleb with his other arm on the way out.

'Does your brother enjoy wordplays?'

'Much too much. They are the only form of humour he attempts, and he does a pretty lousy job.' Brendan slipped his burner phone subtly into Caleb's pocket and spoke to him telepathically. *Message Jaxon. Tell him to prepare a space for a ritual sending and to find an acolyte or hierophant who knows how to send Set back to hell. Once he has it sorted, he should message us with a time and location.'*

'I get the sense you do not like your brother much,' Set continued.

'Ha! That's an understatement. The bastard stole the love of my life. Oh, and he always had it too good.'

'I understand envy and hatred towards one's brother.'

Brendan recalled his knowledge of Egyptian history. 'Do you mean Osiris?'

'Yes. He was always the family favourite.'

'I hear you man. Liam could do no wrong and always got everything he wanted.'

'What form of vengeance have you enacted upon your brother?'

'Are you kidding me? Liam is a powerful warlock and pretty much untouchable.'

'Have you thought about killing him?' Set asked.

'Trust me, Set, I've dreamt of all the ways I could end him.'

'Perhaps I could help. I love enacting vengeance.'

'Hmm… maybe once you've finished with this City, we could go back to my hometown?' Brendan suggested.

Set nodded, pausing to take in his surroundings as they stepped outside the building. 'My word, humans have made some considerable advances in technology.'

'With unsolicited help from their magic friends of course,' Brendan pointed out. 'When was the last time you came to earth, Set?'

'I believe the year was 1038.'

A whistle slipped through Brendan's lips. 'The Middle Ages. That's over nine hundred years ago. You've got a lot to catch up on. For one thing, you see those machines moving on the road?'

'Yes.'

'They are cars and they have replaced horses as the main mode of road transport.'

'Indeed.'

'Also, this country we are in? This is Australia: a large island nation in the southern hemisphere. Most of the human world did not know of its existence back then.' Brendan started leading them toward a nearby unseelie club as he went on about the ways of the modern world, all with a view to keeping Set distracted from Caleb's texting. 'Oh, and dragons were driven to extinction.'

Set's brows rose. 'Really? How?'

'Humans literally hunted them to death. They would have done the same to us mages and the other magical races if we hadn't started using glamour. Most humans began subscribing to monotheistic religion and persecuted anyone practising the old ways. That said, we have reached a new age of enlightenment where religious, racial, and sexual tolerance is growing. Who knows, maybe one day we can coexist with humans openly again.'

They reached the club. 'Well, here is the first stop on our tour. The place won't be busy yet, though, 'cause it's still early.' As they stepped inside, a decent number of fae were already enjoying a drink at the bar. They all turned and gasped. 'Oh right. The glamour spell only works on humans—these folk can see you for who you are.'

'It is of no consequence.'

Brendan was inclined to disagree. Set was a God to these people and the Gods were not known to walk among them and drop into the local watering hole on a whim. *But who am I to argue?*

With a lustful eye, Set made his way over to one of the endarkened sitting in the lounge area. Her eyes widened with shock at the monstrous God standing above her. 'I will start with you,' he announced.

'Excuse me?' she replied with an air of sass.

But Set ignored her words as he grabbed her, eliciting a scream from the helpless woman.

Brendan cringed, but for his plan to work, he needed to keep Set occupied. So, he jumped on the bar and hollered, 'Okay, listen up people. I am Lord Jet, Dark Syndicate Boss, and I bring a God before you. That's right, a literal God. May I present Set, the Egyptian God of Chaos.' He thrust his arm out toward Set for dramatic effect. 'Tonight, I am declaring this bar to be Set's breeding ground. Think of it like a dark Beltane where an actual God will honour the lucky babes. So, ladies, you have two options: either line up to become a willing recipient of Set's lovin' and let him rock your world like only a God can. Or cower in the corner and pray like hell he doesn't turn his attentions on you, but I don't fancy those odds. Either way, none of you can leave here before he finishes with you.'

Caleb stood near the door, shaking his head as he thought, *'I don't like this plan much, Winters.'*

'Well it's the best I've got,' Brendan replied telepathically. *'Would you rather I unleash him upon the unsuspecting masses at a regular nightclub to keep him busy while the warlocks hatch their plan?'*

'Of course not, but I still don't like forcing him upon anyone. Plus, this won't go down well for you in the Syndicate ranks.'

'I couldn't give a shit about the Syndicate ranks. Right now, my priority is saving the world at large from the horrors this God can unleash upon them.'

Five drinks into the night and Brendan decided he better not go back for more else he become too inebriated to banish Set to hell. Surprisingly, over half the women in the unseelie bar had willingly offered themselves up to Set. Brendan could not help but think Set owed much success with the ladies to his own speech, and he felt a sense of pride in his oratory skills.

But as the night wore on and the consenting partners stopped lining up, things took a turn for the worse, and the heavy drinking commenced.

Caleb slumped over the bar next to Brendan, nursing his seventh or eighth drink. 'I know Set's old-school, but this shit is sick and twisted. I could never treat a woman like that.'

Brendan snorted. 'No, but you let *our* woman treat *you* like that.'

'Not cool, man.' Caleb tried to hold Brendan's eyes in a death glare, but his gaze was too unsteady.

'Hey, I'm as pitiful as you. Bridey may not have used magic compulsion on me, but she coerced me in other ways. She did a lot of wrong shit to us and yet we both encouraged it and now we can't imagine living without her.'

'Yep, we're one big fucked up family. Maybe you should change your surname to Hawthorn.'

With a smirk, Brendan leaned in closer to Caleb. 'Are you proposing to me, Thornsy?'

A few laughs erupted from Caleb. 'I'm sorry, but the thought of you legally married to anyone is too funny; although, I could totally imagine the three of us in a hand fasting, but good luck finding an acolyte willing to sanctify our union.'

A moment later, Set stepped up behind them, slapping them both on their shoulders. 'Have another drink with me, men!'

'Gladly,' replied Caleb as he pushed his empty glass forward and threw another fifty down on the bar.

'I'll pass. I've had enough tonight,' explained Brendan.

'What? The night is young, and the alcohol has barely touched your system. You promised to have an enjoyable time with me tonight.'

'Fine.' Brendan groaned as he pushed his own glass forward. 'I never thought I'd still succumb to peer pressure at the age of twenty-one.'

As they clinked their freshly filled glasses together, the phone in Caleb's pocket beeped.

'What was that?' Set's eyes darted from Caleb to Brendan.

'What was what?' Brendan asked nonchalantly.

'The peculiar noise.'

Brendan shrugged. 'Must be one of the machines behind the bar. How are you going with the ladies out there, Set? Have you had your fill already?'

His big burly chest rumbled with a deep chuckle. 'I am far from satisfied, but there is only one damsel left for me to ravish.'

'Why don't you go violate her while Caleb and I work out where to take you next?'

Excitement radiated in orange sunbursts from Set's uber aura. 'You are a better servant than any of those stuffy old dark elves. They never took me drinking and whoring at the taverns like this.' Turning away, Set stalked his last victim.

'Please tell me that's a newsworthy update,' Brendan pleaded as he turned back to Caleb.

Caleb's eyes lit up as he read the message, but his brow furrowed toward the end.

'What is it? What's wrong?'

'They have a place setup, but they don't have enough mages attuned to Aether.'

'Shit! How many more do they need?'

'Two.'

'Wait, did they include you in their numbers?'

'No, but I'm pretty plastered. I don't know if I can do much magic.'

Brendan waved his hand dismissively. 'Shouldn't matter. All you need to do is channel the mana. Tell them you'll do it and get them to ask the bookshop owner in Darlinghurst. They will also need to make sure Tyler is there.'

'Will do.'

'So where are we doing it?'

'High Magus O'Grady's house.'

Brendan gave him an impish grin as he replied, 'Kinky.'

'Your ability to shamelessly flirt in such dire times amazes me.'

'So sue me for feeling horny after the free porn show Set put on for us.'

Caleb was gobsmacked. 'Please tell me you haven't enjoyed the sight of him raping women.'

'Not the raping part. I'm talking about the women who threw themselves at him. As if you didn't enjoy watching that.'

'Maybe.'

'You know, I kinda feel like I've bonded with the bastard. If it weren't for his propensity to take without asking, I'd say it's a shame to send him away.'

Shock spread across Caleb's face. 'You aren't reconsidering, are you?'

'Reconsidering what?' Set had snuck up behind them.

Brendan startled, but swiftly regained his composure. 'Caleb worried I would reconsider his suggestion for our next party destination. But I'm all in.'

Set's eyes gleamed with devilish delight. 'You have another venue arranged?'

'Yes, we do,' Caleb replied. 'We should get going now if we want to make the most of the night.'

'Good thinking,' agreed Set.

They took a taxi to O'Grady's harbour view mansion in Cremorne Point.

'This does not look like a tavern,' Set observed.

The driver cast a wary glance at Set.

Brendan paid for their fare and beckoned Set out the car. 'Because it's not. We are going to a private party. In this day and age, a lot of people have wild parties in their homes, and they are often a lot more fun than nights out at pubs and clubs. The drinking works out a lot cheaper too.'

'Is this your house?' Set eyed the place warily.

'No. It belongs to a friend of ours. Come on.' Brendan tugged on Set's arm to encourage him inside.

As soon as they passed through the wards, Set stiffened. 'This place feels wrong. I don't like it.'

'You are probably reacting to the wards. All mages put those up around their homes. It's nothing to worry about.' Brendan tried to sound as calm as possible, but a sliver of anxiety slipped through the cracks.

Set stood firm. 'You are not being straight with me, Brendan. Why is that?'

'I'm nervous about introducing you to my friends, okay? Some of them can be aloof or even hostile with strangers. Hopefully your divinity will help break the ice.'

After a moment of hesitation, Set nodded and followed them. 'If this is a party, where is everyone?'

'Downstairs, in the basement,' Caleb replied.

Bemused, Set shook his head. 'Modern people are strange.' When Brendan flung open the door to the cellar, Set froze. 'You tricked me; this is no party!' His voice roared at a near-deafening volume. He attempted to back out of the doorway, but Caleb wrapped his arms around Set and Aether flowed from his hands, effectively trapping them together in a forcefield.

'So much for being too drunk, Thornsy!'

With a smug grin, Caleb steered Set into the middle of the pentagram.

The Hierophant cast the circle and invited High Magus O'Grady, Acolyte Carran, Brendan, Caleb, and Tyler to join. After working together to bring the devil to Earth, it made sense for Brendan and his doppelganger to join once more and send Set back to hell.

As the four Aether users worked together to bind Set in celestial shackles, Brendan visualised the fiery pits, pulling the stygian element into his mana conduits. He could also feel the power flowing into him from Tyler—like he had in the summoning ritual earlier—only this time, the connection was stronger. It was as though Tyler's willingness to help intensified their doppelganger bond.

When the time came for Brendan to perform his part, he closed his eyes and spoke the mantra, 'We banish thee Set. You are no longer welcome on Earth. Return to the fiery pits.' After a minute of chanting, Brendan began to tire and Set was still resisting, crying out in pain as he did so.

Set snarled in his mind. *'You will pay for your betrayal, puny mage!'*

Guilt tugged at Brendan's heart, and he felt the need to explain. *'The world has changed too much, and it is no longer acceptable to treat women the way you do.'*

'Bah! Men have grown soft. I should take you with me and toughen you up.'

'Not gonna happen, Set.' Brendan reached into the last of his reserves as he sent a blast of hellfire at Set.

The God retaliated, using the fire to burn the flesh above Brendan's heart.

Brendan yelped and doubled over in pain. As it eased, everyone else fell silent, and he opened his eyes. The middle of the circle was empty, which meant they had successfully vanquished Set. He expelled a large breath and grinned as he glanced around the room. But the others wore apprehensive looks, and when he could not see Caleb, fear and understanding clenched his chest. 'Where is he? *Where is Caleb?*'

True remorse showed in Tyler's expression as he spoke, 'I'm sorry, Brendan. Set took Caleb with him.'

With those five words, Brendan felt the world cave in around him.

Chapter Twenty

Feeling wrecked, Tyler dragged his feet up the basement stairs and into O'Grady's living room. The sight of Samantha sobbing against Shane's chest cut to the bone. The memory of her suffering would live with him forever, along with the guilt he felt for allowing it to happen. 'It's done. Set has returned to the Underworld,' he announced to the room at large.

Jaxon looked up from comforting Tanya. 'Good. You should get some rest. O'Grady is happy to put us all up for the night.' His attention shifted behind Tyler.

Turning, Tyler watched as the others emerged from the basement. O'Grady was conversing in hushed voices with the Hierophant and Acolyte Carran as he led them away, but Brendan had not yet shown his face.

Still wrapped in a blanket, Bridey stood up from her armchair. 'What about Brendan and Caleb?' When Tyler looked at her with silent remorse, her eyes widened. 'No!' Dropping the blanket, she dashed past Tyler and ran down the stairs to the cellar.

'What happened?' Jaxon asked.

'We lost Caleb,' Tyler replied solemnly.

'Oh.'

After crossing the room, Tyler sat on the couch next to Samantha. He needed to touch her, to comfort her. But when he attempted to pull her into his arms, she resisted. 'Sam?'

She shook her head.

'Sam, please. I need to hold you.'

'No.' Her voice sounded aloof.

'I'm sorry, baby. I didn't want any of that.'

Her muffled voice came between sobs. 'I thought you were different, but you are as depraved as the rest of them, as evil as Kek.'

'What? Sam—'

Shane glared at him. 'Quirky, please. I think you should give her some time. She's had an extremely traumatic experience.'

With intense pain piercing his heart, Tyler stormed out of the house, slamming the door behind him as he stepped out into the back garden. When he found a wooden bench a decent distance from the house, he collapsed on it and let out a furious scream. He was not angry with Samantha. It was those Cultists and their Dark Lord who boiled his blood. But he directed most of the rage inward at himself.

After the frenzy wore off, sorrow kicked in and Tyler let the tears come. He cried for the terror Samantha must have felt; for the soul-destroying way that monster had used her; for the betrayal she must have felt knowing Tyler had enabled it all. And he wept for his own loss, because things would never be the same between them. Even if Alannah's life had not been on the line, Tyler's selfish side would not have allowed them to take Samantha's life, no matter how much she pleaded for the sweet release of death.

Shit! Alannah! In all the chaos of the night's events, he had almost forgotten about the assassin sent to watch her. He grabbed the burner phone in his pocket and dialled her number.

'Hello?'

Relief washed over him at hearing her voice, at knowing she was alive. 'Hi Lana. It's Tyler. Are you okay?'

'Have you been channelling cosmic mana? Because I swear you must be psychic. I was thinking of calling you because honestly, I feel like shit.'

'But are you physically okay? Has anyone harmed you?'

Her tone became riddled with anxiety. 'No, why? What's going on?'

'I've had a totally fucked up night. Can I see you? I'd rather talk about this stuff in person.'

'Yeah, okay. I was hoping to see you anyway. Meet at our hotel in an hour?'

'Yes please.' When he signed off, Tyler tuned in to the ley lines. As he suspected, the High Magus had bought property with intersecting lines of power, one of which led south and straight across the harbour bridge. He arrived hastily and made use of the shower in the meantime. When he walked out of the bathroom, wearing nothing but a towel, Alannah was waiting for him on the bed. Her sudden appearance made him jump. 'That was quick.'

'I guess I'm getting better at magiporting.'

'I'd say! Plus, I can see you didn't bother changing first.' His eyes scanned her scantily clad body, dressed in nothing more than a black satin slip.

A sly smile tugged at one side of her lips. 'I put a coat on before stepping out.' She pointed at the black overcoat she had draped across the back of a chair before standing to embrace him.

'What's going on, Tyler? Why did you worry about me? And why have you been crying?'

Clinging tightly to her, another wave of sorrow hit him. But rather than drown in it, Tyler let Alannah carry it away as their lips crashed together and their bodies merged.

A sense of calm set in as Tyler's breathing settled, and he used it to tell Alannah everything about the night.

'Poor Sam,' Alannah said in a soft voice.

Tears threatened Tyler's eyes again. 'It was horrible, Lana. And Damien wouldn't let me look away. It kills me knowing she suffered all that because of me. I desperately need her forgiveness, even though I know I don't deserve it.'

Alannah straddled Tyler, pressing all her weight into him as she brought her face close to his. 'Hey, what happened wasn't your fault. The Cult used you too, Tyler. Sam will come around to see it, but she needs time. I never told you this, but I kind of know what she's going through.'

Tyler's lidded eyes flew open. 'What do you mean?'

'Remember my trip to the big house?'

Nodding, Tyler felt his stomach stir.

'One of the Council's warlocks raped me in prison. The incident turned me into an emotional wreck for a while and I misdirected a lot of my rage toward Liam. Logically, I knew it wasn't his fault, but emotionally it took a while to forgive him, not only for the way he dumped me in the first place, but for the imaginary part he played in letting Clayton defile me.'

'But you did forgive him?'

'Yeah, I did.'

'Yet things won't ever be the same for the two of you, will they?'

Alannah sighed. 'No. But that has more to do with my feelings for Brendan. Speaking of which….'

Tyler brought his hands up from her hips to encircle her back with his arms. 'Is this what you wanted to call me about?'

'Yeah. I need someone I can confide in because the truth of the matter is quietly killing me.'

'Hey, you can always talk to me, and you know I will never betray your secrets.'

'I know. Thank you, Tyler.' She took a deep breath. 'This baby I'm carrying… it's Brendan's.'

'Oh, hell. But didn't your uncle say it was a blessed baby?'

'It is, but Brendan was my only partner at Beltane.'

'I see.' He fell silent for a minute.

'Does this upset you, Tyler?'

'Yeah, but not in the way you might think. I'm sad for you, Lana. I know how much your separation from Brendan has hurt you, and now you're carrying his child. It's gonna make it much harder to get over him.'

'Exactly. And that's where I'm going to need your help a lot in the coming years.'

'Fuck!' Tyler rolled Alannah over, pinning her down as he looked into her eyes. 'What are you saying, Lana?'

'I'm saying I don't want these therapy sessions to end.'

Those were the sweetest words Tyler had heard all day… possibly all his life.

An ominous red glow filled the ritual room as Bridey entered, fearing the worst. The sight of Brendan's hunched form sent her heart lurching into her throat. 'Oh Gods!' She ran to his unmoving body and knelt beside him. 'Oh, Brendan.'

Turning, his gaze lumbered toward her, and she felt a moment of relief knowing he was alive. That was until she saw his red, puffy eyes. 'W-what happened?'

His expression was almost blank as he blinked at her. Shock. He was in shock. The symptoms were obvious even without reading his aura. The mere fact he was letting her read him should have been the first clue.

'Brendan, sweetie, what happened?'

'He's gone.' The coarse, scratchy voice sounded almost alien.

Panicked, Bridey looked up and scanned the room, looking for Caleb's body, but there was no sign of him. 'Gone where? Where did Caleb go?'

'Hell.' Brendan choked up as waves of hysteria set in.

She could not quite make out what he was saying, but she heard something about hell and whatever he meant was clearly the cause of his distress. She tried to subdue her own fears and focussed on calming him. With her attunements, Bridey placed her hand on Brendan's back and whispered soothing words as she poured a sense of calm into him. 'It's okay, handsome. Everything will be okay.'

After gulping a lungful of air, he sat up and focussed on her. 'I'm sorry, Bry. I didn't realise there was a risk of banishing Caleb when I sent Set back to the Underworld. The dark lord dragged Caleb down with him!'

With a sinking heart, Bridey understood what Brendan meant. If they had sent Set to hell and Set took Caleb with him, her beloved boy was currently in the Volcanic Pits, the lowest level of the Underworld, where nether formed. It was where the most wicked souls went. *Poor Caleb must feel terrified.* 'Listen to me, handsome. If you were able to release Set in the first place, surely you can get Caleb out?'

'That was the first thing I thought of, but it's not likely.'

'Why not?'

'Summoning Set took a lot of power, more than I have. I would need to find others willing to help despite the risk.'

'What risk?'

'Releasing Set again.' He leaned into her and brushed a hand along the side of her face. 'I can't believe how close things got for you, Bry. If he'd defiled you, I never would have forgiven myself. And poor Samantha and Tyler. I can only begin to imagine what they are going through right now. I don't think I could ask Tyler to take the risk again.'

'It's okay, sweetness, we will find a way.'

Brendan shook his head defiantly. 'You're forgetting one major complicating factor here: Set is an immortal Celestial, but Caleb's not. What if Caleb can't survive conditions in the Volcanic Pits?'

'We can't afford to think like that, Brendan. Let's try to stay positive so we can focus on rescuing Caleb. Can you keep your hopes up for me?'

He still looked defeated when he nodded, but it was a start.

'Come on. Let's go home and get some rest.' She began to rise.

But Brendan tugged at her hand, pulling her into his lap. 'Wait a sec. I need to hold you.'

'Of course, handsome. Whatever you need.' The warm comfort of his arms was more than welcome.

Pressing into the crook of her neck, he inhaled her scent and traced his fingers along her side. 'Where did this tracksuit come from? I don't recall you owning anything like this.'

'O'Grady's wife gave me these clothes. I lost my own at the Mara building.'

'That was nice of her,' he replied absently, shifting back enough to look at Bridey. Something dark flashed in Brendan's gaze and his eyes filled with hunger. With a swift movement he pinned her down on the floor, right in the middle of the pentagram. 'Although you look much better without any clothes.'

Bridey gasped from the sudden movement. 'Brendan! What are you doing?'

Tearing her pants down, he grinned wickedly. 'What does it look like I'm doing?' When he rose to his feet, Bridey tried to sit up, but he pushed her back down with a bare foot placed on her chest.

'Brendan, have you forgotten where we are?'

'Not at all.' To prove his point, he removed his ritual robe and threw it across the room. When he looked down at her a moment later, lust burned red in his eyes and aura. 'I've always wanted to fuck someone in a ritual circle. Looks like you're the lucky someone.'

Bridey's body flooded with desire at the sight of him standing over her in nothing but a pair of red silk boxers that did nothing to hide his erection. A moment later, the red silk dropped to the ground.

'Remove your top,' he commanded.

With expert deftness, she stripped herself naked.

'On your hands and knees.'

The authoritative tone he adopted sent a thrilling rush to her core. Damien had been right. This was exactly what she wanted from Brendan. Assuming the position, Bridey relished the feel of cool, hard stone pressing into her knees and palms.

Brendan dropped to the floor behind her and without any warning, he grabbed a handful of hair and pulled her head back as he thrust deep inside her. Holding his position, Brendan brushed his lips against her ear. 'You thought you could own me, but you need to understand no one *owns* Brendan Winters. I am the one who *owns* you, Bridey Hawthorn.'

Amazement did not even begin to describe how Brendan felt when Tyler rang, inviting him to visit his home. 'Why?' He laced his tone with scepticism.

'I have a surprise for you. Get over here.'

Brendan accepted the invitation. Bridey had been busy working in her study, so he gave her a quick kiss and took off. It had been two weeks since the whole mess with Set and they had yet to find a safe way to bring Caleb back. But she refused to give up on him, devoting hours every day to studies into the arcane.

After ringing the doorbell of the large Darlinghurst townhouse, he stepped back and waited anxiously.

Within seconds, the door flung open, and Tyler grinned back at him. 'Come in.'

It was odd how Tyler had recently taken to styling his hair the same as Brendan's. *Should it flatter me or creep me out?*

When they stepped into the living room, a fiery redhead looked up at him and gasped. Samantha looked much healthier and happier than the last time he had seen her, and it did wonders for her sex appeal. Her eyes darted between Brendan and Tyler. 'Babe?'

Tyler laughed. 'That'd be me, Firecracker. So, yeah, this is the first opportunity I've had to formally introduce you. Brendan, this is my girlfriend, Samantha.'

Reaching forward, Brendan clasped Samantha's hand and shook it. 'A pleasure to meet you.'

'Likewise,' she replied with eyes fixed on his.

A throat-clearing noise from Tyler broke her gaze. 'So, uh, before I show you the surprise, I need you to promise you won't ask any questions like how, or why etc.'

Brendan cast his dubious glance over Tyler. 'O-kay.'

'Promise?'

'Fine. I promise.'

'Right. Follow me.' He led Brendan up a flight of stairs and onto the first floor. They stopped outside a door. 'I would suggest bracing yourself though. This won't be a pretty sight.'

Vague curiosity shifted to full intrigue as Brendan prepared himself for something grotesque.

'Go in when you're ready.'

With a deep breath, Brendan entered the room. Tanya sat on the far edge of a large bed, and she was in a trance with her hand resting on the crown of a man's head. The heart beating in Brendan's chest became the only thing he could hear. Three long strides brought him close enough to see who lay in the bed. His skin as red as a lobster, blistered from third degree burns, but there was no mistaking the slender body and well-defined face.

A few tears trickled from Brendan's eyes as he perched on the nearest edge of the bed. 'Thornsy?'

Caleb's eyes fluttered open. 'Winters?' he asked with a hoarse voice.

'Christ, Thornsy! You look like shit. And you sound even worse,' Brendan jested as the tears flowed more freely. He grabbed a glass of water from the bedside table. 'Here, have a drink. Sorry it's not the good stuff, but I wasn't able to sneak the whiskey past Dr. Tanya.'

Tanya opened her eyes long enough to roll them, then resumed the meditation in which she was channelling the mana needed to heal Caleb.

With Brendan's help, Caleb shuffled up the bed enough to prop himself up against the pillows. He took a few sips of water using the straw Brendan held for him. 'I guess I'm not the pretty one anymore,' he whispered.

'I'm sure Bridey will happily wear that crown until you get better,' Brendan gave him an impish grin. 'Seriously, it's great to have you back, Thornsy. Bridey and I have missed you something fierce. Can I kiss you if I'm gentle?'

'Yes.'

Reclining on his side, Brendan leaned in carefully to press his lips against Caleb's. He kept the touch feather soft. But Caleb's hand jolted up from his side and grabbed the back of Brendan's neck, pulling him in closer. After wincing from the increased pressure, Caleb deepened the kiss. Even when dry and cracked, Caleb's lips felt incredible against his own, especially when moaning.

'Okay, that's enough excitement for my patient,' Tanya interjected.

Brendan smirked at the tent between Caleb's legs. 'Indeed. I'll let you get some more rest, Thornsy. But I'll return soon.'

''Kay. Love you,' Caleb whispered.

'Love you too.' Brendan rose and left the room. After shutting the door, he leaned against it to find his bearings. *Caleb is alive!* Questions about how Caleb got home and what he'd endured filled Brendan's head. He jogged down the stairs and found Tyler curled up with Samantha, watching television in the living room.

Tyler looked up and gestured toward an armchair. 'Take a seat.' He paused the show they were watching to focus on Brendan.

'Thank you,' said Brendan once he had settled in his seat. 'You didn't have to do this for him, and I know you Council folk aren't usually fond of unseelie.'

'You and he are welcome. It was the least we could do. Unseelie folk aren't usually known to help the Council combat the forces of evil.'

'Yeah, Caleb's pretty special.'

Tyler studied Brendan a moment. 'Are you really in love with him?'

'I am.'

'And his sister, Bridey?'

'Yup. In love with her too.'

Another moment of awkward silence.

'What about Lana? Do you still love her?'

Why the hell is he interrogating me on my love life? With careful consideration, Brendan opted for the truth. 'Even after severing the soul link and trying everything in her power, Bridey could not shake my feelings for Lana. That love runs deeper than any other emotion.'

Tyler did not even appear surprised. 'So why aren't you trying to win her back?'

'Because I can't. There are greater forces at work here, Tyler. Lana's better off keeping me at a distance.'

'I doubt that. Not when—'

'Tyler, please. It hurts me as much to stay away from her, but would you risk the life of the woman you love for your own selfish gain? If being with her put her life in danger, would you continue to see her?'

Tyler stared at him in stunned silence, then shook his head. 'What aren't you telling me, Brendan?'

'I'm not telling you anything that will put your own life at risk. I suggest you stop this line of inquiry before it's too late.'

'Is your life in danger?'

'I'm the boss of a criminal syndicate, Tyler. My life is always on the line.'

With a nod of understanding, Tyler quit his questioning.

'I'd better get going. Bridey doesn't know the wonderful news yet and she will want to see Caleb.'

Brendan had reached the door when Tyler stopped him, 'Oh and Brendan?'

'What?'

'Lana sends her regards.'

The penny dropped and Brendan understood how Tyler was able to bring Caleb back from the Volcanic Pits. 'For her own sake, please don't send her mine.'

<h1 align="center">Chapter Twenty-One</h1>

Five years and six months later.

Sweat poured from every inch of Brendan and Liam's bodies as their swords clashed blow for blow. The duel had been intense, lasting for at least one hour, if not two. But what Liam failed to realise was Brendan had not even attempted mind reading yet.

The moment Brendan dove into his brother's mind, it was easy to anticipate Liam's next move. Liam may have had spent years learning to block Brendan from his mind, but that was before Brendan had mastered his attunement to the stygian element. Bypassing Liam's defences had become a cakewalk.

Seizing the moment, Brendan plunged his blade deep into Liam's heart. He watched with delight as daddy's golden boy fell backwards with a look of pure horror on his face. Leaning over Liam's dying form, Brendan scowled bitterly. 'Good riddance, *Brother.*'

Brendan's forehead was dripping with perspiration as he woke from the vivid dream. Sitting up in bed, he rubbed the throbbing brand on his chest: Set had given him the cartouche shaped scar as a parting gift. Brendan cursed the clock for showing how little sleep he had gotten so far. Not wanting to disturb his lovers who slept on either side of him, he carefully slid down to the bottom of the bed and made his way to the bathroom.

After wiping his face with a cold, damp cloth, he headed into his study to continue working on the latest translation. With all the volumes from the Obsidian Cult's library he had been working through, his Arabic literacy was exceeding that of his Celtic. What he found strange, however, was his ability to read ancient hieroglyphics without need of a reference book.

The subject of Brendan's study was a fascinating analysis of the original *Book of the Dead*, better known to the original elves as *Spells for Coming Forth by Day*. Several spells contained within related to various forms of immortality, including paths to the Celestial Realm. *I would love to get my hands on the original tome!* He wondered where the Egyptians had hidden such a book.

Sensing movement at the door, he looked up from his desk. Caleb slouched against the doorframe, arms crossed against his firm chest, a hint of muscle bulging in his biceps. Every inch of his silver skin shimmered in the dim lamplight. *Fuck! He grows more beautiful every day!* Thankfully, Tanya's healing magic had worked miracles all those years ago, so there was not a single scar or blemish left on Caleb's perfect complexion.

'Hey, what are you doing out of bed?' Caleb crossed the room and moved around behind Brendan, where his hands got to work on the tension in Brendan's shoulders.

'I couldn't sleep.'

'Was it another one of those vengeance dreams?'

Brendan dropped his work and leaned back into the massage. 'Yeah.'

'They're getting more frequent of late. Maybe you should give the Egyptology a rest for a while.'

'You think it's related?'

'I'm almost certain. You must come across the name Set often in your reading. It's gotta be like a big subconscious trigger.'

'Maybe. But if that were the case, why am I not dreaming about the shit Set did?'

'I dunno. I'm not an expert in dreams. It seems likely, considering Set's M.O. along with your own resentment towards Liam.'

'You're probably right. Once I finish working on this book, I'll move on to something different.'

Caleb's hand trailed down Brendan's chest as he leaned forward. 'Did you realise it's after midnight?'

Brendan huffed. 'And?'

'And, happy birthday, Winters.'

'Ah damn. I was hoping you'd forget it was today.'

'Not gonna happen.' His fingernails skirted around Brendan's nipples. 'Why don't you come back to bed and let Bridey and me spoil you?'

'Mm, now that's an idea I can get behind.' Brendan let Caleb pull him up from his chair and take him back to their room.

The scent of violets filled the air as he approached the bed. And Bridey knelt on the mattress, waiting for him with a mischievous glint to her eyes. 'Happy birthday, handsome. I have the perfect gift for you.'

'Is that so?'

Nodding, she handed him a purple box with a silver ribbon. 'This is from both of us.'

Making quick work of the ribbon, Brendan opened the box. But he took a full minute to recover from the shock after peering inside. When words became possible, he looked up at Bridey. 'Are you sure this is what you want?'

'Yes.'

Brendan turned to Caleb.

'You shouldn't even need to ask me. You know I've wanted this for years.'

'I want you both on the floor.'

Once Caleb and Bridey were both kneeling before him, he retrieved the two collars from the box. He inspected them. The rings of delicate silver thorn embellishments suggested a custom job. Brendan fastened the grey collar around Caleb's neck and stooped to kiss him on the head before doing the same with the violet collar on Bridey. Taking a step back, Brendan admired the incredible view. *What a gorgeous pair of subs. And they are mine!*

Unable to contain his excitement any longer, Brendan climbed into bed. 'Get up here and make me feel good.'

Brendan's pair of Hawthorns obeyed his command to the letter, bringing him pleasures beyond his wildest dreams.

To be continued...

What's Next?

Thank you for reading *Winter's Thrall*. Reviews are the lifeblood of authors, and they make a huge difference to the success of a book. Could you please post a review to one or more of the following sites?

Goodreads
BookBub
Amazon
Other bookstores

Alannah and Brendan's stories continue in *Winter's Mother 1,* coming November 2022.

Keep reading for a sample…

Bonus Content

Winter's Magic: Trouble in Paradise (Winters Wedding)

Lord and Lady Ross Winters cordially invite you to attend the nuptials of Alannah Winters and their son Liam Winters…

Things have never been easy for Alannah and Liam, and their wedding day is no exception. All the chaos, calamity, and cold feet leaves their restless guests wondering if the ceremony will even go ahead. Will Liam and Alannah successfully tie the knot?

If you are keen to read this bonus content, you can access it on the 'Freebies' page of my website: www.starlaarts.com

The Winter's Magic Series

A modern fantasy and paranormal romance about secrets, mysticism, empowerment, and the complexities of love.

Winter's Maiden 1
Winter's Maiden 2
Winter's Thrall
Winter's Mother 1 (November 2022)
Winter's Mother 2 (May 2023)
Winter's Bride (November 2023)
Winter's Crone 1 (May 2024)
Winter's Crone 2 (November 2024)

Winter's Mother 1

Most mistakes have consequences. This one has a legacy.

Following the birth of her daughter, Alannah slipped into a deep depression. Many blamed it on the hormones, but they did not know the truth: this precious baby girl was the spitting image of her father, a man who broke Alannah's heart and shattered her soul.

After years of escaping her grief, either at the bottom of a whiskey bottle or in the arms of Brendan's doppelganger, Alannah is finally sober and on the road to recovery when the devil himself walks back into her life. Will his return spell her ultimate destruction, or will they find a way to reconciliation and a second chance at love?

Having escaped sexual slavery, Brendan has become the master of his own universe and Boss of the unseelie underground. Everything is good until work takes him back to Gaeilge Shores where he discovers the daughter he never knew existed.

Old wounds reopen and priorities change when he throws himself back into Alannah's life. And all this family drama takes place amidst an apocalyptic threat. Can Brendan help the Council save the world, and reunite with his soulmate?

Warning: This book contains coarse language, adultery in a crumbling marriage, and explicit scenes, including steamy m/f/f romance, that may upset or offend some readers. It also ends on a cliff-hanger, with the sequel launching in May 2023.

AVAILABLE NOVEMBER 2022.

Keep reading for a sample…

Winter's Mother 1: Chapter One

Sixteen years following the events of Winter's Maiden 2

Glancing at her reflection in the bedroom mirror, Alannah cringed. She studied her cotton unicorn pyjamas and felt the beginnings of a mid-life crisis set in. *When did I trade in the black satin slips for these pyjamas? How am I only noticing how frumpy I look these days?* With a bamboo brush and some concerted effort, she managed to tame her wild bed hair. It had been another restless night.

The house was quiet when she made her way to the kitchen. The silence was unusual, but not alarming. Being a summer Saturday meant Liam was likely at the beach already, making the most of the surf. She turned on the coffee machine and looked across the open plan living space. Her daughter sat at the dining table, watching something on her laptop.

Neve was using headphones which explained the lack of noise. But the sound of grinding coffee beans got her attention. 'Morning, Mum.'

'Morning, hun. I didn't expect to see you up before me on a Saturday.'

'You do realise it's nearly midday, right?'

'Oh shit! Really?' Alannah looked at the old grandfather clock. She had recently acquired the timepiece from an antique auction for a bargain price. 'Damn. I guess I overslept. Did you get yourself some breakfast?'

Returning her attention to whatever YouTube had to offer, Neve shook her head.

Alannah took her fresh brew to the table and sat next to Neve. 'You know, if you want your father and I to show more lenience, you are gonna have to start behaving responsibly. That means looking after yourself more.'

'Spare me the lectures, Mum. I get enough of those from Dad. Besides, I remembered to feed the cat.' Neve gestured at the ball of white fluff sleeping on the couch.

Sighing, Alannah returned to the kitchen. She threw together some avocado and cheese toasted sandwiches. 'Here, eat this.' She put one of the plates beside Neve's laptop, then sat in front of her own computer.

Sipping her coffee, she scrolled through her social feed. Not much engaged her foggy brain beyond some cat memes. She clicked like on a few and went to close her laptop when a news bulletin caught her attention.

'Mum, can—'

'Wait a sec, hun. Come look at this.' She opened the live video feed and gasped at the aerial footage.

'*The Victorian Government has declared a state of emergency. Melbourne residents flock from their homes amidst the City's collapse.*'

'Oh wow! Is that a volcano erupting?' Neve asked. 'It looks awesome!'

'*The dormant volcanoes erupting form part of the Newer Volcanic Province. This disaster follows a series of earth tremors. Experts claim the odds—*'

Alannah muted the sound. 'It's devastating is what it is. Don't forget I spent nine years of my life living in that city. I have friends there.'

Remorse filled Neve's bright green eyes. 'Shit! Sorry, Mum. Can you call to check if they're okay?'

'Now's not a good time to be clogging up the phone towers over there. I hope they've marked themselves as safe.' Alannah's hands trembled as she clicked over to Melissa's profile. Nothing. She looked at Emma's and Cole's next. *Damnit!* None of them had checked in.

'Mum?'

'Mm?' Alannah was too distracted to give Neve her full attention.

'Is it okay if Cat and Fi come over for a bit?'

'Yeah.'

Neve disappeared down the hall. Alannah switched between face-stalking her friends and watching updates on the disaster. The more she watched, the more uneasy she felt about the whole thing. The reports coming from the scientists only fed her suspicions. *Why is a dormant volcano with such low odds of current activity erupting in such a prominent place? Could this be the work of dark mages?*

The issue warranted some investigation, so she sent a quick email to Kieran Lane, the High Magus of her state. She included a link to the newsflash with the question: *Could this be dark magic?*

When Kieran did not reply within an hour, she grew impatient and rang him.

'Yes, Councillor Winters?' His curt tone was typical even after years of working with her.

'Did you get my email, Your Honour?'

'I did.'

'And?'

A loud sigh crackled through the line. 'Why are you asking me about the goings on in another state? You know I don't have any jurisdiction over there.'

'Are you not the least bit concerned for them?'

'I sympathise, sure, but it's not like I can do anything. If High Magus Hanigan has need of us, I'm sure he'll be in touch. Now if you don't mind, I am in the middle of something.'

'Of course. Sorry to bother you.' Alannah hung up and flung her phone at the couch out of frustration. *Sixteen years on and I still haven't earned enough respect from the man.* Then it struck her. *If this volcano business is a dark magic conspiracy, they could hit South Australia. What if I can uncover such a plot and prevent devastation at our doorstep?* Surely *doing so would raise Kieran's esteem.*

With newfound enthusiasm, Alannah dialled her friend Monique.

'Hey girl, what's up? I hope Caitlin isn't causing you any grief.'

'What?' Alannah remembered the girls were over and hanging out in Neve's room. 'Oh right. No, she's fine. Have you seen the news?'

'No. Why? What happened?' Monique's cheerful tone plummeted.

'A volcano in Melbourne. It's all-over social media, so you should check it out. But listen, I was hoping you could hack into your dad's work files. I need some contact details for the magic community in rural Victoria.'

'You thinking foul play?' Monique was always more astute than her father, the High Magus.

'Yeah. Your dad's too stubborn to look into it, so I need to use some back channels to check it out.'

'I'll see what I can do.'

'Thanks.' After signing off, Alannah returned to checking on her friends. A little relief washed over her when she found Emma's update declaring she was fine and out of the danger zone. She continued to wait for news from the other two.

'Well, there's go my plan to fly under the radar.' Brendan huffed as he stuffed his phone back in his pocket. Zipping his small carry-on case closed, he became thankful for the decision to pack light.

'What do you mean?' asked Caleb.

'My flight got cancelled, something about a volcano in Melbourne spewing too much ash into the air. Now I need to magiport there, which sucks 'cause I'm not keen for High Magus Kieran to know I'm in town.'

Caleb's big, dark, soulful eyes looked so pretty when they grew wide with surprise. 'A volcano in Melbourne? Are you for real?'

'Yup.'

Grabbing his own phone, Caleb became engrossed in footage of the volcano erupting. 'I didn't even know we had active volcanos in Australia, let alone under cities.'

'Hmph. We should have paid more attention in school.'

Sardonic eyes peered over the small screen in Caleb's hands. 'You were the one playing hooky all the time. I kept my head down and got the work done.'

'That's right.' Brendan cast wistful thoughts back to their youth. Stalking around the bed, he backed Caleb up against the wall. 'I'd almost forgotten you were a nerd back then. Hm, I wonder... Would I have noticed your beauty sooner if your hadn't buried your head head in books so often.' He brought a hand up to Caleb's face, tucking a strand of long, black hair behind one of his pointy ears. The proximity aroused them both, their dicks tenting against each other.

The pitch of Caleb's voice lowered. 'Perhaps, but then I would have been nothing more than a distraction. A passing fad like all the girls you used back then.'

'Touché. Instead, your timing was perfect. You were like my life raft in a sea of despair.' Brendan drew Caleb's lips into a deep, passionate kiss. When the calendar alarm on his phone sounded, he groaned as he pulled back. After silencing the damn thing, his gaze returned to Caleb's mouth. Subconsciously, Brendan grazed the pad of his thumb along the bottom lip. 'Gods I'm gonna miss these sweet lips.'

Caleb's mouth curled into a mischievous smile. 'Jacob has pretty soft lips.'

'You sly fox.' Brendan laughed. 'You never told me the pair of you hooked up.'

'Sure I did. I told you about all the times I partied with him whenever I paid our hometown a visit.'

'You told me about the gang bangs, but you never related the details of being intimate with *him*.'

'My bad,' Caleb replied with a wry smile. 'I figured you'd assume we fucked.'

Brendan drilled into Caleb's soul with a stern expression. 'You know I don't like it when you leave me guessing. When I ask for details, I want *everything*. The who, the where, and most definitely the how. I am going to have to punish you for such insubordination.'

A slight moan escaped Caleb's lips as his eyes darkened with lust.

With a wicked grin, Brendan stepped back, breaking all body contact. 'I can see how much you want me right now, Thornsy. But you see, punishment is never about what *you* want.'

Caleb's eyes lowered. 'Of course. I'm sorry for offending you, Sir. What is my punishment?'

Seeing his submissive stance sent signals southward and tested Brendan's willpower. It would have been too easy to dish out a few lashings and take him then and there. But what he had in mind would be more fun in the long run, and it would give Caleb time to reflect upon his actions. 'No intentional sexual release until I return home. You will not touch yourself and you will not initiate intimate contact with anyone else while I am away. I'll let Bridey know the deal too, so she won't let you get off.'

Caleb gasped.

'What's wrong, Thornsy? Are you afraid of a little celibacy?'

'Not afraid, more… frustrated. I can't remember the last time I went so long.'

Closing the distance, Brendan reached inside Caleb's pants and gripped his erection. Then he leaned in to press his lips to Caleb's ear. 'If you think this is frustration, how do you think you will feel in two weeks?'

'Ah Gods!' Caleb gritted his teeth against the torture of Brendan's teasing touch.

'Will you be good for me Caleb?'

'Y-yes Sir,' he replied with a shaky voice.

'Good man. Now I want my goodbye kiss.' Embracing Caleb, Brendan kissed him with ardent fervour. Their passion rivalled anything Hollywood ever put on the big screen. He walked out sporting a massive smile and the boner to match. At least he could use magic to control the latter. Although he didn't have time to hide it before finding Bridey in the parlour.

She glanced at his situation and grinned. 'Oh dear. Has my brother left you unsatisfied?'

'Quite the reverse, I assure you.' He dropped his case beside the chaise longue and straddled her lap. 'At least I can do something about mine, unlike Caleb. I forbid him from seeking relief for the next two weeks. Can I rely on you to police him for me?'

'Certainly, Sir.'

'Thank you, Bry.' The farewell kiss he shared with Bridey was much more savage, like a pride lion with his lioness. By the time he left, Brendan considered the merit of Caleb's suggestion. Seeking out Jacob might prove necessary. The pickings in Gaeilge Shores were slimmer after the Council had exiled him. He was not even sure if Bianca would welcome him back in her bed.

EDM blared from Neve's speakers as she sat on her bed with the girls. Clicking next on the photo slideshow, she gasped at the fine specimen on her laptop.

Fiona squealed with delight, 'Oh. My. God. Dorian Pearce is so hot!'

'I know right! And you know what they say about vampire bites.' Neve licked her lips.

'Your parents would have a fit if they heard the two of you lusting after a vampire,' Caitlin scoffed. 'Especially your mum, Neve.'

Neve shot Caitlin a suspicious look. 'Why do you say that? I know my dad can be an arrogant arse, but Mum is more tolerant than most bloodline mages.'

'Didn't she ever tell you about her vampire ex?'

After scooping her jaw up off the floor, Neve questioned her blonde friend, 'My mum dated a vampire? I can't imagine her doing something so sordid.' A giggle slipped out as she thought of her mother letting a vampire bite her.

'She did. He was Dorian's late uncle, in fact. Austin was working for your great-grandmother who was a Lich. Under her orders, he tried to talk your mum into becoming cursed, which freaked her out, so she dumped his arse. But he went crazy and tried to force the curse on her. A big battle ensued where your mum killed the lich, and your dad killed the vampire.'

'Wow! How did you know all this and how have I never heard anything?' Neve asked.

'My mum told me. She was there. I guess the memory is too traumatic for your mum to retell.'

'Hm, I guess.' Neve continued looking at the photos she had downloaded from her phone. She paused when one of the Rowan family filled the screen.

'Mm, Jasper!' Neve and Fiona chimed in perfect unison.

'At least our folks can't complain about his bloodline status,' added Fiona.

'No, but he is a massive slut. I heard he's already slept with half the girls at Gaeilge High,' explained Caitlin. 'And he is a senior! Good luck pinning him down for more than one night.'

Neve laughed. 'I'd gladly pin him down for a night.'

As if on cue, her phone buzzed with a message from Jasper: END OF SUMMER HOLIDAYS PARTY AT MY HOUSE TONIGHT. OPEN INVITATION.

Screaming, she threw the phone at her friends. Then using the breathing exercises Mum had taught her, Neve tried to calm her excitement. *Jasper messaged me! The hottest boy in town sent me personal invitation!*

Fiona gave her a wicked grin. 'Looks like you might get your wish.'

'Will you give up your V-card to the rat? Don't you want your first time to be special?' Caitlin asked.

Neve frowned at Caitlin for throwing a wet blanket over the elation she felt. 'With Jasper, it will be special.'

Caitlin sighed. 'To you sure, but not to him.'

'So?'

'So, you should hold out for someone who will treat you with respect. Someone who appreciates you.'

'Ugh, why are you being such a drag, Caitlin?'

'Because I care about you, and I don't want to see you get hurt. What about Lorcán Ó Máille or Kane Sheridan? They are both hotties and they're nicer boys.' Caitlin grabbed one of the carrot sticks from the snack plate on the bedside table.

'They are in our year level, so they're way too young. Boys mature slower than we do, so you need to pick one at least one year older, two years is even better. Besides, I doubt they even look at girls that way yet.'

A loud crunch filled the air, then Caitlin grinned. 'Trust me, hun, they've noticed us. Don't forget mages grow up quicker than humans.'

Neve gasped. 'You like one of them, don't you? Alright, spit it out, who are you crushing on?'

Caitlin blushed, but kept her mouth shut.

'Oh, come on, Cat. You know we won't tell anyone. Your secrets are safe with us, right Fi?'

'Of course,' replied Fiona with an eager tone to equal Neve's.

'Okay. It's Lorcán. He is so… dreamy.'

Fiona cupped her mouth in her hands to hide the big smile on her face. But the joyous expression was still there when she pulled them away. 'Are you in love?'

Caitlin bit her lip. 'Hardly,' she scoffed. 'I don't even know how he feels about me. The attraction is purely physical at this stage.'

Fiona shrugged. 'Let's go to this party. Then you can both find out what the guys think of you. Plus, it would be a great ice breaker before we start senior high school on Tuesday.'

'True,' agreed Neve. 'So, the big question is, what should I wear?'

Liam hung up his surfboard beside the outdoor shower affixed to the back of his house. Peeling off his wetsuit, he slipped under the warm water. He closed his eyes and basked in the feel of the stream cascading over his skin and seeping into his tight muscles. It was his favourite form of meditation. Then a scream, followed by fits of giggles coming from an upper floor window broke his reverie. 'Curse that girl,' he muttered as he stepped out and grabbed a towel.

Wrapping the Egyptian cotton bath sheet around his waist, Liam stepped inside. He spotted Alannah curled up on the sofa with Luna the cat purring beside her.

She was texting someone, tension swirling around her like storm clouds.

Is she oblivious to my presence, or choosing to ignore me? 'Who are you messaging?'

'Hm, what?' Alannah's attention remained on her phone.

Meanwhile his own attention shifted to the sight of her curvaceous body in a skimpy summer dress. He had not seen her wear anything so revealing for years, and the design looked new. 'Who you are chatting to and why do they have you so worried?'

'Oh. It's Emma from Melbourne.' Alannah finally glanced at him, but she took little heed of his partial nudity, or his growing arousal. 'Have you seen or heard the news at all?'

'No. I've been out at sea all day. What happened?' He sat next to her, adjusting himself in a none too subtle way, although she did notice.

Alannah showed him the footage of the volcano erupting in Melbourne.

'Christ! That's horrible. I'm so sorry, babe.' Leaning in, Liam kissed the crown of her head. At least she did not flinch when he did so. 'Are your friends okay?'

'Emma is. But we can't get hold of Mel or Cole.'

When his hand moved to her back, she stiffened. But he refused to pull away from his wife when she needed comforting.

'Neve's friends are here, by the way, so you should put some clothes on.'

So she did notice. Liam dismissed the thought as soon as it occurred. *Doesn't mean she cares.* 'Explains the squeals coming from upstairs.' He rose and headed into his room, closing the door with a little too much force. The last thing he wanted was for Alannah to feel pressured, especially at a time like this. *But what was she thinking when she put that damn dress on?*

Slumping onto the bed, he eased the towel free. He used it to contain the mess he made when thoughts of his last time with Alannah brought him over the edge. Then he threw it in the laundry hamper and fetched some clean clothes. Dressed in black cargo shorts and a tight, white surf brand t-shirt, he returned to the living room.

'Can I get you something to eat?' he asked as he fixed himself a snack in the kitchen.

'Just a coffee, thanks.'

Concern furrowed his brow. 'Have you eaten much today?'

Alannah glared at him. 'I'm not hungry, okay? What do you expect me to do? I can't exactly conjure up an appetite.'

'Jesus, Lana. I'm worried about you. I can tell you're not sleeping properly, and you've been losing weight again. Why won't you let me help you?'

'Because you can't. Let me work through my own shit, okay?'

'You could see your therapist again,' he suggested, trying to be supportive.

She snorted. 'You have no idea what my therapy entails, do you?'

'Not exactly, no. I know you said he uses unconventional methods. You tend to feel better but after a weekend of therapy, and it's those results I care about.'

Neve chose the moment to interrupt. 'Mum, can I go to Naomi's house tonight?'

'Yeah I—'

'Wait,' Liam cut Alannah off. 'Will her parents be there?'

Neve shrugged. 'I dunno. Probably.'

'Unless you can get me confirmation from her parents the answer is no.'

'But Dad—'

'I won't hear it, Neve. I don't trust Jasper anywhere near you. Rowan boys don't exactly have the best reputation for respecting girls.'

Noticing Alannah's shiver, Liam kicked himself for reminding her of Clayton.

'*You're so unfair, Dad!* All my other friends will be there.'

'So not only are Naomi's parents unlikely to be there, but it sounds like a party. You are most definitely *not* going.'

She gaped at him. 'I hate you, Dad!' Storming off to her room, she slammed the door behind her.

'Fucking brat,' he cursed under his breath.

'Do you have to be so hard on her?' Alannah asked.

'Do you have to be so soft on her?' he retorted. 'She's only fifteen, Lana. Far too young to be going to parties and hooking up with boys.'

'She turns sixteen in July. Have you forgotten what we were like at her age?'

Recalling Alannah's reckless past, Liam paled. He dreaded the thought of Neve following in her mother's footsteps. 'I remember. That's the problem. Especially if she's anything like you.'

Thunder rumbled from inside Alannah as those storm clouds burst around her. 'How. Dare. You.'

Startled, Luna sprang from the couch and skidded along the floor in her attempt to flee the room.

Shit! 'Lana, I didn't mean it like that. I'm concerned about her is all.'

'Right. Like you're worried about me. But there's nothing wrong with *you*, is there?'

Liam froze. 'What do you mean?'

Alannah sighed. 'Never mind.'

'No. I want to know what's on your mind. If I've done something wrong. If I've upset you somehow, I need you to tell me.'

'Do you really want to know what's wrong?'

'Yes. I do.'

A tense moment passed as Alannah studied him. 'You're a lousy lay, Liam. Sex with you is boring. It's why I stopped putting out for you. You don't do it for me.' Her words floored him.

Anger simmered away inside his nerves. 'So what, no sex is better than any sex with me? Is that it?'

A malicious grin formed on her perfect face. 'Who said I wasn't getting any?'

Liam's heartbeat kicked up a notch.

'Would have been so quick to suggest therapy sessions if you knew what they involved?'

Shaking his head, he denied what he was hearing, 'No.'

'Oh, yes, Liam. My therapist fucks me the way I like it because you can't.'

With his blood boiling, Liam took off in a mad dash for the gym where he pummelled the punching bag with his fists. 'Fuuuuck!'

Also By L. Starla

The Phoebe Braddock Books
(Taboo Romance & Forbidden Love)

I Heart Mr. Collins
From Prying Eyes
Crystal's Crucible
Undeniably Wrong (August 2022)

Serial Fiction Boxsets
(Exclusive to Amazon and available on Kindle Unlimited)

Well I'll Be Damned Season 1
The Dark Matter Between Our Hearts Season 1

About the Author

L. Starla is an Australian author who often raided her mother's shelves for any form of fiction she could get her hands on. Her first love was the horror genre, but she owes her love affair with the romance novel to her high-school English teacher, who started her on the classics. Given her earlier reading, magical realism and paranormal romance were a natural progression. Along with steamy romance, these are the genres she writes.

Starla also loves spending her spare time playing tabletop and video games, paper crafting, singing, dancing, and watching anime.

Access Exclusive Content

Join my newsletter to access free stuff like short stories, deleted scenes, fan art, and invitations to future launch events.

Newsletter: www.starlaarts.com>freebies
Facebook Group: groups/l.starlareadersgroup

Follow me Online:
Website & Blog: www.starlaarts.com
Goodreads: L. Starla
BookBub: www.bookbub.com/profile/l-starla
Amazon Author Profile: author/l.starla
Instagram: L. Starla Author
Facebook: L.Starla
Twitter: @LStarla2019